URANIUM!

URANIUM!

by

Bernard Brunner

Author of

THE FACE OF NIGHT

A World of Books That Fill a Need

Frederick Fell, Inc.
New York

Copyright © 1968 by Bernard Brunner

All rights reserved. No Part of this book may be reproduced in any form or by any means without the prior written permission of the Publisher excepting brief quotes used in connection with reviews.

For information address:
Frederick Fell, Inc.
386 Park Avenue South
New York, N.Y. 10016

Library of Congress Catalog Card No. 68-9261

Published simultaneously in Canada by
George J. McLeod, Limited, Toronto 2B, Ontario

Manufactured in the United States of America

For Adlai Stevenson
In Memoriam

URANIUM!

CODA

(November, 1967)

"Do I look nervous?" he asked rapidly. "I do, don't I? A little bit?"

"I don't have to look, I can smell it."

"Yeah? Really? That's bad, very bad. They ought to make a scent, a male deodorant or something called 'I don't care, Charlie.'" Bob Werden's tall pink face seemed to lose its shape for an instant and then he chattered on, nervously stroking his tie and stretching his mouth. "But you will admit it's quite a surprise, him coming to visit the mill like this, out of the clear blue. I hope nothing's rotten in the state of Denmark?"

He glanced eagerly at the man sitting beside him on the plane: unhealthy looking, with very dark hair, a skim-milk face and dandruff sprinkled on his shoulders. "Denmark is fine," the man said ambiguously. "Just fine."

"Crops are good this year again? They got the hay in all right?" Werden joked angrily, to cover the rebuff. "But listen. I got word the Senator is coming and I rush up here from Denver in the middle of the night. I couldn't sleep, I just walked around the airport for six hours, up and down, up and down, like an expectant father." Crazily he reeled into mimicry: he was a midwife, his face was a feminine wobble of dismay. "More herbs!" he cried. "More herbs!" Abruptly he was himself again, moaning, "You saw the way he met me, one limp handshake and then nothing. Brrh!"

Too late, he saw that he'd left himself wide open by almost criticizing the Senator. His damn hysterical anxiety, it caused mistakes. He had to play it tight, go slow, feel his way. He'd picked this little fink out of the Senator's party because he was sitting by himself at the front of the plane, and all he'd found out so far was his name, Lennie Silverman, and that he was ghost-writing the Senator's autobiography.

"Of course," he corrected himself hurriedly, "I know the Senator is a busy man. National affairs and all that, the destiny of the world." That sounded ironical, he decided, and so he added piously, "I think he's a really great man."

The propellers turned over and over, blurring into transparency with speed, and then the runway was flowing and the shadow of the wing, sliding, fell away underneath. The glossy woodwork in the cabin rattled. Far below, gaunt clay hills tipped over as the plane banked westward, and Pierre, South Dakota, dropped behind and sank into the brown land.

"Senator White," said Silverman deliberately, "is a rat."

"What?" Werden said, blank.

"And not just a little one. He's the big, *big* rat. The rat that ate the rat that ate little sister. Super Rat," he said with bitter relish. "The King of the Western World."

In panic, Werden whipped around to see if Silverman had been overheard. Down the narrow aisle the Senator's doctor was snoozing with his head rolled sideways, a bridge game had started between seats. Garbled music from a speaker mixed with the sound of the motors.

"Take it easy," he implored, still wincing. "You never know, I think the copilot is a female spy."

"Super Rat," Silverman said, "and I'm an expert. Back there is the most powerful man in the country, and that includes the President. He's head of the Senate Finance Committee. Not to mention the public works committee that controls all the pork barrelling. So when the President wants something, he gets what Senator White gives him. And take my word, he doesn't give. He trades. And the saying in Washington about that is, he trades apples for orchards."

Wriggling and darting looks, Werden tried to balance the need for help against the danger—and his mind flickered, blinked and flashed with hideous possibilities. Maybe the little fink couldn't carry the ball on the writing job and was on the way out. If so, sitting with him was like kissing lepers. Or he could be a decoy sheep. That was it! Just follow along behind, agree with him, and wind up cut into lamb chops.

"Wait a minute," he fluttered. "The Senator is a good family man, isn't he? And a strong church-goer, no smoking or drinking?"

"Not one beer, even for employees. And very self-improving it is, too. Once upon a time I was a nice, clean, normal American boy—a couple martinis before dinner and that was it. In two short months he's got me up to a fifth a day. I'm hiding bottles in my parachute like W. C. Fields." Grinning ferociously, he steered his sickly face even closer. "But go on, list his other good points. He loves his country as much as his oil company—almost. What else?"

"Ssh! Will you be quiet? Just be patient—the moon is full; I'll let you go out and drink blood tonight." He started a Bela Lugosi-vampire imitation, but Silverman turned a dark look on him and he collapsed. "Well," Werden said unhappily, "you still have to admire the Senator's qualities. He knows what he wants and gets it."

"That he does. He's got forty-five million dollars, a sixty thousand-acre ranch, eleven different companies, *and* an ego exactly the size of the United States and still growing. Do you believe in Anti-Christ? Just look at his record in the Senate: he's voted against the widows and orphans every time." Silverman was gasping with fury, his voice squeaked into the muffling, woolly roar of the motors. "Need I say he's against the nuclear test pact? I've seen the oration the old boy is going to deliver in San Francisco after he stops at your mill. He's saying about Viet Nam what he said about Korea—it's the same old song, music to end the world by."

Werden sat with his red face pressed in his hands. Silverman was no decoy sheep, he was a maniac, frothing at the mouth as he spewed out all the anger he'd had to keep hidden for months, all that he had to put into the biography and all that he couldn't. Now he remembered Silverman's name. Before he'd sunk to ghosting, he'd written a couple of sorehead plays that flopped. The only way to soften him up and maybe get a little help was to take potshots at the Senator, too.

Instead, he found himself mumbling cautiously, "Well, I'm no political thinker. I mean . . . there's something to be said for both—it's a point of view."

"So is pederasty or fascism," Silverman sneered, but then the cramp smoothed out of his unhealthy, clever face. "But there *is* hope, oh world, oh time. White spent two million dollars at the last convention, trying to get the nomination, and struck out with the delegates loaded. Remember? He set up that log cabin in a hotel lobby and passed out coonskin caps—you know, the Daniel Boone image, with a little railsplitter thrown in. And he would have been nominated next time for sure—only he won't live that long," Silverman held up two fingers. "Two coronaries in the last six months."

But Werden wasn't listening. Just because it was the worst possible thing that could happen, he suddenly believed that Senator White *was* a mankiller. his mushrooming terror screamed inside him—you're next! It's all over!

"God damn it," he bleated, almost weeping. "So that's why he's carrying a bombardier on this plane. Abel to Red Rooster, Abel to to Red Rooster; the flack is getting heavier. Where's the target?" His pink elastic face was working, and he was Gregory Peck in *Twelve O'clock High;* he was Van Johnson in *Thirty Seconds over Tokyo,* skittering wildly out of control, his voice babbling, snarling, whining with pain and shock, quavering into song, "Coming in on a wing and a prayer . . ." "Do you know any prayers?"; "Sure I do." And in a moist little sing-song, joining his hands, he lisped, "Now I lay me down to sleep. God bless Mommy and . . ."

Silverman shook his arm. "Snap out of it, soldier. Okay, it's my turn to be chaplain now; let's hear it."

"Huh?" He swallowed painfully. "Okay, sure. I know I can trust you. I even admire you. I wish I was noble and honest and true—sort of. You can't expect too much."

Silverman was waiting but nothing would come out, not a word. He told himself he was being morbid, stupid, but it didn't make any difference how safe it was, or how necessary, he never could bring himself to let go of any private information. It was a disease that had spread and spread in the years of brutal competition until he was eaten away, nerves, guts, brains and all. Gloomily he turned and stared out at the motor slugging in the strong headwind. The desolate countryside slipped under the wing—immense crumpled distances lumpy with hills and torn with gullies and dry watercourses.

"All right," Silverman said disgustedly. "Forget it."

"No, no. Please! You see, Dr. Christian, it's like this." In despair he swelled up and hunched into a kindly simper. "Scpeak up, my childt. Don't be afraid. You don't eat good, und you don't sleep?" Clucking his tongue, he applied a make-believe stethoscope to his own fatty stomach, listened, and then grunted. "Oho! I zee. Vell, I tell you. You haff a baby in your tummy. Sure, I can tell. Tvins, maybe." But even as he twinkled and nodded benevolently, his face twisted and the parody splintered into grief. "What I've got is a knife in my back."

"What you've got," Silverman said, "is bad trouble at National Mining, Incorporated, and the Senator owns forty per cent of it."

"You knew all the time?" He groaned, and the words spilled out; he was telling everything. "This has got me by the short hair, it really has. I bust a nut working up to western manager of NMI, I'm responsible for all three uranium operations, and old J. C. Lochran told me he was stepping up to chairman of the board in a couple of years, which is practically saying I'm the next president. It's like I'm really there at last, no more sweat. Listen, if I get belted now, I couldn't take it. I don't know, every time you hit the ground you bounce a little less higher."

He sat there, a big soft growth in the blue plush seat, getting pinker and softer and dimmer, blurring with terrible memories. "Listen, when I was twenty-two, I was making fourteen thousand a year, and that was real money back in those days. Then wham-bam, the lights go out. But I knew some pretty big people, and one way and another I get into promoting stocks. And I make a bundle of money at uranium and lose it all—boy, you talk about chicanery in this world. So anyway, when the stocks went blooey, I angled myself into the corporation side of it. I wanted a safe, regular life, especially for my wife's sake. Boy, safe! How's that for irony?"

"I hear the Securities Exchange Commission pays you a yearly stipend to stay out of promoting. Is that true?"

"No, not quite. The widows and orphans send me the money directly," he said huffily, very offended. "It means opening a lot of letters but—seriously, though, that's why I've got the bloody sweats. It's in my craw, I can taste it. I'm knocking at that Big Door again— for the last time. And what happens? They built the Wyoming mill in the wrong place—*they,* not me, you understand. So now the area is mined out and we have to ship the ore in from Utah, and there go the profits. Every day I take a bath in my own sweat. And then to top it off, all hell has busted loose at the Enterprise mill. The captive mine that supplies eighty per cent of the mill load comes up with this terrific artesian water problem. My God, we have to bail it out like a sinking ship! Down goes our production. A million and a half a year is going out with the tide."

"And for that kind of money, White would poison a nunnery."

"Don't I know it, and I've just taken the veil." He glanced back at the Senator's office and jerked around again. All at once he reverted to suspiciousness. "Boy, have I talked to you! If you're thinking of telling teacher on me, just remember I'll spill liquor on your nightie and tell him you swore—but I know you wouldn't do that, I was only kidding. I'm practically out of my mind." A small tremor stitched in his neck as he pleaded, "Have you heard anything? What can I do? How can I reach him? I'm good at shining shoes—with my tongue if necessary. In fact, I do a better job that way."

"All I know," Silverman said, "is that one of those oil company execs briefed him, and somebody is going to pay the supreme penalty."

Bob Werden swayed his tall head back and forth, tragically.

"But let me give you some advice, stop looking so scared. The Senator is basically a simple man: he thinks a scared look means guilt *and* inadequacy *and* maybe treason."

Just then the Senator's secretary came up the aisle with the deadly, quiet importance peculiar to Harvard underlings. Werden froze but the secretary went past them, wagging his chunky thighs, and on into the cockpit. In a few minutes he returned. His dumpling face was very grave as he hurried back to the office.

"Mr. Werden?" he called, almost immediately.

"I wonder what's up?" he hissed, jumping to his feet with an electric smile. "Well, here I go, and Justice triumphs again." He walked stiffly down the aisled, his glance sticking to the framed photograph by the door: the President and Senator White at the Senator's ranch, posed with a lunking, powerful, sex-dangling prize bull. There was only one chance, he decided. If he dropped a word about the *real* Lennie Silverman, maybe, just maybe, he could get off the chopping block himself. It was a dirty trick, but the writing job was a short term proposition for him . . .

The secretary motioned him into the tiny, crowded office, hardly more than a flying closet. The Senator opened his eyes and rubbed them, yawning like a tired child. He was obviously very ill. The flesh seemed to be coming loose on his face and his reddened eyes were swamped in limp, purplish lids.

But then his voice came crashing out of that feebleness, loud and hoarse, scraping irritably. "Why doesn't the airport reply to our radio?"

Werden felt the blood go out of his face. Rubbing at the twitch in his neck, he explained that Enterprise didn't really have much of an airport, just a couple of broken-down shacks and a runway or two.

"Why wasn't I informed?" White demanded. "I don't suppose you have the slightest idea how long the runways are? And you didn't bother to check?"

Werden fumbled out of the office without having had a chance to bring up Silverman. And actually he was glad—remembering other crises and other frantic treacheries—that he didn't have this one on his conscience, too. It couldn't have helped anyway.

"I'm defunct," he said as he sat down by Silverman again. "I knew I was dead all along, I could see the handwriting on the wall: *J. H. loves M. L., Kilroy was here, For a good lay call AL 7-4333 and ask for Janice.* I can see it coming," he babbled and deepened his voice into thunder: "Foxgrove, you will find a week's wages at the cashier's desk." Then, in agony, he burst out, "How in hell am I to blame for the airport being abandoned? Coming here was his two-thousand-watt idea, not mine."

"Take it easy."

"Are you nuts, take it easy? I've just been kicked in the jewel box and you say take it easy. Look, you've got to tell me what to do. You're my friend, and boy, I really need a friend today." His pale eyes were woozy and slick, begging. "Do you like me?" he asked.

Silverman laughed out loud. "Really and truly," he said. "Especially when you're Dr. Christian or Baby Snooks." Werden flushed, and Silverman added mildly, "You will admit you're sort of like protoplasm, the way you change."

"That's me, all right," he said, dejected. "Protoplasm. A blob. Mr. Jello. I never thought of it that way." But he was deeply hurt and hate suddenly exploded inside him, murderous. "Now do me one more favor. Just stay away from me."

Silverman merely grinned. Werden moved across the aisle by himself and looked out the window, frowning and sullen. Far down under the beating propeller, the rough brown grazing land was smudged with flying dust. To the north the starved hills and gullies swelled and heaved up into mountains: the Black Hills. Then they were circling Enterprise and the pine-bristling slopes were broken open with old dead uranium mines like unhealed sores, abscesses. Whole canyons were infected with mines leaking pale yellow spills of rubble.

In a minute they were losing altitude, sinking down over a flat-topped butte, and ragged dry pastures were rushing faster and faster underneath. Then the plane settled onto its hurtling shadow, bumping as it trundled down the weed-grown runway.

Henry Knudson, the assistant manager in charge of the mill, popped out from behind the derelict hangar and came scurrying down the dusty wind toward them. Nervously he shook hands with the Senator and everybody else he could reach, including the Senator's bodyguard, and led the way to the waiting cars. Looking at his pinched face, Bob Werden suddenly realized that his own nerves had stopped wrenching and straining. His panic was gone. Somehow Silverman had broken him, finished him off, pushed him over the edge into a deep mournful calm.

The small procession of cars rolled down a hill into the thirsty little cattle town. A corner of buildings in the center of town had burned up years ago and the emptiness gaped like a charred wound. Many of the remaining board-front stores and hotels were silent, locked up and weathering. Looming in the hazy sky behind them was the water tank of the mill, fat-bellied, enormous, bulging on its long metal legs.

Werden had told Henry Knudson to save enough ore to make a good showing, and as they thudded across the railroad tracks and entered the yard, the crusher-tower was grinding satisfactorily, conveyors were spitting ore into trucks, and trucks were backing up a steep incline and dumping fiteen tons of ore at a time. The only flaw was the yawning space where the hills of stockpiled ore had been.

"Damn you! You, Senator White, I mean you!"

They had just climbed out of the cars when a limping, dusty man barged up to them, cursing. He must have been close to seventy, but he was still muscled and powerful, with long heavy arms and brute hands. His grey hair struggled in the cold wind.

"You're making yours, aren't you, Senator?" he shouted. "And the rest of us can go hang."

The man lunged forward dangerously, but White barely glanced up as his bodyguard shouldered between them and roughed him away. The party filed into the crusher-tower. The air was stuffed with noise. Ore went riding up on long conveyors and tumbled into grinding metal jaws, steel troughs snapped upside down. Through a dusty window could be seen the poisonous blue lake of ore washings. Werden knew that the Senator was annoyed at the assault and blamed him and Knudson for it, but he simply wasn't involved anymore. Vaguely he wondered how Sam Bolton had gotten wind that the Senator was coming. Old Sam had been stewing about White for years. At one time he had been the second largest producer in the area, and quite a wolf in his own right too, but then the big, *big* wolves had moved in and made a light lunch of everything in sight, Bolton included. He had even thrown his cattle holdings into the fight for the mill and lost them. Then came the knockout blow—in 1956 the government finally got tired of buying uranium it didn't need and put a lid on production. A cut-off date for buying was set, and quotas were etstablished until then, based on production in 1955. Only Sam hadn't done much mining that year, since he'd had to start over, and so he was stuck with a tiny quota, practically nothing at all. He hadn't taken it lying down, though. He'd even led a group of mine-owners to Washington to argue for the old unlimited purchasing program. Then he'd found out how Senator White had been behind the strikes and construction delays that had caused him to lose the mill. He forgot that he'd been fighting for unlimited buying himself, and he went around spouting how White had grabbed up mills and mines and then pressured the government into extending the cut-off date and buying more and more uranium it couldn't possibly use.

"Yes, yes," the Senator said impatiently. Poor Knudson was rattling production figures into the roaring, acid-stinking air. Huge barrel-sided vats dripped pitchy fluids. Metal blades revolved slowly in grey, sludgy mixtures. "Al right, this is fine," White said, cutting the inspection short.

Knudson trailed after him, making helpless motions at Bob Werden. In the car, he blurted, "I hope the tour wasn't too exhausting. I mean—your heart attack, I hope it wasn't serious, Senator."

"Every heart attack is serious," White snapped. "If it's serious enough, you die." Then he closed his eyes. In the twenty-five miles out to the mine, he opened them only once, to say to his secretary, "I want you to add something to that speech. What this country has to do is export our ideas instead of taking in foreign notions. Develop that— weakening ourselves, and so on."

To Bob Werden in the front seat, it was all unreal: the raging wind, the danger, the Harvard secretary, and the small, tired man in the back who wasn't going to live long. Gravel ticked against the bottom of the car. Disasters of ten and twenty years ago whispered inside him like voices of the dead. The wind was sweeping the hills and sagebrush flats, and far across the empty land, the bottoms of the Cheyenne River smoked with bitter white dust. They rumbled across a wooden bridge. The dry creek bed slashed through red, fleshy-looking clay, and the exposed roots of the cottonwoods along the bank were a horrible red, like blood vessels and torn muscles.

He seemed to be slipping deeper and deeper into nightmare. The plateau was spotted with mounds like great anthills, and somebody said they were discovery holes on blank claims. Way off at the end of the road, ash-colored dumps of clay shouldered up in the blizzard of dust. The mine office was a purple and white trailer squatting by a corrugated iron quonset hut. As they pulled up in front, Werden thought he recognized Sam Bolton's grey panel truck, creeping along behind in the wild dry storm.

Their engineer, Harry Beecher, drove up in a jeep. He had been working out there, sixteen hours a day, for weeks, and his eyes were like red jelly in his dirt-caked, whiskery face. The dust was strangling. Shouting wind-torn explanations, he led them toward the open pit. Oil tanks stood on stilts in the boiling dust. Dry prairie grass hissed and lashed at pieces of dead machinery. Blundering with their heads down and their eyes squinted almost shut, they staggered to the edge of the enormous crater. Radioactive dust whirled up like sulphurous smoke. The sides of the pit broke off straight down, burning red and ash grey, like smouldering ledges of fire. Long yellow streaks, the sign of uranium ore, glowed in the dizzy fall of the cliffs. Far down at the bottom, pumps were chugging and brute-slow earth movers were bailing out the soupy green lake, grunting, squashing in the mud and puffing smoke from their deisel chimneys.

"The pumps can't handle it any more," Beecher shouted. "It's not an artesian spring, it's an underground river. Even with the Euclid double cans bailing it out, we're losing ground."

Senator White looked grim. He told Beecher to get the jeep and, accompanied by two of his oil company executives, went churning down into the smoking red circles of the mine. Knudson whined nervously, "Why did he take those oil execs instead of us?" Werden gave him a vague shrug. He was battered with stinging dust, and his teeth gritted with dirt. He could just make out Sam Bolton hovering in the distance, a dogged and futile spectre, dipping along on his bad leg. He felt as if the cold storm was blowing through his head. Silverman's jeering voice wouldn't stop: "The ninth circle of the Inferno is reserved for traitors, did you know that? They're frozen together and they gnaw and bite each other's heads. Wouldn't it be jolly if the Senator got his balls frozen to Judas Iscariot down there?"

At last the jeep came bouncing and lurching up again and they started back. The Senator, wiping the dust from his glasses, was silent. Even the inside of the car was foggy with dust. The bald plateau seemed to be dim with the smoke of raging fires behind them.

Suddenly the Senator's voice jarred from the back seat, "Get rid of your engineer."

"Yes sir," Werden and Knudson said, at the same time. "Right away."

Werden let out a long, sighing breath and discovered that he was shivering, trembling all over with the shock of relief. The sacrificial victim had been chosen, and it wasn't him! All that detachment, all that calm, flat neutrality, had been nothing but a stupor of despair. Well, he was safe now anyway, home free at last.

And yet, curiously, he didn't feel the happiness he should have. Once in the dear dead days beyond recall, he had made 380,000 dollars with Bert and Wally on one deal, and now here he was, sweating, bleeding inside for a 35,000-dollar-a-year job. But it was more than that: he was drained and sick, used up, and the dreary realization filtered through him that his life had crested and begun to slip downward years ago.

His hands continued to shake, and then he felt a swell of nausea surge up from his stomach. Blurts of acid gushed into his throat. "Stop the car," he said through jammed teeth, and stumbling outside, he bent over by the road and threw up. The two cars following them stopped. Faces stared through the windows. And Bob Werden, the next president of NMI, doubled over in the wind twenty miles from Enterprise, South Dakota, vomiting.

1952

That winter the worst storms of the century hit the West. Mud slides swallowed up homes and streets in California, and blizzards, stampeding over the plains, swept up fifty-foot drifts and cut off dozens of towns. And the war in Korea dragged on, bloody and frustrating, one bitter hill at a time, while the truce talks lagged and Jacob Malik accused the United States of germ warfare. Johnny Ray's "Cry" sold a million copies in two months.

Already in January and February, "I Like Ike" buttons were popping up all over the country, though Eisenhower was still in command of NATO in Europe and not officially a candidate. Tony Bennett was the new idol of the bobby soxers, *The Lone Ranger* was in its twentieth year on radio, and *Quo Vadis*, with Robert Taylor and Deborah Kerr, was making the rounds of the movie houses. But television was mushrooming stupendously: it seemed as if everybody was watching "I Love Lucy" and "Robert Montgomery Presents," and Hollywood was already staggering into heavy losses and reorganizations.

Without warning, Batista seized Cuba. In the sandhills of western Nebraska, a ranch hand ran amok and shot the owner of the ranch and his wife, then roamed aimlessly over the countryside, stealing cars and killing until he was trapped in a burning barn and riddled with bullets by a posse of a hundred ranchers. Pierre, South Dakota, was five feet under water. As the spring sun melted the snowcover, the Missouri and Mississippi rivers flooded and heaved up enormous tides of water that poured over a dozen states, crushing highways and bridges, displacing more than a hundred thousand people and drowning millions of acres.

Estes Kefauver and Adlai Stevenson were battling for the Democratic nomination; Senator Robert Taft was campaigning with skill and determination for the Republican nomination, but Eisenhower's popularity was snowballing irresistibly. Meanwhile the AEC announced a fifth great uranium plant would be built in the Ohio River valley, and a few days later an atom test at Yucca Flat was shown on nationwide television for the first time. All over the West, in South Dakota, in Utah and the Colorado plateau, uranium prospectors were charging into areas and back out again in furious stampedes.

It was a year of terror. Haunted by the atomic bomb and international tension, the nation reeled in a nightmare of investigation. "Loyalty," "treason," "fellow traveller"—the words thickened in the air like ghosts. Communist infiltration of government had become an obsession and Senator Joe McCarthy was one of the most powerful men in America, the high priest of a grotesque modern witch hunt. It was plain that nothing short of war could have prevented the loss of China to communism, but scapegoats in the government were accused of giving China away deliberately out of communist sympathy. The State Department denied Owen Lattimore a passport, basing its action on the lies of an informer, and then had to retract and apologize publicly. Indignant, he called it "midsummer madness" and "government-by-informer," but the pillorying went on. Nobody was safe. Shielded by senatorial immunity, McCarthy accused General George Marshall himself of traitorous motives.

Like an epidemic, the search for subversives and fellow travellers spread into every walk of life, and the list of persons before congressional investigating committees grew longer and longer. It was the age of the loyalty oath, of the smear, of the spy and the book-burner, but a few spoke out courageously. Humorist James Thurber growled, "The blatherskites. The end of American comedy is in sight and the theatre's gone to hell. Who can write when everybody's scared? I hate communism but I happen to be on one of those letterheads with Paul Robeson— and I'm not getting off. I'm not letting any congressman scare me to death." And Adlai Stevenson, refusing to play safe, gravely injured his chances for the presidency by repeatedly speaking out in his campaign against "the pursuit of phantoms among ourselves."

But week by week the infection spread and the fever mounted. The country was swept by crazes. All that spring, panty raids broke out in colleges from Maryland to California, wild riots with fire hoses and shrieks, tear gas, looting and broken windows. Juke boxes wailed "Kiss of Fire." The sweltering summer nights were lit up by flying saucers, hovering discs and streaking balls of light, like apocalyptic signs in the delirious sky. And in Korea, a soldier was found two hundred yards from the nearest dressing station, crying from the bloody sockets where his eyes had been shot out.

I

(June, 1952)

"State your business," the dim old voice shrilled from inside.

"We'd like to talk to you, sir."

"For just one minute?" Both of the young men pleaded through the door of the grey, disintegrating house. They were scorched and dusty, wearing green sunglasses, khaki shirts and shorts, and heavy shoes. Their jeep was standing in the vague dirt road that straggled off to the highway.

"Talk? What about?" Without waiting for an answer, the voice spat, "Get off my property . . . trying to cabbage onto information, that's all you're doing . . . snooping . . . damnable goings on." The ill-tempered voice faded out.

'Fungoo," Stan said, disgusted. "We'd need a wooden horse to get in there. Let's go."

"And walk up and down twenty-five miles of canyon, blind? You're mad." The other young man knocked again and cocked his bearded face, listening. "Is this your famous western hospitality?" he called. "All I want is a drink of water for my tubercular brother here."

"It's no use, Ted. He's heartless."

Ted glowered at the door and said, "I must warn you, sir, that I will use force if necessary—I'll huff and I'll puff and I'll blow your house in."

Struggling with laughter, they prowled around the withered shack, trying to see through the dirt-blind windows and gasping piteously, "Just a cup of water! Please, sir!" The hot bare yard was cluttered with rusting tools, a grindstone and a snaggle-toothed hayrake. Deserted pastures, broken and dry and clotted with greasewood, stretched out under the heat-whitened sky.

At last Stan said, "Come on, let's bazoom out of here. I've got to make my fortune by the end of June. I took a vow."

"That sort of talk is aid and comfort to the enemy, chum. He can be reached, if we bear down with the I.Q." Stan groaned, but Ted held up his hand. "To wit. The old boy is the town history expert and pot-hunter—he's messed up grave sites for fifty miles around picking up arrowheads. All we have to do is let him know we're fellow scientists and he'll—ugh!—eat out of our hands."

"Theodore, you're a genius. We're unstoppable."

"Precisely." Smirking, he preened his thick black whiskers. His sunglasses flashed. "The world—to put it in terms you can comprehend—will be our nipple." Confidently, he pounded on the door and called, "Mr Butler? I don't think you understood us. We're from the dig by the Cheyenne River? Sponsored by the Smithsonian Institute?"

The door screeched open, and a wispy old man peered out, blinking. Little horns of hair curved from his nostrils, and his loose-skinned neck dropped into a yawning, yellowish collar. "The Smithsonian?" he said doubtfully.

"That's correct, sir," Teddy said, brisk, dignified. "We're college students excavating the Indian village on the Cheyenne. This is our day off, and we'd heard of you, of course, and your work."

The old man, fluttering apologies, scrambled to let them in. "You're the ones digging on Sam Bolton's ranch? Well, well." His tiny bleached eyes were shining, and he waved a trembling hand at the two musty rooms jammed with his precious collections. "This is only part of it, there's more out in the barn—The Smithsonian, eh? Well, well," he said, scraping his hands together. "I guess you're thinking that was a pretty strange reception, but I've been run off my feet by snoopers—"

"Think nothing of it."

"Yes sir, this is a pleasure I never expected, boys. I gave up dickering with the Smithsonian long ago. We just never hit it off. To give you the plain facts of it, they never respected me. I've been exploring these hills for sixty years, and I know things they never even dreamed of, but they wouldn't give me a look-in. I was just a damn fool country school teacher to them."

"I understand, sir," Ted said, twitching a wink at Stan. "This is confidential, of course, but the Smithsonian *is* a bit stuffy. Hard to deal with."

"Eaten up with bureaucracy," Stan added gravely. "Simply eaten up."

"God bless you. I sure thank you." Dazed and blissful, the old man resurrected an old suit coat in honor of their visit and began showing off his treasures: a broken gramophone and a pile of hit records from the dark ages; a lamp with a stained-glass shade and dozens of other pieces rescued from homesteaders' cabins; boxes of arrowheads and shattered Indian pottery; gaudy twenty-five-cent souvenirs from Mt. Rushmore; a coyote skin with green marbles for eyes, glowing dustily in the shadows; whole bins of different colored rocks; a stack of *National Geographic* magazines; and at least three pails of fossilized bones.

"Superb! Magnificent!" the boys exclaimed, their eyes wide with

Uranium! 15

sardonic awe. Big and sweaty and tramping, they followed the frail, shrunken little man around as he rummaged in his dusty junk.

"Now here's quite a curiosity," he said. Blowing soft explosions of dust from a chunk of pink quartz, he held it up to the churning light for them to admire. "You'd be welcome to have it. Go ahead, put it in your pocket," he insisted. "You know, this is a real treat for me, talking to professionals like you for a change. A real treat . . . yes sir."

Mumbling in ecstasy, he led them to a miniature stockade of varnished twigs, poking up a grimy tag for a flag, which he asserted was the spit image of General Custer's encampment. "It took first place at the Fall River County Fair," he said proudly.

"Is that a fact?" Ted said. Stan whispered, "Ask him how his pies and cakes did," but Ted elbowed him away and said, "You have a regular museum here, Mr. Butler."

"Well, there you hit the nail on the head, boys. That's my goal, what we're aiming at. All we need is a decent building and someone—oh Charley!" he called.

A ten-year-old Indian boy appeared silently in the door of the kiitchen. Shaggy and brown, he simply stared when the old man told him to say hello to the scientists. Instead of going back into the kitchen, he stayed right there, motionless, watching.

"Charley's helping me," the old man confided. "Since my health broke down, I have to spend the winters at the VA hospital in Hot Springs. He keeps an eye on the place while I'm gone, and when I'm here, I teach him where everything in the hills is and what it means. You see, it's pretty late in the day for me; I don't have a lot longer to go, and all that knowledge mustn't be lost."

"It would be a tragedy," Stan said, and Ted agreed. "We have to think of future generations."

"That's it," he said eagerly, stretching out his veined and shaking hand. "Boys, if you would talk to your superiors and tell them about me. It's all right here, in my head and on those oilcloth rolls you see over there. Charley's a good boy; it beats the world the memory he's got, but there's things that need a scientist . . . discoveries, places . . . you know." He lapsed for a moment. His eyes twitched shut, and the shadows seemed to deepen in his scooped-out face. But then he rallied and said, "I'm willing to prove myself. Anything I could show you boys or explain, I'm at your service. Is that fair enough?"

"Good deal, sir," Teddy said, thinking fast. "Could we take a look at the pictographs in Red Canyon? We hear you're an authority on them."

The old man jumped at the chance. "I'm not bragging on myself, but I'm the only one that knows where all those Indian writings are and what they mean. But the Smithsonian wasn't interested, and what could I do? Just smile and keep on taking it."

"Righto, courage and all that. Stiff upper lip." Jubilantly, they hustled the old man and Charley into the jeep and took off for the canyon. Stan began to sing, "A-hunting we will go," but Teddy elbowed him in the ribs. Pitching in the seat and holding onto his grey hat, the old man kept up a rapid fire of information, trying to impress them. "All this was under water forty million years ago," he said. "It was part of a great big shallow sea with dinosaurs splashing around in the marshy places. Two ounces of brain in a twenty-ton body. I've got some of their bones in my barn."

"You don't say."

"The Black Hills over there aren't much to look at, but they'll surprise you. Yes sir. They were here before the Rockies and the Alps. They were old mountains when the Himalayas were nothing but a swamp. You notice how round they are?" Feverishly, he insisted that they look at the pine-darkened hills off to the north. "You see? That's why the technical name for them is dome mountains. They were pushed up like huge blisters by the molten lava underneath."

"Well I'll be jingoed," Teddy said, but in spite of himself he was impressed. Butler might be feeble and a little bit senile, but he was still a pretty sharp old bird and he might not be so easy to handle after all. And the Indian kid was no help, period. Every time he glanced at little Hiawatha, he knocked against a steady, black stare of suspicion and hate.

As they whipped into Red Canyon, he said casually, "There's uranium around here somewhere, isn't there?"

"There's all kinds of minerals. Feldspar and mica. Alum. The Indians used to come here to cure their animal skins with it." He rambled on about Indians and Teddy looked at him, unable to tell if the old geezer was stalling deliberately or not.

The hot clay road turned pink and the canyon wound in and out, twisting, throwing up high cliff faces of red and yellow above the somber pines. Doves blew up from the sagebrush with a sound like plucked wires. A few dusty cattle, as red as the canyon walls, bumped heavily away from the road, rocking on their short legs.

"Whoa! There's a batch of them right up there." The old man stretched his arm up at the glaring, furnace-red cliff. They stopped the jeep, but he said he had to have a little rest before he started, and fanning himself with his hat, he wobbled toward the shade of some thirsty old cottonwoods by the creek. The gnawed-off grass was spattered with cow plats. He was circling around the trees, muttering and picking at the bark, when he suddenly noticed a homesteader's cabin, hollow and grey in the ferocious light.

"Right here," he said, all excited. "We came out to this very spot, let's see, fifty-four, no, fifty-five years ago. That was it. Yes sir, fifty-five years ago this very month of June was when I got started on the Indian writings. I remember school was just over and twelve of us came out in a lumber wagon and ate our prime here. The country was green in those days, not like now. What a memory, boys. What a memory."

"Swell, that's just dandy." Unable to wait any more, Stan blundered out, "Don't you have a uranium claim somewhere in this canyon?"

"Um-hum," he said vaguely and walked off toward the ruined cabin, mumbling to himself. "Now you've done it," Teddy hissed. "You've snarfed it up good." Anxiously they went after him, with Charley trotting right behind them like a small, dogged shadow. For a long time the old man gazed at the empty door and windows, at the bleached and shattered roof, at the bristling nails squeezed out of the emaciated boards by seventy years of heat and cold.

All of a sudden he pointed at a row of clay daubs tucked under the edge of the roof.

"Wasp nests," he said in a voice they hadn't heard before, ominously fierce. "Each of these little pots is a tomb and a nest at the same time. The female wasp paralyzes a spider and puts it in there and lays a yellow egg on its breast. In due time a tiny pretty little thing hatches out—like a necklace with thirteen beads. Then it eats the blood and the flesh of the living spider. Afterwards it goes into a cocoon, breaks out and finds a mate, and the cycle starts all over again."

Stan and Teddy gaped. He looked wrathfully at them, his eyes like bitter flames in the darkness under his hat brim.

"That's what life is, boys. It breaks your heart to think about it, but it isn't evil, not in the lower forms. You've got to have consciousness for that. It's man that's evil."

He stamped off, a furious scarecrow in his saggy blue suit and bulging hat. They stared at each other, demolished. "You put the old bastard onto us," Ted whispered. "We've lost him, we're down the tubes." But then, incredibly, he was climbing stiffly up the tumbled boulders toward the pictographs! He was gesturing for them to come on!

They galloped to catch up. Left out, all but forgotten, Charley kept stubbornly at their heels. They offered Mr. Butler and Charley a drink out of their canteen, but Charley just looked at them, clenched like a small brown fist. Squatting down in a crease of shade, he waited while Mr. Butler, panting and swabbing at his face, explained about the straggly lines and circles and dots gouged into the rock. "The experts used to believe these marks were a language, like Assyrian or Egyptian," he said in a wheezing voice. "But it's not so. They're a sort of travel map. These spots here are places where the Indians camped . . ."

He wasn't going to get any quarter today, Charley thought glumly. Mr. Butler always gave him a quarter if he remembered everything he'd told him. Sometimes when it was real hard or when Mr. Butler forgot he'd given him a quarter already, he got two quarters. Buzzards drifted in the hot sky, wheeling in great towering circles as they floated on the updraft from the canyon. He aimed a stick at them and made soft bursting sounds with his mouth, cch! cch!, picking them off expertly, one after another. The men weren't watching him. He swung the stick around, slowly, cautiously, and fired into their large, sun-soaked backs, cch! cch! He wished he had the .22 Mr. Butler had promised him. It would be a cinch to run them off with a .22. He was almost as good a shot as his father. Once, a long time ago before they moved to town, his father was meat hunting for the Pine Ridge reservation and he had killed an elk with a .22 by shooting it twenty times in the head.

Mr. Butler finished explaining and everybody climbed back down to the road. Charley looked hopefully at him but then one of the men said, "Do you know of any other pictographs, sir?" Mr. Butler laughed with pleasure and said, "Boys, I'll take you to another one that nobody knows about except me and Charley."

"That'll be great, sir."

Then Charley felt his heart come up into his throat: instead of getting into the jeep and taking them to one of the pictographs down the road, Mr. Butler was hobbling into the little side canyon called Old Woman's Creek. That was where he and Mr. Butler had their claim. How could he be so dumb? Every two or three days he'd been saying they had to finish exploring and staking the creek before somebody found out where their claim was and staked all around it and maybe took the best uranium. But he was always so busy with his Indian writings and stuff that they hadn't done it yet.

Dodging past the men, he tugged at Mr. Butler's coat. "Let's go home," he said in his blurry, smothered voice. "Mr. Butler? Let's go home, huh?"

"Shut your mouth," the old man said crossly.

Charley sank behind again, his furry head down, scuffing his feet. For just a second he felt like he did when there was going to be a fight after school and he knew he was going to get licked, even before the big kid and his friends came grinning out of the deserted rodeo grounds toward him. But then his mind whirled like a cornered weasel, biting and striking out fiercely, conceding nothing. Anybody could tell that these men didn't care about the Indian writings—anybody but Mr. Butler; he wasn't very smart except about his collections and stuff like that. It was the two men against him, and he trudged up the canyon, wary, alert, figuring, the way he had been prowling the back streets of Enterprise since he was six, foraging and scrounging and running errands, stealing when he had to.

Mr. Butler was beginning to totter wearily but Charley knew he would keep going until he dropped. The smell of sage was thick in the oven-hot ravine. A lizard flicked away like a wink in the stones. There was a puff of dust far up the hill and he saw a hawk drive down at a twisting and swerving rabbit, bounce and skid off into the air. The dry creek bed scrambled upward, closing in on them like a red nightmare, airless, suffocating. His mouth was so dry that he couldn't swallow, but he held his place behind Mr. Butler, watching, and when the man with the pack fell behind and stooped over with his back turned, Charley dropped back too.

"Get moving," the other man said. His friend hastily stuffed the Geiger counter back into the pack, but not before Charley had seen it. They scowled at him, their trickling faces swollen and red under their new straw hats. Without a word Charley turned and jogged after Mr. Butler, his dwarf-like shadow running beside him. Sweat leaked into his eyes. The ravine wrenched sideways and ended in a sun-tortured spill of brush and cactus and rocks, like a long, motionless avalanche.

Halfway up on the left side, where the rocks were barbed with pines, he could see the short wooden stakes of their claim. He tightened his fists.

Exhausted, Mr. Butler paused every few minutes for a rest and a drink from the canteen. His face was sick, mottled with dark red blotches, and his mouth was a mud-crusted slot under his skinny nose. Changing his tactics to annoy the men, Charley accepted the grudging offer of the canteen and took big, sucking swallows of the stale, metal-tasting water. The men winced. Finally one of them growled, "Take it easy, Crazy Horse. That's all we've got."

"My name is Charles Trueblood," he said.

Slowly, they worked their way up toward the rim. The stones were hot to the touch. Every time the man with the pack tried to drop back, Charley stopped in his tracks and the man, glowering savagely, started climbing again. Then they were directly opposite the first stake, only a hundred feet away across the quivering light. Charley felt like the inside of his chest was swelling tighter and tighter.

One of the men halted and jacked his hat back from his red face, glancing around. Instantly Charley kicked some stones loose, sending them bounding and rocketing viciously down at the men.

"Hey, watch it, Crazy Horse," they shouted. "Cut it out!"

"My name is Charles Trueblood," he said.

"I don't give a goddamn what your name is. You knock one more stone down here and you'll be a dead Indian."

His black stare didn't change. He scraped the damp hair from his eyes and plodded upward after Mr. Butler, and slowly, slowly, they left the first stick, and then the second, behind. He was safe for the minute, though he didn't see how he could possibly get the men past the claim again on the way down.

The old man staggered more and more weakly as he neared the top. The cliffs looked like enormous banked fires, torn open in red gashes where coals had slipped and caved down. His heart was banging painfully against his scrawny ribs. A stone raked his leg. Dizzily he looked up at the dead tree on the rim, pinned to the burning sky. There was only about thirty feet to go, but he couldn't make it. Half falling against a boulder, he stared blankly down at Charley and the toiling archaeology students, then far across Red Canyon at the crumbling pinnacles and masses of stone, rearing up like colossal statues of kings. The buzzards were like spots of decay in the blinding white sky. His blood roared in his ears and the black spots whirled faster and faster in the aching light . . .

The boys were helping him up to the rim. One of them was saying something about uranium.

He managed to lift his arm and steer it at the heave of the dessicated land, the long lift into heaped-up piny mountains like cinder piles in the sun. "This country is like the Holy Land," he said in a dry scratch of a voice. "The Red Land of the Phoenicians as it was called. All this around here, I've named all these hills. I call this one Mount Sinai, and there's the Mount of Paran, where the Lord came with ten thousand saints. Over there are the plains of Moab, and yonder is the mountain of Nebo . . ."

His body felt hollow. There was a pain behind his eyes and the hills seemed to be moving in the dazzling light, mounding up and sinking like waves. With a cruel effort, he dragged himself over to the pictographs dug into rotting pink stone.

"I didn't tell you the real meaning of the writings," he said hoarsely. "Look, look here. See? This is the Garden of Eden, and here is Cain and Abel." But the joined circles next to the crude square smeared away before his eyes and he turned helplessly to the shadowy forms of the boys. "I can't make it out too good but it's all here. The story of life from the beginning. Jephtha's daughter . . . the bondage in Egypt. Everything."

Clear and faraway and meaningless, a voice said, "Jesus H. Christ."

Blindly he wandered away from the pictographs. His head felt like it was stuffed with fire, and memories of ten and twenty years ago flickered up like pale flames: the day he had found the prehistoric cave, the first boy who was to carry on his work dying at Pearl Harbor, a corporal in the 29th Division. Way off to the north were the hulking cliffs like stone beasts, like statues of gods staring into miles of dazzling light.

"That isn't all," he said in a harsh whisper. "This is the rock in the desert land where the hand of the Lord shall take hold on judgement. Death and hell will be loosed, and power be given unto them over a fourth part of the earth." His excitement gave him a brief strength and his voice rose in a dry, chanting shriek. "Nation shall rise against nation and the sun shall be blackened. Then shall the heavens pass away with a great noise, and the foundations of the mountains be set on fire, and the sea become as blood."

The two young men looked at each other.

"What the hell is he? The Wandering Jew?"

"The professor has blown a fuse," Teddy said, but he was shaken by the deep crack of senile lunacy that had opened up in the old man. His earlier explanation of the pictographs had been so sound.

"This here safari has sure gone to hell," Stan grumbled. Setting down the pack, he gulped from the canteen and wiped his mouth on his sleeve. "Well, what now, genius?"

"Get him back to the jeep somehow. That's all we can do."

Frail and shrunken in his blue suit, he thrashed his dry, weightless hands. His eyes were like holes in the sweaty ruts of his face, and his dry voice whispered of the beast whose breath was fire, of the woman in the heavens who was with child and crying in her travail, of the gathering of the nations to Armageddon.

"That's dandy preaching, Pops," they said. "So let's go, huh?"

Unnoticed, Charley had sneaked closer and closer to them. Suddenly, in one motion, he grabbed the pack and threw it into the ravine—a hundred feet straight down. With a sickening bump, it hit the rocks.

For an instant the boys were rigid with horror. Then they yelled, "You little bastard! You dirty little bastard!"

Charley crouched on the edge of the sheer drop, small and brown, like a hole punched out of the sunlight. They lunged toward him but he made no attempt to escape, and they skidded to a halt, baffled, swearing futilely.

"You're gonna pay for that Geiger—your parents or somebody. You little bastard! That's a hundred and fifty bucks we want from somebody." They wheeled on the old man and shouted at him, whacking their hats against their legs, but he only croaked tiredly to himself. Charley, moving over beside him, stared at them with simple, concentrated hate. At last they gave up in disgust and said, "Okay, God damn it, let's get back to the jeep."

"Go away," Charley said.

"Now look, Crazy Horse—yeah, we know, we know, it's Trueblood—it would be a pleasure to leave you out here, nothing could please us more. So just don't push your luck." But nothing could budge him. "All right, have it your way," they said finally. "You and the prophet can sit there." After another argument, this time between themselves, they left the canteen and went clumping off.

Little by little the clash of rocks and the angry voices faded out down the ravine. Charley sat Mr. Butler down in the shade and waited, squatting on his heels. For a while the old man muttered to himself, trumpets still sounded in his crumbling mind and the world was coming to an end, but gradually the monstrous visions dimmed from his eyes and he was quiet.

"Where did the boys go?" he asked then.

In his breathless jabber Charley told him what had happened.

"Did you see the Geiger counter? It was like ours, you're sure?" He was overwhelmed with disappointment. "Nothing that glistens is gold, is it?" he said drearily. "Nothing at all. The Smithsonian don't care, they were just after the uranium like all the others. I should have suspicioned it, but my mind was so busy—the damned government," he burst out. "I send an ore sample to Rapid City to get analyzed, and the next thing I know it's in the Sunday papers."

But it was only a ghost of his usual indignation, melting in the black rush of grief. The Smithsonian wasn't interested. He was done for.

"They thoroughly well made a fool of me, all right. Did they laugh at me? Doubtless, they did. I was just an old nut to them." It was the final agony to think of them buttering him up slyly, jeering at him while his back was turned, the arrogant young men with their inexhaustible energy, rutting, cheerful, invincible. "I was just a set-up to them. A joke."

Charley said, "They didn't find out nothing."

But the old man was sick at heart, and for a long time he couldn't appreciate what Charley had done. "Why, I led them right up our canyon," he said in despair. "I'm a fool. . . . And you still outfoxed them? By yourself? You're a God's wonder, Charley. A God's wonder." Weakly, humbly, he clutched at the tough, shrewd life pushing up in this little weed of a boy. "I'm wore out," he said. "My day is over but—will you stick with me?"

Charley nodded. "Sure."

The old man dragged himself painfully to his feet and looked down at the shaggy child, drinking in hope from the fierce intention he saw in the sweat-traced brown features.

"You're my trump card, Charley. With you alongside of me, we're not beat yet. No sir. We'll give them a run for their money," he said with all, or almost all, of his former spirit. He put on his hat. "We don't need the Smithsonian, we'll set up our own museum in town. I just have a hunch this uranium is gonna come through for us. Tell you what, we'll stake out the canyon tomorrow if I'm able."

He was faint and his head ached but he took the first broken, pulling steps toward home, two miles away across country. "It's gonna have to be easy stages," he said, "and plenty of them."

"Mr. Butler?" Charley said and scratched himself, mumbling. "My sister's having a birthday party."

He understood immediately what Charley meant, and fumbling in his pocket, he brought out a quarter. Charley's eyes pulsed open and deep with happiness, and they trudged off together through the merciless sunlight, the old man leaning an arm over the boy's shoulder.

II

Teetering up, blundering and grabbing, little Jeffrey reached the handle of the cupboard door and hauled himself onto his bare feet. The door swung open with his toppling weight but he managed to hold on and stagger upright. A wild, witless look of pleasure swam on his face. He patted the shelf and then began to clutch at plates and cups and drag them out, crashing, bursting into pink and white scatters on the floor. His mother darted at him, screeching, and slapped his hand. His mouth pulled down and he howled. Stricken at what she'd done, she cuddled him until they were both comforted and he smiled back at her, his five toofies gleaming in flows of saliva. As soon as she set him down again, he crawled back toward the cupboard, an almost bald little force, making intent snorting noises. "Jeffrey!" she warned for the twentieth time, "I'll blister you." Sighing, she went back to peeling potatoes into a dishpan full of water.

"Vivie runs off and I have to do for everybody," she said, looking helplessly at the clock. The low-ceilinged old kitchen of the ranch house swarmed around her. Dogs panted on the floor. On the radio, Arthur Godfrey was whanging the banjo. Her two sticky-faced blonde girls pattered in and out, squabbled over a doll, and left it on the floor with its dress flopped up over its face and its naked legs sprawled out. Flies whirled in the air. A soft-furred puppy vibrated clumsily when she told it to move and five minutes later was sleeping in tender, infantile abandon right in the path to the sink. A little wet tail of hair hung down from its belly, and her hectic look, flicking over the messy room, found the fresh puddle in a corner.

"You stinky dink! Mamma, he killed my guppy!" Debbie, her eight-year-old daughter, burst into the kitchen, followed sheepishly by her cousin Dean. She had a jar of tiny fish in her hands, and she wailed, "Mamma, he peed in the jar and killed the black one. My favorite one!" The childhood crisis swirled up with outraged squalls and subsided at last, the screen door whacked shut, and then she smelled butane gas: Jeffrey had turned on one of the stove burners. "You little dickens!" she cried and glanced again at the clock. Oh dear, the men would be coming in for noon dinner in forty-five minutes and nothing was done, nothing at all was ready. Almost weeping, she sank down on a chair and picked up Jeffrey and laid her small, plain, tired face against his cheek.

But then the jeep grumped into the yard, and in a moment Vivian Bolton came in and went tearing through the confusion. While she boiled the filling for the chocolate pies, she set Dean to beating the egg whites and Debbie to laying the table. "And get those dogs out of here," she ordered. Jeffrey was penned behind two chairs in a corner and the littlest girls told to keep him in there. Screaming with rage, he crashed himself against the chairs like a tiny cyclone.

Irene yearned to go to him but she knew better with Vivie there. "You see what he's like," she whined. "He run me crazy all morning long, getting into everything."

Vivie gave her daughter-in-law a look of contempt and said, "Cut the potatoes small so they'll cook quicker. We'll mash them."

In less than ten minutes the pie filling was cooling in the shells she had baked before breakfast and she was frying hamburger, swooping around in a haze of savoury cooked beef and onions. Irene looked at her humbly. Even in her dusty bluejeans and blouse smudged on the breasts with dirt, Mrs. Bolton was a great lady. It was her spirit and her flying energy and her enthusiasm, like a kind of glory. Bearing and raising eight children hadn't whipped her down one bit, and she was just as beautiful as she ever was, only dried in a little around the eyes and mouth.

Irene took hold and between them they were almost ready by the time Sam Bolton came in. He dropped an absent-minded kiss on Vivie's neck and sat down at the table, his packed shoulders hanging, his sun-cured face grim with fatigue. Immediately, he was so overrun with children, tumbling and grappling onto him and climbing into his lap, that active little arms and legs seemed to be growing out all over him. The sticky blonde girls put ragged teddy bears and pipe-stem princesses into his hands. Jeffrey, butting out of his prison, crawled across the floor to him with a drooling smile. "Hello there, stud," Sam said, picking him up.

As the sweet fresh life nuzzled and jumped around him, the harsh lines eased out of his heavy jaws and his leaning red forehead. His work-rubbed hands were gentle.

Vivie was quick to take advantage of the opportunity. "Sam?" she said from the stove. "Could you spare me a little time this afternoon?"

"I don't know. I got a load of water out there now, and another one to get. The summer range is about dried out."

"All I want is an hour or so. Sam? Just come over and look at it."

"Umm." The hard strain had come back into his face and he played with the children vaguely.

"Listen to me," she insisted. "There's gobs of uranium over there, I'm sure of it, and it's in the national forest. Anybody can take their pick and the government is paying a fortune for it. They're paying thirty-two dollars a ton for low-grade ore and a ten-thousand-dollar reward for a good discovery! The Rapid City paper said so. Sam? And it don't cost a thing except a little time and a dollar to file a claim."

"Unhuh," he said. "Do you know where those two pieces of pipe went that were laying by the barn? I think I can make a cattle oiler that won't sag."

"Oh *you*!" she fumed. It made her so mad. Here was this wonderful lovely thing, the world was shooting off like stars and Roman candles right under his nose, and he just *wouldn't* see it. She'd been begging and begging him for weeks but it was Sam's nature to do one thing at a time—harder and better than anyone else but only one thing. Right now he was ranching, fighting the drought for all he was worth. By herself she couldn't do much and meanwhile time was slipping away, King Midas's fortune right there and slipping away because she simply *couldn't* get him interested. It was like trying to turn a river . . .

Her hands scurried even faster with exasperation. She made fresh coffee, opened jars of canned beans and tomatoes, and spooned the meringue onto the pies in rich white swells that curled at the tip into hooks, then whipped the pies into the oven. Sam, his large hands plastered on his knees, was brooding in the tangle of children.

"Daddy?" She went over to him and took him by the ears to make him look at her. "Sam, you've just *got* to help me before it's too late. I saw old Zeke Butler and two of those archaeology boys jeeping into Red Canyon yesterday. They're grabbing it all up while you set there on the flat of your butt."

But he didn't answer, and his blind look was more frustrating than a hundred refusals. Her aging lovely face swamped with violence, her brown arms cocked out from her hips. "Well God darn you," she blazed. "It's me, Sam Bolton. I'm talking to you, and I expect to be listened at, old buddy. I mean it, I plainly can't stand it, Sam. There's gonna be a war around here if you keep doing me like this."

He stared right through her spitting attack. She slammed the food on the table and yanked the pies out of the oven. From the wash house attached to the kitchen came a jumble of voices, sloshing water, and the screek-screek of the pump; then her three boys trooped in bringing a dusty breath from the heated land outside, mixed with the smell of sweat and freshly cut hay.

"You been walking the hills again with that Geiger, Mamma?" they teased her.

"I most certainly have," she snapped.

Two of them, Billy Joe and Frank, were good, quiet, hard-working boys, but Pierce was just the opposite, a constant and continuous whiner, and immediately he started complaining about the poor hay crop and the heat and the rattlesnakes. Even as a boy, he wouldn't fight but snitched and whimpered till she despised the very sight of him. "That stinking, rotten tractor," he said, his cooked red face knotting up fretfully. "It wouldn't run thirty minutes before it gave out again, and I had to cobble it back together. The stinking . . . It's enough to give you the bloody piles."

Irene gulped, afraid to cross her husband by protesting.

"I won't have that kind of talk in front of the children, Pierce," Vivie said sharply. "All right, everybody set down."

Sam went to clean up, and while he was out in the wash house Pierce grumbled, "I don't see why he won't leave us have a plane. The Petersons have one, all the modern outfits do. Damn it, you need a plane to check the stock with, instead of busting your guts for thirty miles in a jeep." Frank simply listened to him, apart, sitting in a kind of special atmosphere of his own, but Billy Joe was nodding in agreement. "Just once in my life," Pierce said, "I'd like to see Daddy turn loose of a nickel. Just once. It would break his penny-pinching heart. All he can ever say is bad times and the herd is cut down to the bone till I'm sick to my stomach of hearing it. He's got us rupturing ourselves and sweating off our gutfat . . ."

"That's enough, you shut up that whining," Vivie stormed at him. She might be as mad as the devil at Sam herself but she wasn't going to listen to this. "You're twenty-seven years old but you're not a man, little sonny, and you won't never be one. So just you don't go talking about a man, because you haven't got any right. You smart off one more time, just one more, and you can start packing."

"Maybe I will," Pierce blustered. "I've got a mind to leave out right now, in the middle of haying, and get me a construction job."

"Hop to it," she said, and hurriedly he lowered his head over his plate. During the meal she made no attempt to eat or help with the noisy little children. This new commotion with Pierce had sent her blood running even faster, warming, humming in her ears, and she felt herself lifting higher and higher into dizzy, pounding lightness. Her breathing came shallow and quick. She watched Sam push food into his huge, swallowing mouth.

At last, stretching their arms and lighting cigarettes, the boys ambled out of the kitchen. Sam picked up his stained hat and, just as if nothing at all had happened, put his hand on her shoulder and bent to kiss her cheek.

She smashed the hand away.

Blood gorged his already flushed eyes and he leaned forward with his ragged teeth showing. A great flame of erotic anger swept between them. "Help yourself," she flashed at him, daring him to hit her. She felt light, burning, suspended in high, pure rage. "Go ahead, help yourself. I'll get you back, I guarantee you, if I'm to die for it."

He picked up his hat and glowered at her.

"You sorryass old rancher," she taunted him. "Go play nurse-maid to them old cows. Thirty years of brow-sweating toil and what have we got to show for it?"

"Seventy thousand acres, that's what."

"And one truckload of water. You better hurry up. Go ahead, I bet your old cows are thirsty."

He made a choked sound, then turned and went out with his heavy arms dangling. Slowly the haze cleared from his eyes. He looked at the small tight barns, the cars and trucks and powerful machinery scattered over acres of yard, the horses sweeping their tails in the sun-beaten corral. How could you ask for a finer setup? Vivie was a damn fool. He breathed in the smells of hay and sun-baked dung, of gasoline and dust and chickens, with rising satisfaction. The sound of the tractor starting up drifted from the fields. For half a mile to the river, the bottom land was rustling with cottonwoods and striped golden with windrows of cut hay. It was alive in spite of the murderous dry heat, and the windmill spanked around and around briskly over the low yellow ranch house—not withering into grey ruins like most of the others, but pushing out new additions for his children and grandchildren.

There was thirty years tied up in this. Just thinking of it started dim thunders in his head. Beginning with a little spread of five hundred acres which his carpenter-minister-rancher father had left him, he had fought his way up to seventy tousand acres by ferocious, back-breaking, endless work. It had been cut-throat all the way, too. In the early days some of his cattle, as much as twenty-five or thirty in a year, had been stolen and seeped from ranch to ranch by stockmen in cahoots, then butchered out on the Pine Ridge reservation. But by God, he had never backed down from anybody or anything, and he asked odds from no man. He had bulldozed stockdams and roads, he had cobbled scraps of junk into working machinery and built up the herd in size and quality, and as the dry years killed off the other ranchers, he had bought them up one after another, whether he could afford to or not. Never in all those years had he bought an acre he was ready to buy, but it wasn't in him to pull in his horns and play safe.

Vivie and uranium be damned, both. He wasn't about to let up now. From time to time he had other notions, other dreams you might say, but what were they compared to this? It was like—he didn't know what— like he and the ranch were one thing, like it was the part of the world he had turned into himself . . .

Impatiently, he broke off the slow, groping thoughts that Vivie had set in motion. On the way to the summer pasture, he toggled fences and took a look at the stockdams in the sun-infested gullies. Some of them were dried up so completely that they had faded into the powdery dirt and sagebrush. Others were still fringed with green and held a pitiful nick of water churning with doomed and frantic life—green frogs, insects, squirting black minnows. He would have to find time to deepen the basins with the front-end loader to cut down on evaporation. It ought to be done soon, just in the unlikely event of a rain, but in any case before winter to make full use of the spring runoff of melting snow. The other ranchers could sit on their hind ends and wait for a good soaker of a rain, but not Sam Bolton.

The work eased him, and he began the shapeless humming to himself that was a habit with him. The heat and the powerful light didn't bother him; he moved and lived in them. The water swayed heavily in the tank as he charged the truck forward and stopped to open and close cattle gates and charged on again. He felt better and better. The wheel tracks swooped ahead of him into hills like massive brown waves, like a vast motionless sea bulging and rolling off into the heat-shimmery sky. Far down by the river, he could just make out a green speck of a stationwagon and little dots moving in a scrabble of heaped dirt and trenches: the archaeology boys. Windy growths of dust blew in the dry alkali grass. A rattlesnake was trickling across the road in front of him. Instantly he leaped the truck forward and the wheels went over its back, squashing.

"Twenty-two," he grunted to himself, pleased. It was the most he'd ever nailed by the middle of June.

As soon as he reached the summer pasture, he began checking to make sure that the bulls weren't loafing in bachelor clubs instead of servicing the brood cows. Then he had a look to see that the yearling heifers, who were too young to be bred yet, hadn't sneaked in with the bulls.

"Patience, girls," he said to them. "Your day is coming." Grinning dustily, he remembered Susie, the peskiest crawler he'd ever owned. Now and again, in a lifetime of herds calved and branded, trailed to the summer range and back, and finally sold off, a cow stood out from the anonymous chewing masses. Susie had been one of these. No fence could hold her when she was in the mood and a bull was somewhere in the vicinity. With goodhumored lecherousness he saluted her: a lady of no morals and spectacular perseverence. Another one he remembered was a bull named Old Red. Sometimes stock accidentally blocked a road and had to be shooed off, but Old Red waited on roads with his harem of females and when a truck or a jeep came along, he stood planted in the dung, his tremendous bulk looming in a whirl of flies and sparrows and his curly head lowered dangerously. The courage, the brainless magnificence of the great bull had never failed to move him, and he had always turned the jeep off the road and circled around him.

The wheel tracks got steeper and rougher. The truck pitched, tipped half over with the ponderous roll of the water, and came back up, staggering in the ruts and stones as it fought up toward the empty sky. Pounded and thrown sideways, he wrenched at the wheel. Groaning, the truck made it over the top of the hill and nosed down into a chewed-up watercourse. The water plunged in the tank behind him. The wheels skidded. His eyes were cracks in his sun-flaming face and his chest worked sweatily, but excitement was pouring inside him, streaming in rivers of deep, mindless, slogging joy.

And yet—and yet it wasn't quite that simple. Something was wrong. Usually when he set to work on a thing, he submerged himself in it; he did it so completely that he became what he was doing. But now, somehow, he was conscious of a tiny thread of discomfort, awareness, as if a split had opened up between himself and carrying water to the stock. And it had been there since he left the house.

Damn Vivie anyhow, her pestering had knocked him off kilter. Anybody halfway sensible would have given up after being turned down fifty times, but it only raised her determination. She wouldn't give him a breather, no way at all.

Resentment crammed up inside him again and widened the gap in him. His concentration was falling apart. Anger went through him in hot streams, pressing, itching in his loins. It was just a job now to empty the sulphur-stinking water into the dry stock tank. The dusty cattle shouldered each other and bawled. The flies stung viciously.

Hot and savage, he drove to Enterprise for another load of water. Gusts of restlessness went through him like a sickness. When he'd filled the tank and paid his fifty cents at the little brick city hall, he did a thing he hadn't done in months—he stayed in town afterwards. It was about as unlikely at this time of year as taking a drink of whiskey, and he didn't believe in throwing away money to wet his gullet. A dog panted under one of the trucks leaning into the curb. Bored trainmen loafed on the porch of the white stucco Dakota Hotel. If there was anything that raised his temperature, it was railroad men: the same old run up to Gillette or somewhere, then a twenty-four hour wait to come back, talking idly of tires and sports and nothing at all, yawning over cheap magazines. It made him almighty mad. The whole West was a railroad graveyard of safe, bored men putting in their shifts and waiting for retirement.

He had to do something—something. As he opened the door of

the Western Cafe, he felt his chest stuff tight and his heart begin to pump heavily. Peggy Frye was behind the counter! It wasn't possible, unless . . . Grunting to the other ranchers and men from town, he squeezed himself onto a stool and put his elbows on the counter. The druggist said, "Sure is a hot bugger today, ain't it, Sam?" He grunted again.

She came over to wait on him. "Hi, stranger. What's it going to be?"

"I thought you had retired to married life," he said. "Permanent."

"Oh I have. Cecil didn't even want me to come today but I told him it was only what Mrs. Binder would have did for me, one neighbor for another. She called me last night and said she just wasn't up to it."

"Mrs. Binder has been doctoring for a good while," the druggist said. "She hasn't been what you'd call real sick but she's been doctoring."

Sam was numb with disappointment. To hide it, he took off his hat and wiped the trapped sweat that slicked down his face. "I'll have a cup of coffee," he said. "With cream."

"Ain't you been weaned yet, at your age?" she said archly. The joke was as old as Cain and Abel, but a chuckle came from the slow tough cattlemen, hunched at the counter under their battered hats with plow-shaped brims. Triumphantly, Peggy marched down the counter, flaunting her small, neat buttocks. For six years she had been a waitress and barmaid around town, a divorced woman taking care of her small daughter, when all of a sudden she had up and married Cecil Frye, the manager of the Piggly Wiggly store. Since then she had given up fornicating and had become a church-going housewife. When he'd first seen her behind the counter again, Sam had been dead certain that she and Cecil had parted company, and his hopes died hard. He could feel that she was intensely aware of him. He pressed his feverred look on her legs, her small breasts, her lean pretty face. With exaggerated nonchalance she slapped the coffee down in front of him and then fled to the other end of the counter. While she chatted with the men she flirted her hair and pouted, tilting her head like a girl, but it was all automatic, all a reflex action left over from years behind a counter. Again and again she made a point of talking about the Busy Club at the I.O.O.F., about the missionary society, about Cecil's simply wonderful singing, and every time somebody came in she hurried to tell him, "I'm just filling in for Mrs. Binder, she took a sick spell last night . . ."

Peggy was making herself clear, all right. She was Mrs. Peggy Frye now and not a ranch hand's slut—nor a rancher's either.

And still he couldn't leave; he couldn't accept it. His chest beat thickly with dammed-up passion and he was barely conscious of the ranchers talking: "hard pressed for sure . . . we've not had a substantial rain in two years." The words floated around him in the dense, greasy air.

"It didn't green up hardly at all this spring. I calculate a seventy-five per cent sell-off next year if we don't get some moisture."

"Next year, hell. All the herds is sold down now for want of feed and water. I'm selling off breed stock right now that I was ten years building up."

"Did you hear what Peterson is doing? And not just him, either, but some of the other big operators—he's going to graze his herd out of state on leased pastures."

"I was thinking of that myself," came an old leathery voice. "Only I don't figure my stock is strong enough to take any long trip."

Before the stockmen could relish the joke, the druggist butted into the conversation. His name was George Mencke and he was the town booster, gossip column, and general all-around fatass. The ranchers waited without expression while he said his piece, a pink chubby man with pop eyes and a soft pink mouth curling into his cheeks. "Everybody is feeling the pinch," he told them. "The farm implement dealer is quitting, so is the Chevrolet man, and one of the gas stations has gone bust already. The whole town is getting killed. If it wasn't for the railroads, the hotels would be out of business, too, and they're just hanging on."

There was a silence.

"Well, I guess I'll head out," one of the cattlemen said. "Peggy, will you give me another glass of water first? It's so dry I ain't spit in two weeks."

"I suppose you fellows have heard," Mencke went on. "Amos Putnam has been dropping hints but there's not a buyer to be had. His spread is going begging for a buyer."

The cattlemen stared at him. He blushed and said, "Oh . . ."

"Sam?" Putnam's cousin was standing beside him, his bony face a dark, suffering red. "There's no sense hiding it, Amos was meaning to go see you anyhow . . . Sam, and . . . it's true what he said. Amos would sell very reasonable."

Sam blinked murkily, trying to concentrate. Four thousand acres next to his summer range and he could get them for maybe 45,000 dollars, a quarter of it down and the rest on time. Seventy-four thousand acres! He waited but the surge of exultation just wouldn't come. His restlessness was a delirium now: it was a roaring in his blood like fire, sweeping the ranch and everything else with it. Life wasn't long enough, there were so many other things to do. He had a million plans—those patents on the hay lift and a dozen kinds of tools and machinery; the tourist place he'd bought up in the Black Hills and the ideas he had for improving it, new cabins and a trout pond, even an incline up to the top of the mountain. Lately when he'd gone out to the range in the morning and seen twenty years of work in the first twenty minutes, the feeling had sometimes come over him that the ranch owned him instead of the other way around. Vivie had been scraping on a sore place with those remarks about the ranch, the old hellcat. The ranch was his life—but the patents, the incline—everything was all scrambled together in his mind. He felt helpless, he couldn't seem to get hold of anything.

And there were the ranchers watching him and saying to themselves, look at that Sam beat down the price, will you? He's a shrewd dealer, all right, and tough as a boot.

"I'll see," he mumbled, just to get rid of the problem for a little while. The ranchers went out, but he couldn't see his way at all. Roiling with frustration, he shoved his look at Peggy every time she came near him, battering at her tense, shaky aloofness. Mencke was still talking, talking. The walls of the narrow little cafe were painted a slambang orange. Next to the cash register was a calendar with a picture of a cowgirl, posing her long naked legs under a skim of greasy dust. "That girl of mine," Peggy began to fret. "I told her to come by the restaurant before two o'clock. She's the forgetfulest thing, but you know how teenagers are. Probably she's over at the store, talking to Cecil. He's so proud of her; he just dotes on her like she was his own. Do you know what he gave her for her birthday? A sixty-dollar coat with a fur collar and little pleats . . ."

Even to Sam, who didn't know anything about the Frye household and didn't care, there was something odd about her anxious bragging. And what was she so worried about? She kept looking and looking out the window. At last she saw Lucy dangling along the hot sidewalk and rushed outside to talk to her. Gawky and delicate, wearing jeans and a boy's white shirt slopping out in back, the girl listened with her thin pure face motionless. Then she spoke and Sam saw something frightened, even desperate, come into her mother's face. Lucy scuffed away. Peggy came back into the restaurant, but now she was completely different; she hardly said a word and she seemed smaller, older and worn. She took the cover off the blue water cooler and slipped in another cake of ice. When she turned around, Sam pushed his swollen look at her again.

Her face was like white leather and she obviously didn't even know he was there.

Tormented, he jerked on his hat and went slamming out of the cafe. The wide dusty street was blind with light. His truck stood in the glare, the loaded tank dripping into the gutter, but he could think only of the wild flaming inside him. It was a case of have-to now. Damn it, he couldn't get to Buffalo Gap in time, Ellie went to work at four . . . And Margie Selkirk, who taught the fifth grade, was out of town visiting her folks . . . But Mencke's wife, Helen . . . She might have her craw full of George again and want to bust loose.

He went straight for the drugstore, rocking down the sidewalk at full speed. In front of the Pig Store, a woman with immense freckled arms was hoisting herself out of a truck, her thighs heaving in a firecracker red dress. Lifting his hat without slowing down, he said, "Afternoon, Mrs. Robel."

But she hulked toward him. "How's it going, Sam?"

"Too hot."

He tried to move on. With a sociable air, wiping the sweat off her forehead on her arm, she said, "I ain't exactly cold myself," and proceeded to give the weather a thorough going-over. "I heard the snakes is bad in town again. Every time it gets this dry they come in for the water." Galled and straining, he shifted his weight from one foot to the other.

A look of what he could have sworn was cunning ducked back into her cherryred face. "Say," she said. "Vivie's been doing some prospecting, I hear."

"She gets these wild hairs from time to time," he growled. "And I bear them as best I can."

Mrs. Robel hesitated and bunched her forehead, evidently fresh out of guile. "Has she struck on anything?" she asked baldly.

"So the disease is catching, huh? You've got the itch, too. Well, you'll have to ask Vivie about that. Her and I don't converse on the subject."

She let him go then, and he made for the drugstore. A half-ton truck rattled by, pulling an empty horse van. Across the street by the clapboard post office, George Mencke was standing in a small block of shade; he was talking to the owner of the Ben Franklin store but his look kept sliding off and loitering past Sam. As he turned the corner to the drugstore, halfway to the depot, he caught sight of George trailing along behind at a discreet distance, his fancy black string tie swaying across the front of his shirt. Sam speeded up his thumping, booted walk.

Inside, he shot his glance past the lounging trainmen into the long, cool, dusty spaces walled with shelves of boxes and bottles. "Where's Mrs. Mencke?" he asked sharply.

"She's out back," one of them said. "Oh Helen! Customer!" Sam paced up and down. Through the open door to the back he could see her little girl's head bobbing around a table and her baby jouncing up and down in a teeter-babe. George must be nearly at the front door. The canary sent out a high, trembling whistle. "I'll be with you in a second," she called and then she came hurrying out.

It always amazed him that a grey, drab-looking woman like this, with thick legs and tired shadows in her face, a homely woman, in fact, except for her long rich hair—how could a woman like this be so gay and teasing and bright sometimes? Life just seemed to shine from inside her then. There was a sweet lift in her mouth and her eyes warmed and flickered like light on quick water. She was the only woman friend he could remember a half hour after he left her, and he sometimes caught himself missing her even though they'd broken off almost two years ago.

"Helen?" Desire swelled up inside him and he looked at her, asking with his eyes, urging, demanding.

A dry, tearing sound came from her throat. A shock went through him as he saw the grey shiver in her face. Then it drained, white and sick around the tiny speckling of moles, and she ran back out of the store.

He had only a dim, muddled sense of what happened after that. George came in, asking heartily, "What can we do for you, Sam?" And in order to protect her, he said at random that he wanted some more of Irene's pills but he didn't have the bottle or the prescription number with him. "Some kind of nerve pills, wasn't they?" George said. "About when did she start taking them?" He went back to his files but though he looked and looked, he couldn't seem to locate the prescription. Somebody came in and wanted a chocolate soda. George called to Helen to come make it while he searched in the files. Mechanically, with blind dull movements, she dug out scoops of ice cream and triggered them into a glass, bending and moving behind the ornate old fountain with its tomb-heavy marble counter. There were tears in her eyes . . .

"Why don't you call home for it?" George suggested, with a malice that Sam didn't see then.

He even dialed the number for him.

"What pills? For Irene? We threw that bottle away six months ago," Vivie snapped. "What's going on, old Daddy? You setting out on a rampage again?"

If there was anything she wholeheartedly detested, it was one of his rampages. Generally the worst of them happened in the winter doldrums, when the herds were in close to the house and there was spare time on his hands. Then sleeping with her just whetted his appetite, before long he'd turn up missing for a day or so and if she tore into him out of jealousy, it only stirred him up more. He made her so mad! The old stud bull. There was no telling how many women he'd had or how many children he'd fathered, either. His seed was scattered all over South Dakota, Wyoming, and nothern Colorado.

When he didn't come home for supper, she began to get seriously worried. "I've rode him too hard," she said to herself. She watered the garden, looping a rope of fresh water into the dusty corn and beans and tomatoes. Shadows began to flow out of the barns and fences. The children were playing hide-and-seek in the long yellow light, and Debbie's bossy voice rang across the yard, "I'm the witch and everybody I find I get to put them in the pot." As the dogs and children went running they scattered the chickens around them like scraps of blown white paper. It was so hard to wait. There was more than her feelings involved this time, for if Sam went tomcatting for a week right now, old Butler and Robel and the archaeology boys would leave her miles behind. And other prospectors were starting to trickle in besides. There was one hope, though. The very things that had whipped her this morning, the drought and the ranch, would make it awful hard for him to really cut loose. Why sure, they had too deep a hold on him for Helen Mencke or any other slut to break. He would be back tonight, sore as a boil, maybe, but he'd be back. She could feel it in her bones.

A lovely feeling of expectation, of delight, began to grow inside her. She crossed the yard toward the barn. The old mother cat came toward her proudly with a dead rat spiked in her teeth. Her kittens were in the saddle room, a sweet fuzzy mess tangled together in a box. One of them was lying on top of the pile, breathing up and down with the others, and Vivie looked down tenderly at the slow rich riding of its sleep.

She took down a bridle and went out to the corral. The filly and the mare were both wild, they'd just been brought in off the range, and the mare wheeled away, snorting, a mad slick on her eyes, and stood at the other end of the corral with her head up. But after a while the filly stepped timidly toward the sugar in Vivie's outstretched hand, then skittered away and edged back again. She was a deep clear orange, like burnished copper, with pretty little hooves and delicate legs, and as she tiptoed closer her mane floated softly like a girl's hair. Vivie felt her heart go warm. She remembered the first horse she'd ever broken. She was ten and there was a Fourth of July celebration in town and she wanted to go so badly. Her sister had her own horse, but there wasn't another saddle horse on the place except one that hadn't ever been ridden. So she put a saddle on Doc and led him into a plowed field where he couldn't buck very well, and if he did throw her she'd have a soft fall. Two hours later, bruised and flushed and glorious, she rode into town and tied him up near the park. After that people began bringing her their horses to break, and when she started having beaus, they really taught her how to ride.

The beaus had been pretty numerous, too, until Sam came back from World War I and decided on her. The first she heard about it was when he ran them all off, stomping on one or two who convinced slower than he liked. Then he told her, "You've got two choices, me or nobody."

At the memory, a delicious excitement went through her.

The filly took the sugar with a soft velvety nuzzling. She slipped the bridle over its head and walked up and down, crooning to it gently. After all, she said to herself, Sam wasn't entirely to blame for his rampages. It was his nature in all he did. Just to see him take a reading spell was a sight. Physics and mechanics, novels, Reader's Digests, western and detective magazines, chemistry books—in the quiet winter days he tore into them like a threshing machine, gobbling everything in sight. Then he wouldn't come near a page of print for six months. That was Sam, always doing something, always building something, making something restlessly, never satisfied, seizing one idea after another almost at random. And yet there was something—a greatness about him that she could feel without being able to say exactly what it was.

If she could get him to throw in with her on the uranium, they could beat the world together.

When she came in, shadows were growing up over the smooth brown hills and hunching under the spurs and powerful juts of Tower Rock in the west. The sun was setting behind it in a great silent orange explosion. "Grandma," Debbie said, pulling at her. "Can we stay outside and look for flying saucers? Why not? Where's Granddaddy?"

"He'll be home directly."

She helped Irene to collar the children and put them to bed. The little girls were eating catsup on bread, slobbery crimson to the ears, and Jeffrey was still running amok down there in the tools and scraps of broken toys. The sense of expectation was like a beautiful glow inside her. Bending down to pick him up, she breathed in his sweet sour baby smell of powder and urine and milky plumpness, burrowing her face into his fat neck until he giggled and shrieked. Gradually the house quieted down and the boys went to bed, too. She waited dramatically.

At ten o'clock he banged in looking dangerous and sullen. There were wet stains on his back and under his arms and the wrinkles in his face were parched and dusty, like the ravines and draws that bit into the harsh dry land. She asked him if he wanted some supper. He grunted. Recklessly, while she heated it up for him, she started in again.

"Won't you dig me one little discovery hole?" she coaxed. Actually, of course, she could get Frank to do it for her, but she was bound and determined to get Sam out there and *involved*, not just looking around like a tourist.

"No more," he rumbled. "Give me some slack, will you? God almighty, woman."

"One little tiny old discovery hole? It has to be done inside of sixty days, Sam, or the claim is no good."

His sprouting eyebrows squeezed up wrathfully. "No, damn it, I won't. Now just you hold off and quit pestering me. I've endured all

I'm going to, Vivie. You hear?" Pawing at his eyes, he continued to grumble while he pushed down his food: ". . . damn aggravation . . . miserable damn aggravation."

"Why you bullheaded old thing," she said. "It wouldn't take you ten minutes with the front-end loader. Not five minutes!"

"You just won't quit, will you?" He lunged halfway up before he controlled himself and sat down, breathing through his yellow bear's teeth. Then he said, "Now listen and listen good. I don't have any interest in a pie-in-the-sky deal like that. Not any whatsoever. And if I did, I don't have the time. The trouble with you is, since the children have growed up, you have too much excess energy and nothing constructive to put it on."

"Like cows, huh?"

Her anger was like a sweet fire inside her, charged and rich and lovely.

"That's right, like cows. Like making a living," he said. "We'd be barefoot inside of a year if I carried on like you." Hands on her hips, she asked him exactly what was wrong with a little adventure, just for a change, after thirty-five years of raising a family and doing chores. "Nothing at all," he said. "As long as you don't run me crazy with it. Now I don't want any more damn nonsense. I've no time for it."

"Time!" she said hotly. "You got enough time to rut after them old whores like a stallion." His mouth strayed open and he loomed up toward her, swinging his dusty grey head. She raved. She slammed about the kitchen, weeping. Melodramatically, she let her head sink and her hair tumble around her face. All her reproaches and accusations were exaggerated to twice the size of life, and even while sobs dragged at her throat and her eyes spilled great wobbling tears, she was playing a role, acting for herself and him and enjoying it.

"Damn it, woman." His hands began to twitch.

"You filthy old stallion. Pills for Irene, my foot. You're nothing but a stud bull." Deliberately she provoked him, inflamed him, posed her defiance at his raging glare. She was bursting with delightful frenzy. Nothing he could do had ever been able to tame her, not even taking her over his knees and paddling her or tying her up and leaving her to rant and jerk out in the yard, not even throwing her out of the bedroom, naked, after raping her in a monumental fight that had lasted for three days and nights.

"I'm not speaking to half the women in the country," she sobbed. "I can't even keep track of who I'm mad at!"

He butted past her out of the kitchen but, weeping hysterically, she kept right on his heels. There wasn't a peep from the rest of the household: the children were fast asleep, and the others had learned by painful experience not to get in the way during these collisions.

In the bedroom, he shucked off his clothes and padded out to take a bath. While he splashed around like a walrus in the tub, she went about picking up his dirt-stiffened clothes and complaining, "I don't see why you can't be neat." With very ill grace, she brought him a towel. Suddenly he burst up from the water, his naked muscles and grey hair streaming like Neptune, and hauled her screeching into the tub with him. He chuckled with his water-sleeked face rolled back. Wrapping her in his huge sudsy arms, he held her while she scratched and spit and floundered like a drowning cat. Splatters of soap went flying. The water heaved up, tilting and brimming over until the floor was awash with foamy sluices and runs. Oh, she was so mad! "Leave me go!" she screeched. "My clothes! Oh, my hair!" She kicked and thrashed; she battered him with her elbows, and he lolled easily with her in the warm churn and slosh, cradling her, rocking her back and forth in warm tides while he sang in a goodhumored bellow: "Many brave hearts are asleep in the deep, so beware, bee-ee-ee-ee-ware," rumbling deeper and deeper in his chest.

Then he let her go, and she went fuming into the bedroom to peel off her wet things. Slouching in after her, he stood roughing his head in the towel and singing, "bee-ware, beeeeeeware." His face was curved into a grin like a red mask above his muscular white body thickened with years and work. Her mouth clamped tight. Blazing, she tried to comb out her snarled black hair, each savage tug jerking motion down into her long breasts. His big hands closed on her. Weak and breathless, she fought him again as he lifted her effortlessly onto the bed, gasping and weeping and sinking at last with a moan and sprawling her legs open to him.

"Daddy," she murmured to him afterward. Lightly, lightly, she kissed his chest and nibbled at the damp, coarse, grey hair curling out of the slabs of muscle. "Won't you doze out even one little discovery hole for me? It's just over in Red Canyon."

"Nope," he said mildly, comfortable in the bed with the big heavy furniture sleeping around them. "You can go on raising extreme hell until Doomsday and I won't do it."

"Ooh! You terrible, mean, nasty . . ." She caught a bunch of coarse hair in her teeth and tore it out of his chest. Roaring with surprised pain, he grabbed her and the violent, biting ecstasy started again. Her wet hair squashed on the pillow. Her body warped, hitched, clutching and twisting, deformed with bliss. Luscious warm tremors ran up inside her, spasms of crazed hot sweetness coming harder and harder . . .

Her Geiger counter was equipped with an audio amplifier and it pulsed regularly, every couple of seconds, in her hand. The clicks didn't mean anything; they were only background count from ultraviolet rays and tiny specks of radioactivity everywhere in the rocks, but near the rim of the canyon, she knew, the clicks always came a little faster.

"About there, Sam," she pointed. "But please be careful, don't get too close to the edge."

Nodding, he shoved and pulled at the gears bristling up around his feet, and the loader bumped into position, lowered its steel jaw, and ramming and biting heavily, swallowed a yard of dirt and stones and lifted it, dribbling, into the air. Dust boiled up in the fierce, pressing light. The sound of the motor rolled down into the fire-red canyon, thickening with echoes off the huge walls and spreading out into the pine-smudged hills. Sam worked like a demon. Even before they'd gotten out here, the uranium had started to take hold on him. The mechanics, or rather the electronics, of the Geiger had fascinated him so much that he'd stopped the loader to ask about the clicks. Then he said, "Let me see that thing." He studied the black and shiny metal box, studded with dials and knobs, and grunted, "I've read about uranium some. The radioactivity is matter breaking down, like it was rotting away and leaking out burning particles. And this must be some kind of gasfilled tube—helium maybe. And the batteries put a charge into it—unhuh, pretty sharp. A hell of a good man figured that out."

All she needed now was a little pod of uranium, just a tiny little pod, to make the Geiger kick up a storm for him.

And it was there! As she edged closer to the grinding and dumping machine, the tick-tick of the Geiger speeded up and the needle cocked over on the dial. She held it close to the mound of rocks and dirt beside the cut and the ticking increased, coming faster and faster until it was a delirious scurry of clicks, then a steady z-z-z like a burning wire in the air.

"Sam!" she cried. "Sam! Come here!"

He cut off the motor and swung down in the boiling dust. "I've got some!" she said. "I knew it, on *my* claim!"

The decaying rocks were simply burning with uranium. He knelt down, breathing hoarsely, shakily, and picked up a chunk powdered with yellow carnotite like sweet, fresh pollen. "Give me that thing," he said. Squatting, he held the Geiger counter near it and the wild buzzing swelled and swelled. "By God," he said. "By God Almighty." The whole pile seemed to be ore; the sun-heated rocks were alive with it, like red-hot coals. Feverishly he crumbled a broken rock in his hand and stared at the sulphur-yellow pebbling inside. "By God," he muttered. It was enormous—it was, it was like the surface of a great interior fire, a mountain of fire under his feet.

The Bomb

The theory behind the bomb is relatively simple. Fission is based on the terrible weakness in matter: the heavier an element, the more unstable it is, the more likely to weaken and come apart. Uranium has this ominous instability. One of its isotopes, U-238, is especially precarious, and when it is bombarded wth neutrons it splits apart into barium, krypton, and loose flying neutrons, releasing a spew, a witch's pot of boiling energy. If the neutrons bombard more uranium, the flaming cataclysms of energy become continuous and there is a chain reaction. There is a bomb.

III

"We should've stayed in Utah. We could've at least finished going bust in comfort."

"There's supposed to be a big strike here," Wally said. "It's our big chance."

"Big chance, my sore tail. That's what you said about Colorado and Arizona." Peevishly, Bert Stephens shoved himself farther down in the seat of the swaying, gas-smelling old truck. Wrinkled and dirty and unshaved, he scowled at the flow of brown hills snagged with sagebrush. Sheep, daubed with blood-red initials, huddled on a naked slope. The pastures were ripped with deep wounds of washed out clay. "Look at that—lousy sagebrush meadows," he fretted. "They make me want to puke to look at them."

"There's enough of them to go around, all right." Wally whistled under his breath into the gusty roar of the motor.

"Pick another hymn or quit whistling, will you?"

"I'm sorry. I keep forgetting."

"Damn nation." Wincing, Bert felt at his battered left hand and then put it in his mouth, sucking at the slow ooze of blood from the hurt knuckles. "Are you sure I smashed it against a wall last night? I didn't hit nobody? You think of all the grade-A, steak-fed, martini-drinking bastards in the world and I have to throw a punch at a brick wall. What's the use?"

"Now don't go working yourself up," Wally said. Wally Riggs was a big gaunt man with a carefully pruned little moustache, sitting in a wallow of baggy work clothes. Trying hard to concentrate, he squinted under the curling brim of his hat at the highway sliding dizzily under, turning, running off ahead and stringing away into the empty land. It was more than he could handle, driving and taking care of Bert and being hungry, all at the same time. The steering wheel vibrated in his huge sweaty hands. The rearview mirror, cracked across the middle, quivered giddily against the streaming fields. He was

42

hungry. In the last five months he had dropped from two-seventy to a hundred-ninety-five pounds and he lived in a more or less constant ache of hunger, but today it was real torture. His stomach rumbled and he felt hollow, weak. "What you need," he said, "is some food and you'll feel better."

"You mean, what *you* need is about a peck of potatoes, three hamburger steaks, a malt, and a six layer wedding cake." Wally let out a sigh, and Bert began to chant viciously: "Ham and eggs and buttered toast. French fries. A quart of milk and a dozen chocolate cupcakes."

Wally swallowed in agony. Though he was used to Bert ragging him about food, patting his hanging stomach and saying it was too bad he'd lost the twins, and things like that, they had started out at six o'clock this morning without any breakfast and the mere mention of food was more than he could bear. "Hotcakes and pig sausages, fried nice and brown," Bert sang cruelly. "And a piece of blueberry pie. Ham and beans with mashed potatoes and gravy. Six big fat creampuffs." On and on until Wally, with tears in his eyes, was begging, "Hey, don't. Cut it out, Bert. Please."

"Well, stop suffering over there, then. You're driving me nuts with that starvation look. I can't stand it any more."

"I can't help it, Bert. It's terrible enough to go on a diet, but when you're broke, it makes you all the more hungry because—I don't know, it's just worse. But I'll try to get it off my mind."

Unappeased, Bert scratched himself irritably and griped at everything. His eyes were red and sick, like festering sores, and there was a long tear in his sport shirt printed over with impossible flowers. "Why we ever took to the brush again beats me. Damn this miserable life—and South Dakota, too. I'd just as soon go to Texas and get hung."

Wally's blunt mild face was as tolerant, as gentle as ever. "We'll be there pretty shortly now," he said.

"You strictly don't catch on, do you? I don't want to go to South Dakota. Not now or ever. It's just turning the bread over, and there ain't no butter on that side neither. Besides, we don't have a prayer. I'll take a gambling chance as quick as the next man, but what have we got for chips? A Geiger with two dead batteries and eight dollars and fifty-seven cents—at least that's your story," he said sourly. "You're probably cheating me."

"I wouldn't do that, Bert. You know that."

"Well, it's not enough to do any good. We can't even draw one card with that."

Wally nodded and frowned at the problem. "Then I'll call Bob Werden in Denver and get some fresh money. He'll loan us some again. Cathy is my sister's girl, don't forget that."

But instead of cheering up, Bert began to curse savagely. "Can't you understand? I'm fed up! Through! Try to get it into your stupid head. I'm through with this miserable, sorryass life, wandering around and rooting in the dirt. How much does it take to convince you? We've gone bust in feldspar, mica, silver, and every other known mineral—wearing out shovels, digging holes like a damn gopher all over the western states and never any luck. Nothing." He crashed his boot at the glove compartment again and again. "I'm through! The partnership is dissolved as of now. So divide up the money. Come on, give it here. I want four dollars and twenty-nine cents. Right now!"

Wally had heard this too often even to blink. Coaxingly he said, "Aw, come on, we'll connect, Bert. Just hold on a little bit longer. Our day is coming."

"It is, huh? I'm seventy-seven years old and it ain't come yet."

"Cut it out, you're only thirty-six. That's the prime of life, Bert. That's ten years younger than me and I haven't quit. But no kidding, I have a hunch we're gonna strike a jackpot this time. I mean it. Every dog has his day sooner or later. When you touch bottom, you've just got to come up."

Bert's lips peeled away from his teeth and he was laughing, laughing crazily with his eyes swelling out like pink blisters in his whiskery face.

"What's the joke?"

"Nothing, nothing at all," he laughed. Wally glanced at him, puzzled. At last he wheezed to a stop and said, "You've talked me into it, Old Heavy; I can't answer those arguments. I'm in, deal the cards for another hand, and if you promise not to look hungry, I'll pretend like I don't have a hundred-and-thirty-seven-dollar gut thirst."

"That's the way to talk," Wally said, enormously pleased. Far ahead of them, Enterprise lifted its glinting watertower from a clot of green trees. Rusty signs thickened on both sides. The highway jumped the Cheyenne River, straightened out and widened into the main street of the town. They pulled up in front of the small brick bank. Beside them a scrawny man in overalls climbed out of a homemade truck-trailer stuffed with children and shambled across the street—the uranium rush was evidently on.

"Damn nation," Bert groaned, getting out of the truck. "This is the same town we left. We been going in circles." Hands on his hips, he looked around with disgust. The burning sky seemed to press down on the faded old board-front stores and hotels. The houses were runty and mean, with oil tanks squatting next to them and jerry-built trailers, set on blocks, jammed into many of the scrubby yards. Hot and dusty, the gravel streets broke off in pastures or limped up the appalling, sunstruck hills. "Are we supposed to make our fortune here?" he said.

Uranium! 45

"The whole town put together won't retail for two hundred and fifty dollars."

Just then the sidewalk trembled under their feet, and a dull thunder rolled over them out of the puffy sky. "Now what?" Bert grumbled. "I reckon it's Doomsday. Well, you're the one that knows the hymns, start in singing."

It turned out that the sound came from an army ordnance depot, ten miles away at Salem, where ammunition from World War I was being exploded. "That's a nice touch to start off with," Bert said. "Just dandy. I believe I'll have a drink to get over the shock."

"Bert, you know we can't spare the money."

"All I want is a dollar," he pleaded. His ill temper was suddenly gone and he was charming, puckish, a whiskery and bloodshot boy. "Come on, let some fresh air into that wallet. All right, if that's how you feel. You just broke the hell out of my heart. I always knew it, Bad-eye Richardson was my only true friend."

Wally couldn't resist him when he was like this, and with a sigh at his own weakness, he brought out two quarters. "You've got to promise to eat though," he warned.

"You sure drive a hard bargain, Lard. But all right, I'll eat."

Gleefully he made for the closest bar, skipping a little jig down the sidewalk. Wally hustled over to the Piggly Wiggly store, bought a loaf of bread and a bottle of syrup, and fumbled with shaky eagerness back into the truck. Dousing pieces of bread with the syrup, he gobbled down the sticky brown sops, belching and panting and licking his dribbly fingers. Sweat burst from him into his half-empty clothes. He was so absorbed that he didn't see Bert until he yanked open the truck door. "Come on, pitch in," he said, wiping his hands hurriedly.

"You mean eat that?" Bert's face cramped up with revulsion at the gooey mess on the bread wrapper. "I said I'd eat but I meant food, and that stuff there is not in the category of food. Hellfire, there's plenty of hogs that would starve first, before they'd eat that." But then, with a cunning look, he said, "All right, I'll do it. That syrup will give me the toothache, but I'll eat if you give me another fifty cents. And that's my last offer, take it or leave it."

"I can't do it, Bert, not till we get some more money. We've got the shorts now so bad it's pitiful."

"Okay," he snarled, and proceeded to throw the worst tantrum of the day. "I give up and quit, you big-bellied, dumb sonofabitch. Go ahead and spend it all on peanut butter . . ."

Wally's snub face kniked up mournfully: he was angry. "That's your quota," he said sharply. "You stop that whining. I realize things canker up in you and get you down. Also, you have a gifted mind, and I'm not your equal, but I have to say this: you're acting babyish,

Bert. Now you be a man and stop it." Bert muttered sulkily. "I'm sorry I had to say that," Wally said, "but it was overdue, long overdue. You're going to play out the string like you promised, and as soon as we find a room you're going to eat. Do you hear? I'll get you something that ain't sweet."

Gnawing sullenly at his injured hand, Bert trailed along from hotel to hotel. At the first two they drew a blank. News of a big uranium hit had filled the town, and the only room to be had was a double at seven dollars a day, which was completely out of reach. "We couldn't have got to the Promised Land too late again, could we?" Bert griped. Their last hope was the Prince Hotel, a rickety wooden palace with a gap-toothed balcony perched on knobby poles. Clinging stubbornly to its former glory, it flaunted the only fresh coat of paint in town, a yolky yellow slapped over the withered boards.

"I'm sorry," the lady owner told them. "The only room I have left is a single."

Wally turned away from the desk but Bert said, "That's what we want, ma'am. We generally always take a single, then we cut cards for the bed and he sleeps on the floor." Wally stared: the transformation in Bert was unbelievable, and he was notorious for his unpredictable changes. His short, burly-looking body strutted lazily. His tiny hands tossed off a rakish gesture. His soiled eyes took on a glitter under the sheaf of long hair trained down to conceal his balding forehead.

"I can't allow two in that room," she told him.

"Shoot, woman, he don't mind. He's a country boy used to sleeping out on the ground."

"I really can't," she said, but a smile caught at her shrivelled mouth. She was a hefty woman of fifty-five or sixty with dyed red hair and a loud voice that blasted through the lobby, but she was clearly taken with Bert. "You boys a couple more prospectors out of the bushes?" she asked.

"No, *ma'am,* and I'm surprised to hear you say that. I'm Wilfred Wilkins, the famous boy evangelist of Pocatello, Idaho, trying for a comeback. My partner there, he plays the musical saw and handles the collection. You ought to hear him if the take is light—which it has been. He hollers out, 'Brethren, I'm going to pass the basket again, and this time I don't want no belt buckles and charm bracelets in it.'"

With a delighted guffaw, she pushed the register toward them. "I think I can find an extry cot in the basement," she said. "The rent'll be three dollars a day or fifteen a week." Wally handed her three dollars and she asked, "Does that about break you fellers?"

"I wouldn't say that," Bert grinned. "But if it took a dollar to get around the world, we could just about make it to the top of that next ridge." He was sassy, rollicking. She led them up three flights of stairs to a little room, hardly more than a closet, squeezed under the roof. It was hot and still. A wavy-fronted old bureau stood on worn casters, next to a tin closet. Over the bed the dark wallpaper had come loose and fattened out from the wall like a tumor. "Exactly my style," Bert said. "I always craved to stay in the penthouse suite."

"It's pretty bad," she admitted. "Anyway, I'll have the cot sent up—and, oh yeah, that's the fire escape. In case of fire."

"Where? What? You mean that rope tied to the bed?" Bert sent out a whooping laugh. "You sure somebody didn't hang himself up here? It's a good thing you lost a hundred pounds, Lard, or I'd set fire to this place just to see you pull the bed right through the wall trying to climb down."

She was indignant at first; then she had to laugh, too. "I'll have you know there's regular fire escapes on the first and second floor," she said. "These rooms up here ain't been used till this week in a good fifteen years, since they was building the ordnance depot at Salem. It sure brings back the old times, all the action and the people, the excitement. There's some life in the town again . . ."

Fifteen minutes later she left, reluctantly, and with a beaming smile, Wally pumped Bert's hand. "I bet this suite is drafty in the winter time," Bert said. Buoyantly Wally unpacked the suitcase and the metal footlocker while Bert shaved at the dingy sink. Brushing a dead fly from the dresser, Wally placed a photograph of his wife and two boys in the center of it and stepped back, grave and silent, looking at them for a minute. Bert, his face bearded white with shaving cream, fell to his knees and clasped his hands, worshipping at the photograph.

"Don't joke, Bert," Wally said earnestly. "Five months is a long time not to see your family."

To his astonishment, Bert apologized. He was certainly in the best mood Wally had ever seen, and for no reason whatsoever. He splashed himself from head to foot, then changed clothes and sprinkled some of the after-shave lotion onto them for good measure. "You never know," he said. "I ain't been kissed today, but I'm waiting my chance."

They went down to the lobby and Wally said, "Hold on, I better call Cathy right away." He put in a long distance call, collect, to Mrs. Werden in Denver. With a catch of dismay he heard the tiny, remote buzzing go on and on, and then a metallic voice said, "I get a D.A. on that, operator." He asked his operator to keep trying and pushed out of the booth with false nonchalance.

"She must've stepped out for a minute," he told Bert, but he couldn't help being concerned. Cathy was a frail, nervous girl and she practically never left the house.

Bert shrugged, still with that same baffling gaiety. "You'd best not get your hopes up, Lard. That well has went dry anyhow."

"What are you talking about? He loaned us money before, didn't he? And we always paid him back, even if it took a year."

"Poor old Fats." Bert knocked with his uninjured hand, lightly, against the side of Wally's head. "Open up those gates, will you? What do you think he helped us for? The idea was, if we hit on silver or whatever, he was gonna make a stock promotion out of it. Friendship and loving kindness wasn't in it. I know him, and hell is ten foot deep in Bob Werdens. Believe me, he has wrote us off as nothing but a headache. Don't you remember how you had to crawl to him the last time?"

"I know how you feel about him, but you're too hard on people, Bert. You've got to look for what's good in them. There's good in everybody in this world, Bert."

"Even me?" His scraped red face was mocking.

"Don't talk like that. "You know—well, anyhow—but you *are* too pessimistic-minded. Cathy will get him to grubstake us again, you'll see."

They sat down to wait in the old lobby with its pallid ferns and philodendrons and rubber plants putting out leaves in a wreckage of sagging furniture and dusty geegaws. Two or three other men used the phone. The place was swarming with every known kind of amateur rock collector and prospector—bookkeepers on vacation taking a flyer, leathery men with narrow hips and sun-pinched eyes, men reading government bulletins, and one little fellow with a wedge-brimmed hat who kept telling everybody, "I got three prime claims, all I need is some backing."

"I sure hope we get started tomorrow," Wally said anxiously. "We got to get in on the ground floor this time."

"Right you are," Bert said, laying out a game of solitaire on a wobbly table. Nervous as he was, Wally couldn't help wondering again at Bert's good temper. Why, the last time they had dealings with Bob Werden, he had gone wild with hate and stayed in a terrible bad spell for weeks. The phone rang. Wally rushed into the booth, only to hear that Mrs. Werden still didn't answer. "Please keep on trying," he told the operator. He sat down again and waited, rubbing the back of his neck and shoving his fingers through his damp, light hair. Voices fluttered in the smoky room like caged birds: "hot spot . . . Robel . . . tests out big . . ." Somebody named Robel had hit in Horse Canyon, six miles outside town, and the stampede was on to stake around him, to stake the whole canyon from end to end. The suffering wait dragged on. His nervousness stretched tighter and tighter. The landlady, whose name was Edna Harbaugh, watered the sickly plants. She asked Bert what they were doing and he told her, "We're waiting on a little traveller's aid." Again Wally failed to reach Mrs. Werden, and then again. His heart sank, and minute by minute Bert's usual gloomy talk of defeat that morning became more and more real, sharp, ominous. Wally saw him cadge a cigarette butt from an ashtray and light it up, tip back his raw face and breathe out the luxurious smoke. And for once he didn't reprimand him. It was all too likely that there wasn't any use in breaking his bad habits now.

At 4:30 he decided to phone Bob Werden at his office. He refused to believe Bert's warning and yet, as he put through the call, he could hear a cold edge of fear in his voice. His dry tongue stuck to his teeth.

The secretary said, "I'm sorry, at present Mr. Werden is in New York."

Wally came out of the booth with his head hanging. He stood motionless like a gaunt horse with its back turned to driving snow.

"Up jumped the devil, huh?"

"They're in New York, that's why Cathy didn't answer."

"Okay, so we lost the herd again," Bert said cheerfully. "We can sell the Geiger for enough gas to get home. Don't take it so hard, we'll get another ride on the merry-go-round."

Blindly Wally shook his head. "You don't understand . . . It's got to be now, Bert. . . . I can't think, help me. Help me, Bert, you're smart."

"You won't find no better for brains," he agreed. "Well, let's see. You could take in washing if you had a scrubboard and you wasn't so proud. But the best thing right now is for you to eat. You need a bellyful at a time like this, Sunshine, or I won't be able to trust you near our fire escape. Matter of fact, I could eat the hell out of a boiled egg, myself."

It was so strange. After all these years of taking care of Bert, of encouraging him and keeping him out of trouble, Wally found himself being cared for. It was Bert who bought the food and heated the cans of chili under the faucets in the sink. "Hot and cold is both a hundred and fifty degrees," he said. "Look at that. They must get their water straight from hell in this town. There's enough sulphur and brimstone in it to start another Sodom and Gomorrha."

Wally shrugged like lifting a shoulder under a sack of cement. It broke his heart to see Bert like this, so joking and kind and everything.

"Come and get it," Bert said, banging the canopener against the tin closet, but at the second mouthful he suddenly went dead white and bent over, moaning.

"What's wrong? Bert? Is it your tooth again?"

His eyes flooded with pain and he plunged his face between his knees, breathing hoarsely. Bert's teeth were in awful shape. They were nice enough to look at, but there wasn't a sound tooth in his head and nothing Wally said could persuade him to go to a dentist.

Hunched over in agony, he dug at his back teeth with his fingernail, trying to get the bit of gristle out of a cavity. His face seemed to have melted and run together. "Unh," he gasped. "Man, oh man, that's a sore sucker." Walking around in tortured circles, he pressed his hand against his jaw.

Wally ached with pity. "Aw, that's a shame, Bert. Just when you was feeling so good." He took a half dollar out of his pocket and said, "Here, you better get some liquor. Go ahead, fifty cents don't make any difference now. Get some whiskey and keep it in your mouth, that'll cut the pain."

Bert blundered out, holding his face. Alone in the hot airless room, Wally finished off both cans of chili and the bread almost without knowing what he was doing. Somehow the toothache was the last straw. Bert didn't know it yet but there couldn't be any next time; unless he could come up with an idea, and right now, it was the end of the road. But what? There wouldn't be any mining jobs around here yet, and no other jobs were to be had in these little cattle towns . . . He used to know where Bob Werden stayed in New York but he couldn't think . . .

Slowly, in a mournful daze, he set up the cot and did the laundry, hanging it out on a cord strung across the room. The dead, sealed-off air was smothering. The window wouldn't open. Sitting down in his shorts, he began a letter to his wife: "Dear Esther. Well here we are in Enterprise, South Dakota. I hope you and the boys are okay . . ."

He faltered and sat without moving, his skin hanging like damp rags on his big thick bones. What was the use? There was only one thing she wanted to read, that he was coming home. And that would be it, the end of a seven-year road of hard going. He would carry a lunch pail, and Bert would go back to skidrow and drink himself to death on wine. No! Please, God, no! But he couldn't go on this way any longer, hurting Esther and Ron and Chub. This had to be the last time, he'd promised himself that. Letting her work and stay with her Dad while he went off prospecting—no, it was no kind of life for her and the boys.

She had every right in the world to be bitter. It was a terrible thing, though, to hear her say, "Look in a garbage pail and you find garbage," just because he had run across Bert on skidrow when he was doing a construction job near the Denver train station. Bert was like a beautiful and expensive piece of machinery that he had to fix. Still, he guessed it had been a mistake to take him on as his partner— if only because Esther blamed Bert for it when they went broke and called him a thief to his face for taking money out of the till while he was on a drunk. What he couldn't make her see was that it was *his* fault the company had folded. They were operating on a mighty thin shoestring and three times running, in spite of Bert's advice, he had made a bad bid on a job and lost money.

With a shiver he thought of what had happened then. He found himself a job as a carpenter and tried as best he could to keep an eye on Bert in his spare time. It couldn't be done. For three weeks he disappeared and then, on a cold and windy Sunday in February, he had found him on the post office steps, wearing only a pair of thin cotton pants and a shirt: he was lying face down on the icy white marble in his frozen vomit.

What could he do but bring him home? Esther was not one to make a scene, but it was terrible, the way she said, "I don't care if he is a brilliant man. He's ruining our lives, your life and mine and your children's—oh, you won't listen. He's like some kind of disease you got . . ." Those had sure been bad times. Hoping to make it up to her with a rich strike and to save Bert at the same time, he had taken to prospecting. Between failures he saved money; then off he went again before Bert deteriorated too far. And always inside him, to keep him going, was the dazzling memory of how he'd met Bert: a larking young bum who glanced over his shoulder while he was sweating at a page of figures and who did the whole batch like that, instantly. He was a genius. He was as smart as any of those atomic scientists.

Of course he was hard to control, and after all these years it was still impossible to tell when he would go wild like a shack full of fireworks exploding, or what would set him off. He would do the craziest things, like drop out of sight and wind up three days later in the Denver bus station, drunk to the gills, watching the little puppet orchestra above the juke box, waving his hand as the crazy, spastic little group jerked and wobbled and twitched their broken instruments. Wally had never given up hope, though, that one day he would understand Bert and straighten him out, to boot. It was a vision he had. Like coming out of blinding light into the high cool darkness of a church and way at the end was a great big colored window.

He was hungry again, which made it all the harder to think. His appetite was getting worse every day, every minute—the St. Regis! Like a miracle, the name of the hotel popped into his mind. The St. Regis, that was it, that was where Bob Werden always stayed when he was in New York. They had a chance after all, only a small one maybe, but a chance. He was still grinning and socking his fist into his palm when the door flew open and Bert swaggered into the room with a stocky, freckled girl on his arm.

"Hey!" Wally yelped, jumping up in his shorts with a deep blush. He pushed them outside and scrambled into his clothes while Bert kicked up a ruckus in the hall. Still blushing, he let them in.

"Our troubles are over," Bert announced. "Oh yeah, this is—what's your name again?" The girl batted him affectionately, and he said, "Oh yeah, this is Jackie and she's cured my toothache with her hard-earned money from punching cattle."

"Ber-rt—you devil," she giggled. Awkward and shy, Wally said, "How do."

"Well, look her over," Bert said. "How's this for a woman? She ain't *too* ugly, and she's got the morals of a two-year-old heifer, just what the doctor ordered." Ducking away from her blows, he held out a can of hash to Wally. "Here's a present for you. She gave it to me in return for my affections."

"That's mighty nice of you . . ." Wally began but Bert was already shooing her out of the room with a swat on her rear end. "I and Wally have got business to talk over, honey. You go out and keep an eye on the herd." His skinned red face was grinning, triumphant. "Lard, I mean I have strictly got the answer. But first you better eat so your mind will be clear—and let's get some air in here." Wally told him that the window was stuck but Bert yanked at it, then bashed his boot through the glass, twice, three times, the shatters tinkling down into the yard. "Gee, Bert, you shouldn't have done that," Wally said. Sure enough, in a minute Mrs. Harbaugh was banging on the locked door. "We smelled smoke," Bert hollered, opening the can of hash. "My partner is halfway down the rope and I'm just leaving. You better call the fire department." She went grumbling down the stairs and Bert, with a wink and a flourish, set the can of hash in front of Wally. "Put yourself around that and listen."

"I got an idea too . . ."

"Lard, you're keen-witted but your lack of education is against you. Listen to this. We'll sell Old Paint and go whole hog or none. How's that for a hummer?"

"Sell the truck?" Aghast, he stopped gobbling with the spoon half way to his mouth. "We'll be stuck! It's six miles out to Horse Canyon and six miles back. Now my . . ."

"Hear me out, Sunshine. I found a nice big poker game back of the Cattleman's Bar while I was curing my toothache. There's not a professional gambler among them. Cleaning out that game will be like taking candy from a baby—and I'm good at that. I'll build us up a stake, and then we can take to the brush with new batteries and a full belly. Plus the truck, which I will buy back. Lard, I'll eat that game up. It's a sure cinch."

Wally bolted down the rest of the hash, looking doubtful. "I know you're a mighty fine cardplayer, Bert. You saved our neck a couple of times . . ."

"Fine cardplayer!" he cried, insulted. "I'm the greatest there is. All you have to do is put a deck of cards in front of me and let Nature take its course. That's been our trouble, Heavy, partway measures. You can't get nowhere in this world if you don't take a chance." He blew on his short weak fingers, raring to go. "So you just give me the key and the papers and leave the rest to me."

"You mean now?" Wally gasped. "It's after six o'clock. Everything is closed."

"Sunshine, the car dealer is in the game, and I asked him personally, myself. I can get a stack of chips this high for Old Paint. Come on, cough up that key, my dealing hand is getting itchy."

Frowning, Wally said, "You're travelling too fast for me, Bert. Stand back and give me breathing room to think." Slowly, methodically, he went at the problem. After a minute he said, "I see your point about going to the last notch. This time we have to do it, only not yet. First we try my idea." Bert groaned, but Wally told him how it was going to be. Bob Werden always stayed at the St. Regis, and he was about to telegraph him, right now. No, he wouldn't phone him. He freely admitted that he'd lost his nerve this afternoon, that he didn't have the guts to make a call even if he paid for it. But his mind was made up. If Werden didn't come through by tomorrow evening, Bert could make his play then.

With that, he put on his hat and started downstairs. Bert said, "You understand it'll take our last plug nickel—and he might not be there, he could've gone on to Washington or anywhere and then our dough is wasted—and he wouldn't give us the sweat off his balls anyhow—not to mention you'll starve all day tomorrow, waiting."

"I don't care," he said stubbornly. His face kinked up and he tramped relentlessly down the steps.

"Well," Bert sighed. "I see you're gonna have your way." As they went through the lobby, Edna charged out from behind the desk squawking about the broken window. "Honey, just put it on our bill," Bert said loftily. "We'll be wealthy men by tomorrow night at the latest."

On the way to the depot he continued to coax, but he was good natured about it, resigned. "My goodness, Lard, when you *do* get an idea, you're as proud of it as a mother with brand new triplets." The sun was setting and light poured down the wide streets and up the side of the pine mountain beyond the railroad yards. The evening train to Billings, Montana, had just come through, and cars and trucks were pulling away from the ox-blood red depot, backing up and turning around by a small scummy fountain.

Wally went striding into the dismal station. A round-bellied stove squatted in the center of the waiting room. On a lead-grey wall was a map of the west like a picture in an anatomy book with skin laid back from a tangle of blood vessels and nerves. "You'll be sorry," Bert said. "There won't even be enough money left to buy milk for the baby." Wally labored at the telegram. Just as he finished, a powerful man came slamming in, grimy, his shirt blotched with sweat, and butted absent-mindedly up to the window as if Wally didn't exist.

"Say, Henry," he said. "Take a look and see if a railway express package came in for me. I'm in a hurry."

"Sure thing, Sam. How's Vivie and the family?" The pink, soft-faced clerk showed his beautiful white false teeth in a smile and went pottering off.

"Come back here, you," Bert barked at him. "He's next, right after us." The clerk assured him that it wouldn't take a second to see to Mr. Bolton, and disappeared. Bert was enraged. Struggling with Wally, who was trying to soothe him, he snarled at the man, "You snap your fingers and he jumps, huh? Well, you may think you're God Almighty but you're still gonna wait your damn turn. So just you move back till we're done."

Sam Bolton stood humped and still, his chest breathing in and out and his dusty face slung low. He was obviously thinking of something else. Maddened, Bert cursed at him, then at Wally and the clerk, but Sam Bolton never looked at him at all; he signed for the package and went slouching out. "God damn it!" Bert shouted, his face squeezing close to tears. Impotently, he kicked the benches, the coal scuttle. And all the way back up the street he kept raging, "I don't like it! Nobody treats me that way. I don't like it, I tell you. Why didn't you back me up? Some friend you are, won't back a man up. The bastard looked right through me like I was nothing. I don't like it!"

Abruptly, he whirled and said, "Give me the keys to the truck, I had enough. I'm through waiting right now, so hand 'em over."

Quietly but firmly Wally said. "We're waiting till tomorrow like we said."

"Now! I say *now!*"

Wally shook his head. and he would have made his plan stick except for one of those unexpected things that he feared so much. A lean brown dog went limping past them—and it was bleeding, bleeding terribly, spraying blood from a deep gash in its hind foot. For a moment it stopped to lick the pouring wound, and then it limped on, leaving a great red splatter by the drugstore. Bert stared after it. "That's too bad," Wally said, "but there's nothing you can do. Come on." Bert didn't move.

Two teenaged girls came out of the drugstore, noticed the blood and wrinkled up their faces. "Ish!" one of them said. They tiptoed between splashes, picking up their bare feet skittishly, and crossed the street, giggles flying off with the motion of their elbows. Bert's face was a dark wound. Chewing on his battered hand, he walked jerkily up the sidewalk, following the trail of blood with a kind of sick horror. Frightened, Wally dragged at his arm and implored, "Come on, Bert. Forget it and let's go."

The trail wobbled past the bank, splotch after splotch of wet red. Somehow an artery or a very large vein had been severed and the dog, bleeding to death, was trying to get home. Trembling and lead-grey, Bert gnawed at his hand, hypnotized with anguish and nausea at the staggering puddles of blood. The track wavered into the street, the red splotches drawing up, puckering in the dust like dead flowers. In desperation, Wally hauled him to a stop and suddenly, with a blind lurch, he sank down on the steps of the V.F.W., his head slumped between his knees.

"That's better," Wally said. He couldn't understand, only console. "Easy now, put it out of your mind—also I don't think that's a good idea, biting your hand like that. You'll infect yourself." Bert let his hand fall. Off to the east, the clouds changed from pink to bluish-grey, crumbling, and hill after hill went under, taken by shadows. A dusty car crackled by and turned off a block down the street. Still Bert didn't move. Wally grew more and more concerned. This black depression might last for days, even for weeks, if he didn't head it off quickly.

"Here, Bert. Look!" he said. "Here's the keys to the truck. And the papers, here. Go ahead and play poker." Bert wasn't interested anymore. At last, however, he was persuaded to walk back to Highway Street, and once he was inside the Cattleman's Bar, though he was still pale and dull, he began to look interested when Wally mentioned the game in the back. Jackie bought him a drink. In the next booth a bunch of young men in khakis were roaring jolly songs. A half hour later Bert was in the card game and going like a house afire. As usual the other players sat around the table dead-faced and silent in the fume of light and cigarette smoke; and as usual Bert pranked and cut up like a kid, clicking his fingers, hollering for the card he wanted, and when he dealt, snapping the cards off the deck with a loud pop!

Wally watched anxiously. Bert won a pot and then threw the money back foolishly, and more besides, staying to the last card three times when he didn't have a chance. Again, on the next hand, he hung on stubbornly against an obvious pair of queens. Calling bet after bet, he shoved in the last of truck money warning boisterously, "If I hit this little straight, I'm gonna tear you up." Wally was heartsick. The rancher showed his queens—and Bert flipped over his sole card—an ace. He had aces back to back. Scooping in the chips with a hoot, he said, "Pick up the dead and deal some more."

Then he twitched his eye at Wally, who stared glassily at him with his heart still walloping inside his chest. His head whirling, the strength gone from his legs, he realized that Bert had set it up from the first. He was rowdy and full of horseplay, but his eyes were cold and quick. In two hours he was nine hundred dollars ahead.

Wally motioned to him weakly. His voice came out as a croak: "Let's go, Bert. We've got enough and to spare."

"Why, Lard, you're shaking like a boxcar. Luck is a female you can't have if you're scairt of a social disease. Now you go back and mind the store and don't worry about nothing. A few more hands and I'll own all this around here for miles."

Wally's gentle blue eyes were pleading.

"You old booger," Bert grinned. "I have to win enough to feed you, don't I? Lord have mercy, it's like feeding Napoleon's army. Just look how puny you are. Short rations and long highways have took their toll."

Wally couldn't help himself. Bert felt so good, especially considering the misery he'd just been in, that he didn't have the heart to stop him. "All right, but play careful," he said earnestly. "I'm praying and hoping for you, Bert."

The pressure of watching was more than he could take. He went lumbering outside into the town. The ferocious hunger grew every minute. His nervousness yawned and echoed in a huge cave of hunger. He found himself gazing into a cafe window and yearning at a half-eaten ham: the pink and white flesh swelled out richly from a dry knuckle of bone. Wrenching himself away, he went back to the hotel.

With scrupulous honesty, he insisted that Mrs. Harbaugh hold the Geiger counter. "I don't want you to be losers on account of us," he said. "That counter will just about cover the broken window and busfare for two back to Denver, in case Bert has bad luck. Which he might."

She folded her arms under her sunken breasts. "That Bert is a high roller, I can see that," she said with admiration. "He's like them Las Vegas high rollers."

"Yes, ma'am, he is. He's nine hundred dollars up, but he'll either bust the game or go bust. Personally, I'm shaking in my socks. That's how come I gave you the Geiger. To be accurate, I ain't hopeless or I ain't hopeful," he said. "It's in between. A little more on the hopeless side, I guess."

Sympathetically, she invited him into her room behind the desk for coffee and cookies. He blushed and said, "I'm much obliged, but I'm a married man, Mrs. Harbaugh. Thanks just the same." She called him a darn fool and, rather acidly, informed him that there were two other people there. They turned out to be an Indilan kid named Charley and a stringy blonde girl who was sitting on the floor with her knees drawn up to her chin, working on a crossword puzzle. Her name was Lucy.

"What's a sixteen-letter word for truck?" she asked him. "Starting with R."

"I sure couldn't say," he answered seriously. He placed his hat, seived with airholes, upside down on the floor next to his chair. "Those puzzles are good for your vocabulary," he observed. Unfolding herself

Uranium!

and rolling over on her back with her pencil in her teeth, she said, "Well, try this one. What a *fifteen*-letter word for truck?" Her face was perfectly grave. Ordinarily he would have been jolted to the roots, but now he was blurred and vague with anxiety. His eyes grew more and more vacant as he looked at the potted plants and the baby pictures, a whole raft of them, starting at one day old and going on up, that crowded every inch of space with creamy faces and glinting frames.

"Those are pictures of my grandchildren," Mrs. Harbaugh said from the stove in the back. "My daughter and her husband moved to Tucson last year and it just about broke my heart. But I make do with these rascals." Fondly she looked down at the children sprawled on the dim ferny rug. "These are my babies now."

"Yes'm. I have two boys myself," he said, but for once he didn't even take their snapshots out of his wallet. The cookies, when they finally came, only made him hungrier. Mrs. Harbaugh's gabbling voice dropped right through his mind into a bottomless void of starved worry. Bob Werden wouldn't send enough money even to get their truck back; in fact, all at once Wally knew that Bert was right and that Werden wouldn't send them a dime. He could feel it in every bone of his body. So it was do or die now in the poker game. For a minute he comforted himself with the plan that if Bert did bust the game, they could send a thousand dollars to Esther and maybe win her over, at least partway. But in his heart he knew that Bert was going to lose in spite of his brilliant intelligence and skill.

"This dry spell," Mrs. Harbaugh jabbered on. "It's so bad we can only water the lawn twice a week." The girl had stopped doing the puzzle and was just staring at him with wicked sweetness. The Indian kid was reading a tattered comic book. "I've heard those atomic tests is causing the drought," Mrs. Harbaugh said. "Does that make sense to you?"

"Huh? Oh—That I couldn't say, not being qualified. It sounds reasonable but like I said, I'm not qualified." There was an ache in his stomach. He felt as if he were suspended in a hollow of craving and it was getting larger and larger and larger. He wondered if it was wrong to say a prayer that Bert would win. The children went out somewhere and Mrs. Harbaugh started telling him about the Indian boy and how worried he was because somebody named Mr. Butler was in the hospital. She rambled on about Lucy, some long muddle about her father being manager of the Piggly Wiggly store but she was running wild and Mrs. Harbaugh let her stay here to keep her off the streets. . . . None of it made any sense. His head was thudding.

Getting to his feet, he thanked her for her hospitality and fled upstairs to the fever-hot little room under the roof. He hoped he hadn't hurt her feelings by running off like that . . . He was almost out of his mind with hunger. Suddenly a howl, a stupendous wail like the death-scream of a great animal shocked the breathless air. Wild-eyed, he stumbled pell-mell down the stairs and discovered Mrs. Harbaugh placidly thumbing a button behind the desk: it was ten P.M. curfew. For some mysterious reason the town siren was her responsibility, and it was parked up on the roof directly above their room. Talking to himself, he climbed back up the stairs. Out in the moonless night, dogs were still yowling their answer from the yards of the town.

Then he heard a bumping on the stairs and Bert came rollicking in. Frisky and grinning, he clattered a little tap dance across the floor, his brush of hair flopping on his forehead. Wally's heart gave a jump. He swung off the bed with an eager smile.

"You mean it's okay? Whewh, I put in some rough hours, Bert. Rough hours. How'd you do?"

"How'd you do yourself?" Bert said, shaking hands with him.

"Come on, don't tease me. I'm all in a jangle. Just give me a look at the money so I can breathe easy."

Bert grinned and said cheerfully, "You better take up your belt another notch, son. We are broke flatter than a slice of baloney. Now there's no sense looking like a cheap funeral, Lard."

Wally sat down on the bed. The springs gave deeply under him.

"Son, I had three jacks in a five-card stud game, and four sixes beat me, a seven hundred and fifty-three thousand-to-one shot. And I was dealing, so there wasn't nothing crooked about it." He shrugged humorously and punched Wally on the shoulder. "Come on, raise your drooping head. Tell you what, you can have the bed without cutting cards for it. No good? You're still mad? Damn, you *are* hard to please."

Wally felt as if he had been turned inside out, but it was still impossible to really take it in. The numbness of complete and final defeat, the desolation were still to come. Al he could think of was Bert's amazing good spirits. He was actually humming, and there was nothing faked about it—Bert, who went sick to his soul at the sight of a hurt dog, was laughing over this, laughing! It was the most incredible thing he had ever seen.

"I don't get it," he mumbled. "How can you joke—laugh?"

Bert was more amused than ever. "You don't get it? Son, when that kind of lightning hits, it's really comical. I mean that is *rare*. A ordinary man can't relish it, maybe, but if you think I'm ordinary, just watch this for talent."

And the crazy sonofagun jumped two feet in the air and knocked the heels of his boots together, laughing, laughing in hilarious spasms. Then he went clip-clopping around the room, his scalded face grinning in the weak sour light. "Oh them golden slippers," he wheezed, "Oh them golden slippers, golden slippers I'm gonna wear, to walk the golden street."

IV

At noon the following day Sam and Vivie Bolton were still at it, staking one claim after another. The heat in Red Canyon was stupendous, crushing, but Sam worked up and down the canyon wall, blazing pine trees and gouging marks in the stone with a chisel. His hairy face was the color of the pink clay, his spit was like drying mud. The air was choked with the smell of sun-heated sage. With a grunt he hoisted himself up onto the rim of the canyon and started to pace off the rest of the claim. The orange blooms of the cactus burned like flames in the rotten pink stone. Suddenly his foot came down on a wriggling and lashing dark whip. Instantly, by pure reflex, he kicked at the lifting head and stamped his boot into the flexing, twisting length.

Too late, as he crushed down at it, his tools dangling and jolting from his belt, he saw that it wasn't a rattler at all but a goodnatured, harmless old blacksnake useful in getting rid of all sorts of rodents. Slowly, dragging itself in agony, it wavered toward a bush, tipped halfway over on its checkered side with it long pale belly showing. Sam stepped forward to put it out of its misery. The lag of its crippled body drew up into a weird, off-kilter loop and its head wobbled up, perched on a kinked and broken neck, and it flickered its double tongue at him valiantly. He didn't have the heart to finish it off, and with a jerk of his massive shoulder he went pacing away. Within a few minutes, absorbed in walking off distances and pounding corner stakes, he forgot the pitiful accident.

His dedication was furious, total. He and Vivie even camped out in the canyon in order to start earlier and work later; and by the squirmy firelight he'd read mining law and everything the government had issued about uranium. Not too much was known about it, really. By bad luck, uranium oxide was water soluble and millions and millions of tons had washed out of Red Canyon, down the Cheyenne River and eventually out to sea. All that was left were crumbs, small outcroppings or pockets near the surface that hadn't been washed away. This was the typical pattern for the whole country. The largest ore body uncovered so far in the U.S. was twenty-five thousand tons, most of them ran around one thousand tons or less. Still, at thirty dollars or more a ton, a sizable pocket could make them rich, and up to now he and Vivie had turned up five hot spots, just how big and how valuable they didn't know yet. The big point was *not* to walk up and down the countryside with a Geiger and stake around showings of radioactivity. Most of the good ore was a few feet under the surface and even his new scintillometer couldn't pick up anything deeper than two feet underground.

By using his head a little bit he had come up with the answer: stake by geological formation. Uranium ore was found in sandstone and limestone, any of the sedimentary rocks, and *never* in shale or clay or mudstone. Red Canyon had an average of three hundred feet of red sandstone on a foundation of shale, and so they had been staking what he figured was the better canyon wall, starting halfway up, where the shale ended, and going back onto the rim.

They'd been plugging at it eighteen hours a day for twelve days. All they needed was a little more time, just a little more, and they could sew up the canyon. In a frenzy of haste he took a sight down the cliff and slashed with his hatchet at the trunk of a jackpine, his muscles gripping and shifting under his rolled-up sleeve. Two hundred feet below him on a crumbling red shelf, Vivie was nailing up a discovery notice, a piece of durable white butcher's paper on which she had printed the name of the claim, their names, the date, and so on. She had the new scintillometer which he'd gotten yesterday by railway express, but she dearly loved her old Geiger because it buzzed and lit up like a juke box, and she kept using it to make the preliminary exploration of the claims. He scowled. As soon as he had worked back down to her, he said, "Stop playing with that toy, will you? The scintillometer only has dials, but it's sixty-five times as sensitive. I didn't put out seven hundred dollars cash money for you to let it set there."

"I'm sorry Sam," she said meekly. Her face was gritty and flushed with heat under her straw bonnet with its dangling blue ribbons. Relenting he wrapped his ponderous arm around her and made her take a drink from the canteen. "You're doing a good job of work," he said to her.

"No, it's you, Daddy. I'm so proud of you."

He grumped modestly and took a huge, sucking drink of the tepid water. "I think we both done our share," he said. "Well, as long as I'm down here, I guess we can spare a few minutes for a bite to eat."

Gratefully she hurried to take the sandwiches out of the pack and they settled down in a bit of shade. The air was sick with heat. Even the shadows seemed to be filled with burning particles of light. Vivie, however, was too happy to care. "It's like the first days on the little ranch again," she said softly. "You remember that poor little calf born in the winter and her mother died and I hand-fed her?"

"Unhuh, and old Jensen drove her off in broad daylight and branded her." He snorted. Vivie's eyes flashed in her pink face as she battled over it again, as she went straight to Jensen's ranch, cursing the old thief back to the day he was born, and took her pet back from him. Her wide generous teeth were smiling, and Sam was nodding and grinning, but almost at once there was a frown on his face again. Munching on a ham sandwich, he said, "We don't have enough time, we don't have enough time."

"Why not? Dear sweet lovely Bud Robel has everybody dogging after him in Horse Canyon—except those old archaeology boys, I mean."

"Bud sure has been a godsend. The whole herd of almighty fools went stampeding after him and gave us darn near a clear field. But we won't have it long. Any time now they'll be back here, crawling all over this canyon like ants, staking everything that don't move. If we only had another week, even till the fourth of July, we could have the cream skimmed off. But the Registrar of Deeds at Hot Springs knows about us and so does that lawyer we brung out here . . ."

Then he saw it again. High, high above the rim of the canyon, spiky-winged buzzards were winding down out of the sky like a slow black funnel—down to the dead snake, he judged. But as he watched absently, figuring, worrying, talking, he saw a movement up in the pine-bristling rocks. Then it was gone.

"What's the matter, Sam? Those buzzards?"

"Nothing, nothing." He squatted on his heels, his eyes small and hard in his bushy face.

She said, "I'm so excited, Sam. We're going to be millionaires, I just know we are."

He laughed by splitting his lips and grunting once. "When I start something I intend to lick it, but this ain't simple. Most of them claims won't amount to shucks, for one thing. And we're gonna have to do some real humping. We have to stake as long and fast as we can, then get a discovery hole dug on every claim inside of sixty days—that item can't be let slide, as you saw proved. Then I have to bulldoze roads into here and fix up a wagon drill and test drill all these claims. After that it'll be time to talk about mining. It's gonna run into a lot of expense, too. Nothing I ever bit off in this world chewed easy, but this uranium chews like rope and many a man will be broke and ruined before it's all over. Why those darn fool kids of ours could have us bankrupt before then—selling off stock behind our backs. That Pierce is gonna get his hind end kicked just as soon as I get some free time. And a new pair of keen-toed boots."

But the ranch wasn't real to him any more, and they both knew it. This was the passion of both their lives. Vivie laid her hot pink face on his shoulder and said, "We can do it, Daddy. Then I'm going to get me a new red jeep and a Cadillac for both of us and . . ."

"Do instead of dream," he said, slapping her rump, and back he went to staking 600 by 1500 foot plots in the savage light and heat, tireless, charging.

Then, as he sweated up the jumbled rocks, he heard a little puncture of noise far above him, just a prick in the hot silence, and then a dribble of loose stones. It was no animal, that was sure, and it was no wandering idiot with a Geiger, either. For two days this eerie pursuit had been going on. At first he had brushed it off but little by little it had got to him until now he was uncomfortable about it. And irked, plenty irked.

What tied his hands was that there wasn't time to investigate. Every minute of daylight counted; every claim could be *the* claim that would make them six or seven hundred thousand dollars. The spying was sure a puzzler, though. Who was it? And why was he tracking them? The archaeology boys had been circling their claims—which was idiotic because uranium ore didn't run in veins like gold and silver, but in pods. In the gold-rush days of California and Alaska, the prospectors staked around a rich claim, hoping the vein would run into their property, and the college kids evidently had been reading Jack London instead of the government pamphlets. How could they be educated and be so stupid? Anyhow, it couldn't be one of them. In the first place, they had to dig bones until five o'clock, and to clinch it, whoever was up there was an experienced hunter. Of course, a lot of riffraff had come in lately and it could be somebody else trying to stake around them. . . .

But heck, that didn't hold water, either. A greenhorn staking around them would simply do it, and he wouldn't keep himself so carefully out of sight—but this ghostly, invisible watching without any purpose, it got under his hide.

Again and again he squinted up the towering red pillars, up into the pine-blackened crests heaped in the sky. Nothing. Crickets sawed in the broiling afternoon. Heat welled out of the rocks. By three o'clock, climbing and pacing off and driving stakes at breakneck speed, he had nearly put the problem out of his mind. He was halfway up a stupendous rock face, banging with a hammer and chisel, when a lurking sound under the knock of iron and the returning echoes warned him. There was a skitter of pebbles above him. Then stones whizzed past, rocks the size of fists dropping out of the blank sky and clattering, rocketing down and bouncing hundreds of feet below into the shale. Vivie, thank God, was a hundred yards to the side, stooping along over the pink rubble with the scintillator. He couldn't get any view above and behind the cliff. He started to shout to her to look up there, then saw that she was under a sheer lift of canyon wall, even more out of position than he was.

Now what? He couldn't get up there fast enough to nail whoever it was. For the first time he believed that they might be in real trouble. Possibly the falling rocks had been accidental. Possibly. But the sense of threat smouldered along his nerves, and his eyes roved constantly as he worked. Though he hated to spook Vivie, he had no choice now but to tell her about it. "Keep an eye out," he warned her. "I can't figure this at all but I'm pretty cockeyed sure it ain't good."

The worry kept grinding in his head as he slaved away. His nerves pinched as he heard a sudden tapping down below him in the canyon. A few minutes later a sweating man in a city hat and shoes came into sight, tacking up pieces of paper on trees more or less at random—a complete greenhorn trying to stake shale without cornerposts or anything. Right on the dot at six P.M. the college kids came jeeping along the canyon road; they waved ironically up to Sam and curved out of sight beyond Old Woman Creek. Edgy and irritable to start with, he muttered angrily, "That's about enough of their antics. I got a good mind to run the whole bunch off the ranch."

A thousand feet above him in the pines, something glinted like a stitch of white light in the hot sunshine. It was unendurable. There was no chance at all of getting near the nightmare tracker up there, but he launched himself up the jumbled boulders anyway. Shadows were spilling down from the high, sharp-beaked spurs of rock. Vivie called after him. Stones rattled off from his boots. As soon as he clambered onto the rim, he broke into a stumbling trot and plowed headlong into the pine woods with the hatchet in his hand. A rabbit jolted up in front of him and scampered away in springy bounces. His breath was lurching. His eyes were dazed with sweat. Tripping and reeling through the pine shadows, he lugged to the top of the hill.

Not a thing. The wind-combed pines hissed around him. The rocky slope, littered with brown needles and cones, scrambled down into a narrow ravine. Something twitched the baking greasewood in the middle of it. Recklessly he lunged downward, digging his boots into the dirt and rocks at each step, and rushed into the deep yawn of the ravine. The sides closed in, hot and still. The western cliff wall was in shadow, but sunlight still flushed the other side, burning on the red and orange stone.

He swapped the hatchet to his other hand, blowing hard, his boots crunching in the dessicated soil. Then he began to feel something, feel it through his pores, a presence like an invisible net poised above him in the heated air. He looked up and went rigid: printed on the sunny wall was the shadow of a man standing on top of the opposite rim with a rifle in one hand. Sam threw himself under the overhang of the cliff. It took a minute for the shock to lift and then, cautiously, cautiously, he inched along the wall toward the mouth of the ravine. By the time he reached it the sinister tracker was gone.

He met Vivie coming after him, halfway up the side of Red Canyon. "Go on back down," he said roughly. Pink dust exploded from his boots as he slid and jumped. "Move. Get the gear and come on." He grabbed the pack and the scintillometer himself and hurried her along. "We're clearing out of here and staying at home tonight."

"What about the camp? The sleeping bags. All our food."

"Forget it."

"But what happened?" she kept asking. "You scared me half to death, Sam. What's the trouble?"

"Plenty of trouble," he said, "for that guy trailing us. He's gonna find himself dead." Grimly, as they drove back to the ranch, he told her what had happened. During supper the family waited for him to cut loose about the cattle that had been sold off, but he was too preoccupied even to think about Pierce. He brooded on the menacing shadow stamped on the wall of the ravine. His best guess now was one of the ranchers he had bought out. It was hard to lose everything you had built for ten or twenty years to the drought, and it didn't swallow easy to sell out to a man who hadn't gone under. Sometimes there had been harsh words. These he had accepted in silence but to come after him with a rifle, that was something else again.

The next morning he told Vivie, "You better stay home today. There's no sense in you taking any chances."

She flared up immediately. "Old brother, you can take me along or I'll come by myself in a truck. Or I'll walk if I have to, so just you take your pick."

For a moment his cold, fierce intention relaxed and he gruffed, "I guess there's no use tying you up, you'd just get loose anyhow." Once they reached Red Canyon, however, he was sorry he had let her come. She couldn't be left alone in the jeep, a sitting duck down there by herself, and he was forced to take her with him up the rotting wall of the canyon. Wary, keeping her behind him, he crept to the top of the pine hill that overlooked their last claims.

"You roost over there and stay quiet," he told her. "I think we're here ahead of him, he don't generally show too early." They waited. A crumbled moon was giving its last light into the morning sky. A rough wind, still chilled with night, was blowing the shadows out of the broken-backed hills. "Darn it anyhow," he said. "This mess is slowing us down to a standstill." The thought of the claims they weren't staking, of the precious time going down the drain, was like a white-hot pressure inside him, growing and growing. An hour went by, then another and another. The thirsty draws and ravines emptied of darkness, and the sky was a stunning white. Vast thunderheads shouldered up over the hills in the east like gigantic slow explosions. The machine-gun tapping of a woodpecker began down in the ravine, spattering it with bouncing echoes. Sam fumed, galled and restless. Then a noise scratching in the distance and he picked up the rifle, his face tightening like a trap set to bite shut.

And a mangy old man came toiling out of a heat-shimmering draw behind Red Canyon. Feebly he poled himself along with a stick, up the hill toward them.

"Isn't that old Zeke Butler?" Vivie exclaimed. "What in the world!"

"It beats me." Alertly, snapping glances around and stopping to listen, he led the way down. "What the heck are you doing here, Zeke?" he said. "I heard you were in the VA hospital in Hot Springs. Why man, you're in no shape to go traipsing over these hills."

But as he looked down at the huddle of termbling old bones, he suddenly grunted as if he'd been hit. Why it was crazy. What he'd thought was a sorehead rancher trailing him with a rifle—why it was only this—only Zeke Butler hauling himself along with a stick.

"Well I'll be darned," he said and jacked his hat back on his head. "It's you that's been dogging me for three days, ain't it? Well, I will be darned. What for, Zeke?"

Butler's face wobbled up, perched crookedly on his thin neck. His eyes were dry seeds. "I want my claim back, that's what," he said in a dim scraping voice.

Vivie burst in hotly but Sam hushed her and said, "I thought you understood. Didn't you get our letter? You had sixty days by mining law to dig a discovery hole and you didn't do it, Zeke. The claim had lapsed back into public land."

"And not only that," Vivie said. "You didn't have the right number of corner posts. The law says eight, not four. Also, the paper you nailed up didn't give the name of the claim, either. That's besides the discovery hole you didn't dig."

"You must have got the letter," Sam said. "We sent one to your house. It's all fair and square. I checked with a mining lawyer and even brung him out here with two witnesses. Then I refiled the claim in Hot Springs. I don't gyp or pull fast ones, Zeke, you know me better than that." He unloaded the rifle and slipped the cartridges into his pocket. "But what I can't figure is you trailing me. You purt' near got yourself shot. What were you trying to prove?"

Butler's mouth opened into a tragic hole, accusing. "I was laid up in the hospital, and you stake right over me when I can't protect myself. Those boys from the Smithsonian Institute left Charley and me out here to walk it home, which about finished me off. And then you stake right through me. You call that fair and square?"

"I most certainly do," Vivie rapped.

Sam forced himself to go through it again. "The claim had lapsed a month before you even went to the hospital, so no advantage was took of you. Everything is honest and above board."

"Honest! Above board!" Butler shrieked. "Quibbles, quibbles. Right is right and not those quibbles. What does the Bible say: 'The letter killeth and the spirit giveth life.' But what's that to you? Gobble it all up. Everything. Sure, go ahead."

Sam was itching to get started, frantic. There were probably a dozen prospectors, besides those college kids, in Red Canyon already. "I don't have any more time for your foolishness," he said abruptly. "Can you make it back to your car? Where is it?"

A look of senile obstinacy and cunning came over the old man's face. "I won't tell you."

"You don't have to," Sam growled. "It's back on the plateau; it's got to be. You didn't walk all the way out here. Vivie, you take him. Take him to Hot Springs and let them explain it to him. You can file the last batch of claims at the same time. Drive around back to the canyon and pick up your notes on the way."

"Sure, sure," Butler mumbled. "Get rid of the old feller quick. That's the story."

But Sam was already racing up the hill. At the top, he swept his look over the canyon. Sure enough, far across the emptiness of flaming light, two ant-sized specks were crawling on the shattered red wall, and in just a second a car came lurching along the canyon road, pulling a long straggle of pink dust. More prospectors. The stampede had begun to turn back from Horse Canyon already. Rushing down to the jeep for his tools, he pounded stakes, nailed paper, and scaled up and down the red cliffs in a delirium of effort. He hardly noticed Vivie get the claim descriptions out of the jeep and drive away again.

Two hours later he heard her call and saw her struggling up to him, followed a long way behind by old man Butler, tottering over the rocks in his loose blue suit.

"What now? Why didn't you leave him at his house?"

"I tried to, but he wouldn't let me use his car to get back out here," she panted. Her heat-roasted face was stiff with exasperation. "The old monkey! He threatened to call the police on me, can you imagine? I promised on my word of honor we would bring it back tonight but he wouldn't listen. I could just strangle him. He knew all about our claim being legal, too. I took him to the courthouse and the minute I started in the woman told him, 'I already explained it to you, sir.' " With a sigh she dropped down on a boulder, fanning herself with her straw bonnet. "I'm pooped."

He scowled down at Butler slowly dragging himself upward. "Go back, go on home, will you? And stop crimping us."

"Surely, surely. You diddled me good and proper and now I'll just stand aside and clear the road. God curse you, Sam Bolton, and damn you to hell." Hobbling painfully in the heated rocks, he sent up grey little squeaks of hate. Then he stumbled and went down. His hat fell off. He picked it up and dusted it and put it back on his head but when he attempted to get up, his legs wilted under him. Sam, with a grunt of impatience, went skidding down to him. The old man's papery hands were in motion and he quavered, "Friendship, I'm not speaking of that, but you both were my pupils, both of you. For old time's sake, that ought to mean something."

Sam helped him to his feet. "You don't even know what you're yowling about. It's no prime claim. Why the surface barely tests out at ten-hundredths, that's the minimum the government will even buy. But I'll tell you one thing right now, Zeke. I won't be pushed to give up what's mine. I went to considerable trouble about the claim but it ain't that. All my life I've lived by this principle, I won't be pushed by any man."

Piteously Butler clutched at him. "Don't take it away, Sam. Without it, I'm done for. You might as well put a flower in my hands . . . the museum . . . all I've done in my life will be nothing." His little old eyes were sinking into tears. "Look; here, look. Getting down on my knees, will that help? If it will, I'll do it."

Sam had to catch him and hold him up. "Will you stop that? Come on and stand up like a man. Oh—I'll tell you what. I'll do all the drilling and developing and give you ten percent. You're not entitled to nothing, but what the heck."

To his utter amazement, Butler jerked away. "No sir, by God. Keep your ten percent. Completely do me out of it if that's your intention. Don't toss me a crumb."

"Now listen here, Zeke," he said, controlling himself. "You were a school teacher, so you're not stupid. Look at the facts. Drilling might prove it out to be real good—*might*, I said. Most likely, it won't be nothing but a dud. Anyhow, use your head, man. You know good and well you can't develop the claim. You don't have the equipment or the money, not even mentioning your health and age. Now I'll do everything and give you ten percent off the top. Just to stop this discord. If it comes to mining, which I hope it does, you can set back and collect. If it's sold, you get your cut of that, too. Now what do you say? Further than that I can't go."

"You can go to hell, that's where." And the old man fumbled

back down to the canyon floor, walked slowly to his car and drove away.

"Good riddance," Vivie said and they hustled back to work. The next morning when they reached their claims at dawn, they saw two shadowy figures up on the canyon wall, staking exactly where they had intended to drive their next posts. Scalded, furious, they began to stake on the other side of *them*. It was a desperate race now, a head-to-head battle, and every hour more trucks, cars, and jeeps came hurrying into Red Canyon. The heat was savage. Pale shadows hunched under the decaying red stones. High up by the pines, magpies were clustered on a dead rabbit in a squirming black and white knot. Twice the ground trembled and a dim thunder shook the blazing sunlight as another explosion was set off at the ordnance depot. Sam and Vivie drove themselves mercilessly but the men staking against them were good, very quick and experienced.

"Oh no!" she cried, all at once. There he was again, Zeke Butler, just sitting there, a stubborn wispy ghost down below them in the sun-scorched rocks.

Sam clamped his teeth together. His eyes shrank under his hairy brows. "Leave him set," he said and crunched away over the stones. Ignoring Zeke hour after hour wasn't so easy, though. When they stopped for lunch, they tried to give him a sandwich but he refused to eat or even to take a drink of water from their canteen.

"I wish Charley was here," he mumbled. "Listen, Sam, Vivie? Hear me out."

Vivie snapped, "You had your say five times over."

"Won't even dicker, huh? I'm done for, huh? Don't be bashful, say it right out."

It was no use. They left him there, munching tired curses, and rushed back to staking. Vivie was boiling mad. "The pesky old thing! If he don't quit this, I'm gonna tell him a piece of my mind he won't soon forget," she said, but they both slipped worried looks down at the old man sitting, just sitting in the hot glare. "I made him a fair offer," Sam grumbled. "More than fair. I'll be darned if I let him pressure me. I'm not going to give him the claim just to shut him up." It was sure a mess, though. They were haunted worse than before, by a long ways. He would much prefer danger, anything but this helpless, scolding old crackpot getting weaker and more tired.

Down he went to try to give Zeke some water again. The old man was in a bad way. He was huddled in the rocks and his sick eyes were flaming in deep hollows of shadow. His mouth was like a crack in the dry ground. He was mumbling about wickedness and the lust of concupiscence . . . uncleanness, vile uncleanness. Men were children of evil and they suckled at a beast of fire and God would spare them not. . . . He closed his eyes in their exhausted shadows.

His hands were still. The hot soil around him was living with ants, and there were ants crawling on his limp pants and on his pale, hairless legs.

"You knot-headed old coot," Sam groaned. He glanced despairingly at the other prospectors hard at work, and then he picked up the old man and carried him to his car. "You come behind in the jeep so I can get back," he told Vivie. "You oughta be back in the hospital, Zeke. Vivie will drive you there. What about it? For your sake."

Butler opened his eyes and kicked weakly, light, almost weightless in his arms, like a few dry sticks. "My hat," he squeaked and Sam had to go back for it. All the way to the house, he lay in a crippled sprawl and railed bitterly in dry, weak gasps. "You think you're quite the berries, don't you? A champion . . . well, I've seen better . . . I don't know S from fat meat, I guess I proved that . . . but I know one thing . . . You'll get yours in due time like me . . . and . . . it will be deadly, I assure you."

"Come on, leave us take you to the hospital."

"Be damned . . . to you," the old man said and then the trickle of faint words stopped. His eyes were like dry waterholes. But as they put him to bed, he suddenly opened them and said, "Scared you with those rocks, didn't I?" And a tiny cackle came out of his crabbed mouth.

On fire with irritation and haste, they went tearing back to the canyon in the jeep. "This fracas has cost us at least six claims," Sam groused. "I have to admit he gave it a fight, though. He kept swinging as long as he was able. I admire that." They worked until it was dark and slogged back to the jeep and drove to their camp in a side ravine. Spongy with fatigue, they crouched by the fire slurping harsh black coffee and canned meat and beans. Flames chewed at the darkness, sliced like curving orange knives. The logs were stuffed with fire. Moving shadows grew up behind the two squatting figures, swollen, bulging on the fire-lit stones, and all around were tumbled cliffs and gigantic rock pillars surging up, black, into the night sky. They were too weary to talk. Sinking in great swamps of fatigue they fell into their sleeping bags, feeling as if they were softening, melting into the soft thick padding.

Suddenly there was a blundering crash of branches, a clatter of rocks, and old Butler trembled into the firelight. "Don't do it, Sam," he said, weaving on his feet with his sticklike arms held out. "Please don't do it, Sam. Please." Abruptly he crumpled and sat down.

Einstein and Frankenstein

Albert Einstein was spending his last years at Princeton's Institute for Advanced Studies, sorrowful, haunted by guilt. The genius who was the symbol of the enormous achievements of twentieth-century science, who in fact represented the mind of the world, had become, at the end of his life, the symbol of its bad conscience. The familiar and much-loved old man in baggy clothes walked more and more slowly. The wrinkles under the rambling white hair were deeper; sadness had settled in the gentle eyes peering over old-fashioned glasses.

It was not that he had actually worked on the bomb, but in August of 1939 he had been persuaded to write a letter to President Roosevelt, warning him that the Germans were conducting atomic experiments and had cut off the sale of uranium from the Czechoslovakian mines.

The result was the Manhattan Project. Only after Germany had been defeated did the United States discover that the Nazis had made little progress toward an atomic bomb and by then billions of dollars and years of effort had been invested. The momentum was irresistible. A good many scientists tried to stop the avalanche they had set off, but it was too late; a weird, all-too-human race had begun: finish the bomb before the war ended.

It was a tragedy of errors all around. The bomb had been started in the mistaken fear that Germany would develop it first. Then it was used rashly, on an enemy reeling toward surrender.

Einstein was never to know peace again. Pathetically he insisted, "I really only acted as a mail box. They brought me a finished letter and I signed it." Like so many of his colleagues who had worked on the bomb, he continued to lament, "If I had known that the Germans would not succeed in constructing the atom bomb, I would never have lifted a finger."

In a futile effort to repair the damage, he held press conferences advocating international control of atomic energy; he helped to set up a committee of scientists to inform laymen about atomic power; he made speeches and wrote innumerable letters and protests. But the Soviet government would have no part of international control, and year by year the race in atomic weapons accelerated ominously. In 1949 Russia exploded its first atomic device, Joe One. Early in 1950 President Truman announced that he had instructed the AEC to proceed with work on a hydrogen bomb. Einstein spoke now with a sense of doom: "The armament race between the U.S.A. and the U.S.S.R., originally supposed to be a preventive measure, assumes an hysterical character. On both sides the means to mass destruction are perfected with feverish haste. . . . The ghost-like character of this development lies in its apparently compulsory trend. Every step appears as the unavoidable consequence of the preceding one. In the end there beckons more and more clearly general annihilation."

In despair he tried to absolve himself with his work at Princeton, picking up the threads of his grand but unsuccessful effort to unify matter, light, and gravitation. He even said to one of his assistants that "equations are far more important, for politics are only a matter of present concern. A mathematical equation stands forever." But some of the awful blame was his; he had helped to create the monster and morning after morning he would break off from reading the newspapers and call up associates to say, "I can't stand this. I can't, I can't."

V

The highway out of Enterprise cut the tawny land in half. Birds squirted up as a green stationwagon rocketed along in the July morning; cows jogged out of the way lumpily, brown families of pheasants broke and fluttered into the ditch.

"Bill don't 'low no girlies in our camp," the archaeology boys were bellowing, jammed together at the front of the stationwagon. "Bill don't 'low no girlies in our camp. We don't care what Bill don't 'low, we'll get a girlie anyhow." The song went rollicking into dirty verses: "If we can't get a girl, we'll get a cow," and even worse than that. At the wheel Dr. William Bush, Ph.D., tugged at his green sunglasses and managed to grin. His good-natured red face was beginning, at thirty-five, to plump out into jowls, but his big sweat-blotched hat was squashed up jauntily in front. After all, he reassured himself, the obscenity was really harmless and he enjoyed being teased by the students. Still, he felt distinctly easier when they turned to ragging him with songs about drunkards; he smiled and blushed happily and even added his baritone voice to their yowling—everybody singing together, sunburned and jolly, arms slung over each other's shoulders.

Well, not everybody. The fly in the ointment was Morris and the two boys at the back. They would *not* join in. Slouched down in the lurching seat with their hats angled over their faces, they were deliberately, pointedly sleeping. Or pretending to sleep. He could understand about the boys: they were soreheads, fed up with the digging, the accomodations and the salary, the lack of entertainment in town, everything. If it weren't for the uranium prospecting after work and on Sundays, they would have quit weeks ago. But Paul Cabbot Morris, his fellow teacher, his lieutenant, his second-in-command—there was no excuse at all for him. Treachery, that's what it was. Open defiance. And it was bad for the crew; it hurt the fellowship of the team and it undermined authority. Dr. Bush's only consolation was that the two soreheads hated Morris even more than they hated him. Those finicky standards of his had done the trick, insisting on perfect technique hour after hour in the brutal heat.

"Camptown race-track five mile long, oh doo-dah day," Dr. Bush almost shouted, trying to sing away his dislike. But oh, it was hard work. Mingling with the jolly voices and spoiling everything, absolutely ruining it, was the unspoken opinion from the back seat, like a mocking smile in the air. Dr. Bush had always thought he could get along with anybody but this—this dark, knotty, dangerous, sneering, ugly—Some of the things the boys reported about him! Really!

Item. He'd said that Doubting Thomas in the New Testament was his favorite hero. When there were so many wonderful disciples to choose from, Peter or John, the beloved of Christ. Doubting Thomas! This brought up the grave matter of his influence on the boys. He was unwholesome, absolutely unwholesome.

Item. He was the founder, president, and only member of a club to send money to Congressmen so they wouldn't take bribes in office.

Item. He had stated that mediocrity was 99 per cent perspiration and 1 per cent inspiration.

Item. Now he claimed to have been an ace in World War II! After he had freely admitted only last year that he'd cleaned latrines for most of the war. And in the States at that, in Texas or somewhere.

Item. Worst of all, he had openly ridiculed the expedition as a bunch of pothunters, amateurs who messed up grave sites. In his exalted opinion, the expedition was a combination picnic and treasure hunt. And there it was again, lifting its ugly head, their endless quarrel about the boys staking claims. After hours, mind you, on their own time. Morris was dead set against it and nothing, absolutely nothing could convince him. Nothing ever did, about anything. He was the most insufferable . . .

Sweating into his khakis with the effort, Dr. Bush tried to be generous, tried harder and still harder not to hate, not to hate. Tall electric towers marched across the empty land toward the rising sun. A hawk got up from a fence post. They were singing "The Sweetheart of Sigma Chi," mistily, sentimentally, when there was a swoop in the bright rush in front of him, then a plop! as a meadowlark hit the windshield of the hurtling car and skidded off, dragging a red smear across the glass.

"Got it!" Teddy chortled out of his black whiskers. "Scratch one meadowlark."

Dr. Bush endured this, too. Unfortunately it happened on many of the trips to and from the dig and the boys jokingly called it "improving the breed" and "developing the meadowlark by natural selection." He wished they wouldn't be so callous. But that was youth, high spirited and thoughtless, and perhaps he was too squeamish.

He turned off the gravel road. One of the boys jumped out to open the cattle gate, and they bumped along the wheel tracks winding over the rough, dry hills. The lads stopped singing and began to draw straws to see who would dig discovery holes that evening and who would stake claims. Even the malcontents next to Morris sat up, eager. Pitching sideways in the jolt of stones and ruts, Teddy held out a sheaf of match sticks and chanted, "Try your luck, gents. Step right up." The drawing went forward with groans and joyful whoops. A dumpy boy wearing a red neckerchief held up a long match and cried, "Mother, I'm home. I've escaped from Devil's Island!"

"Harry, will you be quiet?" Stan said. "I'm concentrating. The square root of eleven plus X equals . . ." He shut his eyes and muttering equations fervently, plucked a match from the clump in Teddy's hand. It was short. "No!" he roared. "I've been intercoursed. Foully frigged."

"Here now," Dr. Bush said severely. "No profanity."

Stanley put his hands over his face. "All day long I shovel dirt, and after that I shovel some more. I'm cursed, doomed! I tell you, men, when science betrays you it's the end."

"Buck up. Don't kill yourself, Stan. You've got too much to give the world."

"You think so? I guess you're right. I have to think of posterity."

Morris hadn't said a word since they started out. The only sign that he was awake was the cigarette smoke wavering up around his dark hat as the station wagon took the lift and roll of the land under the jarring wheels. Then, without even raising his hat, he said, "I suppose you all know that when we see something, it's printed upside down on the retina. Then it's reversed back again when it registers on the brain. Well, they gave a twelve-year-old kid a special set of glasses that made him see upside down. In two weeks he was perfectly adjusted."

His unpleasant voice grated to a stop. The smoke from the cigarette in his mouth strung upwards and broke against the brim of his hat.

"So?"

"What's the point, sir?"

"This. I have a theory. We're actually standing on our heads, and the people in Australia are rightside up."

Silence, blank silence. Dr. Bush, blowing a sigh from his mouth, tried to figure out what Morris had meant. It was a dirty crack of some sort, of that he was positive. About the prospecting again, of course. Morris was saying that *he* was right and everybody else was topsy-turvy. Really, the constant friction was too much to bear. Then Teddy, wonderful Teddy, clever bearded Teddy, turned the thrust neatly aside:

"I *told* my mother I needed new glasses," he smirked.

Dr. Bush laughed out loud and all the boys followed suit, guffawing. Immediately he swallowed down his laughter and looked stern, discouraging them. It was unprofessional to side against a colleague publicly, even when the colleague was Paul Morris, and he simply *had* to keep better control of his emotions. Firm measures, very firm measures, would have to be taken with Morris, but in private.

The hills sagged down into the wide, arid flats of the Cheyenne River. Sweeping in a long curve and then straightening, the wheel tracks ended at the old Indian burial ground: a few humps of dirt, a box of shovels lying in the torn earth, and the brown grassland flowing away on all sides under the enormous bare sky. As they stopped, he saw something move near the road sign, NO U-TURN, which the boys had jokingly put up among the graves. Something was moving in the graves, struggling.

"Good Lord, what's that?" he said, jumping out.

"Where?" the boys said, piling out after him.

"Beats me."

"It's not Easter Sunday, so it can't be . . ."

Dr. Bush whipped around and glared Teddy into silence. Then Harry cried, "Aw, it's just a cow. It must've stumbled into one of the graves during the night."

Only it wasn't just a cow. When the boys hauled it out with a merry heave-ho and a hearty shove, all together now mates, it stood by a ridge of dirt on three legs, trembling, with its head sunk almost to the dry grass. The other leg hung down like a piece of dusty rope.

"I thought your orders were to board the graves up carefully at quitting time," he said angrily. Light multiplied on his green sunglasses as he turned from one boy to another. "This is criminal. Absolutely criminal!" He started toward the cow, hoping that the injury was only a sprain, but halfway there the horrible limp dangle of the broken leg stopped him. "This is what I get," he said accusingly. "This is your appreciation for my going easy on you. Just look at that poor animal, just look!" Sheepishly the boys put the blame on each other but he wouldn't hear of it. "I don't want a scapegoat, you're all guilty! Everybody in the crew is at fault—myself included—for trusting you. I want you all to know that I've lost a great deal of respect for you. This is no light matter. I vouched for this expedition to Mr. Bolton personally, and you let me down. He's even been kind enough to let us use a house on his property and we've broken our trust with him. Our moral obligation. Boys, I'm *really* disappointed in you."

It was the strongest tongue-lashing he had ever given them and they hung their heads and looked very sad. "Well," he said, relenting. "What's done is done. We'll have to face the music. Teddy, you better drive over to his home and ask Mr. Bolton to come out here please."

"He's not there," the boys volunteered.

"He's over in Red Canyon every day."

"Yeah, bulldozing discovery holes on his hundred claims, the old hog. He snarfed up half the canyon before the rush came in."

"I don't care about that. Not one iota. Now get him, Teddy, and be sure to—you know, soft-pedal it. Say we're very very sorry and we'll be more than happy to pay for the cow." Teddy drove off and Dr. Bush ordered the boys to get to work. "And if I see any more loafing," he said, "it'll be just too bad. Everybody is going to shape up around here, as of now." The boys, looking humble and cowed, ventured to remark that the boxes of small tools were still in the station wagon. "Then shovel off top soil!" he barked. Stamping away over the dead grass, he grabbed off his hat and wiped his cropped head. The boys had needed that chewing out for a good long time. The whole outfit was going to have to get on the ball, and quick. . . . Not that the incident itself was serious. Even though they'd have to pay for the cow, it was by no means a total loss. It could be slaughtered and kept in the Cold Storage in town to supplement their diet, which hadn't been exactly luxurious.

Then he saw Morris just looking at him in silence—gaunt and dark and bent, with a sallow face that apparently no amount of sun could tan. Instead of wearing khakis like the rest of the crew, he had on a disreputable set of denim work clothes, faded and gaping with holes, the black-painted buttons worn through to the crusty silver pattern underneath. Fierce little eyes probed through those sunglasses of his, relentless, insisting.

"Don't waste your breath," Dr. Bush said peevishly. "I know what you're going to say. The boys boarded up the graves carelessly because they were in a hurry to stake claims. First it was greed and hate and every other vice under the sun and now the discipline is crumbling. The digging is sloppy because they have their minds on something else . . ."

"That's the coroner's report. What are you going to do about it?"

"I'll tell you one thing I *won't* do. And that's stop the boys from staking claims. This country needs all the uranium it can get."

"Billy, Billy, Billy. Isn't total destruction enough? We already have enough uranium to blow Russia as high as the moon."

"Which is exactly where they belong!" But then, rubbing his cheeks with both hands, he said, "Wait, wait a minute. Let's not quarrel, Paul. For once let's not turn this into a worldwide crisis. You're too intense about everything. Relax! Take things in stride, why don't you? What difference does a few more claims make one way or the other?"

Morris's little mouth bent sardonically. "What's one more Jew gassed at Auschwitz? What's one nigger more or less?"

Dr. Bush flushed and his white teeth showed for an instant in his pudgy brown face. "Paul," he said, "you're driving me to the breaking point. You're going to make me do something I don't want to do."

"Oh! The saddest words of tongue or pen: you're fired. Is that it? Speak."

"No, no, don't go off the deep end. Why don't you look at this sensibly? You know as well as I do that strength is the only way to stop Russian aggression."

"I agree, but dig a little deeper like a good archaeologist. Granted that Russia can't be allowed to nibble up countries one after another. But even a ten-thousand-bomb stockpile is only a temporary answer. Any balance of power has to be unstable—more and more uranium, more and more testing of more and more powerful devices, a heavier and heavier balancing of death against death. The world is on a seesaw, half on each side tipping up and down."

"Yes, yes, but as long as they're racing us, we've got to keep up, don't we?"

"But the race has to be kept in the laboratory, Bill, and off the front pages. Otherwise, like as not, we'll wind up in a new kind of dead heat—with both sides dead. This uranium hunting isn't necessary any more, and the craze is just starting. What was a real national emergency in 1947 is growing into a monster. Don't you see?" he said passionately. "It's part of a nationwide emotional avalanche. The whole age is morbid. All the fear caused by the atomic bomb is exploding. Just look at the bugaboo of communist infiltration. People trembling because they joined the Friends of the Soviet Union back in the war when Russia was our ally. It isn't safe to belong to anything but the P.T.A. and the Red Cross. It makes me sick! The country is turning into a lunatic asylum out of pure terror. And congressional vigilantes like Jenner and McCarthy and Velde . . ."

"Stop!"

". . . are building a police state," Morris went right on.

"No! Not another word!" Ordinarily so tolerant and peaceable, Dr. Bush began to shout, "Senator McCarthy is a great American! I won't hear a word against him."

"A great magician, you mean," Morris sneered. "Sawing Miss Liberty in half."

"Stop it, I warn you. He's a great American. He was decorated in combat—the purple heart."

"Awarded for an injury suffered in a bit of horseplay while crossing the equator. Some purple heart."

The boys had lagged in their digging and then quit entirely to watch the two men quarrelling by the graves in the vast emptiness. The steer stood on three legs, chewing at the scorched grass. And all around were vacant pastures and sagebrush and, far off in the light-stricken distance, a few cattle grazing by the shrunken river. Dr. Bush pulled off his floppy hat and shouted, "At least Senator McCarthy didn't claim he was an ace when he was actually cleaning latrines at a Texas Air Force base!"

With an offended air Morris said, "I'll have you know I kept those latrines in spic-and-span condition. They were much admired. Guys would come up to me and say, 'Nice job on the sinks today, Paul,' and things like that. Besides, I *was* an ace."

"That's a lie, and you know it."

"I didn't say I was an American ace. I was a German ace. You're baffled? In flight training every plane you cracked up was counted as an American kill. Five planes wrecked, and I became a German ace. It was then decided that I could help the war effort more in some other capacity." His narrow face was wickedly hard. "What else have you heard? That I said McCarthy was using the flag for a blindfold? No? Ah, then it was Doubting Thomas. That's it. Professor Bush, for a Christian you're maybe just a tiny bit ignorant. Doubting Thomas began the conversion of India in 54 A.D. Now what else? Did your little spies tell you what I said about McCarthy's misuse of funds collected to fight communism? That he speculated in soybean futures with them?"

"Do you know what I think, Morris?" he blurted. "I think you're a pink. A fellow traveller, a communist sympathizer!" His head was pounding heavily, and he was sick with raging hate. Even so, as soon as the words were out of his mouth, he knew that he'd gone too far: Morris stooped more than ever and his dull, uneven teeth lurked inside a ferocious smile.

"Dr. Bush and his portable gallows, huh? All right, I'm ready. All I want is a simple, dignified execution. Your excellency, I freely confess my crimes against the Reich, my only excuse is that I was led astray by bad companions. I die loving der Vaterland!"

"What are you doing?" Bush screamed. "This is a disgrace. Get the boys back to work immediately. Immediately, do you hear?"

With a blood-chilling little bow, Morris wheeled around in military fashion and cranked up his round back as far as he could, a grotesque caricature of an SS officer. "Burial detail, achtung!" he rasped at the boys. "Dig, you schweinhunds. Schnap it up!" They fell to at once, throwing cuts of dirt off their shovels at top speed. Rigidly, his face poked out in front of his turtle-back but his meager arms swinging in short crisp arcs, he marched over to the boys and examined what they'd done. "It shtinks!" he said. Dr. Bush spread out his charts and pretended to ignore him. Spinning on his heel, Paul strutted over to the cow and put his hands on his hips. "Zo!" he said to it. "Perzonally you haff my sympathy, but the weak and the unfit must be

Uranium!

eliminated. Pack your things and kommen-zie. Ve take a liddle trip soon now."

Under his jeering parody Paul was tight with frustration. Then he saw a distant fury of dust rolling out of the stony hills, and in a minute Sam Bolton came up in his jeep, followed by the stationwagon in a storm of grey dust. He was out of the jeep in one stride. Grim and slit-eyed, he brushed past Dr. Bush and took a look at the cow, squatting by the broken leg with his hat pushed back on his head.

"We're terribly sorry," Dr. Bush said. "Of course we'll pay for it. You set your own price on the cow, whatever you think is fair."

"I intend to. This steer will cost you two hundred dollars, professor." He stood up, and his heavy red face was like a fire. "Now collect your equipment and clear out of here. Get off the ranch. Now."

"What? But why . . ." Dr. Bush went grey to the lips under his smooth tan. "I don't understand," he bleated. "Be reasonable, Mr. Bolton. Accidents will happen. I don't understand your attitude. Will you explain yourself?"

"There's nothing to explain. I don't want you on my property any more; I got a bellyfull. And shovel in those graves before you leave; I don't want any more of my stock busting a leg."

Dr. Bush clutched at his arm. "Now sir, now listen." Waves of agonized expression went over his soft brown face. "Give us a chance. Mr. Bolton, I beg of you. This is important work . . ."

Bolton shrugged him away and walked toward his jeep. Dark and stubborn, Paul set himself in front of him. "You're not sore about that steer," he said bluntly. "It's the boys staking claims around you. Be honest about it."

Blood dammed up in Bolton's face. His anger surged and piled up like an almost visible pressure in the air.

Quickly Paul said, "You won't have to put up with them any more. Red Canyon is all claimed. The boys are just staking pasture now, and they have their eye on a roadside camp and the town park."

Bolton let out a grunt: almost a chuckle. He said it was their attitude he didn't like.

"Who does? In the Middle East we'd hire natives to do the digging, but here we have to use child labor. Nobody else will work for candy bars. Come here a second, I want to show you something." He lifted the boards from one of the graves and said, "Now imagine standing in this hole all day long. In this heat. Digging and scraping in tiny little touches. What better punishment could you possibly ask for them? It beats the *Inferno* any day."

"By Dante," Bolton said. "He wrote the *Inferno*. That's part of the *Divine Comedy*."

"Right you are."

The tough old rancher was proud of himself. "I guess you wouldn't believe it to look at me but I've read thousands of books. This archaeology, though, I'm as ignorant about it as that steer." And to Paul's amazement, he peered down into the pit with real interest. At the dark botton was the skeleton of a child, a pathetic handful of bones turned a pale, delicate orange by the soil. The eggshell skull was crushed. Tiny teeth jutted out of the ground. Beads, bright grains of color, were sowed in the small crumbling pelvis, which was stained a brilliant fresh green.

Bolton made a noise of pity. "Copper beads turned that bone there green, huh?"

Paul nodded. "In a way it's a sad business, digging this village. Only one child out of four reached the age of two years. The old women of the tribe did the burying. About three hundred years ago they carried this little boy out here, wrapped in a buffalo robe, and scraped a shallow hole for him. Over there, you see that bit of pottery there? It's what they call diagnostic. Pottery styles change, and we can date them fairly well. Just a second, I want to show you . . ." He got a small tackle box from the station wagon and, reverently, like a priest with his chalice and sacred vestments, he brought out his notebook for writing up the dig and his tools: a whisk broom, an ice pick, a folded measuring stick, paint brushes for twitching away crumbles of dirt, a trowel and a slender grapefruit knife. "The digging takes a lot of patience, but out of it we can reconstruct the past. Between the village over there, closer to the river, and the graves here we can get a picture of tribal life, the belifs and customs and—so on."

He flushed darkly and broke off. He couldn't say what it meant: saving this much anyway of life, keeping it from death.

"I think I'm getting the hang of it," Bolton said eagerly. Dr. Bush, running back and forth in panic, had set the boys to work, and their broad crumpled hats bobbed as they worked in the grave pits, bent over in the windless dust and heat. A meadowlark whistled, light and clear, on a fence post. Intense, rattling off dozens of facts and conjectures, Paul took Bolton from one grave to another. Stan pulled back so that they could see into his pit: locked in the dirt, crumbling skeletons lay together, face to face like lovers. "Notice how their knees are pulled up to the chest? It's the position of a foetus in the womb."

"Unhuh. Is that supposed to mean life after death?"

"Very good," Paul said, delighted. This dusty rancher was a formidable man. The way he had changed directions was staggering, and so was the impression of power, of crushing and irresistible strength in every motion he made. To add to that, he wasn't stupid.

This Neanderthal-looking man with his low, trenched forehead and gorilla arms was intelligent!

He stayed almost an hour before he finally tore himself away. "I'm much obliged to you, professor," he said, holding out a big calloused hand. "One of these days I'm gonna read up on all this. By the way, I'd have that steer butchered off as quick as possible if I was you."

As soon as he'd gone, Dr. Bush went into arm-flailing hysterics. Paul watched in disgust. Camp Rockaway had been saved, but the jolly scoutmaster was still shaking in his suntans about his precious career. "Marvelous!" he was shouting. "Just marvelous. We were within a hair's breadth of complete disaster. Maybe you think because we don't have to get out that it's all right. A mere bagatelle. Well, you've never been more mistaken in your lives. You've played your merry tune, and now you'll pay the piper. Effective at once, there will be no going to town for two weeks."

Groans and protests went up from the boys standing in the pits.

"That won't help one bit. You're going to shape up if I have to put the town off limits all summer." Striding away in pudgy wrath, he drove off to see about having the steer butchered. Hats, curses, tools and canteens went flying out of the graves. "Who does he think he is, Captain Bligh?" one of the boys grumbled. Paul ordered them to get back to work. "Fungoo," Teddy said, but under Paul's fierce, drilling stare he picked up his hat, sourly, grudgingly, and the others obeyed too. Paul didn't like the look of it, though. In a really inspired piece of folly, Bush had done precisely the worst possible thing. Having first run the outfit like the Good Ship Lollipop, he had suddenly clamped down too hard. Some very ugly trouble had cropped up on these expeditions in the past and more was coming now, growing, gaining momentum with vicious swiftness.

But as he dug and photographed and took notes, his grimness slowly left him and he recovered his detachment and sense of completeness. At noon, chewing absently on a sandwich, he walked across the withered grazing land to the Indian village. The earth lodges had collapsed a century ago, leaving great thick rings of dirt wall eighty feet in diameter under the grass. Bush had not the slightest intention of digging the village at all this summer, or the next either if possible, because all he really wanted was the sacks of bones they brought back every day from the dig. What a farce. He was what was politely known in the trade as a physical anthropologist—to wit, a measurer of bones —and except for the prestige of being connected with the Smithsonian, he would just as soon have bought the bones in a dime store and run back to his laboratory at the University to measure them. Archaeology itself bored him; in fact, he despised it. After pleading with him in vain for weeks, Paul had started uncovering one of the earth lodges on his own time. Patiently, patiently, he worked with a trowel on his hands and knees. The dead grass went off on all sides, shivering in tides of heat and light. Sweat leaked into his eyes. What he wanted more than anything in the world was to dig in Assyria or Egypt, or at least try the places here where ten-thousand-year-old Folsom flints had been found, but this was as close as he would ever get, a fourth-rate Indian village in South Dakota. And yet there was absolution in the work, and, digging out here alone in the parched grass and the numbing light, he dreamed down into the earth, recovering the lost and broken life under the dirt. Tips of bone peeked from the soil, round and orange, like fruit growing in the dark earth. At one o'clock he walked back, and all afternoon he and the boys stood in holes with the dead under the flaming sun, brushing and scraping, clearing the poor skeletons tangled in a night of earth. Dust swirled along the trenches. A radio was playing in the graves. The boys obeyed sullenly when he told them to give the cow some water, and a steady fire of ill-tempered remarks crackled from pit to pit. He scarcely noticed. Released, exalted, he was fixed on the still logic of fitting the past together; he could feel it grow in his mind like a shimmering architecture. It was a kind of resurrection. It was a small luminous eternity created out of the stupendous chaos of all that had been born and lived and died.

Just before they called it a day at 4:30, Bush showed up with two men and a truck. The cow stood on three legs, groaning softly. Its dull, white-fringed eyes were bright with pain and a green slobber hung from its mouth. They shot it and cut its throat. Blood vomited from the lopsided mouth slashed into its neck. The grass was drenched, splattered with red spasms of blood, and still the heart in the motionless carcass went on squeezing, squeezing, and the throat welled blood into the red mud around it. The men backed the truck up and let down the tail-gate and two of the boys helped pull the steer up with a rope. The others watched, fascinated.

"Dumpkopfs," Paul bristled. "Haven't you ever seen an execution before? We had to set an example to the other cows. Now board up the pits and load the equipment. Schnell!"

"That will be enough of your Nazi lingo," Bush said. "I'll have you know that this has been the worst day of my life, the absolute worst. What I had to go through to find somebody to slaughter that cow." He was most upset, and on the way home when the boys kept after him to lift the restriction, he said with an air of grievance, "I'm very very sorry but you've got to learn that life isn't child's play. It's deadly earnest."

The rest of the drive was silence. They were quartered in a deserted sheep ranch that Sam Bolton had bought up years ago, and

Uranium! 83

nothing had ever given Paul such a sense of life crowding in and replacing life that had crumbled and gone under. He and Bush had set up in the house, a two-room shack with a gaping empty door, broken windows, and a corrugated iron roof that tapped and banged all night in the wind. A shattered white chamber pot lay in the weeds and decaying machinery. Fifty yards away were the tumble-down pens and the low grey sheep barn where the boys slept on canvas cots. εχ, λτΔ: the derelict walls of the barn sprouted a luxuriant crop of fraternity symbols, and a grisly yellow quarantine notice (SCARLET FEVER: WARNING) had been nailed to the door. Half swallowed up in weeds, a gaunt outhouse leaned in the heavy sunlight. A brash red-and-white sign, tacked to it in happier days, said HARVARD.

In surly haste the boys washed up, gobbled the supper of weiners and beans and grocery store cake, and roared off in the jeep to stake claims. Paul ate a little without noticing what it was, shaved his coarse whiskers and put on an old-fashioned linen suit. Wearing it he looked, with his round back, like an out-of-work violinist, but he marched into the other room and drew himself up, clicking his heels smartly, ready for his nightly turn on M.P. duty.

Bush threw him a nettled glance. His face was blistered with sweat and he was in his underwear, beginning his daily letter to his wife. The iron roof poured heat down like a furnace. The slumping bed was messy with wilted sheets. A few miserable chairs and boxes were scattered around the table of warped grey boards where they all ate. "I meant every single word," he said to Paul. "Any boy that so much as sticks his nose into town, I want you to report him. Is that understood?"

"Jawohl, Herr Commandant."

"Will you stop that?" he almost screamed. Then, closing his eyes, he rubbed his face as if to erase the angry creases. Flies staggered on the table. His underwear was stuck wetly to his sleek little paunch. "Paul," he said after a tremendous effort, "things may not be ship-shape between us but I want to give credit where credit is due. You saved the day with Mr. Bolton this morning and I wish to express my thanks. Even if you didn't do it for me, I thank you."

"Could I take it out in trade?"

"What do you mean by that? It's a snide remark, I don't doubt."

"No, no, no. All I ask is one minute, Bill. You can't keep those restless young studs completely tied up. They need to drink some beer and sing some songs after working all day in this heat. Don't you see? You're afraid of a blowup, and that's exactly what you're provoking."

Bush waited for him to finish, sealed off.

"Are you there?" Paul said. "Speak to me, Rudolph. Are you happy there in the other world? Are they nice to you?"

"Ha-ha-ha. Are you finished?"

"Almost," Paul grated. "It wasn't all patriotism that made you such a red-hot supporter of uranium prospecting. You wanted to drain their energies, use up their free time, keep them out of town as much as possible. And now you've got six grade A, corn-fed Gadarene swine on your hands, complete with devils."

"Brilliant, absolutely brilliant. It's one of your most brilliant analyses. You know something, Morris? The more I get to know you, the more I thank God I'm not an egghead. I do, I really do."

"Amen to that." There was nothing more to be said. He drove into Enterprise. Having made sure that the jeep wasn't in town, he parked the stationwagon on Highway Street, where the boys couldn't miss seeing it, and went to have a couple of beers with Wally Riggs in the Victory Bar. It was a shabby old place. Pictures of registered herefords spread all over the walls in a sort of idiot multiplication, animal after animal after animal all exactly alike ercept for the different brands on their blocky hind quarters. Men, most of them with over-sized hats, were riding the stools with their knees spread out. Pretty generally ignored, a sickly looking fellow was playing an organ near the whirling fan, fingering melodies and singing in a small voice. Wally was in a booth, just sitting there while his partner frolicked around with two women.

"Set down, Paul," he said eagerly. "You're a lifesaver for sure. My own company ain't fit even for me."

All of Paul's frustration came bursting out. "Well, it finally happened, the jolly bone measurer accused me of being a communist sympathizer. It's the psychological gas oven. All you have to do any more is disagree with a super-patriot and you're a traitor."

"He oughtn't to say a thing like that. You're no communist."

"Everybody's doing it; it's the old game—whip yourself into a frenzy and set sail for Troy, attack the Hittites, make the world safe for Sumerians. Only this time you know what happens—Western civilization goes under, the world goes under. Mankind has finally produced its own ultimate test. Repent or perish, by God."

"It don't look good, that's for sure," Wally said.

"Repent of what? I'll tell you what, of being what we are. Ground apes that made good—and evil. Hell, the crisis is as old as life because life itself is the problem. We have to resist life; it all comes down to that."

"I don't get it, Paul. You're against life?"

"You might say it's a lover's quarrel. But I'm serious, resisting it is the only way to save it. The atomic bomb has at least done one thing; it's exploded the delusion that life can go on indefinitely unresisted. Unshaped, uncontrolled."

Wally bunched his forehead, straining to follow him.

"For example," he said passionately, "blind reproduction without sense or discretion. And not just uncontrolled breeding in the biological sense, but this craving to make more and more of *me*, turn everything into *me*, to grab everything in sight for myself and shove aside or get rid of whatever isn't *me*. The evil exploding in the atomic bombs is the evil in all of us, Americans and Russians, everybody. Stalin is *our* evil. The guilt of Nazi Germany was *our* guilt. My God, the things we do in the name of love, the murders we commit as a matter of course in business. My own father . . ."

His lean, sallow face knotted up. In a scalding rush it had all come back to him, the anguish of his father, of both his parents, all they had so confidently expected of him and all he hadn't become, and now the deep hopeless alienation . . . "Say something," he told Wally. "Talk, for Christ sake."

"Me? Talk? Not me," Wally said, with evident fright. "I couldn't contribute nothing of value. If I ever get started I can talk a blue streak but it's only hearsay, there's no knowledge in it." When Paul stared down at the pockmarked table without answering, Wally said earnestly, "You're doing me a favor, I mean it. It's a education for me."

"Crud. I've been out in the desert too long, that's my trouble. What I need is some locusts and wild honey . . . and a new goatskin wardrobe." He finished his glass of beer and said, "Drink up and I'll get us another one."

Wally fixed his eyes on his untouched glass, turning red all the way up to his pale hair. "Could I—could I have a hotdog instead?" he blurted. "As a loan, you understand. You'll be repaid the first dollar we make." His fresh blue eyes were sinking with shame. "I hate to be a moocher like this . . ."

"Hey, cut it out. Come on, you're entitled to all the loaves and fishes you can eat after that sermon you just got." He'd had the impression that they hadn't been exactly prospering but he was shocked, now that he really looked, at the way the skin didn't fit Wally's large mild face. His hair hadn't been cut in weeks, and no matter how often he combed it, it kept coming apart in long yellow straggles. He looked like a starved elephant, his huge clumsy bones bulging in sacks of skin and worn clean clothes.

"I wish you'd stop improving him and fill his belly," Bert hollered over. "I woke up this morning and he was chewing on my foot in his sleep." Flushed and soupy-eyed, he told the organist to play "Don't Fence Me In" and swayed his hand in time to the music. One of the girls in the booth with him rumpled his hair, and he flicked her hand away. "Look out, woman," he said. "If you had perty hair would you like somebody messing with it?"

"That's how we get by," Wally said to Paul in a low voice. "Women can't resist him at all. If it wasn't for Mrs. Harbaugh that owns the hotel—she likes him so she gives us food and lets us live there on the cuff, or I guess we'd be in jail. I always said I'd die before I'd be a moocher and now . . . we sure have hit bottom." He blushed as his stomach rumbled windily. "I don't know, it's like a trance or something. A hypnotic trance. Or a spell. Every day we get in deeper and deeper and nothing ever happens." With a hitch of his shoulder he managed a rueful little joke. "Any angle you look at it from, Paul, we're in a mell of a hess."

"I could get an advance from Bush. How much would you guys need to get back to Denver?"

"Oh no," Wally said hurriedly. "I shouldn't ought to have pestered you with our problems. Don't you worry about us, I mean it. For years and years we've always been setting out to find that old dollar tree and coming back without a cent. By this time we're well used to it. I mean it, Paul, there's no call for you getting upset. Why any day now the mining will start up and we'll be able to pay our debts and . . . leave out for home without owing a nickel."

There was a quality, a kind of gentleness, that came from the big slow humble man with the sporty little moustache parted under his nose. In just a week Paul had come to depend on him.

Outside, the terrible sky was beginning to darken. Beyond the railroad yards, low light sculptured the pine hills, deepened and carved them with cool shadows. The doors of the weatherbeaten Church of Christ stood open and lights glowed in the dusty orange windows. When the siren howled for curfew at ten o'clock, Paul headed back to the camp with a feeling of peace. The stars were clear and quiet over the sheep ranch, like luminous seeds floating in dark seadeeps of infinity.

He noticed that the lights were still on in the barn, and poking his face in the door, he told the boys, "It's time to go night-night. Brush your teeth and don't forget to say your prayers."

The boys made rebellious noises, and one of them slammed down a towel. Teddy, however, said brightly, "Yes sir, just one minute." The door closed with a dry gasp of wood and instantly his elaborate respect blinked out. "The Master has spoken," he sneered, his teeth glinting in his furry black beard. "The Holy One. Warmed-over Jesus."

A colored picture was being tacked up again to the board wall. Stan gazed at the girl naked to the waist, at the creamy ballooning of the pink-tipped breasts. "Boobums," he said ecstatically. "Boobums."

A hefty boy with spike-teeth and a dented jaw shoved him to one side. "Look at the size of them," he breathed. "You can have the delicate young ladies with falsies, I'm a gour*mand*." The other boys crowded around and struggled to get near the picture. The gasoline-pressure lamps gave off a dead-white, metallic light that leeched all

Uranium!

the color from them, drained the faces and the sun-burned bodies wrestling and hauling back and forth. Monstrous black shadows rolled on the walls and roof. Ugly quarrels had been flaring up all evening, and suddenly the horseplay teetered on the edge of a savage fight. The picture was ripped off the wall. Muscles surged and a boy went down.

"Heads up!" Teddy barked. "Knock it off, we've only got a couple of minutes. Quiet!" Slowly the boys broke apart, panting. The smell of their sweat thickened the air still reeking faintly of blood and wool and dung. "All right," he went on, "this meeting will please come to order. So far we have had three plans put forward. One, a general strike. Two . . ."

A tall clumsy boy flapped his arm in disgust. "Balls," he said, "I'm quitting. Split up the claims and give me my share." And refusing to join the meeting, he sprawled out on his cot.

"Larry, Larry," Ted said to him. "I'm disappointed in you. Just think, the blind have Helen Keller for an inspiration, the deaf have Beethoven." He paused wickedly, with his hands on his hips. "I was hoping you could be the same kind of example to the mentally retarded."

"Take that back," Larry snarled, leaping up. "You take that back or I'll bust your face open."

Stan came up behind him, ready to jump him if he moved. "Ignore him, Ted. He's just sulking because he's been refused by the national sperm bank in case of nuclear attack."

For a second Ted thought Larry was going to take them both on, but then he backed off, looking mean. "I was only kidding," Teddy told him. "Let's all take it easy and use the old I.Q. We've got to solve Dr. Fuddy-Duddy but quick."

"Hey, how about this? Any of you guys got any fireworks left from the Fourth? We could do a little testing of our own."

A number of ingenious (and obscene) suggestions were made as to the proper test site, but nobody had any firecrackers left.

"Well, we've got to bust him somehow. One more evening in this stinking barn and I'll go mickey mouse."

"I second the motion," Stan said. "Give me liberty or—something."

"Rum, Romanism, and Rebellion."

"Fifty-four Forty or Fight!"

"It's no use, I can't think," Harry groaned. His nose was peeling, and his sun-inflamed back looked purple in the ghastly light. "Jock," he said, "how long has it been since you saw your girl?" Jock (or Jockstrap, as he was called because he played football) swung his head and looked glum. Teddy grinned. "I saw him trying to figure it out last night." Holding up the fingers of both hands, he said, "It's this many, isn't it, Jock?" Jock shook his fist at him. Harry dashed over to a space between cots and, making a megaphone with his hands like a cheerleader, called for a great big locomotive for the team. Skipping this way and that, crouching and pumping his fist to the right, then to the left, he chanted, "C-O-P-U-L-A-T-I-O-N." The others joined in with emotion. Then, in the uproar, Stanley made it known that he had an important announcement. "Men," he said solemnly, "I've decided to surrender my most precious possession. My virginity." Two or three boys hooted, "Again?" They were all hoo-hawing when somebody cried, "There he is! It's him, officer. The masked terror of sorority row."

"Hold it, hold it." Waving his arms, Teddy finally restored order. "I think I have something. How's this for a strategic move? The silent treatment. No more buddy-buddy, no more Sunday School picnic. Nothing. Just do your work. Don't talk unless you're spoken to and then cut it as short as you can. And if that doesn't crack him inside of forty-eight hours, I'll quit myself, Larry."

A cheer went up.

"Mystic!"

"Theodore, you're the ace!"

Getting down on their knees, the boys salaamed to him, muscles undulating in the phosphorous-white glare.

"Everybody needs a god," he said, fingering the weedpatch on his face. "Worship all you want. I also accept gifts." As they settled into their cots for the night, they thought up crackerjack names for their claims: Aardvark, Oedipus Rex, Finnegan's Wake. Then Teddy said, "Wait! Wait a minute. I make magic, heap big magic." Grandly, with liturgical unction, he brought out a Geiger counter and a chunk of grey-and-yellow rock and held them close together: a stream of clicks erupted from the counter as it picked up the fiery leak of energy from the disintegrating uranium. He cocked his head, listening closely. "The oracle says the gods are angry," he declared. "They ask for a sacrifice. Stan, will you come here for a minute? Now close your eyes . . ."

The door screeched open, and Dr. Bush said indignantly, "Just exactly what is going on here?"

"Nothing . . . sir." With an insolent lack of haste they turned off the lamps, which went out with a loud *pow*, as if they were exploding.

Dr. Bush was annoyed—and just a little bit apprehensive. The next morning the boys went through the routine of breakfast and loading the stationwagon like prisoners of war, and on the way to the dig there were no songs, no cheerful cuffs and elbowings, no jokes. Desperately he started up the conversation again and again; they replied in monosyllables. All morning long they worked in the awful heat without a word, without even turning on the radio. The sawmill lifted a black smudge in the crumpled hills toward town. One of the boys was opening a new pit, and light flashed from the shiny tip of his shovel, wickedly sharp. It was heartbreaking. They were giving *him* the cold shoulder, they were all against *him,* his boys—didn't they understand that he hadn't wanted to discipline them? It was cruel. Why, they wouldn't even meet his eyes! Awkwardly, almost timidly, he prepared to take a photograph of Stan's work. Somehow he had to make contact, break through the invisible wall around him. Aiming the camera down at the jumbled skeleton, he tried the boys' favorite joke: "Now smile," he said. Stan, completely blank, simply waited for him to finish. Blood swarmed into Dr. Bush's face and he fled back to his charts.

At two o'clock dark, powerful clouds started coming up over the hills to the south: herds of clouds moving swiftly down on them, driving, stampeding. The wind was tearing at the naked flats and dust squalls swept across the pastures, spectral tumbleweeds turned over and over. A black-and-yellow bird clung to a lashing sunflower, making tiny squeaking noises, and then it whirled off in the fuming dust, blown sideways by the wind. Lightning flicked like horns in the charging greenish-black clouds. Dust boiled in the grave pits. Quickly Dr. Bush ordered work to stop, but instead of going into a rain dance and whooping jubilantly the boys covered the graves and loaded the tools into the stationwagon without one sign of enthusiasm. Even picking up eight steaks from the cold storage on the way back to camp made no difference to them. They hated him! It was impossible to go on like this—and impossible not to. The Gordian knot had been tied. He knew that he'd been too severe but if he gave in now, the effect on discipline could very well be disastrous.

His heart shrivelled in his chest and he felt like weeping. The rain started: hard stinging drops, bitter cold, shattering on the windshield and hitting the bald pastures with little explosions of dust, like miniature bomb bursts—like strafing machine gun fire from a plane, brief and vicious. And utterly useless. It barely settled the dust it kicked up, and before they reached the camp, the storm had blown over and grumbled away to the north-west.

In icy silence the boys climbed out of the car. He couldn't hold out any more, he just couldn't. "Boys," he faltered. "Boys, you've learned your lesson I think. The restriction is lifted as of now." Hoorays burst out, and they all joined in howling, "For he's a jolly good fellow." Delicious relief spilled through him, a warm sweet happiness that rose up and wet his eyes. "Provided you stay on the ball," he managed to add sternly. "And no getting careless again. Is that understood?"

The Gordian knot had been cut. Supper was hilarious, a celebration. The boys decided to skip claiming for one day, and they stampeded out of the house to get ready for town. "You better go in right with them," he told Paul. "And keep a close watch every minute."

"No thanks. You go." And he stooped away into his room, picked up a book and lay down on the swaybacked iron bed.

Bush went after him. "Why do you act like this? You never lift a finger to help me."

"You built this Doomsday," Paul said, "you can go downtown yourself and watch the Four Horsemen come in."

"Be reasonable, Paul. I can't sit around those taverns, I don't drink!" Morris ignored him and he gaped, helpless. Strictly speaking, he had no authority from the Smithsonian to make him chaperone the boys in town every night. If only, *if only* he had gotten him fired at the end of the first year at the University, when he still had the chance. "You must hate me very much to do this," he said mournfully.

"Not at all."

"Yes, you do. You're against me, you're against everything. You're ruining your life, Paul. Why don't you wake up? I'm serious. Have you ever thought of going to a psychiatrist? The way you're acting—I can't understand you at all. What's your philosophy of life, really? I'm serious."

Paul continued to look at his book. "It's too beautiful to put into words."

Bush felt his face grow hot. Everything about Morris, even his room, filled him with irritation: the stacks of outlandish books on demonology and twenty other obscure subjects; his portable record player and those crazy records that just set his teeth on edge, as incomprehensible as blackboards covered with mathematical equations; the awful seedy clothes hanging from a length of rope; the potbellied fertility stone (which he called "mother") squatting on his footlocker; the crazy modern art taped to the walls, looking like stained glass windows smashed to bits and put back together all wrong . . .

Crimson up to the eyes, he said, "I'll overlook that insult. Don't think I don't know what you're trying to do. You're trying to get rid of me, but this has come to a head. For three years I've been watching you, Paul. And honestly, just exactly what are your plans? What are you going to do with your life? You've written some brilliant articles, extremely brilliant. It would be a simple matter to finish your dissertation."

"I did finish it."

"Forty-five pages," he scoffed. "That's not enough, the entire committee agreed on that. I know, I know, you said all you had to say, but you could easily puff it up to a hundred and twenty-five pages or so, now couldn't you? Then you would be on your way, and I mean to the very top of the heap." Modestly, he didn't mention his own promotion to acting chairman of the department, the 30 percent raise, the Ford Foundation grant in the offing. "It's not too late, Paul. How old are you?"

"Twenty-nine," he said. "Going on thirty."

"That's still a young man. Don't you *want* to get ahead?"

"Of what?" Paul asked mildly. "Of whom?"

Frustration was throbbing, swelling inside him. From the barn, more and more pressing, came the racket of the boys getting dressed to go to town. "It's psychopathic," he cried. "You act like there's something fine and noble about being the lowest man on the totem pole. I think I may reasonably say I'm a success in life, and I don't see one single thing wrong with it. What's more, I firmly intend to be even a larger one. Do you want to know what I think? I think you're deliberately trying to fail! I mean it."

"What's so bad about that?" Paul let the book down on his skinny chest and smiled a sharp little pixie smile that showed his murky teeth. "It's a talent, just like success. You remember the story of the talents in the Bible, Bill. A person's got to use the talents he has."

"We all know you're very clever," Bush said bitterly, "but your actions speak louder than words. You need professional help. You're running backwards, you're making a career of going in reverse. And what are the consequences? Teaching freshman courses for a mere pittance of a salary, living in cheap rooms for the rest of your life. It's not normal! It's stupid! The train of life is tearing along the tracks at eighty miles per hour and you're fighting it, walking toward the back car. And what good is it? What happens when you get to the end of the train? Then what?"

"Get off at the next station and walk back along the tracks."

Bush wanted to scream: Get dressed, hurry up! The boys are about to leave! If only he had told old Archibald Jones not to renew Paul's contract at the end of that first year. Now the power was his, but now his wife—his own wife—was devoted to Paul and wouldn't hear of letting him go. Imagine. The mother of four children and pregnant with her fifth acting like a schoolgirl with a crush on the new French teacher. About Morris! It was enough to make you wonder. But Carol absolutely wouldn't listen, even when he'd pointed out to her that the weird creature was carrying on a similar platonic relationship with at least four other married women at the same time, courtly, urbane, a round-shouldered dandy in a baggy suit, bringing them flowers and gifts to the great amusement (and relief) of the husbands, and then sitting there and talking, talking, talking until three and four o'clock in the morning. In a way it was really a laugh to see this dangerous, odd, crabbed fellow suddenly become a hanger-on, a household pet. It was like having a tame boa constrictor around the house. All the crackpot had to do was finish his dissertation and he could afford to marry a wife of his own, instead of borrowing other men's —or even just stop feuding with his parents and accept some money from them. But not Paul Cabbot Morris.

"Have you ever thought how much you're hurting your parents?" he said. "Have you, Paul? Your mother spoke to me about you, you know, and really I felt sorry for her. I really did."

It was a last, wild, random shot and he could scarcely believe it when Morris stood up and began, slowly and somberly, to take off his denim jacket. "All right, I'll go quietly," he said. "No, no, please, no more. You've convinced me. There are disadvantages even in failure."

He felt rotten as he got dressed and drove into town. There was no mistaking the temper of the boys, and he dragged Wally out of the Victory and into the Cattleman's Bar where he could keep an eye on them. They didn't like it at all. Ordering their silly drinks, creme de menthe, stingers, gin fizzes, anything and everything and the wilder the better, they bellowed out table-thumping songs and practically assaulted the barmaid when she came near them. "Take me, I'm a moth scorching its wings," Harry said, holding out his arms. "Don't mind him," Stan said. "He's just a big, fun-loving sex fiend."

Paul went over to their table.

"Look, guys, . . ." He wanted to say something that would reach them, make a difference to them; he wanted it more than anything in a long time, and all that came out was a lecture barbed with ferocious irony. "You've all heard of Baal, the god of the Philistines. He was a sun god and a sex god, both. There were even statues of him as a phallus with a human head. In the spring they had ritual orgies, processions of priests in women's clothes with their stomachs padded to look pregnant, and men and women had intercourse in the plowed fields to make the crops grow. When the Israelites overthrew Baal, they called him Baalzebub, and eventually he became Beelzebub, the Prince of Devils . . . Have I made my point?"

The boys sat there, enduring him. As he went crouching back to his booth he heard snickers and Teddy chirped, "I've seen the light, men. It's the religion I've been searching for." Paul slumped down across from Wally, and the sense of defeat, of disgust with himself, grew like a dull pain behind the eyes. What a pathetic attempt that had been. Idiotic. He was a goddamn fool . . . The ranchers were disgruntled about the rain and their wry comments went up and down the bar: "I was afraid there for a while I was gonna get wet." "Yuh, that was a real Dakota six-incher, all right—six inches between drops." A gandy gang had come in from repairing the tracks, and they were all drunk and alternately petting and abusing a half-sized man with a red gargoyle's face who was the drunkest of all. Even Wally seemed to be in a trance.

"You look like you're in the middle of the Great Potato Famine of 1847," Paul said. "How about something to eat?"

"Huh?" he said with a start. "Oh—no thanks, it wouldn't be no use, five dollars' worth of grub couldn't hold me an hour. That's how I am when I worry, I get all the hungrier." Paul persuaded him to talk about it and then he said feverishly, "I hate to keep bothering you like this but maybe you noticed how Bert wasn't in the Victory? He's in the back room right here, in the poker game. How he ever got a hundred dollars cash money out of Mrs. Harbaugh to try his luck again, I'll never know. Except he can talk the hair off a dog if it's a female—not that Mrs. Harbaugh is a dog, I don't mean that." He was blotting at his face and neck with a limp handkerchief. "Could . . . would you mind going back there and see how he's getting on? I don't have the nerve to do it myself, I'm twisted up like a dishrag inside."

"Sure thing." Paul checked the game and came back with good news. "You can relax. He's got a big pile of chips and he's whooping and carrying on like the King of the Cannibals."

"That don't mean a thing," Wally chattered. "The last time out he was nine hundred to the good and lost it all back on four sixes. I'm scairt, Paul. You don't know what that does to you. I have grieved about them four sixes ever since. We've lost a scad of things, Bert and me, but that was . . . you see, I didn't figure we had a chance any more and now we do . . . and . . ."

He was almost gibbering with fright and Paul couldn't bring him out of it. Instead, his panic began vibrating inside Paul, too, and the sight of the boys huddling and talking intensely together seemed suddenly ominous. He had a strange sensation of the horrible, the obscene, multiplying with a kind of terrible inevitability. Wally was hunched over, grey and sick. The gandies were still drinking and tormenting the drunken little man. His broad red face was trickly with sweat. He waggled his stunted arms from his keg-like chest and mumbled in a foggy voice, unable to get up. "Hi, little wart," a scrawny Mexcan gandy was saying, over and over. "Little wart. What's wrong with that? You're smaller'n me, and they call *me* wart." The dwarf lurched out his flipper arms and his tongue rolled loosely in his open mouth. Tears leaked from his bulging, red-veined eyes.

"Sir? We're going over to the drugstore." Teddy was standing by the booth, crisp with sham respect. "Got to buy toothpaste, etcetera etcetera."

Paul nodded. He was on the alert, though, and when the boys didn't return in twenty minutes he said worriedly, "Come on. The Joy-Through-Strength Club is loose." They legged it toward the drugstore. The storm had veered around, and huge clouds lumbered across the lemon-colored west, black and shouldering. The stop light over the highway swung back and forth. A truck loaded with hay went by in the flying dust, a tarpaulin surging and beating in black waves on the yellow bales.

They plunged inside, and with a big gulp of relief he saw the boys actually drinking Cokes at two of the marble-topped old tables. In the center of them was a thin young girl who couldn't have been more than fifteen, and they were jostling each other and competing for her attention. He and Wally sat down at the fountain and Wally put away three milkshakes in one glazed, hysterical, belching rush. Paul was completely mystified; he didn't even know whether the boys had just met her for the first time. Probably they had. It looked harmless enough, and yet—why was it?—he couldn't get rid of that queer feeling he'd had in the bar. Mr. Mencke never stopped talking for a minute about the uranium rush. "Yessir," he said. "In two weeks I've just about gone out of the druggist business, I'm selling those Geigers so fast. Over eight hundred claims have been filed in Hot Springs already, it's a fact, and the boom is only starting. The government is sending down a geologist from Rapid. This town never seen this much excitement, why talk is so hot I can walk into the cafe and pick up a good Geiger reading in there." He laughed, pink and soft, with his girl's mouth. The wind pushed at the dark windows. Wally grew more and more desperate.

"I got a hunch that Bert has went bust," he said miserably. "He can't quit while the game is still going and sooner or later he'll get hung up in a knot hole again. I can feel it, Paul, I can feel it . . . Would you . . ."

He looked so forlorn that Paul didn't have the heart to refuse. "Okay," he said. "You keep an eye on Quantrill's Raiders for me." But he hated to run the risk, he could feel it was a mistake, and even before he hurried out of the Cattleman's Bar and saw the empty space where the jeep had been parked and heard Wally's stuttering cries, he knew that he had lost them.

His headlights tunnelled ahead through the blowy gloom. At every corner swaying arc lights pitched the street back and forth in flailing shadows and trees. The sky over the mountains to the west blinked steadily, black on white. If they did anything to her . . . Of course they *could* be merely driving around with her but it wasn't likely, not with this wind, not in an open jeep. But where could they take her? The park was out of the question; the police car, as the boys knew very well, patrolled the town every hour. They wouldn't dare take her out to the ranch, and getting her into a hotel was impossible. Then where? His wheeling headlights splashed over a half dozen monstrous gasoline tanks, over weeds and a rotting shack, and then settled on the gnawed dirt road along the railroad tracks. The strings of boxcars were chunks of black growing together. The black heavy thrust of the feed elevator went up into the flickering sky.

At the highway he turned back into town, sweating, riddled with a sense of doom. She didn't have a chance with them, she didn't have a chance. For ten precious minutes he drove up and down the short streets, bumping into hilly pastures at the end, backing around with a crash of raked gears and tearing on. The little frame houses huddled their glows behind the lunging trees. Then he thought of the water tower and drove up the long wind-blasted hill with the whole western sky splitting white, cracking everywhere in crazy shatters like a sky of glass. Shaggy clouds, apocalyptic black shapes, loomed in sweeps of wild light jumping all over the mountains and sky. Jarring and swerving back down the hill, he tried the deserted school on the edge of town. Another blank. But then he noticed the abandoned rodeo grounds on the other side of the football field: ruined wooden pens and runways, corrals, and the black mouth of the grandstand yawning, deep and empty, on a weed-choked track.

His stomach clutched inside him as he saw the jeep pulled up next to the derelict pens. He leaped out. Timbers creaked in the cold wind. A chain dangled and clinked on a post. Some horses were quartered in the pens and he could hear a hoof set down and see the whisk of a tail behind a fence. He wrenched the gate open: shadowy forms broke for the corners of the pen, trapped.

"You bastards," he said. "You dirty bastards, picking on a high-school kid. Which one of you held her down?" Weak and mushy with horror, he asked her, "Are you okay?"

She was still trying to get on her jeans. His eye flinched from the slide of white skin as she tugged, hitched them up her thin legs and over her frail, pathetically childish hips. Brushing back her hair, she buttoned her blouse on the unfilled little pouches of her brassiere.

"Don't be so dumb," she said. "Nobody held me down."

He stared.

"That's right," the boys joined in, taking heart and crowding forward to argue. "She came here of her own free will."

"We didn't make her do anything. Isn't that right, Lucy?"

"Permit me to give you a few facts," he said, pulling himself together. "Gang shags with a fifteen-year-old girl are statutory rape if you're twenty-one. Two of you qualify there. And all of you qualify for expulsion from school at once."

"But sir," they babbled, eddying around him in the shadows and flittery light. "You wouldn't do that! Sir, give us a break. She won't bring charges against us—will you, Lucy? Please, sir," they said abjectly. "Our whole lives are at stake. Don't report us. We'll stop prospecting, as of now. Whatever you say."

"I'm not a blackmailer," he told them. "Get the hell out of here. Beat it, I don't want to look at you."

Imploring him and blurting extravagant promises, they trooped slowly out of the pen. The wind sucked at the board fences. The smell of manure seeped from the next stall. He was sick with loathing but already his cold rage was beginning to falter, his horror at what they'd done was staggering into a new horror. He asked her where she lived and without a quiver she said, "311 B Street."

And by God, she sat there beside him, a cheap pink wallet instead of a purse in her lap, and she was as calm, as self-possessed—where were the muddy tears? At least a flushed defiance—something. But there she sat, like a girl being driven home from a dancing class, and once in a while she touched the frayed tassel of hair on the back of her neck, and her thin straight body was like a stem for her clear face—and she had done that! It was appalling.

When they drew up in front of the house, she waited for a moment—slyly, he could have sworn it—and then said, "Well? Aren't you going in and tell *everything*?"

He swallowed. He didn't know what to do any more.

She slid out of the car and before she closed the door and walked off, she leaned in and said, "I don't live here anyway."

VI

The Bolton boys were haying two miles up the Cheyenne from the ranch house. The heat was suffocating in the hay bottom and the cottonwoods along the river stood motionless, dull green in the broiling light. Grumbling and cursing savagely, Pierce was building stacks with the hay lift. It was a home-made contraption, a tractor stretching out a heavy iron neck and a yawing mouth with ragged teeth and a thick metal tongue to dump the hay. Grinding along in a churn of powdery dust, he lowered the huge maw to the stubble and pushed it into shaggy piles of hay while Billy Joe helped fork them in. The engine racketed and coughed pale blue deisel fumes. Every time Pierce raised a load up onto the stack the little tractor was pulled forward off its rear treads, down, down, tilting dangerously, and when he yanked at the lever and four hundred pounds of hay tumbled out, the tractor staggered backwards, the ponderous jaws sawed up and down in the sky, and he was slammed hard against the metal seat.

"Stinking, rotten, lousy junk heap," he fumed. "It's gonna kill me off one of these trips, but Daddy wouldn't buy nothing new. Oh no, he's got to cobble it together out of coat hangers and old bedsprings."

If there was one thing he hated and despised anyhow it was haying. His back felt like it was broken in six places already, and it was only ten o'clock. The heat was poisoned with oil and dust and the dense, sweetish smell of hay. As he hitched the clumsy lift around, heeling almost over with the weight of the hay, his sun-drugged stare reeled past Frank, who was fencing in one of the stacks to keep off the cattle when they wintered along the river. Fifteen hours a day suited Frank just right, fifteen hours of putting out salt cake and protein, haying, repairing equipment and spraying for ticks, *plus* hauling water now that Daddy had got the uranium bug and left them to do everything. At no increase in their percentage, naturally. They still got their same old fifteen percent of whatever the old man felt like marketing, which was mighty damn little these days, while he did nothing and hogged the big share for himself. They would be better off as hired hands, much better off. As it was, they busted their guts for board and room and very few extras, with never a bit of sayso in the operation—the way Daddy had lit into him and Billy Joe for selling off six lousy head of stock, it was humiliating. If he ever found out what they had done with the money . . . But maybe it would be better if he did. Let him find out, let him raise holy hell and be damned to him; they had to make a stand sooner or later. He had a gutfull of always being the underdog and never, not once, not one time in his whole miserable life, getting a single taste of happiness. Why had he been sent off to agriculture school for two years if he was going to be treated like help?

Billy Joe lifted a wad of hay and jumped back in the same motion, swiping down at a rattlesnake with his fork. He beat it into mangled, bloody shreds and hollered, "Hey, Bubber, did you see that? It just laid there and never striked nor nothing. See? It's got two bumps in it. It must've et a couple gophers."

"That's very interesting," Pierce said sarcastically. "Have you got any more interesting facts and statistics? Don't worry about turning my stomach or nothing."

Short and jug-eared, his bare arms stuffed tight with muscle, the boy gaped at him in confusion. "But it just laid there, Bubber."

Pierce's chunky red face squeezed up and he bawled, "Will you kindly shut your mouth? My nerves are tore up enough without you carrying on like a idiot." Jerking irritably at the lever, he rammed the hay lift toward the next puny heap. It grew hotter and hotter and the discontented pressure inside him increased. The haylift pounded him cruelly, shocked him, wrenched him until he was breathless and torn with pain. The huge swallowing mouth took in hay and rocked it toward the big loaf-shaped stack that bulged up in the hot sky. Curse his father and curse this rotten stinking putrid life. He ought to have left out years ago like Hank and Gary . . .

Gradually he became conscious of a blundering scuffle of dust on the hill toward the ranch: it was his father's jeep. "Looks like God is paying us a visit, get ready to bow down," he said venomously.

The jeep stopped and Sam Bolton rocked toward them, grizzled with harsh white dust. He spanked at his hat and pants, took a swallow from their water jar and said, "You remember that fifty foot of cable at the Baird place? I know it was there two years ago."

Pierce felt his insides go cold. It was just his luck, his cursed hellish stinking bad luck. The old man was cobbling together a drill for his uranium claims, and of course he happened to need a piece of cable from the bought-up ranch where they'd hid the plane. But why wasn't he raising sand and busting wind? He couldn't possibly have missed seeing the plane, not in that old barn without even a door that they used for a hangar.

Frank said he'd taken the cable last winter.

Bolton nodded and stood around talking. He scratched his crotch. He lifted his hat and scratched in his damp grey hair. Almost as an afterthought it seemed, he looked at Pierce and said, "I told you, boy, no plane. Get rid of it."

Then he went back to his jeep in his shingle-butted slouch and drove off.

Pierce's face was a crimson smear. "Did you hear that? Like we was ten-year-old children. Jesus God, I ask you." Swerving around, he ran a few feet after the jeep screaming, "You murderous natured old bastard! We're not selling the plane, not now nor ever. You can have this frigging ranch if you don't like it, and welcome."

In an agony of fright, he turned toward Frank. "The Petersons won't buy back the plane, they already got a new Cessna," he babbled. "I'm lost! I'm dead and buried! Billy Joe is safe, he's not twenty-one, but Daddy will fire me and Irene and the kids off the ranch. He's merciless hearted." Frank simply stood there under his wingy hat, lean, dusty, flat-bodied, chewing quietly at a plug of tobacco. Pierce held out as long as he could, then blurted, "All right, so what if I can sell it in Denver? It ain't right. We're entitled to that plane. And we need it to cut down our work load, we're so short-handed it's pitiful. Talk to him, Frank. He respects you as a man and as a rancher, and rightly so. I know you don't like the notion of flying and I dearly thank you for keeping quiet about the plane . . . but would . . ."

His voice trailed off. He could feel everything he said fall into that deep, remote quiet. The man wasn't human. He was thirty years old and bachelor wasn't the word for him, he was a hermit. Practically the only time Pierce ever saw him even mildly sociable was when he played the guitar for the kids of an evening, plunking and singing to them through his broken nose, and even then he was somehow by himself, smiling at them out of a kind of silence. Nobody could get through to Frank, not even the old man, but he had to do it somehow, and right now, or he was lost and ruined.

"Frank? Look, Frank, forget the plane, dearly as I want it. It's the whole deal I'm talking about, all the way around. We don't necessarily have to sweat our guts for pennies. Daddy can't afford to buck us if we stick together. It's the God's truth, Frank, he's so tied up with uranium he won't never get loose, and he wouldn't trust hired hands to run the spread. I'll tell you what," he added eagerly, "you throw in with us and you can run the outfit—right, Billy Joe? It's only fair, you're the oldest and you're the best cowman."

Frank let him have his say, as distant, as untouched as ever. He leaned aside once, quietly, to spit a mouthful of brown juice.

"Damn it, all I'm asking for is fair play. He's strangled us all our lives, he's never given us nothing but the shit end of the stick—if even that. He could at least give us our own brands and leave us build up our own individual herds. But not him, he wants slave labor out of us."

At last Frank spoke. "It's his ranch."

"His ranch! It's ours too. We sank our heart's blood into this place, but do you think he gives a small goddamn? He's no father to us. I'll tell you what he is, a stud bull. That's all he is, the whore-hopping old—he's fathered bastards from a radius of a hundred miles around. A man like that has no feelings for his children. A stud bull ain't a father."

"That's true," Billy Joe said. "A stud bull ain't a father."

Frank gazed down at his calloused hands, quiet, detached. Wild with frustration, Pierce called him a traitor, accused him of having a secret deal with the old man to inherit the whole ranch for himself. Frank looked up, his eyes like flakes of metal under the brim of his hat, and then walked off toward the haystack he was fencing. "Judas Iscariot!" Pierce shouted after him. "Judas Iscariot!"

He dropped down on the treads of the tractor and put his face in his hands.

"Hey don't, Bubber. Cheer up."

"Cheer up!" he exploded. "Can you give me one single reason for cheering up? Can you?" he demanded. "Everything I put my hand to goes sour. What's the use? I wish I was dead of the bloody piles." His face kinked up, and he spewed obscenities.

"I wish you wouldn't," Billy Joe said. "It's wrong to swear, and you've done nothing else all morning long." His face, between the little fists of his ears, took on that special look it always got when he tried to save Pierce, earnest and sweet and sort of complacent. "You know, if you would go to God with your problems, Bubber, you wouldn't be turned away. There's a revival meeting on this week at the church. His Blessing is waiting for you."

"Don't waste your breath on me," Pierce said tragically. "Leave me go to hell and burn. I'm damned here and in the hereafter, both."

A vast sorrow came down on him and he worked with a dragging heart in the delirium of heat and hay smells, and snakes twisting out of forkfuls of hay, leaking brown in the stubble, drawing up from their coils and sputtering their dry rattles. At noon when they went in for dinner, he brooded at the table, mournfuly refusing his food. His parents weren't impressed. A soon as the meal was over, Sam went off in one direction and Vivie in another, carelessly ignoring him. He drooped into the bedroom and lay down. Timidly, Irene asked him if she could bring him a piece of pie or something."

"Pie. That's a big goddamn help," he said. "If you saw Jesus

Christ on the cross, you'd cluck your tongue and see if He wouldn't like a bite to eat."

Billy Joe leaned his head into the room and said, "Bubber? We better move out, Frank's waiting in the truck."

Without taking his arm from his eyes, he said, "I'm not going."

He could feel them gawping at him, thunderstruck: words like that had never been heard in the house before. In a moment Billy Joe came near and said worriedly, "I don't know . . . Daddy won't like it, you laying out of work."

"I'm sick!" Pierce screamed at him, sitting up with a choked, red face. "I'm wore out and sick. Can't a man even be sick around here?" Flopping down again, he rolled toward the wall and didn't move until Billy Joe had left and the truck had rambled away. Then he got up, muttering, and began to rummage around in the dresser. His daughter Debbie tiptoed into the room and said, "Can I go visit Dean in town? Can I, Daddy? He's brung his pony in and we're gonna sell rides. Dad . . ." Irene jerked her out of sight, grabbing at the same time for Jeffrey who had wobbled in, his little sausage legs forced wide apart by his diaper. "I'm sorry, honey," she said abjectly.

"Where's the goddamn whiskey?" he shouted, getting red again and throwing clothes around. "Never mind, I found it." Sitting down on the bed, he stared gloomily at the bottle. Irene scurried in with a white porcelain basin and closed the door. "Get out of here," he bawled at her, his face cramping, and tipped up the bottle. His eyes gushed water. He shuddered and gulped at the burning in his throat. Then his stomach lifted greasily, bunched, and he vomited the whiskey into the waiting basin, bucking up off the bed with gargling moans, cursing as he sucked frantically for air. Irene held the basin and, after each of the hacking spasms, wiped his face with a damp cloth. "Every time," he panted in despair. "Every miserable stinking time. It's piteous when a man can't even get drunk. Piteous!"

Afraid to say anything, afraid even to croon soothingly to him, she dabbed at his face with the cloth. He crammed more whiskey down his throat and gagged it back immediately—over and over, retching with flooded eyes and damning his fate. Irene sobbed. "Forget it," he said with mournful satisfaction. "I'd just as soon vomit my guts and die."

He sagged back onto the pillow and she turned on the fan and closed the door softly. But he felt nauseated, his head thudded sickly, and a tired rattle of dishes came from the kitchen, mixed with a dim commotion of children and dogs. One of the little girls let out an anguished screech. "Cut out that damn racket!" he bellowed. Irene shushed the children but he dragged himself out of the bed, muttering bitterly, "Can't a man have peace anywhere in this world?" He changed clothes and announced that he was going to town. "If Daddy asks about me, tell him—tell him I went to the doctor in Hot Springs." Debbie kept pestering him to let her come along and he grumbled, "You better hurry up, then."

She threw her arms around him and hugged him good and hard, then dashed off to pack, her dress flying around her skinny legs. A soft glow of pleasure filtered into his melancholy, and on the way to town he listened to her excited chatter hungrily, greedily. "Dean and me are going dibs on the money from selling rides," she said. "I'm saving up."

"Is that so. For what?"

"I'm just saving up," she replied nonchalantly. He had never spent much time with her before, and he slid cautious glances at her hard, little-boy hands and her dainty face, the pure white ribbon tied in a bow on her perky curls. She was losing her front teeth and from time to time, talking away at a mile a minute, she gave him an empty smile that grabbed at his heart. With her, scratching around in a home made wire cage, was her pet white rat, Randy—sent by Uncle Henry from Caspar, Wyoming—and a metal suitcase that bumped against her legs.

He consented to have a race with her in eating a lifesaver. "The first one through wins," she said, giving him one of the thin white halos of candy.

"Wins what?" he asked her.

"Just wins!" she said, looking at him as if he were too slow for words. "Ready, on your mark, get set, go!" And she crunched down on the candy with her back teeth, chewing like sixty. Her eyes were shining. He was dazzled: it was like a revelation. For a little while, for a few minutes anyway on the trip to town, he could forget the old man and the tragedy of the plane, released into her sweet, simple world. The gaunt pastures skimmed by. Ahead of them clouds were coming up over the pine mountains, soft and white, floating toward them like great soft angels.

She won and laughed with delight. "There's a boy in school, his name is Charley Trueblood, he's an Indian, and he ate a whole box of crayons on a dare," she informed him impressively. Then she noticed Randy springing onto the sides of his wire cage with a strumming noise like a hand raked over a guitar, and bending down to him, she took him out of the cage and sheltered him, cuddled him maternally in her lap. "Were you scared?" she cooed. "There now, that's better— only don't you pee on me!" Looking over at her father, she said, "He tickles. Like electricity."

"Unh." His stomach practically turned inside out at the sight of the red glass eyes and twitchy nose, the bearded white sides, and the bulging red testicles, as large as small plums, lolling under the base of the long, all-too-snaky tail. But he didn't have the heart to say anything; she was so crazy for animals of every description, puppies, kittens, bunnies, even a pet antelope that had grown up and raised no end of hell.

"He's a boy," she confided seriously.

"Yeah. Sure."

"I think he's lonesome. I'm going to write Uncle Henry to send him a wife."

The bald, scaly tail curled on her knee like a snake. Queasily he speeded up the car. The road plunged down a long hill and swerved. He cut the wheel sharply, they leaned in the seat and the suitcase tipped over, and he felt a clawing at his arm: Randy, dumped out of her lap and flung sideways, was scrambling onto his shoulder. "Get it off me!" he screamed. The nasty skittering tickle reached his neck. In wild-eyed panic he tore at it, bashed it away, wrestling the wheel with the other hand and braking the car to a stop on the very edge of the ditch.

"God damn it! God damn it! You almost killed us!" he said hysterically.

She wasn't even looking at him. She picked up the dead animal wailing, "Randy! Randy!" Her face pinched together and she began to cry, holding it in her arms. Great tears swelled out of her eyes and ran down her cheeks. All the angrier because he was wrung to the heart at having hurt her, he spluttered over and over, "We nearly got killed! Don't you understand?" With shocking rapidity the rat was changing in her huddled lap: the sharp red feet were fading, and the testicles had drawn up into its body, the red eyes were glazing over, dimming to pink, to a dull and soiled violet, to a membrane-like grey. It was awful.

"I didn't mean to . . ."

"You did too," she sobbed, twisting away from him. "I'm gonna tell Granddad."

"You're gonna what? Whose kid . . ." he strangled. "What kind of a . . . All right, by God, he can have you, you're none of mine." Rigid with hate, he drove her to her cousin's house and, without a word, dropped her off in front, still crying and hugging the dead white thing in her arms. Scowling, he parked the car on Highway Street and stamped into the back room of the Cattleman's Bar to play poker. His reckless fury chilled, however, when he found out how steep the game was. It took fifty dollars to sit in—just about every cent in his pitiful checking account—and the bets were running two, five, and ten dollars and more a card. One hand of five card stud could finish him off. He saw back cautiously, turning over hand after hand, waiting for an absolutely sure-fire cinch.

The men sat like moles in the scummy light. Cards rattled together, skidded through the air and dropped on the weary green felt, chips clicked and voices said, "The Jack is high . . . the Jack bets two . . ." It was a rough, mean game, nothing like the little sociable games in the pool hall. To every effort of his to be friendly, the players responded with a bare grunt, and that included neighbors of long standing like old man Peterson and Lee Stark, the car dealer, and Fred Claussen, a veterinarian with a ranch on the side who had known his father for twenty years. He felt out of place, jittery, intimidated. The only exception was a crazy lunatic from out of town named Bert. He had a rubber knife and a toy pistol, which he called his "cap buster," by his stacks of chips, and when he lost a hand he put the pistol to is temple dramatically, wept, "goodbye, cruel world," and pulled the trigger: click! Then he guffawed, purple-faced, his hair slopping against his forehead, and said, "Okay, deal. This war ain't lost yet." Still wheezing and chuckling to himself, he took a handful of chips and went at it, driving, raising on every card. He hit a second pair on the last card and whooped, "Up jumped the devil!" Pulling in the chips with both hands, he gloated, "Come to Daddy. As the old lady said when she peed in the ocean, every little bit helps."

It was plain to see that the other players hated Bert, and just for that reason Pierce said cordially, "I wish you'd pass a little of that luck this way, sir."

Bert went on stacking his chips, humming "When it's Springtime in the Rockies."

Pierce flushed a dull red under his dress Stetson. Silent now, he waited for his chance and at last he got it: a king on top and another, rich and solid, in the hole. His heart began to struggle, his eyes flicked around the table to be sure that no ace was showing. With a wet and trembling hand he put two one-dollar chips into the middle. Bert dropped out but three other players called. On the next-to-last card Claussen paired up sevens and now it was his bet. He had a sun-dried face and a sunken upper lip filled out with a grey moustache. The light broke up on his hard ridgy hand as he clattered a stack of chips, picked it up and let it fall a chip at a time and shaped it again into a small red column. Then he detached three of the chips and flipped them in. "Sevens bet fifteen dollars," the man who was dealing said. The others folded. It was Pierce's turn. He glanced into Claussen's flinty look and away, quickly. He tried to concentrate: a pair of sevens . . . was that all Claussen had or did he have another pair to go with them? Or a deadly third seven in the hole? His head was going around and around. Blindly he shoved three of his precious five-dollar chips into the pot.

"He calls," the dealer said. Cards sliced out of his hands, one to Claussen, one to Pierce. "No help . . . no help. The sevens bet."

Claussen said, "How much d'you have there in front of you?"

Shakily, his hands quivering, his mouth as dry as alkali dust, Pierce counted the chips and said, "Twenty-nine dollars."

The men sat in the frayed smoke and light, watching with neutral faces. The ridgy hand moved and chips splayed into the heap, blue and red and white. The dealer said, "The sevens bet twenty-nine dollars."

Pierce felt himself shrinking into a knot of fear. The possibilities whirled giddily and muddled together: his kings beat the sevens, if that was all Claussen had . . . but Claussen must have noticed that he'd laid back, waiting until this hand, so Claussen *had* to figure him for kings . . . but maybe it was a bluff . . . His mind seemed to be melting, dissolving into grey fear, and somewhere away from himself, a hand that wasn't his hand turned his cards over.

Claussen scooped in the pot.

"You had more than them sevens, didn't you?" Pierce asked with a painful attempt at a smile. Claussen didn't even do him the courtesy of answering. And suddenly the awful suspicion crystallized, froze into certainty: he had been bluffed out. He was sure of it! Oh no, no, no! Sick, horrified at what he'd done, he played stupidly and lost the twenty-nine dollars on the very next hand.

"Give me another fifty," he said to the house man.

"I'm sorry, Mr. Bolton, but you'll have to get an okay from the boss."

"Who do you think I am?" Pierce stormed. "A drifter? Or a hobo? My Daddy can buy and sell this whole rotten town, you included." He swung around to the shrivelled old rancher next to him. "Mr. Peterson, sir. How about you? . . . Mr. Claussen?" Every single player he knew let him stand there and beg in vain. "Neighbors," he said bitterly. "Some fine neighbors you are."

Just then Bert said, "Hold on a second. You Sam Bolton's boy?"

"You damn stinking right I am. Not that it looks like it around here."

"Sam Bolton, the famous cattle king? He says 'frog' and everybody jumps? *That* Sam Bolton?"

"That Sam Bolton, and you better believe it."

"I do, I do. And personally the name of Sam Bolton is good enough for me. You just set yourself down there, Junior, and write your check out to me, Bertram J. Stephens."

The same man had snubbed him not forty minutes before, and now he was saying, "It beats me how these men can call theirselves Christians, treating you like that." But Pierce didn't care a plug nickel about the why or where of the fresh money; he reached for the messes of cards and shuffled them clumsily, his straining face pebbled with sweat. For nearly half an hour he hoarded the fifty dollar stack, waiting, waiting, and then plunged disastrously. "Ain't that a pill?" Bert said. "Who'd of figured him for queens?"

"Give me fifty more. No, make it a hundred."

Bert obliged him, and a few hands later obliged him again, just as cheerful as a day in May. Pierce thanked him lavishly, beginning to hate him. He was on the verge of tears. He lost again and leaped up in agony. "Nothing! Not one smell of good luck," he cried. "Who'll change seats with me? I've got to break this dry spell someway. Come on, you've got my money." The stonefaced men didn't move. A big contractor from the ordnance depot let out a mouthful of cigarette smoke.

"Suits me," Bert said, gathering up his chips.

And immediately he began to win in Pierce's old seat.

"I should've stayed where I was," Pierce said, utterly wretched. "I gave my luck away when it was just starting to turn. I'm the most unfortunate human being there is."

"Where there's winners there's got to be losers," Bert said. "That's what playing marbles is." Scraping the cards together and then clattering them into each other, he slicked them around the table to the players. "Look out, gentlemen," he said. "They say a man is no good if he can't win on his own deal . . . The ten is high. Bet like you live, son, to kill." The freezing stares of the other players only amused him, only made him worse, brassier, even more loudmouthed. "Look at that," he cackled gleefully as he hit aces. "Now ain't that a dinger and a half. I told you I'd beat the snot out of you." When the pot was large, he'd run out of the room in the middle of the hand and yell, "Ray? Come here." Then he'd shake hands with an ugly pint-sized man with eyes like a toad, shout to the bartender to bring his lucky charm a drink, and come tearing back to the table hollering, "I raise. Twenty more—no, make it thirty. And gentlemen, unless you were brought up by a gypsy with one tit and the evil eye, I seriously advise you not to call." He was in a crazy sort of ecstasy and not just because he was winning: he actually liked the risk, enjoyed it, lived for it. Pierce was appalled. Why, why, *why* had he come here? He hated gambling, hated it bitterly.

"Looks like your little red wagon has broke again," Bert said to him. "You want another stack?"

"How much do I owe you? Four hundred?"

"Four and a half. You want fifty more?"

"No, it wouldn't do no good. The way my bad luck is running I could play to Doomsday and not win." He got to his feet, then hesitated. "About those checks, Bert . . ." All at once a new and desperate idea struck him. "Bert, you're a gambling man, Bert. Double or nothing, how about it? One cut of the cards."

Bert told the houseman to shuffle the cards, and, loafing on his tattooed arms, nodded at the deck. "It's your lick, son."

Pierce felt weak, lightheaded, giddy. He cut the cards and looked with scared eyes: a nine. Easily, almost disdainfully, Bert cut and turned up a jack of spades.

"God damn it!" Pierce choked. "Once more."

The cards slithered and jumped together, lay in a smooth block. The ring of faces, watching intently, seemed to float in the stale, thick light. There was a heavy churning in his head. Biting his teeth harder and harder, he put his hand out toward the deck . . . and faltered. All at once he knew he was going to lose, he was failling, falling into bottomless dread.

"Stop swallering your heart and take a pick."

He snatched at the cards. He was staring at the deuce of clubs, the lowest card in the deck. With a sob he tore the card in half—and saw Bert turn up a measly little four of diamonds. A four! Violently he swept the cards off the table, fluttering and spinning onto the floor.

"One more time," he gasped. "Give me a chance. What do you say? One more."

Bert's rowdy horseplay had disappeared. Even and deliberate, he said to Pierce, "You owe me eighteen hundred. I'm telling you straight out, this is the last time."

"All right, all right. Where's a new deck? Give it here, I'll shuffle it myself." He scrambled the cards, fumbled them around, and set them down in front of Bert. "You first. You go ahead."

The hollowness yawned deeper and deeper inside him. He couldn't breathe. Bert cut and rolled his palm up. With a shock like a noiseless scream inside him, Pierce saw the ace of diamonds. He mashed his face in his hands. "Cut," Bert told him, and he turned up a five of hearts. The men eased back in their chairs, talking. "Oh my God," he moaned, scribbling the check. "Oh my God. Oh my God help me."

"It's after closing time now," Bert said to him. "I'll take this around to the bank on Monday. Say about noon. You tell your Daddy that."

Pierce walked out of the back room and through the tavern. His life was over. The only consolation was that it served his Daddy right; it would bust his skinflint heart to pay out 3600 dollars to save the precious name of Bolton. Even in his mushrooming horror a fierce pleasure at that would not be smothered, and he realized that he'd intended to get back at the old man all along; the intention had been there like a bitter little fire deep inside him. But he was finished. There would be no forgiveness. They would be thrown out with nowhere to go and not a penny to their name except what he could get by selling the Piper Cub. Somebody spoke to him. The long stretching light caught in the bone-white antlers nailed up over the door of the barber shop. Across the wide hot street, Cevil Frye was locking up the Piggly Wiggly supermarket. Pierce had no idea of where he was walking or what he was going to do, only that he couldn't go home. Ever since he could remember he had been terrified of life, and now at last his worst premonitions, his blackest and most awful worries had all closed in on him at once.

The doors of the gaunt frame church were open and the clank of a piano and a singing garble of voices spilled out onto the dusty sidewalk. He went in eagerly. The hand-planed wooden pews were crowded with sweating people, and at the front preachers were hugging each other and shaking hands, young children squirmed around and paraded to and from the toilet, a sallow girl was jouncing somebody else's baby while it bumped its round head against her and smiled wetly, and all the while the piano pelted hard flat sounds into the harsh, laboring voices.

The squalling hymn ended, finally, and a preacher said, "I'm here to shine a little light on you, praise God. I'm *glad* I'm here in God's house." Grunts answered him from the pews and he raised his face, a greasy and radiant young man, and asked, "How many people here have requests? Hold up their hands." All over the congregation hands bristled up in the hot orange light that soaked through the pointed orange windows. "All right, just you bow your heads and tell God what it is you want. They aren't any troubles too big or too little for Him." A great babble of prayer went up; eyes were squnched shut; hands groped toward the blind wooden ceiling; and the piano bonged into the mumbling, wailing voices.

Pierce looked around, wishing he'd never come in. It didn't mean a thing. Here he was, discouraged in his very soul, and he couldn't even get a little religious comfort for his suffering. It was disgusting. He kept thinking about the plane, about the way his Daddy and Mother hated him, and the ace of diamonds slid up in Bert's rolling hand—red and sharp like the red knife in his Daddy's hand when he was castrating stock.

During the love offering march, as the congregation was filing up and putting their contributions into a basket, Billy Joe caught his eye from the other side of the church and nodded happily and gave him his born-again Christian smile. Pierce looked away with a grimace.

Then a blushing young man was called out of the choir and presented with a check to help pay his expenses at ministerial school. And how everybody carried on over him! One of the men in the choir was weeping. A lard-faced woman stood up and made a speech, the pleated dress over her chest working like an accordion. "Wayne has been such an inspiration to me personally, and his Mother and Daddy too. He's had some wonderful training behind him and we're all praying for him to make it through and work for the Lord in His vineyard." The young man kept his head bowed, as pink as a bride, blushing sweetly while he lapped up the love and the praise. Pierce hated him. Then one of the ministers poured still more flattery on the smug, safe, pinky boy. "Wayne is gonna be a great man of God, I'm just sure of it. I'm *glad* he loves God like he does." And beaming at the people, he called out, "Don't you love the Lord?" A raft of pious voices responded, "Yes, Jesus. Bless you, Jesus."

Cut off, all by himself in his misfortune, Pierce watched a boy and girl come forward out of the choir and sing a duet, "Fly away, fly away to *Jee*-sus," twanging their jews-harp voices while, behind them in the corner, a balding man fought the piano. His desolation grew heavier and heavier. "That was mighty fine," one of the preachers said. "Now we're really getting warmed up good.' Amen's spattered up, ecstatic blurts from all over the church. The sunset had left the puckered orange windows and the preachers sunken face was grey in the forlorn light. "My friends," he said, "I'm glad God is blessing us and moving in our midst tonight. Rejoice in the Lord for His help is great." The old woman next to Pierce sat with her flabby belly hung like a broken cradle from her spindleshank bones. Her face was lifted, lifting the slack fall of her neck, and her tiny eyes were closed in their sockets. Her thready voice was praying, and something moved in Pierce, just faintly stirred in the blind, heavy gloom. The words from the pulpit were gentle, pulsing softly:

"Don't be afraid to let Jesus work. I've knowed Him to shake a man before he ever got down in his seat. Just let the Lord have His way and this can be the night. It *will* be the night, and my friends, the blessings you will have. Accept Jesus into your heart and at that minute you're a new person entirely. There's no weakness and no misery of this imperfect world that won't be part of *His* glorious perfection. And you will be born again with His eternal Power."

Tiny lost bleats came from the old woman. They seemed to fill his head like birds, little white birds, and he knew that the call was for *him*, that the words were aimed at *him*, that the blessings were there waiting for *him*. But there was something inside him that wouldn't let go. He strained at it frantically. His sorrow was a huge lump in him, swelling, a huge bulging agony.

"What Jesus done for me, He will do for you. Here and hereafter both. On that millenium day, you'll be right there with Him. The wicked shall be under your feet and you shall judge the world with Him."

People moaned around him. The voice rang like a great iron bell, "And heaven, it'll be perfect. There won't be no tiny babies that died in infancy there, nor any old people, nor hunch backs and people with deformities, but everybody will be in God's perfect likeness in glory. Forever."

It was beautiful. He could see it lifted above him, all white, like a dazzling white radiance, and he longed to give himself into that whiteness, so transparent and light and warmly shimmering. He shuddered. The heaviness inside him was unbearable. He was struggling, bunching up in torment, and then he bucked over in the pew, torn open inside, and Jesus was pouring into him, gush after gush of weltering sweetness, pumping up and flooding him with spasms of the sweetest happiness, and he was panting, "Oh yes, yes Jesus, yes," and the warm sweet tears were all over his face.

VII

As soon as Pierce handed him the check, Bert cashed in his chips and strolled out into the bar. Wally was crouched in a booth, haggard with fear and hunger and thirty-six hours of sleepless waiting. "You lost, huh?" he croaked. "You lost, I can tell you lost."

"Mash potatoes," Bert said. "Pork chops and gravy. Four T-bone steaks smothered in onions." His tired, stubbly face was portentous as he ticked off the delectable items. "Corn on the cob and fried liver. Peach pie a la mode." Then he was smiling, chortling triumphantly. "And you can have them all, Old Heavy. Come on, get off your butt and we'll tour the cafes and restaurants of quality. I'll have you fat and sassy in no time."

Wally looked at him doubtfully. "Bert, if you start in tap dancing and singing 'Golden Slippers' like before—I'll never live over that. What was it you run head-on into this time, a full house? Something busted you."

Grandly, like a bloodshot and rumpled magician, Bert pulled wad after wad of money out of his pockets and heaped them on the table in front of Wally. "Cast your eyes on that. Now say this travelling medicine show ain't back in business," he crowed. "I told you I was peerless."

Wally gawped stupidly at the money. The hard knot of worry was coming loose painfully, and he felt dazed, unreal, watching his hand clutch and quake in the tangled bills, tens and twenties and fifties. He tried to count it and broke down, trembling all over.

"I knew you couldn't count that high, you old booger," Bert laughed. "There's seventeen hundred and forty there in cash. Go ahead and salt it away, you're the treasurer. Only just promise not to wear the numbers off by stroking and smooching them too much. All I need is a hundred to frolic with and . . ." The pint-sized little man was gabbling up at him excitedly, thick and low, like a blue fireplug in a dirty blue shirt. Bert tossed him a fifty dollar bill. "Here's your cut, short stuff. You can get drunk enough on that to be six foot tall . . . temporarily." For just an instant the hilarity had blinked out of Bert's soiled face, but then it was there again, like a light blazing in a dingy hotel room, and he swaggered away to the bar. "A little service here," he said. "I'll have a jug of your finest, grade-A, pasteurized bourbon. The honeymoon has started."

"I were lucky for him," the little man told Wally proudly. "I were always a lucky charm. Once I blew on Sammy Mandel's hand and he won eleven grand in one night. He give me a new hand-tailored suit to my specifications and a straw hat." With his stubby fingers he jammed the bill carefully into his cut-down work pants. His bulging eyes were swimming in juices and his foggy voice came like blats from a broken little horn. "I ain't drinking this fifty away, no sir. This fifty will take care of my problems." Wally stared at him. Marching on his short legs, he went over to the gandies who had been petting and teasing him for hours. "You and me," he announced. "We're through. I've broke off all connections with you." Bashing away their hands, he came back to Wally, squat and ugly, stumping along with grotesque, dirty pomp. "See what I mean? I've broke off all connections with them. They're low-type riffraff. Winos and such people. I only signed on as a cook's helper to take a trip West." His eyes bugged, red and wet, and he smiled a gummy pink smile at Wally. "It were for old time's sake. In the former days I travelled all over the West and Canada with the Royal Universal Shows. It were a good life, too. Colonel Casper and myself—he was only up to here on me—we had an act. We'd come out jumping and running around and acting crazy— like this!" Waggling his bitty fingers by his ears, pop-eyed and grinning, he whirled and capered around the floor to demonstrate. "I were very fast," he puffed. "I could stop on a dime in those days."

It was like something in a gaudy carnival dream. Wally held onto the money, blank and light-headed, and gaped at the bragging, strutting, unfinished little creature, like a child with a hideous man's face and a powerful chest. "Look here," he puffed. "Here's a flip." And launching himself into the air, he flopped heavily on his back, waggling the tiny nubs of his arms and legs like a maimed bug. The gandies and the ranch hands hooted with laughter. "I'm out of practice," he told Wally, scrambling to his feet. "But give me a half hour's practice and I could do it." Turning around angrily, he spluttered at the men, "Shut up! Shut up, all of you!"

Goggling and waving his short arms, he toddled away. Only then did Bert come back. He ripped the seal from a pint of whiskey, swung it up and took three epic swallows. "Whoo-ee! That's better," he said. "I hadn't drank for a day and a half and I thought I might've lost the hang of it. Let the partying and carrying on something dreadful begin."

"Wait—hold on," Wally said. Pulling himself together, he packed the money into his wallet and buttoned it securely into his back pocket. "Before you start honkytonking, Bert, we oughta pay back Mrs. Harbaugh. We owe her the best part of a hundred and fifty dollars, plus the hundred she bankrolled you in the game with."

"What? Pay her back?" Bert roared. "Oh well, if you're gonna be honest, I don't know. My goodness, Lard."

Wally smiled at him, blinking his slow, sweet blue eyes. "That's your joke, Bert, I can tell. I wish you'd give it to her in person, instead of me. It would please her very highly. And say a few nice words along with it."

"How about if I start off with a banjo solo? All right, all right, I won't hinder you in your high ideals." He took another swig of the whiskey and dried his mouth on his arm. "Yay, Lordy, I feel the spirit moving in me now."

"Boy, Bert, I tell you . . ." Now, finally, it was beginning to take hold in him, the wonder of their good fortune. They were free, they were safe at last, for a while anyway. Blissfully he discussed getting the truck and the Geiger counter back, and the opportunities still to be had in the area. Then he hesitated: "Bert?"

"Yeah, you can send Esther a couple hundred bucks."

"Huh? How did you know I was going to ask that? You sure can read my mind. I'd greatly appreciate it, though. Esther has had a hard time of it herself. I'll tell her the money is from you and maybe —you know—she won't be so set against you."

"That's always possible," Bert said with a straight face.

"I think so, too. It only just takes time." He kept feeling better and better: he was brimming inside, he was flooding with delicious relief and happiness. "Boy," he sighed. "I told you our luck would turn . . . everything . . . I can sleep tonight. Like those times we paid off Bob Werden. I admit he let us down the last time like you said he would, though . . ."

Bert merely grinned at him and said, "Let's go get you some groceries, Lard. I intend to build you up till you look like a pregnant hippopotamus," he chuckled. "Again."

They strolled outside into the twilight. Wally felt again at the luscious bulge of his wallet and threw delighted glances all around. "The town don't even look the same any more," he said. "Hey, what about if before we eat, let's go look at the truck." Bert said, "It's your party," and they walked buoyantly past the green park with its bit of water, its World War I cannons and its tubby little bandstand, like a white and yellow clown in the trees. Beyond the grey pens of the auction barn, and far beyond that, the sky was a red glory above the black slabby buttes. "Whewh!" Wally said. "I don't hardly know where I am,

I feel so good. We were purt' near licked that time, but we came up kicking once more—thanks to you, Bert. I'm proud of the way you come through for us. Awful proud."

"Naturally."

With an elegant flip of his hand he brought out two cigars, and, puffing luxurious clouds of smoke, they stood looking at their truck in the shabby lot. Bert patted the fender and said, "Easy there, Old Paint. We'll be around for you Monday morning."

They were sauntering back when Wally stopped dead in his tracks, an awed expression on his face. "Guess what. I'm hardly hungry at all, and I didn't even have supper! When I think, the hours I put in just making up menus when we were flat broke, and now I finally can eat my fill of anything and everything, and it don't mean all that much."

Bert looked sober and said, "I was afraid of this. It's a bad symptom, Wally. I hate like fire to tell you but hospitals and doctors can't do much for you either. You've been partnering with me too long, you're getting complicated." Whooping, he slugged Wally on the arm and rollicked up the sidewalk, pounding a dance with his worn boots, the cap buster and the rubber knife stuck under his belt. "I don't care how I look," he warbled, "I'm gonna get my picture took."

Wally lumbered after him smiling fondly, adoringly. Bert was so comical and everything, and so gifted. It was worth any amount of pain, any kind of heartbreaking defeat to save him.

At the stoplight, instead of going on to the hotel, Bert abruptly veered right toward the depot and stopped, his tattooed arms folded on his chest, his whiskery face curved in a grin. Across the street was Mencke's drugstore, and Mrs. Mencke was out in front passing the time of day. As usual six or seven dull, empty railroad men were clustered around her, clinging to her for life like a bunch of ticks. Without her chatter and teasing, Wally sometimes thought they would all just dry up and blow away. She had borrowed a bike from some kid and she was teetering up and down the sidewalk like a girl, holding her dress down, primly, with one hand while she pedalled along. Her plump country face was radiant.

"Damnation," Bert said, "Now *there's* an outdoor sport I like. I just believe I'll take a spin myself."

He tossed away his cigar and ran a comb through his hair, then lounged across the street with careless arrogance and sat on the fender of a car. She came wobbling and giggling by. He said, "Can I have a turn, little girl?"

She jerked a startled look at him, almost careened off the sidewalk, and pedalled away in full flight. Bert winked a red, boiled eye at Wally. When she came back, reluctantly, avoiding him with a scarlet face, he said, "All right, I'll give you a dime to ride it—and two bus tokens, cash on the nail." She was not flirting, though. She seemed to be frightened half out of her wits. Rigidly she kept going past the old square-fronted buildings, all the way down to the depot, and got off the bike near the small fountain. Bert, looking like a tramp, but cocky and gay, shouted raucously to her, "You're sticking pins and needles in my heart!"

Wally said, "Let's go, you're scaring her to death."

Blithely Bert preened the comb through his hair. "If this hair gets any curlier," he said, "I don't know."

At last she gave up hope that he would leave and, with her head drooping, walked the bike back to the store. Letting it clatter in a sprawl on the sidewalk, she shrank into the bunch of railroad men. They glowered at Bert.

"That's no way to ride a bike," he told her. "Watch this." And away he skimmed, doing tricks up the street: he swooped this way and that and rode with no hands, he turned and reeled back down the sloping street with his legs spraddled out on both sides, gulping at the same time from the pint of whiskey. Back he came, stunting all the way. His wild "yippee!" echoed off the fronts of the wooden stores, and for just a few seconds it was crazy and beautiful: Bert flying along on the bike, light flickering off the spokes and everybody watching, and silver cloud blooming on the pine mountains beyond the lines of dark red freight cars. Then a battered car started up by the fountain and he swerved to get out of the way, jarred, and catapulted over the handles into the street.

Wally galloped to him like a frightened mother. "Are you all right?"

"Damn," Bert said, picking himself up. "Throwed again. Did you see that thing buck? My rodeo days are over." As he limped back to the drugstore (with Wally pushing the bike behind him), he groaned, "OOOeee, but I'm crippled up. I must've left a yard of hide on that road." But when he gave the bike back to Helen Mencke, he straightened up, borrowed Wally's hat for a moment and tipped it gallantly to her. "I thank you, little bitty girl," he grinned.

Then he slapped the hat back on Wally's head and strutted up the sidewalk. "Fortunately, the whiskey's not broke," he said and paused for another belt. "This is dry country around here for a fact. Yes sir."

"Ssst! The goat wagon!" Wally said, nudging his head at the police car parked by the bank. "Hold it down, will you?"

Humming and clicking his fingers, Bert peered into the gritty frame dimestore and discovered the owner at a desk in the rear, still going over the Saturday receipts. "Open up!" he hollered, beating on the door. The town policeman drove by slowly, looking. "Please!" Wally hissed, but he couldn't be reasoned with. He forced the owner to let them in and bought three bunches of glass roses, burning like coals of ashy fire among their dusty glass leaves, their twisted wire stems embedded in roundbellied white vases. "Beats hell out of a garden," he chirped and gave them a shake to make them tinkle. "If there's anything boresome, it's looking at a dead flower. Plus, these give out a tune." He shook another ghostly shower of clinks out of them and then handed the vases to Wally. "Here, you better carry these. I'm a little down in my back."

Wally was not only bewildered but annoyed at the waste of good money, and he obeyed in frowning silence. It was hellbent foolish extravagance, he muttered to himself, that's what it was. But then they went into the hotel and he could have sunk through the floor with shame because Bert, bowing with rakish magnificence, presented the flowers to Mrs. Harbaugh.

"I picked these for you along the tracks," he said.

She went pink with pleasure. Holding them under her pouchy face, she actually sniffed at them like real flowers and then laughed at herself, hefty and loud but all soft with emotion. "So you won, huh? I hope you separated them from every penny they had." Beaming over the sprays of tinking red shells, she lifted the flap of the counter for them to come in.

"It was a Sunday school picnic," Bert said. "They was overmatched." He told Wally to pay their tab in full and added loftily, "Give her another hundred to go along with it."

"No sir," she said. "I won't make a nickel profit out of you boys. It's a treat to see you take some of those old coots over the high hurdles. It's no surprise to me, either. I can tell a high roller when I see one." In a perfect delirium of happiness, she wedged the glass flowers between the baby pictures and the potted plants. "There!" she said, with a catch of a smile at Bert. "Look at me, I'm all out of breath. A woman don't get many gifts any more at my age."

"Don't talk like that," he said. "You can't be a day over seventy-five."

"Oh *you*!" She insisted that they have some cookies she had just baked up and started in about the parties she had gone to as a girl, country jamborees in one-room schoolhouses, with families from thirty miles around driving in by horse and wagon, and fiddle-playing and dancing until morning . . .

"I'm full as a frog," Bert said after three bites, and off he went to shave and clean up. Crestfallen, she sat by the ruffly lamp with her wee brown dog slithering over her flabby breasts and licking at her face. She looked old. The lamplight picked up gleams from the pink scalp under her wispy dyed hair.

"You have to understand," Wally said sympathetically. "He's ripe for a howler of a celebration. And when he gets on a tear like this, well, I'd rather handle nine outlaws sometimes than him." After a moment's deliberation, he gave her his wallet. "I wish you'd hold this. We'll probably both be in jail before midnight."

As soon as they walked back into the Cattleman's Bar, Bert snapped up a girlfriend of his named Florence and started enjoying himself in earnest. "Look out, sugar," he whooped. "I got beans in my belly and love in my eye." Wally sat down with his book and a package of gingersnaps. What he wanted most now, what he craved, was sleep, but he hung on faithfully, ready to quiet Bert down, to fight for him if he got into a brawl, and to carry him home when the time came. Oh, but he was sleepy, though. Mr. Mencke, sporting an I LIKE IKE button, was talking loudly to two men in business suits. Several cowhands were crowded around the dwarf, laughing at something. "Kiss of Fire" squealed from the juke box, and then Peggy Lee's mambo version of "Lover" came roaring out and swamped the room, drowned it with a noise like a highballing freight train in a tunnel. He blinked sleepily at the page, drifting, sinking into the muddle of voices: ". . . communist menace . . . struck a hot spot that made their Geiger go wild . . . my wife tells me I'm off my rocker, but I can't seem to quit. Once that prospecting urge gets ahold, it's like you're hypnotized . . ."

"Hey, chaperone!" Bert was grinning down at him. "Here I am, acting rowdy, and you're not even registering a protest. Let's get on the stick, buddy." He reached for Wally's book and dropped his mouth open in pretended astonishment. "You mean you're still on page eleven? Lord have mercy, you've been plugging at that thing for six months and that's all your progress?"

Wally smiled placidly. "It's slow going, all right, when you're stupid like me."

"*An Outline of History* by H. G. Wells," he read from the cover. "Masterpieces Book Club. Damnation, Lard, this is a back *buster*!" Opening the book he turned over the pages, shaking his head and snorting sample items: " 'Life began as a slime, as a sort of sub-life that slowly and imper-ceptibly took on its distinctive qualities.' Oh this is a hummer. 'Reptiles . . . Mammals . . . ground ape with increasing consciousness.' No sir, this ain't healthy for you, Lard, nor that gravedigger you hang out with, neither." Boisterously he waved for Florence and Jackie to come over. "Take your pick," he said. "This is Shadrack, this here is Meshack, and—where the hell did the other one run off to?" Wally reminded him that he was a married man. "All right," Bert groaned. "Have a ham sandwich."

The women joined them in the booth, and Bert rubbed his cheek against Florence's arm. She was a wide, easy-going woman with smooth laps of plumpness under her chin. "Move in a little closer, where you can give me a hug," he ordered. "Aah, that's better. Ain't it about time you bought me a drink?"

"Me buy you a drink? With all your money?"

"Can't spare it, sugar. I'm giving all my fortune to a home for girls like you." He guffawed and threw Jackie a ten dollar bill. "Get us some refreshments, dear heart."

Though he shuddered at the rate Bert was spending money, Wally drank a bottle of beer to be sociable, and then, because it was a great day, a second and a third. He began to feel woozy and gazed at Bert's capers with a drowsy, contented smile. Then, across the buzzing room, he saw that the ranch hands and gandies and prospectors were tormenting the little man. One of them knocked his drink over and pretended to apologize. Trickles came from his bulb eyes. They fawned on him, sympathized with him, stroked and petted him, winking gleefully at each other all the time. Wally felt his comfortable happiness drain away. He had noticed before, while he'd been sweating out the card game, how little Ray seemed to bring the worst out of everybody; even the lavish presents he kept getting were tainted somehow. A long-nosed man with red hair was tricking his fists at Ray, feinting and jabbing lightly, in an effort to get him to spar with him. Ray, muttering irritably, waved him away. The man faked twice and slapped him hard. Garbling with rage, Ray flailed back with his stunted arms, hopping up and down and climbing into the air to pummel at the man's chest. "Thatta boy! Get him, Ray! Chop him down to your size!" the men cheered him on, and there was something in their laughing faces—it wasn't exactly the tight, greedy look that people got when a fighter was hurt in the ring or when a stock car spun and crashed into a wall—it was—all he knew was that it made him feel ashamed and sick.

He slid out of the booth and elbowed his big hulk through the men. Ray was kicking futilely with his tiny chocolate-colored shoes. Sweat glittered in his thin hair and on his gorged, oozing face.

"All of you get back," Wally said in a choked voice. "I'm telling you, stand back or I'll knock you flat." The men looked at him viciously. He grabbed Ray by his small calloused hand and led him back to the booth. Hoisting himself up into the seat, he took Florence's drink and slurped it down, holding the glass in both hands like a child, sucking and slopping with his muzzle pressed into the opening and his eyes closed.

"Ah, that were good," he sighed. "I'm thirsty as never before. People, they got me all turned around in my head. You understand what I mean?" He held out the glass in his hands and said, "I'll take another whiskey if you'll be so kind, thank you."

Bert looked sullen. "Well move," he said to Wally. "Get off your butt and get him one."

"Okay, you don't have to bite my head off. I'm going."

Bert didn't say anything more and, bewildered, Wally went for the drink. The ranch hands over by the empty stage gestured at Ray to come back and held up full glasses of whiskey and beer to entice him. Wally turned angry scowls at them all the way back to the booth and tried to find out from Ray what his plans were. Both Florence and Jackie were ogling and whispering. "You're pretty cute," one of them said.

Ray set down the empty glass, making smacking noises, and his swollen bestial lips smiled sweetly. "You're fine-looking girls," he said in his marshy voice. "Very attractive. I don't see much beauty any more these days . . . I were doorman at the Blue Poodle in Chicago, once. That were a good life. I wore a blue pinstripe suit and a chauffeur cap and my spiel were, 'Come right in, come right in, the show is just starting. The world's most beautiful girls.' And so anyway . . ."

He lapsed into muttering as another whistle came from the men.

"You mean it was a strip tease place?" Jackie asked with awe.

"They were very good strippers at the Blue Poodle," he assured her. "I made up to twenty dollars a day with tips for calling cabs and so forth and so on. The business men from outa town, it were their place to have fun. Or they could hire them for stag parties, too. Also they could go to the back or get the girl to—you know what I mean, right at the bar. They had their fun, you betcha, and the sky was the limit for money. Every girl had a nice shape and nice bumpers—excuse me again, I'm not very good at polite company. And they turned on different colored lights and the three-piece band was playing. Laa-dee-da," he crooned hoarsely. His toad's eyes were half closed and his bloated little arms, tied off in miniature wrists and hands, swayed and bent languorously and writhed, performing a lewd, crippled dance in the air. "Laa-laa-laa."

"Why don't you for Chrissake shut your mouth," Bert said. His face twisted in the soiled darkness.

Wally frowned. For some reason, Bert's high spirits had suddenly curdled and gone sour. "Take it easy," he said to him, and to Ray. "Hold on and set down, everybody is friends." He grasped that Ray was the trouble, though what (if anything) the Blue Poodle had to do with it was more than he could make out, since Bert wasn't exactly straight-laced, to put it mildly. Meanwhile, Ray was about to leave in a huff, and Wally cast about anxiously for some way to keep him from going back to those men.

"How about lining up a hotel room, Ray? You quit the gandy gang, so you'll need someplace to stay. You haven't blowed that fifty bucks, I trust."

Ray fumbled his thumb-sized fingers in his pockets and came up with a filthy handkerchief, some crushed cigarettes, the melted remains of a Hershey bar, and two combs. "It's gone," he said dolefully. "I lost it, I guess."

"Gone!" Wally bawled. "Look some more. Fifty dollars!" He went through Ray's pockets himself. The little man was blinking sorrowfully. All at once he sniffled and pawed at his eyes with his tiny fist, like a dirty child who has lost the grocery money on the way to the store.

"Get out of here," Bert ripped at him. "Go on, get out."

"I were a lucky charm for you," Ray said.

"Bert!" Wally cried. "I'm surprised at you." Slewing around in high indignation, Ray stumped away. Wally put out a big hand to stop him but he swung his fists and kicked wrathfully, spluttering, "Lemme alone . . . People . . ." Wally turned back to Bert, full of reproach, and then he saw his face: it was like a red, open wound.

Frightened, he said, "Forget it. Let's clear outa here; let's go over to the Victory, Bert. Florence? Jackie? How about it?"

Bert didn't answer.

The men welcomed Ray back with loud shouts, slapping him on the back and grinning like apes, and though he was still grumpy with them, he condescended to accept a bottle of beer. It was useless to think of getting him away from them any more. Bert was tense, restless, silent. He couldn't take his eyes away from Ray as, winking slyly, a prospector with a green-and-white shirt clasping his long torso handed Ray a glass of bourbon. He swallowed thirstily. Then his eyes bulged out, red and hideous, and liquor burst from his mouth in strangling, coughing spasms. Shaking with suppressed laughter, they mauled him on the back, on the pretense of helping him get his breath. Bert was staring and staring.

"As a favor to me," Wally said. "Come on, huh?" The redhaired man, with a great show of commiseration, brought Ray a half-pint of whiskey. He clutched at it and attempted to peel the seal off. His fingers, sticking out from his hand like sprouts from a potato, clawed and scratched in vain. Furious sounds came from the pink gulch of his mouth and tears spread out, glistening, in his pulpy cheeks.

There was a queer slickness in Bert's face. He walked over to the sniggering men, and both women tagged along after him. Wally was cold with the memory of how Bert had looked when he followed the hurt dog down the street, as if he'd been hypnotized by the horrible red splatters of blood. Then other things that had happened in seven years began to come back, to sprout and shoot up murderously in his head. To think, only twenty minutes ago they had been so happy . . . He felt as if he'd stepped through ice into freezing black water. Across the room, a mouth crammed with teeth barked open. Ray's dribbling face popped out from behind a long sag of gut in a green workshirt.

Uranium! 121

The dead, abandoned stage by the smirking men was like an open jaw filled with shadows.

"Bert," he said, pulling at his arm. "I beg you. As my friend . . ."

"Get off my back," Bert snarled, and the look on his bruised grey face was worse than any punch. The strength went out of Wally's legs. In despair he hunched down in the booth. He watched Bert go to the bar and purchase a fifth of bourbon and hold it, uncorked, in front of Ray. The little man snatched at it, but Bert drew it back, making some sort of condition about giving it to him. The girls left. Wally had never felt so alone in his life. He wished that Paul was around to help. He wondered what had happened to keep Paul and the boys out of town on a Saturday night. Whatever had happened, it was his fault on two counts: if he hadn't been so jittery he'd have noticed that the girl was Lucy, and he'd have warned Paul; and if he just hadn't asked Paul to check one more time how Bert was doing . . . Ray was stuttering now and holding his arms out toward the bottle, and something was going to happen, something cruel and terrible that he couldn't prevent.

Jackie returned, carrying a blue dress, and Ray disappeared in a knot of scuffling men. A spotlight flushed on over the grimy stage. Wally's stomach came together as he saw the men lift Ray and heave him up onto the boards, floundering inside the blue billows of the dress. For a minute he stood there in the gluey light, blinking out at the hoo-hooing crowd. The skirts of the dress puddled around his feet. His red snout was varnished with sweat and light. Behind him on the wall, his shadow ballooned as big as a man. Wally felt the grey thickening in his head and the men were laughing and Bert was gnawing on his hand; then Wally couldn't look at him any more.

The juke box spewed music.

And Ray, struggling and trampling in vast, shapeless drapes of blue rayon, paraded back and forth in the mildewed light, wagging his short haunches and flowing his hands along his chest and hips to the shouts of "Shake that thing!" and "Take it off!" Curses rumbled out of his mouth. Repulsive, pathetic, a little nightmare of pain, he sashayed up and down the stage. He tripped in the drag of the long sprawling skirts, recovered, and tugged at the zipper of the dress as he tottered along in clopping, oversized women's shoes. There was a small avalanche of blue, and he was standing there in an undershirt and a pair of Army surplus shorts, grinding and bucking his low hips with one hand behind his head. Wally felt sick. It was more like a jerking agony than a freak show take-off on a naked woman dancing, and yet the men were clapping and yelping, "Take it off!" Why didn't the bartenders stop it? Then Wally felt the blood go out of his head. Bert was climbing up on the stage with the bottle. His face was all slippery and his chest was working heavily. He yanked at Ray's muggy undershirt, at his shorts, and suddenly everybody was staring at the huge, erect, prodding sex of the little man.

There was a sort of gap, as if everything and everybody had stopped, fixed for all time in a shameful dirty picture, and then Jackie whirled and ran out and some of the men, with sheepish faces, began to edge away. Now when it was too late, a bartender came to break it up and switch off the spotlight. Ray went off with the bottle. Bert was still on the stage, motionless in the shadows.

Testing Grounds, Yucca Flat

An hour before dawn, the Nevada desert six hundred miles away glared with a blinding flash, and a ball of fire three times as hot as the sun burst up into the sky. The third series of atomic tests was in progress. Just eighteen years before, in the summer of 1934, Enrico Fermi and his associates had begun an experiment in which they fired neutrons at uranium. They were trying to create element 93 by adding neutrons to the nucleus of uranium, number 92; instead, a swarm of fiery dwarfs popped out, inexplicable, burning with radioactivity. At the time Fermi had no idea what was happening, but the unnatural copulation was spawning half-sized monsters.

It was five years before they were identified: the uranium atoms had deformed grotesquely under the microscopic cannonading, growing longer and longer, pinching in at the middle and then splitting apart in a storm of unleashed energy. The devil in matter had been let out.

Then, like a chain reaction, had come war and the first atomic test outside Alamogordo, the ruins of Hiroshima and Nagasaki. Now the tiny radioactive dwarfs were a monster of fire and smoke forty thousand feet tall in the bright Sunday morning air.

VIII

An hour later Ray was stumping along in the grey, sparrow-fluttering dawn. The streets were empty. A deisel snorted in the freight yards. As he steered himself down the sidewalk toward the tracks, the sparrows blew up in front of him, stuck to the edge of the store fronts in the red sky, and then dropped, one by one, like leaves falling, back into the gutter. The Denver bus from Rapid City heaved around the corner from the highway and drew up in front of the Black Hills cafe. The driver threw out a roll of newspapers.

On impulse Ray made a run for the bus, his eyes popping and his rubbery cheeks blowing in and out. Then he remembered that his fifty dollars was lost. He slowed down and came to a stop. It was too bad. Denver was a nice town. Plenty of enjoyment to be found in it.

Rolling his ponderous head dejectedly, he toddled on toward the depot and the freight yards. His feet stumbled under him. The sky was a great bruised purple and yellow and red over the dark mountains. The fountain by the depot steamed into the chilly air. When he reached the tracks he sighted blearily down the long files of boxcars, trying to make out whether the orange work cars of the gandy gang were still there, parked outside of town under the buttes. His eyes sagged shut and opened again. It was too far anyhow; he couldn't navigate that distance in his present condition.

Then he noticed an Indian boy fishing in the pond in the park and he wobbled over and sat down with a grunt. "My feet are acting up something terrible," he said. "Hey, Slim, do me a favor, you got young eyes. Can you see, are the orange cars still down the line?"

"Sure."

"Thanks a thousand. I'll be moving along in that case, get my old job back. They'll be pulling out pretty quick . . ." He broke off and rubbed his drugged red eyes. "No . . . that's not what I was gonna do. But . . . I lose track, that's my trouble. You know what I mean?

I forget things. I use to have a fine memory before liquor turned me boogey. That and people, they don't leave you alone."

The boy went on fishing, brown and shaggy in a net of moving light. He was standing on the bridge to the little island with a picnic table, and all around him in the clear silence the trees dripped bird sounds and pieces of shadow. Two ducks boated on the pink water, pulling glass-black triangles behind them. The red and white cork sailed under the bridge, sailed in one place on the rocking water, up and down and up . . .

Ray blinked his eyes open. "Hey, Slim, what town is this?"

The boy, surprised, looked at him and then said, "Enterprise."

"Enterprise. I'm sure lost. Man overboard this time for sure." He frowned, groping at a muddle of shame and bitterness inside him, groping. "People mess you up, you know what I mean? Well, I'm coming to bat now. Before I leave this town, whatever it is, somebody is in for a bad surprise . . ." And he trailed off into murderous grumbling.

The boy pulled in the line, shucking off droplets in a glittery spray, and put another worm on the hook and dropped the line back into the pond. An evil smell of sulphur came from the fresh, rosy water.

"People. If you look inside of them—not everybody, though. Some people is good. I give a man a drink once, and three years later I met him on the street in St. Louis. You know he recanized me right away? He bought me a pint and said, what kind of cigarettes are you burning? I said Pell Mell and he said, bartender give him a pack, make it two packs . . . I'd die for people like that."

He found some battered cigarettes in his pockets and asked the boy to light one for him. "I can't handle it now myself. In my condition. Have one yourself." The boy accepted quickly, and they stood together on the bridge, looking down at the cork and smoking. "What's your name?" Ray asked.

"Charley Trueblood."

"Mine is Ray, pleased to meet you. Let's see if you're as tall as me." Standing on tiptoe he measured himself against Charley, back to back, cutting his hand along the tops of their heads. "About even-steven, I'd say. It's a pleasure talking to you, I don't have to keep looking up to see who it is . . . for a change."

Smoking like an expert, inhaling and easing the smoke out through his nose, Charley said, "My father drinks a lot, too. My mother threw him out; she gets two hundred and forty dollars from the government every month." Once he got started he could talk a person's ear off, and he knew everything about the town. "You see them tree stumps over there? A beaver done that. The sheriff trapped him and killed him, but four dogs got trapped first."

"You don't say." Ray spit on his hand and greased Charley's fishing line for luck. "I'm a lucky charm," he said. "Or just the opposite, whichever way I want. I blew on Sammy Mandel's hand and he won eleven grand in one night. Or I can jinx somebody if I want . . ."

He frowned again, straining to remember, to make out what was hurting in the sleepy tangle in his head. Even when Charley landed a nice perch, he was still discontented. "Somebody sucker-punched me last night," he muttered. "Or something. I need a nap to clear my head. You know where I can lay down in a safe place? You know, not in public."

"Sure, I know lots of good places." He rolled up the line on a stick, and dangling the perch by the tail, led the way past the bandstand and the old cannons pointing at the famine-grey hills. The sun whitened the faces of the shabby buildings across the street. Throwing the fish away, Charley took out a metal slingshot and snapped pebbles at telephone poles, at hubcaps and signboards, at a burly tom cat prowling off into the weeds. Ray had to work hard to keep up. "I'm outa shape," he puffed. "Where we headed? I forgot."

"You're gonna take a nap."

"That's right, I just want a little nap. I'm all turned around at present."

In a minute they reached the manure-smelling pens of the auction barn. Bales of hay were warming in the sweet early light, cattle bawled. Charley ripped a stone at a sparrow perched on a grey post and it was gone, erased without a sound, without even a flutter of wings. Ray gaped at the spot, like a puncture in the sunshine, where the bird had been sitting.

"Hey! What did you do that for?" he damnded. "I don't appreciate that."

Charley wriggled his shoulders and mumbled at the ground.

"That were a nice bird," Ray said. His bulging red eyes were angry. "Go bury it at least."

"What for?" Charley said in a sullen voice, but he scaled over the rails into the pen and scuffed a grave for it in the dirt and crumbling cow plats. Ray was unappeased. In an effort to make it up to him and win him back, Charley showed him four shark's teeth which he had in a Bull Durham sack and said, "I know where there's some dinosaur bones." Ray lugged along the path toward the railroad tracks, breathing hoarsely. "That were a nice bird, though," he muttered.

The path sank into a tunnel under the tracks. It was deep and thick with echoes and cold stinks, and there was a faraway peep of light at the other end. The floor was wrinkled with dry mud like very old skin, the walls were scribbled with generations of lost initials and dates. "This is our club house," Charley said. "Nobody can use it except my gang. There's a swinging bridge on the other side, you wanta see me swing on it?"

"So what?" Ray said testily. He picked up some tattered newspapers, spread them out and let himself down on them. Charley squatted nearby and said, "This is a good place, huh?" Ray grunted. "I'll keep watch so no kids or anybody wakes you up." After a minute, in a small voice he said, "I need a quarter pretty bad."

"Huh?" Ray said, opening his eyes. "Yuh, sure. A bargain is a bargain." He jacked himself up unsteadily and searched in his pockets, yawning his mouth open on ridges of innocent pink gums. Eventually he found some change and counted it out. "Twenty, twenty-one, twenty-two—that's all the more money I got. I owe you three cents."

"That's all right."

"Credit," Ray mumbled and capsized onto the newspapers. From farther and farther away came the boy's voice, "When Mr. Butler gets back, I won't need no money from anybody. He'll be out of the hospital pretty soon. He wrote me a letter and he's just about back on his feet, I'll be seeing his old car in front of our house any day now . . ."

An enormous eye grew brighter and brighter, a string of crashes came toward him like a giant walking, and he sat up on the crumpled newspapers. The Indian kid was crouched in the mouth of the tunnel, a folded-up little shadow in the dazzling hollow of daylight, and a freight train was switching thunderously overhead.

"I watched for five hours," the kid said. "You feel better now?"

Ray staggered to his feet. "Boy, I were dead for sleep . . . Let's see, your name is what?"

"Charley Trueblood," the kid told him. "Did you forget the town, too? It's Enterprise."

"Yuh, that's right. Yuh." He knitted his forehead at the lost intention inside him, the hatred he couldn't pin down; then it faded completely away and he said, "I'm dry as a dog. But to start, I gotta get me a hamburger or a sandwich so I don't get D.T.'s."

Before he set out on his rounds, he washed up at the fountain by the depot, first splashing away the green scum and the candy wrappers and then shipping up bits of water onto his face and over his hair. "Comb it, will you?" he asked Charley. "It just sparkles when it's combed." He handed over one of his combs with the warning, "Part it straight," and stood motionless, drapes of water sliding down his hideous face, while Charley arranged the long, wet, colorless hair in hollows and waves on his pink scalp.

"Now I'm ready for action," he said, and brushing his draggled clothes, he started out. Mencke's drug store was still closed but men were lounging on the streets and on the porches of the hotels. Church bells clashed in the endless void of light. In less than twenty minutes he collected a dollar and thirty cents simply by walking around. With the arrogance of the freak, the scapegoat, the victim, he waded along the hot bright sidewalk, his man's head swerving waist-high past the large bodies, his tiny hands clenched, his low hips coming around with each step. The sheriff beamed from across the street and called, "Hi, Ray." Four or five hands pressed money on him and voices boomed down, legs as big as trees moved around him. "You sure can shake it, Ray," somebody said, and he felt his hair scrambled roughly.

"Hey!" he said, skidding around and recovering his balance. "I don't appreciate that." With an irritable grump he accepted a half dollar from the man and rolled on, an angry little nightmare exactly the size of the squat and crippled shadows of the men. Scraping sorrowfully at his hair, he peered at his round distortion in the hubcap of a parked car. "Would you comb it again?" he asked Charley. "It's spoiled."

In front of the Western Cafe, he said, "Come on, I'll buy you some sinkers and coffee."

"I can't," Charley said and looked down. His soft, slurring voice was very small: "They don't like Indians in there."

"They don't! Screw 'em, we'll go to the Black Hills Cafe then."

Charley shook his head. "They don't like Indians there either."

"What's the matter with everybody? Bastards. I suppose they don't like colored people either . . . People . . . The best man I ever knew were a colored man."

Still muttering to himself, he entered the muggy, fly-buzzing little joint and vaulted onto a stool at the counter. "I need something solid. Gimme some buttermilk," he told the waitress. "A glass of buttermilk."

She brought him a carton and poured it into a glass. He doused it thoroughly with salt and, opening a big empty mouth down into his body, slopped at the sludgy whiteness with his eyes closed, gobbling and smacking noisily. "Ah, that were fine. I'll take another and a couple of sinkers for my friend outside."

"That'll be forty cents."

"Credit," he said in a surly voice.

"You can wind Mrs. Binder around your finger but not me. So just fork up. See that sign on the wall?"

A man down the counter, hunched over a platter of ham and eggs, said, "Put it on my check, Eloise." He was a longnosed fellow with loose red hair and acne nicks in his cheeks. "You should've saw the show he put on last night, Eloise. Best stripper in town, ain't you, Ray?"

Ray gave him a bulging, stupid look. Slowly the numbed memory was coming alive, terrible, writhing inside him, and the blood thickened in his face. "Shut up!" he squealed.

"Hoochy-coochy," the man laughed. "You know, for a little guy you're really hung."

"Shut up! Shut up! Shut up!" He hurled himself off the stool and butted out the door. His veiny eyes bugging, he jabbered incoherently at Charley, "All right, there comes a time, and this is it. Once and for all, you understand? This favor I'm giving back double. Triple." Plowing down the sidewalk, sloughing off hands and voices as he went, he reached the Cattleman's Bar. It wasn't open yet and he kicked wrathfully at the door with his doll's feet.

"What's going on?" Charley said. "Don't kick any more, you'll hurt your foot."

"Listen, I got to locate a certain party, and when I do . . . it won't be light and easy, I promise you that. Now listen, there's two of 'em. He has a partner, a great big tall guy, but the one I want, he's smaller built. And he's a Fancy Dan with women. I'll wait here."

Charley's mud-colored face was a blank.

"Pay attention!" Ray said, exasperated. "He's a gambler, a hotshot gambler—with my help, too." At the thought of that, he slipped into baleful mumbling. "Bert," he said, recovering. "That's his name, Bert, and he won a bundle last night. Now that oughta be sufficient."

Repeating the scraps of information to himself, Charley went off at a run. Ray sat down on the front step of the bar. There were smudges of white cloud in the vast burning sky. Blotches of oil stained the empty parking spaces. He felt at the torn underwear under his clothes and tiny whimpers came from his mouth.

Ten minutes later Charley came tearing back and panted, "It was easy. He's at Mrs. Harbaugh's, his name is Bert and his partner's name is Wally." Greedily he snatched at the coins Ray gave him and said, "Come on, I'll show you. He's in room 301."

Scowling in a glaze of sweat, Ray stumped beside him to the Prince Hotel. "I'll take it from here," he said, and toiled up to the third floor, carrying his feet from step to step and hauling himself up on the rail. Outside the door, he stood for a minute with his eyes shut and his fists bunched tight, whispering hoarsely. Then he knocked.

"Yeah?" a voice said from inside.

He turned the knob and followed the door in. The big man was polishing a pair of shoes with a glum expression that broke into pain when he saw who it was. Bert swung around from the window, his eyes going little in his sour face. "What do *you* want? Clear out, beat it."

Hate boiled through Ray's body, gushed like acid into his throat and eyes. A ghastly smile jerked at his scooped-out lower lip. "Hello," he said.

The next thing he knew, the big man had set down his brush and led him out of the room. "You better stay away," he told him gently. The door closed behind him, but Ray knocked again, stubborn, absolutely determined. Years of frustration and impotent rage had crystallized into this one hate. "Bygones be bygones," he shouted through the door. "How about it? Last night, forget it and shake hands. Stuff like that, it's an old story to me." The big man came out again, looking sadder than ever, and escorted him all the way out of the hotel.

Ray stamped up and down the sidewalk, goggling his pop eyes and swearing.

"What did you do?" Charley asked. "Did you fight him?"

"Lemme alone." He took a lunging step off the curb and walked right into the path of an oncoming car. Charley grabbed him and pulled him back, struggled with him.

"You want to get run over?"

"Lemme alone. Lay off, I'm fed up with you." Shoving Charley away, he mumbled, "When I'm through, he'll wish I'd went after him with a German Luger." Then he sat down on the curb and covered his thick, leaking face with his paws. The men on the hotel porch were grinning and making remarks.

"Look here." Charley brought out the treasures he'd purchased with the money: a red top, a mad-scientist comic book, and something which he slipped into Ray's hand, a small round mirror. "Now you can see to comb your hair," he said.

"Lemme alone," Ray said, but the unexpected present from the boy made a clear cool place in his flaming hate. Little by little, he quieted down and pretty soon he took a peek at himself. "It'll be a very handy item," he said, tucking the mirror away. "I hope you'll look over what I said. I was outa my head."

"That's okay, you want to see me ride a horse? That's how come I needed a quarter. You get three rides for a quarter, come on."

"I gotta stay here," Ray said. However, he couldn't resist taking another look at himself in the mirror, and one of the loungers on the porch called, "You're *perty*." With a black glare at the laughing men, he said, "All right, let's get out of this vicinity . . . temporarily. He won't be coming out till the taverns open."

"That's not till one o'clock. Come on, so we can get first turn or we'll have to wait all afternoon. It's Dean's horse but him and Debbie are partners."

On the way, he showed Ray a wild goose penned in a back yard, then shinnied to the very top of a cottonwood tree and brought down a lustrous green bead. Nonchalantly he broke it open and exposed the shocking white worm, lewd and blind, which was cradled inside it. "I can walk the top of the railroad bridge, too," he bragged. "Everybody else is ascared." People were coming home from church, families in cars, ladies in polkadot dresses, three crisp little girls wearing straw hats with tails of red ribbon, and so Ray and Charley kept to the alleys and back streets, fellow exiles puffing on the same cigarette and strolling along. As a mark of special favor, Ray asked him to tie his shoelaces for him. "Good and tight, if you please—no, no, loop 'em underside over or it's bad luck."

"Hawks is bad luck too," Charley said, and they swapped information about luck. If you didn't want something to happen, you said, "trouble, trouble, go away," and scratched behind your right ear with your left hand; a cross-eyed man was a jinx; if you saw a white horse and didn't say "zit!" right quick, it was bad luck. In spite of the terrible burn of the memory inside him, Ray couldn't help feeling somewhat better. Cooking smells drifted from the boxy houses and trailers sheltering in tree shadows. A mongrel dog frisked up to join them, and then a boy glazed over with Sunday clothes, then two stringy roughnecks with a jar of grasshoppers.

"Lemme see that top," Ray said to Charley. He wound it carefully with the string and whipped it onto the sidewalk, reeling in an orbit like a small red planet. Quickly, deftly, he snared it in a loop of the string and flipped it up into the air and landed it, miraculously still spinning, on his horny palm. The boys were dazzled. He caught it on the back of his hand, rode it down his bloated forearm, and even, after two or three failures, made it run along the string in the air, shuttling back and forth under his smiling gargoyle face.

"I can put a lighted match out in my mouth, too," he said proudly.

The boys were his. While they waited for Dean and Debbie to finish Sunday dinner, they hung around by the old stable in back and took turns squinting through a hole in the door at the horse lashing its tail in the manure-smelling dusk. More and more children collected, and except for a little girl who ran off bawling in fright, they all flocked around him, wide-eyed, respectful, competing for a word or just a look. He arbitrated squabbles. He broke it up when two of the boys, egged on by the others, squared off and taunted each other, circling fearfully in the hoof-bitten dust. When the boys with the grasshoppers put yellow paint in the jar and everybody jostled to watch the slow, sticky, roiling blobs, he scolded them and took the jar away. Until Debbie and Dean came out, he was like a little king and Charley, as his sponsor, lieutenant, and minister-in-chief, swaggered grandly beside him.

Then Dean led the cow pony out of the stable, and everybody watched Debbie feed it lumps of sugar and sling herself up and wriggle into position on its bare back. Her elbows posing, her pigtails bouncing on her back, her heels clouting the barrel sides of the pony, she rode at the head of a small procession of children, tilting her head occasionally to take sips from a bottle of orange pop. Almost forgotten, Ray tramped along contentedly in the pack. He was accustomed to attention, and this was far better than running the show: this was happiness. Something eased and unclenched inside him. In the long years since the Royal Universal Shows had folded in Canada, he had forgotten what it felt like simply to be comfortable. Now, truly, he was away from the kindness, the patronizing smiles, the insistent voices and the booze, the practical jokes, the hands in his hair—away from the world of big people.

Having made a triumphal circuit of the block, Debbie hiked her leg over and slid off the horse. "Now who's first?" she said. "All right, everybody get in a line behind Charley. In the order they came." The children began shoving and quarrelling shrilly: "Cheater!" "I was *so* here first." "You were not; was he, Johnny?" "I was too." Meanwhile the horse, shuddering flies off its side and sweeping its haunches with its tail, cropped at the sheared grass next to the garbage barrels. "No pushin'," she said, bossy and smug. "Everybody get their money out. Anybody that uses swear words can't ride; and that means you, Buzz Farley." Charley leaped, scrambling, onto the horse; and she warned him, "Just once around the block and no stoppin'."

Ray watched from the background, contented. Then, all at once, as she and Dean were dividing the money that had come in so far, he caught her black eyes looking at him, just a peek at first, but then again, longer this time and alive with interest. Testily he snubbed her. Charley finished his ride and immediately fell in at the end of the line. The pony thudded off down the alley with another boy, naked to the waist, shaking on its back and saying, "Giddyup."

He could feel her coming nearer. He could smell her orange-pop-and-sweat smell.

She sighed. "Boy am I ever roastin'," she said. "Did you ever see such cheaters? Yesterday Jerry Olson rode the horse away instead of going around the block . . . Are you a real dwarf?" she burst out.

"So what?" he grumbled. "That's a question I don't appreciate."

But to his astonishment, she said, "There's lots of stories about dwarfs. Did you know? They live in the ground and they have gold and silver mines and precious stones. They're magic! Sometimes they're called ga-nomes."

"Yuh, I guess so," he said, mollified, even pleased. Little tiny girls usually ran away or started bawling as soon as they laid eyes on him, and the older ones—well, the less about that the better. It was nice to mean fairy tales to somebody. A very welcome change.

When the horse came plodding back with its small rider, she told Dean to handle the business for a while: she was busy.

Fuddled with bliss, Ray tried to follow the tale of a little man named Rumpelstilskin and a girl who was ordered by the king to weave straw into gold or be executed. Rumpelstilskin helped her do it, but in return he made her promise to give him her first-born child. "Only he gave her one chance. If she could tell him his real name, he wouldn't take away her baby."

"It's a nice story," he said, baffled.

"It gets even better, just wait. Then she got married to the king and had a baby and Rumpelstilskin came to get it. She begged and pleaded for more time until at last he said all right. Night and day she travelled all over the whole kingdom and the king sent out messengers to hunt for strange names. On the very last day she got news of a tiny little man dancing on a moat and singing, 'Today I bake bread.' Well, in the song he told his name. But when he came back to her, instead of saying the name right off, she asked, 'Is it Caspar?' 'No!' he shouted and jumped up and down and laughed with glee. 'Is it—' I forget what name it was, and he laughed harder than ever."

Debbie's eyes were shining and bits of loose hair tipped on her flushed, excited face. "Then she said, 'Is it Rumpelstilskin?' And do you know what happened? He got so mad that he ground his teeth and got redder and redder and bang! he split right in two, and one half went right through the ground, down into hell. He was the devil hisself! But I don't mean you are."

"Sure," he said. "I use to have nice teeth. They were white as pearls." He felt pretty bad about the matter, but she showed him the gaps and saw-edged nubs of teeth just starting to come through in her mouth. She was a nice girl. He wished he could do something to please her. He wished he hadn't lost his Silver King harmonica because spinning a top wouldn't be very interesting to a girl and neither would the match trick. Each time she left to boss the rides he was afraid that she would stay with the others and his heart gave a big bump when she came back and plunked down beside him in the shade. Her hair was like gold. There were holes in her tennis shoes with the knuckles of her bare toes sticking through. Two hours went by and still he couldn't bring himself to go. The rest of the world, even Bert, even what had happened in the tavern, seemed a thousand miles away. He wanted just to stay here like this.

"Oh pee," she said all at once, and sprawled a bright orange tongue from her mouth. "Here comes that old Barry Engleberg."

A boy of about ten, small and neatly put together but with heavy round glasses staring on his face, was poking down the alley with an elaborate air of carelessness. He had on an immaculate dark suit and a black baseball cap, set too straight on his head. Every few feet he stopped to loft a ball into the air and catch it, inexpertly, in a brand new leather mitt.

"Everybody hates him like anything," Debbie whispered. "He's a snitch and a crybaby. You know what he did? He peed in his pants right in *school*!"

Socking the ball into his glove, he halted a step or two from the boys in the bald light. "If it ain't Einstein Engleberg," they greeted him. "Einstein Silverstein Finkelstein Picklestein." He waited until they grew bored, then edged into the group. Stealthily, one of the boys dropped to his hands and knees behind him, another pushed his chest, and over he went with a flop, arms battling the air. They yawped happily. He squinted around until he found his glasses; then he went after the ball and stood in a timid heap, dusting nervously at himself. "Well, haul ass outa here," Dean said.

He seemed to have come apart; his glasses were slipping on his face, his cap was crooked. "Here's my dime to ride Lady," he said to Debbie.

She gave him a contemptuous look. "Are you *deef* as well as goofy? You heard what Dean said."

"Why can't I? Anybody with a dime can ride, that's the rule."

"Because you can't, that's why. You'll fall off and bust your goofy head."

"I am not goofy."

"You are so."

"Okay, what's eight times six times eleven and add a hundred and twenty-five?"

"Who cares?" she said snootily. "You're still goofy!"

"It's six hundred and fifty-three," he said, blinking through his dusty glasses.

Then he turned away. She put out her orange tongue at him and gave Ray a satisfied smile, but he only mumbled to himself. He could feel the pain, suspended for hours in dreamy wafts of happiness, drop into his chest. In the alley, Charley slithered off the horse. It bit at the nagging flies, nosed them away, and vibrated its straggling black mane. Immediately another kid was boosted on, and, it set off once more, smacking puffs of dust from its treadmill hoofs. The boys were playing keep-away with Barry's baseball, dodging, tossing it to each other at the last second as he bore down on them in hopeless rushes.

Debbie was giggling into the bowl of her hands.

Ray struggled to his feet and marched away, swearing under his breath. Charley yelled, "Hey wait up," and came jogging after him, but Ray waved him off. "Go your own way, lemme alone." Charley dropped behind, a small brown shadow trailing him. "Stop bird-dogging me," Ray said furiously. "Shove off!" When Charley still hung on, Ray pulled the mirror out of his pocket and smashed it on the sidewalk. "Now mind your own business," he said. Charley looked at him for a second, brown, shaggy-haired, expressionless, and then he abruptly cut off through a mangy yard.

Ray aimed himself at the Cattleman's Bar, muttering. At each cross street, the humped bare land came into the town. A tricycle was overturned on the sidewalk. Across the hot gravel street, a girl in a red dress was kneeling on the sidewalk, hunched over a coloring book, scribbling intently, and his heart gave a terrible pull and the fluids thickened in his eyes. But he kept going.

Then there was fierce white sunlight all around. His face was at the level of stomachs and the flies of pants, voices battered at him, arms like the sails on windmills swept at his hair. A man with decaying teeth said, "Come on, Ray, let's see how drunk you can get." Ray lowered his head and plowed past him into the bar. "Where's Bert?" he said. A man wearing a white straw hat pressed down on his ears gave him a quarter and said, "Gimme some luck for the poker game, Ray." Ray blew on the man's hands and went through a little rigmarole, but as the man walked off, he spat on the floor and whispered hoarsely, "Lose, you sonofabitch. Bust your guts." Somebody gave him a drink. His head felt like a firecracker had gone off in it, but he hadn't forgotten. A limp spotty face came wobbling down at him, grinning between hairy ears. He was in the Victory Bar. Bert wasn't around but his sidekick was there, the big guy, looking like a funeral. Ray latched on to him and groped at the conversation, groped for some kind of a lead. "Why do they act like that? Why?" the big man kept asking, and a guy named Paul said something about birds pecking a hurt bird, and maybe saints get rid of it, and so on and so forth.

"Shut up," Ray mumbled. "You big nose, shut up." His head was full of smoke. He hurt inside like an aching tooth. A sickly man was playing the organ, and in a rage he duckwalked over to him and sputtered, "That's enough, Big Nose. Hang it up. You don't have the talent for it." His drugged look floated over the pictures of identical steers, over the big meaty backs of the men at the bar, and dropped on Bert sitting by himself. Now at last he smiled. He went across the floor in a tottering charge and swarmed and rolled up the stool next to him. "Bygones be bygones," he puffed, wavering out his hand. "Shake on it, and be a sport."

IX

"But it's not true," Wally said to Paul. "Most people ain't that way."

"Oh yeah? And what they do to Ray is only one example. Did you ever look at the faces of the crowd that gathers when some poor sonofabitch gets out on a ledge ten stories above the street? They ask questions and look up; they gasp when he totters and almost loses his balance—but you know what they secretly want. Their guts are itching with it."

"No!"

"And when the priest or the minister talks the guy out of it, and the firemen put away the net, the spectators have been known to boo and shout 'coward!' So help me. Ask yourself this: why would people want to read about five children burning to death? And what's more, read about it over their morning coffee, complete with pictures of the mother weeping on her knees." Remorseless, Paul kept on, nasal and gaunt, crouched over in his old-fashioned linen suit. "Death for breakfast," he said, "a little rape and suicide with your cornflakes. Newspapers like that are only pandering to the ugly little thing inside all of us. We can pretend it isn't there, but it's there all right. Greedy, lewd . . ."

"Don't say things like that."

"But after all, how much can you expect of a former fish? The foetus *does* have gills at one stage. The soft spot on a baby's head *was* once an eye watching for the killer diving from above. Movie queens and bishops and girls in summer dresses—everybody carries a tiny vestigial tail at the end of his spinal column. The blind red thing in the womb struggling to become human—even seventy years isn't time enough. Why do you think the devil is pictured with horns and a tail and cloven hoofs?"

With a stricken noise, Wally pushed himself out of the booth. Paul went after him and caught his arm.

"I'm a bastard," he said. "I guess I'm feeling lousy about the boys and what happened . . . with that girl. I'm sorry. Sit down again and I'll be the life of the party. I'll recite my award-winning piece, 'Yes, Virginia, There is a Santa Claus,' or 'Miracles in a Zoo.' " Wally didn't move. Tugging at him, Paul said, "It's much admired, Wally. I've brought hope into the lives of thousands with it. I describe various miracles in ringing tones: the Kreutzer Sonata, Abe Lincoln, Galileo . . ."

Wally stood with his perforated hat in his hands, his jaunty little moustache looking more incongruous than ever on his sad face.

"Isaac Newton? No? Well, let's see. I can also recite 'The Boy Stood on the Burning Deck' and 'The Cremation of Sam McGee,' both spellbinders." Wally was staring off at the organist, who had quit a few minutes ago in a huff when Ray insulted him but who was now sending chords into the racket again and singing, "Oh You Beautiful Doll" in a scrapy voice.

"Oh I know, it's something on the lighter side you want. Watch this!" And he began a crab-backed shuffle which he meant to be a buck-and-wing, vaudeville style, in time to the music. The linen suit flopped on his jigging bones. Then he bowed and said, "I'll be back tomorrow with more fun for the whole family."

Somberly he left the bar. He shouldn't have done that to Wally; the poor guy was in the dumps as it was. Head down, he walked across the street to buy some shaving cream before he went back to the Jolly Scoutmaster and his troop. Damn them. The whole glee club sucking around, pea-green with fright that he would tell Bush, and Bush smiling his jowly smiles and saying, "I told you they would shape up. You can't even complain that they're prospecting." The inevitable Geiger counters were lined up like modern ju-ju's in the sun-beaten window of the drugstore. But inside it was high and cool and dark, and he was very fond of the old marble-topped tables with their wire legs and the magnificent soda fountain, that baroque masterpiece, that altar among soda fountains, with its mahogany and marble and its petals of stained glass crowning the soda fizzers.

All of a sudden he felt the blood climb into his face, and his look skittered off wildly to the shelves of dusty boxes and bottles. The girl he had caught with the boys, the Sweetheart of Sigma Chi herself, was sitting at one of the tables with her face in a book.

She raised it for a moment and gave him a casual glance, without a sign of shame or even defiance, then returned to the book. His throat was stiff. He had only the vaguest consciousness of going past her. A man with a sun-reddened face and a haircut shaved down to the white skin above his ears was waiting at the counter. Mrs. Mencke was on the phone; she was trying to reach her husband so he could fill a prescription. Her baby was crying in the back. It was ridiculous but he was horribly shaken up, and not just with embarrassment and disgust either. She scared him, that fifteen-year-old chippie scared the hell out of him. Not so much because she had taken the boys on, but because she could seem so damn unruffled about it.

Mrs. Mencke hung up the phone and said, "He'll be right here, excuse me a minute." Her slippers hitting on the floor, she made for the back to see about the baby. "No rush atall," the customer called after her. In the display case, locked in still air, were bed pans and enema syringes, limp red rubber gloves, ghastly trusses with straps and buckles and heavy leather knobs. Little by little, he recovered his sense of her trivial repulsiveness, and with it some of his poise. He squeezed a thin hard look at her.

She was chewing on a piece of ice and reading her book—it was Wally's book, Wells' *Outline of History*!

He couldn't believe it. Granted that she wasn't the idiot girl or anything like it, still, the *Outline of History!* She had to be faking, she must have seen him coming and opened it at random to impress him. But why? She had no conceivable reason, and besides, to all appearances she was miles deep in the book. Her forehead was propped in her hand. One of her sandaled feet, spotted with red toenails, was hooked behind a leg of the chair. Without lifting her eyes, she groped for another silver crumb of ice, slipped it in her mouth and chewed away, her shredding pink nose aimed steadily at the pages.

But he could still see her with her blouse unbuttoned, jerking her pants up her frail white legs . . . H. G. Wells was impossible, the two things just didn't fit. Oh yeah? He was really comic, he was. In spite of the girls he had known with a straight-A average and a diaphragm in the dresser drawer, he still cherished the idea that intelligent girls were at least *close* to virgins anyway. He was almost thirty years old and he thought like that! Hell, at fifty he would be the same; the illusion had fossilized inside him.

Which left him right back where he started. Was she the lady or the tiger? Or both?

Mr. Mencke came puffing in and set to work on the prescription. The girl—Lucy, that was her name—went on reading. Either she was the greatest con-man and actress since George Bernard Shaw, or she had completely forgotten that he was there. Her knees bouncing together, the tip of her thumb in her teeth, she looked like a student priming for a final exam with ten minutes to go. It was fantastic.

Approaching her table was torture, but he had to know. His deep little eyes drew in even further; his narrow face inked red. Curtly he asked her if that wasn't Mr. Riggs' book.

She pulled up, flamy with scorn and disappointment. "The Masked Avenger strikes again," she said. "Take it, take your old book. But I didn't steal it. Mr. Riggs left it here."

"No, no, I didn't mean that. I was just asking."

With the merest tuck of her shoulder she found her place on the page again, stranding him there. It was a jarring snub and he started to say, am I supposed to turn into a pillar of salt or something? Then he changed his mind and said, "You like the book?"

"Naturally." She didn't even look up, but then her enthusiasm came bursting through and she said, "Hey, what about the Et-ruscans? Did they just disappear?"

He was staggered all over again. "Well, the Romans wiped out the Etruscans pretty thoroughly," he said. He asked if he might sit down and plunged in eagerly, "But we do know they buried their dead with very complicated resurrection ceremonies. They had strange rites, they had funeral feasts with the dead man's bones anointed in oil and set on a throne. Then the bones were put into an urn with a stone face, dressed like a doll—about this high. But the most fascinating thing is the mirror that's almost always found in the graves. "You see . . ." Suddenly, he caught himself and flicked his eyes toward her, completely defenseless. This was what he loved and if she was bored, even if she was just uncomprehending—but her face was open, drinking, and her eyes were dark. Her hands were very still in her lap.

He could almost have thanked her. "You see," he said, "the Etruscans believed that a mirror gave an image of the soul. If you think about it, there's a primitive logic in the idea. The reflection is *you*, only without the body, so it must be the soul. Hence the mirror in the tomb. A mirror was great magic for ancient peoples, and some of the old mystery is still alive. Take the superstition that breaking a mirror will cause seven years of bad luck, or the custom of covering the mirrors in a house where someone has died. Without the mourners having the least idea why they drape the mirrors."

The answer darted out of her: "Because the soul might get caught in one of them!"

"Right!" he said. Her excitement was beautiful, beautiful. She reminded him of Sam Bolton when he'd come out to the dig about the steer and become interested in the work. But she was so much more astonishing and touching: a sordid child with an utterly unexpected longing to know things, listening with a wide delight in her eyes.

"That's what history gives you," he said intensely, "the sense of connection. Emerson called it longevity. You can see that Senator McCarthy's investigations are the Salem witch trials all over again. And Hitler Germany was another Rome, another religion of the state with a dead culture. It's a fact that Prussia, the heart and soul of German militarism, never produced a significant work of art, and as for Rome, it had no tragic drama at all, the satire was mediocre, the only epic is a flabby imitation. But there were plenty of speeches and no end of falsified history. Their idea of entertainment was ten thousand pairs of gladiators fighting to the death in a single set of games."

It must have been beyond her, much of it, but she listened with a sort of thrilled intensity, and talking to her, fierce with the passion of it, he saw what he meant come alive in her sharp, peeling face: the tremendous *was* of life, the legions marching into Gaul, Athens, the Phoenician traders, iron wheels and dead cities and barbaric queens buried in copper ornaments, Assyria, the flayed skins of forty thousand human beings nailed to a city wall, dynasties rising and crumbling, trampled under by new dynasties, and lines of captives strung on a rope bored through their shoulders, Cyrus the Great, slain youths tied to dead horses impaled on stakes around the grave of a dead king, Alexandria and the broken statues of Praxiteles—all that was shattered in the blood and rape of human history, all that was lovely and had to die, and all that death could not easily destroy. The plays of Sophocles and Galen's researches, the beautiful mind of Nicholas of Cusa conceiving that infinity has no center.

"Who was he?" she asked. "Tell me about the dead youths on horses, tell me—oh, oh, I'm ten minutes late already. Mrs. Harbaugh is going to evening service and I have to watch the desk." She reached for the book. "Tell Mr. Riggs I'll leave it in his room. I'm employed at his hotel. House dick."

Grinning he said, "Are you sure you can carry it?"

She picked it up and lurched over sideways, panting her tongue out; then she smiled at him and legged it out the door, throwing a good-bye to Mrs. Mencke in the rear.

He drove back to the camp in a daze of excitement, still lifted, still absorbed, his eyes dreaming away from the changes of the dry horizon, the cattle lined out in the evening pastures going toward a water hole, a solitary ranch house. The scattered patches of cut hay field along the river glowed in the shadows like windows full of yellow lamplight. He eased the stationwagon down the ruts to the tattered ranch house. Through the door he could hear Bush and the fraternity hotshots having a bull session, and so he walked up onto the stark plateau. He was still abstracted anyway, deep in the past, the iceberg depths under the visible tip of the present, and time, time flowing under everything, seadeeps of time.

Two deer went bounding away over the sagebrush in astonishing light soft jumps, like ballet dancers, and then the pastures and the cracked hills in the distance were quiet all the way to the mountains rooted in the horizon. It was growing dark. A mile to the north a colossal rock jutted into the sky, scarred and battered, tilting on the roll of hills like a great ship sailing toward infinity.

To make a meaning out of twenty billion meanings, out of all mankind since the hairy submen squatted around fires in dumps of bones and putrefying flesh. The stupendous numbers who had found themselves in the world and lived their lives out in good luck and bad, scrambling and pressing forward, inventing gods and praying to them, marrying, growing old, generations climbing over each other into death. He had not exaggerated to Wally. The cruelty and ruthlessness were there, but so was transfiguring idealism, and sacrifice, and love . . . There was the anonymous devotion of the medieval stone workers who raised cathedrals like architectural mountains . . . There was selfless creation . . . Bach, in Leipzig, composing *Jesu, Joy of Man's Desiring* . . .

Gradually the crowding excitement subsided into a pleasant weariness, still mingled with the receiving face of the young girl.

He was aware of a strong, insistent sense of responsibility for her.

How noble of him, to be sure, how splendid—and how ludicrous. The pathological crusader. And what, old Templar, was the Holy Land this time? A lecherous child, a depraved high school kid with intelligence. That, of course, was his weakness. He could resist the pleasures of the flesh (on his good days), money, the opinion of any number of people, and so on indefinitely, but he was a sucker for a quick mind. It knocked him over, even in advertising men, in atomic scientists, in convicts doing ten-to-life. It was an obsession. Like the thought of cheese to poor Ben Gunn, marooned these many years.

Only it wasn't so funny. The memory of Mrs. Bush was throbbing inside him—Carol Bush, another of his disastrous crusades. Week after week, month after weary month, he had watched her change, become dull and harassed as she was beaten down with the exhaustion of four babies in six years. When he'd first come to the school she had still been lively, bright, hungry to learn things, eager. But inevitably she had been drained by all that life demanding from her all the time, the tender sweet little lives scrapping and crying and needing crayons and naps, and Cindy was due at the pediatrician's at three and Bill Jr., had to be picked up at kindergarten, Jimmy was beginning to fret in the playpen, and meanwhile there was lunch to fix, the laundry to send out, and off in the living room another stormy howl went up. It was only at night after the children had been put to bed that the old radiance would come back in her tired face; then almost imperceptibly that, too, had faded and become less and less frequent. Her mind shrank into a knot of drudgery.

What galled him was that it was so unnecessary. For a long time he suspected that Bush was to blame, that he was consciously or unconsciously killing off her superiority, crushing it out of her with childbearing. Then he had grasped that she herself was the cause.

"What do you think you are? Mother India?" he said. "Why don't you create, for God's sake, instead of just multiplying? Any guinea pig can do what you're doing, and the lower you go in the scale of life the worse it is. A queen bee is just a captive organ to lay eggs for the hive and nothing else. But at least that idiot multiplication has a purpose; it does insure the survival of the species. But you're not a goddamn turtle, you don't have to lay three hundred eggs so one turtle will live through to maturity."

Instead of throwing him out, or getting sore at least, or breaking into tears—something, some kind of reaction—she went around the living room tranquilly picking up toys.

"Okay, so we'll play house for a while. You be the mommy and I'll go off to work." He picked up armfuls of toys and unloaded them into a box in the kitchen. Next to the refrigerator was a potty chair half full of yellow urine. A bloated Teddy bear was flopped against it, one of its flat glass eyes hanging by a string.

"Now the mommy sits down real quiet and listens," he said to her. "All right, you don't give a damn what's happening to you. Did you ever think of the bravado of imposing life on a human being? The responsibility to that life you've made? Giving birth to children only begins with the physical act. It takes years—fantastic patience—thought —and even then you might fail. You can't play Mrs. Peter Cottontail, not with human beings you can't. You have to *control* life in order to perfect it. Three kids would keep your hands full. Why, you don't even have time to listen to them any more, much less to read them fairy stories and stuff like that."

"I guess you're right," she admitted, but her long skinny face, worn and blotched under the eyes, was curiously turned in on itself. "I'd sort of like to have one more girl, though."

"The cavalry has arrived too late again, huh?" he said sardonically. And sure enough, in a couple of months Bush told him that Carol was going to have another baby. The fifth in seven years. Even while he'd been giving her the old Malthus rouser she had been sinking into another rich glut of pregnancy, growing more and more abstracted, fixed upon the secret inside her which nobody else could understand—the unique repeating itself endlessly. It was hopeless: it had always been hopeless. Once at a New Year's Eve party—and how a New Year's Eve party depressed him anyway, all those people in party frocks and suits methodically setting out to go native, in cold blood for God's sake, to have a little orgy by the numbers. Once at a New Year's Eve party, she had blithely confided that she felt she wasn't "doing" anything when she wasn't pregnant.

In the last two months before the spring term ended he had almost stopped going over there.

But he had not forgotten, and the half hour in the drugstore had been like those lost first evenings all over again, quick with excitement, shining. More than anything else, it was the look on the kid's face. He loved the look on students' faces when they were really getting it, sort of breathless. A lot of classes were a fat nothing, but sometimes it would happen: the faces would come alive, the arms would begin to spring up with questions, and outside the windows, maybe, the snow was feathering into the strong dark trees and it was warm and chalky inside, and with every minute the feeling was growing, growing like music in him and in the class, growing until he couldn't sit at the desk any more but had to pace back and forth with the sheer exaltation of it. And when the bell broke it off, when the last student had straggled out after the last question, something was left with him in the silent classroom, a sense of completeness and perfection. A kind of small eternity.

What choice did he have? "Let the Barons sware oathe and raise each their severall power, both of men and of armes, that the Holy Land be delivered." Unfortunately, it was less like the mighty campaign of 1095 and more like Easter of 1212, when thousands of children came down out of the mountains into Italy, singing hymns on their way to Jerusalem to help the Seigneur Christ. They had no arms and they had no money, and no miracle happened to part the waters so that they could walk to Palestine. The fortunate ones ended up in brothels. That about expressed the flavor of the enterprise, and the odds, too. A fifteen-year-old bum was not a hopeful prospect, no matter how bright she was. And yet he had to help her somehow. It must be the rapture of windmills and lost causes.

All he knew about her was that she worked at Mrs. Harbaugh's hotel. He had to know more, and Mrs. Harbaugh could certainly help, but the thought of approaching a stranger made him almost physically ill. And how could he, an outsider who had only been around for three months, ask anybody about the girl? What could he say? He couldn't reveal what she had done without injuring her and the boys. And how could he explain his interest? All he had to do was tell the truth, say that he'd seen her reading H. G. Wells, and the sanity hearings would begin at once.

But there was Wally. Wally lived in the hotel, and he could introduce him. Buoyed by this thought, he went into town the next day immediately after work—and couldn't find him.

Bert was in the lobby of the hotel making a phone call. Except for Ray, who was snoring on the sofa, the only other people in the room were two railroad men facing each other over a checkerboard in the syrupy light. Bert hung up the phone and came stumbling out of the coffin-like booth.

"Where's Wally?" Paul asked him.

"Damn if I know."

Paul hesitated. "Could—you introduce me to Mrs. Harbaugh?"

"You mean old Edna? Nothing simpler, buddy, she's one of my protegees." Suddenly he brought his pufiy face around and looked at Paul, then leaned back with an amused expression. "Well, well," he said. "You want something, and I mean you *want* it. The blood is up your nose. True or not?"

A little dazed at Bert's shrewdness, Paul nodded.

Without bothering to ask what it was, Bert said, "Tell you what. I'll flip you for it, heads I do and tails I don't. A philosopher like you oughta be able to see the point of that."

The hostility in that sodden face was numbing. It was all the worse because there was a curious kinship in the dislike, as if they were twins, left handed and right handed. Invariably Bert walked away from any conversation with him and Wally, a sneer warping his mouth, and yet that, too, only confirmed the likeness, the painful bond between them. Hate confirmed it.

Bert's hand snapped and the quarter spun up in the air and clinked dully on the carpeted floor; it was tails.

"Tough titty," Bert called. "Looks like there ain't no Santy Claus." And he stood there in the sticky light with his hands in his pockets and the flap of hair bouncing on his forehead, coughing with laughter.

Paul went outside. Then, as he turned down the hot sidewalk, he caught sight of a woman in the yard behind the hotel. It had to be Mrs. Harbaugh. His hands began to sweat but he had to answer that laughter; miserably he stooped toward her. She had filled an old metal stock tank with water and it was squirming and jumping with small wet children. Over them a tree let down butterfly bits of sunlight and shade. A skinny boy with muddy, sagging underwear was climbing back into the shrill tangle riding up and down, throwing off twinkles of water and slopping waves over the low sides of the tank. And Mrs. Harbaugh, her white hair grown out under a dingy halo of dyed red hair, was looking on with a yearning, surrendered face.

Sweating, he introduced himself. He laid it on thick, described himself as a professor and all that crud, and said he'd been impressed by Lucy's intelligence and wanted to arrange a scholarship. It was the best he could do.

To his surprise she was cautiously friendly, then almost confidential. "I could use some help with her, to tell you the ruth. I do what I can but sometimes I get the feeling I don't have the right touch. Seems like I'm a day late and a dollar short every time." And she told him that Lucy lived with her in the hotel, helping out with the rooms and so forth, because she didn't get along at home. The best thing would be to go see her parents, their name was Frye and they lived over on Fourth Street, third house from the corner.

It wasn't much but it was a start. Immediately, before he could panic, he drove to the Frye house. From inside came the jangle of a piano and a mediocre baritone voice, oiled heavily with self-esteem, singing, "Jee-sus Say-vyor, Pi-i-lot me." He knocked and a long-faced man, knobby with muscles, peered at him through the screen door. His bald head was porous and uneven, like a grapefruit. The ingratiating smile went dead on his face as he saw that it was nobody from town. "Can I help you?" he said, in the tone he reserved for his customers from the Indian shacks near the depot.

His dry tongue scraped over his teeth but Paul identified himself and said, "Mrs. Harbaugh and I—could I have a few words with you? About your daughter."

Frye looked like he'd been fired at through the screen: his eyes stiffened and he went back a step, dragging in his breath. Then he recovered and hurried Paul inside. The pompousness of the small room was discouraging: imitation lace and brown Victorian plush, a paper doily with scalloped edges on the square oil stove, thickly patterned walls jewelled with glassy photographs, mostly of Frye himself. His wife lagged doubtfully in the door to the kitchen.

Before Paul could speak to her, Frye was blustering at him, "Now you listen to me, professor. I was coming out there myself but you saved me a trip. You keep them boys of yours out of Enterprise or I'll have them locked up. I have a daughter to protect—she's my wife's child but I'm her legal parent, and I'll protect her like she was my own blood." His flimsy grey lips were trembling. "We have always held our head up in this community, and that's my intention, to keep it that way."

"Good—fine—I agree," Paul said but Frye was going wild. He must have seen her tear past in the jeep with the boys, or been told about it and put six and one together . . .

"As long as the girl bears my name, she will be protected to the hilt, professor. To the hilt. I've spoke to the sheriff about you people, and he told me steps would be took. The entire town is riled—disturbed. We extended the hand of hospitality to you and what do we get in return? Hanging around taverns and whistling at women and racing that jeep, it's not safe to go out on the streets anymore. Maybe that's customary in your university but we're different hereabouts." And, in the grand manner, he dismissed Paul. "Now if you don't mind I have some practicing to do."

"Hold on, don't I get a turn? Give me a chance for God's sake."

"*If* you don't *mind*."

"Okay, okay. I'm going." On the way out to the car he could hear Frye yelling at his wife, completely out of control, and hear her start to sob. The whole idea had been stupid, doomed from the beginning. All he had found out was that she had dropped out of school and that she had a stepfather—who wasn't even a wicked stepfather. He was only a pretentious jerk, and a rather pitiful one at that. In fact, his vanity was actually helpful to the girl because he'd give her every advantage, if only for the sake of his reputation in town. And he wasn't even capable of bullying her. Paul thought of his pale, jittery, discontented eyes and he was sure of that.

But what was wrong then? Why, for example, had she dropped out of school? He was as far away from understanding her as ever.

The answers, if there were any, could only come from her now, but he was too tired and shaky to think of hunting for her. Fence posts ticked by. Dead rabbits lay squashed to bloody rags on the highway. Frye yelling at his wife had started him off, and he kept thinking of the carefully masked and polite but hopeless division between his own parents, between the dedicated business man and the bridge-playing, sherry-drinking woman with her 300-dollar hats from Nieman-Marcus . . . her hoarse voice and the scars on her upper lip and cheeks where skin cancers had been removed . . . his first night in boarding school when he was eight. He had arrived a week early and he was alone in the echoing house with a tallowy old lady who gave him a gingerbread man with eyes of green jelly. He didn't cry or anything but in the night, very cautiously, very quietly, he had snapped off the masts on his toy sailboat and methodically torn the red sails to pieces.

And yet there was still the girl; there was still a chance if he could encourage her and win her confidence. He worked badly the next day, bent over in the shallow grave in the monstrous heat and light. Mice had eaten out the skull, and it fell in when he touched it. The frightened boys worked like slaves but he knew the change was worthless; it was a defeat and the girl had become the only answer to it. Could he find her?

He needn't have worried about that. An Indian boy slipped up to the stationwagon as he was parking it by the bank and said, "She wants to see you."

"Lucy? Good, fine," he said, jumping out. "What's your name?"

The boy looked at him with the still, expressionless eyes of the hunting cat and led him to the door of the Black Hills Cafe. Country music whined and tinkled out of a juke box. Men in rough khakis and bib overalls loitered at the counter. In the back, a gross cook with hips standing out like shelves was frying sausage. Lucy beckoned him over, sitting in one of the wooden booths with a low-built, muscular boy.

"Here's your book," she said, pushing the H. G. Wells toward him.

"Did you finish it already?"

"No."

It was the light, cruel way she said it that crushed the breath out of him.

"Please close your mouth," she told him. "You look like Buck—

I'm sorry, Bucky-Ducky, I didn't mean that." And leaning over, she dabbed a kiss on the boy's cheek. Paul picked up the book. "Just a teensy second," she said to him. "Buck, this is a professor, and he's taking a survey, like. Tell him, is it good?"

"Is what . . ." Color flooded into his beefy face. "Hey! What's the idea?"

"I told you, he's taking a survey," she said. Paul could feel the rigidness in his own face, and he caught the sly, needle-sharp look she darted at him. What was going on, for God's sake? She was deliberately stabbing him, cutting him up. "I reckon I better be going," Buck mumbled, getting out of the booth in a hurry.

"You might as well," she said. "Visiting hours are over anyhow." Crimson to the ears, he paid the check and tromped out. "But you don't have to go, do you?" she said to Paul sweetly, laying her skinny face to one side. "Let's us have a nice talk. I'll sit here and you tell me some more great thoughts. Like Sunday."

Raging lights burned in his close little eyes. He hesitated and, at last, just because she wanted him to slink out, he ordered a cup of coffee and sat down across from her. But he felt stupefied, turned upside down.

"Buck is kind of feeble-minded but he's cute," she said.

"Suppose you tell me what's going on?"

"Nothing, I just wanted to have a nice talk, that's all. You want to hear *my* philosophy? Take sex," she said airily. "A person is silly to be a miser about it. Someday you'll wake up and you're old. It's like saving money and finding out the bank went bust."

"You better let me do the great thoughts," he told her. "Tell me, just when did you start going into your piggy bank?"

But she wasn't so easily demolished. "Would you like to hear about the first time?" she snapped. He held his hands up in front of his face, and she said, "I was going to ask you, how is Teddy? And Stan? They're not around anymore."

He should have expected this by now, but he wasn't ready and he felt his bitter strength failing. Why was she doing this? Why? "At least you know their names," he said finally, but she was rummaging in her purse. A woman's red mouth was lipsticked on her almost emaciated face, and her slender neck was lassooed with cheap, flesh-colored beads. Her blouse was the color of overripe strawberries. "You can stop worrying about your precious boys," she said. "I have a full schedule anyhow." And to prove it, she dug out a compact that Buck had given her and bragged about somebody named Arvid who would leave his wife for her any time she said the word.

"Okay, I believe you. You've brought sex within reach of the average man."

Undeterred, she went flipping through the snapshots in her pink wallet. "And this here is Kenny," she said. "He's in the air corpse now."

"I suppose he took potluck too," Paul said, jeering at each picture in turn. "Um-hum. Another child molester?"

She compressed her mouth, wavering for the first time, and he followed up brutally. "So much for your trophy collection, I guess there's nothing left to talk about *except* the first time. I get to tell you about mine first. Well, sir. Once upon a time I was in military school, and there was this dentist's wife in town who used to say dirty words for the sheer pleasure of it, like Paul Verlaine—since you want culture, he's a French poet who holds the world's indoor record for immoral behaviour. His mother, by the way, had her three dead babies bottled in alcohol and kept them in the house. Anyway, this woman . . ."

"Oh shut up! And keep out of my personal business, will you *please*? If there's anything I mortally hate it's somebody with nose trouble."

"So that's it," he said and whistled. All this had been her charming way of getting even with him for talking to her parents. "I'd hate to see you get really mad. You'd hang the children, wouldn't you?"

"What's the complaint? You wanted to know everything, didn't you? Well now you've got a noseful and maybe you'll leave me alone." She flicked her red-tipped fingers, witheringly. "Goodbye, old professor. Disappear somewhere."

"Wait a minute. I'm sorry about that," he said. "I know it didn't work out, but I didn't *say* anything to him. You don't think I'd do that!"

"You didn't have to, dear professor. Cecil is having a hemmhorage every ten minutes and taking it out on Mamma, and they're *both* threatening Mrs. Harbaugh with the electric chair for leaving me stay with her. That's what your nose trouble has done. So kindly just disappear, huh? Make a hole in the air."

"No."

Susage smells and a nasal female voice coming from the juke box.

"Now look," she said, "I mean it. Stop haunting me." When he stayed where he was, she slid out of the booth herself, her eyes flaming. Politely, he held the door for her and tucking the book under his arm, followed her out into the blinding light.

"It's back to Mrs. Harbaugh, I guess," he said evenly as she went loping into the street. "She and I are going partners on you."

"I don't give a happy goddamn," she said, but she dragged to a stop. Her frail shoulders heaved up and down. "Can't you save somebody else, for yip's sake? You're fouling up my entire life. Mrs.

Harbaugh! E-e-e! If she hears one more word about me I'll be living in a boxcar."

Gently he steered her around and walked her down the sidewalk toward the depot where a half dozen cars were waiting to meet the evening train from the east. At the hot, belching fountain they turned off into the coolness of the great cottonwoods on Front Street. Railroad houses crouched by the dirt road, ox-blood red. The trees made deep hollows of shade, suspended, quivering, and all around in the dead stillness the light was burning on red holly-hocks and coarse dusty pumpkin vines, oil tanks, piles of square-cut black railroad ties, a blistered orange work car.

She gaggled along with her head bent, kicking her slummy tennis shoes and dangling her purse. When the trees ended they sat down on some planks in the shade of the feed elevator. The tall galvanized iron shed gave out a sweet grainy smell and there were fresh spills of corn and oats on the ground. A white butterfly zigzagged away toward the freight cars. Soberly, rubbing her chin on her knees, she said, "Mamma and me should never of come here. We use to live in San Francisco, Salt Lake City, all over. It was neat. There's a park on Telegraph Hill where we went sometimes, you can see the Golden Gate Bridge and the fog and the big wine tankers going by. We only moved to this icky town because of my aunt, and then she died and Mamma married Cecil. I told her not to. Mamma is actually very level-headed, except about men. She gets so infatuated you wouldn't believe it. She acts like Cecil is the benevolent ruler of the universe or something. When they have fights and she throws stuff at him, she always misses. On purpose!" Her face came around, delicate, quick. "Did he leave you smoke?"

"Smoke? Sure, I think I smoked a cigarette there."

"That's a big honor, you don't *know*. He's got this obsession that smoke hurts his God-given throat, he's got a whole scientific theory about it. He's mean as a snake, too. I couldn't stand any more, so Buck and me ran away to Grand Island to get married—that's over in Nebraska. Only his parents came and got us and when I came back, Cecil told me to pack my bag." She jerked her shoulder, picking at the polish on her fingernails. "End of story. I lived with Charley and his mother for a while and then I moved in with Mrs. Harbaugh."

"Nice try," he said quietly, but he was very disappointed. The honesty had been there only to get him to swallow the lie. The childish lie.

"You don't believe me?" she said, apparently dumbfounded. "But it's the truth!"

"You couldn't pass for eighteen right now, so you couldn't have gotten married," he told her. "And your mother wouldn't let you be thrown out into the snow, even if Cecil would try it. Which he wouldn't, he's too worried about his reputation."

"Well he did!" she insisted stormily. Then she began to cry—and the tears were a swindle, too, he could feel it. The train had pulled up at the station some time ago, and now its horn blatted down the tracks and the deisel came lumbering past them behind its round light, blasting them with oil stinks and heated winds, followed by grim old coaches with tiny windows, pulling each other on the shaking and clanking rails. The train shrank out of sight into the cindery hills and at the highway crossing the bell stopped clanging, the jumping red light went out, the guard arms hitched unsteadily up.

She began to speak in a small, tragic voice. Kenny, her only true sweetheart, Kenny, whose picture she had showed him, had died in the Korean war. The vulgar sentimentality of the lie was disheartening. The half hour in the drugstore seemed infinitely far away, like a half-remembered dream, and a weary sense of futility spread through him.

She cut her eyes sideways to see how the story was going down.

"I know how you feel," he said. "Now that Kenny is gone, nothing makes any difference. Are you coughing blood, too?"

"I didn't think you'd believe that one," she said. He started back toward his car, and she came along with a chastened look on her face. The sun had dropped into the hills and off toward Wyoming, glimmering carlights trickled on the vast shadowy land. Sharp black buttes were cut out of the orange sky. "You're right," she said after a minute. "Cecil didn't throw me out. But I can't tell you what happened. It wouldn't do any good anyway."

Cynically he waited.

"You see," she said and her voice wobbled theatrically. "You promise you won't tell anybody? Or do anything, promise?" She was holding her purse very tightly. "Well . . . Cecil, you know . . . When Mamma was at work, he . . ."

"Raped you," Paul finished for her, breaking into jagged laughter. "And you were scared and you closed your eyes and held onto your dollie while he was doing those awful things."

This time she was really furious. "It's true," she said with her fists clenched. "It's true. He did *so,* whether you believe it or not."

It was the same old pattern, and yet, because he disliked Cecil or because she didn't cry this time, he almost believed her. Almost. Somewhere in the welter of falseness and self-pity and acting there might be part of a truth. But before he could say anything, she broke down. "You're right," she said, looking away. "That wasn't why I left or anything."

For the first time he felt a lift of hope. It wasn't much, only a few lies cleared away, but it was a beginning. The cottonwoods were filling with darkness, taking it up from the ground, and lights were blooming in the little houses. A dog gruffed from a shadowy porch. The first stars were pricking through, bright silver.

"The night with the boys," she said in a low, flat voice. "I've slept around with men but I never done a thing like that, ask Charley Trueblood if I did. I don't know what happened. I get to feeling sad and I do nutty things . . . I don't know why."

X

"Mr. Butler! Mr. Butler!" The old man had just hobbled out of the clapboard post office with its wind-shaken flag on top. Charley hurled himself across the street, flailing his arm, and dropped in beside him with a breathless "Hi."

"Here you are! Well now, this is first-rate." Under his high-domed hat the old man's face gathered up with smiles, and shifting his letters and rolled newspapers under one arm, he took Charley's hand in his cold, scrawny hand and shook it. "I was just this minute calculating how to hunt you down. Come on, we've got a plenty things to do."

The boy bobbed along beside him, talking eagerly in his rapid mumble. "I got your letter from the hospital. I went out to your house three times to make sure it was okay. Are you well now?"

"I'm passable, passable," Mr. Butler said, smiling again. "My high-stepping days are over, but I'll manage." As he started the car he asked, "How's life been treating you? Catch me up on the news. You've doubtless been fighting."

Charley shrugged. "It's tougher on the reservation. There's lots tougher fights there." The old man wasn't satisfied, however, and Charley looked at him. It wasn't like Mr. Butler to talk about stuff like this; he believed in making every minute count because he was so old. He was about seventy or eighty years old. He wouldn't even buy anything new because it didn't have memories and he mightn't have time to give it some. "Not much happened," Charley said. "I only have seven teeth on top now. I pulled out a loose one yesterday with a pliers. It didn't hurt much."

"Well, well," Mr. Butler said with the same vacant cheerfulness. "Any other news?"

Wondering more every minute, Charley told him about his mother buying a car for seventy-five dollars and about riding Debbie's horse and about Ray, who was a grown-up man but no taller than he was and who drank more than his father did. "He's okay, though, when he ain't crazy."

"Is that so?" The old man guided the car along the highway at fifteen miles an hour, his spotted hands holding tight to the steering wheel. The loose fender strummed. On the other side of the river he turned off the highway toward the cemetery. The dirt road plodded through greasewood pastures, broke down in stones and clay, and then crawled up the naked hill sprinkled on top with gravestones like a jaw with a few worndown teeth. Getting stiffly out of the car, the old man said, "Bring the water jug, will you?" and shuffled toward the graves of his wife and the soldier who had died at Pearl Harbor. It was windy and hot. Dust fumed like brown smoke over the graves. To keep off the cattle, a barbed wire fence had been strung around the small field of stones.

Charley pulled out the weeds and splattered water from the five gallon jug. In a few seconds the dark wet blotches paled over with dust. The old man, holding his hat down on his head, stood for a long time staring at the headstones crusted with sparkles of glass and mica. His nose was carved to a fine point, and he looked as fragile and weightless as the empty shell of a bird's egg. "Those were almighty fine days," he said at last. "We tramped every inch of this country, the three of us did. I'll never forget when we found the cave, I felt like the Lord had laid his hand on me." The wind flapped his suit as he gazed off at the dead hills and the cloud-high horses of dust riding over them. "The dreams we dreamed then, Charley. The dreams we dreamed."

The boy, eyes slitted against the stinging dust, hands in his pockets, stood on one foot and then the other, watching a hawk sail away across the river toward the glinting water tower above the town. He spit expertly. As usual he didn't bother to listen, and yet, without comprehending, he sniffed at the faint crackling words uneasily, suspiciously, like a small animal circling a buried trap.

"It takes a lot of faith to keep going," Mr. Butler said. "There comes a time when you feel your eyes have been opened and what you see . . ." His voice flawed and broke and his adam's apple throbbed in his wilted throat. "But this is no sort of talk for young ears," he said with a smile. "Let's make tracks for home, we've got a plenty things to do."

On the way down the hill he said, "Promise me you'll take care of the graves, Charley."

"Sure. Where you going?" he asked, prickling up.

"Nowhere, nowhere," Mr. Butler assured him, but Charley was positive now that something bad was coming. He tightened himself the way he did before a fight. There was a feeling inside him like a weight in his belly and, surreptitiously, he scratched behind his right ear with his left hand and whispered, "Trouble, trouble go away." When they drove up to the house, Mr. Butler went inside and began searching for his ballpeen hammer. They couldn't find it and after a while, muttering to himself, he went out into the blowy yard and picked up a round stone and some rusty nails. Dust hissed over the bare clay and blew like fine ashes around the grindstone and the rotting machinery. Tottering against the wind, his sparse white hair licking like flames on his head, he beat his way to the barn. "There's a treasure here, a treasure beyond price," Mr. Butler said. "Well . . ." And, briskly, he nailed the door shut.

"What are you doing?" Charley demanded.

"Nothing," Mr. Butler told him with a bright, warped smile. "Let's keep moving. No sense poking around at it."

Clenched with fear, Charley followed him to the house. There were streaks, like ragged brown icicles, in the glum wallpaper. The ceiling had been smoked into black circles by oil lamps. The old man puttered over his dusty relics more and more weakly, his lips munching in his bloodless face, his deep-socketed eyes closing for seconds at a time and his hands lying like withered leaves on trays of jade, onyx, and quartz, and when he took out the first of the oilcloth rolls on which he had copied every pictograph in the hills, he stopped completely.

"Are you okay?" Charley asked him.

"As fit as can be," he said, blinking and coming to. With a show of energy he opened one of the sixty-foot rolls, inscribed with patterns that looked like spilled intestines. A strong smell of oilcloth fouled the long-shut air. Then he stopped again, kneeling rigidly like a wax man. The tips of his collar bent up under his chin.

"I'm wore out, Charley," he said slowly. "Whipped clear down to the bone. This is almighty hard to say . . . you see, my health isn't up to it any more and I'm obliged to go back to the hospital this evening. I'm only out on pass for this one day to wind up everything. I'm shutting up shop for good."

Charley's breath stuck. "You ain't coming back? Not ever?"

With a brave smile the old man continued, "Don't take it so hard. You can step into my shoes when you're older."

"But why do you have to? You said you were okay. You did."

The old man's face was like a shrivelled rag, wrung with another terrible smile. "Everybody has to go under at last, Charley. A person never figures it'll come his turn but it does. There's always youngsters coming up and coming up and sooner or later you're at their mercy . . . And that's it."

"Our mine," Charley said. "What about our uranium mine?"

"Now get a hold on yourself. That's just the clincher exactly. I couldn't bring myself to tell you but we don't have that mine anymore. It's gone and out the window. You saved the day once but an old geezer like me, I'm too outclassed to keep saving indefinitely. I didn't handle the claim according to correct mining procedure, as laid down by law, and it was slickered right away from us."

"We ain't gonna be rich?"

"That's about the size of it," the old man said, standing up feebly. "I know how you feel, it hurts till you purt' near can't endure it. That's the worst of it, coming so close and missing. But there's no sense pulling a long face over it. Now how about a smile? I sure could use one from you, Charley. It's the end of the line for me, a bed in the hospital and the hobby shop and waiting for my ticket to get punched." The skin hanging from his chin quivered and stretched and collapsed again. "Don't look like that, don't. I can't take it. I figured strong on that claim myself . . ."

But he was completely mistaken about the stare Charley was giving him; there was no anguish in it and no despair. The news had hit him like a swinging fist, but he picked himself up instinctively and fought back. "No," he said, meaning that he refused to believe it, to accept it at all. The claim was theirs and they were going to be rich.

With a wheezy sigh the old man returned to his treasures, squatting by the strip of unrolled oilcloth and poring over the unravelled sprawl of lines, curlicues, dots. "This is the whole story of the migration down from Alaska after they crossed the Bering Straits from Russia. The Smithsonian never heard about this one, no sir." For a moment he was triumphant, even gleeful, pecking his face and cackling reedily; then he grew sombre and said, "It's up to you now. You have to keep watch on all this and don't forget anything. Do I have your word on that? I'm counting on you. If you let me down, it's all gone—poof! Fifty-five years of my life."

Brown and shaggy, the boy hunched his shoulders under his ears, dumbly resisting. He hadn't heard a thing.

"It's a golden opportunity for you, Charley. When you grow up you can make a real tourist attraction out of this, the cave and the writings and our collections." With fumbling hands he wound up the oilcloth and took out a second roll. "This here," he said, pointing at a shredded flower of lines. "You remember what this means, don't you?"

The boy stared at him.

"Come on, come on. Why you can rattle all this right off."

Sullenly the boy kept silent.

"Son! Son!" Trembling, he pointed to a run of loops like unspooled wire. "What's this one? Snap out of it and think."

"I don't know," Charley told him.

A screech came from the tragic hole of the old man's mouth. "You're lying! You know and you won't tell me." He wavered to his feet, clawing the air. The earthcolored face of the boy remained the same, hard, small, utterly without expression; it was the face of a hunted and hunting animal, innocent and ruthless. Capitulating humbly, the old man held out his hands and said, "I didn't mean to light into you like that, Charley. I'm so damnably wrought up, I'm not myself. Be nice to the old feller, will you, and give him something to hold on to? How about it?"

The boy looked at him, unmoved, and the old man saw the last tatters of his life dying in the shut brown face.

"You're punishing me because you think I quit without a fight," he said. "That's it, isn't it? Well you're dead wrong. Sam Bolton finagled us out of the claim on technicalities, but I went to the last notch. Yes sir. I come out of the hospital and fought him to a standstill by myself. You weren't to be found so I did what I could till I was played out entirely. They had to drive me to Hot Springs, I was so near done for." He sniffled piteously.

Charley watched the tears drain out of the old eyes with contempt. Last year, when he was sneaking into a pasture to ride a horse, he had lost his balance and ripped his chest open on the barbed wire, and *he* hadn't cried. Mr. Butler didn't have any guts. When he bawled like this he sounded like an old sheep.

"Where's the Geiger counter?" he said. "I'll find some more mines by myself." Fresh tears welting his cheeks, Mr. Butler confessed that he'd left it in the car and that some rascal had stolen it. Charley was silent with anger. After a minute he said, "I want the paper for the mine. Give it here."

"The claim paper? It's not worth a tinker's damn, Charley. But if you want it . . ."

The old man took it out of a cardboard box, and Charley snatched it away. He believed in the paper. Now he consented to answer questions about the pictographs, the arrowheads, the bones, and Mr. Butler thanked him damply and said, "God will bless your life for carrying on for me." Charley gave him a scornful glance. He conceded nothing, admitted nothing, and what he was counting on now was the cave. Mr. Butler loved his cave more than anything, and just because it hurt so much to leave it, he was saving it for last; he might not be able to give it up. Silent, crouched on his heels, Charley waited until Mr. Butler had looked at everything, counted it, blown the dust off it, and talked about it. Finally, with clumsy knocks of the round stone, he nailed the house shut.

"It's in your hands," he quavered. "The whole shebang. Well, let's block up the cave mouth and be done."

The wind had stilled. A black storm front had spread like a stain above the buttes to the south and then stopped, blotting up half the sky in the swollen light and heat. Mr. Butler lifted his face, pulling the cords tight in his limp neck, and muttered something about a sign. On the way to the cave, Charley kept watching him for traces of excitement and returning hope, but all he did was mumble to himself about some old horse and a rider whose name was Death and the sun becoming black as sackcloth of hair. Not even their plan to buy the cave from Mr. Bolton and run a road to it for tourists could bring him out of it. His hat was on crooked. He halted the car on a winding jeep road near the national forest, took a flashlight out of the glove compartment, and they walked the last five hundred yards along a dried-up stream bed. Locusts clicked. The scraps of shadow glowed inside with heat. A dead cow, its eyes gone and ants trickling in and out of its mouth, lay in the baking rocks.

Doddering past it without a glance, Mr. Butler flapped his arm up at the side of the gully, half way to the top: in one layer darker than the rest, knobbly bones poked like blind hands out of the clay.

"There's scads of 'em," he said with a flicker of spirit. "Not your ordinary buffalo bones, either. They're *bison antiquus*, the ancestor of the buffalo, I looked it up in a book from the University of Nebraska. This was what they call a kill-area for hunters ten thousand years ago or more, but the Smithsonian doesn't deserve to be told about it. No sir." His eyes glittered in the fissures of his old face. "Sakes alive, if they knew this spot existed, they'd have fits."

The gulch shallowed. They were getting close to the ragged hole in the sagebrush and boulders, and Charley's heart skidded, picked up speed. He didn't like to go in the cave. It was dark in there and it smelled funny, a little bit like the tunnel under the railroad tracks but older and deader, and if there was any wind at all, whispery noises and rumblings came out of the deep places in the back. Mr. Butler had told him that the Indian who had showed him the cave called it "the breath of the world." He dragged his feet unhappily even though Mr. Butler was starting to feel better. "Son," he said impressively, as he always did, "this is where they lived. A hundred centuries ago."

He stooped into the hole, and Charley forced himself to go after him, down a wreckage of clattering stones, down into a great hollow of darkness. It was cool and musty. Their footsteps were absorbed in floury dust and the dung of bats. The silence was old and strange, a secret underground stillness, and then Mr. Butler said something and his voice went off into deeper and deeper shadows, rolling, bouncing far away into channels of bottomless darkness. He washed the beam of his flashlight this way and that. The crumpled walls were powdered with yellow. Bats were stuck to the ceiling in patches like mangy fur, and Charley, watching them shift and move a little, felt his skin draw up in icy prickles. All at once there was a whoosh and a battering, a dark rush of wings, and an owl blundered out of the cave through the tiny hole of light. Charley's heart was socking against his ribs.

"We gave him a scare," the old man chuckled. "Just think, Charley. The darkness in here is a million years old. Gives you a feeling, doesn't it?"

The thin stream of light spread on a wall, blackened with smoke and scratched with magic pictures of antelope and hump-backed buffalo, then slipped down over flints and broken bones, the silvery ashes of ancient fires. He kicked at a scatter of basket shreds, matting, and colored beads. "This here is late stuff, two-three hundred years old. But come over here, and don't forget a word now. I dug here off and on for five years," he said, shining the flashlight down into a pit terraced with layer after layer of dirt and bones and rubble, dropping away into darkness. "Remember, each and every one of those layers is older, the further down you go. In New Mexico they've found a cave used by what they call the Folsom Man. He's calculated to be ten thousand years old but this cave has that one beat. Primitive man migrated down from Alaska along the Pacific coast and the rivers . . ."

There was a rustle behind them. Charley turned and caught sight of little eyes like bright pin pricks in the shadows. Was it a lizard? A cave rat? His heart fluttered, his breath seemed to come harder and harder, and he couldn't hear what Mr. Butler was saying. The entrance was the size of a penny. A sound he had never heard before came out of the darkest holes in the back; it was like dead people whispering to him.

"Pay attention!" Mr. Butler rapped, his voice doubling over and over with echoes. "They've found the flints he used but nobody has ever found *him,* the Folsom Man himself. That's what those archeologists are hunting for. They won't find a darn thing but it's here, Charley right down in that pit," he gloated. "The bones of the earliest human beings in North America. Think of it! The Smithsonian boys would give their eye teeth for this."

Charley's look probed fearfully into the echoing shadows. Never before had he had any sense of what was *in* the cave. A cold sweat greased his whole body. At last when he was just about to run for it, no matter what, Mr. Butler had enough and they were outside again, blinking in the familiar hot light.

The old man's exaltation leaked right out of him, though, and his strength with it. His head rolling on his weak neck, his breath coming like a faint pulse, he sighed and went back against a boulder. "Oh Charley, Charley," he cried, "why weren't you around? I looked for you all over and I couldn't find you. We might could have saved it together."

"We ain't licked," Charley said.

"Son, son, I know you're spunky, but you have to face facts. Sam Bolton is the winner; we can't dispute that." And yet, in the very center of his despair was something waiting for hope to renew itself.

He gazed at the small mongrel figure and once more, though not as strongly as in Old Woman's Creek after Charley had out-foxed the college boys, he felt hope grow erect inside him. "Could we still make it?" he said. "You think we could?"

"Sure."

"Maybe you're right at that. I don't believe Sam Bolton is so all-fired sure of himself as he made out. He offered me ten per cent of it after I read him his pedigree, and Sam Bolton doesn't give away one per cent of anything. Yes, by George! We'll just threaten *him* with lawyers for a change and see what happens. Why if we can even haggle him up to a fifty-fifty split that might be sufficient and to spare."

Charley pulled in his breath and for half a second it was pure glory, pure happiness; then his shrewdness took over and he said quickly, "Let's go see him right now."

They scrambled down the creek bed to the car and drove to Red Canyon. The pink road worked hard on the canyon floor, climbed and turned and fell off sharply. Cattle were lying down under a gaunt cottonwood tree. On both sides, the cliffs were the dark red of decaying carcasses. A mile from Old Woman's Creek, as the canyon widened and the high ledges sank away, Charley's quick eyes picked out a new sign, BOLTON URANIUM CO., KEEP OUT, and a raw bulldozed road going off to the canyon wall in the heat-shimmering distance.

"Right here, right here!" he said and jumped out to open the gate. Mr. Butler bumped the car along the strip cut through the sagebrush, looking more and more doubtful. "Keep on going," Charley said. A hundred yards ahead of them a white house-trailer squatted on the ground, glaring in the light like a welder's torch. There was a heavy Mack truck loaded with ore beside it. Mrs. Bolton was perched up there on the yellow and pink rocks, busily whacking at the bigger chunks with a hammer. Mr. Butler braked the car to a stop when they were still fifty yards away and peered irresolutely at her. Then Sam, his mouth open with a shout they couldn't hear, came hurrying toward her from the cliff, she clambered down, and they both got behind the truck.

"Come on," Charley urged. "You got to."

Just then the car shook under them, the air was stunned, and while a dull rumble heaped up and up into the sky, a huge slow collapse began in the red wall of stone: part of it shuddered to pieces, rippling and falling, pouring down into the rising clouds of pinky-yellow dust. A new wound lay open in the fleshy red cliff. Poisonous orange fumes of cordite drifted away with the colored dust.

Mr. Butler seemed to be paralyzed. Charley tugged at him frantically, but his mourning look was fixed on Sam Bolton, who grabbed up a scintillator and made for the smoking pink rubble, shoulders crouched and ape arms dangling and swinging. Caught up in a mindless fury of work, he hadn't so much as noticed that they were there.

Charley opened the car door and tried to push him out.

"No, no, it's a lost cause," the old man said. "Sam only offered me that ten percent to get me out of his hair whilst he was staking claims. I don't have the get-up to tackle him any more and he wouldn't listen anyhow. I'd appreciate it if you blocked up the cave when you get a chance. I can't bring myself to do it."

Charley couldn't get through to him at all. Sagged behind the wheel like a thin rag doll, he stared straight ahead with eyes that looked past everything. "You know, I cursed Sam Bolton before, damned him to hell, but I was wrong to do so, son. He's no worse than anybody else and better than many. We're none of us clean, we're all rotted sepulchres under the whitewash, myself included. How can God listen to our prayers? How can He stand it? One of my pupils—it must be twenty years ago, but it's stuck in my mind. She prayed night and day and went to every service, and what was her reason? To get to be a drum majorette. God smiled, doubtless. But we pray for what we want and what we want is—millions and millions of prayers rising to God constantly and the most respected of them is selfish." He bunched his mouth, whimpering sarcastically, " 'Take me to heaven, Lord. Let me live forever and ever. Me. I'll be good, Lord. Is it a deal?' What value is charity or sacrifice from such as that?" he demanded.

"You can't quit, Mr. Butler," Charley said. "You promised."

The old man's face was a skull draped with limp skin. His nostrils were stuffed with white hairs and his voice dropped to a whisper like sand powdering against rock in the wind. "I loved her so dearly. Clara . . . She was my wife, Charley, and she was on her deathbed, dying of tuberculosis, and I didn't kiss her on the mouth because I might catch it. It's true, I swear it. Who did I ever really love in seventy-odd years except myself? I'm every bit as bad as Sam Bolton. Homo Sapiens," he snorted. "The entire lot of humanity is evil and vile, it's so miserably corrupt that even the mercy of God cannot avail. Why even His only begotten Son couldn't save us. The story is covered up in the gospel of John but read St. Mark, 15:33: 'And when the sixth hour was come, there was a blackness over the whole land until the ninth hour. And at the ninth hour Jesus cried out in a loud voice, saying, "Eloi, Eloi, lama sabachthani. My God, my God, why hast Thou forsaken me?" He was shedding His blood for us, Charley, and God rejected Him. His precious blood, and it was like unto the sacrifice of Cain, in which the smoke of the burnt offering rolled along the ground instead of mounting up to heaven." The sad vision flamed in his eyes, and he said, "We are all damned, all of us, lusting and hurting and killing each other. Well, we've got the killing down to a high science now and sooner or later we're going to destroy ourselves with those atomic bombs. And who can say it's not fitting and proper?"

The words meant nothing to Charley except that Mr. Butler wouldn't try after all. And there was Mr. Bolton, scuttling along under the cliff and holding the counter to the red stones. Charley put his whole being into one look of hate: he would do anything, kill Sam Bolton if he could.

Without saying good-bye he got out of the car and started toward a break in the canyon wall. The hot sagebrush sizzled with grasshoppers. Mr. Butler called to him, but he preferred to hike six miles back to town rather than accept a ride from him. He went a few more feet, then turned and yelled, "I'll forget what you told me! I won't remember nothing! I won't watch your house, neither."

He didn't look back any more.

The claim wasn't lost, he told himself, it wasn't lost, and nothing could ever change his mind. Mr. Butler was chicken, and he hadn't even given him a quarter. It wasn't fair. All the way back to town, trudging the last four miles along the railroad tracks, he kept thinking about the quarter. He had to get one somehow. The need itched in him, burned like the sting of a wasp. Lucy was always teasing him about wanting a quarter, but he really had to get one now, more than he ever had in his life. He had to.

If it had been earlier in the day, he could have helped the drivers of the big trucks unload at the Pig store and the taverns. The only one who delivered late was the 7-Up man, and he came on Fridays. Padding into the drugstore, he asked Mrs. Mencke if there were any prescriptions he could take to somebody's house. Then he hung around the nickel-and-dime game in the pool hall, hoping that maybe a player would toss him a nickel when he won a pot. Tonight they were all too stingy, though. Ordinarily he would have gone home, accepting what had come philosophically—you got licked or you didn't, you lost or you won—but today was different.

Only the two taverns were still open when the curfew siren wailed at ten o'clock. There were more customers in the Victory so he folded himself up in the next doorway where the cop car by the bank couldn't spot him. Once, he remembered, a drunk had given him half a dollar. He'd skipped supper and he was pretty hungry. To kill time he practiced the match trick he'd learned from Ray, lighting the match, quickly gluing it with spit to the end of his tongue, and rolling it into the little cave of his mouth to put it out; he burned himself every time, though. After a long time there was a commotion, and five or six men in boots, work clothes, and hats with rolled-up brims came slamming outside. In the center of them, boozy and drooling, was Ray himself.

Hopefully Charley eased out of the shadows. "Hi," he said to Ray.

"Where's Bert?" Ray asked the others mushily. His tongue stayed between his blubbery lips when he finished the words, and great hiccups clutched at him as he fumbled along the sidewalk. "Where's my harmonica? If I find out . . . who stole . . ."

"Little but mighty, huh?" one of the men said. "I bet the Indian kid here can take you." Charley moved his head back and forth, inching softly away. "Hold on, kid," the man said. "There's a buck in it for you if you can lay him out. Hell, he can't hardly stand up."

"Unh-unh." He darted a look up the black empty street; the cop car was off somewhere on its rounds.

"Here's the buck, right here," the man said, spinning a big round dollar off his thumb and catching it. The other men were working on Ray: "What about it, short stuff? Let's see how much of a man you are." "You been bragging all night what a hard rock you was."

"I were strong in those days," Ray mumbled. "Me and Colonel Casper had a boxing act. Three rounds. He were smaller'n me but he could go. We had regulation-size gloves and my robe had "Champ" on it on the back." His pink face melting on his burly neck, he wobbled among the men's legs, hiccupping and smiling with memory. "I swung like this and he took a backwards tumble . . . and so, back and forth."

"That's the ticket, Ray. A little exhibition."

"Exhibition. Like the old days." He rubbed his eye with his fist and tipping from one side to the other, came up to Charley and planed his stubby hand above their heads the way he had that morning by the pond. His eyes were red and wet in his drifting face. He didn't recognize Charley at all. "Even-steven," he said. "It's a deal. No rough stuff, exhibition."

"I don't want to," Charley said. "It's me, Ray. Ray?"

The little man drew back and launched himself forward, his short flipper of an arm sweeping the dim light a yard short of Charley. The watching faces broke open with laughter. The momentum of his swing took Ray half way around: he teetered and rowed his arms, and slowly keeled over into the street. Whooping and staggering together, they hoisted him up and back onto the sidewalk. His muddy look found Charley. "If that's how you feel," he panted. "All right . . . to the finish."

He butted forward with sightless pop eyes, swinging with all his might.

"Hit him, kid, or it's no buck."

Sidestepping the charge, Charley reached out and tapped Ray a couple of times, just touched him, and then he felt the side of his face go numb. The salt taste of blood was in his mouth. He was lying on his back. Tears stabbed into his eyes and scrabbling to his feet, he struck back at the swaying little man, hit him while tears choked his eyes, hit him again and again and again.

XI

Moving like a bulldozer, Wally rammed into the circle of men. Shadows peeled off and went over backwards, his bone-cracking fists plunged with his ponderous weight behind them. Somebody hit him from the side. A heavy coin clinked to the sidewalk and Charley, with a dive between the trampling boots, scooped it up and slipped like a small brown ghost into the darkness. Grimly, but without hate, without any personal feeling at all, Wally churned through the tangle of drunken men, clubbing them down. One of them pulled himself up from the sidewalk, sagging on his legs, blood squirming from his nose, and started a roundhouse swing. A five-gallon hat went spinning away. Heavy workshoes scuffled. Wally brought his fist down like a boulder and the man sank to his knees, then slowly rolled over on his back.

There was a click, a blink of icy metal: a ranch hand was coming at him with a knife, steering it back and forth, wickedly, as he closed in. "Commere, sonofabitch," he said. "I'm gonna let the juice outa you." Wally kicked him in the stomach and the solemn punishment continued. There was no pleasure in it for him, no blood lust, no savage thrill of vengeance, and he neither expected fair play nor gave it. Blood poured from a staring face. Methodically, he hammered his fist into it again. The only man still on his feet took off toward the depot in a hopping, pitching run with one shoe missing. Wally went after him. Before he could collar him the man screamed and dropped to his hands and knees, but with the same grave thoroughness Wally kept smashing down at him until his squeals stopped and he lay still.

"I warned you fellers time and again," he said, sucking in his harsh breath. He couldn't feel anything in one of his fists, and his shoulder hurt. Cranking it painfully he limped back and picked up his hat, then went over to Ray who was sitting in a drowsy heap on the curb. "Up you go," he said, carrying him to his feet. One of the men he had punished was holding onto a parked car, gagging. To the spectators in the doorway of the tavern he said, "I'm done asking you to leave Ray alone. Stay out of his vicinity and don't buy him no more drinks. You hear?"

"Colonel Casper and myself," Ray drooled. "He were only up to here on me, but he could really go."

"Come on." Towing him along by the hand like a child, Wally got him back to the hotel. The lobby was empty and the clammy breath of a water-cooled fan came down the dim, creaking hall. "And so, anyway," Ray mumbled. "Do I have to go to bed?" Now that they had a heavy wallet, Bert and Wally had moved from the attic to a large room with two double beds on the first floor, and Ray had his own cot next to the radiator. With motherly patience, Wally removed Ray's chocolate-colored shoes, his pants, his shirt, and made him lie down. "In your schooldays is the time for sleep," he objected, but already his doped and leaky eyes were shut. "Where's Bert?" he asked, and then he was snoring.

Wally stared down at him, rubbing his massive shoulder. He was still completely at a loss. How could Bert switch like that and not only allow Ray to hang around but insist on taking him in? It didn't add up at all. Ray was a constant and continuous millstone around their necks. It was plain hell. It was like the torture Paul had told him about, that fiendish thing some king in the *Aeneid* had thought up: you were tied to a corpse till you died in its rotting arms.

And why did Ray keep hanging around, for that matter? He stuck to Bert like a little burr, but once—he must have been seeing double—once he thought he saw Ray making faces at Bert behind his back, leering at him with murder in his heart. It sure was a puzzler.

What he wished and prayed for was that Ray would go away, anywhere at all, just so he was out of sight. It wasn't his fault, poor little guy, but he was hideous now as never before; he was like a sin made into flesh and bone. And yet, what difference did it actually make? If he never laid eyes on Ray again, he still wouldn't be able to forget what Bert had done. He dreamed about it—the smear of the spotlight on the mouldering stage, Ray stumbling around in the billowy dress, the clomp-clomp of the women's shoes he was wearing on the dusty boards, his ugly face red with pain, his hips swaying while he cursed into the hoots of laughter, taking it off; and then Bert, looking all glassy and strange, climbing up there and ripping at Ray's soiled underwear . . .

It haunted him. He was forever trying to accept it, to cover it over, to explain it away or at least cut it down to endurable size. Once more he made all the allowances he could think of. Bert felt bad about the matter. And he had a good heart underneath; in fact, when he did somebody a kindness he never mentioned it like most people would and got sore as blazes if he was praised. Once in Denver he'd given every nickel they had to an old pensioner selling tomatoes in Capitol Park, saying, "It's your turn for some luck, buddy." Most of all, there was that curious helplessness about what he'd done, as if he'd been hypnotized or something, the way you scratched at a sore and couldn't stop.

Wally sighed with defeat. At the very moment that Bert had saved their partnership, he'd threatened it as never before . . . because he had to be able to forgive Bert in order to go on, and the only way to do that was to understand why he'd done it.

And all the while the picture of his wife and boys stared at him like a reproach from the bulgy-fronted dresser. Ever since Saturday, despite the money he'd sent Esther, his guilt about coming to Enterprise had been getting worse. Ray was breathing like a motor that needed grease. The screen on the open window was ashy with moonlight. Outside, the town was still and the mountains stood like black herds in the pale, decaying light.

Maybe Esther was right, he told himself, and Bert *was* past helping, like a crazy jigsaw puzzle that wouldn't come out. There was just one thing he knew for certain: the Ray business was only a part of the problem, and in order to understand that he had to understand everything, how Bert ticked.

It was a large order. He had bad habits galore but that wasn't it. For one thing, there was his wild and woozy partying. Bert didn't just honky-tonk and get drunk like a human, he tore as much of the world as he could reach completely apart. Take what had happened in Utah. When they had been close to starving, Bert had fed the mice in their room with cheese and other stuff from his plate. He even gave them names, like Duchess and Mike. Then one day he killed every one of them. There was blood all over the place when Wally came back, and the last mouse was thrashing around with a fish hook baited with salami in its stomach and Bert on the end of the line. "I had to put them to death, Lard," he said. "There wasn't enough calories to go around."

It would be a whole lot simpler if only Bert was worthless, instead of being a genius.

Or take his restless spells, when he couldn't stick to anything for ten minutes at a time and the least little thing seemed to tear his nerves to pieces. And going haywire, coming completely unwound without warning, for no reason whatsoever. He was like a bomb that could go off at any time. But maybe the most frightening thing, the hardest to handle anyhow, was his sad moods. Then it seemed like the whole world was a dead loss to him, and nothing, not even liquor, could raise his spirits. Sometimes it appeared that Bert didn't do anything like other people. Not one single thing. He was a born lady-killer, with girls aplenty around him at all times, but even here he wasn't like other studs; he couldn't live without women, lots of women, all petting him and smooching with him and fighting over him and calling him up day and night on the phone. Wally knitted his slow, gentle face. Now that he had described it to himself, just surfacely of course, it didn't seem so peculiar. There must be something he was missing because who else but Bert would come back to his room, where a woman was waiting for him, with another woman on his arm and say, "Myrtle, I want you to meet Genevieve. That's not your name? Well goddamn, introduce yourselves then. I give up and quit." And stretch himself out on the bed as calm as you please.

With a shock Wally discovered that he was eating. While he'd been struggling to come up with an answer, he'd taken a can of pork-and-beans, hacked off the lid, and started wolfing the cold, tomatoey beans with a spoon. Thoroughly ashamed of himself, he put the can on the dresser, but his mind kept straying back to those beans and before long, instead of thinking about Bert, he was having a debate about wasting good food. He finished off the can.

About then Bert came in and began, quietly, to take off his shirt. Wally looked at him. He wasn't depressed or even muddled with liquor; he was just quiet. When last seen he'd been jitterbugging and raising an uproar in the tavern, and suddenly he was back in the room, hours ahead of schedule, as sensible and well-behaved as anybody.

"I hear you chastised the very hell out of some ranch hands," he said in a conversational way. "I'd hate to see you get onto me, Lard."

Wally watched him climb into bed before he answered. "I hope not, too, Bert."

In the morning Wally waked up first and lay for a few minutes meditating on what strategy to use with him today. Light crept over the door, over the directory of churches and civic organizations. On the way was a calendar with a comical picture: a cowboy hanging onto a plaster merry-go-round horse as if it were a rodeo bronc jolting with its head slung down and its legs going in all directions. At the end of the hall the toilet flushed with a gasping sound.

He decided to be offhand about it, to take it for granted that Bert would come along with him. "Bert?" he said, shaking his arm. "It's high daylight already, let's get some breakfast."

"You go on, Lard. I believe I'll eat tomorrow." He groaned when Wally shook him again but then he sat up, yawning and feeling around for his socks. Wally was encouraged. "Damn nation," Bert said, parting his toes to look at the terrible crumbling, the deep red cracks in the scaly skin. "Look at that, will you? I believe that's why the army gave me a dishonorable discharge, they couldn't cure this foot itch. That and falling in love with the colonel's holstein cow."

Earnestly Wally said, "You ought to doctor it. I keep telling you."

"Can't no remedy cure it," Bert said. His tone was cheerful, though, and without further urging he got dressed and shaved. Ray was still asleep, his mouth wide open like a pink chute. At breakfast Bert consented to eat two doughnuts, which was a record for him, and Wally's hopes went up still farther. As soon as they returned to the room, he hurriedly collected the Geiger counter and the rest of their gear and said, "All right, let's head out. There's still some wonderful opportunities, Bert. Everybody is just setting on their lease and hoping for somebody to come along and explore it for them and do the developing. We can practically have our pick for a ten per cent royalty."

Whistling a jaunty tune, Bert sat himself down at the table and took a fresh sheet of stationery from a pack. "Much as I hate to, I guess I'll have to stop finessing and get severe," he said. "Bad-eye Richardson would of done it before this."

Wally almost threw down the gear. "Bert, it's not any use and you know it."

"Hold on just a second." In a moment he turned around and said, "I think this'll stir up some results. Listen to this. 'Dear Sir: Seeing you won't negotiate, I am forced to get my just rights some other way. Beginning as of tomorrow, one of your steers will be shot each day till the debt is paid in full. Yours, Bertram J. Stephens.' That's what you call high diplomacy, Sunshine. Stalin and Truman couldn't do no better."

"Bert, you got to stop this. Day after day, calling the ranch thirty times a day, you even get your girlfriends to call, and you haven't so much as contacted the old man yet. It's idiotic! The Bolton boy is flat broke and his daddy won't honor the debt and that's all there is to it. The banker told you himself he was acting on Mr. Bolton's personal instructions. You're just going up against a stone wall. A gambling debt ain't legal and you can't never in the world collect it. I grant you that you're within your rights—what's owing is owing. But if they want to be like that about it, pestering them ain't gonna help."

All Bert did was wink at him. "Old Heavy, you just watch Bertram J. Stephens lick the hell out of this problem. I'm counting on that money for my dowry, so I can marry and settle down to a life of comfort."

"This is no time to joke, Bert. I mean it. It's foolish to kick up a fuss, but the main thing is, we can't afford to get sidetracked now. It's caused us to lose three prime days already. We've got enough money to give prospecting a real try, and you go off on a tangent that's just wear and tear for nothing. Prospecting is why we're here, not anything else."

Blithely clicking his fingers, Bert savoured his letter once more, then put it into an envelope and addressed it. "I'd bet you dollars to doughnuts this works," he said, "except you think food is too sacred to bet." His red and yellow shirt was open on his chest; his face squirmed with amusement under the flop of hair on his forehead. It was nearly impossible to budge him when he was like this, whimsical, gleeful, bursting with outrageous capers, but steady and hard and cold underneath. "Now there's no need to frown up like that," he said. "When I set my mind to something, it's strictly in the bag. Because I ain't nothing but pure hell on strategy of all kinds."

Wally's somberness only deepened. "We can't just lay around like this, we have to get to prospecting. You can hector the Boltons between whiles, at night, if you have to."

"My goodness, Lard, you don't realize the amount of calculations I have to do," he grinned. "It's a full-time job." Ray woke up and asked him if he was going to play cards, and Bert told him the same thing. Grumbling to himself, Ray stumbled into his clothes, his eyes still glued almost shut. "I'll be back in a couple hours," he said and went out to make his morning rounds. Wally stood brooding. The washing machine in the basement was beating like a worn old heart under the floor. Suddenly he felt a finger jab into his stomach and grunted. "You old booger," Bert laughed. "You're putting on weight, I do believe. If you don't watch it, you'll be swole up like a dead horse again. Tell you what. Why don't you prospect by yourself to stay in condition whilst I negotiate some more."

"It's no good if you don't go too. You know that."

Ignoring the ominous note of sorrow in Wally's voice, Bert went bouncing out the door. Wally lumbered after him, frowning. "First off, I have to make a little phone call," Bert declared. The girl Lucy was down the murky hall, stooping by a snowdrift of used sheets and pillowcases. Bert said gaily, "Hey, sweetie, what's your name, loan me a dime to call my mother, will you?"

"Could I talk to you for a minute?" she asked, looking very serious. The small light from the linen closet touched the ends of hair shredding around her face. She hugged a pair of ironed sheets in her skinny arms.

Bert puffed out into his woman-conquering posture, sassy and strutting. "Permission granted," he grinned. "Only first hand over the dime, sweetie. Then you get to ride the roller coaster."

Instead of being charmed right off her feet, she said in a freezing voice, "I'm sorry, I don't have any change. What I wanted to ask you is to please leave Mrs. Mencke alone. She's not the flirty type, and she gets so unhappy. So please, kindly don't."

He was shocked by her unconcealed distaste, and hurt. "I wish I could stay away," he snarled. "But I can't resist her and she can't resist me."

"Great big bad stud, ain't you?" she said. "Ho-hum. What you need is a thumb and a blanket."

Hate scalded Bert's eyes. "Ain't that a pill?" he managed to say to Wally. "Come on, I just believe I'll make my call from the drugstore instead of the lobby." Wally didn't move: a bulk with hanging arms by the stairs. Then, slowly removing his hat, he turned back toward the room. "I'll see you in a little bit, then," Bert said. Squinting in the awful light, he went down the sun-tranced street to the post office. The pine mountains looked bruised in the hot emptiness miles away. As soon as he'd mailed the letter he made a bee-line for Mencke's drugstore.

"Pleased as all hell to see you, ma'am," he said to Helen, who was waiting on a gaunt man in stiff, new, funeral-blue denim. She blushed and went rigid with alarm. Bert dialed the number of the ranch, identified himself as a cattle buyer and asked for Mr. Bolton. Pierce's wife fluttered and said, "None of the men is home, Mr. Stephens." He cursed her cheerfully and then, undismayed at still another failure, loafed to the soda fountain and waited for Helen to be free. Every time he thought of the contempt in the girl's eyes, he felt poisoned and wild. He had this to do, too, now.

"I'll have a chocolate sodee," he said when she crept behind the counter. Prim and nervous, avoiding his mirthful look, she opened the flap-door to the freezer. "My partner tells me they're the best in the West," he purred, "so don't hold back on the ingredients, little girl."

"I heard you only drank whiskey," she said daringly and went redder than ever. Her hands flew as she squirted chocolate syrup onto the egg-like scoops of ice cream.

"Where'd you hear a lie like that? My gracious, woman, I was on that telephone not two minutes ago trying to bring truth and grace to a hardened sinner. I'm in the evangelical and temperance line." Hands bunched under his chin, he watched her hiss in the carbonated water and slap the soda in front of him.

"Well, go ahead and drink it."

"I will, I will," he said, without even glancing at it. "But it don't hardly look like enough. Fix me two more and I'll make an ice-cream social out of it."

"All right, I'll do just that." She gave a toss of her head and made him two more sodas. Her mousy face was vivid, quick, and this time she brought her eyes up to meet his. "Start in drinking 'em, I dare you," she said with her hands on her hips. "You're scared to."

"Don't get personal, woman. I'll drink 'em, just give me a minute." With a genuine quiver of nausea, he stared at the creamy tan swells of foam, alive with swarming bubbles, that puffed over the top of the glasses. "Looks like it would make a pretty fair worm cure," he observed, "but for just pleasure—tell you what. You drink some and I'll rub some on, how's that? Couldn't nothing be fairer."

She broke into laughter but at once, possibly because the loafing railroad men had begun to notice, she ducked back into stiff reserve. Bert hung around for an hour, while the ballooning sodas slowly collapsed and sank into thick muddy slop. Then Mr. Mencke bustled in, out of breath, with news of Sam Bolton for the railroad men. Bolton was loading a freight car with ore to ship to Rifle, Colorado. Vivie and Sam were doing it themselves—they were even living in Red Canyon in a trailer.

Bert left the drugstore in a trance of concentration. It was clear now why he hadn't been able to contact Bolton by phone. Furthermore, a man digging and shipping uranium ore wasn't going to be easy to distract. Nothing less than a stroke of genius would do; in fact, it might take five or six of them to scorch his tail . . .

A little after twelve o'clock, Wally stopped pondering about Bert and began to wonder what had happened to him. Coming out of the hotel he halted in his tracks, incredulous. Automatically his glance had flicked at the glaring desertion of Highway Street as it bent toward the river—at the Church of Christ and a few houses, the two flaking pumps of an abandoned gas station standing in the weeds, the veterinarian's house and pasture, and a grey shrunken building that had once been a cafe. There his glance caught, frozen to a huge pink splotch on the side of the cafe and a capering figure with a pink brush. Bert was painting it pink! Gathered round was a fair-sized audience made up of old pensioners, railroad men, two of his female admirers, and boys with bikes and dogs.

"It's a beauty, huh?" Bert said as Wally came chugging up.

"What in the name of fire do you think you're doing?"

"Lard, what this town needs is some prettifying. It gets boresome looking at grey shacks." He was wearing a checkered cap, set at a cocky angle, to keep off the sun. Exuberantly he dipped the brush into the can, lifted it out with a flourish (still rivering from its tip), and walked a gorgeous circus-pink stripe along the weathered boards. "If you think that's good," he said, "watch this one. I'm gonna make my reputation with this lick." The women went into fits of laughter. His shirt and pants were splattered, his hands were pink, and the ground looked as if pink Easter eggs had been thrown around and trampled into the dust. In one of his hind pockets was a bottle of turpentine and in the other a half pint of whiskey. "Yessir," he said, stepping back to admire the dribbling pink blear. "I saw some paint jobs in my day but this flat wins."

Wally couldn't help laughing. "You don't have a bit of sense, Bert."

"For some things it don't take sense, Lard. It takes practice." He plastered another gaudy patch on the crumbling building and paused for a drink, narrowly avoiding a swallow of turpentine instead of liquor. "Woo-ee, that was dangerous," he said, winking gleefully at Wally. "The horrors of strong drink ain't nothing to turpentine. I *know*." He waved his brush to the police car as it went by, flecking himself with drops of paint like melted strawberry ice cream. Unbelievably, there came an answering honk from the car.

"How come he didn't stop you?" Wally asked. "Don't somebody own this?"

"It's Edna Harbaugh's," Bert said. "She wants to fix it up to rent out, what with this boom on and everything. Naturally I volunteered, seeing as she helped us out."

Wally could hardly believe his ears. "Bert, this is the nicest thing you've done in I don't know how long." Mightily encouraged, he offered to help and asked if Bert would come out and prospect a little bit afterwards.

"Old Heavy, it's a promise," Bert said. "Word of honor." Wally went tearing off to buy another brush and borrow a ladder, and as Bert jauntily splashed and daubed and streaked the building, he came along behind him, blending the mess into a smooth even coat. "Damn if this ain't artistic," Bert said. He looked through the front window, smoky with dust, smashed in one place and plugged with rags. Intricate parts of an electric motor were scattered on the floor. Dead glints came from glass and stainless steel coated with grime. Wires, like exposed nerves, poked out of the soiled darkness. "This will never do," he said. With great pink swipes he painted the window; then calling Wally over, he laid down his brush and posed grandly, cap in hand. "Kinda looks like me now, don't it?" he smirked. "You know, pink and perty?"

"Bert! Can't I take my eyes off of you one second?"

"Shoot, the window is broke anyhow, I was just being playful." In high good humor, he blotched and blobbed paint on the walls, drank, joked with his girlfriends, and from time to time sent ferocious messages out to Bolton, paying five dollars a trip to a prospector who was low on funds. "Now don't pout up, Lard," he said. "This is all diplomatic with no disagreeableness or nothing."

All at once, however, he tired of the job. "This has about got me winded," he said. "Besides, much more out here in this sun will spoil my schoolboy complexion." He sat down and wouldn't get up—until he saw Pierce Bolton come driving into town in a truck. Instantly he was on his feet and painting hard.

Pierce swerved to the curb, gawking with his mouth open. "Daddy won't like that," he told them. "I'm serious, Mr. Stephens. He won't like that atall."

"This is Mr. Bolton's building?" Wally said, aghast. "Bert, I'm ashamed of you. You lied to me."

"True," Bert said airily. "And it ain't the first time I lied, neither."

Wally was very angry. He should have known better, he should have seen right off that this was just another way to plague the Boltons—another piece of crazy senseless pestering. Stupid, that's what he was. It was awful to think such a thing, but he found himself doubting all he had ever believed about Bert, all he'd ever hoped to do for him. Gravely, very gravely, he listened to the talk.

"Daddy ain't nobody to fool with," Pierce said, "and I'm not saying that to scare you. Ask anybody that ever butted heads with him."

"Junior," Bert said with a pleasant smile. "Your big trouble is plainly clear. You're chickenshit. Tell me if I'm wrong. You mess your britches every time your daddy comes near, now don't you?"

It was a mean thing to say, and coming from a babyish person like Bert who ran for cover at the first punch, it was doubly bad. Wally's mouth thinned to a grey stark line.

And Pierce took it! "Go ahead," he said tragically. "You know I can't protect myself or spite you in any way, so enjoy yourself. Go ahead, pour it on if that's your wish. Shame me before my neighbors." It was disgraceful, and Wally herded him toward his truck. Bert lolled along, his cap tipped forward over his eyes. "That paint job will just mean more torture for me," Pierce whined. "When Daddy hears about this he'll take it out of my hide as usual, that's all. But as far as getting any money, Mr. Stephens, you're sadly mistaken about that. The stinking lousy skinflint—" Pettishly he spewed insults against his own father until a frown from Wally jerked him to a stop. He was a sorry sight indeed, alternately cringing and griping and bewailing his fate. As a last resort, he offered to sell his airplane and give the eleven hundred dollars or so to Bert not later than next Wednesday. "A gentleman's debt between the two of us, sir, with that for a down payment. Will you shake hands on it? All I ask is some time for the balance and don't aggravate my father."

Wally said, "It sounds fair, Bert. He's going his limit."

"Ssh!" Bert said, his finger on his lips. "You're just my conscience, Lard, not my lawyer." To Pierce he said, "Thirty-six hundred cash on the nail, Junior, or face the consequences. Which I hate to even describe."

Pierce's face twisted out of shape and he wailed, "But I can't! Sir, I'm only asking you to be Christian. I'm sick, I'm so nervous I can't go on. I came near to being killed on the haylift this morning, I mean it. That's why I had to lay out of work again, and that'll make him even more merciless when he finds out. Sir, as a Christian thing to do—I don't know how much you're religious minded but please! This has scalded my guts till even prayer don't hardly help me."

Bert wasn't nasty; with the same smiling and dreadful good temper he said, "Can't do it, Junior, I'm allergic to being gypped." Even when Wally volunteered to give Bert the entire eleven hundred and wait for his share, he was inflexible. And suddenly Wally whirled with shock, as if he had almost fallen into a dead mine shaft and, hanging onto the rotten boards, looked down and down into mouldering rusty shadows: he had realized that Bert was not interested in the money at all, or in Pierce. The first night in town, when they'd gone down to the depot to wire Bob Werden, and Sam Bolton had brushed them out of his way—it was the old man Bert had been after from the beginning.

His confusion deepened with numbing quickness. Bert was not a man to forget or forgive; still, after all this time, to persecute somebody for such a trivial thing, for a little careless push! This campaign of pestering had not come about by chance; it was shrewd and deliberate revenge. He had waited his opportunity, then sucked Pierce into gambling for high stakes in order to get at his father. It was frightening. And beneath that, bottomlessly deep, were other things, horrible and very sad. They were completely beyond him . . . except that he had the strangest feeling Bert wasn't even tormenting Sam Bolton so much as he was tormenting himself.

"It's a dog's life at the best for me," Pierce continued to plead, but at last he cursed them both venomously and drove away. Bert was laughing like a fool.

"That's enough," Wally said, grim. "Whatever is haywire with you is too much for me to figure out. But I'm done asking and begging you to do right. Today is Thursday. You have till Saturday morning at seven A.M., sharp. Then if you don't start to prospecting, and I mean full-time with no dragging your feet, I'm done with you."

"I've got it!" Bert said triumphantly, just as if Wally hadn't said a word. "Damn if I'm not a smart chicken." Flushing, Wally watched him rollick up the street to the office of the small weekly newspaper that served the whole county; then he went back to painting the cafe. Though it would still be an eyesore when he finished, the least he could do was make it neat. The thirsty wood drank up paint by the gallon. He was alone in the blast-furnace heat except for an old collie panting in the shade, its tail spanking the dust when he came near. What choice had he had except to give Bert a deadline? And yet, minute by minute, he grew more terrified. He'd handled it wrong. Bert was too proud to give in to an ultimatum, and whatever chance there'd been to get him to cooperate was gone, completely out the window.

On the other hand, he couldn't back down from his word either, because there was no denying its justice. The deadline had to stand.

By six o'clock that evening Charley and several other boys, for a dollar apiece, had splashed the entire town with handbills. WARNING TO ALL AND SUNDRY, they blared, SAM BOLTON WON'T PAY HIS DEBTS. THIS IS A PUBLIC SERVICE ANNOUNCE-

MENT (signed) BERTRAM J. STEPHENS & CO., INC. "That'll blister him," Bert gloated. "Bolton don't know what he's up against. He's been playing checkers with amateurs." This new outrage should have hardened Wally's determination; it didn't. In spite of his anger, in spite of the slow patient hours and days of thought, all building to one inevitable judgement, he was not prepared for the anguish he felt. It was like a steady seep of blood inside him. Dumbly, opening and shutting his big hands, he watched Bert saunter out for the evening and long after midnight, long after Ray was snoring in his cot, come stumbling back in, scratched and bleeding. "The rest of the wagon train was scalped," he mumbled. His red sodden eye winked and then he flopped down.

Heartsick, Wally put him to bed. Who would take care of him after tomorrow, who would hold him together? But it was more than that; he loved Bert as a father loves his child, his only son. No matter what was wrong with him, how could he give him up? Bert was brilliant and funny and—everything he wasn't and could never be himself.

And on Friday he was more extravagant, freakish, and full of pranks than ever. Among other things, it was his way of saying that he hadn't the least intention of giving in. He walked around with a water gun, squirting people and shouting, "Cover your eyes! It's got carbolic acid in it. I blinded three dogs and burned the ninny off my best girl so far already." Wally lost count of how many times he ate. All day the light outside seemed to lie like a burning weight on the low frame buildings. Night came, pulling the sun into the hills, but the air was still like heated wool. Insects boiled in the street lights. A car full of noisy ranch hands tore up and down the streets, honking and taking the corners on two wheels. Wally was in the sweltering cafe, spooning in gooey peach cobbler with absent-minded ravenousness, when he happened to look out the window and see Bert and Sam Bolton at the corner by the dry goods store.

He went out the door and pounded toward them. Bolton was ambling forward, into the glow of the street lamp swirling with insects like a spring pond full of spermy life. Bert, a beer opener in his hand, was raging, "I'm gonna stick this in you and leave it there," but he was backing up in terror.

"Take him, Wally!" he yelled as he saw Wally come running up.

"Mr. Bolton," Wally said, "you lay a hand on him and it won't be good for you."

They were all enveloped in a formless multitude of whirling, biting, mating, dying bugs. Wally could scarcely see Bolton and he pawed at his eyes, one arm pulled back like a battering ram.

Bolton gave a snort. "I haven't hit a man for fifteen or twenty years. That your partner? He's sure excitable. I can't get him to hear me out, so I guess I'll have to tell you." Stubble-faced, his dusty levis sweated white under the arms, his hat leaning back on his head, he spoke his piece while Bert swore, entreated Wally to get him, and scuttered back out of range. "First off, we might as well get one thing straight. You're not getting any money at all from Pierce, what he gets from selling that plane is going back into the herd where it come from. I can appreciate your disappointment. You'd like the money and Pierce was a darn fool as usual. Also, it's only fair to tell you I don't feel myself obligated. In the first place, he's growed up and his debts are his business. In the second, card players are beyond my understanding. Gambling is not my notion of making money, and the way I see it, a gambler has no call on me." Goodnaturedly, almost humorously, he swatted at the insects and spat a few of them out of his mouth.

Wally looked at him with respect. He could tell a man when he saw one, and this was much of a man.

"You think you're a bad sonofabitch," Bert snarled. "Well, you're not immune from being taken. As you will find out."

"I'm talking to your partner." Bert went half mad at this, and for just an instant Wally thought he would make a rush with the beer opener. Bolton, however, went on talking. "You see if you can get him to think it over. I'd pay you boys for the job on the cafe if your motives were kinder, but those handbills, now. You vilify my reputation any more and I'll have to take another line. Maybe I would've already except I'm busy and I hate like heck to waste time on a blowup . . ."

"Busy!" Bert shrieked. Crazed glitters slid on his bloodshot eyes, and his starched face was grey in the insect-roiling light. "Going to be the bigshot mining king, too, huh? What's the matter, ain't being God almighty for fifty miles around enough for you?"

You think it over," Bolton told him, and went swaying off toward his truck, his arms dangling from his great sloped shoulders.

"God dammit," Bert sobbed and abruptly, before Wally could prevent him, bashed his foot into the window of Kearley's dry goods store. The plate of glass split, cracked everywhere in jigsaw pieces, and fell in on heavy work clothes, boots, five-gallon hats pierced with air holes. Wally didn't even reproach Bert. He simply let his hands drop to his sides, limp, while the snowstorm of insects swept all around him, hitting him, stinging his face. The stoplight pulsed red over the vacant highway. He didn't understand what Bert said at first; he was only conscious that his slogging blood had speeded up, that it was flowing, running with miraculous relief, deliverance. Bert had said, "Let's get to prospecting."

XII

At seven o'clock in the morning, dead insects lay in small grey drifts under the street lamps. The old frame stores with their false fronts were wrapped with light and in the alley behind the drugstore, sparrows pecked at yellow horse droppings. Pink and haunchy, George Mencke came out into the small backyard carrying a half-empty tow sack in one hand. As soon as the dogs spotted him they set up a frantic baying and leaped back and forth in their wire pen, spotted and lanky, their long ears dangling and their muscular tails in motion.

"Shut your dirty traps," he murmured to them. Before feeding them he hosed the turds from the concrete runway, then washed out their drinking pans. The water pressure was down further than he'd ever seen it, and only a weak gush, a dribble, came from the nozzle of the hose. After he'd put out the pellets and they'd been gobbled down, he scratched the dogs gently behind the ears, examined them for ticks and checked their paws, talking all the while in a caressing voice. "You filthy bastards," he crooned. "You think you're too expensive to kill, don't you? But you're wrong. One of these fine days I'm gonna turn a shotgun on both of you." Their long white carnivorous teeth gleamed in purple fringes, their tongues dripped and slobbered, their stinking breath poured over him.

As quickly as possible he shut the wire door and took a deep breath of the lovely clean air. For a moment he was himself. The hills were pale soft bulges at the end of the alley. A bird winged overhead, fragile, delicate, its flight like a tender bit of song. Pottering over to the fence, he began watering the coarse red hollyhocks, but he was unlucky: Helen's brother, Bud Robel, came rattling up in his truck.

"What brings you into town at this early hour?" he asked, guiltily letting the hose fall. If only he'd been watering the dogs instead of flowers. It made such a bad impression. "Come in, come in, the coffee's on the stove," he said too loudly, too hospitably.

"Morning, George. Just dropped by, I have a little business at the garage." He was courteous enough, he was pleasant, and yet there was something in his clear simple eyes, a wry patience perhaps, that meant—everything. The dogs were barking madly and jumping against the wire. A smile curved into his face and he squatted down by the pen, a small leather-brown man wearing overalls and a khaki shirt with ragged holes at the elbows. "How's it going, Blue? How's the old boy, huh? Howdy, gal. Whatcha say, honey?" They wriggled and whined adoringly, and the long collapsed dugs of the bitch swayed under her like tassels of black skin. Opening the door, he stroked them and took their muzzles into his hands, speaking and handling them with a warm kinship that made them go crazy with joy.

"You wait and see," George hissed at them when Bud had gone inside. "You'll get it. A load of buckshot right in the face." But he knew it wasn't the dogs he hated so much as the hunting. Bloody fur. The rigid body of an antelope bouncing in the back of a pickup truck. Dead pheasants shattered into wet red feathers. Twenty-five years of guns and dogs and game, a long martyrdom of slaughter, of swift graceful things crumpling in the sights when he pulled the trigger, of talk about bags and limits and the words coming out false every time. He would never be like Bud, who hunted as naturally as a mountain lion and who ate what he killed, enjoying the rank sinewy flesh that even some hunters admitted they couldn't stomach. He would never be like Bud. Down inside he was still the terrified boy in Scouts who had run away and thrown up in the woods when they skinned the rabbit.

Pushing down his nervousness, he went in for breakfast, determined not to make another mistake. Bud was Helen's favorite brother, and she was waiting on him hand and foot, all excited and gay. "I was so in hopes you'd come," she kept chattering. "Bacon and eggs? We've got to fatten you up, Buddy. You're looking as poorly as that herd of yours."

"Just a little coffee. Black," he said, smiling at her.

"Honestly, look at him, George. He's downright puny." Nothing would do but to fry him some eggs at least. She was commonplace and frumpy, her hair was in curlers and a housecoat slopped around her feet; and it made no difference at all now that Bud was here. She was charming and bright, radiant. "You *would* have to catch me with my hair up," she said.

"It beats some ways I've been caught," he observed.

She giggled, and George laughed out loud to show his appreciation. Bud, swinging his leg as he sat and smoked, allowed himself a sly grin, and George decided it was safe to relax a little. The baby Therese, all milky softness, was kicking her legs in the high chair and dabbling her oatmeal with a spoon. Sandy was parading up and down in the morning light, a balloon stiffening out and sinking from her mouth, her hair in silky tangles and her panties showing under her little dress. Eggs spluttered in the frying pan, blistering up around the yolks. The canary sent out squeaks and bubbly trills. Wiping her hands in her apron, Helen left the stove to cover it up with a cloth again, explaining to Bud, "George says we have a off-key bird, and I don't want to spoil his breakfast. You sure you won't have something besides toast, George?"

"No thanks." All at once he was afflicted with a spinal, base-of-the-brain worry. Helen was being just the tiniest bit too nice, too considerate, too sweet, and his nerves began to prick with subtle messages. He watched her uneasily. The eggs were cooked badly as always. Bud, reminded by the jam on his plate, was telling for the fiftieth time about the hornets. He was fighting in the hedgerows of Normandy shortly after the landing on D-Day, everything was in bloom, and he was putting marmalade on a hardtack biscuit and shooing away the yellow-jackets—all but one, which got him on the tongue just as he bit the cracker. "You should've saw that tongue of mine swole up," he grinned. "I couldn't close my mouth for two weeks."

It was beyond belief, George thought ruefully. Fighting all through France and Germany, getting wounded twice, and this was what Bud remembered. Imagine. But that was Bud Robel. He'd fought when he was told to fight, killed when he was told to kill, and forgotten it. The man was almost completely without mind or imagination. What he remembered about the buzzbombs the Germans had sent over England was how the RAF pilots had nudged them around with their planes and sent them put-putting back across the Channel. He thought that was funny. Imagine. He was that unsensitive. And yet he was somehow great, great as George knew that he himself could never be. Bud was brave without trying, the way a fox terrier is brave, and at the same time there was a dignity about him, a self-possession that commanded respect. George envied him with his whole soul, even knowing he was superior to Bud in many things. He was flattered when Bud so much as noticed him. He studied him and copied his every gesture—the way he used obscenity, with an inoffensive naturalness that George could never exactly hit—the way he ate, devouring his food hungrily but not coarsely, attacking it with a sort of clean masculine delicacy. To be like that you had to be back in the Garden of Eden.

"Served you right," Helen told Bud fondly. "As long as you're here, take off that shirt and I'll mend those elbows. A 'stitch in time' don't apply any more, it would take higher mathematics." Bud shook her off, his face smiling in curls of luminous smoke. She continued to harass him about it, her commonplace features glowing with affection, beautiful. Then she seemed to catch herself and turned to George. "It's an act of mercy, honey."

"You don't have to defend yourself," he said indifferently. But he was wrung with an icy shiver. Preoccupied with the state of the uranium boom, he hadn't been paying as much attention to her as usual; now the vague unrest of the last few days crystallized inside him: with cold fixity he realized that she wast in love with somebody. It was Sam Bolton, it was Leroy Jackson beginning all over again. And poor Helen, silly and childlike Helen, in her guilt and remorse (because she didn't want to slip, she really and truly didn't) was trying so hard to please him that she was even giving less of herself to Bud.

Couldn't she understand anything? Would she never be able to grasp that it was a sacrifice he couldn't bear? Withdrawing from them entirely, he blew up Sandy's balloon for her. The dark red pouch expanded with his breath, swelled, grew paler and paler as it thinned until it was the loveliest, translucent pink. In ecstasy Sandy whirled it up over her head, swatting at it with her little hands and jumping up and down. Whap! it exploded. Her mouth howled open, tragic. Doing his best to console her, he thought he detected a warm sweet stink coming from Therese's diaper and put his hand inside it to check.

"She's dirty," he said to Helen, reproachfully. "I've asked you fifty times to put her on the potty chair at breakfast. She never fails to do this."

Instead of snapping back at him, Helen lowered her face submissively and took Therese out of the room to change her. His pink face grew pinker. It was a submissiveness, a loyalty to him in front of her brother, that he didn't want now. That he detested, in fact. An instant later his nerves were crackling with new signals of danger: Bud was looking strange. Now what? But he hadn't changed the diaper himself! Surely it was within the province of parenthood to feel inside a diaper. But no, he had blundered again. Stricken, he saw Bud get to his feet.

"The mine," he said quickly, before Bud could say goodbye to Helen. "I was meaning to ask about your famous mine. How's it coming? Riches galore, I hope."

"Afraid not. I sunk a shaft about six feet into the cliff but it's a narrow shoot of ore and it's pinching off. That's the way your outcrops go, mostly washed away."

"Is that so?" George said, clutching at him. "I thought it was doing so good."

Bud rubbed the back of his neck, anxious to be off. "I'm closer to losing my hind end than getting rich. A few hundred ton of low-grade ore is my guess. After expenses and shipping costs I'll show a profit on it and that's about all." Not roughly but firmly he pulled away and called to Helen, "I'll see you, Sis."

She came rushing back into the kitchen, carrying the baby. "You don't have to go yet, Buddy. Please."

"Set down and have some more coffee," George urged. "How about your other claims?"

"Well, they say a fella could hit hisself a jackpot, but from what I've saw I'd swap the whole works for two brood cows and a plug of tobacco." And chucking Helen under the chin, he walked out.

For a moment the quiet rejection left George empty, feeling helpless and collapsed. Then he was churning with the dreadful news of the mine. It was another serious blow to the uranium boom, and the report would be all over town before tonight and all over the state in a week. The boom was failing, dying every day, every hour, and he was frantic to go out and keep it alive somehow. Nevertheless, punishing Helen mournfully by sacrificing himself, he insisted on washing the dishes and vacuuming the living room before he opened the store for the day and sallied forth.

On the sidewalk he folded a pinch of snuff into his lower lip. It was a nasty habit, snuff, but even the smallest details of dress and talk and action were important. Or so he had always thought. His secret dream was to ride the train clear to Chicago and hear grand opera just once, but he knew he would never dare. Dear God, the things he had done—not to be admired or popular—just to be taken for granted, to be not disliked. The fights in school, flopping down with a wail at the first punch and picking himself up somehow to get punched some more. The white-hot terror when it was his turn and he galloped the horse across Swinging Bridge, the loose boards clattering and jumping under the wild hooves, the steel cables raking first one of his legs and then the other as the long skinny runway yawed hideously from side to side. Why hadn't it been enough? His family had homesteaded this country; his father had owned the drugstore before him, and still nothing had worked. Not his professional standing, not making himself expert in cattle and markets, nor his devoted service in every single community function. A lifetime of the most gruelling and terrible frustration, all because his parents hadn't let him go off to be a medical missionary but insisted he take over the family business in this godforsaken town.

The only happiness he'd ever known had been during the boom. The excitement! The fabulous rumors! There'd been people from out of town to talk with and show the ropes to, and his articles in the Enterprise *Gazette* had been very highly praised. Overnight, everything he had pretended for thirty-two years had become true. Sweetest of all, the people who counted most in town had changed their tune; they wanted that cash register to ring, and it was George Mencke, little Georgie Porgie puddin'an'pie, kissed the girls and made them cry, who could help them.

And now the boom was dying and it was like his own life slipping away. Not a soul from out of town was in sight except for a truck from Rapid City fixing the broken window of Kearley's dry goods store. The slab of new glass flashed painfully into his eyes as the men slid it, cautiously, off the bed of the truck; the tarpaulin over the racks of glass hung limp. One after another the shabby trucks and cars of the prospectors had shrunk down the highway and disappeared, heading for North Dakota or Canada, where new strikes had been reported. The old days had come back. There was Cecil Frye, in his white apron, going into the bank for the day's supply of change. Homer Larkin was sitting in his chair outside the barber shop and Mrs. Perkins was sweeping out the hardware store, her broom spitting dust into the empty sunlight. A truck carrying water went by and then the street, walled with grey sham fronts, was still.

No, he couldn't resign himself to it. He'd had a taste of real life and he couldn't go back. There was only one hope left, actually—Sam Bolton's shipment to Rifle a week ago. If it tested high enough, interest in the area might possibly return. What did it matter that Bolton had mounted Helen as carelessly as a stallion in a pasture? Bolton was rich anyhow; another fortune or two wouldn't make any difference. What really worried him was the attitude of the Atomic Energy Commission. As soon as the shipment left, he'd alerted Mr. Farragut, the AEC man in Rapid City, but Mr. Farragut was frankly otherwise occupied. He was all steamed up about the north Dakota lignite fields now and in fact he'd been just about to leave on a flying visit to them. Even a top rating for the shipment might not be enough.

The thought made a yawning hunger, a vacuum inside him. He just *had* to do something. But it was no use going to the newspaper office and asking Ed Reilly again if he could write one more article on uranium. He was back to "News Around Town," the all-too-familiar run of items like a meeting of the Busy Club and a pancake supper by the American Legion Auxiliary.

In desperation he went into the Victory Bar with its moulting eagle perched on a beer sign, its gallery of stock brands, and its group of faded pensioners mumbling the idle days away. Although the shot of whiskey burned like lye-water in his throat, he could at least get rid of the awful snuff for a while. "This Korean war ought to be settled by atomic bombs," he began fervently. "General MacArthur himself has said it straight out. And with all those new uranium plants going up, a great amount more of uranium will be needed. We're in the greatest crisis in our country's history—will Russia or us go under? Look at all those Commies in government, which we haven't rooted them all out yet by a damn sight. I tell you it's a frenzied pace."

The downy old heads nodded, the faces like shrivelled bladders were interested, impressed.

"Every bit of uranium that can be found is necessary; it's our life's blood. And I'm not even figuring in the peacetime uses. We're in an age of great scientific discovery. You take vitamins. And chlorophyll. Dyanetics, where we're pushing psychology clear back to . . . before we're born. The peacetime uses of uranium will be fabulous, and the Black Hills area will play its part. Why, in a few years all our cars will be run by uranium. It's the fuel of the future. Electricity will be a thing of the past."

"That's right," one of them cheeped, and all the others shifted their empty, gaseous flesh and looked alert. Wilted skin hung from their chins. Their brittle hands were as light and dry as twigs. With crushing weight the futility of what he was doing pressed down upon him. He couldn't keep the boom going this way, and there was no satisfaction in talking with the same old geezers, beached on a sunny mudbank of memories and small talk and whiskey. Trainmen and pensioners, that's what he was back to. It was horrible.

To be what he had been, just once more before it was too late—could he pull it off? The craving was too much for him, and he waddled in the direction of Lee Stark's Motor Sales. Already the delicate clouds were melting in blue heat. The deserted highway ran out over the hill beyond the auction barn, bone white. Strings of orange flags drooped over the used cars. As usual, several unoccupied business men were standing around in the cement and glass showroom, next to the stubby green Chevrolet. He knew the sort of thing they were saying, "Our period of feast is over with" and "We're running on three legs again," and he knew that he wasn't welcome any more. His breath shook with fear but he scraped together a careless air and sauntered in.

"Harvey," he said with his pop eyes blinking and a smile on his red lips. "Pete. Howdy, Jim." Hands in his back pockets, bluff and hearty, he observed, "It's gonna be another hot bugger, looks like."

Only the barest grunts answered him. Impatience creeping in the slack red folds of his face, Harvey Perkins turned away to blob a mouthful of tobacco juice into the pail of sand. Where was their gratitude for all his services? They had no appreciation at all. Even a very popular subject, the nomination of Eisenhower for President, failed dismally. He lost his head completely and did the stupidest thing he could possibly have done: he lied.

"I have some good news for all concerned," he announced. "That shipment of Sam Bolton's, it's tested out sensational." The reaction was all he could have asked for. "I know, our hides have been nailed to the fence so often I can hardly believe it myself," he said. "But we're going places now, and that's my sincere belief. Investment money will be coming in to develop the area, and I mean big money, by the ton. Over thirty million was invested on the Colorado Plateau last year alone."

"By God, we might still get some of the gravy ourself," Harvey Perkins said.

"I sorta figured all along the letdown was only temporary," Jim agreed. "I just had a hunch."

Gluttonously he fed on their enthusiasm, filled himself to bursting in an orgy of longed-for recognition. He was alive again. What he'd said could very well be true, too, and with evangelical fervor he told them, "If we beat the drums hard enough we can do it. We'll become the uranium capitol of the world. That's my slogan."

"Hey, Lee," the men shouted. "Hightail it out here! Hurry up!" In due time, looking preoccupied and annoyed, Lee came out of the garage in back, a piggy-faced man with mean little eyes that didn't quite match. George felt a tremor in his heart. Ever since grade school he'd been scared of Lee, and he wasn't the only one, either. Lee pulled the wires in town; the mayor and the Chamber of Commerce were in his pocket, and so were plenty of other items he'd taken a fancy to. He openly said, "I'm for Lee and Lee only," and behind his back everybody swore he'd steal the flag right off the pole, but they were mighty friendly to his face.

While the men were still babbling he wheeled on George and said, "I seen Sam yesterday, and he didn't mention it. What's your source of information?"

"The AEC man in Rapid," George said, quailing. "Mr. Farragut. You remember, he paid us a visit. I called him long distance. Honest I did." He felt the guilty blood surging into his face.

The uneven little eyes were fixed on him, canny poker player's eyes, estimating. "Georgie," he said, "you wouldn't be telling us a fib, would you?"

"I swear it, Lee—my solemn word . . ." Then he went to pieces and fled, shamefully. It was the most awful disaster of his life. He must have been insane to lie, and then to break down instead of sticking to his story at least! Oh God, the humiliation. He would never be able to face them again. He was already a laughing stock on account of Helen, and this had finished him. He was done for.

Half out of his mind as it was, he saw Pierce Bolton's daughter, fussy and prim, a little mother in pigtails, parading her doll buggy up and down in front of his drugstore. Sure enough, the buggy was overloaded, sunk down on its flimsy springs, and the canvas side bulged out like a heavy womb. Waddling into a run, he saw his own child, Therese, in the buggy.

"You idiot!" he cried. "How many times do I have to tell you? It's not safe!" Snatching up the baby and whirling around, he ran smack into the half-sized gandy who had been hanging around town. An ice cream cone plopped on the sidewalk. "Hey, watch out!" the little man growled. In a frenzy by now, George spluttered, "Watch out nothing, you watch out. Did you pay for that cone? I didn't think so. You're a bum."

He stormed inside and gave Helen a tongue lashing, then rushed into the back with Therese wailing in his arms. Helen followed him, but he told her to take care of the store. An hour later he was still there, refusing to leave the back except to fill one prescription. The strength had gone out of him. It wasn't only the men he had lied to; he couldn't bring himself to face anybody. Ravaged with bitterness, he listened to the railroad men, who all worshipped Helen, trying to cheer *her* up: "Look at that, Helen. The kid's got a little dog in the buggy now." "With a bonnet on it and everything." "Look, she can't get it to lay down." The feeling of doom thickened with every hour, and his heart seemed to beat slower and slower. "It's so pitiful," a girl was telling Helen. "He was just about halter-broke. Now he won't leave me come close to give him some sugar, he spooks when I'm ten feet away." With a shudder he realized she was saying that her new saddle pony had just been gelded. In other days he would have been out there, sick to his stomach but saying carelessly, "You can't have a rough horse, Jessie May. You have to gentle him, and it don't hurt to amount to anything." At least that was over; he didn't have to pretend any more. The grisly branding and castrating every year at Bud's ranch. Mother cows bawling for their calves from outside the corral. Blood and alkali dust. Severed testicles cooking on the open fire until the skin blistered and popped open. Then the munching faces, his stomach wrenching with nausea as he chewed with a show of relish. "Ah, good old prairie oysters," he would joke. "They sure help your you-know-what." Dear God, at least that was over, too. How he hated them, Stark and Perkins, all of them, but especially the hard dusty cattlemen who looked at him reflectively and then let their eyes slide past him. They could all go to perdition as far as he was concerned. He was through.

Picking up the phone, he called long distance to the AEC office in Rapid City, praying that the lie wasn't a lie, that somehow the call could make it come true. Mr. Farragut was back from North Dakota, the busy voice said, but he was out for the day. Was there any message?

"No, no thanks." The only comfort he had left was the children. Sandy was eating peanut butter from a jar, her face an oily brown smear. "Come here, Daddy's girl," he said, and gave her a bath and put a clean dress on her, going all soft and woozy at the feel of the live little body between his knees. He changed Therese then, holding her tiny feet up and sprinkling her with powder, smoothing it on the delicate little cleft where she came together. His heart brimmed over with the sweetness of them, but he couldn't escape; every time a customer came into the store he flinched, and his helplessness was like a moan inside him.

"What *is* the matter?" Helen asked him again.

Gently he pushed her comfort away. "I'm fine," he said. "Just fine."

When deliverance came he thought at first that Harvey and the others had believed his lie after all, or more probably, that they were trying to make capital of it. Ed Reilly phoned him just before five o'clock and asked him if he could do an article, quick: Sam Bolton's shipment had the AEC higher than a kite.

"Well," George said, "there's rumors but—are you sure?"

"Does fourteen thousand for that shipment sound like a rumor?"

George sucked in his breath. Glory burst upon him, exploding geysers of beautiful color and fire. He could scarcely hear what Reilly was saying, something about the major wire services—a follow-up for the Rapid City papers—Farragut—pictures of Bolton he'd taken at the county fair. It was true! It had come true, the whole crazy lie, all of it and more! His head swimming with relief, he did his best to grasp the sort of thing he was to write: spectacular new find, production in the area increasing rapidly, the thousands of claims staked since Zeke Butler's original find. "You have all the details," Reilly said, "you're the uranium expert."

"I'll get going on it this minute, Ed. Only too happy to render a service."

By working his head off he managed to get the story and pictures on the 9:30 P.M. bus for Rapid. And the byline was his! George Mencke, Enterprise correspondent! Already news of the shipment charged the air, and as soon as he strolled into the Black Hills Cafe he was surrounded and pelted with eager questions. "It's no will of the wisp," he assured everybody. "We hit a royal flush this time." It was just marvelous. Not only was he at the center of great affairs once more, he didn't have to worry about a scandal any longer. Helen could whore in the main street and hardly be noticed with a uranium boom going on.

Most reluctantly he left the cafe and started home. Insects whirled in the pond of light around the street lamp. The curfew siren howled into the streets and alleys of the moon-silent town. Suddenly he found himself wishing that it wasn't Sam Bolton who had struck it rich. Fourteen thousand for one shipment, and he had over a hundred claims out there in Red Canyon. The wealth of King Midas was his, and who was paddling the canoe for him, who was helping to make him a celebrity as well as a mining millionaire? George Mencke, that's who. Breaking his neck for a knot-headed rancher with a big prod. Now that the boom was underway again, he realized that it *did* make a difference, that it galled his very soul for Bolton to be the heavy winner. Words and phrases from the article he had written began to rankle inside him— "leading citizen," "one of the foremost ranchers in the state" . . .

Tormented, he went down the alley to the back of the store. The hounds whined and padded back and forth in the kennel. Now his discontent started reverberating with something else, with the knowledge that Helen was in love again. His blissful triumph shrivelled and sank into cold memories. It wouldn't be hard to discover who the lucky man was; she was so simple, so completely incapable of deception, that he wouldn't be able to avoid finding out.

Opening the door he found her, with this painful new devotion, scrubbing the floor on her hands and knees. Her dress was hiked up and knotted on her thighs. The kitchen still smelled of sauerkraut. "Did you make conections with the bus?" she asked, but it was a poor attempt at naturalness. She was greyer, more lusterless than ever, dwindling into remorse for what she hadn't done yet.

"I'll finish up for you," he said quietly. "Give the rag here."

"Please couldn't I? I'm almost done."

Though her self-punishment exasperated him—there was a perfectly good mop around—he did not reproach her. Firmly he took the rag from her hands and mopped the rest of the floor himself, then polished the shiny new monster of a kitchen range studded with dials and controls. As always she had forgotten and hung the scissors from the antlers on the wall, and as always he banged his head against them. A scalding gush of hatred went through him before he was able to control himself. Very quietly he put the scissors in a drawer and went into the bedroom.

Damp and pink from a bath, she was sitting at the dresser mirror and combing her hair. Her housecoat was half open on her breasts and they swung and wobbled deliciously as she dragged the comb through her hair.

"It was a nice article," she said with just a trace of confidence: she knew that no matter how he felt she drew him, drew him irresistibly to her soft gentle body.

"Thank you," he said in a formal voice. He noticed a broken chocolate, oozing pink cream, on the rug by Therese's crib. Stiff with unspoken grievance, he dropped it into the wastebasket, but when he turned out the light and she lay in a pale foam of moonlight, waiting, a soft craving melted through him. Humble, pathetically anxious to make him happy, she closed her eyes and offered him her mouth. Trembling a little, he kissed her softly and nuzzled his face in the moist channel between her breasts, nuzzled against the soft ripe curve of her belly, joining his mouth to it. How happy he was when she was pregnant. The rich swelling of her breasts and womb, and, at last, the first tiny movement, the first ticking of a little heart. He was losing himself, he was blurring and dissolving into her, becoming her naked softness.

She sighed and clung to him, her breath beginning to quicken.

Then he pulled himself away. The effort it required was agonizing but he detached himself and sank back.

"What's wrong?"

"It's no use," he said sadly, punishing her, watching the emotional shock quiver all through her. "I can't—knowing you don't love me."

"How—how can you say that?" she gasped, but her eyes were despairing. With mournful satisfaction he watched her sacrifice of herself go dead, her silly hope of easing her conscience go dead. A tearing sound came out of her mouth. With stumbling hands she tried to drag the sheet over her nakedness, as if it were obscene.

XIII

The air compressor grunted in the broiling canyon. Whirring metal screamed against stone. In a furious ecstasy of effort, his ragged teeth biting together, Sam Bolton leaned his weight into the drill, sinking it deep into the soft pink cliff. The vibrations of the drill went through him, hammering, battering at him, numbing his bunched muscles, and his face was a hairy and dust-caked mask with red eyes glaring through narrow cuts. At last he pulled the drill from the hole, and dragging it along at the end of its long nose, slogged down to the boxes of dynamite beside the oil barrels.

"You ready for lunch? Vivie yelled to him from the door of the trailer.

"I'll pull the round first. While the cordite clears off, I can eat." Oblivious of her and of the man from the East, he sat down on a coil of rope and attached the blasting caps to fuses, then went toiling back up with the fuses draped around his brute neck, his back pockets bulging with sticks of dynamite. The churned-up red earth gave fleshily under his boots. At the base of the great wounded cliff, he squatted and pierced three of the sticks and laced fuses into them: they looked like three enormous sperm with wiggly black tails. Next he stuffed two sticks into each hole, tamping them in tight with a wooden pole, ramming them home like charges in ancient cannons, and then he shoved in the "primers," as the dynamite sticks with fuses are called. A black tip dangled out of each hole like the tail of a rat. He worked carefully because blasting the cliff was a tricky business. The charges had to go off just right, one at a time, and if they were too heavy, the explosion threw thousands of dollars worth of ore from hell to breakfast. Not only that, but the cliff was as rotten as an old whore in places, and even a perfect shot might send tons of rock sliding down and bury the ore, diluting it beyond hope of recovery.

His work-knotted hands working deftly, he spliced "spitter" fuses of graduated length to the black tails and shouted down to Vivie and Mr.

Lytton, "Get behind the truck!" He touched off the first hole, the tar-soaked cord fizzing little white stars as the fire ate slowly in, and then the second one. While he was lighting the third, he heard an evil hiss and saw the point of fire, gushing sparks, dart into the second hole. He must have hit the dirt instantly, by pure instinct, before there was a stupefying triple concussion as the second charge went off and took the others with it, shattering the cliff face for twenty feet. The air was still vibrating. The stench of cordite burned in his mouth and nose. He was lying under a wreckage of broken rocks. Then Vivie and Mr. Lytton were running toward him through the blur of dust and yellow cordite fumes, and Vivie was helping him up, her face distorted with fear, and he was supporting himself against a bulky stone. His ears were still full of the explosion, roaring.

"All right, I'm all right," he told her groggily. "I'm all right." His smoke-and-grit-soiled face was swaying and there was a branch of blood in the gaping tear in his sleeve. Lytton was coughing into a handkerchief held over his mouth. "The second fuse," Sam said. "That danged thing went zip! and then the fun started."

His head was clearing, and he could hear Vivie sob, "I was just sure you were dead, Sam. I just knew it." Hugging against him to reassure herself, she caught sight of the blood. "Your arm, Sam! You're hurt!"

"Only a scratch," he snorted. "I'm in need of a few repairs, though. We'll declare a short recess." Nudging his head in the direction of his stained and rusty hat, he said, "Get me my chapeau, will you?" He clapped it on his head and stumbled down to the trailer. Clumsy, groping, he spilled so much water pouring it from the ten-gallon cream can into a basin that Vivie grabbed it away from him. Slumped in a chair, he let her wash his face and dress his arm. "I'm still deathly ill," she said over and over again.

"Unhuh. Mr. Lytton, there's no use wasting good minutes. Suppose you fire away."

"Now? In your condition? Are you sure? Well, U.S. Mining and Manufacturing is opening an atomic materials division, and what I'd like . . ."

Without the slightest intention of selling, Sam let him say his piece. After all, it was flattering to have a man come clear from New York just to dicker with him, and he wanted to find out what a big corporation thought his mining operation was worth. Also, not being the type to sit still, he had plowed right through the glory into more work, and here was a chance to savour his achievement for a few minutes. "Have a bite to eat with us?" he broke in cordially.

"He says he's on a special diet," Vivie said.

"I'm not a well man," Lytton apologized, and Sam could see it was true. His smooth young face, under thinning silver-alloy hair, had the fragile, almost transparent delicacy of pink china, and his meagre shoulders sank away from his neck. He chewed tensely at one piece of gum after another, wrapping the wads in tissue paper and slipping them into the pocket of his black silk suit. Out of politeness he accepted a cup of coffee, but the first sip pulled him up from his seat, choking.

"That's sagebrush coffee," Sam chuckled. "You boil the grounds till it starts corroding the pan." A few cuts and bruises didn't bother him, and he folded pieces of unbuttered bread in his fists and dispatched the beans and canned meat with prodigious zest. Naked to the waist, massive, whiskery, he looked like the God of the Old Testament in a good humor. When Lytton said the mine was a shoestring operation, Sam laughed amiably. "The shoestring is fourteen thousand dollars thicker than it was."

"Okay, you made a good buck, sure, but from a corporate standpoint its popcorn money," Lytton said. "To get this sandlot game into the big leagues—I mean no offense, Mr. Bolton—let's face it, it'll take a couple hundred thousand dollars for equipment and exploration and development. Why break your back for one blue chip? It isn't worth it. I'll have the engineering boys come in for a survey—at no expense to you whatsoever—and you'll be under no obligation. But I'm sure we can come up with a most attractive figure. Fair enough?"

"Nope," Sam said, eating.

"And that makes two of us," Vivie crackled.

"It's to your advantage a hundred per cent," Lytton insisted. "Look at all the test drilling you get for nothing. With no strings!"

"I don't want your engineers messing up the ore bodies," Sam rumbled. "Furthermore, I can't spare the time to watch over their shoulders while they drill."

"Now wait a minute," Lytton said, taken aback. "You'll get a fair and honest estimate, man. What do you tihnk I am, a burglar?"

"I'm not saying that. Let's just say, human nature being what it is, I prefer not to tempt anybody too severely. I may be sort of unsophisticated, but I didn't build up a seventy-thousand-acre ranch without knowing a few things."

Lytton wagged his china face. "Some people," he said. "They see a fishhook in every piece of pie. Look at the risks you take, you could have been killed this morning . . ."

But it was time to get humping again. Hoisting his arms and stretching, Sam told Vivie to find him another shirt. "Mr. Lytton," he said then, "I'm obliged to you for your interest but Vivie and me are riding this one out. We're enjoying ourselves too much to sell out at any price. And that's about the size of it."

"Enjoying himself, he says! All right, I believe you, getting blown up is fun. Now you believe me. Fun is fun but so is money. All I ask is, don't give me an answer. Chew on it for a couple of days, okay? Just keep the door open that long."

"No!" Vivie barked at him.

He turned up the palms of his hands as if accepting defeat, and they thought they were rid of him. However, he showed up again the following morning, smiling, indefatigable. Vivie was in town at the time, getting six barrels of gasoline, and Sam had neither time nor inclination for another spiel. A shovel gripped in one hand, he was moving in a gorilla-like stoop over the tumbled rocks that he had blasted yesterday, fanning the scintillator back and forth and watching the needle swing and fall back, tremble, spurt up on the dial. With his grimy, trenched face lowered, he circled and experimented with one direction and then another, tracking the hot ore like a bird dog, and finally set the scintillator down where the arc of the needle was greatest. Then he shoveled out a crumbly brown rock as big as the head of a bull, which he lugged in his arms to the steel mouth of the front loader. "I thought I'd get in touch again," Lytton said, tagging along after him. "You're a busy man so I'll make it as brief as possible . . . " Rummaging in the slag heaps of stone, Sam felt his breath stick as the needle kicked up to one percent, the highest it had reached yet, and he dug straight down, his shovel clanging against rock, echoes snapping off the tremendous loom of the scarred cliff face, multiplying. In a swollen frenzy, his blood driving inside him, he glutted himself with the rich ore, tracing it eagerly, ferociously, and ripping away at the burning heart of the mountain. When the front loader was full he ran it down to the ore pile by the caterpillar tractor he had bought, dumped it, and came grinding and squealing back uphill in a fume of acrid dust.

"Mr. Bolton," Lytton said after an hour of this. "Do you realize what Red Canyon could mean to the Free World?"

Sam put down the shovel and then the scintillator. "What was that?"

"I'm not kidding, the ore from your claims could tip the scales in our favor against the Russians. Now wait, by yourself it'll take years to get the uranium out of your holdings but that's a bagatelle. If sizeable production is gotten out of this batch of claims, it'll open the whole area up. All the big corporations will get on the bandwagon. Ultimately hundreds of thousands of tons are at stake."

Without a word Sam sat down on a pile of rubble, the branched wrinkles deepening by his eyes. The red clay in front of him, torn and wheel-scooped, was like a spill of lava under the drilling sun. And the canyon wall went up, ledges and splintered crags, rock slides and grey-orange layers, like a colossal furnace glowing through its ashes. Lytton watched him, chewing tensely. Sam took a drink from his canteen, trickling water into his whiskers, and absentmindedly held it out to Lytton. His eyes were almost shut under their hairy brows.

"You're either ignorant or a darn fool," he said at last, "or one of the smartest men I ever come up against. Or maybe all three. I know the ore in this canyon, mister, and I test drilled every likely claim I have. What we can do, me and Vivie, five of your crews together couldn't do." Then he erupted dangerously, "And I don't like implications I'm not loyal to my country."

"I didn't mean that," Lytton said in dismay. "My God, the idea never entered my mind."

"I'll put out enough ore to lick the Russians myself," Sam growled and crunched away. In a few minutes he heard Lytton's car drive off but the next day, incredibly, he was back again, as distinguished as ever with his heat-lacquered invalid's face, his bowtie and his carefully polished shoes, apologizing and waiting, waiting in the incandescent shade of the Mack truck for Sam to spare him a minute. Vivie was so mad she could have spit, and every time she passed by she laid her lips back from her teeth like a wild mare; Sam merely went on working.

"Look, I don't want you to blame me for yesterday," Lytton persisted. "I was just fishing a little bit. A gambit is a gambit, man, and I tried it on in good faith."

"Whatever that means," Sam grumped. He was bent over the open motor of the front loader. "Hit it again, Vivie," he said. The naked engine turned over with a groan when she pressed the starter, then came to a stop. "The son of a gun is gone, looks like," he said.

"Give me thirty seconds," Lytton asked. "I've got a brand new proposition—don't look at me like I got a dead fish in my pocket. You said you'd test-drilled the most likely claims yourself. Okay, I'll put my head on the chopping block and we'll use your figures. We'll go over them together and work out something."

"I swear," Vivie said. "As if we didn't have our hands full already."

Then Sam lifted his shaggy and oil-blotched face from the motor. "Can't set you a price," he said. "No man can set a dollar valuation on a hundred and forty-seven claims at this stage. Best thing you can do is call in your dogs and go home."

"And good riddance," Vivie yelled after Lytton as he beat a retreat to his car. That evening after supper she spoke her mind at considerable length. "It's sinful the way you let him go on, Sam. Why don't you run him off of the property? Setting there, watching you like a winter-starved buzzard. He gets me all in a jangle every time I lay eyes on him. All he wants is to separate us from our eye teeth."

She was washing dishes by the light of a lantern while Sam sat on the block of wood that served as the front step of the trailer. He was smudged with fatigue and his clothes were stiff with greasy dirt and sweat. The red and pink walls of the canyon, twisting away into the piled mountains, were bleeding softly into the hot summer dusk. "I know that's his intention," he said at last. "But that's his job, to get our batch of claims . . . And he's a battler, I'll say that for him. He's a real competitor."

"Pooh," she said, banging tin mugs and dishes.

However, his mellow tolerance was wearing thin. The AEC man was also getting in his hair, and Lytton harassed him most of the next morning: "It wouldn't do any harm to look over your test figures, would it? I'll put plenty of icing on the cake, Mr. Bolton, I promise you. . . . Look, I made a mistake waving the flag the other day, okay. I'll lay it on the line. Let's both of us admit our self-interest and start from there, that's the free enterprise system in action."

Chafed, Sam told him there was no figure and there wouldn't be one. He had problems. The front loader would be out of commission for days, and in the meantime he'd have to make do with the truck. Then the scintillator went on the fritz. The muscles above his jaws tightened under his dirt-clogged whiskers, but Lytton, as quick-witted as ever, had gone before Sam could tell him to make tracks for the road. Instead of tinkering with the scintillator, Sam clambered slowly up the side of the canyon and sat for a long time, brooding and still, looking off like Jehovah at the sun-tortured mountains. A hawk lifted against a current of air, towering above the rock shoulders and pine-spiked ledges. Vivie's voice drifted up to him, calling. A click-click-click came from the trees beside him, like a huge clock being wound. He knew that Lytton was only the beginning, that there would be more and more offers from groups of every sort, and at the prospect something formed irresistibly inside him. The thirty years he'd put in on the ranch were unreal, were beside the point. Only this was Life. It was time to burn his bridges.

Without a qualm he sold the ranch to his boys. In one way it was a kind of nominal deal because they didn't have to put any money down and because he set the payments at the same percentage of the gross he had been drawing all along. On the other hand, even while he was being fatherly and benevolent, the habits of a lifetime were still in effect. He drove a hard bargain on the price, and to protect himself against laziness or mismanagement, he froze the payments at their present level in spite of the drought. That would keep the boys hopping.

What he hadn't expected was the howls that went up from the rest of the brood. There were letters from all over three states, phone calls, and even visits from the five kids who had been left out. The cafe (now as pink as a birthday cake) in which he'd set Marie up in business years ago was recalled with bitterness. Hank and Gary went so far as to demand the sawmill and his property in Custer. Sam was astounded.

They seemed to think he was arbitrary, capricious, and downright cruel because he gave what and when he pleased. It had never occurred to him that he *owed* any of them a thing. He'd made his by a lifetime of sweat, and they could make their own or go without. Inheritance? Providing for his flesh and blood? Darn foolishness, that's what it was. "It's my ranch," he told them brusquely, "and I'll do with it as I see fit."

Nor was the proposition entirely pleasing to the three boys at home. Frank was agreeable but Pierce and Billy Joe looked as sour as alkali water. "Do you know how long it'll take us to own it?" Pierce groused. "Thirty-five stinking, lousy, putrid years—if we last that long. It's piteous! We're just your slaves like before, only worse. The ranch is a cross on our back now and we're tied to it!"

"If you're discontented," Sam said without rancor, "you don't have to put in. You use your own pleasure about it."

Beyond that he didn't bother to discuss the matter. As soon as the papers were signed at the lawyer's office in town, Vivie let out a big whoop. "We're off with the wind," she cried, and on the way back to the canyon she made up a song, "Goodbye cows, we're going to leave you now."

She was like the girl he'd married, singing beside him with the strings of her straw bonnet dangling under her vivid face. "It's a change at that," he said, "scratching at rocks instead of grazing stock on 'em."

"It's wonderful, Sam! Just load a truck with old sandrock you lived around all your life and it's worth whole bushels of money. It's like a miracle. I'm buying that red jeep out of the very next shipment money."

Lytton was waiting for them, and with considerable satisfaction Sam told him what he'd done. "That oughta make my position clear," he said. "If I were you I'd pack up and move on."

"Yeah. Well, thanks for your time anyhow. I can't say it's any big shock, I knew I was on a horse with a wooden leg." He dabbed at his face and neck, chewing disconsolately. "The payoff is, I'm in no position to recoup. For God's sake, let me learn the uranium business from you, Mr. Bolton. You're the master. Forget about the deal, I laid a ten-pound brick and that's that. The thing is, here I am, picking up leases with the aim of starting production, and I can't find my way across the street as far as uranium is concerned. I'm flying blind."

"What about your engineers?"

"That's just the point exactly. We all need a white cane and a dog. Even a professional geologist is starting from zero on this, it's so new."

Sam scratched the back of his neck, unwilling to be distracted by anybody.

"I won't bother you, I swear to God. I'll stay out of your way, and if I make one single solitary proposition, you can cut my throat." It was a shock to see a distinguished-looking young man like this holding his hands in front of him like a street beggar. "I'm not asking for a free ride, Mr. Bolton. I'll make myself handy. I can pick up your gas and supplies and run errands, whatever you say."

Sam shrugged and went back to work. The truck labored and spun its wheels in the churned-up clay, tipped its back and poured waterfalls of ore onto the stock pile, rolling sound against the dead mountains. In the gargantuan struggle he often lost all consciousness of Andy for hours at a stretch; then he would notice him, and if it could be done without slowing down, he explained as he went along. "See, you sort of feel your way with the scintillator. The big thing is, you have to avoid diluting the ore. If you're not mighty careful, you can mine right through an ore pod and recover only ten or twenty per cent instead of ninety. That means a shovel instead of a dozer." He tossed Andy a chunk of ore, almost toppling him over. "Sorry, I forgot you're not very stout—but look at that. You'd miss that completely with a dozer."

Andy soaked up every word. "It's an education," he said. "Technology, that's what I need. Technology."

The instruction itself was a success; Sam liked to talk uranium, and even Vivie conceded that Andy behaved himself. She came to take his presence for granted. And yet, whenever Sam had a spare minute to think about it, he regretted allowing him to stay on. Under the surface, under his honest desire to learn about uranium, the fanatical sonofagun was still trying to make a deal. It was the weirdest thing Sam had ever witnessed. As far as Andy was concerned it was a silent but life-and-death battle, a fight to the finish—only there was no opponent. Sam was fighting the canyon and nothing else, while Andy was conducting an imaginary campaign, full of ingenious tactics and complex maneuvers, like a sick madman. He suffered agonies trailing after Sam in the furnace-hot canyon. His delicate old-maidish skin dried out. His lips chapped and split open. His hands trembled when he took out another piece of gum. The pressure to get moving, to line up some other claims, or at least to join his engineers in Colorado must have been something awful, but every morning he showed up as regular as the mail. "Put the fatted calf back in the barn, Hiram, it's only Lytton," he joked feebly, ill and haggard but hanging on like grim death, giving no sign of the tension inside him except for the endless chewing, chewing of his jaws. Not once did he complain or break his word not to make a proposition, though he was clearly strained to the very limit. It was heroic, senseless, laughable, pitiful, and Sam didn't know what else. Devilish, maybe, if devils were stupid.

In a few days the ore body in *Calamity Jane* was pretty well exhausted. The nearest likely claim was two hundred yards down the canyon, almost at the top, and Sam started putting the caterpillar tractor in shape, building up the worn treads with a welding torch, so that he could bulldoze a road up the canyon wall. Armored with heavy gloves and goggles, he humped over the hissing blue center of fire. It flared like a miniature sun, throwing off sparks like comets, blazing planets, galaxies of fire streaming from his hands.

"What's up?" Andy inquired, shielding his eyes. When Sam told him he said with awe, "Man, you talk about versatility. There's nothing you can't do."

"A rancher has to be a master cobbler—and so does a miner." Taking a break for a minute, Sam pulled up his goggles. "You wear out a set of treads on a cat and it's twenty-six hundred dollars right there—and this sandrock is like emery. Expenses would eat me up in no time. Take a bit for that wagon drill there. It costs fifty dollars, and it lasts one day if you can't weld new burrs on it." His voice didn't show it, but he was pleased by Andy's profound admiration. "You're a fast learner yourself," he said.

"It takes more than intelligence to be a success," Andy said with a drop into gloom. He was wearing a fancy summer hat and black sun glasses like holes sunk into his face. "You have to have that drive, that inner motivation. Plus a high level of follow-through. So sayeth J. W. Hatfield, Second Philistines, verses eleven to thirteen."

"How was that?" Sam said. "Hatfield? Philistines?"

"J. W. Hatfield, he's the board chairman of U.S. Mining. J. W. Hatfield," he intoned sardonically, "the self-made man, and I mean *self-made*. God had nothing to do with it."

This was mighty strange coming from a loyal organization man, and with amazing bitterness Andy continued to take shots at J. W. Hatfield, cynically reciting his mottos: "The man with warmth of personality has a wealth of power at his command" and "The positive thinker will be the Pied Piper of any situation."

"Which brings up the subject," he added with sour relish, "of who's playing the role of the rats." Stranger yet, he was still faithful to a job he despised. The hard-hitting businessman was coming apart, melting like wax, and bits and pieces of some other man were showing through like silvery framework—without affecting his set goal at all. He was still after Sam's claims, heart and soul.

At last Sam was driven to ask, "If you feel like that, why in heck are you working for U.S. Mining?"

"Because when I sell out, I sell out to the walls. What I say to myself is, what's the good of being a halfway collaborator? Some guys when they sell out, they keep selling out to every fink they meet, but not me. What I say is, you made your decision, now live up to it." And he meant every word. His face, rubbed by fatigue and heat and illness, was held high with bleak dedication. "It's not just my own bread I'm trying to butter. I put out a hundred and fifty per cent for U.S. Mining, day and night. Insomnia? I've got it. Ulcers? You name it and I've got it. But I put out."

"You're a jackass," Sam said bluntly and forgot him in bulldozing the road. The huge deisel motor bellowed and puffed blue smoke from its stack. The monstrous blade in front, a ramming steel wall, pushed waves of scaly grey shale and rock ahead of it, crunching forward and reversing in a dry snowstorm of pink dust. Clay chunked off the massive tank treads. Yard by yard he angled upward, cut off a scraper full and pushed it over the edge, cut and pushed. It was no job for a greenhorn; it took nerve and considerable skill to buck the dirt and rocks over the side of the road, sheer off into the air.

Andy sank farther and farther below, a limp despondent figure sitting by the mound of stockpiled ore. There was nothing for him to learn and nothing to hope for and still he hung around, whipped down to the bone but unable to leave. Pretty soon, crazily, he spent most of the day watching a fight between ants. "Don't knock it till you see it," he said, and the next day after lunch Sam stopped for a look. The terrible silent battle was still going on. Oily black specks trickled out of two pustule-like hills and fed into the struggling mass on the hot sand. It squirmed and roiled slowly, sending up a faint stench and glistening hideously in the light, as thousands of tiny creatures ripped and bit and pinched, severing mandibles, legs, abdomens. Maimed and dying ants were fastened to amputated heads and bodies. Other ants on both sides carried off the dead, tugging, dragging the corpses away into jumbled piles. Sam was brought up short in spite of his hurry and preoccupation, but he said, "Well?"

"Well there it is. The whole mish-mash, New York, London, all of it. From individual people up to big companies and countries, all scrambling to get theirs or keep it. Ants even have special soldiers, just like countries, did you know that? That's global warfare down there. I'm not kidding."

"You're coming unglued," Sam told him, but the words fell flat. He had the queerest feeling of uneasiness, of muddy chaos spoiling his exhilaration.

"No listen! You asked me how I could keep at a job I didn't respect. I'll tell you why. Because it's all peanut butter, man. In an insane asylum, you go bub-bub-bub."

The eerie warfare went on at their feet, soundless, incomprehensible, ants tearing each other to pieces in the hot sunlight. Andy looked at him, smiling.

With a growl Sam slouched away. The powerful cat worked in a thundering haze, dirt heaved up on the blade and sluiced off over the edge, boulders moved with shrieking discords, a dark pine tree trembled under the shock of the steel blade, leaned back and went down. The seat and gear handles vibrated. The air was saturated with deisel fumes and the smell of hot grease and metal. In a few minutes he had become what he was doing and was clear again, whole.

It was necessary to switchback up the mountain, climbing higher and higher until the canyon road was a piece of string and he was level with the rip of somebody's mine in the ragged pink wall far across the heat-swimming light. Higher, the heaped mountains looking charred and black with pines under the metallic sky. He had no sense of personal triumph over Andy, only the mighty exultation of battering at the mountain, the splendor of roaring energy.

And then the shelf of a road he had cut out of rotten stone caved under the treads. The mammoth cat slewed and canted sharply, throwing him off balance, away from the safety of the gouged wall, carrying him with it out over the steep-dropping rubble. For a second it hung there, heeled halfway over. He jumped into nothing. He went numb. And there it was, looming up there, huge and yellow, stones cracking off the treads and skipping down. Then, slowly, it tipped on end and plunged past him like a ship going over Niagara Falls, tons of metal hurtling in a torrent of crashing rocks and trees, in stones as big as houses, tumbling, avalanching down into the canyon.

The roar went on and on and on, tides of sound coming back off the canyon walls and crashing together. He couldn't make out where he was, he couldn't move. After a while he was conscious of his own hoarse breathing and a towering cloud of dust, like smoke from a forest fire, going up into the sky. Little by little he forced his way out of the stunned blankness. He was lying on the switchback road, thirty feet under the shattered level and not five feet from the motionless cataract of broken stone the cat had left behind it. He still couldn't feel his left leg. Then he saw that it was oddly twisted and that blood was wetting the pants, gumming the fabric to his skin and leaking into one of the tread marks punched in the dirt. . . .

Five days later, sitting in a wheelchair in the Hot Springs hospital, he signed over his hard-won holdings. For 90,000 dollars cash, U.S. Mining took a six-month lease on the 147 claims, with an option to buy for 160,000 dollars more. Andy had learned enough to be a real horsetrader. U.S. Mining was to have the stockpiled ore as part of the deal, and in six months, while the engineering boys went over the claims, a mining crew would be making barrelfuls of money for the company. Nevertheless, Andy haggled over every point; twenty times he must have said, "Let's kick that around some more," and he ridiculed the idea of buying Sam's equipment. "Are you kidding?" he yelped. "That stuff is all held together with rubber bands."

Sam had been shaved and his strong, deep-cut face went as red as hot iron. He stared at his leg, fattened out with plaster and propped in front of the wheel chair on a raised shelf. "It don't matter," he said at last. "It saves us dickering over the price." But when Andy seemed to expect the drill figures as a matter of course, Sam said curtly, "You're buying uranium property, not my brains and work."

Nothing in his life had been as painful as this, and Vivie had taken it so hard that she had gone off in tears. Abrupt, speaking little, Sam finished the business as quickly as possible.

"Whewh!" Andy said, sliding the contract into his briefcase and patting the leather side. "It was a rough break for you, but this I needed. Was I ever on the hot seat! I was on the verge of a nervous breakdown, no kidding. Every day was like another ten pounds on my back, and New York was sending me these wires, putting the hot poker up my derriere. I could've made plenty of quickie deals but I hung in there, I knew you had the three with the apples."

Feeling numb, Sam rubbed his forehead with his calloused hand. From the hall came a confused bustle of visiting-hour noises, voices, the scuffing and tapping of feet. A woman with pale weak legs showing under her skirt went by the door, hugging a pot of flowers tied in a satin bow. A neighboring rancher, whose daughter had lost her baby, stuck his dried face into the room to say hello. Sam nodded.

"You're a wealthy man," Andy reminded him. "And with capital gains you can keep most of it, too." He made a circuit of the room, glanced through the window at the wide shadowy porch, and came turning back with his nibbling old-man's walk. After almost three weeks of agony he could finally go, but he couldn't seem to tear himself loose. "Don't begrudge it to me, Sam," he said. "Look at me. I'm only forty years old and look at my hair. Prematurely grey. I could be taken for a man of sixty, and inside I'm seventy if I'm a day. And do you know what I am, how far I've got? A twelve-thousand-a-year field man. Not exactly what you'd call a top exec, huh? But if your batch of claims comes through like it should, I'll be in Belden's shoes when he moves up to Vice President. Division Manager for Strategic Materials, that's not too much to ask out of life, is it? Faust got more."

With a mirthless noise he drew a metal flask from his pocket and unscrewed the cap. "Go ahead. It's the best."

"I'm not a drinking man."

"Neither am I except on days when I'm a hero." He pulled a chair behind the open door and sat down, stretching his legs out with a sigh. "With your permission I'll just relax and spread my toes for a minute. It's the last straw, lifting the festive cup in your room, I know, but I'm feeling kind of lonely. How about that? I go for a touchdown and I feel worse instead of good. The price I paid emotionally, you wouldn't believe it." He raised the flask, glimmering weakly in the half light like his tinsel hair. "Well, a toast! To Andy Lytton, the peanut butter king."

Though Sam wasn't listening the disillusioned words struck up vibrations inside him. It was a sonofagun to lose out after a fine start like that. He had figured strong on mining those claims himself, very strong. And he didn't like to fail at anything; that was what hurt the most. "I wouldn't have sold if I wasn't going to be off my pins for so long," he said, almost to himself. "Even if I could get around enough to hire a crew on my own and teach them the tricks . . . But what the heck, I never was much good at delegating authority anyhow. It's not in my nature."

His mind was a scramble of broken plans, ideas, dreams. He felt lost. And Andy was no help at all, sprawled behind the door, holding a crazy sad little party of his own. The first mouthful of whiskey had made him drunk; his face had thickened and lost its fine lines; his voice was mushy. "Let the cup of cheer go round," he muttered. "Thou has been overcome, O God of Israel, and Thy temples are overthrown. Understand, I don't deny I needed the score personally. Not at all. You see, I'm a forty-year-old man with a mother—otherwise known as the Sow That Eats Its Young. Speaking of my mother, you don't happen to know of any antiques, do you? She collects antiques, rooms and rooms full of 'em, everywhere you look more antiques. You should see her. Sam, no kidding, you should cast your eyes on her. She's like the fox that ate that Greek kid's insides out. You know? The poor kid, think of him. Never complained, not one single word, and where were his insides? Gone. Eaten up completely."

In just minutes he had dissolved into a mumbling wreck. Exasperated, Sam told him, "The party's over."

"Sure, sure. Whatever you say." Obediently he drifted to his feet and came over to shake hands. "No hard feelings, I hope. I was ordered to bring in your head and so naturally . . . that's business . . . As J. W. Hatfield, Vice Admiral, U.S. Naval Reserve, has said so brilliantly, and I quote. Quote: 'Don't take any prisoners.' Pithy, that's what that one is. Pithy." His dull-silver head veering dangerously, he pulled himself up to attention and saluted the porch and the mountains. "Mission accomplished. All present and accounted for, sir." Steering the flask into his pocket he paused to say, "You know where you made your big mistake? You became necessary to corporate fulfillment. And that you must not do. Never. It's a rule. But I'll say this, you really threw me for some losses. Man! I was fourth down and thirty yards to go. But in the immortal words of J. W. Hatfield, 'The successful man risks twenty yards to go for a touchdown and makes it.' That's me, Andy Lytton, All-American—okay, okay, I'm going."

Briefcase under his arm, he meandered toward the door, stopped and came back once more to apologize, breathing whiskey down at Sam. "I hope you'll overlook it, not many days like this. I'm finally on the way up at last—of course, quality will count in the long run. As

J. W. Hatfield has so pithily put it, 'The kind of man I want is like a fine watch.' Listen," he said, wavering closer. "Tick-tock, tick-tock. You hear that? Is that a twenty-one jewel movement or not?"

Lacerated almost beyond endurance, Sam watched him go out into the hall, still ticking unsteadily. His leg was hurting him and he felt more and more lost. He should have thrown Lytton out on his ear as soon as the papers were signed; the man turned everything into a bigger muddle than it was already, made it seem senseless. Savagely he gripped the worn, rubber-tired wheels of his chair. After only five days the inactivity was beginning to gall him, to itch and canker in him until he was half crazy, bursting with frustration; and he would be laid up for weeks, months. At the thought his balked energy pushed up violently, with stupefying pressure, mushrooming the chaos he was in.

In agony he wheeled himself out onto the porch and rolled up and down, up and down, his eyes burning under his ragged brows. The hospital was one of the long abandoned spas set on the cliffs overlooking the bubbly sulphur springs that had made the town a famous health resort fifty years ago. The late afternoon sun flamed on the great lion-paws of an eroded hill. Rock ledges, spurs, huge stone hulks broke off and tumbled down to the crumbling buildings scattered along the river. Spreading over an entire hill was the Army cemetery by the VA hospital, thousands and thousands of identical white crosses lined up like platoons still in formation. The mountains were dry and flinty. For the first time in his life he really looked at the mountains, standing desolate in infinities of light.

Without knowing it he had stopped wheeling himself back and forth. He was aching with the realization that there was nothing he could set his hand to, nothing to shoot at. He had always been an active man, going wide open summer and winter, and then, without warning, he'd been chopped down, left with nothing to do. The sense of disorder, of emptiness, was terrifying; his whole life suddenly seemed futile, and he found himself asking, what was there? What did all he had done mean? What did anything mean? Though he hadn't had the time for much church-going, he considered himself a religious man. But the questions would not be answered. They were still alive, sinister, crawling inside him like the ants that Andy had showed him. He could still see Andy smiling at him, his black sunglasses like holes in his face . . .

It was getting late. The last visitors had gone, and from a window at the end of the veranda came the smell of supper cooking and a rattle of dishes, a singing commercial on the radio. A nurse held open the door and wheeled in a senile old codger with a tottering face; it rolled to one side and he gave Sam a brainless, drooling smile.

He *had* to do something. In a week or so he would be discharged from the hospital, and then what? He would be worse than useless on the ranch even if he hadn't sold it to the boys. There was the tourist trap which he'd bought up in the Black Hills; but he wouldn't be able to do more than putter around while his leg healed. What could he do to plug up the murderous emptiness?

The sunset was red between the mountains and shadows were beginning to fill the ravines and draw in behind the hills, cooling and shaping them. The Greek-columned summerhouse down by the spring was small and pure against the dark water. Sam scraped his calloused hand against his jaw, groping. It was a great serious land in the gold and twilight, and, unaccountably, it gave him a feeling . . . as if something he'd forgotten was coming back, some kind of experience that he'd had . . . He could always go on a reading rampage, of course. Sometimes he'd gone through two or three hundred books at a stretch, anything and everything he could get his hands on. But a thousand books wouldn't be enough to fill the emptiness opening all around him now. He had to have something more . . . a feeling . . . the feeling he'd had when he talked with that archaeology fellow: Paul—what was his name?—Morris. That day when he'd gone out there about the steer and gotten interested in burial customs and the past, religion and so on, looking down at the pitiful bones in the pits.

That was where to start. That's what he would do, write and ask him what books to read about it. Yes, by all that was holy, that was the ticket.

XIV

"Tears," she announced, "have the same amount of salt the sea had a hundred million years ago."

Paul blinked and said, "Have you been crying?"

"Oh you," Lucy snapped. "Don't you get it? We carry the sea around inside us."

"Easy now, don't let education go to your head," he teased her, but he was full of tender delight at her charming airs. "Well, sometimes a person feels philosophical," she said pompously. She had been feeding the ducks in the town lake; now she fell silent, her skinny face dreaming at the smooth water that held the darkening yellow sky in its surface. Scorched clouds cooled in the west. The last boys with fishing rods went trooping away past the bandstand and the ducks came out of the water and walked over the grass making throaty noises.

"Speaking of tears," he said, "seven hundred million years ago the North Pole was in Arizona, and the whole world was under water. Three billion years ago the moon was ripped out of the earth and thrown into space, leaving a hole that's the bottom of the Pacific Ocean. It's a good thing we don't have much imagination; we're surrounded by infinity. Stars eight hundred thousand light years away—what does that mean? Nothing, that's what. The farther out the telescopes reach, the more abstract everything becomes. Imaginary. Fictitious. All those universes of mathematics, from quantum theory to space-time curvature and negative infinity. And inside us the same bottomless nothing opens up and we have Einstein telling us that matter itself is abstract —that you and I are fields of energy."

She didn't answer but what he'd said was beautiful in her face: not the thought itself so much as the intensity of it, the shining fervor of it, ecstatic and rich like desire. Her rosy mouth was parted a little and her slender neck was so young and unprotected . . .

"What can a poor little field of energy do in a spot like that?

Uranium!

I suppose the best way to begin is the way Pascal said: to think well. I don't mean you have to be a genius. If that were the case, Voltaire would have been an admirable man. Pascal himself was a first-class bastard most of his life—one of those boy wonders, as vain as the winner of a beauty contest because he was a hot mathematician and invented the first computer. It took illness and a religious experience to turn him around. After that, believe it or not, whenever he felt he was enjoying praise he pressed his elbows into a nailed belt he wore around his body."

"Ick! That's gruesome."

"So is his famous wager. Either there is a God or there isn't. If He doesn't exist, all you lose by being a good guy is fifty or sixty years of discomfort. And if He does exist, you win the eternal jackpot. Conclusion? Bet Christian, the price is right."

"You're very sarcastic, aren't you?" she said.

"No, no." His undernourished face was hard, fanatical, as he explained what he was after. Religion was a step in the right direction but you had to keep walking. It was a much more difficult world without the consoling idea of God, but life had to be confronted; the human predicament had to be faced without illusion. With the last lie swept away, with the last and most comforting hallucination gone, to outstare the lunatic infinities. To accept the fact that when we die we have never happened at all as far as we ourselves are concerned—to accept it and go on anyway, without despair, without even melancholy, and create into the void. Create beauty, create sanity and order, create a meaning in the face of universal nonsense and futility. And there was something else. The slow and almost invisible improvement of life as a whole comes not just from the Platos and the Montaignes, whose work shines down the centuries; it comes from all of us—for example, the nameless peasants who died in 1381 and 1524 fighting for personal liberty, hundreds of years before there was a chance.

But still there is death. Well, then, there is death and extinction. Death absolves us all, and from it comes the beautiful kinship of the dying, and sacrifice, and love.

It was dark and his words seemed to merge with her and with the darkness, the bales of hay gleaming like chunks of gold in the pens of the auction barn and the solitary jackpine beside it on the hill, lifting its tattered branches into the burning rubble of stars.

"Somebody must've hurt you very much to make you so sad," she said naively.

He gave one jagged laugh, then checked himself. Once again he'd been expecting too much of her, dazzled by the clear bubbles of intelligence that streamed up, astonishing and lovely, from the gum-chewing blankness of adolescence. "That's where I got this squint," he said. "Looking at the world through a hole in the dike."

"Seriously. How come you aren't married? Don't you have any girls?"

"Not pretty ones. They have to be over forty, preferably with a moustache and a limp." Grinning, he kept slipping away from her questions, and with an intoxicating little kick at him she pouted, "You won't ever answer me anything." Her hair was like sunshine in the net of tree shadows. Springing to her knees, her hands on her hips, she pushed her face toward him and said threateningly, "You might as well come clean, buddy. We know you're the Kissing Bandit."

They laughed together, but he could feel her earnestness and he shrank at the necessity of talking about himself. "Okay, okay," he said ruefully. "Well, here goes. The Short and Simple Annals of the Rich, Chapter One. How I got to be a grave-digger. The truth is, Miss Ophelia, I've always been a digger. When I was three years old, my father found me trying to dig up the devil in the back yard. Later on I discovered you don't have to dig for him. Am I boring you? I hope? I warn you, like all great works of art, I'm sort of dull in places. Honest." Sweating with reluctance, he went on, "Chapter Ten. Courtship and so forth. The post-debutantes in Chicago drew straws for me, and I found myself engaged to a fine, wholesome girl of excellent family. Only the reception was to be at the Saddle and Cycle Club, and I always fall off horses. So what could I do? I called it off." Grabbing his wiry hair, he said, "I can't do it. It's indecent exposure, for God's sake."

"Don't bother," she said, looking straight ahead.

It was crazy but all at once he wanted to tell her, painful as it was, he had to tell her if it meant tearing the words out of himself. "You see," he said. ". . . have you any brandy? You see, it was all part of the system. It was taken for granted I would go into my father's business, to wit, eight or ten supermarkets, and well—you know, food makes me nervous. No kidding, it does. All my taste buds fell off when I was ten . . . I hate to eat, even. All right, that isn't it. I guess I don't have any will-to-power in merchandising canned goods. And that's the truth—partly. You see, I kept thinking of those poor bastards in their one-man grocery stores, bleeding to death because there was a Red Giant supermarket across the street. Christ, it's embarrassing to say stuff like this."

The worst was behind him, though. Of course the anguish of the past, of his parents' disappointment, was still fierce inside him, and yet there was a sweetness, too, in telling her about it. Over their heads the tree was a deep well of green. Waves slipped loose from the bank, tipping and falling into each other, and the ducks boated in pairs on the pale water, towing wakes of black and silver behind them. "This lovely posture I have," he said. "Every military school I went to— hup, two, straighten up Morris—made my back a little bit rounder."

The way she smiled, listening with head laid to one side and her fingers stroking absently at the branch of hair on her neck, pulsed inside him like magic. She laid her thin, calloused hand on his.

He stiffened and a rush of awareness went through him, a flaming sense of her soft exposed face, her stringy throat, the peeping breasts under her cotton blouse.

As gently, as quietly as possible he took her hand away—and saw the pain bite deep into her like broken glass. "Are you toying with my affections?" he tried to joke. She sat without moving, her face a stricken blur in the shadows. A simple rejection, the shame of it, would have been bad enough, but he knew that in her mind he had rebuffed her because of what had happened with the boys in the rodeo grounds, because he was disgusted, because he thought she was "dirty." She seemed to be more and more haunted by it, and he couldn't do a thing; he couldn't even tell her that he understood why she had gone with them. She still hadn't moved. As long as he looked at it from his own standpoint it was simple: she was practically a child and anything except a teacher-student relationship was ridiculous and unthinkable. But as soon as he considered her too, it became fantastically muddled. He wasn't even sure why she had put her hand on his, whether she'd been hoping to see that he wasn't repulsed, or whether she'd merely been feeling sympathetic about his early sorrows, or what. He wished he hadn't just lifted her hand away . . .

"The dig is closing up for the year in a couple of weeks," he said awkwardly. "I'll be leaving and I hope—I want you to promise me you'll go back to high school."

"I'm turned sixteen," she said sullenly, and he raged at himself for bringing up the subject at a time like this. What the hell was the matter with him? She was ready to balk at anything, and if she did stay out of school, she would inevitably drift back into her old promiscuous, wandering life. "Be reasonable," he said. "You're very intelligent, for God's sake. Don't throw it away." She didn't answer. And then, as if the chance of persuading her weren't small enough already, he realized it was time to rout the boys out of the tavern.

"Excuse me for a minute," he stammered. "Don't go away, please. I'll be right back." He hurried off without telling her where he was going. Unfortunately, she knew anyway. The joy boys, damn them, though they were still too frightened to prospect or even to dig discovery holes on their claims, had recovered enough confidence to come into town almost every night for beer and a spot of fraternity song. Without ever saying a word about it, Lucy and he kept out of their way, but the boys were like snickering ghosts, inescapable, sly, tainting everything. They were poisoning her mind with despair right now while he went to send them home.

"The group therapy is over," he told them harshly in the tavern.

"Aw, but sir. It's Saturday night."

He stared them outside into the jeep and said, "Teddy, you be the half-breed guide and lead the expedition back to camp."

As soon as the tail lights swerved out of sight down the highway, he ran back to the park, dead certain that she would be gone. Then he heard the shatter of water, the whack of beating wings, and saw her moodily feeding the last of the bread to the ducks. Black heads and necks snaked from the shimmering surface. "You've simply got to go back," he insisted. "I realize most of the work will bore you, but it's the discipline and stability of going. Don't you see?"

Cold, inaccessible, she flipped pieces of bread and watched the black wet struggling in the water. "Don't make any plans," she said.

"My God, I know you're upset—look, I'm sorry if I hurt your feelings, but you have to understand, I'm full of inhibitions. Hell, I used to take showers in my underwear at school." In spite of the distance in her face, he forced a grin and said, "Come on, give me another chance. I'll hold hands with you, I'll sing Act Three of *Tristan and Isolde* if you want."

"Oh kiss my elbow," she said. "You really think my heart is broken, don't you? For a college professor, you are stupid, Crumley. *Stu*-pid."

"Fine, great! If that's not the reason, then what is?" He pulled her around and put his hands on her thin shoulders. "There isn't any reason to drop out. You don't even have to live at home. Mrs. Harbaugh says you can stay at the hotel and go."

Twisting herself out of his hands, she said, "If you're too dopey to figure it out, *I'm* not going to tell you." She turned and walked toward the bandstand, the laces whipping on her ragged tennis shoes, and he went after her, arguing, demanding. She closed her eyes and sighed with exasperation, then put her hands over her ears. "Stop, stop, STOP! If you don't shut up, I'll scream my eyeballs out! How do you think those snotty girls act? Their snotty mothers have told them not to breathe the same air, and anyhow they're all scared pea-green I'll take their goopey boyfriends away. Which I could do if I didn't want to upchuck at the sight of them. Creeps! Each and every one of them think they're going to get into my frilly pink panties. They come up to me and give me this pimply *charm* with about eight whiskers on their face."

There was a stiff pain in his throat. Headlights splintered on top of the rise, glared, and dipped down into the town, coming past the two old cannon aimed at the dark-lying hills. A freight train was switching in the yards.

"Now," she said, "are you going to drive me to Mother's or am I going to walk?"

"Sure, sure," he said, all his plans for her in ruins, but in the stationwagon he said grimly, "I didn't realize what it meant but—I know it's too much to ask, but you've got to go anyhow. There's no other way."

"Shit."

They drove to the house in desolate silence. The curfew siren wailed. "I'll see you tomorrow at noon," he said, looking at her anxiously.

Without bothering to answer, she went inside. There was nobody home and she knew that Cecil and her mother had been fighting again because the kitchen was a shambles: a half-gallon can of syrup was overturned in a sticky brown puddle, dinner plates were smashed, and the chubby plaster wishing-well lay on its side by the stove. Indifferently, she wandered into the living room and flopped down at the piano. "April Fool," she cried gaily, and answered in a deep voice, "But my child, it's August fifteenth." "I know," she said, "but I have leukemia so I'm having April eight months early. Ha-ha-ha." She pecked at the keyboard, idly at first, walking her fingers up and down at random; then she pretended to play and thrust her hands into the blind keys, losing herself in a wilderness of incoherent chords, jangles, lurching runs and falling crashes down three scales. Passionately, tragically, she plunged her hands into the keys. Now she was a brilliant young concert pianist dying of an incurable disease, though no one in the vast hall knew it except the impressario. She was giving her last concert, and, while an audience of thousands sat enthralled, her wasted fingers clanged out her sorrow and her defiance. She finished and let her head sink, her hands drop to her sides. Tumultuous applause thundered in the silent house. For her encore, playing the despair within her that nobody knew about or could help, she touched the keys softly, tenderly, making sounds as pure, as tiny and delicate as heart-beats, and everyone in the huge audience was spellbound at her marvelous performance . . .

Her mother's footsteps clattered on the porch, and the screen door was flung open. "Why didn't you come when I called?" she whined. "I been all over town looking for you." When Lucy didn't answer she said, "Did you see the kitchen?"

"Yes, Mother."

"It's the complete end this time, I told him to get his tail out of here," she announced, her eyes starting to dribble. "Look at me, I'm shaking like I have the chills. I'm so upset I don't hardly know my name any more." Breathing in sobs, she went out into the kitchen to fix a cup of coffee to settle her nerves, talking all the time. "Just look at this mess. Oh, I'm so tired. The minute he came home he got onto me, and nothing I could do was right. I keep a nice house for him; I cook his meals and do my level best . . ."

Lucy sighed, plunking at the piano. Her mother always had the whimpers after a racket with Cecil, and it made her so sick; it was always the same old putrid thing. Cecil took one of his fits, and her mother yapped at him and threw stuff in his general direction till he popped her one where it wouldn't show in public. It was all too putrid.

"He's got no call to hit me with his fist," her mother wailed, coming back with the cup of coffee. While she was out of the room, Lucy noted drearily, she had rumpled up her hair to make herself look more pathetic. "He's rotten mean and always has been, and I'm not going to dirty myself with him any more."

This, too, had been said so often that Lucy didn't feel the tiniest flicker of hope. She gazed down at the dark reflection of her fingers, melting in the blank whiteness of the keys, and the voice of her mother scratched at her, frantic with the same old terror: "I mean it! My nerves can't stand it, we're total strangers from now on. Look at me, can't you? You could at least stop monkeying with that piano."

Lucy bashed her hands at the keys and swung around, dangerous. "I have to do *something*, Mother. It just so happens I'm not in the mood for this old poop tonight. It's totally putrid."

Her mother started to bawl, of course. With growing desperation Lucy looked at the bunchy curls shaking on the bowed head, the sweat beading the coarse hair in her armpits and the violet flush of broken veins in her legs. "This time it's different," she blubbered. "Somebody at the store told him he wasn't going to be elected to the board of deacons at the church, and you know how hard he's worked. It means everything to him. He was practically out of his mind, I should have realized it instead of being so mean." She raised her smeary face and said, "He's over at Mr. Bailey's right this minute, trying to find out for sure. I seen the car in front of his house."

"I thought you were out looking for me," Lucy said cynically.

"I was! A lot of the time. It's the end, I just know it. If he don't get on the board, he'll leave me *and* the town. His heart is so set on it."

"Goody. Tell him bon voyage from me."

"Sure, that's right, you selfish thing!" her mother squalled. "It's fine with you if we live from hand to mouth in furnished rooms while I work myself to death waiting tables. It don't affect *you* one particle. Well, you'll find out yourself someday, a woman can't live like that. A woman's got to have a home and a husband to give her life a meaning. It's her birthright."

Lucy felt the old life close tight around her, smothering. "Mother," she said in despair. "We've been through all this forty-three thousand times."

"This time is different. If he don't get on the board he won't even come back for his things. I know it."

Scornfully Lucy said, "You think he'll go and leave all these beautiful pictures of himself behind? The entire holy shrine? Not old Cecil."

"It's all right for you to laugh, but a woman can tell these things." She sniffled twice, clutched at her scraggy neck, and then brought it out, the same miserable old request. "Honey? I'm so deathly ascared. Won't you go and bring him back? I can't live without him."

Lucy made a disgusted blurt with her mouth. "You can get better than him with three boxtops and a quarter."

"That's a dirty mean way to talk," her mother shrilled. "I happen to love him with all my heart. And we could make a go of it, him and I, if it wasn't for you. Your wildness is the bane of his existence. It's constantly on his mind." Lucy felt it coming, and the sweat pricked through on her upper lip. She knew her mother believed only what was pleasant and ignored everything else; she had seen her blandly refuse to admit what had happened between her own daughter and Cecil, and yet it came as a fresh hurt every time. "Why can't you and him be friends?" her mother whined. "It ain't as though he wasn't good to you. Look at the coat he gave you—and what did you do with it?" Lucy slumped her elbows down on the keys, and instantly her mother went back to supplication, begging her to go after him, to make it up with him, promise him anything, promise him to live at home and keep her word this time, at least till he got on the board.

"Couldn't I just take poison instead?" Lucy sighed, but the old weakness stirred automatically inside her, the old habit of love. It was her responsibility to make this childish, fretting, troublesome creature happy. Grownups were so disillusioning, anyway. You expected them to be, well, better than you were, smarter and wiser and everything, and they were just older. "All right, all right, for yip's sake. Just do me one favor, will you? Don't say God bless you, honey."

She wriggled away from the sweaty arms.

"I'll clean the house while you're gone, honey," her mother babbled. "Oh, I look so awful—I wish you'd wear a dress *once* in a while. At least comb your hair."

Hunching down with her hands in her pockets, she scuffed outside. It was too putrid to come back to this, the same old scene, and it would happen again and again; it would go on for ever and ever and ever. Paul had been very shocked, but she hadn't thought about going to high school, either. It had all been like a daydream, and then pop! went the something or other and Mother was saying, "make it up with him, honey" . . . and she would never get to go to college or talk to Paul again or anything . . . If there was a God he was like Alfie, the whiskery old idiot who had lived down the street in Salt Lake, sitting on the front steps and blowing soap bubbles, puffing them out of the wire loop in streams, up in the air, so pretty and light and

transparent, floating like tiny rainbows in the sunshine, floating away.
She waited in the car outside Mr. Bailey's house.
"Oh, so you decided to toss me a crumb, huh?" Cecil said when he saw her. He climbed into the car, splattering her with the same old worn-out profanity. "That sonofabitching Bailey," he said then. "Would he tell me a thing? I sat there for two hours and didn't find out nothing, and he's the one that decides, too. I'm up shit creek without a paddle and who put me there? You did. You hotass little bitch! You! If I don't get on the board it'll be your doing," he ranted.
Bored, she held out her hand for the keys. It was the same old nothing, a chewing out which she endured stonily, in contemptuous silence, and then a few vague promises. It was like a sacred ritual or something. She always drove the car, for example, because he was having too big a seizure to watch the road. In a detached way she watched his skinny lips as he gibbered at her, swiping at his sweat-oiled bald head with a handkerchief.
"Mr. Bailey is going to wonder if we don't get going," she said.
Hastily he handed over the keys, and she slammed the car forward. "Watch it, will you?" he said, and started in about her and Paul. "That's why I'm sucking the hind tit, you and that professor fellow. It ain't rough enough, oh no, you have to whore around with an outsider, a man that sticks out like a sore thumb." The lost, hopeless feeling was so bad she was afraid Cecil would notice, and clenching herself into one hard thing, she concentrated on the gravel street sliding under, the headlights sweeping as she turned and bursting over the thin naked trunk of a tree, over a scarred lawn, a child's swing hanging crooked. And then, although she was straining not to listen, she was aware of something different in the usual threats and abuse, a sort of jagged edge in the "forever trying to make some headway" and "I'm wore down to the bone" and "you and your mother are gonna wind up in the fucking street where I found you." She realized that it wasn't the same tired old mad scene. Her mother, for once in her life, had been right! The singing grocer was actually on the verge! If he wasn't elected to the board of deacons, he would really and truly chuck it all, job (complete with apron and five-year pin), town, and Mother. He would just drift out like he'd drifted in and take his marvelous voice to Montana or somewhere. Well, well, said the bullfrog.
"I swear to God I don't know what to do any more," he said.
"Why don't you sing something?" she suggested. "Like 'Danny Boy' or 'The Alphabet Song.'"
The effect was quietly spectacular. She had never spoken back in these reconciliations or whatever they were, and he simply came to a stop for a second, blank, and then began his tirade all over again from the beginning. She parked the car in front of the house and, in

spite of her sadness, in the very center of it, listened with something like amusement.

"Fee-fi-fo-fum," she said in her deepest voice.

While he was blithering away, her mother came out on the porch and waved to them ever so gaily. Then she went back inside, giving them a chance to finish "arrangements."

"You little pissant," he hissed. "I'll tend to you."

"Well, look here." She peeked inside her blouse and smiled down at herself. "Hey, Cece, there's time. Let's do it now." His long face looked as if she had thrown boiling water into it, and with her sexiest little giggle, starting at her neck, she traced her finger down her body, down the shallow place that separated her small breasts, and down between her legs.

That really busted his balloon. Leaping out of the car, he made for the house. She stuck out her tongue at him and then, for good measure, screwed up her face and thumbed her nose. The guided tour of her points of interest had been for her own personal satisfaction, not to push him over the brink. As long as there was a chance of getting on the board he would never leave town, but she had a plan that would take care of that, a plan complete in every detail. Paul was gone anyway, all that was gone, and at least she would have the consolation of getting rid of Cecil. Savage with loathing, she remembered how she herself had accidentally caused the marriage in the first place. Her mother and Cecil were going together and one day when her mother was at the cafe, old Cecil had showed up and . . . she had let him. She didn't know why, she had just let him. It wasn't the first time with a man or anything, and not much of it had stuck in her mind, thank goodness, except his scared, greedy hands and the absolutely nutty thing he did afterward. He asked her to make him a cup of coffee, and he sat there complaining about his unfortunate life, in deadly fear she would tell on him. For about two hours that was all he did, moan. If she hadn't been feeling so ishy and disgusted with herself, she would have laughed in his stupid face. A week later, before she knew what was happening, he had gone off with her mother and come back married. Out of pure fright! But now, if her plan was successful, she could rectify the whole putrid mistake and get her mother back.

Wearing her most truly humble expression, she walked into the hysterical quarrel in the house. Cecil practically had Angora kittens right there when he saw her.

"I'm sorry," she said with her face down. "I'll come back home if you want."

In about ten minutes Cecil stopped hollering and her mother quieted down into weeping. "Can I use your hatbox to bring my stuff back?" Lucy asked her. "My suitcase won't hold everything." Twiddle-dee-dee, step one of her plan completed. Upstairs, though, she felt kind of crazy and sad. Putting down the hatbox and her panda, she sprayed herself with her mother's huge bottle of Shalimar until she smelled like the Garden of Allah. Then, standing in front of the mirror, she slung out one hip, tucked in her chin, and threw out her chest—creeps, no! She wadded a handkerchief in each cup of her brassiere and, loosening her hair and shaking it down over one eye, arched herself into another pose. "Darling, you are ravishing," she murmured. "You're irresistible—as long as you don't catch cold and need a hankie." Giggling, she picked up her velvety panda, which lay sprawled against the hatbox, ogling her with its glass button eyes. "Noodles! I'm ashamed of you," she lectured it severely. "I know the evil thoughts that are going through your mind. You're wicked, you're going to *hell!* You'll *burn!* Do you hear?"

She thumped down the stairs. Shrewdly she accepted a ride from Cecil and then, at the door to the hotel, when he said he'd wait for her, she told him, "Mrs. Harbaugh is asleep, and I can't just *disappear* without telling her. I'll come home tomorrow after I finish the rooms. Promise."

Cecil didn't like it one bit, but she held up the panda and cooed, "Say bye-bye to the nice man," and strolled inside to pack. Step two completed.

At ten-thirty the next morning, Mrs. Harbaugh went off to Sunday service, and at exactly five minutes to twelve, lugging the hatbox and her suitcase and wearing her best white cotton piqué dress, her terribly innocent straw hat with the blue ribbon and her white gloves, she struggled upstairs from her room in the basement and went outside to wait for Paul. One of the men loafing in the chairs in the shade said, "You missed the train, honey. Where you going?" She stared off at the sun-dazed, empty street and said, "I'm running away to Nome, Alaska."

Heat swelled into the shade. By five minutes after twelve she was fidgeting, picking at her dress, tensing whenever a speck trickled out of the curve in the highway. Every single time it was just an old car creeping past the pink nightmare of a cafe Mr. Stephens had painted, and creeping past her with light flaking off the chrome and the windshield. The men kept pestering her with good-natured but absolutely brainless remarks. Then two grade school girls bounced by in crisp Sunday dresses, hats and patent leather purses flying, and her heart pinched with fright: was the service over already? Maybe they were from the Baptist church. Paul had to show up now, now this very minute. The voices of the men lapped around her, the long bare street was drowned with light. And then the stationwagon grew out of the curve, and there was Paul, in his dear old suit and his green sunglasses, braking the car to a stop in a blast of dust. She piled in with the bags.

"Hurry up. Turn right at the next corner and hurry!"

"Hey, what's the deal?" he said, doing nothing at all. "You running away to join the gypsies?"

"Charley and me are going to visit Mr. Butler at the VA hospital, if you'll be so kind. Now will you start?"

"Charley and *I*," he corrected her. "Okay. But why the bags?"

She rolled up her eyes in exasperation. "I'm taking my lunch," she said. "Will you *kindly* start the car? We have to pick him up *now*."

As the men in front of the hotel craned to see better, Paul removed his sunglasses and laid his elbow on the steering wheel. "All right, let's have it," he said. "What kind of gunpowder plot are you cooking up?"

"It's no plot! Charley misses him, and I thought you could drive him to Hot Springs. Oh you!"

Beak-faced, his eyes frowning, he said, "Couldn't you make up a better lie than that? Like you're going off to look for the Northwest Passage or something? Let's all be rational; I understand how you feel..."

"For yip's sake, move! Start the car! We'll talk it over on the way!"

Paul refused, and refused again. Pressing her cheeks in her hands, she cried, "You *have* to!" Neither of them saw the jeep with two of the boys in it until there was a shout and the rasp of skidding tires. The grimy red jeep was backing up in the center of the highway, swerving through a scurry of dust from the wheels, and Teddy was on his feet, bearded and hairy-legged, hooting, "I spy!" Paul and Lucy sat there. Stan, at the wheel, was cackling, "Oho! Getting a bit of the goodie yourself?" The dread of weeks and weeks had fallen upon them without warning, and Paul gaped helplessly at the khaki figures capering in the white horror of light, doubling over with exaggerated glee and pelting them with jeers: "Nasty doctor!" Sliding one index finger down the other, Teddy chanted, "Shame, shame, double shame." The door of the stationwagon slammed and Lucy, stumbling with the bags, ran back into the hotel.

The blood rose hot into Paul's eyes and he started for them, but flapping satirical goodbyes at him they sprinted off in the jeep. He drove back to the camp, reeling. What kind of fantastic scheme had she dreamed up? She was a devious little creature and it had been nothing as simple as running away, of that he was certain. Stan and Teddy must have suddenly decided to drive in for something—damn them. He and Lucy had been living with their sniggering invisible presence for so long that it all seemed like another morbid fantasy, something he'd imagined out of worry, and it took an effort to realize how bad things were, and not just for her.

The stationwagon jolted to the rim of the heat-filled swale where the abandoned ranch buildings were scattered like bones slowly disintegrating in the acid light. He drew up in front of the grey shell that had been a house, and a few minutes later heard the jeep crunch down the slope, footsteps scuff, the door to the sheep barn where the boys bunked whack open and shut. Bush was cheerfully doing his laundry in the other room. The radio was blatting the news: in the election campaign Adlai Stevenson, who was losing ground steadily, had made a speech urging patience and the spirit of negotiation with Russia, and meanwhile, in Los Angeles, a cheering crowd had heard him blasted as an egghead with Communist sympathies. Overseas, a plane with twenty-four persons aboard was overdue at Cairo and presumed to be down . . . Lying on the clammy bed he did his best to read but the air was suffocating and the corrugated iron roof sent down masses of heat that pushed upon him, soaked into him. His head felt swollen, and everything was slow and indistinct, his sense of time was dissolving; his thoughts seemed to melt and blob together. Then he heard a hsst! and opened his eyes: one of the boys, Harry, was standing at the empty, glassless window. His sunburned nose was mottled pink and red. His bulky shoulders were glistening. As Paul stared he drew his face up on one side in a knowing wink, then popped out of sight.

Paul was shaken. The brief second had had the terrific vividness of an hallucination but he knew that it had been real enough, and that they would be back.

There was nothing he could do, either. He would get the full treatment; they were going to tie him to the anthill, and what was left of the expedition would be eaten up with him. Explanations were completely useless; the appearance was every bit as fatal as the reality. His moral effectiveness was gone, shot to hell, and his authority with it. The boys were loose again. And they wanted blood too, his type-O blood, for having been so badly frightened. They were in no position themselves to say anything to Bush; however, there were other ways, and they had plenty of Yankee know-how.

Sst! Now Teddy was at the sun-blinded window, grinning at him like a bearded young satyr. He put a finger to his lips, lifted a rolled-up paper and spilled it open: it was a full-color picture of a girl with naked breasts. Nodding like a fellow conspirator, he disappeared.

And all the while Bush was dunking underwear in a pan of suds and humming along with the radio. Paul turned on his record player and concentrated on the angular notes beginning to assemble around him, to form an ascetic logic like the purest mathematical equation. It was no use. Lucy had wrecked everything, the little idiot! Even as he was raked with anger the deep pull of concern about her grew stronger, dragging at him. Whatever her silly plot had been, it was swept away and she was caught like he was by that searing minute in the station wagon. It must be impossible for her, already tortured by what she had done with the boys, then rebuffed by him last night and in despair about high school. The undertow of concern kept growing, became a torrent, a swelling river of anxiety.

He scarcely noticed Jockstrap at the window, goosing the air, tickling it, stroking it obscenely. His face poking out even farther from his round back, he went through Bush's room without a word of explanation and raced the stationwagon up out of the ranch yard, grinding and slewing in the ruts. He had forgotten his sunglasses and he narrowed his eyes in the overpowering light. Off in the lurching distance, in the hills as dead and scorched as the moon, the cloud shadows were small lakes of coolness drying away. It seemed incredible now that he could have left her and returned to the camp. As soon as he turned onto the highway, a red-and-white bull which had broken out of the pasture went lunking along in the center of his lane, its cantaloupe-sized testicles dangling, and he had to swerve wildly to get around it. At the top of every rise was another long discouraging stretch of empty road, curving away through the baked dirt and greasewood. The light streamed and streamed into his eyes. In a field close to the river a haystack bulged up like a shaggy head pushing out of the ground.

And Lucy was nowhere in town—not in the park, not in the drugstore or the muggy little restaurants. His worry about her was like physical pain. Everywhere there were strangers, drawn by the news of Sam Bolton's sensational ore shipment; they were very different from the first influx of grubby hill-walkers with their Geiger counters. These were men in expensive business suits, men smoking cigars, mining engineers and speculators buying leases and forming combines. His eyes felt as if they were being crushed with light. Dazed, his breath staggering, he went into the hotel lobby. Three well-fed men were talking excitedly about some mining corporation. Mrs. Harbaugh was not at the desk, nor in her room behind it, and all he could think of was to ask Wally if he knew where Lucy was. But Wally and Bert were prospecting seven days a week now, and just as he feared there was no answer when he knocked.

The commode gurgled in the open toilet across from the linen closet. Next to him was the door to the basement, and remembering that her room was down there, he opened the door and pounded down the steep wooden steps. There were piles of soiled sheets, womb-like tubs and water dimpling in a tank, old-fashioned washing machines with roller wringers, a mangle open like a mouth in the wet shadows. Opposite the furnace was a doorway spilling cornmeal-yellow light.

His heart swamped and worked heavily as he saw her lying on a discarded bed, under a basement window milky with sun-filled dust. Her face was small and dull. She didn't look at him when he asked what sort of plot she'd been hatching up.

"Hey, don't let it get you," he said. "Teddy and Stan don't matter. The hell with them, they just wanted a small public execution because I'd scared them. It wasn't you they were after." Her face was muffled, lifeless. He sat down on the edge of the bed, his voice groping, "There's something else we have to get straight. What happened on the rodeo grounds, that doesn't matter, either. I mean, I know why you did it. It was because you hated all that . . . and how you were living. Remember when you told me how you got sad and did nutty things, and you didn't know why? Well, that was the reason."

All she did was turn her face away. He could feel the misery in her stiff clenched body and he couldn't get through to her, make her see that it didn't matter. "You have to believe me," he said. "When I didn't hold your hand last night, it wasn't that at all. You have to believe me. It doesn't make any difference!" But it did make a difference; it made so much difference that there was nothing else. He had to make it all right, he had to prove it was all right. Almost roughly, he pulled her face around, and her eyes were wide open, dumbly looking at him, and it was as if he were sinking into her eyes . . .

"I'm sorry, I'm sorry," he kept saying. They were lying in deep yellow light, and her dress was squashed up under her arms. Shakily he pulled it back down over her legs. "Christ, I didn't mean for this to happen."

She covered his mouth with her hand, but he jerked away and sat up with his head sagging. "What are we going to do? What are we going to do?"

"I can let you out the back door," she said. "Mrs. Harbaugh never comes down here."

"No, no, that's not what I mean." Over their heads the wooden floor creaked with tromping steps. Rubbing his face with both hands, he said aimlessly, "What were you after this noon?"

He didn't care any more what she had been scheming. In a stupor of remorse he heard her say that she had been trying to get rid of Cecil. They were to have parked by the church, waiting for Charley, just as service let out, and there she'd have been with her bags and everything, and after a scandal like that Cecil would never in the world have been elected to the board of deacons. Then he would have gone away. "I thought I might as well have that at least," she said. "I didn't have nothing else."

It was all a blur, and then he heard her say in a small voice, "I'll go back to school for you."

He raised his head and saw that she meant it. Overwhelmed, he reached out and touched her face. It was soft and open in the light like spring sunshine. He was confused, remorse aching in sweet avalanches of tenderness and gratitude. There was hope for her again—out of this! "I don't know," he mumbled, but then, thin and large-eyed, she crept into his arms and this time the slow grave act of love was like absolution, forgiveness.

XV

All the next morning at the dig they continued to give Paul the slow death. Brown grass ran off to the horizon under a flaming sky. The hats of the boys rode up and down as they crouched in the graves, measuring, taking notes, peeling the flesh of dirt from the tangled bones—and, while Bush sat over his reports in the stationwagon, needling Paul with fiendish skill.

"This is your roving reporter," Stan said, standing up in his pit with a flow of burnished muscles. "What, in your opinion, is our number-one national menace?"

Teddy stroked his brushy whiskers. "No question about it, young man. Frigidity."

Gurgles and blurts of laughter sailed out of the graves. Stan said, "I see, sir. And what is the solution to this vexing problem?"

"Young fellow, we all have to pitch in," he said in a crusted, old fogey's voice. "The people will have to be educated, hit them with slogans: SEX *CAN* BE FUN!" He sliced a quick glance at Morris who was bent over in a pit, his gaunt face blotted a dull red. "START NOW! IF YOU'RE BIG ENOUGH, YOU'RE OLD ENOUGH, JUST LIKE POTATOES."

"Thank you, sir."

Teddy smirked and doffed his hat to the horsey laughs coming out of the pits. He was as keen as mustard today, if he did say so himself. Dr. Fuddy H. Duddy looked up in the stationwagon, frowning mildly, and they hustled back to work, their roasted backs buttery with sweat, strips of muscle flexing as they scraped and picked with a great show of zeal. Meadowlarks flared away like big locusts out of the grass. Nighthawks perched on fenceposts, on shovels and ridges of dirt, and a hot wind gradually covered the half-naked boys with a fur of dust. Whenever a cloud slid over the sun for a minute, they sprang to their feet and bowing down to the ground, stretched out their arms in thanksgiving. "The sun god is angry and scorches the earth," Teddy said. "Has anyone here done something naughty?"

He looked past the boys to Morris, inquiring.

And the once-great man took that, too, his head lowered, reflected light from his grapefruit knife slipping across his chest as he cut at the dirt. Once again, Teddy felt a prick of disappointment in his swaggering triumph, but his loyal followers were waiting expectantly. Thumbs in his pockets, he sauntered with a superb air to the five-gallon can of water, swallowed a few mouthfuls, and on the way back stopped beside Harry, who was sitting crosslegged in his pit and tossing bits of dirt with his spatula.

"You better come to the station with me," Teddy said, crisp and official. "We want to ask you some questions."

Heads and shoulders popped up, and Harry, his eyes blown out in simulated fright, said in a faltering voice, "Me? What for?"

"Never you mind. And don't try to bribe me. You know my philosophy: an eye for an eye. Tit"—and he let down one eyelid significantly—"for tat."

"It's a case of mistaken identity, officer! I have my faults, but I never—why I'm the best friend a girl ever had!"

Sniggers and leering voices flew out of the pits: "Sex maniac!"

"Babette, you tell on him!"

"Yeah, tell what happened under the railroad bridge . . ."

Thump! A shovel with a tip as sharp as a butcher's cleaver flashed through the powdery light and plunged into the hump of dirt two feet from Harry's head. The boys froze. The blood emptied from Harry's blistering pink face. While they stared Mr. Morris came stooping over the piles of loose soil, lean, humped, his lips pulled back viciously from his grey teeth, and while they continued to stare, he yanked up his shovel and went back to his pit. Bush, of course, hadn't noticed a thing. Jovial, sunscorched, bustling, he climbed out of the car and said, "Who's ready for the camera?"

A silence fell over the young men toiling in the light and the hot whisks of wind. That shovel had been no warning; it had been hurled from twenty feet away blindly, murderously. Even more stunning than the near-miss was the fact that it was Morris who had tried to kill one of them—solitary, fiercely-disciplined, abstract, unphysical Mr. Morris. At noon they made sandwiches on the tailgate of the stationwagon and ate them stiffly, without any of the ordinary wisecracking and horseplay; then Morris trudged off to dig the village by the river and Bush, looking perplexed, drove away to get the mail.

"Bro-ther," they all burst out together, "He's gone mad dog!"

"That shovel came like an ax, pow!"

Still shaken by the close call, Harry kept saying, "Frig him." The air seemed to be on fire. Except for the pits and the heaped dirt there was only the endless dead pasture and a hawk sliding in the hot wind, banking, the white insignia showing on its sharp black wings. "We're whipped," Stan said gloomily. "When I think of all the claims and the juicy joy he did us out of."

"Like hell we're whipped, let's read him that goodie-goodie thing, Ted. You know, that Egyptian stuff about life being centered in the sex organs and all that about those sacred orgies. Those bunches of women roaming around with statues of Osiris with his dong worked by strings. That'll psych him right of his shoes."

"Take gas, will you?" Ted said. "You saw him throw that shovel, stupid. I might be able to bear it if he chops you in half, but he *could* miss and get me."

"I mean when he doesn't have a shovel close by, Ted."

He was hooted down. "Tool up that mammoth intellect, Jock."

"Hey, you guys hold him, and I'll engrave the Lord's Prayer on his itty-bitty skull."

They were all raw and savage from the long, sun-fevered months under Paul's relentless eye, and what they really wanted was October, homecoming, and the first fraternity hop; in the meantime Paul's head would do. "How about it, Theodore?" they chorused. "Come on, you're the brain."

"Stay loose," he said. "Daddy Warbucks is on the way." He pressed his temples with the tips of his fingers, while they made the humming and buzzing sounds of a mighty intellect in action, but actually he wasn't dreaming up a new piece of strategy. The truth was that he didn't want to hack up Mr. Morris any more. With a twist of sympathy, of regret for what he'd done, he looked across the simmering grassland at the tiny bent figure digging the village. Kook, screaming weenie, oddball—that's what they called him, but grudgingly, in a Sherlock Holmes and Dr. Moriarty sort of way, he had always admired Morris. He had a terrific I.Q., and some of the things he did were rare, absolutely rare, like saying he was left-handed because it was more poignant and celebrating weird feasts like Bonfire Day and the Gypsy Fair and the winter solstice. The man was a real ace, damn it, and personally he had enough of pounding lumps on him. But Stan and Harry and the others were crowded round . . . the best he could do was make it as easy on him as possible.

"We better not push Morris too hard," he said to them. "He's armed and dangerous. What we need is something subtle. Something . . . Chinese."

"Stick bamboo shoots under his fingernails and set fire to them, huh?" Stan said. "Say, that's good." Everybody jumped around, whooping and clucking to each other, "Velly fine, velly tophole."

Holding up his hand for silence, Teddy said, "Gentlemen, I trust you all remember the look on Morris's face when Dr. Fuddy crushed that skull with his shovel? What does Morris hate more than anything? What does he hate more than Harry hates a virgin?"

"Potting out!" they shouted rapturously.

"Cor-rect. Therefore, this afternoon we will commence operation potout. We will not only dig like amateurs, we will set new lows for speed, dexterity and endurance. This won't be easy for you, but do try."

Their enthusiasm was heartwarming. When the lunch hour was over they dawdled and goofed around in the pits. "Oops!" Stan cried, "my hand slipped. I didn't mean to!" Teddy frowned down into the trench. "Dummy, you've choused right through the pelvis!" And gleeful shouts came from the other graves, "Welcome to the breakthrough club!" "Another first, Stan." They diddled away the whole afternoon and Morris never so much as glanced at them; the ruthless perfectionist didn't seem to care what they did. "Is this important?" Jock said, holding up a bead, and they chorused, "Throw it over your left shoulder, Jock." In the end it was Bush, not Morris, who complained, and they rode back to the sheep ranch feeling let down, disgruntled, outwitted somehow. Teddy's reputation as a mastermind had gone down thirty points, and he had to think fast. "Gentlemen," he said as they splashed and spluttered at the squeaking pump, "I have it! Let's dust off the old Geiger counter!"

"Hooray!" they yelled.

"Stout fellow, Ted."

"That'll put itch powder in his bridal outfit." Naked, hollering and rollicking, glitters of water flying from their burnt shoulders and backs, they wrestled and pummeled boisterously and cuffed at the sluices of water from the pump, bashing waterfall-blasts of spray at each other.

"You're a great inspiration to me," Stan said, his hair and face streaming.

"I realize that," Teddy said. "Don't forget to put this in your diary."

They made the announcement at supper and rushed off to prospect and finish digging discovery holes. Paul didn't even look up from scribbling an answer to Sam Bolton. At any other time the strangely pathetic letter saying that he was laid up with a broken leg and asking for the names of books that meant something would have touched Paul to the heart; now, however, it was as unreal as everything else, as having thrown the shovel, as the malevolent parody of digging the boys had put on, as the whole brutal day in the numbing light and dust. He was suspended in a sort of mindless hollow, and things happened as they did in a fever, very clear and emphatic and meaningless. The darkness inside the shack was riddled with light coming through the windows, between the boards and the sheets of metal roofing. He didn't so much remember her as continue to drink in the sweet freshness of life breathing out of her. There was a constant pressure in his throat and chest. He was restless. The need to see her, to be with her again, was a craving that raged inside him like thirst.

When he saw her waiting for him by the pond in the town park, he expected the tightness in his chest to ease. Instead, he went across the hot grass with his heart drowning and his breath stopped, hardly able to get any sense of what was happening.

She had tied her hair back. Her face, high and light on her long neck, was grave and looking into him.

"Say something intelligent, for God's sake," he said to her. "A magic word or two to get me out of this bearskin . . ." The words crumbled and lost their significance. Her eyes were soft and deep. He took her hand and they walked through the tunnel under the railroad tracks to the swinging bridge and out along the creek. It was green here, and there were wild roses in the weeds. Sunflowers caught at their legs. A small wind stroked her face. The trees flicked and chirped with birds, and they lay down on his coat, and her face and her thin girl's body were printed with quick leafshapes. Her eyes were uncovered into warm depths, and breathing hoarsely, he held her face like a flower in his yearning hands.

"I can't keep doing this," he choked, but she kissed him into silence. The guilt, and the feeling of chaos and unreality with it, were carried away in the reeling brightness and then they were lying together in the simple light and the faraway calling of children. He was released from the complexity, from the iron-hard years. He was free. He had never felt so alive and whole. There were soft little clouds over the pine mountain, and the sky floated the bits of whiteness, like drifts of orchard blossom, toward them.

She laid her face beside his. Her breath washed lightly against his cheek as she sighed. "I feel so nice."

He said something disconnected. Over them the tree let down butterfly bits of sunlight and shade.

"Will you be coming back next summer?" she asked, and there was a childlike and beautiful devotion in the way she volunteered to live at home as soon as he left. "But I can't move till then. I couldn't see you with Cecil on guard at all hours."

Monday, Tuesday, and Wednesday. For three days, until it all shattered and crashed into horror, he was lost in happiness, racing and simple. Her fresh moist face lifted toward his. Killdeers piping as they swooped over the creek and delicate bird tracks in the fleshy mud. The broken dam of stones that some boys had made, spurting sweet runs of water over the colored gravel. The breathing wind. The blows of his heart against his chest as he tremblingly uncovered the gawky bones of her hips and the little puffs of her pink-tipped breasts in the thick cream of light. The indescribable richness grew and grew, and warm sweetness pulsed in him after he left her and all the next day, sluicing with the pour of his quick blood, and when he met her again it surged up tumultuously, swelling inside him, bursting like innumerable buds into delirious white ecstasy.

Then on Wednesday night, inexplicably, the boys didn't come into town after they finished prospecting. When he drew up in front of the ranch house, he saw them through the gutted window, hulking around or slumped at the plank table in the acid light of the lamps. Something was wrong. Bush was pacing up and down and flogging his chubby arms.

"Teddy's missing!" he almost shrieked when Paul came in. "Completely disappeared! I'm just sick." The shock took Paul in the stomach. In the merciless flare of the gasoline pressure lamps everything—faces, underwear drying on a string, the reports and the bible on a chair— was singed black and white. Harry, his look dipping away, said that while he was shovelling a prospect hole, Ted had taken the Geiger and gone off to explore a little. An hour later he hadn't returned. It had been nearly dark by the time the boys assembled, and they had been unable to find any trace of him.

"We thought he might be down in the canyon," Stan said, and they began quarrelling.

"I told you, stupid, it's all staked."

"That's right, he wouldn't go there."

"Well, he wasn't on the plateau . . ."

Paul looked hard at them, suspecting another and more ingenious torture. But they were shaken and glum, frightened, and if there was a plot Teddy hadn't let them in on it. A foreboding, a presentiment of tragedy seeped into him.

"And I thought I could bank on you," Bush lashed at them. "You let me down. I'm at the end of my rope, absolutely at the end of my rope. All summer long, the things I've had to put up with—that cow you let fall into a pit. You've been derelict in your duty, every single one of you, and this is what comes of it. There's not a bit of rhyme or reason in something like this happening. It's a travesty!" Then his face bunched up, and he moaned, "Oh my God, oh my God. Why did this have to happen now? With only a week more to go." The boys shuffled and looked down. His rubbery shadow stretched and then collapsed on the peeling wall scribbled with names and patched with any kind of wallpaper, blue and red, faded rose patterns and lines of yellowing green plants. "It's the end," he said.

"I'd better contact the sheriff and get a search party organized," Paul said.

"What?" Bush bleated in horror. "Sheriff? What for? Nobody can do a thing as long as it's dark. If he doesn't turn up tonight, which

I certainly think he will—Teddy is a strong and intelligent boy—why then we'll start looking for him ourselves as soon as it's light."

"We need help, Bill. There are miles of canyons and mountains, and anything could have happened. He might have broken his leg . . ."

"Scare talk, that's all I ever hear from you, it's your specialty," he blustered. "The odds are still in our favor, Ted's probably spending the night at some ranch. In any case, we have more than enough people right here to conduct a search."

"Then I'll get the sheriff myself."

"Stanley, get the keys from the stationwagon and bring them to me. I'm in charge here, in case you've forgotten, Morris. Now that's enough of such nonsense, the subject is closed." Suddenly—and this unnerved Paul far more than the hysteria—he was full of authority and fatuous confidence. "What we need to do is not lose our heads. Let's see. Boys, you take the jeep and drive back there right now. Chances are he's hiking it home this very minute."

The boys piled out the door, anxious to do something, anything rather than simply wait for morning. With a calm but energetic air, Bush took out a map of part of Red Canyon, which they had drawn and marked with the location of their claims, and began to split it up into segments to be covered by various members of the party. It was preposterous, it was pure self-hallucination built on mortal terror of publicity which might damage his career.

Paul felt his control sliding away, tearing loose in waves of contempt.

"There," Bush said, looking with satisfaction at the pencilled map. "Do you know what this is?"

"Let me guess. Is it the first chapter of *Crime and Punishment?*"

"Now listen here, Morris," Bush said, his voice going up into squeaks. "I'm fed up with these smartalecky cracks. This is the absolute payoff. Here I am, doing my best as director of this expedition to get us off the horns of a very serious dilemma and you—but I'm not surprised," he said sorrowfully. "You have never once extended a hand of help to me the entire summer, and now you have your revenge, don't you? I was the one who was in favor of prospecting for uranium, so *I'm* to blame. I know how your mind works, your attitude is perfectly obvious. Let me boil in my own oil. That's it, isn't it?"

"I *am* trying to help. Give me the keys to the stationwagon, you damn fool."

"No! Absolutely not! I told you the subject was closed, and I meant exactly that."

"You'd better open it again, Bush, for your own sake as well as Teddy's. Because that rope you said you were at the end of is around your neck," Paul said cruelly. It wasn't a question of saving Teddy any more. He was flooded under, swamped with frustration and disgust. Bush yapped at him in furious outrage, his plump face cut open on snarling white teeth, and he ripped back mercilessly, for the sheer pleasure of wounding him.

"Rope? Is that so?" Bush choked. "We'll just see about that, we'll just see. In case you don't remember, Morris, I delegated the responsibility of those boys to you. As soon as they set foot out of this camp, they were in your charge, and don't forget it."

Swept with hate, Paul had no sense of stumbling away into his room and flopping onto his bed. His heart worked heavily and he was exhausted and shaking. It had never happened to him before, to run amok like that, and as his weltering and crowding blood slowed down he felt dirty, fouled. Bush's blaming him—the accusation, in the sense Bush meant it, was too childish to consider, but what about the real circumstances? No, he was clear there, too, because the boys had been set in motion by seeing him with Lucy in front of the hotel on Sunday, and that had been a perfectly innocent meeting. Anything since then between Lucy and him had no bearing on the matter. He wouldn't accept any blame for this. None.

The actual causes were numerous and intricately linked together: revenge and greediness and high spirits, that gang shag in the rodeo grounds, the adventurousness of ramping young life, and just plain bad luck. And what was the result? There were any number of optimistic explanations for Teddy's absence, but more and more he had a sense of doom. Teddy, the most brilliant and vital of the boys . . . The thought crept like a cold little wind in his head: was he dead?

It was almost midnight when the others returned—without Teddy. Bush told them to get some sleep if they could, and before long the lamps in the other room popped into darkness, and Paul knew that Bush was on his knees in there, praying. Now, too late, he had a vivid sense of what it must be like for Bush, to be plunged without warning into sickening danger, into a frantic effort to save what had been his without question for so long. Paul could imagine his feeling of injustice. He had always worked hard and done the best he could. What had happened? Why should it have happened to him? And Paul knew how strenuously he was trying not to think about his career while the hideous threat grew and grew, and the consequences swelled with cancerous rapidity.

"I was unkind, Bill," he said. "I'm sorry." And struck to the heart, he heard Bush begin to sob. The wind shifted around and poured through the old clapboard house, the withered boards groaned and the sheet iron roof slapped and slapped, maddeningly. It was getting chilly. Under his worry about Teddy a sense of failure, of dissatisfaction with himself, throbbed like a toothache.

Before sunrise they all drove to the spot where Harry had last seen Ted. Raw-eyed and shivering in the wind, they stood by the lumpy mound of clay and stones, and Bush rattled out directions. His hat flopped and strained at his clutching hand. Although there were purple stains under his eyes, he managed a kind of maimed briskness as he said, "Work your way out from here for two miles and then come back. I want everybody back here by noon, is that understood?"

Dust stinging into his face, Paul picked his way along the canyon rim. The wind blew out of the north; the pines hissed in the thirsty rocks, and beyond the distant blurring plateau the dawn was grey and cold on the hills. Naked boulders piled up and up, then broke off, plunging into a crooked side canyon which took an hour to cover. Grass licked at the stakes of claims. The heaps of dirt and stone by the discovery holes smoked in the wind. Fighting for air, his eyes gritty, his hands red with cold and his legs failing under him, he scrambled five hundred feet up a wind-scourged slope and there was Red Canyon again, a sheer drop of burning orange and broken spurs of pink and cinder grey, glowering below him like the crater of a volcano. Away down in the whirling dust a bulldozer was ramming and backing off, and a crew of ant-sized men were loading trucks with ore.

"Nothing? Not a sign?" Bush croaked when he staggered up to the huddled group at twelve-thirty. For a second his mouth, rimmed with a crust of dried mud, stayed open as if in a soundless cry. Then, after a ghastly effort, he said, "We're not licked yet, not by a darn sight. Teddy could be in town or he could have got a ride back to the camp by now if he spent the night at a ranch."

Paul looked carefully away from his hectic and defiant glare. Silent, inwardly afflicted, he receded into the group of mute and fearful boys. The stationwagon bounced with the tipping and sinking road, the windshield wipers fanned away sheets of powdering grit. Teddy had not been seen in town. And when they returned to the camp, the house and barns were empty in the clay yard fuming with wild dust.

"Oh my God," Bush said, his eyes goggling in a mask of dirt. "This is serious, we have to decide on a course of action." But before anybody could speak he let his hands drop in despair. "All right, all right," he said in a dull, shredding voice. "You win, Morris. Get the sheriff."

"I don't win," Paul said. "Everybody loses in this game. And I retract my criticism for not getting him right away. I don't think the delay will matter."

Bush brightened up. "We certainly had to cover the immediate area first. All right, since he's not there, he must have wandered off into the national forest. That means he's all right, so actually the odds are more in our favor than they were."

By the next morning more than forty men had turned out to help: ranchers, townspeople, railroad men between shifts, and rangers from the national forest with jeeps and walkie-talkies. The boy scouts joined in. Mr. Mencke, the druggist, set up headquarters in the fire station. Women from the various church groups not only supplied hot coffee and sandwiches but found clothes for Bush and Paul and the boys, who were completely unprepared for weather like this. In one August day the temperature had dropped from 104° to 37°, and the wind was so strong that livestock could not be shown at the county fair—and this, they were told, was not at all unusual.

Knotted up with the cold in spite of the borrowed sweaters and jackets, they fought their way with the ranch hands and other men through miles of national forest. A terrible wind was flying off the hills and dragging the stark brown plateau. Paul had no doubt any more about what they were going to find, and he walked toward it like a damned soul, carrying inside himself the obscure self-reproach, the oppression that was more than guilt at having cut Bush to pieces. Mercifully it was dimmed for now, smeared away in a haze of fatigue and numbing torrents of wind. The slope lurched up into a sky like frozen grease. His mouth was pasty with dirt. His wind-torn eyes were leaking. In one of the pine trees rocking dizzily around him, a hawk sat motionless on a dead branch, spectral in the driving blizzard of dust.

"You sure look done for, Paul. Now don't give up hope yet." At some point in the day, he didn't know exactly when, Wally had fallen in beside him, big and gentle, plodding along in a hunting cap and a quilted red jacket. Paul was aware of a little spring of comfort flowing steadily from him. He was evidently concerned that Paul understand why Bert hadn't joined in the search. "He's not any account on something like this, you know. He looks stout but he wouldn't last an hour up and down hill. . . . You wouldn't believe how he's changed, Paul, it's miraculous. He's not shirking, and he don't raise ruckuses any more. It's all prospecting with him now and nothing but."

Paul must have said something because he seemed satisfied. The next day the Indian kid Charley came padding along, hunched in a dirty corduroy jacket. "I'm a volunteer," he said. "Last year I helped fight two fires." The theory now was that Teddy had tried to make it back to the camp across country and accordingly the search turned to the range land, most of it part of the Bolton ranch, on the other side of Red Canyon. A cold wind still blew out of the shaggy sky. Dust ripped from the blow-outs and smudged away the winding jeep trails. Sheep crowded together like an outcrop of boulders on a clay hillside. Some time during the afternoon there was a false alarm in another creek bed, buzzards draining slowly out of the sky in the grey wind.

Late in the day, Wally stopped in his tracks and said, "It's a sure cinch he ain't this far, Paul. We're on a wild goose chase."

"Sure, nobody could get lost here," Charley said. His pants flapped on his skinny legs and he wiped his hand under his drooling nose.

"I suppose not," Paul said. A few dusty steers were bunched in the draw. The wind was letting up, he noticed absently, and the bare distances were coming back into focus. There was nothing to do except return to the claim and start over, but that was . . . practically conceding the worst. In silence, they trudged back to Wally's truck, their heads bent automatically as if the wind were still pressing on them. They bumped and struggled to the highway and rolled past the mouth of Red Canyon, wide open like a vast hemmorrhaging womb beyond the stony pastures. When they pulled up near the claim, a frozen orange sunset was sinking into the hills, and the stillness, after three days of blasting wind, was somehow appalling. A sense of imminence came over him, cold, smothering. The fierce red gullies, the silver-black clouds moving away, the grey stump of a mountain, the still pines—everything was glass-clear and mad. Only a few hundred yards from where Teddy had started off, the rotten, fissured stone tumbled suddenly into a dry stream bed, and Wally said, "We better have a look. This rock is awful bad."

"That's Old Woman Creek, see there?" Charley said, pointing toward a humpbacked cliff at the edge of the sky.

"Unhuh. You and Paul take a look downstream." The rocks were raw, harsh, split-off, broken. A cottontail flipped away from in front of Charley, and the brown weeds let down small showers of dust where it disappeared. In a few minutes he was shouting to them, and even though Paul had known it was coming, known it with fixed and icy certainty, he felt his stomach grab and his head fill with sick thuds.

Charley was gesturing excitedly, triumphantly, at a hand sticking from tons of fallen pink rock.

"That's a shame," Wally was saying. "I'm sure sorry, Paul."

Together they uncovered him, clawing away the rubble from the stiff, distorted arms and legs. There was dirt in his mouth and whiskers and there were bits of dirt in his murky blue eyes. Charley leaned to one side and spat, his brown face expressionless, and then dug out the Geiger counter; weeks later Paul remembered that that was the last he had seen of it. By the time they reached town with the body it was pitch dark and the search parties had gone home for the day. Mr. Mencke, fluttering expressions of sympathy, said he would notify everybody and volunteered to go out to the camp and break the news to Dr. Bush. Since there was no mortuary in Enterprise, Wally and

Paul had to drive the body to Hot Springs. It bumped rigidly in the back of the truck under an old army blanket, frozen in the wild sprawl of a man falling out of a plane, one leg bent under and the arms flung out in a frantic grasp at nothing. A thick shoe protruded from under the blanket.

Without warning, irrationally, the lurking self-accusation of the past few days was uncovered, frozen in the pitiless light of this death, and he saw the whole relationship with Lucy, the minute and almost invisible slipping from talk and encouragement to talk which had somehow become a kind of lovemaking, to the Leibestod in a laundry —no, it couldn't be sneered at. To intercourse with a girl scarcely older than a child. The tiny slip had become a headlong downhill slide. But it was almost impossible to see where he had gone wrong, where the sensuality of ideas had turned into crazed sensuality. Even the first time in her room had been an act of pity, an attempt to release her, and yet, in only three days, it had twisted into violent, biting ecstasy.

Christ! he was still lying to himself. It had been impure from the very first. The admiration of her mind, the concern, the desire to help had all been tainted, mixed with the flash of white skin in the rodeo grounds as she tugged the jeans over her frail, pathetically childish hips. A secret greed, a secret thirsty expectation, had itched inside him from the beginning. Unconsciously he had gone into town looking for her that Sunday when he'd found her in the drugstore reading H. G. Wells. The intellectual dialogue itself, those intense and beautiful conversations, had been partly a way to possess her, to make her his as no other man she knew could. And the first time in her room, the compassion, the effort to release her: what of that? All very high-minded and touching . . . partly. And then those three days of ecstasy —of somnambulism. Almost deliberately he had abolished himself in anonymous sensuality, hidden himself in non-thought. Morris, the man in the imported English hair shirt, the man of reason, reduced to the urgent flows and thirsts and stinks of the body.

And so the children's crusade, modern style, had wound up once again in the bordellos of Italy and Constantinople.

Because there was no conceivable justification for having intercourse with her. To control the physical act, to exalt it, to transfigure the blind juicy life of the organs, had always been a basic idea with him, and the plain fact was that years of asceticism—broken by falls from grace with the university librarian, that withering goddess of horny sophomores and instructors too poor to marry—had crumbled into lust. How easily he had succumbed to life, the beloved and invincible antagonist. After years of passionate effort, of denying and denying life in order to perfect it, he had surrendered in the oldest and simplest way of all. Ah, life like a woman with soft arms . . .

The rattly, gas-stinking old truck groaned up the dark mountain in long switchbacks. The rear-view mirror, split in half, shivered like a wind-beaten puddle. Wally whistled tunelessly. Under the curving road, down in the river valley filled with blackness, a few lights glowed like fallen stars.

And in the back of the truck, vibrating as the wheels thumped and rolled, was the body of Teddy under an army blanket. He'd said to himself that he would accept no blame for that, none. But hadn't he been guilty *before it happened,* guilty in his heart of precisely the thing the boys had taunted him about? "I spy!" he heard their hoots again. "Nasty doctor!" "Shame, shame, double shame!" Fantastically, he had gone back to the hotel that very day, blinding himself (again partly, always partly), and the ultimate irony had come to pass: he had made the taunts come true! Objectively true, at least. And then, even more fantastically, in spite of their continuous ragging he had gone back day after day and made the taunts truer still, and truer.

The warped body slid back and forth as the truck swayed through a turn. Some of the awful blame for it was his.

And there was more. The betrayal of himself had spread to other betrayals, to throwing the hatchet-sharp shovel at the boys, to massacring a weak and anguished Bush in an orgy of cruelty. The first madness had spawned others with evil swiftness—if in fact they weren't the same thing at the bottom: Hiroshima and the bellow of a rutting bull ape, the rank and musky smell of tomcats in alleys.

But in spite of knowing all this, in spite of the bitterest sorrow and self-condemnation, he longed to see her again, craved to see her, to have her naked in his arms. Even while Teddy's body scraped and bumped in the back of the truck! It was sub-human. The supreme disciplines of his life had melted, and like a fallen Adam, years afterward, stumbling into the Garden of Eden, he had entered the universal paradise of spring, birds nesting and lovers walking hand in hand, grasshoppers locked together in drugged and beady rapture. And he didn't care! Absolutely nothing mattered except this delirious sweetness, not even her welfare. Didn't matter enough, anyway, and he suffered tortures in the next day and a half, unable to get into town alone to be with her. All he could contrive was a hurried ten minutes while Bush was on the phone with Teddy's parents, but he comforted himself with the prospect of seeing her while he stayed on by himself to finish breaking the camp, returning the rented jeep and packing the equipment and the numbered sacks of bones for Bush to measure and analyze.

The boys left. The body was returned from Hot Springs, and he drove Bush to the depot to accompany it home to Teddy's parents in Kansas City. Cars drew up beside them as people arrived to meet the noon train for the east. The coffin, in an unpainted wooden crate, waited on one of the iron-wheeled carts. The sun blazed on the metal handles.

Uranium! 231

A hundred yards down the files of boxcars, by a low peeling warehouse, a conveyor was belching uranium ore into an open gondola. Bush alternated between red-eyed silence and a kind of spurious carrying on, giving instructions about this and that. Children edged toward the wooden crate, fascinated, nudging each other, and Paul could almost hear their heartless and innocent whispers, "There's a dead man in there." "No fooling? Boy!' Some of the townspeople who had been involved in the search stopped by the stationwagon with condolences, a sack-faced woman with black beads dribbling along her neck, a hard shrunken man in a sweaty hat. Bush looked more and more drained, but Paul went through the ritual with inflexible courtesy, remote, absent, waiting to be released. Eleven fifty-five. The train was due in five minutes.

"It shouldn't take you more than a day to finish up," Bush said for the third time. "Plus three days more to drive back to school."

The words—like everything else, like the lean faces tucked in the shadows of flaring hats and the rumble of ore and the light pressing down on the huddle of cars by the blood-red depot—meant nothing at all to Paul. He yearned toward Lucy, dizzy with the pounding in his chest. They would have at least two, perhaps three, days before he left, and at the thought his heart began to run away, light, happy. She would be sitting beside him in the glut of sunflowers, their hands would be just touching, and then she would rub her cheek on his shoulder and draw his face down to hers . . .

"Howdy!" It was Mr. Mencke, folksy and plump, leaning his dumpling face to the window on Bush's side. "I can't tell you how sorry I am, Dr. Bush. And you, too, Dr. Morris."

Up the street across from his drugstore, some kind of office was being opened: a man was laying paint on the rusty clapboard, and the knock-knock of a hammer echoed down the hot sunlight.

"Thank you," Paul said. "You were more than helpful."

"You're as welcome as can be for any little help I give—you don't have to get out yet, Dr. Bush. The train is late as per usual. The saying around here is, on the last day it'll be twenty minutes late for Judgment." His smile wiped away as quickly as it formed, back into doleful sympathy. "It's been a heartbreaker for you, I know. And I can imagine the chore it'll be, telling the boy's folks. I sure don't envy you."

Bush sat in crushed immobility.

Paul thanked him once more, stony with dismissal, but Mencke went on and on, bug-eyed, perspiring. "Maybe this will help out a little, Doctor. I was just having a word with Mr. Wassburger, the Atomic Energy Commission man. He's opening that office there. The government has finally saw the possibilities here, which are tremendous, as I said all along. Well, be that as it may, I happened to mention your tragedy to him, and between us we come up with a thought that might bring at least some peace and comfort. That boy laying in that casket is a martyr. He was trying to help his country when he died, and he gave his life for America as sure as any kid dying in Korea. Or Nathan Hale."

It was ludicrous, macabre, the final flourish to the chaos and horror of the past week. Paul made no comment. To suffer fools was the habitual posture of his life, and, like an instinct, a reflex action, he felt the distance and irrelevance of everything snap back into focus.

He saw the pine crate on the cart.

Poor Bush grasped at the comfort. "That's right, you know," he said. "If you think about it, he laid down his life for his country. He was doing his part . . ."

Paul clamped his teeth together, and a muscle pulsed in his sallow cheek. He felt himself set dark and hard again—against the flourishing uranium boom, against a world he did not fit, against himself. Somehow he would push down the breathless cry of longing. As soon as Bush left he would get Lucy started for home and school; he would say goodbye to her; he would return to camp and load the stationwagon; he would head for the University. The tearing pain he felt at losing three days with her was an act of faith, the first stone placed upon stone. Somehow he had to construct himself again, rebuild the interior fortress, the citadels of the mind which he had betrayed.

XVI

"You don't understand," the AEC man said to her. "We're here to assist the prospector and the miner. For example, we assay ore samples and help out with technical problems. I couldn't take you into a mine even if I did have the time. Added to that, the former Bolton mine you're talking about is an open pit operation. So there isn't a shaft there to go into."

"Any mine will do," the old woman replied. Ten minutes after the train came in, she had hobbled into the AEC office like a faded photograph come to life, musty and dim, a withered girl shoving her feet along with slow, crippled motions. Her blotched, skinny hands were knotted up and distorted with arthritis. "Harriet went down into a mine in Colorado last summer," she said, "and it did her a world of good. She can even drive a car again, you ought to see her bat around now."

Her face, streaming wrinkles, lifted to him with a terrible bright smile that showed her wintry teeth.

George Mencke, who had trailed her in, said, "I told her it was no use but she wouldn't listen, Larry."

Once more the AEC man went over it. "There's no medical evidence for uranium helping any kind of a disease, lady, not any at all. I hate to tell you, but you're on a wild goose chase. You have the word of the United States Public Health Service for that." Drab, patient, careful, he put the serious words together. His eyes were blue and direct. Small rudimentary ears cropped out under two batches of neatly combed hair.

"Surely," she said to everything, her mind shut tight upon her single dream. "I didn't believe it myself till I saw how much better Harriet was. The improvement, it's simply miraculous, like a fairy tale. To add spice to it all, she's so shackle-brained I didn't believe she would ever do a sensible thing. Her husband died quite young, you see, and sometimes, frankly, she's not quite all there. The poor thing, she's talking of a golden wedding anniversary—with her husband in his grave for forty-one years."

He winced, looking at her warped hands dangling a black purse. The tender protectiveness and devotion he lived with expanded and took her in, but there was nothing he could do for her, not a thing.

"Lady, you have to take the bitter with the sweet," he said earnestly. "These fads or crazes or whatever you want to call them, they go around like wildfire. The early part of this year we had a rush of elderly folks asking for ore samples. A rumor had spread around the entire country that if you wore one around your neck in a little bag, it would soothe rheumatism. Eventually it got so bad the Commission had to put out an order restricting distribution of samples to bona fide prospectors."

Shocked, he watched what he'd said become a new hope lurking in the nets of wrinkles on her face; she crept toward the crates of ore samples in the window.

"Hold on! Lady! I told you those are restricted." The shrivelled mouth twitched open; the cracked and hairy lips pulled back, and she squeaked insults at him personally, at the AEC, and finally at the government of the United States itself. "You don't mean that," he said severely. "You're disappointed is all." Scraping to the window like a crippled bird, she snatched up a chunk of ore and clutching it triumphantly in her crabbed fingers, labored outside into the sun-blank street.

"Should I get it away from her?" George asked him.

"No, let her go," he said. "I'll make up the piece of ore out of some I have at home. Hope sure springs eternal in the human breast, doesn't it? But it's getting serious, how many sick people come to every hot new area. I haven't kept track but there's more and more of them all the time. The worst one was one that had cancer of the liver. That was bad." He lapsed into silence. He thought of the sunken yellow face and the limp hand on the gay Indian blanket. He said at last, "But the principle is still the same. Publicity is necessary to stimulate atomic development, and you naturally stir up unfortunate people like that, too. The national welfare comes before the individual."

"You darn right," George said with enthusiasm. "The old hag. She ought to be locked up instead of catered to."

Larry Wassburger sat down stolidly at his desk and even managed to take a sip of coffee from the thermos cup by his half-eaten sandwich. But the words, spoken though they were in all innocence, burned through him like acid. He'd confided in George, but he hadn't mentioned that Blanche had said almost exactly the same thing last night. A sense of crisis, of desperate need, closed down upon him, and he looked without seeing at the familiar picture of President Truman, the posters, topographical maps, and Geiger counters. A mound of brochures and pamphlets still lay under an olive-drab tarpaulin.

"This is the seventh headquarters I've been at since 1947," he said slowly. "That's me, a rolling stone that gathers no moss."

George understood immediately what he meant. "Don't worry," he said, "it'll be a fabulous boom, Larry. And I'm not saying that for myself or the town, but you. In all sincerity."

"No, it's for the good of the United States," he corrected him, but all the same he was warmed and grateful. In the few days since he'd arrived, they had become about as close as you could get. It wasn't only seeing eye-to-eye on every subject, or George helping in whatever way he could, and not just to butter his own bread, either. Somehow George had sensed the anxiety he lived with, and a more understanding and sympathetic person he had never met. Since then, whenever the worry had piled up too high, it seemed like George was there to take part of the load.

"There's no harm in you getting a lift at the same time," George insisted with utter devotion. Georgie Porgie, puddin' and pie, Georgie the boy who had wet his pants at school, Old George the lonely and disliked town booster, George Mencke had found a friend. Sweetness plashed into his soul. Tactfully, delicately, his nervous pop eyes watering with compassion, he alluded to the sorrow that Larry had unburdened to him, and to him alone. "If you can settle down for a while, it'll make all the difference to your wife and . . . family. You said so yourself. You have to get out of those rented apartments and a here-today-gone-tomorrow life."

"I know. For the good of the kid especially, I need to light in one place and right away. That fire scared the daylights out of me," he said heavily. "The way I see it, Farragut told me I'll stay on if the office is expanded. But the thing is, that means a buying station and a crew, some secretaries, probably another field man, somebody for public relations—the complete works. And for that to happen, the area has to prove out." Laboriously, a word at a time, he had defined the frightful predicament. If he was going to save the child, he had to give the go-ahead for a buying station, but he couldn't in conscience make a commitment like that until he was absolutely sure. "Right now," he said, "I'd have to call this an area of interest. That's the verdict so far. Maybe it will, and maybe it won't. Time will tell."

"I'll see if there's anything new around town," George said. "I heard there's a flatcar loaded with equipment coming in. That's a good sign."

He bustled out, and hunched at the desk in the tap of hammers and the smell of paint, Larry began studying ore sample reports. There were only a dozen so far, too few to make a judgment with. Time, it would take time to build the picture, to determine the size and importance of the ore deposits and project the future output. Bud Robel came in and applied for the government production bonus—this was a plus, but his mine was small, and he had stockpiled ore for a good long while before getting enough to ship. A family on vacation drove up with the idea of prospecting and camping, and patiently he explained what sort of rock might contain uranium and made their cheap Geiger stutter at a piece of ore for them. But all the while worry seeped into him until his mind was filled again with the smoke gushing down the stairs, and Anne and Eric were coughing and crying in the hall, the baby buggy was trembling with every tiny bleat, and inside the apartment Blanche, her hair in tangles, was filling a pan of water at the faucet and running into the bedroom and splashing it on the burning bed. The charred and sopping mattress had fumed for hours afterwards in the backyard while the quarrel broke out again and again in the smoke-tainted little rooms, leaving him at last, at two o'clock in the morning, exhausted and grim with concern. Would something go wrong again today? The thought was like a steady noise in his head.

Through the window he could see a pink Cadillac parked in front of the bleached storefronts. A big Texan wearing hand-tooled leather boots with sharp toes, a creamy gabardine suit, and a fifty-dollar Stetson hat raked back on his head, was leaning against it and talking to a corpulent man with a diamond ring winking on his white, pulpy hand. Eagerly Larry grasped at the sight. When that type of vulture showed up it was a mighty promising thing. They could smell uranium, it seemed like. Pray God they were right this time.

On the way home he imagined twenty disasters but his little girl was waiting for him at the top of the stairs, her hair curled into long spools of red and her flaggy-blue dress crisp and fresh. He let out his breath with relief. She was so beautiful standing up there, as clear and sweet as a picture in a fairy story. His bruised and cherishing heart swelled with devotion, and he pledged himself to her all over again.

"How's my sweetheart?" he said, going up the stairs two at a time.

"Daddy, Daddy!" she cried in ecstasy—and then her flawless loveliness seemed to break down, the pure white lines of her face distorted slightly, her dark blue eyes wavered, and her dancing feet hitched just a trifle as she flung herself into his arms. Love, all the more love, stormed his heart and with his face all in smiles he carried her into the air. "Did my girl miss her daddy? Give me a kiss."

He hugged Eric too and said hello to the baby who was lying on her back in the crib and kicking her feet. "Thanks, Blanche, for dolling up my girl," he called into the kitchen. "How'd it go today? Better?"

"The new mattress came," she said. "The bill is on the dresser."

"Fine," he said in a hearty voice. Anne grappled onto him hungrily, asking, demanding to sit in his lap, and beaming down at her he reached into his coat pocket. "Look what I brought you, sweetheart." While she tugged and pouted at him he unwrapped a small tin merry-go-round with cut-out horses caught in the middle of their gallant prancing and a tiny rigid flag, the stars and stripes, flying on the peak of the roof. Winding it up with a key in the bottom, he said, "Watch now, sweetheart."

"And what about Eric?"

Blanche was standing in the doorway to the kitchen. Her voice was waspy, and grievance pinched at her thin nose and her sullen grey eyes. "Did you get *him* a present? I didn't think so."

"My gosh, I forgot. It only cost a half a dollar, honey." Hastily he promised little six-year-old Eric two quarters, three quarters. Blanche threw him a scornful look and set the table for supper in grey-lipped silence. Under the reek of sauerkraut the air was still bitter with the smell of the fire. A dreary feeling came over him. In a cheerful tone he said, "Now then, kids," and set the toy down on the stringy carpet. The bright tin horses went around and around, wobbling crazily on their tin platform, and the flag on top turned its blade-stiff faces one after the other. Anne watched for a minute; then her vagrant attention drifted away, and flopping against his knees like a rag doll, she insisted on sitting in his lap. Sprawled on his legs, she rolled back her lovely face and ogled up at him, pulled at his arm and babbled to him with her clumsy tongue. A pang of desperate love took his heart. Nobody except him really *cared* about her, and the poor dear kid was starved for attention. When he looked away for a few seconds to wind up the merry-go-round for Eric, she snatched at him ravenously and forced his face back toward her, making the cluttered words about anything that meant she needed him.

At supper he cut up her weiner for her and pampered her into eating, all the while keeping up a cheerful line of talk to Blanche. "Naturally I can't afford to get trigger-happy about a buying station, but it sure looks awful good. It's my bet that before long we'll be able to rent a house and send for our furniture. Then everything will straighten out, you'll see."

"Eat your hot dog, Eric," she said crossly.

He was glad when the meal was over and he could escape to the living room. Folding Anne into his lap, he read to her from a primer about a little boy who helped George Washington beat the British until she tired of it and dabbled the pages away with a whimper. "All right, that's enough reading," he smiled. "Do you remember what three and four is?"

"I want a horsie ride," she said.

"Sure thing, Princess. But first, tell me what three and four is." One by one, he patiently coaxed the answers out of her while she slewed back and forth on his legs and squirmed and slung her pouty face against his chest. Still, he told himself as he lifted her onto his back, they had made some headway, only a little but some. Slow and sure won the race. "Giddyup," she squealed joyfully, and around and around he went, her strangling arms locked on his neck.

Querulous wails rose from the crib. Blanche, her mouth still pressed together ominously, changed the baby and gave her a bottle. He wanted to tell her that he understod how rough it had been for her—the weathering little cattle towns and the rented rooms with their sickly wallpaper and huddle of worn and dirty furniture. And Anne, always the problem of Anne. Blanche was about at the end of her strength; the truce of last night was deteriorating already, and how he was going to head off a showdown he didn't know.

"Horsie needs a rest now," he told Anne. She hung on, pulling at him, and so he lugged her with him over to Blanche, who was settling the sleepy lump of baby in the crib. "Keep your chin up, honey," he said to her. "Come on, where's that famous smile?"

She gave him a tired nod, but as soon as they had put the children to bed Eric set up a howl: his piggy-bank was missing. "Anne!" she said furiously. "You bad girl. Where did you hide it?"

"Hold on, wait a second now. We at least ought to look around before we accuse anybody."

"You know good and well Eric guards that bank day and night, he's at that age. She stole it!"

The cankered hate in her voice was frightening. Quickly he said, "It's not worth fighting over, let's forget it. Here, Eric, here's two dollars. That ought to cover it with interest, and the three quarters I promised you besides. Okay, fella?" But Eric didn't want the two dollars, he wanted his piggy bank, and Blanche backed him up and fired away resentfully, meanwhile petting away his tears. "I tell you she's more than I can handle, Larry. She does it on purpose!"

"Not in here," he said sternly. "She understands what you're saying." Fierce with love, he made Blanche leave the bedroom and closed the door. "The child can't help it, she's upset and nervous, and I don't want you punishing her. It's unfortunate but it can't be helped. Please, honey, she's our sacred trust."

She turned her back, but the look that came at him out of the mirror was sharp with antagonism. "Do you realize she could have killed us all yesterday? Do you? I can't ever breathe easy." She elbowed him away and whipped around, her eyes sparking. "I can't leave her alone for ten minutes, she'll find some matches or do something else terrible. She's not all there and you know it, she's ten years old and she's like a baby. I'm just so tired of it. I can't go on, my teeth are jittering from morning to night. Today she stole Eric's money, yesterday it was the bed."

"That's water over the dam," he frowned. "We agreed to drop the subject."

"I don't care! Maybe we did get off light that time, what about next time? I mean it, there's no cure except to put her away."

Fury churned up inside him and he shouted at her, "Don't you say that! Don't you ever say that again, do you hear?" His heart was staggering, but he forced himself to speak quietly. "All right, let's both cool off. Cease fire. Honey, it won't be long till we're settled—"

The door opened and Anne waded into the room in her pink pajamas, holding out a crayon in her fragile hand. "Did you bring me a present?" he smiled, stooping to accept it and stroking her red curls. "Thank you very much." Ever so gently, ever so tenderly, he enticed her back to bed with promises of another horsie ride tomorrow. Bitterness scalded him as he thought of the countless times she had brought her mother little presents—a piece of string, a pretty stone, anything to get her notice—and how Blanche never so much as glanced at her. Sometimes he could hardly believe that this was the wife who had loyally worked to get him through the School of Mines, the wife who had stuck to him through thick and thin. She even pretended not to understand what Anne was saying. Once—he would never be able to forget it—she had hacked off all the child's hair simply because she wouldn't sit still to have it combed. And she wouldn't admit that there was the least hope, even though the specialist in Minneapolis had said it was partly emotional. Even though the improvement in her had been absolutely miraculous while they were in Utah.

There were angry cramps at the corners of his mouth when he walked back into the drab living room. He sat down on the couch. The mirror wrenched at her face as she moved around, fretting. "It just makes me sick, Larry. Sick! You let that child gobble you up. You give and give and give—and for what? I tell you I can't take it another day. I mean it. The minute my back was turned, she . . ."

"Your back was turned!" he exploded. "Horseshit!" This was his only word of profanity and when he used it he was lost in fury, completely out of control. "Your back was turned, all right. You were asleep or watching television, I know you."

"How *dare* you say that to me!" She began to cry.

"And I know how you treat her, too," he shouted. "You set her in front of the TV all day long and tell her to be quiet. I know exactly what you do, don't you think I don't." All the dreadful things they didn't say came spewing out, like sewers popping their lids and vomiting evil-smelling sludge during a flood. "You didn't take her with you to the grocery store today either, did you? You left her here by herself. You're ashamed of her! That's why you won't ever go to church with us. Isn't it?"

"Yes!" she screamed, flinging up her wet face. Her teeth were showing, and he could see the fillings and the grey stains around them in the enamel. "Yes! I'm ashamed of her, I'm ashamed she's mine! She's a freak and I hate her! Now you know," she said with a kind of triumph, driving the words in like nails. "And so I'm a monster, what about you? It's Anne this and sweetheart that till I want to puke up my insides. *Her welfare comes first, she comes first in everything*—just like you talk, talk, talk about your sacred duty to your country. I'll tell you one thing right now. You don't love me or anybody else in the world. Just her! Nobody else counts. You'd blow up the rest of mankind for her."

His eyes were gorged with raging blood. He fired back, "You know what I think? I think you *want* her to do things like that—set fire to the bed. You figure that'll push me into having her put away."

Long after the battle was over and she was in bed, he sat doubled up in the open window and stared, his shoulders hanging wearily, at the night-filled park across the highway. The bandstand gaped, empty. A solitary car whispered by. The two ancient cannons pointed up into a sky salted with fine, bitter stars. The showdown had settled nothing after all; she hadn't left him yet and he was more determined than ever that he wouldn't send Anne to an institution. Those people couldn't give her the love and care she needed. Only he could save her and he was going to save her, on that he took his oath. A handicapped person could be helped, sometimes even to a normal life, if you settled down and worked at it long enough and hard enough. He had all the faith in the world in that kid.

However, the pressure to set up a buying station was crushing now, and the next day it increased still more from an entirely different source. Mr. Lytton, the field manager for U.S. Mining, came trotting into the office, pink and suave and gum-chewing, a briefcase snugged under his arm. Larry sat back from the geologic map he was working on. His job was partly public relations and though he disliked all high-powered talkers and fancy executives, he did his best to look agreeable and friendly. Lytton asked him to have lunch with him and his mother. Larry put him off solemnly, eager to be of service but more than a little wary, suspicious.

In an offhand way Lytton said, "How soon do you expect to set up a buying station?"

"That depends, Mr. Lytton. The outlook is very good. I think we're progressing toward an area with a very bright future."

"Sure, sure, but like when?" he said impatiently, chewing. He leaned forward, his grey hair saturated with light from the street. "I'll make this short and to the point. We have a sackfull of money tied up here and we expect a reasonable return on our investment. That's only fair, isn't it? We're taking some tall risks, remember, and we're not in this for our health. It's a dollars and cents world in uranium like anything else. Now I'll be frank with you, we've got to squeeze the water out of the operation. New York is screaming bloody murder about shipment costs."

"The Commission pays six and a half cents a ton-mile up to a hundred miles."

"What the hell good is that on a shipment to Rifle, Colorado, man? You need pitchblende to show a decent profit."

Larry said, "I can see your point, Mr. Lytton. Naturally you want a maximum profit and just as soon as the tonnage warrants . . ."

"I don't have to tell you this is a national emergency," Lytton said, shifting smoothly to another argument. "The country is in danger and you want all the uranium possible, don't you? The nation that controls most of the uranium rules the world and the destiny of the world is in its hands. Am I right?"

"Yes sir. That's so."

"All right then. The expense of shipping ore all the way to Colorado isn't hamstringing just us, but everybody. A lot of ore isn't being mined for that simple reason—especially the lowgrade stuff."

Larry pecked at the desk with his pencil, avoiding Lytton's look. He went out into the field every day, and he knew that Lytton was lying: little operators were stockpiling instead of shipping, and the lack of a buying station, at least at this stage, was not hurting development. On the other hand, U.S. Mining was unhappy, and business, especially big business, had to be encouraged if the area was to be developed. It was true! He had to give the go-ahead! His treacherous heart surrendered at once, and it was agony to hold back, to counter with the knowledge that U.S. Mining wouldn't pull out lightly or easily with an investment like that. He needed the same thing so badly that every argument convinced him, every bit of evidence seemed to be the proof he needed.

"What can you lose, man?" Lytton said persuasively, switching again. "If the area produces big it's a feather in your cap. If it goes blooey, well, that's uranium for you. Nobody'll blame you." When he didn't reply, Lytton said, "You have to think positive, man. You and me, we both have to score some points."

The argument itself didn't mean a thing to him—words—and yet the temptation to give in was awful. By sheer instinct he muttered the formula, "I'll do whatever else I can, evaluate your ore . . ."

Lytton blew out his breath in disgust and switched again. This time his petal-red face wilted into distress. "You understand, this isn't going to help you with Jerry Farragut," he said. "I don't like to go over your head but the wheel-squeaking on the cart has to stop. Grease it takes and grease I'm going to get."

Instantly he felt the grinding pressure ease up: he was safe from himself, temporarily at least. "If you want to go over my head, I figure that's your privilege," he said stolidly. "But according to what I can see, the area has only proved itself partway. That's my verdict so far."

Lytton picked up his briefcase with a shrug. Larry expected something menacing from him and he was flabbergasted to see him smile ingratiatingly. "We're on different teams on this but no hard feelings between us. Okay?"

"No sir. No hard feelings." The door closed and he went back to his mapping, sleeves rolled up on his arms tattooed with a blurry eagle and the words U.S. MARINE CORPS. Only then did he notice the oily discharge of sweat that soaked his hands, his whole body. For a few critical minutes until Lytton had threatened him, he'd been on the verge of betraying his responsibilities. Even now, after being pushed so unmercifully, the worry scraping at his heart went on arguing for a buying station. He caught himself hoping that Lytton would succeed, would be able to talk Farragut into giving the green light.

All that came of it, however, was a memo asking for yet another progress report. The decision was still his to make, and conscientiously, scrupulously, he balanced capital investment against the number of mines, balanced the quantity of stockpiled ore against the fairly low grade of most of it, and he waited, waited. Little by little the boom made headway, the tonnage crept up, another mine was opened, but he was plugging hard until eight and nine o'clock at night, and without his care Anne was growing steadily worse. She didn't speak as clearly and she pouted more, and when Eric started to the first grade after Labor Day, she went into a very bad tailspin. She tried to go along, fumbling her Sunday dress out of the closet and jabbering piteously. Then she stoped eating. One night Eric proudly recited the "pleasure legions to the flag" for him, and the next evening he came home to find Blanche in the worst tantrum yet.

"The little snot pushed Eric down the stairs!" she blazed. "And just look! When I tried to spank her, she bit me! Look, she drew blood!"

Anne whimpered and hauled at his arm, wrenching his heart with the garbled sounds she was making. "I've got an idea," he said. "I'll get somebody to give you a hand with her, Blanche." With the kind help of George Mencke, he found the widow of a railroad man who looked like the answer to his prayer; then Blanche discovered that she gossipped to the whole town and fired her. He went heavy and slack inside. For the first time he doubted whether he could hold out long enough. On Saturday afternoon a middle-aged stockman slammed into the office, his eyes narrowed to angry blue creases in his sun-cured face. Tipped forward by his boots, he advanced on Larry. "Some sonofabitch calling hisself Dakota Something-or-other has started mining on my ranch without so much as a by-your-leave."

As Larry feared, it turned out that he didn't own the mineral rights to his land. Larry did what he could to pacify him but he would not be consoled. "It's theft, highway robbery. My father homesteaded that land in nineteen-five," he said, "and it's my land, by God. I've put my sweat into it since the day I was old enough to bottle-feed a lamb."

When he finally left, Larry went back to his one-fingered typing feeling battered and weak. More and more he had a sense of painful necessity. The welfare of the nation required that so many people get hurt—the hundreds and thousands who had lost their shirt prospecting and mining, town after town infested with the gambling and vice that always came with a boom, the old and the sick coming from all over and, as often as not, getting swindled besides with some kind of fake uranium treatment . . . He was getting morbid. He took a sip of cold coffee and set down the thermos cup. For some reason the hollow sound made him flinch; then he remembered. The Japanese in the South Pacific used to start the mechanism in their hand grenades by knocking them against their helmets before they threw them. When you heard that peculiar clock! in the jungle at night your blood stopped: you knew that the grenade was somewhere up in the steamy air, flying toward you. He hadn't thought of that in years, he was getting morbid all right.

Later that afternoon, walking out to his car, he heard a clattering and saw, up the bright sidewalk, three boys walking on tin cans tied to their shoes. They tottered and banged along in a Frankenstein lurch, their arms balancing out—and all he could see was the loose-hinged drag in Anne's walk. A crack seemed to open in his heart. Outside the Victory tavern he bumped into the half-sized man who was the mascot of a couple of prospectors; as always, he was drunk. His tongue rolled in the wet red ditch of his mouth, and he staggered on his short legs. "Freak," he heard Blanche say again. "She's a freak and I hate her."

Another week went by. The mill reports on the last three shipments were only so-so. He couldn't make up his mind; he didn't know what to do. He lost confidence in his own judgment and his spirit crumpled; he began to chase rumors instead of plodding through reports and exploration data. One day George Mencke puffed in with a hot new tip: his own brother-in-law, Bud Robel, had hit a fabulous vein of carnotite in his mine. Larry hurried out there at once. A ponderous yellow cat was thundering in the narrow tunnel, the air was fouled with blue deisel fumes, two light bulbs spread faded glows in the hazy air. Up on the seat of the cat, Bud laughed when he heard of the report. "I found a little shoot, about two bushels or so, that runs half of one per cent. The rest of this beats getting kicked in the hind end, but not by a hell of a lot."

Larry gaped in disappointment, his fists dropping open at his sides. It was almost nine o'clock by the time he reached town, parked his car in front of the office and trudged toward the apartment. A pregnant cat, moving portentously like an old queen, walked across the sidewalk in front of him. Guitar music twanged out of a tavern. The blinking stoplight at the intersection dripped liquid red from car to car down Highway Street. The metal siding on a garage had corroded at the bottom into fringy tips like a sinister new growth.

"Hey!" A truck had braked to a stop beside him, piled high with ore, and somebody was shouting, "Mr. Wassburger! Hey!"

It was those two prospectors, and they wanted him to look at their load. Fagged and lifeless, he said, "I'll take an ore sample tomorrow."

"Damn if that rhymes," one of them snorted. "Listen here at this." Swinging out of the cab, he clambered up onto the load with a Geiger counter. Larry reluctantly went over. The steady mutter of the audio counter picked up speed, stammered and gibbered wildly as the little fellow hopped all over the pile of ore. His grimy face, sprouting a ragged beard, split wide open and he crowed, "I thought that would make a believer out of you. You want it or do I sell it to the Russians?"

Larry told himself to be cautious, to protect himself against still another disappointment, but a shock of hope went through him and his blood began to stream and thicken in his head. "Bring it to the office," he said. "I'll check it with a scintillometer. How much do you figure you have?"

They made a U-turn in the highway and rattled back to the office. Larry checked the load himself, poking around, plowing deep into the ore, turning it over and holding the scintillometer over the chunks. His breath sucked through his teeth when he saw the needle lay all the way over on the first scale, then on the second. He twisted the knob to the third scale: the needle plunged all the way over and stuck. He stared at the yellow rocks which seemed to smolder in the street light. "Why—why," he breathed, "it must be three per cent or more. It's impossible."

"I told you, Lard. I told you we were gonna have to get some bigger pants pockets," the small man chuckled. He grabbed the hat off the other's head and launched it into the air, then started tap dancing, beating up the dust with his clopping boots and whooping gleefully. A crowd of men had gathered around them.

Wally told Larry, "It's one for Ripley, all right. Bert bought some leases on the plateau from those college kids before they left town, and he would have his way, there was nothing for it but to look at them leases regardless if no ore had ever been found outside a canyon," he said, pumping his big fists with excitement. "Well, we was driving over this plateau and we had the Geiger beside us on the seat and it started talking, it just jumped all over. I figured something was wrong with it so I changed batteries, but it kept right on talking. So we walked around till we hit the hottest place and set it on top and went to digging. I figure the pod has at least one more truckload like this." Standing in the lamplight, he swung his arms in great arcs.

"Where on the plateau?" somebody in the crowd asked.

Bert winked a bloodshot eye and gave them a toothy grin. "Out there somewheres." He looked around. "Where's my lucky penny? Where's Ray, the little old rascal? Drunk as an owl, I reckon. We had to luck out all by ourself."

Larry still couldn't believe it. "Well I'll be darned," he said. "Out on the plateau? Well I'll be darned. It's geologically impossible; it's a plain and simple miracle."

"Nothing to it," Bert said.

"Fellows, I'd like to shake your hand on it," Larry said. "You know there's a fortune right there in that truck."

Wally said, "Bert figured it out on the way in. He says it'll run twenty-five thousand for the two loads."

"If it don't make at least that," Bert said, "I'll eat Lard's belt. And I'm allergic to cheap leather." Running over with laughs, he said to Larry, "If it's all the same to you, we'll take it in one-dollar bills. Not for my sake. Lard here likes to count 'em."

Larry shok hands with both of them again. "It's the greatest single pod in the history of U.S. uranium," he said reverently. It was wonderful. New life was pouring into him, gush after gush of blessed relief. The weeks of anxiety were over and Anne was saved, his darling girl was saved. "Tell you what. Drive around to the back and I'll take that load right now and lock it up in the shed. We'll just start a buying station here and now, informal, till we can set it up officially."

XVII

Their credit was unlimited, and the first thing Wally did was send for Esther and the boys and rent a house near the school. He was the happiest he'd ever been. Seven years of hard going were over—seven years of failures at prospecting, months at a time of separation from his family, and most of all, guilt at hanging on to Bert when he was getting worse instead of better.

By the time they had delivered the second load to Larry Wassburger, the whole plateau had been alive with prospectors, and in less than three days it had been staked and gone over with a fine-tooth comb without a nickel's worth of uranium showing up. "Now ain't Mother Nature a pill," Bert said. A strange, inward look came over his face, and, refusing to scratch at some low-test claims they had in the canyons, he borrowed all of Wassburger's geology books and sent for more. "You fix up your love nest," he said to Wally, "while I lick the hell out of this uranium problem." The fact that he'd had only three years of high school didn't perturb him in the least, nor did Wassburger's insistence that there was no answer to the mystery. "All it takes is the knowledge and some thinking," he grinned, "and on thinking I'm a hummer."

And so while Bert pored over books a half a foot thick, and smoked, and lay on his bed at the hotel and stared at the ceiling, Wally and Esther fixed up the four-room shack which had been the last available house in the crowded town. Together they painted and varnished and mended the torn walls with plaster and fresh new paper printed with flowers. Afterwards, whistling contentedly as he sawed, he made shelves for the mighty volumes which kept coming from the book club—Voltaire and Dante, Machiavelli and St. Augustine. The sawdust was buttersweet and yellow on the sagging floor. Esther wasn't much of a talker, but he could tell that she was pleased at having her own place again, and she didn't stop and hold her side the way she used to, pressing at the little tug of pain that she was afraid to see a doctor about. Quietly, but with obvious satisfaction, she hung the rack with her antique spoons on the wall and arranged her collection of fancy china in the glass breakfront. Just as she finished, the new curtains filled with light like a comb of milky-golden honey, and the wonderful feeling inside him welled up and overflowed. "I was starving to see you and the boys," he said, coming up behind her and wrapping her in his ponderous arms. She laid her small, greying head against his chest. "We'll make up for lost time now," he said.

On Saturday he took the family to Kearley's department store and bought new outfits for Ron and Chub and persuaded Esther to try on a navy-blue silk dress. While she was in the cubby-hole under the stairs, he breathed in the smells of dry goods and leather and washed wooden floors. He beamed when she stepped out, pale and stiff, picking nervously at the drape of slick cloth and protesting that it cost too much.

"Heck, you're married to a man of means now," he said. And added: "Thanks to Bertram J. Stephens."

She didn't say a word, and he didn't expect her to. After so much trouble in years gone by it would take considerable time and effort to make peace between Bert and her. It was victory enough when she agreed to keep the dress. Blissfully he took her and the boys for a drive in the truck. The furnace-hot summer had cooled into fall, gold and fine. All along the river the cottonwoods were changing color and the creek beds were brim-full of moving yellow trees. Afterwards he showed them around town, commenting on everything. "It sure has perked up. When Bert and me first came in, the total population wasn't six hundred, and that was counting the cats and dogs." Now the streets were busy, and there were three new uranium company offices; actually they were tin-roofed wooden shacks built in 1880, but they were gorgeous with new brick and glass fronts trumpeting names like Western Minerals Corporation. At the end of Front Street, across the railroad tracks, a hill of ore had grown up at the buying station, and a truck, canted backwards, was dumping out more tons of yellow rock. "Our ore is in that pile," he said with pride. "You know, Bert and me are regular conversation pieces around here. Our pictures was even in the newspapers all over the country."

The check for the ore arrived on Monday—$27,760. "How's that for rewarding our pocket book?" he said to Esther. "Our half of that is fifty times what Bert took from the till, and more besides." In ecstasy he hurried to the hotel with the good news.

"Un-huh," Bert said without interest. He was sprawled by his bed under a green lamp, his eyes boring at Clark's *Principles of Geology*, and scattered around on the floor were a dictionary, brochures, pamphlets, government releases, and more books.

"Bert? I borrowed five hundred dollars to get my family here; what's my share with that took out?" Bert turned a page and Wally said, "Bert, come on to the bank and we'll open a joint account. You can spare that much time, can't you?"

"You go ahead, Lard. I'm setting on these eggs, and I got to hatch them out." He told Wally to leave some money with Mrs. Harbaugh for expenses and sank back into the book, intent, brooding down at the pages, oblivious of Wally and everything else.

An angry mumble rose from the other bed and Ray sat up, his eyes red and swimming. "Shut up," he spluttered. "Shut up, shut up." Ever since they struck the pod he had been like this, bad-tempered, grumbling. If it hadn't been so pitiful it would have been funny. He had been blowing on gamblers' hands for so many years that in his fuddled mind there wasn't the least doubt that he was a lucky charm. The poor little bugger had actually been trying to hex Bert for what he'd done, and he couldn't forgive himself for passing out that day and letting him get lucky.

He toddled along with Wally to the bank, kicking the sidewalk and muttering, "I made a miscue . . . I got all turned around and I made a miscue."

And yet the grotesque, whiskey-soaked dream of revenge bothered Wally less and less all the time. Bert was a new person entirely. Of course he had started prospecting to butt heads with Bolton, but Bolton was out of it now and Bert was working as never before, using his brilliant mind at last instead of drinking and going into moods. In the face of a turnabout like this Wally couldn't go on doubting him. Day by day the scalding memory faded, the riddle of his cruelty lost its strangle-hold, and the need to understand him, to forgive him, grew fainter and fainter. He believed in Bert again.

As soon as he had deposited the money, he doled out a few coins to Ray and went home to try some more diplomacy on Esther. She was mopping the kitchen floor. He stood in the doorway, big and earnest, the words catching a little in his sweet, scarred mouth. "I don't blame you for being suspicious," he said. "All I ask is for you to see him now. His hellbent streak is gone completely, honey. He's straight as that table-top there."

She wrung out the mop and slapped it down on the linoleum, neither objecting nor scoffing, just silent.

"I always believe in a man being entitled to another chance, but this time it's only what Bert has coming. He qualifies for another chance." After hesitating he came out with it: "Supposing I invite him to supper? All right?"

"Whatever you say."

"You mean it?" he cried, scarcely able to believe how easy it had been. It took more convincing than that to get Bert to agree. At first, without glancing up from his book, he said, "Hell no, I won't! You're trying to get me killed, Lard. You tell her I'm doctoring myself for worms and thank you kindly anyway." In the end he consented to come but then he tried to back out of it. When he did show up, shaved and dressed to the nines, with a box of chocolates under his arm, he whispered to Wally in fright, "I messed my britches already, Lard, and the fun ain't started yet." As a matter of fact, it *was* pretty strained on both sides. Bert and Esther were so polite that it hurt. After supper Wally played the old wind-up Edison phonograph that he'd put in working order, and everybody listened while the squeaky, mourning voice, as tiny as a kitten's, warbled out of the wooden throat: "The green grass grew all around, all around . . ." On the way back to the hotel Bert groaned, "Damn nation, that housewarming raised whelps all over me." Still, everything considered, Wally was more than satisfied. The ice had been broken. Doubtless it would take some fine handling, but his old dream of friendship between them was coming true at last.

But then, just when everything was going so well, Bob Werden blew into town.

"Bert?" Wally said, tiptoeing into the room. Annoyed, Bert looked up from his book and said, "He just now went out."

When Wally explained that Werden had asked to have lunch with them, there was a silence. "I'm not too fired up about it myself, but we can't just shun him, Bert. The man done us a lot of favors until he got his fill. Look at it his way, we must have got mighty boresome to him, and we *was* a bad risk."

Coming partly out of his trance Bert said, "And why do you figure he's here, Sunshine? Just a social call?"

"I guess he's . . ." Wally came to a stop, frowned. "I don't know. Why?"

Bert laid the book down and said, "You persuaded me into it." Wally blinked at him, uncomprehending, and he cuffed him lightly, affectionately, on the ear. "You old booger. Werden seen our picture—now do you get it? I'll just come along so he don't get you to thinking apples is gold nuggets."

Wally rocked his head, abashed by his own stupidity and warmed by Bert's new kindness. "But what if he—maybe he'll put you into a tailspin. He has an awful bad effect on you . . ."

"Shoot," Bert said, snapping his fingers, "it's my chance to study human nature."

Werden was pacing up and down in front of the Black Hills Cafe, large and soft in an expensive topcoat, a fuzzy green Alpine hat perched on his head. His face went from impatient stretching to delight at seeing them, then to religious seriousness. "Congratulations," he said, fervently shaking their hands. "I nearly went out the window when I heard the good tidings. Boy, you talk about the golden fleece, you really found it. Wally, how's Esther and the family?" Skittering from one topic to another, he ushered them inside. The air was drenched with food smells; chewing and talking men bent over plates. Bugging his eyes at a scrap of meat cooling in grease, Werden asked, "What's that, pemmican? You mean they fry it? Let's sit here in this booth. I wanted to get in touch earlier but I had my finger in some other pies." His face sliding into an expression of horror, he doubled under three of his fingers to make them look amputated. "This little piggie went to market," he said in a wee voice, "and so did this one and this one."

Before Wally could make sense of it, he was complaining about the poor transportation to Enterprise. "I came the last ten miles by stagecoach, for Chrissake." Instantly he was dramatizing a stagecoach full of people: "Marshall?" he cried in a schoolmarm's voice, "aren't those Indians?" Arrows spunked into the woodwork. The brave cowboy suddenly doubled up with an arrow in his stomach. "Don't worry, ma'am," he gasped, "it's just a flesh wound."

Wally was completely adrift. While he and Bert had coffee, Werden, perspiring, dispatched three pieces of coconut cake. "Bert, you're looking very good, no kidding. Prosperity must agree with you. How's the family, Wally?"

He never stopped talking. His formless pink face became different things all the time and his hands were just as fast, sprouting dozens of gestures which withered away as soon as they appeared.

"Okay, so I'm a putza," he said out of nowhere. "I feel very badly about that wire I sent you. So help me, it's been on my mind. I know, you think I let you down, I betrayed you. Listen, you should see a *real* Judas. The Judases I know, boy! Some of those guys, all I do is see them coming toward me, and I don't even bother; I just stoop down for the cross and say, 'One, two, three, upseedaisy. Okay, let's go. Has somebody got the nails?' "

Instantly, sensing Wally's disapproval, he said, "I don't mean I'm Christ, Wally. Far from it. I'm not even Jewish—there I go again," he grimaced. "I'm sincerely sorry, Cathy says I'm a disgrace, and your sister Mae says the same thing—when she'll speak to me. And they're right! Anyhow, *believe* me, I wasn't trying to throw you guys to the wolves. Here's the story, and it's the honest-to-God truth. At the time you sent for more dough, I just couldn't do it. I don't mean the money, a couple hundred bucks like that, who cares? But at the time my back was against the wall! They were tying a handkerchief over my eyes, and I'm trying to remember what brand of cigarettes are longest, and all of a sudden I hear somebody hollering, 'Hey mister? Mister, can you give me a nickel?' And I'm busy *dying!*"

Wally said, "You mean you was too busy. That's all right."

"You forgive me? Really? Say, that's really great," he cried, holding Wally's hand. "I don't deserve it. I'm a schmuck to do these things," he said woefully. "To my friends, too. I feel like I've just eaten my young. I don't know. I'd like to be a human being, I really would, but

Uranium! 251

it's too late. I'd give two hundred and fifty dollars to be a boy again—okay, two-seventy-five, but that's my final offer." And he laughed nervously, turning his blobby pink face from Wally to Bert and back again.

Wally had seen Werden do this before, and painstakingly, over the years, he had figured it out. Werden's attacks of conscience were partly an honest feeling, partly a habit, and partly a way to square things. Actually he was being straighter when he twisted around and began making fun of them. Wally was very uncomfortable. Half afraid to look, he glanced at Bert's thin-eyed, expressionless face. He'd been wrong to drag Bert into this, and he hoped and prayed he wouldn't go to pieces.

"So are we friends again?" Werden entreated them, smiling. "For old times sake?" He swung his face toward Bert. "You forgive me too?" Much too clever to let Bert answer, and perhaps snub or insult him, he went right on, "Here's where I make it up to both of you. This is it, the *big buck!* How much have you taken out of the mine so far?"

"Twenty-seven thousand," Wally said. "A little over that."

"Terrific! Let's see . . ." After a moment's calculation he announced, "I can make you a hundred and fifty thousand apiece with that mine and no sweat. I guarantee it. I know the brokers in New York, and we can incorporate for five hundred thousand—three hundred for you and one hundred for me and one hundred for them."

"But there ain't any mine," Wally told him. "It was just a pod of ore we . . ."

"Don't kid me." For an instant Werden turned ugly. Then, afraid he'd gone too far, he sweated into a joke: "A pod is something with seeds in it. I'm an expert. Me and Luther Burbank used to compare thumbs at UCLA."

"I'm serious. It was a piece of float about the size of a room and that was all."

Werden's voice was injured. "Sure, sure. Now when you're a winner, I'm out, huh? Et tu, Brute. I staked you for years, and this is what I get. Now when I need a score—certain matters have gone to pot that I was counting on. Certain very big matters." Morbidly secretive as always, he wouldn't reveal exactly what matters had gone to pot; all he would do was hint direly about wolves and Benedict Arnolds. Then his eyes went blurry-blue, and he said, "You could listen to the proposition anyway, couldn't you? Give me a look-in—either that or buy these pencils."

"Pencils?" Wally said.

"Come off of it. Don't con *me* now." Angrily he took a swallow of the vile, sulphur-tasting water: his eyes bugged and his hands went to his throat. "Ough! What's in this? Hemlock? I knew you guys were sore but hey!" Without a break he slipped into a performance of Socrates and the cup of hemlock, laughing it up and accusing Wally and Bert at the same time.

"I don't know about all that," Wally said, "but we'll ride you out there and prove it."

As they were crossing the highway to the truck, Ray toddled up and demanded to go along. Werden patted him on his bulging head and said, "How old are you, little boy? Forty-seven?" Ray scowled, "I don't appreciate that," and knocked away the dime Werden held out, grinning. Wally assured Ray they weren't going prospecting, but he wouldn't believe it and tried to squeeze into the cab with them. "Bye-bye, your mother is calling," Werden said impatiently. "She wants you to feed the elephants."

More and more solemn, Wally headed the truck out of town. Brash new billboards had sprung up among the rusty road signs. The grey shanty of a grocery store across the river was selling curios and candy-bright rocks and renting cheap Geigers at five dollars a day. They cut off the highway toward the plateau. Werden began to apologize at top speed. "I believe you about the pod, or whatever it was, Wally. It's just that I got the bloody sweats, you know? I was counting so much on the deal, I couldn't let go." Talking and talking into the silence, he looked out at a small herd of steers, ready for shipment, bunched around a wooden loading chute and then at the endless hills following each other off into the pale brightness. "You can sure see a long way out here, can't you? Of course, in country like this being blind isn't bad either."

He smiled at them hopefully. Neither Wally nor Bert made any comment. The truck staggered over the plateau dug up with prospect holes like a monstrous prairie dog village. They stopped at a pit gouged out of the scrub grass and rock. Werden walged cautiously to the edge and peered down. "Sloppy job," he said. "Very careless. Either those gravediggers get on the ball or out they go." His face wriggled with smiling disappointment. "What I'm saying is, I believe you. It's no mine."

"That's what I told you. We got a couple low-grade claims in the canyon and that's all."

"Wait a minute," Werden said, all excited again. "How stupid can I get? That's the way to the crown jewels. Bert, you listen too, commere. Here it is, the grand coup. We'll set up a company and put out brochures with your picture and the press release on the cover. Inside we discuss the future of the uranium industry, world crisis, *and* twenty-seven thousand plus in profits so far this year. From *all the mines,* you see? The whole operation. It's perfect."

Bert leaned against the truck with his hands in his pockets, as if he hadn't heard, but the blood darkened in Wally's mild shallow face. "I don't intend to take nobody down the river," he said severely.

"What are you talking about, down the river? That's how stock is issued. With the fresh money, you can buy more claims and equipment, whatever you need to put some muscle in the operation. Then if you hit a good vein, or whatever it's called, okay give three cheers, all the pipsqueaks get dividends; the stock goes up, the SEC apologizes to me personally—listen, the investing public is in this for a quick buck, they're not mailing the money to a home for unwed mothers. It's more than they deserve, to get somebody honest like you, busting a nut for them. So where's the boat ride?"

Bewildered by the rapid-fire arguments, Wally glanced to Bert for help. Bert shrugged and said that two hundred thousand seemed like a lot of overhead in a five-hundred-thousand-dollar issue.

"That's right," Wally said with a look of gratitude. "Plus, the whole proposition is too much of a long shot, the way I see it. There's many a lemon and very few oranges in uranium. It wouldn't be fair to ask people to put their money in something this risky."

"It's hot money," Werden insisted. "They want to take a flyer, so let 'em."

Wally lumbered toward the truck. "We're going back."

"You mean no? Wait a minute, let me spell it out for you: M-I-S-S-I-S-I- . . ." He giggled despairingly, then snatched at Wally's sleeve and said, "Please?" Wally climbed in behind the wheel. On the way back to town, Werden threw up his hands and said, "Okay, be a straight arrow, I admire you for it. I really do. How about a lead to another mine? A good one, I mean, with nothing hokey involved. There's a block of stocks in it for you . . ."

By this time Wally was almighty mad. He let Werden off in front of the cafe without a word of good-bye. As Bert got out at the hotel, Wally said to him, "Knowing a man that long, I ought to've known he was a rascal. I'm not very smart."

"Invigorating, wasn't it?" Bert grinned. "Human beings are mostly bastards, and Bob Werden is really human."

"Anyhow, you're not knocked off kilter and we're quits of him and no harm done." The air was cool and bright, and Bert was standing there in his second-hand leather jacket, a trickle of cigarette smoke by his face, and just then a loaded hay truck came bulking past them and spread a sweet alfalfa smell over the dusty street. "Bert?" he said. "We've touched bottom many a time . . . well, I just want to say, you're finally showing me what a man looks like."

"No charge whatsoever, Sunshine." Already drawing into himself, the wave of his hand going absent-minded, he hurried inside to hit the books again.

They were not quits of Bob Werden, however. With the house in good shape and Bert studying all day long, Wally started mining by himself to keep busy and make expenses, and while he was out digging in the canyon Werden made a spiel to Esther. Utterly unsuspecting,

Wally came in after dark, washed up and sat down to a plate of cabbage, fried pork, and potatoes which she'd kept warm for him. The boys were watching television in the living room. She was canning a bushel of tomatoes that she was afraid would "go" on her if she didn't put them up that very evening. The air was moist and sticky-warm. Pans were steaming on the stove and the jars and lids tapped and clinked in boiling water.

"I don't see what you have against Bob's proposition," she said without turning from the stove.

"Bob Werden? Has that pesky sonofagun been after you? I'll tell you what I have against him—the cut-throat. I don't generally like to say anything against a man but he's crookeder than a barrel full of snakes. How Cathy could've married him is a mystery to me. The man could hide behind a corkscrew, honey. What he's after is to sell a half a million dollars worth of stock on nothing but two bread-and-butter mines and our reputation."

He might as well have been talking to the stove. Her eyes shut in by her glasses, she stepped past him and dropped more of the tomatoes into boiling water, then into cold water, to loosen the skins. After that she pierced the dark red bellies with a knife, slipped off the skins, and propped the handfuls of veiny, dripping flesh into a bowl. The skins were like membranes on the newspaper in her lap. Her hands and forearms were red.

"You could go back into construction," she said then. "You could build Bob's new dude ranch near Phoenix for a starter. He said so."

"Esther, I'm surprised at you. The man is a slicker and that's only a bribe, plain and simple. That's all it is."

As before, he failed to make any impression on her. They were in the middle of one of their strange, cold, slow-motion quarrels, made up of a few bare statements and long, long pauses. Holding her side from time to time, she packed the raw tomatoes into jars, prodding out the bubbles of air with a spoon. The red bodies flattened against the jars with a sucking sound and took each other's shape, dull, identical. He couldn't understand what was behind her blind support of Bob Werden; however, from years of experience he knew that asking would only close her up, maybe for days or weeks. He waited.

"At least Bob Werden is a gentleman," she said after a while. "Not somebody with occupation unknown."

She meant Bert by that. She aimed to leave him behind. With all that money, she figured, Bert would be a man of leisure and wouldn't need caring for any longer. He looked at her, shaken. Her lips were clipped together. Her flat breasts showed in the neck of her dress as she bent over and, holding down the floating tomatoes with one hand, spooned sugar and salt into the jars: small white mounds that soaked and sank into red . . . And if such was her aim, it meant—he felt as if he had been slugged in the stomach—it meant that she had joined him here in order to fight Bert, to get rid of him once and for all. She hadn't come around in the least, she would never come around to liking Bert or even to accepting him as a business partner—and he'd been so sure he was making headway.

"All I want is credit where it's due," he said. "Have you suffered any harm from Bert since you come?" The words disappeared into her silence. Rubbing the back of his neck helplessly, he watched her seal the jars: lay the rubber-edged lid on each, slip on the ring, screw the cap down. There was a whole list of things he wanted to tell her—that Bert wasn't shirking, that he was studying hard to make them all rich, that it wasn't necessary to ride herd on him anymore. But she didn't care about any of it.

All at once he saw her more clearly than he ever had in his life—placing the jars in the indestructible old pressure cooker with its handles and twist-down clamps and its dial like a single idiot eye on top, and doing it with such an earnest expression, with a grave ritual of movements for everything, even to the last wiping of dried juice from her elbows. It was just like her to slave for hours canning tomatoes when canned tomatoes were dirt cheap and when she hadn't even raised them herself. The pity of it wrung his heart. She never let anything go or threw it away; she ate the left-overs on all the plates, she saved, she cleaned, she patched. It wasn't that she cared especially for money; she only wanted to keep what was hers. And that included him, all of him, with his boots and hat thrown in for good measure.

"Honey?" He took her damp, scoured hands in his, and breathless with hope, she litfed her heat-flushed face. Then she understood and sat down without a word. The light made a blank stare of her glasses.

Sadly he carried his plate to the sink. A man had to do something beyond himself, or at least die trying to do it, and more than ever he knew that for him it was salvaging the booze-soaked, laughing bum he'd met on Skid-row in Denver. It was the mountain he had to climb. Bert was worth a hundred of him, and now especially, when Bert was taking hold at last, he couldn't turn his back on him. He believed in Bert.

Ironically, the very next day his faith was put to the grimmest possible test. It was Sunday, and after church and dinner he took a walk uptown to pay Bert a visit. The room was dark. Surprised, he asked Mrs. Harbaugh about him, but she had just come in herself. A few minutes later he found Ray throned on a stool in a restaurant, irritably munching at a hamburger. As soon as Wally came in, two of the men near Ray edged toward the back, nervously adjusting their roll-brimmed hats. "Did they bother you?" Wally asked, looking at them.

"Go away," Ray grumped. "Don't mess with me."

"All I want to know is where's Bert. Did you see him?"

Ray sprayed profanity and bits of food, accidentally knocked his hamburger to the floor, retrieved it and went on eating—chewing with his hard gums, packing the food into his squashy cheeks and changing it around, swallowing. His leaky eyes brimmed with some kind of fresh grievance.

It took ten minutes and all of Wally's change to get it out of him: Bert and Bob Werden had driven off in a car and left him behind again.

Wally felt a tremor in the heart. "You're crazy, Bert and Bob Werden?"

"Beat it, you big nose," Ray spluttered. "Go on, hit the street." He mumbled something about crazy people and his eyes wept with venomous feeling.

Outside among the loitering men, Wally came to a stop like a blind man, hunched over, looking straight ahead at nothing. What reason could Bert have had—except a bad one? For a terrible moment his confidence shrivelled, his old fears pricked fiercely at him, and everything that had been settled hung in the balance again. Then he pulled himself together: he believed in Bert.

Striking out firmly, he crossed the street to the hotel and stationed himself in the lobby. To pass the time, he began a letter to Paul: "Everything is fine on this end. Maybe you saw our pictures in the papers. Bert and me made a pretty good strike, I mean Bert did. He did it all. Lucy is fine and doing first-rate in her school work . . ." A half hour later he found himself staring, sightless, at the carefully formed words and gave up the letter as a bad job. Why had Bert gone off with Werden? Doubtless it was to some mining property. But Bert hated him too much to make a deal, no matter how much money there was in it. There had to be some explanation. Restlessly he checked Mencke's drugstore and then patrolled slowly up and down Highway Street. In the veterinarian's yard, the leaves let go from the trees, one by one, and lay like scraps of dried brown leather in the grass. Four, five, six times he passed the pink cafe that Bert had painted to spite the Boltons. Scowling with effort, he pushed away the thought that the leases were in Bert's name and that as far as the law was concerned, Bert was free to deal with Werden on his own if he pleased.

When he noticed the taverns had opened, he refused even to look inside them for Bert. A group of men were talking in front of Perkins' hardware store. One of them, a man in soil-grey work clothes with a strangling belt buckled under the weight of his belly, was saying that two of the miners were forming corporations. Bud Robel was one of them! Wally froze as the ominous motion started in his head: Bert was in Helen Mencke's good graces, to put it mildly, and she was Bud's sister. If Bert had gone crooked on him, if he'd taken a block of stocks for steering Werden to Bud Robel so he could set up a stock deal on that sorry little mine . . . If Esther was right after all . . .

No! He wouldn't believe it! Bert would never do a thing like that. Every step he took, roaming from one end of Highway Street to the other, was a determined act of faith. The sun had gone behind the hills and a wind blew out of the yellow west. Beyond the used car lot, beyond the garage and its rusty scatter of wrecked cars, a lonely arclight shook on top of a bare hill. When, across from the vet's place, he finally saw Bob Werden, it was like a hallucination. Bob Werden was on foot, tottering along the edge of the highway in layers of dusty moonlight. His natty green hat leaning to one side, his collar askew and his coat flapping open, he came reeling toward Wally.

"The fink!" he croaked. "The back-stabbing fink!" Obscenities came blowing out with his exhausted breath. "The rat set me up . . . said he knew of a prospect and left me in the middle of Siberia . . . Where's the car I rented? I'll tell you this. If he stole it he's going to jail!"

It was something to behold. A big smile stretching his sporty moustache, Wally let his fists come apart in relief. It was something to behold, all right. Suddenly, in the middle of some extreme bad language, Werden switched around and with a slavish smile said, "Okay, okay, you guys have got your pound of flesh—you got enough to open a butcher shop with. So let's call it even. Now will you listen?"

Wally hunched into laughter, bellows of glorious laughter. "You got off lucky," he said. "You'd best leave it at that. If you wasn't Cathy's husband I'd do worse to you."

Still smiling, he made for the hotel. Of course Bert had been in his room for hours, bearing down on the books while he had been pacing up and down the street. The tremendous vindication of his faith left him dazed and foolish with laughter. "Werden just come hoofing it into town," he told Bert. "And it was something to behold. It done my soul good."

But Bert hadn't heard him. "Damn nation," he said to himself. "It's there somewhere close. And I'll crack it. I can feel it, like a card you draw to a full house and you know it's there." He glanced out of his deep-tunneling concentration. "I had to mess him up a little bit, Lard, to keep him from pestering me. I should've shot him."

"You sure outfoxed him, and that's going some with a high-powered man like that," Wally said with bungling adoration. "He's just not your equal. There's not a man I ever heard of that is."

A frost moon was shining in a great visionary halo as Wally walked home to supper. Children's voices drifted in the air. There was a pleasant smell of smoke from burning leaves and the bronze trees glowed in the street lamps like stained glass windows. Children were running and crashing through the pools of fallen leaves. He stopped for a minute to watch them cover a boy with heaps and handfuls of leaves while he lay still and grinning, with his scrawny arms at his sides. All of a sudden the mound quaked and trembled from end to end, the children squealed with delight, and he burst up from the ground in a shower of leaves—yellow leaves streaming from his face and arms, flying all around him in the shadows.

XVIII

Pierce Bolton was blissful, too. The Lord had been extra kind since he changed his ways and accepted Jesus into his life. Not only had Bert Stephens stopped torturing him, but the old man was out of the way at last. Now they had the say-so, now they were the respected cattlemen, and just as soon as beef shipping was over, he and Billy Joe went in together on another plane, not just a second-hand piece of trash but a spanking new four-seater which they tied down in the pasture near the ranch house until they could move the barn from the old Baird place.

Proudly he said to Frank, "Is she a beauty or not? Ward Peterson says it's the equal of theirs or better."

Narrow-hipped, hard, quiet, a knot of tobacco in his cheek, Frank looked over the dashing red-and-white plane roped to iron stakes in the ground. "How much did it run you?" he asked presently.

"Never mind, it was within our pocketbook," Pierce assured him. "Don't you worry about that payment on the ranch. I fully intend to pay Daddy off, if it means taking food out of my children's mouth. When I make a bargain I hold to it." Charitably he didn't say what a hellish mean bargain it was, the sort you would expect from a cruel-natured man who had sweated the blood out of his own sons, who had made his fortune from the disaster of other ranchers, and who was widely known as the greatest whore-hopper in the West.

As a matter of fact, he didn't believe his father would dun them for the money at all, not because of any benevolence but because he was so fired up about that tourist trap of his. Likely he wouldn't think of them for a year or more. Daddy did only one thing at a time and at present his head was full of plans for a trout pond, building an incline to the top of the mountain and such schemes—all this with a badly broken leg.

Which was God's punishment on him and it served him right. It would be just like him to wake up one fine morning and start bellowing for his money, expecting to get blood out of a turnip when the drought was so merciless and the herds were sold down to practically nothing. However, it would do him no good. Laid up as he was with that leg, he *couldn't* take the ranch back and run it, even with Frank to do the heavy work, and he was far too pennypinching to hire help.

For the first time in his life Pierce was holding the aces.

All he had to do was pacify Frank, who continued to bring up the matter of the payment. Instead of telling him that the ranch was their birthright, or that Daddy was already fat with uranium money, Pierce shrewdly changed the subject to the steer gather and winter feeding. Then he had a brilliant idea: he suggested flying to Elder, Wyoming, for a cattle auction. Frank jumped at the chance. He might not feel rich enough to buy but he dearly loved to look.

And so, as soon as they'd finished the chores on Thursday, they dressed up and lit out for Elder, the plane bouncing and lifting like a kite from the brown pasture. Before turning toward Wyoming, Pierce made a circuit of the ranch, swooping over dry hills and the flats by the river speckled with their cattle.

"You see?" he yelled to Frank, buckled in the front seat beside him. "Any time we want to check the herds now we can do it in ten minutes. Or say we want to go to a stock sale, it's a matter of half an hour to get there."

Billy Joe backed him up a hundred per cent and pretty soon Frank said, "Could be."

From a man like Frank this was very encouraging. If he could be made to see the advantages of a plane and go in with them on it, then, since it was already paid for, he could send Frank's share of the cost to Daddy as part payment on the mortgage. This would quiet Frank down as well as guard against any kick-up by Daddy, and there would be satisfaction all around.

"It's a good flying plane, too," Pierce said enthusiastically. He began stunting to give Frank a demonstration of his skill (and scare him a little, too). Two thousand feet under them was Red Canyon, its pine slopes and angry cliffs pocked with new mines and scratched with zig-zagging mine roads. Pulling the half-moon steering wheel back into his stomach, he roared up the nose of the plane and whee-ed as the motor stuttered and coughed, the propeller slowed, and the plane sank backwards under them sickeningly. Frank went grey. Chuckling in triumph, Pierce gave it the gas again, then banked steeply to the right. The sky and the trough of canyon below them tilted sharply, rolled half over, and Frank was hurled sideways in his seat. His Sunday Stetson fell off and he was staring down through the side window, suspended over two thousand feet of nothing.

"I bet you never bulldogged a steer this tough," Pierce gloated boyishly. Levelling the plane before Frank lost his temper, he chortled, "I bet you swallowed that plug of tobacco."

"Damn near."

Billy Joe poked his face between them and beamed, "You should see him do barrel rolls. I vomited my guts the first time."

Frank recovered his creamy dress hat, and still snorting with laughter Pierce opened the throttle. They were high and free, up in the floating clouds, in sky above sky. A mile away another plane swam like a minnow in blue lakes of heaven. Hills like heaps of ashes shifted and slid under them, dessicated patches of hayfield and pasture tied together with roads, a town like a fistful of pebbles.

Pierce took the occasion to work on Frank some more. "This is our chance, Frank. Our whole life we've been hemmed in constantly, busting our backs from sun-up until dark for scanty wages or none. With never one single kind word or a thank you. Plus Daddy is thirty years behind the times. We have a free hand now to lighten our load and make the ranch a showplace if we want to."

All around them as far as they could see, the sky was littered with small drifting clouds like fragments from an explosion. He took the plane up another five hundred feet. Off to the left, across thirty miles of empty space, he saw a thunderhead mushrooming up into the blue, a bloated and sinister growth in the sky, humpbacked, deformed, with lifting brute shoulders of white and grey. Fortunately, the doom shape was nowhere near their course.

In a minute the cloud scraps around them cleared off, and just slightly to one side underneath, the highway to Elder threaded between the hills. Only then did Pierce notice the sky ahead bulging with solid grey. Already, he perceived nervously, the clouds had overrun the mountains behind the town, blotted out the peaks with rolling grey and black. The wind increased. Lightning ripped out of the bottom of the advancing squall line.

"Looks like it's raining over there," Billy Joe said with interest.

Frank was watching, too, and he said, "Hope it comes our way."

Pierce glanced at them with bitter scorn, then turned his attention back to the clouds spawning and driving down out of the mountains. It was a pitiful spot to be in. He didn't want Frank, especially, to think that he was chicken-hearted; on the other hand, he didn't like to take chances of any sort. Only a few miles ahead of them, still sitting in peaceful sunshine, were the town and the landing strip, tucked in front of the foothills. The watertower gleamed in the pure autumn light, so close. But the sky was full of wind, the plane sank and bounded upward, the propeller down in front of him whipped around and around heavily. He hesitated, veered off from the town lying now like a vision in slants of golden light, then changed his mind again and tried to make the last couple of miles before the squall hit.

"That stinking, miserable, rotten weather reporter," he fumed. "He ought to be—he's incompetent, he ought to be hung as a public service."

Frank made no comment, but Billy Joe said, "Oughtn't we to go back, Bubber?"

"Shut up!" he bawled. "I'm flying this plane . . . You're an idiot, you've got the mind of a . . ." The mountains were gone, lightning stabbed from the onrushing greyish-green scum. The wings seesawed badly in spite of his terrified efforts and the plane, shuddering from end to end, moved more and more slowly against the shoving headwind. With each second the spastic hitching of the wings grew worse, and then the plane was overpowered, held in one place, plunging and bucking futilely. Witchblack clouds rode toward them; the town went under. Slamming his foot on the pedal, he swerved the plane around and made for a blue corridor of open sky.

"Did you ever see such cursed rotten bad luck?" he said tragically. "Can't even go to a stinking cattle sale without misfortune. It's piteous." His face was a crimson smear. His heart caught with despair as he saw that in the few minutes he'd delayed, it had become too late to turn back: the narrowing sky was sucked up in front of him, the first spit of rain broke on the windshield, and an instant later they were swallowed up in a whirlwind of rain. "I can't see nothing," he babbled.

Far off, his voice almost lost in the mushy roar of the engine, Billy Joe was praying. Pierce tried to pray too, looking at the rain-plastered windshield. The splashes were big and ragged. They melted the smeary fans which the wipers kept reforming in front of him. After a while he was aware that drops were leaking down from the roof and splattering onto the wheel in his hands, that his lap was soaked as if he'd wet his pants. A brand new plane, too, he thought sorrowfully. They had rooked him as usual. Aimlessly, hypnotized by the repetition, he watched new multitudes of raindrops come alive on the windshield, flatten and go under the sweep of the wiper. On every stroke it left behind a welt of shattered drops and erased it coming back. He was very tired, so leaden that he could barely keep his eyes open and his hands on the wheel. This was it, the end of the line. In a few minutes they would be just an item in the paper. Soft waves of melancholy, of gentle resignation, went through him, and he listened calmly to the vicious crack of hail against the plane and stared at the white flicking of it against the drowned windshield, stared at the huge thing taking shape in front of him, swelling faster and faster, lunging, ramming him with such force that he was brought surging up in his safety belt, and ramming him again, again, twisting him, throwing him upside down.

There was no sound except the spatter and lash of rain. He was hanging face down over the instrument panel, his eyes opening and closing and opening on the sight of the rain-blobbed windshield, on branches and wet green fans of pine needles. Frank was talking to him. There was a bump, a fumbling at the buckle of his safety belt, and he found himself sprawled, limp, on the windshield. His head throbbed painfully but he was too far away, weak and dreamy to protest. He allowed himself to be pulled out of the plane, lifted and set down. The clay was greasy with rain and prickly with brown needles and pine cones. "You rode that old heifer down pretty good," Frank said to him. "Come on, let's get you out of the wet."

It was one of the first nice things Frank had ever said to him and he almost broke into tears with gratitude. He was hoisted to his feet and led under a pine tree, where the three of them huddled in the plop, plop of big cold drops. His muddy pants stuck to his legs. Fifty feet away in a grey dream was the plane, flipped over on its nose and plunged deep into the trees, caught like a fish in nets of torn branches. One dripping wing, ripped completely off, was raised like a skinny arm toward the sky; the other was crumpled under. The propeller and motor was crushed against a burly trunk. The plane was a total loss, he concluded without the least emotion, and there wasn't a penny of insurance on it. A tickle crawled down his neck. He brushed at it and his hand came back red with blood.

"Am I hurt?" he asked Frank.

"Not to amount to anything. You bumped your head when I unhitched you."

"Oh."

"The Lord was sure on our side," Billy Joe said devoutly. "We had His blessing or we wouldn't never have made it."

The squall passed over and they helped him down the skidding rocks and over the dead logs, into an abandoned clearing. Blowy sifts of rain glimmered in the sunlight. The soaked brown grass was spiky with seedling pines. Not far from the grey, ruined house and barn were a few gravestones, fenced in with barbed wire. Suddenly Pierce could see everything, feel everything. "We nearly got killed," he said in awe.

'I won't contest that," Frank said. "Let's keep agoing."

Sopping wet, muddy, his fine hat blotched with rain, he plodded forward. But Pierce stood wide-eyed and trembling. "We were as good as dead and buried," he said.

Billy Joe waited beside him, bobbing his head. "It was miraculous, Bubber."

The air was misted with rain shimmers and the sky was steep with white clouds. Seeds of rain glittered on the barbed wire by the worn and nameless stones, glittered and fell. "Life is just a brief moment anyways. We're all of us going to be here only a short time."

"That's right," Billy Joe said.

"We got another chance," Pierce said. He felt something pulsing in him, working inside him. It was the memory of the night he'd wandered into the church because everything was wrong with his life, and the old woman beside him had raised her wrinkled face, her tiny sunken eyes closed in prayer, and the voice of the minister was beating inside him again; his sorrow was pressing like a great lump of agony, and then he was released, delivered into white glory, beautiful white glory.

"Sure, I made a place for God in my life," he said to Billy Joe. "But I only went halfways. I been lukewarm, and the Lord spits that kind out of His mouth."

"What do you mean, Bubber? You're a true Christian now."

Frank had wheeled around and started back impatiently but Pierce didn't care. He was living over the few minutes when the young man had been summoned from the choir, blushing meekly, and given a check to help him through ministerial school. Ever since that night he'd been unable to get the incident out of his mind and now he saw why: the Lord had been working on his heart all the time, camping on his doorstep, and he hadn't understood. Now he knew and it was like a trumpet speaking to him. A great wind of glory went through him and the clouds were strong angels standing at his right and left hand.

"I know the way I have to go," he told Billy Joe. "This accident was for a reason, to bring me to my senses. It was for a purpose, a very serious purpose. The Lord delivered me to be a faithful witness to Him and work in His vineyard."

Billy Joe's spread-eared face was open with wonder. "You mean —be a preacher?"

"I mean it sincerely. Are you with me or not?"

"Can I? You mean it? I been so wishing to go," he said in a quaking voice. "This is the Lord's blessing for sure."

Emotionally, Pierce shook hands with him. Now, truly, he was born again in Jesus Christ and his heart was set free. When Frank asked him what in the hell was going on, he answered without flinching, "We have a hunger to serve God in a better way. We're going to be preachers."

For a second Frank looked at them as if he thought their brains had been knocked loose in the wreck; then he said quietly, "What about the ranch?"

"We'll help you in the summers, the heavy work is in the haying," Pierce said. "With the herds so small, there's not much else to do. Anyhow, we likely won't be able to start till the January semester."

And Billy Joe added, "You ought to live closer to Jesus yourself, Frank. It was a warning to you, too. At the Judgment Day it'll be serious."

Frank let that pass without comment, and he did not refer to the matter again as they tramped to the highway and caught a ride back.

Pierce, however, was not intimidated. Filled with a new and joyful strength, he faced all the difficulties ahead with confidence. In order to cut down on expenses, Irene and the children would have to be left at home. This was easy enough because Frank needed someone to keep house for him and in his silent way he liked the kids. The real stumbling block was cash. All but a few hundred dollars, hardly enough to set a decent table till they left, had gone into the plane, and they would have to pry it loose from Daddy. But even this didn't cow him. Hard and tight-fisted though he was by nature, Daddy was religious minded enough to go off for a day at a time by himself to feel closer to God. With the help of the Lord he could convince him.

That very night he said to Frank, "Billy Joe and me are going up to the lodge tomorrow to talk to Daddy."

Frank merely said, "I'd be obliged if you'd help me with the weaning first. The brood cows are drying up and starting to lose weight."

Pierce agreed very unwillingly. Next to haying, this was the chore he despised the most. The breeding herd had to be driven into the corrals by the ranch house and the cows put in one corral and the calves in another as far away as possible. All day and all night the cows kept up a heartbroken bawling for their young ones and the calves milled around in the fuming dust and blatted back. Nobody could talk or sleep, and his nerves were in extremely bad shape by the time the calves could be driven out to winter grass.

Red-eyed and irritable, he started for the lodge with Billy Joe. "If I never see another cow it'll be a hundred years too soon," he grumbled. "I wasn't cut out for such a life. Stinking, rotten animals." It was hot for October, too, up close to the 90's, and that didn't improve his temper any. While he roared the car down the empty highway, Billy Joe, leaning half over on the curves, read the morning paper out loud: Senator McCarthy had said on nation-wide TV that Adlai Stevenson would continue his Kremlin-directed policies if elected president . . . the British had exploded an atomic device of their own in the Monte Bello Islands . . . the Norwegian committee had announced that no Nobel Prize for peace would be awarded this year . . .

"Will you kindly quit?" Pierce shouted. "You always insist on reading everything out loud. Every single thing! You read the label on a can out loud! It scalds my guts."

"I'm sorry, Bubber. I was only thinking, there's a great need for prayer in the world today."

But Pierce wasn't listening. Once when he was three or four years old he'd found a ladder going up to the roof of the barn. It seemed a mile up there, it seemed all the way to the sky. Rung by rung he crept higher and higher, the ladder quivering under his hands and feet, the ground sinking farther and farther away, and all at once the ladder heaved up and down, vibrating like an enormous rubber band. He snatched at it and looked down into the rocking emptiness under him: his father was shaking the ladder to tease him, and chuckling! He screamed, holding onto the flopping rungs for dear life, and then he was falling, falling—smack into the gigantic hairy arms. Laughter rumbled in the deep cave of chest under him, but he couldn't stop screaming. At first Daddy had tried to comfort him; then the smile had sponged off his face and he'd walked away in disgust.

"We never had no luck in any dealings with him," he said disconsolately. "We won't get penny one."

"Sure we will, Bubber. If we just put God in front and go ahead, we'll make it."

"I hope so." But though he did his best to stay confident, strong, the bottomless feeling kept growing. The jeep-ride by the lake was shut down, the restaurants and curio shops were closed. The highway bent sharply and then the Mount Rushmore faces stared, bone white, in the empty blue sky. Ripples of fear went up and down him as he stopped in front of his father's lodge.

He whispered to Billy Joe to let him do the talking, but even before they got out of the car he could see that the old man had problems of his own. Swinging his plaster leg and setting it down, sweaty, stripped to the waist, he was dragging a garden hose toward a vacuum cleaner lying on the rusty lawn. In the trout pond a hundred feet from the lodge, fish were leaping out of the water and swimming around in erratic, crippled circles and zigzags.

"Got to get air to them," Sam was muttering. He had reversed the hose of the vacuum cleaner to blow air instead of sucking, but the extension cord wasn't long enough to get the cleaner anywhere near the pond. In a fury of effort, he taped the unequal hoses together, and they strung the garden hose to the pond and held the end under water. A feeble slosh of air went in. The fish kept dying: two thousand trout which he'd bought and was raising for tourists to catch for their dinners next season. The whole surface fluttered with gasping, threshing fish. Here and there a trout burst up from the sickly water, flailed in the air and splashed down again.

"It's the hot weather," Sam said, pulling his forearm wearily across his face. "They're suffocating. The lack of oxygen has the same effect as on a human. Brain damage." The two mismatched hoses came apart with a spewing noise. His strong discolored teeth showed in his bristling face and he squatted on one leg with the white log of the other thrust out and jammed the hoses together in his great paws. "Here, let me help," Pierce said eagerly. They taped the hoses together again, and this time Sam kept the joining gripped in his hand. But the small rill of air that bubbled into the pond was practically useless. "Where's that damn fool Vivie?" he exploded, looking down the highway. A half hour later she still hadn't come back with the extension cord and the small watery world struggled in the convulsions of death. Trout twisted up into the air, flashed in mad spanking jumps, and fell back into the bobbing, slowly tipping litter of dead fish.

Sam stood on one foot, slumped over, his brute hairy face hanging, and gazed somberly at the pond. "They were pretty little creatures," he said. "Their organization ain't much higher than the worms they feed on, but their speed and grace was pretty."

"It's sure a bad setback," Pierce said, coming as close as he dared to the old man. He was making some progress as a companion in misfortune when his mother drove up, almost hysterical, with a coil of extension cord and another old vacuum cleaner. In a matter of seconds the cleaners were gurgling and frothing air into the pond, but only a few of the trout were still alive, their brains and nervous systems destroyed, hanging and jerking insanely among the floating corpses.

"Oh Sam, it's terrible," she cried, pressing her cheek against his shoulder. "The highway store was closed! I went all over the whole county. It's such a shame, all those beautiful living things!"

"It's piteous, all right," Pierce joined in.

Her face snapped around and she put her hands on her hips. "Just what are you two doing here anyway? Billy Joe? Don't you have nothing to do either?"

Billy Joe scuffed his feet and looked to Pierce. Quailing, he said, "It's not anything important. It can wait for another time."

"You wasted a whole day already coming up here. Out with it!"

Just the tone of her voice turned him inside out. She had always despised him, and he dearly wished now he had tackled Daddy while she was away. "Mamma," he said as bravely as he could, "Billy Joe and me have reached a decision. We decided to dedicate our life. We're gonna be preachers."

"Goodbye and good luck," she said. Her strong legs, sheathed in blue jeans, were wide apart and her pink corduroy shoes were planted in the gravel. "Anything else you want to say in conclusion?"

It was humiliating. His face hot, he glanced toward the old man but he was brooding down at his dead trout. The fight went out of Pierce then, and he merely went through the motions of asking. "All we need is enough money to see us through ministerial school," he mumbled hurriedly and promised that they would help Frank on holidays and during the summer. "And God will bless you if you do," he concluded.

"That's right," Billy Joe said. "He will."

"God! What do *you* know about God?" she blazed at Pierce. "You little weasel. Religion has got to a pretty pass if *you* get up in a pulpit. What both of you need is a good swift kick in the right place."

"Sorry you feel like that," he said with dignity. "Let's go, Billy."

Then Sam hobbled around, his matted face scowling above his chest crowded with damp grey hair. "Seeing as you're here, suppose we have a few words about the payment you missed. You shipped weeks ago, didn't you?"

"Yes sir," Pierce said, scared and blinking. Why, why had he been fool enough to come near the old man and remind him of the mortgage? "We're squeezed something fearful by this drought, as you well know," he flustered. "And it's getting worse instead of better. But you'll get every dollar owing, you can depend on that."

"Get Jim Kirk on the phone, Vivie. Tell him I'm taking the ranch back." To Pierce and Billy Joe he said, "You wasted that money. If you try to sell off breed stock to make the payment I'll have your skins. Understand?"

"Wait—sir," Pierce stammered. Inside him, the little boy who had been shaken off the ladder was screaming again, screaming.

"I'd run the two of you off without a cent except for Irene and the kids, and seeing you're barely a man, Bill." Glowering in his whiskers like Jehovah, terrible in his anger, he made known his will: "We're parting company. Pierce, I'll *give* you the old Dickenson spread. That's a thousand acres, free and clear. And you can have the Baird spread alongside it, Bill. And twenty head of stock apiece. I started on less."

"I'm on my way," Vivie crowed, and skipped like a girl toward the lodge to call the lawyer.

Pierce bleated, "And what about the other sixty-eight thousand acres? What about them?"

"Frank's a good cattleman. He can hire some help and make a go of it without you. Since you can't hold up your end, I'll leave him run it until I die and then he gets all of it."

"Jesus God! That's not fair! We worked as hard as him, you're playing favorites against us!"

The old patriarch rooted in his sweaty hair and rumbled, "I'll give you a week to clear out of the ranch house. You can patch up the Dickenson place by then."

"But you can't! Daddy!" he wailed. "Please don't! On bended knee I ask you. Forget what we said about going off, it was just a wild hair . . ." He flailed his arms, then held them out in abject capitulation.

Sam limped away from him, swinging out his plaster leg and following it with his body, poling himself toward the lodge. Blankly Pierce stared at the massive log structure, caulked with white cement, and the pine-furred mountain humped behind it. He felt Billy Joe take his arm, draw him away toward the car. He heard Billy Joe talking while the voice grew shriller inside him, lost, helpless, screaming as it had in the card game when Bert Stephens, his cold eyes almost contemptuous, had rolled up the ace of diamonds in his hand for thirty-six hundred dollars. But this was far more awful; this was the end. One minute he'd had twenty-three thousand acres, with pasture and hay fields along the river, and the next he had a thousand acres of goat pasture next to the national forest. And a broken-down privy for a house. And no water at all. He would have to truck water, even for cooking and washing, all the way out from town.

The scream wouldn't stop. He said feverishly, "We're tied hand and foot, Billy. We can't even sell the dirty stinking dirt pasture to go off to school. The bank has foreclosed mortgages up to the hilt. It's so land-poor Bailey won't even mortgage anything."

"Don't take it so bad," Billy Joe said, starting the car. They crunched onto the highway. The shabby white tourist cabins for the lodge were locked up and still. "If we have the Lord on our side, we don't have to worry," Billy Joe said. "He'll provide, you'll see."

"He's done just great up to here," Pierce said. "We dedicate our lives and look what happens. From here on out it's bust our back forever and no extras."

"You shouldn't always look on the bad side, Bubber. We could work our way through school."

"No, it's no use. When I'm whipped, I'm whipped. We lost both ways, we lost the ranch and ministerial school too. A real nice reception that was," he raged, his face a wet red mash. "Daddy don't care a plug nickel for us, guts, brains, and all. We don't fit his plans, so naturally it's a short good-night to us. We can go hang and he won't lose a night's sleep over it neither, you can depend on that. You know what he actually done? I'll tell you. He disowned us! The ranch is our birthright and he disowned us. Like Isaac done to Esau."

Pines flicked by on both sides of the unspooling highway. He talked faster and faster. Only in this way could he choke back, at least for a little while, the scream which was going on and on inside him, getting louder, pushing toward his throat.

November 1, 1952

At 7:15 in the morning, the first hydrogen bomb was exploded on Eniwetok, one of the Marshall Islands in the Pacific. In reality it wasn't a bomb at all but a hulking sixty-five ton machine, with its own freezing apparatus, housed in a large shed. Observers saw an orange fireball swallow the mile-wide island and rush up into the morning sky, dragging a huge boiling cloud of vapor and disintegrated rock behind it. A sinister thunderhead reared into the stratosphere. Where the island had been was a hole a mile long and 175 feet deep in the floor of the Pacific ocean.

It was as if four million tons of T.N.T. had been set off at once. The awesome fission bomb, the type dropped at Hiroshima and Nagasaki, dwindled into insignificance. "Super" as it was called, used that sort of explosion merely as a trigger, to fuse atoms of hydrogen, creating a roaring furnace of energy like a small sun. The man most responsible for this stupendous weapon was Edward Teller, but he was not present to see the fulfillment of his efforts. The "father of the H-bomb" had sullenly refused to attend the test. As the shock wave rumbled across the Pacific ocean, he was waiting tensely by the seismograph at the University of California, his eyes fixed on the speck burning in the center of a photographic plate.

His whole life had built to these breathless minutes of waiting: his youth in Hungary and Germany, tormented by racial persecution; the flight to this country and the years at George Washington University, absorbed in the problem of the thermonuclear changes in the stars. Then the war, the Manhattan Project. By 1942 all he could think of was a thermonuclear bomb. Obviously it couldn't be built before the war was over but it had become his great intellectual adventure, his vision, the mountain he was bent on climbing. Nothing else, not even the crash program to get an atomic bomb before Hitler did, could divert him from it. While his colleagues at Los Alamos worked, he limped endlessly over the dry hills and clanked at the piano and built the bomb in his head, over and over again—a stiff, brooding man with furry black eyebrows and an artificial foot, his mind swarming like a deep cerebral womb, spawning ideas one after another in feverish growths.

When the Japanese surrendered, Los Alamos stopped production like a war factory and the scientists scattered to their old laboratories. But Teller hung on, stubborn, obsessed with his "baby." He begged the new director of Los Alamos for development of a hydrogen bomb or at least for refinement of atomic explosives, and when he was turned down, he went to the Air Force and asked what weapons they would like. They told him, "The bomb we have now is precisely what we need." Enrico Fermi kept urging him to come to the University of Chicago, arguing that the war was over and it wouldn't be pleasant to stay there and work on weapons, but Teller shook him off impatiently. However, the United States was about to present the Baruch plan for U.N. control of atomic energy, and the very idea of weapons development was repugnant to everybody. Teller had no choice; he went to Chicago. There he waited doggedly for times to change, waited.

And gradually hopes for peace slipped away; the Russians exploded their atomic bomb, and the tempo of the arms race speeded up, and the spiral of doom tightened another turn. Suddenly his crooked dream had become a national necessity: the United States had to keep ahead of the Soviet Union or, at the very least, stay even. Unexpectedly, the hydrogen bomb proved to have appalling technical difficulties, but the fertility of Teller's mind was incredible. In less than a year, in February of 1951, he came up with a brilliant new approach.

Then, even before it was realized, he twisted his success into agony. Passionate and irascible as always, he quarreled about how to produce the bomb and quit to start a whole new weapons laboratory at Livermore, California. The result was a catastrophe. The fantastic creativeness of his mind was also its weakness; it lacked discipline; it was almost useless without the control of a seasoned collaborator. Without this help he turned out one humiliating failure after another while the Los Alamos scientists jeered at him and triumphantly put together the bomb he had fought for so long and actually made possible.

Angrily he refused to watch "Mike" tested. Instead he went to Haverland Hall at the University of California to witness his sour victory alone. Huddled in the room over the seismograph, he watched the burning point which a thready beam of light made on the photographic plate. From across the Pacific, surging under the floor of the ocean, came the shock wave from a flaming planet a thousand times as powerful as the bomb dropped at Hiroshima. It took fifteen minutes to roll halfway across the world to him. Then the white dot skittered in a crazy dance and he knew that "Mike" had been a success: Edward Teller had climbed his bitter mountain into world-wide fame.

And terror had been multiplied by one thousand.

XIX

It was 7:30 in the morning, bright and viciously cold. Only a truck or two moved on the wide, deserted streets. Telephone wires moaned in the wind, and the canvas awning on the old beauty shop, now converted into a mining office, bellied out and then emptied with a sound like a gunshot. In the cafe, men in fur caps and padded jackets were feeding on oatmeal and fried potatoes and eggs, weak hot coffee, and flapjacks with a side of eggs bleeding their yellow yolks into sticky brown syrup.

"Holy Toledo!" the waitress said when she saw Bert. "Are you ever up early! Where's little Ray, sleeping it off?" Bert asked for some coffee. As she set it on the counter, her red perfumed mouth smiled at him and she said, "Will you do me a favor?"

"No."

"Oh you *thing*," she pouted.

Her mention of Ray had started the men talking about Nature's blunders, two-headed calves, calves born with no tails, blind calves with their hind legs missing—monstrous births of all sorts. Bert, however, brooding inside himself, heard none of it. He had been up most of the night, straining at a topographical map he'd gotten from Larry Wassburger at the AEC office, which marked every reported outcrop of uranium in the region. To no avail. There was no trend, no pattern to the deposits except that they were usually found on the eroded rims of the canyons. Always they had been just about entirely washed away. And yet, since uranium was water soluble, it had to have been carried in underground water. It stood to reason that a lot of it, millions of tons of it, must be left somewhere deep in the ground. But where? He was lacking just one piece to the jigsaw puzzle. New possibilities jumped in his mind incessantly, theory after theory, only to shrivel up and fall apart, but he kept spawning new ones. It was a passion, an obsession. His imagination was on fire with the stupendous problem, the answer to which beckoned, just out of reach, like the answer to everything.

At last Helen's brother, Bud Robel, drew up to the curb in a panel truck smoking white exhaust fumes. Leaving his dog in the cab he came into the restaurant, a small ropey man pulling his gloves off with his teeth. He was constrained, brusque. "Give me a minute to thaw out," he said to Bert and settled onto a stool. While he slurped at a cup of coffee he told a story—to the men chewing over their plates, not to Bert—of how he had waked up one Sunday morning in Butte, Montana, with the strangest feeling, as if somebody was in bed with him. No, he was by himself, but the tag on the key in the door was swinging back and forth. In a second the hangers in the closet began to clink together, the floor was shaking, a glass was dancing around on the table. "I'll be damn if it wasn't an earthquake," he said, and the men nodded and chuckled.

Then, in a different voice, he said to Bert, "Let's take off."

In complete silence he drove out the highway, his black ragamuffin dog snuggled beside him. In other days Bert would have reacted with violence to his hostility; now it didn't touch him at all. The cold white sun flared over the pine hills, and wind hissed in the loose windows. After a while Bud said, "I don't know as I understand what you're after, exactly."

"You and me both."

"Helen said you was studying on uranium and if I would take you out to the mine. Only I don't see the value of it. You intend running a shaft into a cliff yourself?"

Bert slid further down in the vibrating seat, his hands in the pockets of his leather jacket. "I'm just trying to hatch out an idea I got."

This reticence, far from offending Bud, evoked a cautious approval. He puckered his clear squinting eyes, worked the toothpick around in his mouth for a minute, and then spoke out: "I wouldn't want any more—any trouble to happen to Helen . . . Any running around. Her husband is a horse's ass but still I wouldn't."

Bert was genuinely surprised. "My friend," he grinned, "there's more than one way to fornicate. And uranium is a hell of a lot more invigorating than females—no personalities intended."

Bud let out a snort of amusement—and relief. "You are sure snake bit, for a fact," he observed. After that, the silence was easier, and as he skidded the truck down the twisting road into Horse Canyon he warned the dog, "Say your prayers, Black, this could be it." A derelict orange school bus hulked on the rock apron outside the mine. This was his shop. Inside, it was a regular hawk's nest littered with bone-like tools and engine parts, iron pipes downy with pale dust, cartons of dynamite, naked red barrels. Swearing under his breath, he started the balky generator to light the mine, then hustled outside and dragged the tarpaulin from the mouth of the tunnel. It was warm and dim in there and it smelled of deisel fumes and blasting powder. Lights, strung on a wire spiked into the low ceiling, dusted a yellowish glow over pieces of heavy equipment clogging the passageway. They squeezed past, their shoes plunging in coarse, deep, mushy sand. Ahead of them another corridor fed into the tunnel, which opened at the end into a wide hollow, thick with shadows and smells: the foul stomach of a digestive system spreading in the belly of the mountain.

"There she is," Bud said. "If you have any questions along the way, don't hesitate. I got to put out some ore." And he plodded off, bandy-legged in his slouchy overalls, coughing.

Bert was on his own, discouragingly on his own. In a moment he was overwhelmed with the thunder of engines, like a huge black avalanche of sound crashing over him—Bud was moving the ponderous machines out of the tunnel. Battered and reeling with the noise, Bert tried to concentrate. Somehow, somehow, he had to find out how uranium *acted* underground, and this was his only chance. Frowning, he examined the scarred and crumpled walls, foot by foot; they were brown and porous, with streaks of yolky yellow and orange: sandstone. This was only what he had expected, however, since in this area uranium was found either in limestone or sandstone . . .

Light burst into him, roaring. He shrank back against the wall and Bud rumbled by on the caterpillar tractor, riding up there under the ceiling with his dog perched sedately beside him. He crunched to a stop in the cavern and hopped down. Already the air was soiled with deisel fumes. The bulbs were weak knots of light. Bert felt his head begin to ache with the nauseating blue stench, but he slogged down the tunnel to where Bud was working.

"You miserable sonofabitch," Bud was muttering to himself. Rapidly he went over the six or seven tons of rock he'd blasted loose the day before, laying a scintillator here and there, like a stethoscope, on the radioactive mound of ore.

Bert said, "Will the baby be all right, Doctor? Tell me the truth."

Bud tossed him a chunk: as brown and crumbly as hard-packed coffee grounds and seeded all over with yellow uranium. "Looks like glory hallelujah, don't it? But it'll have to go like hell to make the ten-hundredths minimum. And me with fifteen thousand in stock in my closet."

"Why don't you sell?"

"I just wish I could. The stickler is, Mr. Werden told me not to sell for six months so I don't break the market."

"Chum," Bert said, "the last man that listened to Bob Werden, they ain't found his head yet."

"You're personally acquainted with him, I hear." He turned it over in his mind, then snuffled the phlegm out of his nose and spat. "Could be he *is* roping me in at that, but I have to abide by my word. A man has to abide by his word. Anyway, I'm on salary, so it's not entirely a dead loss."

"Sell the damn stock! He's unloading his, or has already."

"I can't, but I thank you just the same." In gratitude, instead of going back to work he opened up: "I don't know as it'll help, but here's what I done. I begun with a surface outcrop on the cliff and followed the lead straight in. Mostly the ore pinches off awful quick, but this time it kept agoing. It was a stringer about two foot thick, and I stayed with it. Is that any use to you? I don't guess it is."

"Maybe. I don't know." Snapping his fingers he scowled at the rough walls, prowled down the corridor and came tramping back. "Am I completely crazy? It looks to me like you dug out an underground stream. The stuff travels in ground water, that's a known fact, but this —was it like a solid little stream of it?"

"Sure. It was of pore richness, but you hit it right on the head. You see here, this cave we're in? It was sort of a duck-pond, like, off to one side." He pointed a grimy hand at the juts and slashes of sandstone over his head. "See? You can see the riffles in the rock, right there."

Bert's breath quickened, his eyes drew in to feverish slits, and he squashed back and forth in the sand, tense, flaming with exitement. It was alive inside him now, the germ of the answer, and it kept adding to itself, developing in his mind. Since uranium had concentrated in underground rivulets, what he had to find was the pattern, the old lines of flow in this particular layer of rock. That was all he needed, and the answer was right here in the mine, maybe just a foot or two away . . .

"Well, if you'll pardon me," Bud said finally, "I have to put out a dividend. You'd best come along. I'm going to cut the lights so I can start the ventilation. Otherwise the deisel fumes will kill us off when I run the cat."

His frail hands clenched, Bert trailed like a sleepwalker after Bud and the dog. Outside, they clambered into the chilly truck and battled to the top of the cliff over the mine. Pine-bristling hills heaved up all around. And there was the blower, a white metal toadstool in the morning sky. Hooked onto it was a gasoline engine, which Bud cranked by jamming a hand drill, shaped like a large blunt pistol, into a slot in the front. "Come on, you sonofabitch," he gritted. The motor shuddered with the spin of 230 revolutions per minute, groaned, belched one blue burst—and quit. Bert looked on, sightless, his hands hanging and the wind flipping his long hair. How could he read the pattern of the dead streams, the deep-buried stone channels a hundred, two hundred feet under the surface? There must be a way. Bud

Uranium! 277

breathed on his numb hands, and puffing steamy curses, rammed the drill into the engine again, and suddenly it was puttering, the exhaust chimney was fuming into the clear frozen sunlight, and the fan was whirling in its metal hood, taking huge volumes of air into its round mouth.

"Watch out!" Bud shouted and caught hold of Bert, dragged him back as he fell toward the hideously swallowing mouth. "Watch yourself, that bastard'll pull you in and chop you into hamburger!"

Shrinking away, he stared at the blur of knife-edged teeth which had just missed taking off his arm. He was wide awake, shivering. His head was full of cold wind and the icy vision of his severed arm and hand, his fingers chewed into bloody stumps. His chest surged in and out painfully.

"Look here," Bud said. Holding his arms up cautiously, he stepped close to the sinister black hole: instantly it grabbed his overalls, sucked his legs against the hood. Jerking himself free he said, "Yup, it's nothing to fool with. Every now and again it gets a bird and spits the pieces down into the mine." Bert's face was bluish white. Telling cheerfully about the time he'd gotten a shower of feathers on his head, Bud wrestled the truck back down to the shop. Bert slumped on the bench with his head on his fists, unable to think of anything but the amputated hand. His shocked nerves vibrated with the pounding of the generator. The warm, gasoline-smelling air made him sick.

"It was cold as hell up there," Bud said. "How about a cup of coffee?"

Bert rolled his face back and forth, mumbling, "My hand, I nearly lost it."

"Which one was it, your writing hand or your scratching hand?" Bud inquired.

Bert flamed up with anger; then he saw the eyes and mouth curl good-naturedly in the leathery face and realized that Bud was teasing him out of sheer lack of imagination. What hadn't happened didn't exist for him. Sunshine as simple as milk lay on the engine parts scattered on the table. As he puffed on a cigarette, sipping coffee from a thermos cup, a kind of peace came from him, a breath of the pure unconscious quiet of animals, and Bert felt it soak deep into him, soothing. He stopped trembling. He began to grope for the shattered pieces of the problem.

"I guess I'll run the kitty now," Bud said, and while he hauled ore out of the mine, Bert looked and looked at the winding tunnels, at how they changed direction, how they joined and bulged out into the cave. One thing was sure. The lines of flow were not anything like the creek outside which had eaten down from the surface and through the older sandstone layer he was in. But it was impossible to breathe any more. The air, in spite of the powerful ventilator, was a murderous haze of exhaust fumes and radioactive dust. Again and again the giant caterpillar tractor ground past him on its riding steel belts, dirty cogs revolving, the thunder of the engine multiplying off the walls and flooding his chest with vibrations. In desperation he stood directly under the ventilator—and was all but knocked down by the blast of cold air and stinging grit.

He staggered outside but the idea, the vision, was taking shape inside him again, growing almost of itself, and it drove him back into the strangling tunnel. Deep in the cavern at the end, Bud was cleaning off the ore face, bending and swinging in the poisoned light, his shovel clanging on stone. "Sure is sour in here, ain't it?" he said cheerfully. "It'll make you sicker'n a pregnant pig if you ain't used to it."

"This canyon," Bert gasped, "does it run parallel with Red Canyon?"

"Yuh, just about. They're both just about straight north-south."

The smoke seared in Bert's throat; his eyes watered; his head thudded savagely, but the solution was forcing itself out of him; it was pitiless, a swollen pressure building up and up in waves of cramping agony. It was unbearable. He lunged over to where the tunnels joined.

"Damn it, it's got to be! The big tunnel to the outside is only a side branch . . . And this here other one, that looks like a feeder, it has to be the main channel. It breaks off but it's got the feel of it!"

"Could be."

Panting harshly, he lined himself up. His teeth sprouting out of his lips, his eyes squeezed almost shut, he rotated back and forth with his arms out, estimating fiercely, calculating, allowing for the bend of the tunnels and extending them in his mind, farther and farther, reaching for the drift of the ore, reaching . . .

"I got it!" he burst out. "The groundwater goes like this. From northeast to southwest, at a halfways angle to both canyons!" His sooty face was wild with triumph.

"That's it?" Bud said drily.

"*It,* buddy. I got blackjack! Twenty-one!"

Bud coughed and spat out some dust. "You do say. If you'll pardon my plain words, you *are* snakebit."

"I'm much afraid he's right," Larry Wassburger said. "You just don't have enough to go on. First off, ore bodies as rich as those washed away exist only in theory, and they'd be two or three hundred foot underground." His drab, honest voice plodded through the racket of typewriters and the quick smacks of the duplicator at the rear of the office spinning off government releases. "It's a needle in a mighty large haystack, Bert. Even knowing the general direction the ore follows, you'd still have to have a crystal ball to tell where to drill a hole. My advice is, stick to digging the outcrops."

"You see?" Wally put in anxiously. "He says no and he's a qualified expert. Why, we couldn't touch one of them big drill rigs for under fifteen thousand. It takes a slew of equipment, too, and it all costs like fire—the bits alone are sixty dollars apiece, and don't hardly last but a few hours. We'd be pore as Job's cat again in no time."

And Larry said, "You listen to your partner. It'll run you between fifty cents and a dollar a foot to drill a hole, and that's over and above your initial investment. Two sizeable outfits in town have gone broke already, just from shallow drilling on their property. To show you how darn rough it is, the Commission is going to initiate a drilling program of its own to help test out the claims. And you want to wildcat at random, clean out of the canyon! Sink three hundred-foot holes, completely blind!"

"See there?" Wally said.

Bert lounged in a chair by the desk, his clothes still reeking of deisel smoke. On his face was the same glittery look he'd had when he ripped to a stop in Bud Robel's truck, jumped out and stretched his arms, and said, "Damn if all that thinking didn't make me hungry, Lard. You got anything in that lunchpail fit for a future tycoon?" It purely gave Wally the shivers. Bert wasn't budging in the least, and that money in the bank had come awful hard. He dreaded being a pauper again . . . Which was exactly what Esther was hoping and praying for, of course. He didn't dare to think what she would do if Bert blew the twenty-four thousand they had left.

"You let that lucky hit you made go to your head," Wassburger said to Bert. "Lightning doesn't strike twice in the same place."

"For me it does," he grinned.

"Don't get me wrong," Larry said patiently. "I take my hat off to you for thinking of the direction of the groundwater. Only there's no way to put it to good use. All right, let's say you pick an outcrop where the canyon is hot. Then what? Those outcrops don't go twenty foot into the cliff before they pinch off. So you deep drill back of the canyon—but how far back? Two hundred yards? A mile? Ten miles? There can't be but a scattered ore body or two, if any at all. It's like looking for a raisin in a cake as big as—I don't know what. You could drill ninety holes and not get a wheel-barrow full."

"Correct," Bert said, as imperturbable as ever.

"And don't forget another thing. This is a volcanic region and the strata are all torn up. There's slump and faulting everywhere. Which means that your ore direction won't be consistent or continuous—and there goes your one and only chance in a million."

"True as the Bible," Bert said and his live eyes glittered out of his sooty face. "Except for one thing. Me. About the boys who wrote the books I can't speak for certain, but *I know I'm good*."

His confidence in himself was stunning. He flicked a wink at Larry and strolled out of the office, his back arched, drawing a dirty comb through the flap of hair on his balding forehead. Wally lumbered after him down the gaunt cold street. "Farewell and goodbye," Bert said to him. "I hashed it over with that expert like you asked me to, now you make tracks for Denver and buy that rig. Meanwhile, I'll take Old Paint and look over the terrain."

"Bert," he faltered, "you know I'll throw you against anybody for intelligence, but—you're bucking the entire Atomic Energy Commission . . . and . . ." And then he broke off. It came to him that that wasn't the point at all, whether Bert or the geologists were right. He had to string along with him regardless, win or lose, to the very bitterest end there could possibly be, for this was the Bert he had believed was possible in spite of every disappointment. This was what he'd worked for for more than seven years; the watch he'd picked up on a Skidrow street in Denver was working at last, the tiny precise screws all in tight, the jewels glowing red in their sockets, the balance wheel pulsing live movement into the interlocking discs like a miniature perfect universe.

"That's better, Sunshine," he said superbly. "And don't you worry your head neither, because I have it all envisioned out in my mind. We're gonna be the biggest shots there is."

"Okay, spin it," Bert said. Wally switched on the motor. A barrage of noise rocked the decaying hills around them, and the fifty-foot derrick, mounted on the bed of a powerful truck, began to shudder in the ice-grey sky. The pipe inside the derrick whirled faster and faster, throwing off oily slivers of light, and the triple-headed bit gouged downward, metal slurring discordantly on rock, then settling into a high-speed whine. The fire and brimstone smell of friction-heated rock came from the hole.

"Well, good luck to us," Wally said devoutly. It was the eleventh time he had said this in the week they had been wildcatting on the other side of Red Canyon from the plateau—so far without the slightest effect. The air compressor snorted, and the long, snake-like hoses twitched, swung out from the derrick and banged back against it, hissing. At the base of the whirring pipe, a cover-cup of steel jutted out a side pipe which streamed and squirted the cuttings into a bucket. Wiping the back of his grease-blackened glove under his nose, Wally glanced at Bert for some hint of his feelings.

"What's the outlook for this hole?" he finally yelled. "Any better atall?"

Meditatively, in slow motion, Bert let himself down against the curving steel blade of the bulldozer. His face was gnawed red by the wind. Soiled woollen underwear stuck out of the sleeves of his jacket. Taking Ray's harmonica from his pocket, he inhaled and exhaled aimless wheezes lost in the racket of the engines. Just then there was a small commotion travelling across the roughed-up pink clay, and Ray, goggling and spluttering direly, snatched his harmonica out of Bert's hands and stumped back to the fire burning in a rusty barrel. Wally tightened his lips, but Bert's eyes, after a dull blink of surprise, were again fixed upon nothing in particular, upon the sun glowing palely in a frozen scum of clouds. In a minute he lapsed away down the stony watercourse in the pines, the loose sole on his shoe flapping and catching as he went.

"That wasn't nice," Wally said in a stern voice.

Ray, swaying over an empty wine bottle in his lap, gave him a malevolent glare and said something about music soothing the savage beast but if anyone thought he was a beast . . . He subsided into brainless mumbling and his ponderous head drooped, his gargoyle face settled on his chest, and he was asleep by the barrel of flames: a squat ugly nightmare, rancid with the scabs of dried food and liquor, snoring with his slack mouth blowing in and out and yellow light jumping over him from a hole in the crumbling side of the barrel.

But there was no time for him. Every two-and-a-half feet the bucket had to be emptied, and meanwhile the pipe was sinking in the derrick as the bit chewed deeper into the hillside. Wally cleaned and greased another length of pipe, shut off the engine and screwed it in place; and the drilling went on. Dust powdered in the sheepskin collar of his jacket, dust clotted his jam-red eyes and grated in his mouth, dust went through his clothes to the skin, and the motors battered him with noise and the spinning pipe knocked in its slot in the derrick until the whole truck shook. At a hundred and ninety feet down the cuttings showed little chips of petrified trash and wood, which meant that he'd hit an old stream bed, and now he practically stood over the bucket, his eyes locked on the boiling witch's stew of dust, looking for yellow, waiting for yellow. Days ago the number of blanks they'd drawn had proved to him that Larry Wassburger was right; he knew that they were goners for sure; and still the compressed tautness came, the skidding breath when he squatted over the piles of cuttings with the Geiger in his hand.

Fourteen clenched minutes. Then the motor stuttered and changed speed, the drill spun unevenly, and in a few seconds pulverized shale began to spew into the bucket. He stopped the motors. His ears still roared like the mushy whisper of the fire and the wind-hissing pines. Far away, beyond the gullied hills heaping up into mountains, there was the throb of an engine, the cr-rump! of a blast at a mine.

"Wrong number again, huh?" Bert had come back.

Wally nodded, trying not to look reproachful—as if Bert would have noticed or cared. He was fagged out and kind of sore, anyway. Then he heard an idiot chuckle and saw Ray, like something in a mad-scientist comic book, laughing with pleasure. It was just too much. Day and night the little bum hung onto Bert, grubby, vain, demanding, guzzling wine by the pint and throwing tantrums if he wasn't given more immediately, drooling lecherous stories about his sexual prowess and talking endlessly about Colonel Casper and their act with the Royal American shows. And without fail, somewhere along the line, he garbled about Sammy Mandel and the twenty-three straight passes he'd made with Ray blowing on the dice for luck. Because he was still hell-belt for revenge; in his half-witted, muddled brain every blank they drew was due to his superhuman powers. It was too much.

"You darn little skunk!" Wally said, bearing down on him with the vague idea of turning him over his knee and spanking him.

Quietly Bert said, "Leave him be, Lard." Of course it was plain why he kept Ray around and coddled him; he was still punishing himself, or whatever he was doing, and it was just fortunate he was so lost in calculations that he didn't notice Ray for hours at a stretch. Already it was as though he had gone back into himself and shut off his eyes. Safe from punishment, Ray taunted Wally gleefully, hopping up and down and waggling his stub-fingers by his ears, and with a sigh of frustration Wally started the backbreaking job of taking up the drill. Bert, as usual, drifted away and stood gazing down the spilled stones of the watercourse at the gorge filling with cold shadows. Over the stark ridges the sky looked as if it was burning down. Right then the motor behind the derrick conked out.

"Can't you give a person a hand?" Wally shouted at him. Amazed at himself but unable to stop, he heard himself raving, "I'm played out, I tell you. I'm played out."

Bert turned around like a sleepwalker. Then he snapped his fingers and said, "Damn if I don't think I have it this time. We'll punch one across the gulch there tomorrow."

Wally just dropped his arms. After half an hour he got the motor going by himself. The next day he punched a hole where he was told. At two hundred and fifteen feet down the bit broke off. He drilled again and missed. And then again. He lost track of the number of holes he drilled and every day it grew colder, the grass stiffened, the last leaves were paling and falling and deer moved across the highway in the frost-colored dawn. Then the first snow smoked down out of the grey sky, and though it blew off into the gullies and finally evaporated, the temperature scarcely ever rose above freezing any more and the equipment broke down repeatedly. His numb hands stuck to the metal and tore and he didn't notice it until they warmed up and he felt them burn and saw the blood soaking into his gloves. Once the Geiger began to jabber over the pail of cuttings only to go silent again.

"Interesting, huh?" Bert said.

Wally was too crushed to answer at first. Then he said, "I can't make it, I just can't, Bert. I tell myself we don't have no chance, but I want it so bad—we been prospecting for a long time but it never got to me like this. It's like I'm sick. I can't sleep for worrying how rich we might get—and how pore we're getting."

"Never fear," Bert said. "This here Easter egg hunt will yield."

"So you keep telling me. Meantime we're spending money like it was wallpaper. We're near our limit, Bert. We're just about tapped out. It's a tossup whether we'll be froze out or go bust first."

But he wasn't listening any more. It was just as rough as Larry Wassburger had said it would be. The geological formations were all scrambled up; whole mountains had rolled, lurched up and tipped the layers of rock, and sometimes entire valley walls had slumped down so that a structure would be exposed on one side and three hundred feet underground on the other. The difficulty of it, instead of discouraging him, filled him with a relentless driving fury. And day by day the problem of tracking the deep, long-filled underground channels became more and more abstract until it was beyond definition, mystical. Thoretical possibilities so remote that they were intuitions more than anything else formed in his mind; combinations linked and scaffolded together, exact and beautiful, burning with fantastic symmetry—and collapsed. And once more, while Wally ran the rig, he walked the drab November hills, alone in a world of scraggy bushes and pines, grey broom-grass and stones powdered with frozen light. Rawfaced and coughing, stiff with cold but intensely alive, he studied the rotten cliff faces and the boulders scabbed with orange lichen a million and a half years old. Hunched in the wild, he dreamed down into the ground, dropping the net of his mind into oceans of geological time, the earth wearing down an inch a century, the Rocky Mountains (fourteen thousand foot waves cresting hundreds of miles behind the first small swell of the Black Hills) heaving up and crumbling, weathering away seven times in the slow, millenial change of the earth's crust over its core of molten rock. The mountains became wrinkles in the loose hide of the earth. And he dreamed down and down, feeling for the underground flow, creating imaginary structures which might or might not be part of the real world. For once in his life the exhilaration of the gamble involved meant little or nothing. It was more like Columbus, like an astronomer searching the cold depths of interstellar space. It was a lust to pierce the unknown, to solve the mystery no matter what.

It was a marvelous intellectual game, too, a sort of ecstatic mathematics which filled his days and nights with meaning. Wally's jitters didn't touch him; he had a sense of infallibility, like magic. He *knew* he was going to hit, and it was all conquest; it was achievement so great that his mind seemed to expand and fill everything. It was Life.

"Poke a hole there," he told Wally. They were on the other side of a high splintery rock called the Devil's Needle, near the edge of the National Forest, where the hills pelted with black pines sagged down into naked grazing land. He pointed to a crease between two smooth, soft-looking hills and Wally bulldozed a makeshift trail over there. The pipe in the drill rig whizzed around. The swollen prod of the drill went in.

"Well, good luck to us," Wally said once more, his mouth fuming in the cold, and only seventy feet down they got a bang on the Geiger. Wally went rigid. "It's talking!" he cried. Bert folded his arms but his weary eyes were blazing. The drill motor coughed smoke. The pipe revolved at blinding speed. For eight solid feet the Geiger ticked faster and faster, ticked like a runaway clock, and the needle quivered around five-tenths percent, five times the minimum.

"It's a miracle of God," Wally said huskily.

Bert grinned. "It's strictly homemade, Lard. Other parties didn't have nothing to do with it. We'll knock off for a bite to eat and then you punch a hole about down there by that tree."

Wally protested. He was completely done in, and the wind sweeping down from Canada numbed like novocaine. "Let's just stake this and come back tomorrow. It looks like it's coming up a blizzard, Bert."

"Nope. We got to outline the ore body before we're up to our belly-button in snow. But you're right about filing claims, we have that to do, too. Today." Easily, confidently, he directed where to drill—first across the creekbed, then halfway up the gullied hill by the brush choked opening to a cave, then over in the sagebrush pasture. Every hole was hotter—.7 per cent, 1.8 per cent, and finally an unbelievable 4 per cent at the center of a wide pool deep under the wind-lashed brown surface. The cuttings spurted like yellow fire, like a jet of burning phosphorus, and it was pure glory, pure achievement, Napoleon and Caesar and El Dorado, the pot of gold at the end of the rainbow.

Only when they were scooping the best cuttings into sacks did Bert notice barbed wire on the next hill. Some half-assed rancher had not kept his fences in repair and without knowing it they had gone through a two-hundred-foot gap from the National Forest onto private land. Wally was close to tears. "It's all for nothing. For nothing. The whole richest part is on somebody's pasture, and we don't have but the edges."

"It's a stinger, all right, but we still have a good play if we move fast. Let's see. You fold down the tower on the drill rig and I'll get that dozer outa here. Come on, hit it!"

For nearly an hour it was a stampede of wild horses and a cyclone hitting the church picnic rolled into one: Wally taking down the derrick and then scraping and smoothing the torn clay (gory red like blood-soaked sheets) around the drill holes, snow dusting around in the violent wind, and Bert wrestling the wheel and grinding gears as he hurried equipment into a side canyon in the National Forest. It was fortunate that Ray had passed out in the cab of the old truck because they were going to need absolute secrecy. Charging the drill rig into a whirling haze of snow, Bert was suddenly picked up and hurled forward onto the steering wheel; the rig plunged like a ship in a typhoon and heeled half way over. Stacks of pipe went clattering. Hoses and worn-out drill bits flew in every direction. It took only one look to get the bad news: he'd hit a deep pothole in the canyon and snapped the front axle. The rig was out of sight, though, and without a second glance he went stumbling around the wind-blasted hill to hammer more stakes. By the time he was finished he was too exhausted to help lift the bags of cuttings onto the truck. Wally's eyes were choked red; his hands were stiff, and the leak from his nose was frozen into his little moustache, but he stooped carefully to bed the sacks down in the back, plump and sweet and new.

"If they ain't perty now," Bert panted. "Pass out the cigars, Lard."

But Wally was looking worriedly at the sky. It had stopped snowing, and only a thin grey membrane lay on the rumpled patches where they'd drilled. "You think it'll be all right?"

"Why naturally. This is weather for reindeer, boy, and nobody'll be out here in the wilderness. Not to mention, we're due for more snow."

By 4:30 they were rattling down the mountain into Hot Springs to file the claims. Ray toppled sideways on the curves and burbled indignantly without opening his eyes. On the outskirts of the town, under the great rock face castling up and up, was the Greek-columned summer house and the sign: WORLD FAMOUS KIDNEY SPRING. A frail man pottered along with a jar of the so-called medicinal waters cradled in his arm.

"Made it with twenty minutes to spare," Bert said. "And whilst we're at the courthouse we'll find out who owns that dirt pasture next to our claims, and tomorrow we'll buy us a chunk."

"It had better go at a bargain," Wally said. "Because all we got is fourteen hundred dollars and a busted drill rig. I wish you hadn't busted it. I know it was accidental but still . . ."

"Lard, you have a case of the perpetual fidgets. Plus you're setting up as a thinker, which is strictly not your specialty. Now you just relax." Tattered hair falling into his eyes, he opened the lunch pail, polished off the last sandwich and beat on his stomach with his fist. "That helped. Damn if I don't feel jubilation within me."

Wally laughed out loud. "You know, it was like God Hisself had His arm around us. Another week more and our hides would've been nailed to the barn door. I about had heart failure every time we hit another dud."

"'Shoot! I couldn't miss. Nature's a woman like any other, Heavy. All you need to do to get in her bloomers is learn her ways and not take no for an answer." Lounging back with his hands laced behind his head, he looked out at the town nursing at the warm little river. Stores and clinics. A brownstone hotel piling up above the block-long shelf of its porch, massive, royal. Misty glows coming out of windows and . . . and it shouldn't have happened, not when he was feeling so good, but something or other like it was always happening. "God damn it," he said angrily. "God damn it! Why don't they keep sonofabitches like that off of the street."

"What was that?" Wally said. He was backing and wedging into a parking place near the courthouse. "Like what?"

Bert swallowed. There, being pushed along the sidewalk in a wheel chair, was a patient from one of the hospitals. He or she—whatever it was—consisted of a humpty-dumpty head, like a monstrous egg on a pillow, and a few scraps of body tucked up in a yellow blanket. But what was awful was the face. It was as if the expression had run off the dim sallow features, slid off them like water, exposing the wide idiot blankness underneath. And the thing was spinning along the sidewalk in the most ordinary way, propelled by an anonymous-looking nurse.

Then it was gone, reeling jauntily out of sight, but it was still inside him, the deformed and bloated thing that was a human being, only it was more like a rotting jack-o-lantern drooling light from the sunken cuts of its eyes and mouth, and Wally was asking him what it was all about, shaking him by the arm. He rolled his twisted face away. All the half-healed wounds inside him had burst open again. Wally said he wouldn't be a minute and lumbered at top speed toward the courthouse; and there was Ray, snoring beside him with his scoop-mouth open, hideous, hideous. All these months Ray had been like a bad tooth which he pressed continually with his tongue, feeling the pain dig in and spread, dig in and spread—but a little less each time, dulled by repetition and then by all that studying and figuring. Now it was back, like the first sick minutes on the stage afterwards. His breath climbed into hurt gasps. The toothless mouth blew open in a cough and Ray scratched himself in his sleep, breathing gummy sounds, and the smirking faces crowded around, the man with red hair bought Ray a half pint of whiskey and his nubby fingers scraped futilely at the seal while they all laughed, big tears muddled out on his cheeks and the pain was like the frantic squirming of angleworms when kids put salt on them for fun and the membrane-like skin dissolved into oozy, melting agony, and then Ray was up on the stage, up in the mouldy light, floundering like an angry puppet in yards of blue dress . . .

Just in time, just barely in time, he pulled away and flung himself out of the truck and started walking. The river steamed into the cold night. The little summerhouse was empty. When Wally found him and led him back to the truck, asking over and over what had happened, he looked away in grey-lipped silence. As Wally was maneuvering the truck out of the parking place he said, "Well at least I filed the claims all right. And one of the Bolton boys owns that spread. A William Bolton, you ever heard of him?"

Gnawing at his hand, Bert stared out at the sliding darkness punctured with lights.

"I told you not to do that," Wally said. "Come on and think about our problems instead. Supposing this William Bolton agrees to sell, which I wouldn't bet on, what happens if he wants cash?"

After a while Bert said, "When I was a kid—I guess I was about twelve or thirteen—my mother had cancer and she'd been at the hospital for a long time. The hell with it . . ." But he couldn't stop the memory. They had let her come home for Easter and she was so thin, she didn't weigh more than seventy pounds. The two of them had sat in the front room by the coal stove and the light from the flames came through the isinglass windows onto her face. The other kids were too small to know what was going on and they were in the kitchen dyeing Easter eggs. After all these years he could still smell the vinegar . . .

But he forced himself to go on. At ten o'clock the next morning he and Wally were in Edna Harbaugh's room off the lobby. "Don't look so down in the dumps, I'll swing it for you," she boomed. Leaping to his feet, Wally shut the door on the drone of voices outside. "My big mouth," she apologized. "When I whisper you can hear it clean across the county. But like I was saying, Billy Joe won't be no problem. Him and Pierce are both in a tight corner out there—depend on Sam Bolton for that. From what I hear, they're living on credit and trucking water every day and meantime there's a considerable hay bill owing. That's enough and to spare, but also for good measure, Billy Joe wants out of ranching. He wants to be a preacher."

She was in seventh heaven at another chance to help Bert, and she fluttered here and there in front of the plants and the photographs, getting primped up to pay a call on Billy Joe. Her tiny yapping chihuahua trotted about under foot. "It's so thrilling," she said, touching her dyed red hair at the mirror. "I feel—you'll laugh at me—like I was . . . starting over."

A blush went up her face from her wilted throat. She peeked at Bert in the mirror, but he was sunk down on the sofa with his hands plunged in his pockets. There were purple stains like bruises under his eyes. He was watching the chihuahua rub itself against her gnarled ankles. It was a fatty little waddler of a dog, with short dainty legs at four corners. As it leaned and stroked against her, its rows of dugs hung and dangled obscenely—pink, dry, scaly flabs of mammary skin. And he couldn't stop looking at them. It was one horror after another now; the sick thing inside him was awake, viciously awake, feeding on whatever came along.

"Not atall," Wally said to her. "Now don't dicker too hard. Don't get robbed, but don't dicker too hard."

"Trust an old sheep rancher," she said. "I'll get that thousand acres for twelve or thirteen an acre, fifteen at the outside. And terms for as long as you want. Billy Joe will jump at the down payment. If I'm not back in town with him in an hour to draw up the papers you can shoot me." She muscled into her coat like a man, but then she let her hands sink and her dress rustled like dry leaves. "You know, I wish my Sally and her family really was coming up here to ranch on that spread. I miss her and the baby so much." Then she recovered with a smile and said, "But it's a prime story you dreamed up, Bert, and I'm the exact right middle man to bring it off. I mean it sounds real true from me, you boys not being ranchers or anything."

Every time the dog sat down, the bottom pair of dugs bagged pinkly out of shape on the rug. Its large, human-looking eyes let out a slow continuous flow of gluey fluids that streaked the fur on its face.

"Hey you!" she hollered at Bert. "Wake up, the British are coming! Aw, you don't look a bit good. The pressure has been too much, ain't it? But it'll soon be over, I promise. I'll go to beat the band."

"Unhuh," he said remotely. He heard their serious voices confer for a minute; then she was saying, "You be good, honey," to the dog; then she was waving at them out of her dusty Ford and driving off.

"The drought is sure on our side," Wally said. "I thought land was way higher than that. Why even if she can't get terms, we can fix the rig and sell it and the rest of the equipment for enough to pay cash."

Bert shivered in the icy draft under his jacket. There was still a white shadow of frost by the cars and telephone posts. The glass-clear air trembled with shocks of noise from a conveyor moving ore at the buying station. Black Thanksgiving turkeys were pasted in the window of the Piggly Wiggly store. "Yeah," he said.

"There's only one thing, Bert. I want it so bad I can taste it but —I'm not sure. Heck, I don't know, is it honest? I know it was your thinking that makes the land valuable, of course. Without that it would be just dirt."

"You go on home," Bert told him. "I'll call you when she gets back."

He sat down in the lobby over a game of solitaire, bemused, shrouded in himself. Ray came in twice, demanding to know why they weren't out drilling. "We're busted," he said each time, and each time Ray's face swam with gloating satisfaction. Some railroad men were talking about Eisenhowers's landslide victory, about Stalin, about the Korean war, about the H-bomb which had been set off a few weeks ago in the Marshall Islands, but the hole inside him sucked in the voices and the mindless building of cards and the hours of waiting and was still a hole, as raw and empty as ever.

"Where's Edna, do you figure?" one of the men asked. "She didn't blow the noon siren today." At 12:30 the door scraped open. She came tromping in, and even before Bert looked at her he could tell the verdict. With all the finesse of a two-ton truck she signalled him to follow her and practically ran down the hall to the back steps. Her face was hectic. "Everything went smash," she quavered. "It's all a hashed-up mess. I'm so sorry!"

"Run it through for me. You can shed tears afterwards."

"I don't know how it happened—you're gonna be so mad at me . . ." He merely looked away at nothing until she went on: "I didn't hardly get my piece said before he started raising hob. I mean Pierce did. Not Billy Joe. Like I told you, Billy Joe is living with him and Irene and the little ones in that old shotgun house. It was filthy dirty and so cold! Every single one of the children were coughing—I mean except for Debbie. She's going to school in town, so at least she's spared . . ."

She caught herself and said, "I'm sorry, my head's in a rattle. Billy Joe jumped at the chance, just like I said he would. But what I forgot is, Pierce runs the show. What I can't feature is how he done it. Right off the bat he smelled something was up. I didn't give it away, I swear I didn't, Bert. I was just as natural . . ."

"All right. You set his hair to prickling and then what?"

"If I didn't know better, I'd say he was a mind-reader. And mean! Billy Joe is a very likeable boy, but Pierce is the *meanest* one person! He butted right in and dragged Billy Joe over in a corner and started hissing at him to beat the band. Billy Joe was saying it was the answer to their prayers, and Pierce was saying it wasn't beans for an answer. I heard that much. And Irene, she just set there, of course, and Pierce was hollering at the kids to shut up and whispering and throwing looks at me. He was sure something was up but he couldn't tell what. I could see uranium go through his head and then he gave up on that because he's miles from the canyon. But . . . I guess I must've looked too eager. I must've gave it away somehow. Because—I'm so sorry, Bert, I guess I had the shakes, I wanted to help you so bad. He come back and said, we're selling both ranches together or none. With house and stock included. And he wants thirty-five thousand, which is high but not sky high for both spreads. The hitch is, he wants it in cash! In times like this! He said something about going in comfort or not at all. It seems him and Billy Joe both want to be a preacher, and here I always thought Pierce didn't have a religious bone in his body."

Bert took it in silence, squeezing his lips with his fingers.

"I told him he was clear out of his mind. I told him, you might as well ask for the moon, Pierce. But he wouldn't even haggle over it." And then she blurted out that she had lost her head and actually handed over the fourteen hundred dollars in return for a receipt and his gentleman's word that she had thirty days to scrape up the rest. "There's where I went wrong," she faltered, putting her wind-ravelled hair back from her face. "But I didn't know what else to do! I should've just turned around and went home, but I could tell he wasn't gonna change his mind, and I was afeared somebody else . . . Here's the receipt."

Bert's eyes had slitted. Jamming the receipt in his jacket pocket, he went slowly down the back steps. Frost-seared leaves filled the stock tank where kids splashed in the summer. It had clouded up, and the bare trees scratched the grey sky. Still without saying a word, he set fire to the rubbish in the basket and watched the flames, acting swiftly in the wind, chew up the cartons and paper and burst through the wire sides.

"I shouldn't never have gave him the money," she said pathetically. "I didn't even think of making sure it would be returned if the deal didn't go through. I guess I done wrong every way possible."

"Just about." Biting at his thumbnail, Bert watched the windy licks of fire melt the air over the basket. The difficulty of buying the spread had doubled, tripled, multiplied out of sight. Fixing the drill rig wouldn't turn the trick now, even if they dared to take the chance of being spotted by Pierce. They had to have the entire $33,600 and quick. Immediately. Her handing over $1400 on terms like that must have made Pierce dead certain he had something, and if he went snooping over those hills, if he discovered the drill holes . . .

"Snow," he gritted at the blowy grey sky. "Snow, you bastard."

"You mean there's a chance? Oh Bert!"

"Lady, it's not as good a chance as a harelipped whore has of making high society—and there ain't none at all if he guesses who you're fronting for. Even if I do raise the money, he might not go through with it. His gentleman's word is a bad sign. He most likely figures he's setting on oil at least."

"Oh he didn't suspect *you,* I'll take my oath on that . . . Bert? Do you forgive me? I'd sell the hotel except it already has two mortgages . . ." She stretched out her hand, and her age-loosened face was trembling. He patted her absentmindedly on the rump.

When Wally heard what had happened he blinked his eyes and his big rough hands fell open. "Looking like a cheap wake ain't gonna help," Bert said. "We're out of the frying pan anyhow and that's partways. Just leave me handle it—and keep Ray off the street. I don't want him talking to anybody."

His mind was turning, turning over possibilities. The first was Lee Stark, the car dealer who played a tough game of poker. But Stark wasn't having any, thank you; he'd been stung on a batch of leases, and he wouldn't hear the word uranium in his showroom. Now who? Andy Lytton at U.S. Mining? Bert was halfway to the shiny new quonset hut opposite the grain elevator when he decided against it. Lytton was a company man to the core and U.S. Mining didn't go partners with small fry; Lytton would insist on drilling the ore body himself and then insert the knife and bid against them.

Well, the bank then.

Taking the best sack of cuttings and the Geiger counter with him, he walked into the shabby red-brick building and asked to see old Mr. Bailey, the top man. He was told to have a chair outside the cubicle which passed for a sanctum sanctorum. While he figured out the best lie for the occasion, he let his eyes run over the genteel bustle around him. The women customers were dressed up in their Sunday clothes. A plaster swordfish leaped on the wall behind the tellers' windows. The chunky steel door of the vault was small but glittery. Everything considered, it wasn't much of a bank, but it was still enough like a church to get by.

In due time Bailey showed himself in the door of the cubicle.

Sitting at the carved wooden desk, he looked more like a poorass country preacher than a banker: string tie and grey suit, bushy eyebrows like sagebrush grown down almost to his eyes, a lean and solemn face—dry, as if the dry harsh years had burned him down to the sinews and bone. He shook hands with a stiff, formal movement and said, "What can I do for you, Mr. Stephens?"

Bert plopped the sack on the desk and made the Geiger babble over it. "That's four per cent you're listening to," he said impressively. "Forty sweet times the minimum. Look at the scale. And there's an ore body of it ten times the size of this bank! Which I will take you out there and prove to your satisfaction—right now. This minute if you want." This was where truth left off and the other part began, but he was dead sure that he could fool an amateur into thinking that 4 per cent cuttings came from the holes on their claims. "And all the cash we need is thirty-five thousand to get into production."

'Umm," Bailey said. "You know, we're not willing to plunge too much on uranium. You find a hot spot one day and the next day it's gone." It was all a set piece he'd said so many times that it came out like a chant, dry and old. "Your gold is the same thing . . . very much so. All these new promotion companies, we steer clear of all that."

Restraining himself, Bert said, "Okay, I know it's hard times so I'll lessen it down for you. I and my partner own a fifteen-thousand-dollar drill rig, plus a blade and a truck. We'll sign it all over to you, and you won't have to risk but only ten thousand. On a sure bet, too. Okay, okay, to sweeten it some more, we'll cut you in for a percentage for yourself."

In the same dry voice, he gave Bert the routine answer: "First I'd have to look at the machinery, but we might loan you three or four thousand on it. Mines just aren't good security, though."

In a fury Bert raked in his pocket for some change, intending to throw it on the desk and tell him, "here, play with this but be sure and don't lose any." But he didn't have a quarter to his name and so he was denied even this small satisfaction. It was enough to discourage anybody—anybody, that is, except Bertram J. Stephens. Because he had it behind him now, the thing that had happened in Hot Springs, and all the things it spawned, like a bloated white termite imprisoned in an underground nest, popping out eggs at the rate of one a second until it got old and the other termites killed it. If it wasn't behind him, it was at least buried deep enough so he could think of something else. The situation was damned bad and deteriorating by the minute, for every time he propositioned somebody and missed, he increased the likelihood of Pierce hearing about it. But his mind was alive with fresh, quick-springing strategies. The great quest wasn't over, after all, and he was compressed, intense, fighting hard again.

He had climbed back to the surface of life.

And as he pushed out of the bank with the sack and the Geiger, it began to snow: salt-white particles that multiplied in the wind, scoured the huddled storefronts, washed in thin white waves over the street. By morning three inches had come down and the buttes lying in the cold sky were as grey as slabs of ice. "Well now, if that ain't a help to poor sinners," he chuckled to Edna. "And it's free for nothing. Yesterday I'd of sold my soul for this snow if there was any takers. If I had a soul."

Wally showed up to ride herd on Ray, but even his dumb agitation had no effect. "I'll cook up something or other," Bert said. "I'll get up that money if I have to sell my body in the common street. That ought to bring in seventy-five cents right there."

Silent with disapproval, Wally took a seat by the soiled bed where Ray was burbling snores.

"Excuse *me*," Bert said mockingly. He chewed on his thumbnail, considering. "I believe it's time for our Sunday shot. Mister Robert Werden."

"Werden!" Wally bleated. "That man's so dishonest he turns me sick to my stomach. I don't like it, Bert. It makes the whole business seem dirtier than ever. I'm not speaking of Pierce; it's not his land we're after, and he's acting bad himself. But that other boy, Billy Joe, we're trying to pull a gyp on him—to some extent, if you look at it one way. And Bob Werden . . ." He broke down into frowning, hunched forward with his massive hands on his knees.

"Correct me if I'm wrong," Bert said, and his eyes were freezing. "It was you that dragged me off of Skidrow, remember? I had strictly quit life, remember? Retired and quit. Turned in my resignation. Well now I'm back into it, and I don't intend to finish second. Do you grasp that, Sunshine? You had better. Now here's the philosophy of it and you're old enough to hear it said. In this imperfect world you can't do doodley shit without people like Bob Werden. Exactly how does anybody make it? All them Horatio Algers, all them inspirations to boyhood, all the poor and unwashed of every description that climbed to the top. You think it was hard work that done it and maybe a little genius thrown in, huh? Well it's not that simple. If you ain't born with it made, you have to connect with the bastards that can give you a boost up. And around the gravy pot is where they hang out."

Wally's sack-face went down and down.

"What busts my tender heart is I'll have to make him rich. That's what I hate. But there's strictly no help for it." Clicking his fingers, he prowled back and forth in the chilly room. "The other tiny stickler is he won't come within three hundred miles of us. And if we go to him, he won't listen to a proposition if we *could* get past his secretary. He'd just think it was another trap. He'll never in his life forget me leaving him out there in the brush to walk it in. Not Bob Werden." But to state the impossible was merely to attack it: he tilted back his face and held it there, his mouth open, his mind ticking like a room full of clocks.

Then he was grinning. "I've got it, Heavy! Fifty-two, little seven! Damn if I'm not a smart chicken. With all due modesty, I have to say it—where other people's smart leaves off, that's where mine begins."

In the drugstore he told Helen, "It's your decision. Either help me some more or tie a rope around my neck." She did not like the idea of guile, trickery, or subterfuge in any form, but he mixed persuasion with large spoonfuls of Dr. Stephens' Nerve Cure and Tonic for Female Complaints. "Shoot, there's no harm in telling a small harmless little fib, is there? It ain't as if I'm breaking *all* the ten commandments. Yet."

"But still it's not right. It's just not."

"Lord have mercy. You expect to catch the devil with sermons, woman? You have to be shrewd, crafty, cunning, *and* a better liar than he is."

They were standing by the oil burner with its black stovepipe thrusting up and dividing like the branches of a tree across the ceiling. It was necessary to speak carefully, not only because of the loiterers at the front but because of Pierce Bolton's daughter Debbie, who was at the soda fountain, spinning herself around and around on a stool to make herself dizzy. Down near the floor, Helen's baby was scooting around them like a tiny juggernaut, eating a piece of candy.

"Bud mightn't like it," she objected.

"Me with six busted ribs, and you don't even care," he said, cocking his face. He was excited, sure of himself. Nothing could stop him now. "All right, don't relent, but just remember, you're killing our love. Down the trail of broken hearts I go."

"I wish you wouldn't say things like that," she said. The blood was like a hurt in her cheeks.

"I guess you're right. Now that our engagement is broke, I don't have the privilege." Grinning, he watched her flinch and whip around to the baby, which had slathered chocolate all over its face. "Therese! You little pig!" she cried. Going to the fountain for a rag, she made the face custard-smooth and white again. He could tell that she wanted very much for him to like the baby, and so, leaning down into the smell of sweetish powder, chocolate, and wet diaper, he forced himself to be cute with it. The little creature whimpered with a thumb hung in its syrupy mouth.

"Don't suck on that thumb too hard," he said. "You're gonna need it someday."

Out came a bawl. Grievously disappointed, Helen snatched the baby into the air, and shaking it like a girl shakes a naughty doll, carried it howling into the back. Debbie went flying past, her coat flapping around her gawky legs, to ask if she could take care of her, please. In a little while Helen appeared again, painfully hesitant, peering timidly from inside herself. "I swear, she's acting like a perfect hellcat these days," she sighed. "It's that new tooth she's getting, that's the trouble."

"Might be," he said. Unless it just runs in the family."

A smile slipped out, shining. It was like a soft light glowing inside her plain, mole-flecked face. "Bud's changed his mind about you," she said. "He didn't want to take you out there, but I made him. Now he says you're all right." She hesitated. "Can't you please tell me what it all means? I won't tell a soul."

"Ssh! There's too much audience around."

Keeping her voice down, she said, "I'm to send a telegram to Robert Werden, care of Western United Enterprises, National Bank Building, Denver. And say to come out here on the double."

"Correct," he said exultantly. "And sign Bud's name to it. Werden will think there's a strike in that two-bit mine and come tearing out here to diddle Bud out of his stock. Bob Werden wears shoes so the Lord can't keep on his trail but I can read his mind from here."

"You look poorly, Bob. Like your jockstrap is too tight," he was saying two days later.

"I must be losing my marbles," Werden griped. The truck swung off the highway and he grimaced at the hills turning their stark contours, bald, frozen. In a scurfy pasture a small herd of cattle breathed steamily at him. "How many miles out are you going to leave me this time? You're playing Russian sleigh ride with me. Leave them behind on the steppes for the wolves, the old men first and then the women over forty."

"You take another sniff of that again," Bert said, plunking the bag of cuttings and the Geiger onto Werden's briefcase. Just as he'd predicted, Werden had swallowed the bait. He'd been more than slightly unhappy when he discovered the trap, naturally, and before he would believe that Bud hadn't sent the wire, he had to hear it from Bud himself. Morbidly suspicious to begin with, he didn't put any faith in the samples until Bud tested them with his scintillator and whistled, and even then he went on screaming, "Quisling! Judas!" But he was used to double and triple crosses, and underneath the venomous accusations his naked eagerness contracted like a gland. He wasn't taking any more risks, though, and he'd insisted that Bud, as his partner of sorts, lay off work and come along to give him expert advice. So there they were, the three of them, grinding along a dirt road in the National Forest. Eerie clouds lay on the empty land. The pine-black slopes were sharply drawn in the cold, transparent air.

"Yeah, yeah, I know," Werden said without switching on the

Geiger. "This time there *is* a mine. I have the treasure of King Tut within my grasp and all that, but I really don't have the money to put up! I honest-to-God don't! A lot of things have happened, Bert. They bombed me on that dude ranch deal!"

"Now ain't that a shame," Bert said.

A look of hate poisoned Werden's face but—characteristically—he subsided a little. Any kind of reasoning or flattery, any kind of softness was a mistake with him. He pushed and pushed hard, but if you pushed back he folded up immediately. For about thirty seconds, that is. At least a hundred times he'd reconciled himself to the trick and agreed to look at the drill holes, and every time that skittery and itching thing, his mind, reversed itself and back came the complaining and the air of grievance—as it did now.

"You have the grave already dug for me, don't you?" he said. "Hey, watch it, will you? My piles!" he hollered at Bud as the truck took a bump. "Now Bert, I mean it. It isn't that I mind another kick in the chromosomes, but I'm busy. I don't have the time for this."

"That's a nice hat you have on," Bert remarked.

"What? What was that?" He whirled around, red to the eyes, and his hand went to the green Alpine hat he was still affecting. "Well, there's mountains around here, so what's the complaint?" he snarled, and yodelled angrily. It did Bert's heart good. For once in a blue moon his feelings and the correct strategy came to the same thing. "Boy, this is too much," Werden said. "You stick it in up to the trademark and then you make with the satire. This is too much!"

Bending forward to clamp his look on Bud at the wheel, he said, "Don't fail me today. This schmuck is a real threat to me, and you have the know-how on this stuff. I'm counting on you. Don't forget, it was your sister that helped him give me the shaft, so you owe me that much . . . Right?"

Bud, who thought the fake telegram was funny, anyway, and who was pretty sure he'd been swindled on the stock, gravely steered the truck into boulders and ruts to shake up Werden's hemorrhoids. Werden stretched his neck in agony, waiting for an answer.

"I didn't reach you, huh?" he said. "Okay, Helen Keller, see if you can hear this. If this rat here uses me for a piece of cheese today, your stock won't be worth ten cents. I'll see to that. Personally. It'll be confederate money, understand me?"

Robel spoke to Bert: "He don't trust nobody, does he? A snake must of bit him on the ass when he lowered his britches."

"I didn't mean it," Werden said, capitulating at once. "You're an honest man, I can see it—without my lantern, even. Seriously, Bud, I trust you. I'm sincere about that, really sincere." When Bud's smoky face remained distant, he practically went into convulsions. His plump blue eyes were smudgy, his mouth worked pathetically. "If you'd lost the money I have, you'd be shellshocked too. Look at the sweat on my hands—in weather like this! Ever since it happened I've had this dream. I mean this nightmare. I dream the bathtub is full of nickels and dimes and quarters, and they're all running out the hole and I can't stop them! You talk about pure, unadulterated torture! I haven't taken a bath since!"

He laughed miserably. "Do I talk too much?"

Bud slewed off onto a bulldozed trail that Bert indicated. Frozen weeds scraped against the side of the truck. A dead antelope was slung over a pine stump, rigid in webs of dry grey snow, and Werden goggled at it, fluttering his soft hands. "Hey look! Hey, that's a bad sign. It's an omen! Oh well," he said when they made no comment, "what's another fiasco? I'll still have enough left to buy a violin and a tin cup. Can you train a poodle to be a seeing-eye dog?"

In ten minutes they plunged and slogged past the abandoned drill rig. Around the stark grey hill were brownish-grey distances cold with wind: Billy Joe's spread. "The first hole is right under the brush there," Bert said and limped off toward the boundary of the ranch, the sole of his shoe flapping. The icy wind carried the faint crack! of a deer rifle from three canyons away. The shag grass, the rocks and starved dirt were smoothed with snow—with no sign of wheel tracks or footprints anywhere. Bert clicked his fingers, elated. Werden, trailing behind him, shivered in his alpaca topcoat and grumbled, "This is a dandy walk in the snow but hey, I'm freezing! Brrh!" Eyes shifting from one of them to the other and back, he gibbered, "Hello, hello America, this is Admiral Byrd." Static crackled and buzzed and his voice emerged again, remote, squawky with outrage: "Byrd, B-Y-R-D. From Antarctica! You remember, the expedition! What's wrong down here? The goddamn penguins have got in the oatmeal, that's what's wrong. Can you hear me? The oatmeal!"

Bud was letting out foot after foot of heavy wire, lowering the phallus-shaped probe into the test hole. Attached to the other end was a scintillator. Unable to restrain himself any longer, Werden rushed back to him and said anxiously, "What's the verdict? Is it good?"

Crouched on his heels, Bud twiddled the knobs on the scintillator. His eyes leaked with the cold. His mouth fumed. "You're quite the berries," he said to Bert. As each hole rocked the needle all the way over on the top scale, his wind-gnawed face grew more and more impressed. "You sure have made a believer out of me," he said.

"It's good? It's here? You're sure? Honest?" Werden kept asking. "How much do you guess is down there? Give me an estimate."

Bert said, "There's a million and a half down there. And much as it pains me, I'l give you a third for sixty thousand cash, to buy the land and open up with."

"You're on!" Werden said, putting out his hand. "I'll have the money for you inside of two days."

It was more than a good deal for Werden, it was getting twenty-dollar bills for pennies, and yet Bert had that cold feeling at the base of the spine which meant a harpoon was on its way. He ignored the outstretched hand and his eyes narrowed, as sharp and thin as razor blades under the flop of hair on his forehead. Then he took out his jackknife, a rusty thing with one of its wrinkled sides fallen off, and showed it to Werden. "It seems I got to set you straight, Bob. You're not screwing around with widows and orphans this trip."

"What's that? What's the idea?"

"This here pig-sticker is the idea. As you'll notice, it's dull. It'll take me ten minutes to remove your balls with it but I'm willing to invest the time and energy."

If he'd tried that with somebody like Bud he'd have gotten the jackknife stuffed up his nose, but Werden wasn't Bud Robel. His elastic face slid out of shape with horror and his hand went to his crotch, quivering. "Don't *talk* like that!" he cried. "I never intended anything hokey, Bert. I swear it! I don't even know who owns the land, so how could I buy it myself?" Then he got on his high horse and said, "If this is how you feel, you can count me out. I don't want anything to do with you. At any price."

"No you don't," Bert said. "You don't have any more option. I proved my story, now you reach for your wallet—and don't look to Bud for help. Because I'll sic him onto you and he'll flip you over and stomp your face."

"I might at that," Bud said.

"Traitor!" Werden shrieked. "I bet you conned me about those holes, Robel. You finks set me up—no! I take it back!" he said hurriedly as Bud looked at him. "I believe, I believe. Bert, the deal is still on, okay?" As they drove back to the highway he attempted to make peace. "Maybe I did have an idea of evening the score back there. We're both putzas, okay? This is no time to have a hassle, with the golden fleece right in front of us." And in a flicker he was standing on the deck of a comic-strip galley, Jason, shouting, "Row, you schmucks, faster! Put your backs into it!"

Bert said, "I want the money today."

"Okay, okay, but listen—just as long as there's no hard feelings. Please? Let's all get rich and marry the heroine and live happy ever after, okay? Or even better. Let's get married and keep the money in the family. Can you cook?"

Suddenly Bert felt his wild excitement run out of him. It wasn't the falseness in the squirming jokes, but the little kernel of honest embarrassment and shame in Werden that got him, and lying back on the seat with his his face averted, he watched the faded highway store slip past, weathering and plastered with signs behind its dusty gas pumps. It took a wintry act of will to recover even some of his alertness and purpose. In front of the bank, Bud left them to sit in the Victory Bar and get drunk and dream of ore bodies burning like the deep belly of a volcano with four per cent uranium oxide. Bert didn't have to ask him to keep quiet. His eyes small and cold, Bert stayed right with Werden while he had Bailey call the First National Bank in Denver to clear the checks; then he shoved Werden into the hotel room with Wally and Ray and handed the cashier's check for $33,600 to Edna.

"You done it!" she exclaimed. "Oh Bert, you done it! But there's rumors around in spite of everything. I never said a word, but people keep talking about a big hit and *you!* I'm so scared. I just know Pierce won't go through with it."

"Probably not but I think there's a play for it anyhow. Keep working on Billy Joe. Pierce will butt in, but say, 'You gave your word, Billy, and you don't want to go off to serve Jesus with dirty hands, do you? That'll get him in the tender place, and Pierce will have to go along or be stuck with his thousand acres of sagebrush."

"I never seen anybody to match you," she said. "Never."

He started her toward the door. "I ain't any better than other people,' just smarter. Now get along."

With that he turned and went down the unlighted hall to the room. The next few hours made him want to puke at first—before the dull, paralyzed feeling came back, the feeling he'd had watching the highway store slip past and dwindle into nothing at all. Werden kept griping, "What's wrong with me making some phone calls? I got to keep in touch!" Then he switched to Edna and began moaning, "*She'll* cross us, I can feel it, Bert! *She's* the big threat now." Bert told him to shut up or he'd have Wally bust his snot-box. Then Werden had another wild hair: stock. "We can make three times as much this way," he said, all his overworked pores wetting with enthusiasm. "Here's how we do it. Boy, if motherhood was this easy, every American girl under sixty would have triplets." At this point, for the first and last time, Wally spoke up: "No stock," he said dourly and went back to page five of *Thoughts That Have Shaken the World* or something like that. And then Ray, who was starting to mutter and butt toward the door, had to be anesthetized with whiskey. Bert put his foot up on the windowsill and stared out at the cold yard and the peeling side of a house, at the ghosts of smoke revelling into the grey November afternoon. The sunset was like a lonely ranch house going up in flames miles back in the frozen brown hills. It was close to five-thirty before Edna burst in and threw her hefty arms around him, sobbing with happiness.

"Okay, okay, sign the property over," Werden told her. "Bert, I'll call my lawyer and we'll nail it down."

"You'll call hell," he rasped. "You'll get your tail out of town. Now, this minute. Hire a car or something. Walk. I can only look at you for so long before I want to cut my throat." Werden hollered foul and insisted on at least a preliminary agreement, properly witnessed and notarized, but Bert said, "We'll do all that later. Wally's my conscience, and he gives you his word. Right, Wally? So goodbye and pleased as all hell to have did business with you. You hurry back with your hotshot lawyer and a hundred and twenty-six nifty paragraphs of fine print with a piece of barbed wire in each one."

Werden rolled up his moist pink palms in surrender. "Boy, you're a shark, you know that? I'll be lucky if I don't get blitzed on the contract myself. And I always figured you for a loser. Boy!"

Bert pushed the door shut on him but it took most of a pint of whiskey to get the taste of Werden out of his mouth—and to really feel what he'd accomplished. In due time each scorching mouthful was doing its job and his good spirits flared up, grew into a raging bonfire of triumph. For one absolute moment, celebrating with Edna and Wally in her room behind the desk, the torn darkness inside him seemed to knit and he had solved everything, all the ills which flesh is heir to, all the dying and being born, all the despair, all the equations with no answer, all the mysteries from the time the first baboon became conscious enough to sweat at night and pray to a chunk of stone he particularly favored.

"Damn if I didn't do it," he said to Wally. "I made it up to you, too. True or not? A drunk old stray like me."

"I guess so," Wally said, looking down at his cold cup of coffee.

But Bert was floating above all that. Rakish, irrepressible, he stamped his feet at the tiny, wet-eyed dog. In terror it scuttled behind Edna's legs. The loose sole of his shoes got in his way and he ripped it off, then trampled his feet again, laughing as the dog bounded into her lap and burrowed under her shapeless breasts. She implored him to stop. His eyes swelled, and whooping like a crazy man, he stamped at the old floor until the concussions set the room vibrating, pots and leaves and sculptured gilt frames, and the glass roses that he'd given to her swayed and clinked together like thin bells. "The seismograph in Los Angeles picked that one up," he wheezed. "Now for a small toast: To a good long pull at Lady Fortune's left titty." Raising the bottle, he finished it off with a spouting, bubbling, glugging pour and then dropped one eyelid in a wink. "Partner," he said, "Let's us go out on the town. Tie down our hats and let 'er rip."

"No thanks, Bert. I'd better be getting home."

"As you please. Be that as it may, it ain't much of a town but still I'm going out on it." He jumped up, clicking his heels together, and then patted Edna on her beefy shoulder. "Don't wait up, dear heart," he cackled. "I'm going out with a deaf-and-dumb girl from the Pine Ridge Reservation and something like that naturally takes time."

"I still don't see what I could've done," Wally was saying at ten o'clock. "The whole thing was his brainchild, not mine. I only come along for the ride . . . And when you think how much it meant to him, too . . . He earned that money, Ray. If ever anybody earned it, he did."

Ray's veiny eyes were doped and slow. Scraping his clipped-off fingers in his hair, he mumbled, "I'm drunk, so please excuse it. Anyhow . . . I'm checking out on the first freight. Easy come, easy go."

Hour after hour had passed and still Wally hadn't gone home. The cafe was almost deserted. On the pastry shelf were slices of pie with pale scorched crusts: blueberry, gluey brown apple, pumpkin dried to the color of mud and cracked open like the desolate country outside. The carcass of a turkey left over from Thanksgiving, stiffened into rags of meat and brown skin on a cage of bone, sat in the opening to the kitchen. "I'll have another hot turkey sandwich and a cup of coffee," he told the waitress. "And give me one of those pieces of pie. Blueberry."

Ray said, "I'll have a chili." None too pleasantly, the waitress reminded him again that they didn't have any chili. "With crackers," he said. "I like chili with crackers. It's my favorite." When she made a gesture of disgust he grumped irritably, "And hurry up about it." He was in no mood to be thwarted. From time to time when the realization of Bert's prosperity became too much for him, he would splutter gummy curses and swipe his fists at the air, helpless, his eyes weeping in his ugly boar's face. A minute or two later he would be speaking sorrowfully about Debbie and how nice she had been to him. Wally knew that he wasn't listening, wasn't interested, and wasn't able to think straight in any case; but maybe that was the kind of audience he wanted.

"But you take it from another angle," he said, "and the whole deal was fishy for a long time. I told Bert he had to start prospecting or I was through—which he did, but it was only to get bigger than Sam Bolton on acount of some disagreements they had. And you know what I done? I accepted it at face value, when I knew better . . . Compromises, more and more of them, worse ones. I'm a weak person, Ray . . . I was scared Esther would kick up a fuss and leave, too, if she found out Bert had blowed every penny on drilling." He fell silent, looking down at the bits of the hot turkey sandwich he'd gobbled absentmindedly, without even enjoying it. Then he burst out, "Ray, I wanted the money myself. It's hard to feature, but the itch was there inside of me too. Somewhere along the line it stopped being just Bert and saving him. I guess this is the worst thing I ever done in my life. I put up an argument but not much of a one. I was only dragging my feet. I left him do the dirty work and took my share of the profits. Right now, I could still tell them, 'I'm out,' but I can't do it. I'm that weak."

Ray was saying to himself, "He were too much for me. His luck were too much. And so . . . Well don't be sad and mopey, that's the way."

"Maybe you're right!" Wally seized on the random words. "Nothing can be done about it now. If I pull out or not, it's the same. Besides, what harm was done? Just the opposite, in fact. It'll help my family. And Bert. The Bolton boy will get to be a preacher, too, which he mightn't of. Anyhow, what difference does that much more uranium make?" For just an instant he faltered and then went on. But he had been hit, like a murderer's blow on the skull, and he kept talking only by a kind of momentum, the way the heart goes on beating for a few seconds after the brain has been crushed: "Why one of these days the peaceful uses of atomic energy are going to take over, you'll see. It's the power of the future . . ."

His voice ran down, stopped. Up until now he hadn't thought of the talks he'd had with Paul as applying to *him,* the letters he'd received as applying to him. Placid and admiring, he'd read the crackling pages about government by fear, about hysteria and blind nationalism. Sagely he'd agreed that life had come at last to its ultimate crisis in infinite power set against infinite power, and agreed that Russia and the United States were only the beginning, that in thirty or forty years, if the world lasted that long, any number of other countries would have nuclear weapons, too. On rockets! And he'd sympathized with Paul about the defeat of Adlai Stevenson and the "egghead rebellion"—not that Eisenhower was a bad man, only mediocre and passive, allowing McCarthy on his campaign train, for instance, even though he hated him and all he stood for . . . But now he saw the rest of it. Paul had been plugging away at *him,* telling *him* to quit. Trying to cast out one devil, anyway. Only he'd never thought they'd actually hit like this, and the problem of Bert had been so pressing . . .

Then somehow it had happened. It had taken terrific effort, it had taken Bert's magnificent intelligence and unbelievable hardship for both of them, but they had succeeded in adding their bit to the damnation of everybody.

And there beside him in the soupy light was Ray, drunk and croaking to himself on the stool, flipper hands waving, eyes bulging, deformed—something you looked away from, something you pretended wasn't there. But he was there all right, like a twisted dream come to life, like the nightmare of his own evil.

And the consequences of it. There he was, a goggling freak, a half-finished little monster, like an atomic mutation. The shape of things to come.

Fumbling down from the stool, Ray made it out the door, veering from side to side, wobbling on his plug legs, and turned toward the freight yards. Shamefaced, Wally ordered ham and eggs and a side of potatoes and went on eating.

December 2, 1952

(Columbus Day, Modern Style)

Forty scientists assembled under the stands of Stagg Field at the University of Chicago. They were marking the tenth anniversary of the first self-sustaining nuclear reaction. On a raw, windy day ten years before, Enrico Fermi had led the great breakthrough, conducting the critical experiment from the balcony of the squash court under the stands. With him were about two dozen scientists. Below them on the court was the pile of graphite blocks and cylinders of uranium, looking like a huge flattened beehive. As the last control rod was pulled out, a little at a time, the counters ticked faster and faster, whirring like runaway clocks. Needles leaned farther over on dials as atoms, blasted with neutrons, split apart spouting radioactive energy and more neutrons. Fermi bustled around watching the instruments, making calculations on his sliderule and calling out orders. It was a glorious moment for the small, homely man with the enormous mind and the childish ego: on hikes it was always Fermi who carried the largest pack and reached the top of the mountain first, explaining that he never got tired because his heart was "custom made"—it was Fermi who could see farther than anyone else because his eyes were also "custom made"—it was Fermi who had to be first even in parlor amusements and who tormented his wife and associates with humiliating question games. Now he stood at the center of history. Late in the afternoon he shouted down, "Pull it out another foot," and said to Dr. Compton, the director of the project, that this was going to do it. Released at last, white storms of energy boiled in the cylinders. The counters stuttered frantically. He checked his slide rule once more and smiled in triumph. "The reaction is self-sustaining," he announced. "The curve is exponential." After a half hour the control rods were thrown back in, pushing down the unleashed fury, and a bottle of wine was produced; Compton rushed off to telegraph, "The Italian explorer had landed in the New World."

And all through the hectic days of building the first bomb at Los Alamos, it was still pure conquest, pure achievement. Fermi hooted at the conscientious scruples of his colleagues. "The thing is superb physics," he insisted blithely. After the first test the triumphant telegram went off to Truman and Churchill at Potsdam, "Baby is satisfactorily born," but as Fermi looked at the tornado of fire and smoke that swept up into the sky, he was so shaken that he was unable to drive the car back from Alamogordo. The brilliant voyage, he was beginning to realize, was a voyage into nightmare. In 1949, as a member of the General Advisory Commission of atomic scientists, he argued against development of the hydrogen bomb, calling it "an evil thing considered in any light." But President Truman's logic was unanswerable: "Can the Russians make the thing? And if so, how can we help making it?"

Scientific discovery was a one-way trip; there was no going back. And now in the winter of 1952 as the scientists returned to the scene, the festivity had something macabre about it, and they celebrated nervously, defensively. The New World of Enrico Fermi might blow up at any minute.

XX

Bert's spectacular discovery made the front page of the Rapid City paper: "The Atomic Energy Commission has confirmed the most sensational find to date," it trumpeted. "Larry Wassburger, manager of the Enterprise office and buying station, announced the strike at a press conference yesterday, adding that its worth is of untold value. The heroes of this truly epic saga are Bertram Stephens and Walter J. Riggs, who were wildcatting on a section of the Bolton ranch . . . purchase details not disclosed but . . ."

Sam Bolton felt the blood ram into his chest. "Commere, quick!" he shouted to Vivie, his eyes sucking in the hymn of praise to Stephens and Riggs, "colorful personalities who arrived in Enterprise with only $4.29 and struck it rich. . . . The ore-finding techniques employed by these farsighted and resourceful men have completely changed the picture of our country's resources, according to Mr. Wassburger, and are of importance to the future of the entire free world. Other large strikes, using their techniques, are expected to follow."

"Get a move on!" he bellowed at her. "Did Frank call you? What in thunder is wrong with him? Look at what Pierce and Billy Joe done! Those two ignoramuses let themselves get buffaloed out of a fortune!"

Vivie grabbed the paper. "Oh no!" she wailed. "I told you not to *give* them anything, Daddy. I knew it, oh I knew it. We should've run that no-good Pierce off years ago, and Billy Joe don't have the brains of a chicken."

They closed up the tourist lodge and set off for the ranch in less than an hour, but the boys had already lit out for the Bible college in Sioux Falls. The details of the transaction, when he dug them out, only poured gasoline on his blazing exasperation. To get taken like boobs! Not to see that something was fishy when they got a cash offer in times like these! And over and above that, they had betrayed him. He had paid for those spreads with the sweat of his brow, and they'd known they weren't to sell. Finding uranium on his land was a thing of blind

305

chance, of course, but the irony of it, after all his prospecting in Red Canyon, was not easy to swallow. And that Bert Stephens, that little jughead, had done the finding was not exactly to his taste either.

Still, it was past remedy now, he told himself, and, though he didn't relish doing so, he had to hand it to Stephens. He was a smart little rascal, a darn sight too much for those gullible numbskulls he had raised. The best thing was to count his blessings, and they were numerous: he still had most of the $90,000 he'd received for his claims, and U.S. Mining was obligated to pay him $160,000 more when the option was up. He still had the lodge and the ranch, the sawmill, and property in town. Come right down to it, he had lost nothing but a couple thousand acres of dirt. And yet—for some reason his chagrin persisted; he felt damaged, smaller, as if *he* had failed.

For two or three days he sat around the ranch house, muddled, brute-heavy, growling. There was work enough to be done—Frank was running the spread with only one nephew to help—and in spite of his bum leg he was able to lend a hand; but he did nothing. The books he'd been reading gathered dust in the bedroom. Vivie said, "It's sinful the way you're brooding, Sam. What about those stock dams you were going to deepen?"

"Leave me be, I warn you," he told her. The quarrel which followed ended in the usual rape, which utterly failed to quell the volcanic roiling inside him. He took to staying in town all day, bored and idle, dissatisfied, caning himself along from the post office to the Western Cafe to the barber shop, and sooner or later, to the drowsy checker game in the firehouse-city hall. Such was his daily fare. The town itself was moving ahead; the hotels and cafes were well populated and the stores were doing a land office business. Only *he* was inactive, paralyzed in a monotonous round of talk and trivial errands—he who had been going like a house afire all his life, doing, battling, creating and procreating. Somehow he had come to a stop.

Standing around with ranchers in the winter doldrums, old timers on pension and railroad men between runs, talking about the temperature, about the poor snowcover, about the horse auction coming up, about nothing. Snowlight came in through the window of the post office and glowed dully on glasses, false teeth. The grate blew out heat and a man with a hanging neck said, "that kid is still in the hospital. The quarterback that got the brain concussion in the game against Lusk. I'll never forget, we had the ball on the five yard line, first down, and couldn't put it over . . ."

More and more, however, the trance-struck, mumbling hours began to flicker with news of the outrageous antics of the new mining millionaire, Bert Stephens. A man with fallen cheeks and a munching smile said, "He's blowed more'n twelve thousand dollars already. First off he got outfitted in a hundred-dollar Stetson hat, hundred-and-fifty dollar boots, and a wardrobe full of suits. Every one custom made. He purt' near bought out the store."

"So I heard, too. And wasn't that Cadillac something? It was something to behold. Colored a high purple. With air conditioning. You know what he said when he bought it? He said, 'Now that suits my personality.'" And his mouth dropped open on brown slivers of teeth, laughing.

"It suited him to a tee, that feller. And when he wrecked it, he didn't give a hoot neither. All he done was hang a OUT OF ORDER sign on it and walk off."

Every day, it seemed, there were new tales of his capers: he had given a thousand dollars apiece to Bud Robel and Edna Harbaugh; he had tipped the one-lunged war veteran who played the organ in the Victory Bar a hundred dollars to pay him his favorite tunes, "Blue Boy" and "Money, Marbles, and Chalk." Chafed and frowning, Sam listened to the men in the barber shop, sitting like lively corpses in the smell of hair tonic and the buzz of the clippers, their embalmed faces nodding and smiling as they corrected each other, added fresh details. "Yessir, it's in the man's nature to whoop it up. His partner now, he's just the opposite, but Bert Stephens likes to whoop it up."

"I seen this one myself. He drinks Scotch and soda out of a quart mug, and last Saturday he throwed a party for his whole crew. Eighteen men!"

"He likes to whoop it up, all right. And he's got girls aplenty. Half a dozen women is pulling hair over him and he's taking 'em all on in rotation."

"He sure outclasses the field."

"He's comical, too. You know what he calls whiskey? Groceries!"

"Speaking of groceries, did you hear about that trailer he bought? He filled the freezer with steaks for a cross-country party. But he forgot to plug it in and they rolled into Salt Lake stinking like a dead horse."

Wheezes and chuckles of appreciation rustled along the row of men and one of them added, "He looked in a mirror and said, 'I ain't never seen a millionaire before.'"

"And wasn't that some hunting trip? Him and his buddies went tearing down the highway as drunk as they could be, shooting at telephone poles, powerlines, and anything that moved. Somewhere along the line he crept up on Russel Hanson's herd, fell in a stock tank, and right from there started blazing away. Got a brood cow, too, and they brung it home roped on the hood like a deer. For his partner. He said, 'I'll shoot 'em and you eat 'em, Lard.' That's what he said. His partner has an appetite, you know, and he was joking him . . ."

Sam burst outside in a plunging limp, crashing the door shut behind him. Celebrating was one thing but that was going overboard; the man was a crackpot and he was good and tired of hearing about him. He looked around. The afternoon was dry and cold. Christmas trees were stacked against the side of the Piggly Wiggly store, tied in bundles. Strings of unlighted bulbs hung in motionless sags over the street. There was nothing to do, nowhere to go. To fill the gaping hours somehow, he took a run out to the sawmill. A conveyor belt for the scrap angled up from the corrugated iron building to an iron furnace fifty feet high, smoking into the sky like bees pouring from an immense hive. Inside the mill, oily chains jerked in the screaming air, logs and boards rode away on belts, a machine grappled logs to its side and drove them through the tearing teeth of a high-speed wheel. Men with fingers gone, with bandaged hands, worked in a stink of resin and the shriek of saws. Roy Wilkins, the manager, caught sight of him and hurried over looking concerned. "Nothing, it's nothing in particular," Sam said. "I was just passing this way."

"How's the leg, Mr. Bolton?"

"Coming along, I guess." He swivelled around on his cane and got out of there. For a while he made a show of examining the stacks of lumber; then, as a last resort, he peered through a vent in the side of the furnace. His face and eyes seared. A pipe forced air into the fire, stirring up a whirlwind of flames, and red furies gushed out of the burning hill of sawdust. Heaps and piles collapsed like a bombed city, and smouldering masses of ash and embers were swept up into the firestorm; sparks swirled like a fierce orange blizzard in the superheated air. But it was only a temporary escape; Roy was watching him from the mill, bewildered and uneasy, and there was nothing else to see.

He drove back to town feeling more caught than ever, more futile, restless, galled.

And when the Enterprise *Gazette* came out on Friday, at least half of it was devoted, one way or another, to puffing Bert Stephens. The pictures, which even a simpleton could tell were faked, especially got under his skin—pictures of Stephens and his partner looking at chunks of ore, supposedly judging them with the naked eye, pictures of Stephens using a Geiger counter (kneeling in a handsome pose and holding the counter like a prize leg of mutton at the county fair), pictures of Stephens at the wheel of a front-end loader; Stephens; Stephens. The crowning piece of hokum, however, was the editorial proclaiming him "the Columbus of a new era of golden opportunity dawning for our community." That really peeved Sam, and he had a right to be peeved. At least part of the credit belonged to *him*. After all, *he* had been the first substantial producer and developer in the region.

But nobody remembered that. He just had to sit there and grit his teeth while the whole town, the entire state of South Dakota, reverenced the little cuss and doted on his antics. The single exception was George Mencke, and he had his own reasons, his own private grudge. It was common knowledge that Helen was sweet on Stephens—for that matter,

Sam didn't exactly find that pleasant himself—and all day long George went from place to place, speaking against Stephens and getting the cold shoulder for his pains. Unfortunately, it didn't take him long to sense Sam's feelings about Stephens and to try to form an alliance with him! Georgie Mencke, who used to trail him around town to protect Helen from him, and now waddling up, ingratiating, tactful, submissive, with another choice tidbit about their mutual enemy. Sam swung his greying head. "Stop plaguing me," he growled with dull, blood-gorged eyes, but an hour later Georgie was there again, tiptoeing closer.

Then, at the horse sale, unexpectedly, his banked-up frustration was raked into flames. He'd been waiting thirstily for the event, and he came to the auction barn early to enjoy the corral talk beforehand and take in the pungent sights and sounds. Hoofs thudded in soft dirt. Weathered ranchers, as gaunt and plain as the land, were settled against the railings with their curled hats shoved back. "It's a good using horse," Peterson was remarking. "Plenty of color, too." Feeling released from the useless days, Sam limped genially up to them. Tail-switching animals moved in the pens. A shaggy head suddenly careened in the half-light, live ears poked up. The air was rich with manure and hay smells, and from down the line of stalls came the great blubbing breath of a stallion. Sam talked more than he was accustomed to and looked over the entire assortment of stock, from the unbroken colts, snorting and shying off in beautiful swift breaks, their slender haunches flowing along the fence, all the way down to the beaten old slaughter horses. Just as the chant of the auctioneer was about to start, it happened. Amos Putnam, who had tried to sell his spread to him last summer, observed, "You sure missed the boat on that one, didn't you, Sam?"

"Huh? What was that?"

"The strike on your ranch. You missed the boat on it."

He scratched behind his ear, standing humped over. "I think somebody gave you a distorted story, Amos. It was the boys' spread to do with as they pleased. They got singed in the deal, not me. It was none of my affair."

Amos let out a mouthful of tobacco juice. Then he said, "Whatever you say, Sam."

"Well I do say. As for that Stephens," he found himself rumbling, "I got no kick against him. He was more than a match for them and that's that. I bear no grudge."

Five or six cattlemen were spectators. Their lean, cured faces were expressionless under their brims rolled to a point in front, but he could feel that they were enjoying themselves, having the time of their lives. A fog of maddened blood came into his eyes and, blindly, dragging his leg in its metal brace, he pulled himself outside into the cold. Beyond the frozen creek the pale winter sun was caught in the naked cottonwoods. A string of ore cars backed slowly in the freight yards. He hadn't expected sympathy—of the hundreds of persons he knew, some of them neighbors of forty years' standing, there was not one he regarded as a friend, an equal with whom he shared his thoughts and dreams—but their sly pleasure at his misfortune took him by surprise. Maybe he had been too occupied to get close to others, or maybe it was his nature to keep to his own people; whatever the explanation was he still couldn't help feeling hurt. And almighty angry. He must be an object of amusement for three hundred miles around. The more he meditated on it, the more it fevered in his blood and the more his unexpended energy heaped up and up, swelling the erotic frenzy battering and bludgeoning inside him. Margie Selkirk had never come back from that visit to her parents, and Ellie in Buffalo Gap had taken up with a man who wanted to marry her. It was the fleshpots of Denver or nothing, and for two days he rampaged and coupled like a centaur in a spring orgy—and returned unsatiated, in torment, but stuck more deeply than ever. Try as he might, he couldn't accept it, couldn't set himself to anything else. Now he actually looked for the little cuss, waited for the sight of him swaggering along in his fancy duds, spoiled and sassy, accompanied by his pack of stooges, or tottering out of a tavern with a bottle of whiskey in each hand. Now, instead of hobbling away in wrath, he listened in helpless lust to any and all reports of him.

Even from George Mencke. The podgy man with the mouth of a girl commiserated and deplored, made references to the circular which Stephens had put out about Pierce's gambling debt, and every few hours, it seemed, came up with another of the stories making the rounds: "He set up office in the Cattleman's Bar! In the telephone booth! Would you believe it, he nailed a sign up on the side, WESTERN STATES MINING CO., OFFICE HOURS NINE TO NINE-O-FIVE!"

His face was a pink pudding of indignation.

"Well, the telephone company wouldn't stand for *that,* never fear. They came and took away the booth."

"That's his affair," Sam said shortly, though his soul was crazed with bitterness. The way Stephens had duped his boys now seemed like a sharper's trick—drilling the land on the sneak and then buying through a middleman, Edna Harbaugh, who had thrown in with that drifter to hoodwink two boys she'd known all their lives. Working his massed, powerful shoulders up and down, he stood in the stinging swarm of gnat-like words, caught like a bull mired in quicksand.

"Busting wind and raising sand like that," George said. "It's not right."

"Let him. He's the cock of the walk. Let him be the big shot and splurge if that's his pleasure."

"Well it passes my understanding how the sheriff puts up with him," George said. They had stopped kibitzing the checker game and moved over by the ancient fire engine, gorgeous with red and gilt, which had come tearing up to the smoking ruins of ranch houses for twenty years. George had an irritating habit of wiping specks off it with his handkerchief, but at the moment he was too upset to do any housekeeping. "You take his latest frolic. If that doesn't top them all, I don't know. He climbed on the kiddie horse in the Pig Store, absolutely pie-eyed, of course, and rode it till it went on the fritz—the thing kept bucking like a runaway washing machine. The check-out girl had to pull the cord to stop it. Cecil Frye would never have stood for that, but he's disappeared into thin air, did you hear? For no rhyme or reason. I really feel sorry for his family. Well anyway, the girl didn't have sense enough to file a complaint! So *Mister* Stephens got off scott free once more."

"Just so he don't provoke me," Sam growled. "He can disturb the peace and act childish all he wants."

George went home for lunch and Sam found himself, as he did at least once a day, staring unhappily at the quonset hut office of U.S. Mining and Manufacturing. It was a raw windy day, and the sky was blowing around, rough grey and blue. More and more he regretted that he'd sold Andy those claims. It had been the worst mistake of his life.

He was aware then that Andy was waving through the window, beckoning him to come in. Rather sourly he limped across the street.

"Entrez!" Andy beamed, holding the door open. "You're just the people I want to see. How's the leg?"

"It's fair."

"Glad to hear it, glad to hear it." He treated Sam like the chairman of the board, steering him between metal-gray desks and sputtering typewriters to his office. He was the same gum-chewing Easterner with the elegant head and the face like pink wax, maybe a little more fragile looking and tired. With quick, deferential swoops and touches he put Sam in a chair by his desk. "Are you ready to go to work?" he smiled.

"Heck no, I'm through with uranium. That was yesterday's dream."

"Still not receptive," he said, disappointed. "No kidding, I really want you on the team. Your savvy—man, you're fabulous, you know that? At least come to lunch. We'd both love it—my mother is here now, you know." Sam agreed. Just then the phone rang and what he heard must have been pretty annoying because he said sharply, "You figure it out, that's what you're getting paid for . . . Oh all right, I'll be there in an hour."

He set the receiver down, looking harried and ill. "If you won't you won't, but you could really take the weight off me, Sam. Mull it over anyway. The paper work alone is murdering me and not only that, I have to mine the damn ore and drill too. Oh well, as J. W. Hatfield says, 'successful effort is total effort.' You know, I've got the feeling he blames *me* for that hit by Stephens and that other guy. I'm putting out the carloads of ore but I can just see him in that office with all the ship models and the paintings of *other* famous sea captains, dictating something like 'a setback is just the opportunity for a comeback.' And believe me, he's not *purring,* he's *waiting* for me to top that discovery. No kidding, that was some development, though. It was a real eye-opener. The jury is still out but I can feel it, the big picture has changed. Say, how about this? How about handling a drill rig for us, working along those lines? Out of the canyons."

Sam felt all his thwarted and tragic blood go hot, pressing.

"Okay, okay, you're not interested," Andy said swiftly. "I'll make do with our engineering boys—otherwise known as the three blind mice. I just wish I knew what that guy used, a ouija board? You talk about magic. I'd like to see him with loaves and fishes."

His eyes glaring like slots in the door of a furnace, Sam hoisted himself to his feet. "You better hurry up if you want any legerdemain. Because pretty shortly now he's gonna get his tail kicked. Him and all his toadies together." He started toward the door in his dropping stride, rumbling incoherently about crooked deals and gyps.

"My God! I forgot it was on your ranch, Sam. I got so much on my mind. I realize that's no excuse, but it's true." He squeaked and hopped around him with that appalling shamelessness of his, like a U.S. senator going down on his knees. "Listen, forget the job, just come home with me to lunch, that's all I ask. I'm in a bind like you never saw. I mean it, I'm at the point of no return. The old bitch, three divorces she's caused me and now she's hanging around my neck like an albatross. You don't know what I go through, Sam. The grief I take. She thinks I'm gonna drive her to Hot Springs to buy some more junk, and I have to go out to the canyon! Be a friend and get her off my back for a little while . . ."

Mourning for his lost claims, Sam was far from disposed to help Andy with his family problems or with anything else. On the other hand, the claims were gone anyhow, and the dead afternoon stretched in front of him, desolate, endless, and his nervous fury was like a brush fire spreading inside him. He went.

And before five minutes were up, he realized the blunder he'd made. Andy and his mother squabbled, told him hair-raising things about each other and fought to get him on their side. "He makes me so tired," she told Sam. "You can see how grouchy he is. Now I have gas on my stomach, it puts gas on my stomach every time." Hissing and grunting like an old turkey buzzard, she served an elaborate meal of roast beef and three vegetables, not a scrap of which Andy even put on his plate. He sipped two glasses of milk and looked depressed.

"Sour puss," she said, a small withered woman sending up clouds of cigarette smoke.

"Did I tell you about the praying mantis?" he asked Sam. "The male has to sneak up on the female or she'll eat him before he can make love to her. If he's quick and lucky, she only eats him afterwards. Or during. She chaws away on him during copulation. The head and thorax are gone and the rest of him is still having a honeymoon, banging away."

"Is that your only topic of conversation?" she said haughtily. "Nasty bugs and I don't know what all?"

"Tonight," he said with relish, "I'm going to tell you about opossums. The litter is born with twenty naked and blind little things and only a dozen teats for them in the pouch. That's how the world goes, it's every opossum for himself."

"Isn't he tacky?" she said to Sam. "Why does he fill his mind with trash like that?"

"Because," Andy said, more to himself than to her, "it's all that keeps me afloat. The thought of my fellow creatures."

Sam had had about enough, but before he could reach for his cane Andy had gotten up from the table and said, "I have to run, Mother, but Mr. Bolton would like to look at your treasures."

Her ancient lizard face flicked around, ravenous. "If you really like beauty," she said, "I can show you a thing or two." Her wintry jaws parted in a smile, enticing.

"I don't have much time to spare. . . ."

Andy ducked out and Sam found himself in the airless, overcrowded house with a sleepy Siamese cat and an old woman. He was trapped. Moving like a musty old sheep, she showed him through the precious debris of a hundred lives, miscellaneous pieces of china and tarnished candlesticks, a butter churn falling apart, a lamp with a fanged serpent curling up its metal base, a crude painting of two hunters and a dog with insane eyes. Oriental rugs were piled two and three deep on the floors. The crumbling stucco house was stuffed to the walls like a royal tomb, like a chamber of the dead in one of the books he'd gotten from that professor, or, to put it more exactly, like a cross between a museum and a lunatic asylum. What in heck was she after? There was no basic reasoning in it. He could see the use in the thousands of machinery parts he saved, but this—it was chaos, a junk heap of senseless acquisition with a square gas stove welling heat in the center of it. He felt compressed, suffocating—and uneasy, the way he'd been in the hospital after he'd bunged up his leg and before he'd gotten started on that ancient history and philosophy and religion, two hundred dollars' worth of the highest brow books he'd ever laid eyes on, but once he'd gotten into them, darn good reading. Well, that was yesterday's dream too.

"Isn't this lovely? I think it's so lovely." Jabbering incessantly and pecking at him with her crabbed fingers when his attention wandered, she dug through box after box of plunder: trinkets, moldering fabrics, seventeen kinds of monogrammed silverware. Her stiff black dress hissed when she moved. With evident pride she led him to a painting called "Maternité," cracked and discolored with age and set off by a lumpy white frame that reminded him of curdled milk. The old harpy's face hung in drapes of skin. Her lower teeth stood like dead sticks in the foul wind of her breath. But she was alive, violently and insatiably alive, nodding and smiling with her face to one side and fingering her necklace of dull green stones, telling him about the Chinese bed she'd had to leave behind in Connecticut. "And most of my china, too; you never saw such china. This is only a fraction of what I have. My son calls it my loot and I don't know what all. It's unworthy of him, but, of course, his health isn't what it should be. He doesn't sleep a bit well and half the time, if he *does* eat, he'll go straight into the bathroom and heave it back up. He frequently says I'll outlive him, and I'll say this, I always have had good health."

Huge discharges of impatience spilled into his balked and plunging blood. He lost track of what she was saying; then he heard her exclaim, "Oh! Now isn't that a pity. It's broken! They say you lose one day of your life for everything you break. Do you believe that?"

The words seemed to hang in the air, suspended like the flakes of stirred-up dust, and he wasn't sure how long it took them to reach him. He was shut in a horror of smothering heat and worthless litter—figurines, a decomposing rag doll with a patchwork face, gewgaws. There were a few long straggling hairs on her gristly legs. The legs knotted with each step, and the knob of hair on the back of her head bobbed in front of him, and now she was jabbering about her son; he laughed at her because she was frightened every time a hearse went by. "The things people say, anyhow," she sniffed. "When I was six, the next-door lady said I was homely. She died not long after." Her small birdlike eyes were fixed on him. She was inquiring how old he was; she hoped that he didn't think she was nosey. She was seventy-one herself, seventy-one last June sixteenth to be exact, and she hadn't a scar on her. "I've never had a single operation," she said. "Once the doctor told me to get my appendix out, and I took a trip instead. And while I was in Florida I found this!" Triumphantly she pointed to a cracked oaken screen bristling with carved archers, seige guns and castle turrets. His lungs were blocked, he couldn't get any air, and there was still more to be looked at—boxes and boxes of dusty bric-a-brac, acquired without sense or discretion, vases with delicate girls flowering on the sides, damaged red glass, iron statues, anything and everything that she had been able to lay her hands on, more and more and more . . .

"My apologies, Mrs. Lytton," he burst out and limped for the door. Her voice hopped and fluttered after him, clutching: "It was so nice! You must come again tomorrow. . ." Snow picked at his face. The sidewalks were ice-scabbed and bumpy. The streets were brown streams of ground-up snow and dirt, and where they ended in barbed wire fence and sheds, snow-grizzled hills bulged up in wave after wave, as if they were about to flood over the small town. He was conscious of a feeling of inevitability, of blood-hot expectation. On the windows of a decaying house the plastic weathershield, blown to pieces, licked like grey flames in the wind. Frozen laundry hung upside down on a clothesline. Some boys were playing war around a horse barn, sneaking up and throwing make-believe grenades and dodging back with shouts of "Ka-boom!" Their clear, excited voices came through the whisper of dry snow.

"Mr. Bolton, Mr. Bolton!" Just before he reached the corner by the bank he was hailed by Peggy Frye's girl, Lucy, and the Indian kid who hung around with her. She chewed down a mouthful of potato chips, daintily gobbling the salty, greasy, blistered flakes, and said, "Hello."

He flicked his head and kept moving, hauling his crippled leg, but she tagged along beside him, her thin shoulders hunched inside a boy's jacket. "It's business," she said. "You know that place where your daughter used to have a cafe? The cute pink place?"

"I do." He recalled the paint job, another of Stephens' damnable tricks, and again he had the feeling of imminence. There was no hurry, however, quite the contrary. With a positive feeling of luxury, he stopped to let her have her say. The Indian kid stayed back, his hands stuffed in his pockets, drawn up like a tiny rattlesnake.

"Can I rent it?" he said eagerly. "I mean, Mother and me, can we? There's business for another cafe with all this boom going on." Snow powdered on her cheap scarf, on her face turning smug as she added, "Mother and me have to make it on our own now; you probably heard that. Promise you won't rent it to anybody else for a week, till I can raise some money to open up with."

"Where's Cecil?"

"He died in surgery, I'm sorry to have to tell you." She giggled and licked a grain of salt from the corner of her mouth. "I don't know where he lit out to. To the Far Beyond, I hope. Do you promise?"

It occurred to him, looking at the lean alleycat girl he'd brought candy to when he'd been seeing her mother, that Peggy Frye was available now. And that here was an opportunity to get re-acquainted. The great male potency welled up inside him again, heavy, pressing, but he didn't have time for that now. He nodded his promise, already limping past her.

"Goody! Thank you, Mr. Bolton!" Her dancing voice fell behind him as he pushed into the Cattleman's Bar. He hadn't been in a tavern in years, and he stretched his lips from his yellow stallion's teeth uncomfortably. "I'll have a soft drink," he told the staring bartender. Guitar music splattered like hot metal. Grey light settled out of the air like ashes on the scaly old counter, on hands and soiled hats, and thickened in glasses of urine-yellow beer. In the long mirror, burning with red Christmas tree lights, he could see Bert Stephens, lolling in a booth with his toadies and sycophants, evidently on another toot. "Hey you! Gertrude, Emily, Ralph, whatever your name is," he said to a broken-down ranch hand. "Take these boots out for a shine, will you?" Stretching out his feet with a royal air, he had the boots pulled off. The peaked and whiskery alcoholic hustled outside with them.

Sam opened and closed his bone-cracking hands. But he hadn't hit a man in over twenty years and even now, even with his soul a burning mass of anger, he didn't see how he could strike the first blow.

The door opened with a sweep of frozen air and a mineworker tromped in, rawfaced and coughing, smacking the snow off his cap. Stephens evidently had noticed Sam because a change came over the merrymaking: it was stagy, it was consciously and maliciously exaggerated. Reclining at his ease, a cigar tilted up in his mouth, he told the woman with him to get off her Wyoming tail and order another round. "And give the dear folks at the bar another of what they're drinking." Sam refused the 7-up the bartender set in front of him. Over in the booth Stephens reeled to his feet, a flamboyant figure in a peach-colored shirt with fringes across the chest and back, and loudly accepted the thanks of a grateful nation. His mug of scotch careening in the warped green light of a beer sign, he proposed a toast: "To the bigshot mining king," he said in a gloating voice. "Me!"

It took Sam a few seconds to place the words: they were what Stephens had snarled at him during their disagreement on the street back in the summer. And it was no coincidence, for as Sam wheeled half around on the stool he was jabbed by a trailing foxy look from the booth, followed by contortions of laughter. It was too good to be true! The rascal was playing right into his hands, deliberately provoking him! Bloodshot and shaggy, his arms hanging from his deep shoulders, he let the insults from across the room accumulate, his blood surging faster with every sly look, every snigger, every boisterous bit of comedy. The damned little cuss was riding high, bragging and showing off and humiliating his toadies, but he wouldn't be for long. They'd had one skirmish already and Stephens had run like a jackrabbit. This time he wouldn't have that chance, and his partner wasn't around to back him up.

His head grew heavy with intention, and he watched Stephens order the freckled lumpy woman to hold the mug full of scotch, then the beer chaser, to his mouth. "My mother told me never to lift nothing heavier than a petticoat," he guffawed.

"You *thing*," she pouted. "You don't love me."

"Woman, I repudiate that. I love you lock, stock"—he smirked, patting her ample stomach—"and barrel." She slapped at him, taking good care to miss. He put on a serious expression and said, "No, I mean it. I need the love of a good woman. Three or four of 'em."

As soon as the ranch hand, sprayed with snow, came stamping back in with the boots, Stephens proceeded to make what he said was the largest cocktail of all time. Everybody gathered round the glass fruit bowl. The bartender cooperated with sickening alacrity. Chesty, his hair tumbling over his eyes, his little hands strutting in the air, Stephens bustled around in back of the bar, selecting bottles and calling out orders. The buckle on his belt ignited with red glints from the Christmas lights. The fringes rippled on his shirt. "It's the experiment of the century," he said. "You folks had better stand back, I think the sonofabitch is smoking." He checked the taste once more and smiled in triumph. "Sorry I can't reveal the formula," he announced. "But Doctor Stephens' Cureall is a secret." The outsiders and even the hard taciturn ranchers laughed appreciatively, and, standing in the center of the crowd, Stephens raised the bowl with both hands and began swilling it down in one gurgling, spilling, tottering, throat-drowning inundation. The onlookers were applauding. There was a red slick on Sam's eyes. His nostrils sucked air and distended like hairy pouches.

"You look like you got a bellyache, old man." Stephens was taking to him, wiping his mouth as he steadied himself against the bar. Sam went for him, charging without his cane in an off-kilter, hobbling lunge. And as he jammed forward, all of his flaming energy released at last, he had a wonderful sense of recovery, of freedom after the helpless days and weeks, a sense of perfect completeness. He was himself again.

Stephens' drinking friends abandoned him and he backed along the bar, weaving but moving as fast as he could. His gaudy shirt and pants were soaked with liquor. His face was a boggy red. "Nobody wants him except me?" he yelled. "Okay." Raging and groping backwards, he crashed glasses and bottles onto the floor between them. Sam crunched after him. All at once Stephens reversed himself, staggered forward and threw a roundhouse swing that swished the air a foot-and-a-half short and, as Sam made a grab for him, followed his wandering arm to the floor and lay there like a pile of wet circus flags.

Bellowing, Sam picked him up and shook him. The limp draggle hung from his hands—whether playing possum or dead drunk he couldn't tell, and it didn't make any difference; either way he couldn't hit him. The frustration of it was awful. The blood hate which had been multiplying inside him for weeks was pushed back in, and he stood there in the great fire of his agony. Slowly, quietly, as if he were being very careful, he let the sodden thing down on the floor.

December 25, 1952

Christmas came on with the nasal whine of "I Saw Mommie Kissing Santa Claus," sung by frecklefaced Jimmy Boyd. It had been a hard year, and it was ending badly. Mau-Mau uprisings flared again, and terrorists chopped an old Englishman to bloody pieces in his bathtub. An FBI agent called on Mrs. Roosevelt, asking about the loyalty of John Foster Dulles, picked by Eisenhower as Secretary of State. Abraham Feller, Assistant Secretary General of the United Nations, killed himself in despair over the U.N.'s inability to end the Korean war. Breaking away from his wife with the tortured cry, "It's no use," he plunged headlong from a twelfth story window. In the remote towns of southern Quebec, the devil was reported at dances, wearing white tie and tails. A man with a deformed right eyelid died in the gas chamber at San Quentin, his left hand sagging open to show the tattoo HARD LUCK. In a frenzy of killing, he had murdered six people in three weeks and when arrested said, "I hate everybody's guts and everybody hates mine." Werner von Braun, our rocket expert imported from Nazi Germany, announced the possibility of man-made satellites. He assured us that "if we put up such a station first, we could dominate the world."

Early on Christmas morning, Russian troops in the French section of Berlin machine-gunned a West Berlin patrolman named Herbert Bauer, and a pitched battle raged over the dead body for half an hour. But the year closed with a little seed of hope to cherish and make grow. On the day of Bauer's funeral, a Communist policeman edged up to a West Berlin patrol with a wreath hidden under his overcoat and whispered, "For your dead one."

XXI

The train from Omaha was slogging through the sandhills of western Nebraska in a snowstorm. It was four days after Christmas and the rattling, drafty coach was nearly empty; across the aisle a drunk was snoring in a rumpled heap, his slack cheeks giving in and out with every breath; a gnawed brown apple core wobbled in the trash under the seat. Greasy and tired after fifteen hours of travelling, Paul let his book slump into his lap and stared out at the whirling snow. It was an unusual thing for the West, a wet heavy snow that plastered the cropped grazing land and clung to the roots. The light was creamy with the spawning, colliding flakes, and the little cow towns blurred and thickened, the stark trees puffed out, the roofs and dirt roads went dim in the frothing white. Up on a hill a concrete schoolhouse was losing its gaunt lines in the swarm of snow. Already the train was more than an hour late, and his impatience, the need to see her, was like a steady fever in his eyes and head. The last few days had been very bad but they were behind him now and Lucy had the money she needed to open the cafe.

It had been a rough time, though. Knowing the penalties involved, he hadn't accepted any money from his parents in ten years and it had been an evil choice: should he ask his father or his mother? And just because he loved his father so intensely and hated to see the unspoken plea in his eyes, he'd wired his mother at the ranch. Hoping for a stay of execution, he'd even told himself she might be so taken up with Yuletide festivity that she would just send the money, but she caught the next plane from Dallas and barged into his apartment, hoarse-voiced, autocratic, and worried. Her face was coated with powder to conceal the scars of skin-cancer operations. She pressed her sherry-tainted mouth against his and, rummaging in her purse all the while, said, "Are you all right, Paul? You don't look it. What do you need the money for?"

He twitched his shoulder. "I'm underpaid? I got a tip on the stock market?"

"You don't have to tell me, I didn't expect that much. Is there a cigarette in this place?" Sucking smoke into her lungs, she asked him how often he wrote his father. "The cold cut king" she called him. "I know you've always blamed me for the divorce, don't deny it, but I can't talk about cold cuts for more than twenty-four hours, I just can't. He doesn't need you either, you know. He has a dozen children. All stores."

He refrained from any comment. Her wide red mouth squeezing with distaste, she gave her attention to the two grubby rooms in which he lived: the narrow bed against a wall of books, the tropical fishtanks filled with more books, the record player, the shelves of pottery and artifacts, and his most precious possession, a scarred and pitted fertility stone, three thousand years old, with a bestial face almost gone and one worn hand splayed on its pendulous stomach. "How about that? Isn't that great?" he said, and forgetting himself in his excitement, he told her how it used to be soaked with bloody sacrifices to make the crops and babies grow.

"How interesting," she said.

Everything she saw scandalized her, wronged her. She looked up at the Japanese fish-kite, five feet long, hanging from the dreary ceiling, and cried, *"That* hideous thing! Won't you *ever* get rid of it?"

"What for? It's quiet, it doesn't need any attention, and it's immortal. What more do you want in a pet?"

"Don't be silly." Marching into the kitchen, she inspected the contents of his refrigerator. "Cheese, grapejuice and crackers. Is that *all* you eat? When was the last time you had a decent meal?"

"You sound like my mother," he said. Struggling to keep his detachment, he stretched himself on the bed and contemplated the paper fish lying in the air. At times like this, indoor kite-flying was the only thing to do.

"I'll send you some decent furniture," she said, coming back into the room. "You live like a renegade priest, Paul, I swear you do. It's unhealthy. I *wish* you'd stand up straight, too, your posture is worse than ever. Are you a homosexual?"

Here they were again, at the same place on the merry-go-round: grandchildren. The woman who had gotten rid of him when he was eight by sending him off to a boarding school was now fifty-seven herself and developing a red-hot maternal urge, and every wrinkle she saw in the mirror, every cancer scar, made her that much more determined. Diagnosis: the old immortality itch. "Remember," he said to her, "this is the season of peace and good will. Let's try to keep the X in X-mas anyway."

"It's all very well to make jokes but we've got to find *some* solution for you."

"For God's sake," he said, "you make me sound like the Jewish problem. Be patient, will you? I'm just waiting for Miss Right to come along. Cross my heart. As a matter of fact, I have several excellent prospects in mind. Let's see, there's Annette, Yvonne, Marie, Cecile . . ."

Up to this point, by deflecting her with silence and hiding himself in irony, he had been able to hold his own; now, however, she said, "I thought what had happened last summer would have taught you a lesson."

He laid his arm, very slowly, over his eyes. It was apparent that she had been to see Dr. Humbug before coming to his rooms. He knew the sort of report Bush must have turned in to the Smithsonian, and certain little frowns and shakes of the head had led him to understand that, to make his punishment complete and perfect, his contract at the school would not be renewed next year . . . There were bits of dirt in Teddy's hair and dirt in his still blue eyes . . .

"Leave the money on the desk as you go out," he told her.

"I'll do no such thing," she said. "I'm not giving you one penny. You have to be brought to your senses some way."

"Fair enough," he said. "Just get out of here. The Judas hunt is over."

The episode had left him with a feeling of disorder and self-reproach, as if he had betrayed himself in some way he couldn't define. A baby was crying at the front of the coach, a piteous bleating, mindless and rapid and urgent. Outside the window dabbed with milky fingerprints, the flakes were swirling and pooling in the updraft from the train, and the lean hills were softening away, fading into the whiteness of the sky. Everything—jeep trails, dark knots of sagebrush, cattle bunched by a fenched-in haystack—the whole landscape was drowning into a single glut of white, anonymous, universal.

His father, of course, had wired him the money immediately and without questions, without pressure of any kind. There was no defense at all against this and so, bringing his gift of myrrh, he had taken a train to Chicago to spend a few days with the Jolly Red Giant and other problems. The firm had grown enough to try a few holds with A&P and the other large chains and the advertising boys were creating (to use the word loosely) a new image for the Jolly Giant. To wit: no longer a feebleminded strong man beaming and waving from the sky but a friend, a real live supermarket Jesus who cared about *you*, personally. Meanwhile, there were negotiations with a shopping center going up in the suburbs, the manager of a west side store couldn't carry the ball, and the shopping cart problem was getting out of hand.

It just wasn't his cup of tea, and neither was his father's assistant,

Jack Harris. What a bunch of rotters he was, chock-full of energy and loud opinions, the type of bastard who gave waiters a hard time and really expressed himself by going first class on a plane. What frosted Paul the most, though, was the way he made a contest out of everything, and before you knew it you were infected, too, and a round of golf at ten cents a hole somehow turned into a battle to the death.

In fact, none of this was his cup of tea. What he wanted was a bigger and better Boston Tea Party, right now. Everybody he met got his ideas out of the same newspaper, watched the same programs on television, bought the same car and believed in peace of mind through insurance, whored after the executive position above him, and dreamed (oh consummation devoutly to be wished for) of owning a home on the North Shore, in Wilmette or Lake Forest. It was run-sheep-run living. It was the man on the conveyor belt, the man with the briefcase moving up in the world, up, up toward what? Toward those vast dumping grounds for the old—Florida and Arizona and California, and burial in a 3000-dollar bronze casket half the size of a Cadillac. A hundred years ago Kierkegaard had called it the "nothing" of mass society, and young Sören hadn't seen anything. Year by year the lumps of life had become more immense and the people in them less differentiated, less individual, less conscious, less human. They were sliding backwards, back into anonymous units, cells in the collective organism.

Life had to be resisted on this level, too, if it was to be saved, if it was to have meaning. And yet, more and more there was his father. It wasn't only the yearning to please him, the feeling of obligation, the pathos of his broken hopes for his son; suddenly, in the few months since Paul had seen him, he had grown old. The muscles in his body had let go, the weight of seventy years pulled down his stomach. And, when he spoke, his voice was fuzzy and his adam's apple throbbed like a faint pulse in the skin hanging from his neck. He forgot things. He took a nap in the afternoon, something he'd never done before. On the last day of the visit, however, he'd come shuffling out of the bedroom after only a few minutes, and Paul had felt a deep wince of sorrow, almost of fear, at what was coming.

How could he say it? My God, I can't live by the numbers, I'm only on three-and-a-half?

For a few moments, sitting there in his slippers and grey woollen robe, his father was silent, fallen within himself. Then, instead of saying, "You haven't changed your mind about taking over, I suppose," or trying to involve him in company matters, he drifted back to their vacations on the farm in Michigan when Paul was a boy. "You remember, it must be twenty years ago," he said. "That pet pig of yours. What did you call it?"

"Little Orphan Annie," he smiled. "Even after it grew into a three-hundred-pound boar, it was still Orphan Annie to me. You brought it home as a suckling for Christmas dinner, but I wouldn't let you butcher it. I fed it every day myself, too—when I was home, I mean." It caught at him with unexpected emotion, the memory of the dark, sallow-faced boy holding a pan of corn and the lewd white pig with red eyes snuffling toward him in the mud.

"Yes, that was it. You didn't know it, but every time you went into the pen I held a rifle on that murderous bugger from the upstairs window."

"No kidding," Paul said softly. "You never told me." The years scaled off and they were chuckling together about the summer when he was three or four and a great snow-white goose had chased him whenever he went into the yard, its wings raised like the sails of a windmill, its saw-toothed beak wide open and hissing dreadfully, its bristly tongue vibrating, its snake neck flexing back and striking as it pecked at his arms and legs. But under their voices, quick with pleasure, under the laughter, there was something lost and melancholy. A constant flow of emotion went from him to his father, like a wound of love. The windows of the Lake Shore Drive apartment were fashionably tinted and they stained everything yellow, reduced everything in their yellow atmosphere, like a single idiot gaze fixed upon the blobby pink Christmas tree, upon the expensive but anonymous furniture, picked out by some decorator, trite and depersonalized—stained the face of his father, aged into deep lines and slackness, as if the bones underneath had lost their fine architecture.

"Are you sick or anything?" he asked, painfully moved.

"The doc gave me a clean bill of health," his father said with an effort at vigorousness. "But when a man gets to be seventy, it's time to get your head out of the sand and look at things." His hands moved restlessly to his knees. The skin on them was almost transparent and raised in bluish welts by the veins underneath. "Afterwards," he said, "after you're dead, if it was like a memory floating around, then I wouldn't mind. Or gradually fading away, even that. Like rock crumbling . . . But nothing, nothing left—what's it all for then? What's the use of anything? Take Julius Caesar, or anybody else. Whatever the history books say, they're just names. Nothing."

"Look at it the other way," Paul said, but the stiffness in his throat made it hard to talk. "Look at the suffering that's cancelled out, too. The millions of human beings born without a chance, and all the others who get smashed along the way. I mean, the losers get even, Dad. It's useful for some winners I can think of, too. Go ahead, take Julius Caesar. A playboy with some very ugly habits who was bankrolled to the top by his creditors. After one battle he crippled ten thousand Gauls for life by cutting the tendons in their legs. Or a more modern example. Would you want a man who used convicts with machine guns to break a strike to live forever? If you think about it, death is the only thing that makes life possible."

His father didn't care about that. "And what a man has built," he said. Then his voice came apart, dissolved into the whisper of traffic twelve floors below. "Paul, if I can't pass it on to you . . ."

The desperation, the despair in the unfinished words riddled his heart. For the first time he grasped the immensity of his father's tragedy. After all, the old man was great in his way, and though it was true that he'd forced small grocers to the wall, for more than thirty years he had given to his stores the driving, complete, twenty-four-hour-a-day dedication and passion that had painted the Sistine chapel and enabled a janitor with the hobby of grinding lenses to build the first microscope. Eleven stores—they were not what mattered, it was the magnificence of the effort which had gone into them. And he understood how his father felt; it mustn't die with him, it mustn't mean nothing. To make something that death couldn't destroy: the aspiration, even in the form of a chain of stores, went through to the deepest part of his being. How could he deny his father? Refuse to give his life a meaning, no matter how much it cost? Even though that meaning was trivial from his own point of view.

Surprised, he'd heard himself say, "I can't, Dad. I can't." Even now he could scarcely believe he'd said it; it must have been by a kind of habitual posture more than anything else. Crossing the Dakota border the train came out on the other side of the storm. The winter daylight had gone and darkness carved out the silver roofs and chimneys of a little town, clean and definite in the blur of motion. Miles and miles away under the running of the black horizon, the solitary light of a ranch house was a clear glow living in the darkness.

And yet he couldn't block out the memory of his father getting slowly to his feet. The acquiescence on his face had been as heavy as sleep. It weighed on him, and adding to its mournful burden was a sense of failure. Though apparently he had acted as usual, though he had made no promises or concessions about his way of life, he had a feeling of damaged integrity, a feeling of having given ground, compromised what he had never compromised before—without so much as the consolation of having made his father happy.

But all that was behind him now, and ahead of him, only a few miles ahead, there was Lucy. One thing at least had been accomplished by her call for help: it gave him a legitimate reason to come out here, it was something that was not his burning need for her. He was released, at least partially, from the months of ascetic discipline, from one letter a week to her—relentlessly held down to platonic affection and talk of this and that—from the cheerless Thanksgiving which he had spent by himself simply because he'd wanted so badly to visit her. Day by day, stone by bitter stone, he had rebuilt those inner citadels which had come crashing down in the summer. In fact, he would have gone straight back to school from Chicago if he hadn't been absolutely sure he could keep the relationship under control. All he wanted was to see her. To see her skinny face open and drinking when she listened, the way it had been in the drugstore after he'd found her reading Wally's book. The trailing silky-fine hair on her neck. Her eyes uncovered into warm depths . . .

Finally the train shuddered to a stop and there, next to the station, was the little fountain steaming and squirting into its basin. The cold stunned his hands and face. All the way up the street, snow, frozen as hard as crushed glass, glittered on parked cars, on trucks, on the edges of the blank-faced stores and mining offices. The last car meeting the train pulled away, wheels crunching and red tail lights blearing the exhaust fumes pink. He should have wired her. His heart banging under his ribs, he looked in the drugstore and then in the Black Hills Cafe. Wally was at the counter, bent over a huge lump of white cake. He had put on some weight, and a blue silk tie spread down the front of his brown workshirt. Well hello, Wally said, and no he hadn't seen her today. From the constraint in his voice and the way he turned back to his plate, Paul could see that he didn't want to talk about the famous strike—didn't want to speak to him at all. "Okay, okay, I'll never darken your door again," Paul said, stooping away. It was a pity about Wally, he thought, but nothing was real except his need to see her. Where could she be? Should he go to her house? After the reception he'd had there last summer, he doubted that her mother would be very cordial, in spite of the money. Down the vacant highway, the flags strung over the car lot flipped and twisted, leaped like fish smothering in the cold air. Headlights slashed open the darkness and then he felt a jab in his back.

"Don't move! This bottle in my hand contains nitroglycerine," her voice said. "Give me the combination to the safe or I'll blow us both up."

"12-29-52," he said, dropping his suitcase and swinging around with a laugh.

She showed him the tiny bottle of dime-store perfume, giggling. She was wearing a car coat with the hood thrown back, and the light from the street lamp gathered in her smooth yellow hair and made a small summer around her head.

"Zo!" he puffed, opening the bottle and sniffing. "Fraulein, this what you haff here, it iss not nitroglycerine. It is rocket fuel. Mit the formula of this, ve can rule the vorldt!" The hard sticking in his chest had melted in delirious relief and tenderness. He hardly knew what he was saying or that she was taking him to see the cafe. The double sense, the consciousness of seeing life as he lived it, had dissolved away. The scrawny fir trees leaning in oil drums for decoration, the creak of their shoes on snow, Christmas tree lights shining in bristly halos and the delicate frosting of her breath around her face—it all came together in a happiness pure and single.

"Do you need a chef?" he asked her. "I'll work cheap. And the Duke of Windsor said my Irish stew was yummy."

Full of crazy brightness and joking, he followed her around to the back of the pink cafe. She led him to a small room jammed with boards and paint cans, the door of an oven, a shapeless pink rug in the corner like flesh sliding together, a spare refrigerator, rags, an old cane, a bed and an oil stove, and, bulking above everything, a mammoth player piano, tall, thick-bodied, varnished almost black and adorned like a sarcophagus or an altar with columns and elaborate scroll-work.

"Very nice," he commented, looking around. "It's a dungeon fit for a queen!"

"It's real spooky, isn't it? But Mamma and me are gonna fix it up and live here. To save on house rent."

They went into the front and he said, "Hey, you're about set to open. If you need any more money, remember your friendly loan company stands ready to help."

She gave him a smile but something about her set an uneasy motion going in his heart. Something was not right. There was a subtle difference in her, he could feel it. And yet, when he asked her if the player piano worked, she was her old self again, eager and enthusiastic and charming. Opening the small doors above the keyboard, she hooked a roll of perforated brown paper to the cylinder inside and, seating herself with the flamboyant air of Liszt, posed her hands elegantly above the keys. Then she pumped the rubber-treaded pedals with her feet and the yellow and black keys fluttered by themselves, ghostly, and the withered twanging and plinking of "In the Good Old Summertime" sifted out of the ancient body.

Then there was a hitch and the same note repeated, repeated, repeated.

"Oh fish!" she cried. "It always does this." She shoved harder on the pedals but the identical note kept coming and coming, mindless, rapid. Suddenly the notes were pouring out at random, streaming from the old sides, and then with a frightful crash all the keys played at once. It was like the inside of a lunatic's mind. Shaken, he told her to put the piano on manual. And just to get rid of the feeling of chaos, he sat down next to her and struck a few chords, placing his hands carefully, awkwardly. The old clunk was out of tune and all he knew about playing was what he had taught himself on long dark afternoons in military school, but he could get by enough to show her a couple of things about modern music, some of the dissonances and odd intervals and how they built into lovely angular forms.

"The idea is . . ." he said, and discovered that she wasn't listening. He let his hands fall to the cracked and discolored keys. Her high light face on her long neck was dull and muffled-looking, withdrawn.

"All right," he said. "Bring out the bull, I'm ready."

"What do you mean?"

"I mean, just tell us your story from the beginning, young lady. I mean, what the hell is the matter?"

"Nothing," she said. "Honest!"

The chilling falseness with which she widened her eyes made him despair. "Will you cut that out?" he grated. "It's a hell of a long way from the soul to the eyes."

And it was getting longer all the time. Instead of being offended or angry, or at least bursting into tears, she lapsed back into herself again, pale and lifeless, picking at her fingernails. He was scared. He had to get through to her. His hands fumbling anxiously, he unfastened his suitcase and took out the book he'd brought for her. "The other two wise men missed the train," he said wryly, giving it to her. "But here's mine."

"Thank you." It was a splendid art book with lustrous colored plates, and buying it had just about put him into bankruptcy. After an indifferent glance, she laid it down. He was crushed. During the long trip out he had imagined again and again how he would explain the paintings to her. Tell her what Feininger had said: "I have to destroy Nature before I can rebuild her again." Show her the dark and gold shatters that slanted and came together, piled up into a cathedral, and make her feel the rich interior tensions in the jagged forms, growing like soundless music, and all the while the exaltation inside him would rise, rise like the cathedral with the beautiful intensity of her listening . . . And it was no use even to try. The light from the naked bulb overhead seemed to press the darkness into the muddle of odds and ends around them. She sat with her face turned down, separated from him, inert.

"Hello," he said, making his voice flat and tinny. "That is a recorded message. How are you? That's fine. And how's the family?"

She smiled at him but her heart wasn't in it. When a car went by on the highway, its headlights flashed through the dark restaurant in front, glass-hard, sharp. In desperation he caught her hands and said, "Look at me! For God's sake, give me a bullet to bite or something, and tell me what it is. Are you worried or what? Is it Cecil? Your mother? What is it?"

"Nothing," she said. "I told you, there's nothing wrong."

Anguish tore his voice and he no longer knew what he was saying. He had to reach her somehow; he loved her. Breathing in tortured gasps, he put out his hand, shakily, and touched her pale closed face, touched it all over like a blind man. And when it happened—when it happened, she squirmed against him expertly, slipping her tongue into his mouth and wriggling it like a little fish. She rode and pumped her belly, she moaned at exactly the right time, and then they were lying side by side in the limp, clammy sheets. Her ribs lifted and sank. The delicate accumulations on them, her breasts, were tipped with a pink so pale and undefined that they seemed to be made of air and pink sugar, like bits of cotton candy. And above that heartbreaking loveliness her face, on the grey pillow, was utterly self-possessed, utterly impersonal. In a moment she got up and with her back turned to him, dressed beside the stove, shivering a little. The flamy light from the burner lapped on her thin legs.

"So much for understanding through orgasm," he rasped.

He sat up and his eyes were parched and aching. Once there had been the breathing wind and her girl's body printed with leaf shapes in a glut of sunflowers. That had been merely unforgivable; this—this was like looking at dirty pictures. Her lewd whiteness and the frenzy in his gaunt and hairy body—God! And they were farther apart than ever. How could he have thought that was a way to reach anybody?

His throat filled with sourness and he said, "You know what Ghandi said? He said his only sorrow was that he'd known the pleasures of sex. That's a little gem of Eastern wisdom that just came to me."

He started pulling on his clothes, then lost track of what he was doing and caved down on the bed. His teeth were chattering with the cold. A shiver caught his back and shoulders like a spasm. "Why the hell did you—oh forget it," he said.

"Why did *I*?" she flung back at him. "Just a teensy second. You were the one that was hard up, not me. I was doing *you* a favor."

"A gracious and kindly action, and I thank you. Tell me something. Is there such a thing as a fallen man? Because I think I've just come to a bad end."

She had refastened her hair in a rubber band and shrugged into her coat. "I have to get home," she told him. "Mamma needs company, now old Cecil ain't there. Lock up when you go, will you?"

And before he could say anything she was gone, just like that. He was demoralized, in ruins. What could have happened in the few days since she'd asked for money? How could she have turned around so completely? Why? Why? The questions beat inside his head like the snagged roll of the player piano, repeating, repeating.

Mrs. Harbaugh let him spend the night on a sofa in the lobby. The next morning he ate some gluey, undercooked pancakes, then another order of them, and wandered around for paralyzed hours, in a daze of panic and sleeplessness, waiting for her to appear. The brightness of the day was like metal and the shadows were empty and cold. A truck moved out from in front of the Red Canyon Mining Company, grinding toward him through the pinkish mush of dirt and snow. On the other side of the freight yards at the buying station, thousands of tons of ore lumped under a dirty skin of snow, and the rumble of gondola cars unloading was like a weight filling into the air. The door of a tavern opened, vomiting fiddle music and beer stinks, and Bert Stephens maneuvered himself outside, wearing cowboy boots and a crumpled tuxedo with a gold lamé shirt. The smell of death came out with him. The very sight of him made Paul long for Lucy, Lucy naked in the dirty sheets, Lucy any way at all. It was nearly ten o'clock. Was she staying at home to avoid him? Down a side street that ended in the railroad tracks, Sam Bolton was pushing along the sidewalk in a ragged limp. Paul went after him to see how he had liked those books. Bolton came to a stop and, putting his weight on a rubber-footed cane, stared moodily across the street at the office of U.S. Mining.

A cane ... Paul felt the memory of the room behind the cafe like a heaviness on the brain. That wasn't—that couldn't be the same cane he'd seen in the boards and rags. Or was it? He couldn't be sure. Anyhow, it didn't prove a thing, he told himself. Bolton owned the cafe and what could be more natural than for him to be around there while it was being painted and cleaned up? But even as he devised explanations there was a shrilling in his head, a fog came into his eyes, and the thought of the cane kept pressing like a growth inside the skull, pressing harder and harder.

His mind was a blind jumble. Sam Bolton and Lucy. He looked without seeing into an open garage where a stooping, long-armed mechanic was using a blowtorch. The roaring spout of flames was yellow and orange. He looked at a stallion tied in a horse van, a powerful old animal with heavy genitals and a low-slung belly, puffing steamy breaths and stamping restlessly. He had no doubt that he'd stumbled on the answer, and by the time he found Lucy and led her grimly to the frozen little park to have it out, the cruel fact was already part of him.

She admitted it right away. "I didn't sign no contract with you," she said sulkily.

His head wobbled up, off kilter, and he made a dry sound in his throat. "I don't understand. You weren't just passing out free samples."

"Oh for yip's sake! Do we *have* to talk about it? This is so putrid." She mucked around in her purse and came up with a letter: his. "Here's your money," she said. "Thanks, but I don't need it now."

He felt the blood like a hemorrhage in his face. "You might as well keep it," he said after a few seconds. "Buy a cookbook with it or something. To keep my memory green."

She kicked at the snow impatiently. It had all been for nothing, for nothing. The betrayal of himself with his parents, the miserable surrender last night, all of it. In spite of his rigorous efforts, the compromises of last summer had spawned others, multiplied disastrously . . . And before he'd even set out to get the money, before her letter had reached him, she had already given herself to Bolton instead. It was the worst moment of his life. Slowly, dragging himself in agony, he walked beside her. The chain clanked on the empty flagpole. The bandstand was snowed under. Near the frost-rimed weeds that marked where a trickle of steamy water went into the pond, the carcass of a duck lay in the snow: a red foot, wings, a chewed rib cage and the rope of a headless neck. According to Charley, she said, a weasel had gotten it. Paul didn't answer.

"Oh go ahead and curse me up and down," she burst out. "I don't give a happy goddamn. Cecil got the foot itch and took every penny with him. I couldn't wait for weeks for you to *maybe* send the money."

"Foot itch, huh? You scared him out of the state, if not out of the country. I don't know why I didn't see it before."

"So what if I did?" In a sullen voice she said that she'd gone home and started back to school, hadn't she? "I was so good it was ridiculous. The least I could do was turn off Cecil's faucet, I had *that* much reward coming." They were standing by the half-frozen pond. Ducks rode in the small clearing by the ditch, their breasts dividing the winter sky that quivered on the water. Crossly she threw a chunk of snow to them, as if it were a piece of bread, and watched them race toward the splash, circle in the futile rings going out, and suddenly rear up at each other with wings thrashing. "Well I *did*," she said. "So I gave birth to this plan. I was gonna go to the minister and tell him about—you know. Only I didn't have to, I only told Cecil I was going to, and he went glup. Like I was Count Dracula and I was going to bite his neck and suck all the blood out. Then I had to make it up to Mamma, she was hysterical for *days,* and I thought of the cafe . . ." It was a typical scheme of hers, naive and full of guile, and at the end of it, hideous, was Bolton and Lucy.

No! He couldn't reconcile himself to it. He couldn't accept it. "Sam Bolton and his portable Maypole," he rasped. "Love potions and aphrodisiacs at reasonable prices. Orgies a specialty. Will you use your head for about two seconds?"

"Yes sir, Master."

"Why do you think he honored you with his attentions? Because your mother was being true to Cecil, that's why. You practically said so yourself. My God, it's all the same to him, Little Bo-Peep or the fat lady in the circus. He snapped you up like he does everything. One after another, whatever he happens to get his paws on." The crumbling darkness in his mind was in flames. He hated Bolton, hated him as he'd never hated anybody.

"You're all wrong," she said. "I love him."

It was idiotic, childish, degrading. Her thin face was held high and her lovely deep eyes, the eyes that darkened and went deeper when she listened, flashed with the superb fire of a thousand corny melodramas. And still he craved her, craved her nakedly, frantically. Stormed with jealous blood, he would have killed Bolton if he had the chance, anything to tear her away from the old satyr.

"You know all he's doing? All he's doing is taking it out in trade . . ." Then he stopped himself, trembling. She was tormenting the ducks with pieces of snow again. Beyond the ice-locked pond a line of ore cars jerked and screeched in the yards.

And the silent hopeless struggle went on inside him. He tried to remember what Bolton was—incessantly moving, changing, dominating and possessing, unconscious of anything but immediate purposes but always magnificent, too, and infinitely sad. Life, making more and more life, and more and more death.

He tried to set himself against that—in himself. Tried not to sink into the anonymous universal pattern of life.

Tried and failed. Human responsibility, the counter-movement of the spirit, the authentic posture of mankind: they were just words: he couldn't feel anything except hate. But he twisted himself around somehow. He made a step, and then another step. Then he was walking back to the hotel.

February, 1953

Lucille Ball was beginning a nation-wide pregnancy on the "I Love Lucy" show and plans were announced for a coast-to-coast delivery. Women were wearing Mamie Eisenhower bangs. Hollywood's newest weapon in its life-and-death struggle with TV was the 3-D movie that hurled nightmares at shrieking audiences: spears and arrows whirled out of the screen, wild animals came thundering, horrible monsters heaved up, snakes crawled out of holes right into the pink cellophane glasses.

In Europe, huge tides burst over England and the Low Countries, sweeping away whole towns and shattering docks and ships in the worst flood since the Middle Ages. People everywhere were grumbling, "This crazy weather is the fault of those atomic bombs." The first large-scale "breeder reactor" went into operation at Arco, Idaho, "breeding" fissionable U-235 out of non-fissionable U-238. The effect was to multiply all the uranium in the world by one hundred.

The voice of doom was selected—the voice that would make radio announcements in the event of atomic attack on the United States. It was the warm cozy purr of Arthur Godfrey.

Like a deadly twister bouncing across the country and settling down, the hunt for subversives swung into the colleges and universities. When Albert Einstein cried out against the attack on intellectuals and called for resistance, Senator McCarthy promptly denounced him as "an enemy of America." A reader of the *Christian Century* sent in his subscription with a loyalty oath attached for the editor to sign. It seemed to be the action of a crank but it was actually a storm warning. The Protestant churches were next in the path of the congressional cyclone. The

American Legion forced the withdrawal of Charlie Chaplin's movie "Limelight" because of his political opinions. Even the Amateur Athletic Union added its wheezy breath to the whirlwind by turning its fund drive for the 1956 Olympics into a sinister crusade. "We must have a concentrated effort by the people of Amerca," it bleated. "We must beat Russia."

XXII

The lights had been turned off in Legion Hall. In the center of the room was a slide projector, a little box of burning white that leaked out of its back and sides and sent a glowing shaft, spermy with cigar and cigarette smoke, up to a screen on the stage. There, at the end of the stopped beam, like a mis-shapen red foetus, was a badly focussed view of some mines in Red Canyon. The rows of men on folding chairs were lumps in the semi-gloom. The flags and the paintings of Washington, Lincoln, and Eisenhower were drained of color by the phosphorescent glare, leeched to dreary greys and blacks. And the dead voice went on in the bare, echoing hall.

"Definitely I'd say we're off of the ground now," it droned. "We're definitely airborne." Step by step, methodically, painstakingly, Larry Wassburger had given a history of the uranium boom in the Black Hills, beginning with Zeke Butler's first discovery while looking for Indian pictographs, and now he was taking a look into the future. "What with aerial prospecting and deep drilling, I don't see any limit to our growth. Experience is the best teacher and we're learning fast. As for the erection of a mill to process the ore, I have been asked to make some comment about that. Several towns are in the running. As members of the Chamber of Commerce, you're naturally interested in this town winning out, but I have no definite information at this time. The construction of a mill for this area is under consideration, but as to either location or timing I couldn't say."

Masses of darkness toppled on the walls as he changed the picture on the screen. "Moving out of the vicinity for a few moments," he droned, "the newest area of interest is the lignite fields in the northern part of the state . . ."

"You bastard!" somebody in the audience said. "I figured you'd get around to that."

"What? Who's that?" Voices boiled up, the lights blinked on, and Sam Bolton was bearing down on him, shaggy, bull-footed, irascible. "Beating the drum loud enough to wake the dead," he said at the top of his voice. "Working up another rush and the government won't buy the damned ore."

"Now hold your horses," Larry said.

Car dealer Lee Stark's jowly face was contorted and he was rapping his gavel and calling for order. "Larry's our guest, Sam. He spared us some of his valuable time . . ."

"That's right," somebody else said. "No sense getting on the prod, Sam."

Swaying forward on his cane, he shouted, "I came here to say my piece and I'm saying it. I put thirty thousand dollars into lignite leases, and I might as well have chucked it down a gopher hole. You atomic energy people publicize the area and just accidentally don't mention you won't buy the ore till you find a way to get the uranium out of it. Why didn't you warn us? Now there's swindlers up there selling fake ore extractors to the suckers with mines. But what do you care?"

Everybody at the meeting was standing up, chairs scraped and fell over, a dozen men were hollering at Bolton to quiet down. "No, he's got a right to speak," Larry told them. "Just a minute—hold on." His tall cropped head leaning forward, he said to Sam, "It's true that the processing of lignite is a problem that hasn't been solved but . . ."

"In other words, you mean I'm stuck."

"*But* extensive laboratory work is going on night and day by the Commission and also the Bureau of Mines," he said earnestly. "And nothing was hid from the public. There was nothing fishy about it, Mr. Bolton. Everything was done in a perfectly aboveboard way."

Sam flapped an arm at him in disgust. "What you're saying is, I didn't read the fine print. You're a servant of your country, Wassburger, and that means the people in it—or ought to." At this, practically everybody lit into him: "You made your pile out of uranium, Sam," and "You can afford it, your wallet is bulging," and "You're accusing the United States government. Jew-Marxist talk, that's what it is!" Grabbing a chair to steady himself, he took hold of his cane like a club. His breath raked through his broken yellow teeth. "Who called me a communist?" he shouted. "Who said that? I'll pitch him out a window." Larry Wassburger came to his defense, regretting, deploring, but Sam told him to go to the devil and limped out of the hall.

It was twenty-five below and the air caught in his throat and lungs. The stoplight by the bank pumped spouts of red into the night like a severed blood vessel. Down in the freight yards, fires were blazing under the switches to keep them from freezing. Beaten, he thought dizzily, rooked out of thirty thousand dollars. Trying to get back into uranium, he had lost a third of the money he'd gotten for his claims and made things that much worse. There was no end to it; the misfortune would go on breeding more and more of itself until it devoured him, guts and all.

Slowly and painfully he went up the wooden stairs behind the cold storage and grocery—he and Lucy were using the room up there since her mother had moved in behind the cafe. She greeted him, smiling with her hands behind her back. "No, you can't kiss me for a nickel," she said.

With a grunt he let himself down on the bruised sofa, unstrapped the brace from his leg and rubbed the welter of itching scars in the thick hair. His head was still pounding and his nerves were like tangles of white-hot wire.

"You're late," she accused him pertly. "I put seven curses on you and now I have to take 'em off."

He made no answer, massaging his leg. She flopped onto the bed and pouted into a magazine, and for a while the only sounds were the sharp crack of her gum and the breathy whispers of the gas stove. "You could say *something*," she said then, thumbing the wad of gum under the windowsill. "You act like this is the place where elephants go to *die*." He picked at his eye, scowling, and half-penitently she came over and touched the rough hair growing on his neck. "Daddy Bear," she said. "Old Daddy Bear."

"Daddy Bear, hell," he said savagely and shoved her back on the bed. Her legs went loose and open and his great crude strength fell on her. Her mouth was forced apart. She could hear herself moaning far away and then she was swept under. He left her splayed out on the bed, shuddering her breath with her eyes closed. The plash of sensations prolonged itself, subsiding to little tremors that rippled and sluiced under her skin, and then she was groping and coming up, all blurry and melted but coming up to the surface again.

Her lips felt swollen and numb. Her breath slowed down and she opened her eyes, her drugged body still welling softly. He was stretched out next to her, staring absently at the ceiling. She gave a sigh to attract his attention, and when that failed she reached out, almost timidly, and let her hand rest against him. He didn't even pat it. A pang took her heart and threatened to burst in her throat and eyes. She might just as well be a pink hole in the air. Besides, the way he made her feel when it happened. Always before it had been a thing *she* had done, regardless of whether it was nice and she felt romantic and everything or whether she was in one of those stinky moods when it all curdled. With Sam, though, it was like the Johnstown Flood. Or Niagara Falls. Actually she didn't feel like herself at all in his company. He didn't have *any* sense of humor and he practically never just had a conversation with her.

About an aeon and a half later he got up, put on his britches and shirt and started reading the *paper!* If she didn't do something she was going to disappear. She went over to the bureau, completely naked, and began talking to her velvet panda, Noodles. "Did you get the ransom note?" she said crazily. "Well if you ever want to see your little child again, stay near the phone and wait for instructions."

He kept on reading.

"Oh! You're so aggravating!" she said to him.

"You better get for home."

"Sam, no!" she cried, in full retreat. "I didn't mean that. Are you staying in town? Let me stay here then, come on. I'll tell Mamma I was at Edna's." She might as well have been asking a boon from the Sphinx. Taking her time about it, she sulked into her clothes. At the door, however, she said humbly, "I'm going now. The morning rush will be over by ten. Can I come then if I'm real careful?"

To her surprise he nodded and said, "Goodnight, kid," but her happiness didn't last to the bottom of the snow-plugged steps. A shadow moved inside the shadow of a ratty old shed and she knew that Charley, in spite of the extremely severe temperature, had been standing out there the whole time she'd been inside.

The small shadow drifted away toward the Indian shacks. "Hey wait up," she said, racing after him. He slowed to a walk, grudgingly, kicking sprays of snow. "Wait a sec. Here," she said, going into her purse for six of the horror cards that came in packages of bubble gum. But though he was saving them up and had over fifty different ones already, he only stuffed his hands deeper in his pockets and backed away. "These are new ones," she said enticingly. "One of them, look, his flesh is *bubbling!* See? And one eye is hanging by a *thread.*"

His burnt-sugar face showed no expression. Then, disdainfully, he sent a needle-thin squirt of saliva between his front teeth.

"You're wasting your spit," she informed him loftily, but it was hard to get the words out. Just the way he stood, hunched together, carefully avoiding her look, was a reproach. Day after day after day, forlorn and indomitable, he hung around outside while she was with Sam. In spite of the fact that they had been like Damon and Pythias for years, he just *wouldn't* understand, or forgive her. In his pocket was the dirty and flattened claim-paper that old Zeke Butler had let him have. Even though Sam Bolton didn't even own the stinky claim any more, he was Charley's deadly enemy for life. According to Charley, Sam had stolen their mine. At least forty-three thousand times she had explained to him that the claim hadn't been legal, but he was absolutely *fanatical,* and simply because she went with Sam she was automatically Public Enemy Number Two. He wouldn't take quarters from her or let her call him "Chief" anymore, or anything.

"Do you want the cards or don't you?" she said. "Last chance, get a cocklebur in your pants."

He dragged the snot into his nose, hopping up and down to keep warm. There was nothing at all in his brown face. Before she could bring herself to tear up the cards, he turned and dog-trotted away, running on his cold, meager shadow.

"We're blood brothers and you can't quit," she yelled after him. "Ha-ha, too bad." His white breath dissolving like cotton candy, he ran through the frozen light by the depot. "Your old claim ain't worth the paper it's printed on!" she yelled.

The fires lashed under the switches in the yard, licking up the darkness.

She let the cards drop in the snow. Maybe he would pick them up tomorrow when she wasn't around. It was all so morbid. Helen was practically her bosom enemy, too, and when she deigned to speak at all it was, "You're throwing yourself away on Sam Bolton." And the only reason her mother didn't know about it and have six fits was because she was still in deep *mourning* about Cecil. She acted like a widow in India about two minutes before she went to a fiery death with her husband's remains. The cafe didn't mean anything to her. As a matter of fact, she said that it was a sin and a shame how the cafe was keeping Lucy out of school. In practically the very same tone old Cecil had made famous, for creep's sake. And yet she wasn't sorry about Sam. He was quite elderly, besides being married, and she could feel in her bones that sooner or later he would switch to somebody or something else, but you didn't love somebody because they were suitable. And when you loved somebody, what mattered was to *mean* something to him. If she could just get him to care for *her,* Lucy. It was awful to be just a female to him, the whole stupid entire sex.

Her best chance, she decided, was to talk about Stephens. If that didn't make a dent on Sam, then nothing would. "What a goop that Bert Stephens is," she said the next morning. "Florence and them start drooling at the mere mention of his name, and he isn't even a *man*."

"That's a tender subject," he said shortly. "I'm out of the picture and he's in, and that's it." But the fury inside him was like a banked fire, shivering, beginning to slide open on throbbing red caves of flame. "A national reputation," he growled. "That piece in the Sunday supplement with him standing in front of the ore pile at the buying station, like it was his!"

"Did you know he's hired himself a publicity man? Some *nut* from the east?" Kneeling beside him, she offered him her hate, stroked his hand and laid her cheek on his knee to show her sympathy. And saw that he didn't want or need her at all; he was lost in harsh reveries that had no place for her. Before long, grabbing his sheepskin jacket and his cane, he went pitching out of the room without so much as a fare-thee-well.

She tried simply everything: telling him stuff that had happened in the cafe, asking him about current events, cheering him up, and as a last and final resort, deliberately getting him sore: "Did I make you happy?" she said afterwards, lying beside him in the shallow bed. "Just a teensy weensy bit? In that case, couldn't you say yum-yum then? or *something?*"

He made a non-committal sound.

"Was it better than with Mamma?"

That brought him up on one elbow, his face absolutely livid. Then he sank down. "I don't want any fracas with you," he said. "My leg is giving me enough heck as it is."

She felt more and more blue, and she found herself doing these nutty things. She wrapped herself in one of the curtains, gave him her most ravishing smile, and said, "Guess who? Don't bother, you'd never get it. It's Miss Nobody." He shrugged, and except for the grind of traffic outside and the ker-chunk! of the meat cleaver in the cold storage downstairs, there was silence in the small room with its ruck of hand-me-down furniture. Slippers and shoes, coke bottles and clothes were scattered around. A long cord wriggled over the worn Eden of the carpet and went under the bed. "Ding-a-ling!" she said brightly. "You better answer; it *could* be important."

Bored and lonely, she put on her coin bracelet and jangled it until she was three-quarters out of her mind. She wandered over to Noodles and said in a deep voice, "You double-crossed us, Mr. Abercrombie. No use lying about it, the place was crawling with cops. You will never see your little Susie again." Sam didn't even *look* at her. She stuck out her tongue at him and wandered to the lopsided mirror, glimmering with winter-grey light from the window, and stared and stared at herself until her dark reflection wavered, sinking away like a slender tree shadow in the icy water of a pond. She wished she was nine years old again.

And out of nowhere, the thought of Paul came into her mind like small, sad music. She hated Sam, really and truly hated him—those bristles in his nose, the funny muff of grey hair around his head where his hat stopped. The next time he put his hand on her arm, she elbowed him away and said, "That's *sacred*." He looked as if he was going to go berserk. "I'm not in your harem," she said frostily. "Go away. If I even hear the word 'sex' again I'll scream." It was so humiliating. She simply couldn't resist him, and all the while she was cutting him into little bitty pieces, her body was going its own way, softening, giving itself into his powerful arms, her flailing head drooped and came around, and it was happening again.

When he lifted himself from the bed he pulled on his denim work clothes and gazed with sightless, vague eyes down at the street. He didn't feel any better. The loss of his claims was still like an infection, a virus burning in his bloodstream. Without much interest he noted that there was a uranium treatment clinic in the defunct bathhouse across from the park. The Cattleman's Bar was now a nightclub and casino with roulette and dice tables like Reno or Las Vegas. Along with fresh money and new jobs, the scum of creation was coming in, he thought dully. But with each day that passed it was more difficult to care about anything, to keep active, even to go to the post office for the mail. Bits of his past life tumbled over and over in his mind: cleaning out a rattlesnake den in a cave when he was eight or nine—foul, choking air and the baby snakes, just born, squirming away into cracks and holes. The time a mouse died in the piano and smelled to high heaven and nobody could locate it. Doughnuts frying in bacon fat and his mother praying with two other women, why or exactly when escaped him. He remembered his father dying. Always, even before his mother had died in childbirth, his father had waked up first, shaken the ashes out of the grate and started breakfast. This particular morning, when he opened his eyes, nobody was stirring and he couldn't understand why. So he went into the other room and his father was lying there. He was warm but at the same time he was cold. Scared, he didn't think to take his pulse, just lifted up his eyelid. And he was dead. Funny he should think of that now.

The girl went back to the cafe for the noon-hour trade and after a while he lugged down the street to the post office. The snow cover had about gone. Out beyond the frozen trickle of the river the windy range country was hazed with blowing dust. A car drawn up to the curb was rotted underneath like a tooth. As soon as he opened the glass door of the mailbox, he caught sight of the letter from U.S. Mining. The calendar said February 9th, three days before the lease was up. Resignedly he opened the envelope.

There was no certified check in it. His eyes bleared away on stiff, ungainly phrases, "in pursuance of" and "notification of non-renewal."

He swallowed his breath. Jolting away from the boxes, he stood reading the letter over and over from the beginning, from the New York postmark to the jaggy signature of S. W. Belden, Andy's boss. It was no use; his mind kept rejecting the words. Though he'd read many a lease and contract, suddenly he had lost confidence in himself: he was just an old dirt rancher and he'd gotten tangled up in technicalities. Why, U.S. Mining was the second largest producer in the region. They wouldn't turn loose of his claims like that, not with an office set up and equipment brought in and crews on the job.

Blundering and weak in the legs, he made for Andy's house. Andy had been laid up for a week with the flu, but by the Lord Harry he wasn't too sick to give him a plain yes or no. His claims back and $60,000 to boot! The motor of a car gasped and kicked over and the loose bumper vibrated up and down. The decaying chrome was like ice breaking up, water beginning to jump over stones. His chest was struggling. It did no good to hold back, to caution himself that a letter might not be binding in court; his blood was flowing, running like the red, clay-heavy water of a spring flood.

At the last second, on the porch of the small stucco house, he decided to play it close to the vest in case there *had* been some mixup in New York. "How's your son?" he said to Mrs. Lytton. "I heard he has the flu."

"Flu, my eye!" she said. Catching his arm in her sharp fingers, she complained, "This happens all the time. There's nothing in the world wrong with him, he's just babying himself." The draped wrinkles on her face changed and took on an antique coquettishness. "I have a bone to pick with you, Mr. Bolton. You didn't come back like you promised."

The door opened and Andy came out of the bedroom wearing a blue silk robe. His waxy pink face was no more exhausted and ill than usual. "How they brought the good news from wherever it was," he said cynically and lowered himself onto the couch.

Sam didn't know what he meant. "I just come by to see how you were getting on," he said.

Closing his eyes, Andy said, "That's fine, Mother. You can go now. Mr. Bolton isn't here to look at your junk."

"Grumpy Gus," she hissed at him. "What do you know about it? At least he's a man that makes use of his God-given powers instead of having a breakdown at the least little thing."

Andy kept his eyes closed in their sickly hollows until she had left the room. "So you got the word," he said.

Glory, a storm of glory rushed into him. "I got a letter from New York."

Querulously Andy broke out, "That goddamn cat! Do you hear it?" From the next room came an anguished twanging like a jews harp struck over and over and over. "It never stops. Day and night it never stops. The goddamn thing is in heat."

"The letter, is it legal? I mean, you know . . ."

"It's legal," Andy said wearily. "So relax. You're the new peanut butter king. The claims are yours."

Sam limped back and forth, whacking his hand against his leg and panting, "By God, by God . . . But how come?" he said. "I don't see the logic of it."

"It wasn't my decision," Andy said. "Personally, I still believe in the property, but the scorekeepers in New York added it up and turned thumbs down. A hundred and sixty thousand more is a tidy sum, you know, and they figured it wasn't an economical proposition. You have to look at it from their viewpoint—dividend results and so forth. The drill reports weren't that terrific, and you should've seen the bugs in the mining operation! I kept it afloat, which I never could have except for the education you gave me, but it wasn't anything supra-supra. It wasn't even in the same league as Stephens. So . . . while I close up shop here they'll take the show to Utah. It's stupid because my information is that the mill will be located here."

Curiously, as he spoke the fretfulness left his voice and a sombre but gentle resignation took its place. "I'll get the meat hook over this but I been giving it a lot of thought, Sam. The way I see it, I don't have the survival qualities for top management. The exec has to not only live with competitive tension, he has to actually benefit from it, and that I can't do. In a nutshell, I guess anxiety just isn't a creative thing with me."

Sam wished him luck and left him sitting on the purplish sofa in his silk robe. There was a kind of peace in the way his hands lay on the cushions.

"Oh Mr. Bol-ton," Mrs. Lytton said voraciously, but he told her that he had to get off his tail and start humping again. The sky was pouring under an east wind. The flag over the post office was streaming its folds. He drove back to the ranch at seventy miles an hour, slammed along the swooping wheel tracks into the yard—and then loitered into the house as casual as anything.

"Well look at what walked in," Vivie said, her eyes snapping. "You decided to pay a social call, huh? You can just turn around, old buster, and go back where you came from. Go back to your herd of females."

Undisturbed, he went to the stove and got himself a cup of coffee. "Afternoon, Velma," he said to his son Hank's wife, who was visiting with her little girl. Velma, ducking for cover, mumbled a hello over her shoulder.

"I know you ain't here because your conscience hurts, because you don't have one," Vivie said.

He regarded her with mellow good humor, rubbing his sleeve across his chin. She tore into him like a cyclone. In the background the crumby, tangle-haired baby was chasing around in a pajama top, naked from her fat tummy down. Vivie told her to hush up and she replied stoutly, "I'm being Jack and the Bean-stuff." Vivie said, "Come here, you little devil," and she scratched herself between the legs and blazed back, "No!" Sam broke into snorts of laughter. Vivie yelled to her mother to come and get her and be quick about it, but in no time the baby paraded back into the kitchen, guzzling milk from two bottles at once, and leaned back against Sam's knee bumping softly, gulping like a fish. He waved her mother away. "She's one too many for you," he chuckled at Vivie, and all the while the glory kept rising and rising in him.

"You old whoremonger," she spat at him and went through her

entire catalogue of vituperation; he sipped his coffee and enjoyed the fresh new life bobbing against his leg. "Are you sick or what?" she said all at once. "You're not yourself."

"Why so?" he said innocently. "You're the injured party and you're naturally going to air your grievances. Go right on. Proceed."

"Sam Bolton, you just better tell me. What *is* it?"

"You might be interested at that," he grinned and showed her the letter, relishing her disbelief, then her rapturous questions. She couldn't resist putting the bee on him again for his indiscretions, but she was too thrilled, too intoxicated with the wonder of it to stay mad for long. "I could skin you alive," she said. "Oh I feel so good. You suppose they messed *everything* up?"

"I was just now going out for a look. There's got to be some explanation more than what Andy told me. It don't make sense."

They found a crew still at work, pecking away at a shattered pink cliff, getting the last dollar's worth out of the option, so they drove farther down the canyon and scrabbled over shale and piles of rock grey with scurfy snow, over lacy animal tracks and oil stains, over tires and broken machinery and bulldozer trails battling up to walls of dynamited red stone. And by God, it was comic! Only eight or nine claims, and those not the best, had been mined at all. In one place a four-foot outcropping had been diluted by at least ten feet of waste rock, and again and again the crew had dug right through the ore bodies instead of following them as they squirmed into the cliff. Picking over the littered boulders of another fiasco, they stopped short as the dial of the scintillometer fluttered in breathtaking spurts: the mangled rock and clay was alive with radioactivity under their feet!

"There's sure some dumb people in this world," he exulted. "Hurry, hurry, that's what they done, and fell flat on their face. They got their big tonnage, all right, but mighty small profit."

"How could they? It's sinful the way they messed up good ore."

"I'll tell you. Andy was a good enough hand, but he had to spend most of his time pushing paper in the office. It was just fortunate, that's all. The good Lord was with us, Vivie."

He waved his frozen, clay-stained fist and they climbed up to examine the drilling. It was, if anything, worse than the mining. The crew had constructed heavy-duty roads for their large rigs and sunk holes half way to Hades in neat, senseless patterns. It must have cost the company several fortunes. "What they done was lose on the peanuts what they made on the popcorn," he laughed. "I doubt seriously if they made their ninety thousand back." To finish off the comedy, a week later the news drifted back from Utah that U.S. Mining had bought an exhausted property for $1500—and was blowing huge sums on it while the whole area howled.

His jubilation was a tornado whirling inside him, uncontrollable.

Though his crippled leg was aching and giving at every step, he had to bust loose. Looking to make sure that the U.S. Mining crew was still out of sight up the canyon, he took a shovel to the soft cliff face near a butchered mine, and only a little to the south he found a luscious yellow pod eight inches under the surface. The scintillator, when he held it close, registered 1.6! "By God," he muttered hoarsely, shakily, swinging his arms and driving the shovel into the stone. The crash of the shovel mixed with the rumble of bulldozers across the valley and the echoing WHUMP-Whump-whump of an explosion, filling him like the innumerable clashing vibrations inside a great bell swinging and spilling out torrents of sound. It was glory, glory. The outcrop widened and widened as he went in. He threw back his wind-cut face, his mouth open as if to take in the cascades of debris, the road, and the creekbed submerged now in shadows, the sky-ramming spurs of pink and rich orange in the late light, everything in the canyon.

"We're going to make a comeback like you never saw," he said then, and it was like swearing an oath. "But we'll have to go like heck, Vivie. We're a long ways behind Stephens."

" 'Course we will," she said, hugging him. "Nobody can't lick us!"

"We'll give him a good fight anyhow, bum leg and all. There's enough ore right here to cut down the gap."

XXIII

"Bert! You're giving me a heart attack! Bert, please!"

"Ssh! I'm travelling incognito." Roaring down the midnight highway, drunk and laughing, he hit the brakes and reined, hobbled the Cadillac to a stop. "Whoa! Easy now," he said, stroking the dashboard, patting it. Then he spurred the car forward again and leaned sideways toward her. "Give me a little kiss and a hug to go with it."

Holding onto the seat to brace herself, Helen Mencke raised her face toward him, mousey and radiant.

"I'll count to six. Five, six. That was your last chance to go steady."

Instantly the car reared up, lunged and pitched, and she was flung, squealing, half out of the seat.

"Hey there, boy, easy. I been in the saddle all day." He soothed the top of the dashboard.

Giggling, she darted a kiss at him and said, "What in the world's got into you? You been so down in the mouth, and for no reason. There wasn't nothing would satisfy you. Being big stuff like you are would satisfy anybody else, but I swear, look at you. You were poor as beans and no sooner did you get rich than you were saying, I finally have got there and where the . . . heck is that?"

Yipping and ya-hooing, he sent the car up to seventy, then eighty miles an hour. The highway rivered under them and slid dizzily, twisting, tossing up a cinder-grey hill and falling off into a valley, empty in the moonlight for miles ahead except for a tiny pair of moving tail lights. The lights became a half-ton truck, banking sharply in a curve of the road. Bert raced beside it, fishtailing on the gravel shoulder and swerving back alongside with a shriek of tires. His muddy red face was alive with gloating pleasure. Across from them, the startled rancher flicked a glance from the cab of the truck. "You're going to scatter us all over creation," Helen cried, but her breath caught with scared delight, her heart skipped like a jump rope at his daring, and she went meek with awe as he called back over his shoulder to the truck which was slowing up farther and farther behind, "I'll scrub paint with you anytime, buddy. This car don't know anything but run."

"You crazy," she said. "What's it all about? Here I practically die because you have to be told Sam Bolton got his mines back and it makes you cheer up! I only done it because I thought it would be better hearing it from me. I could've swore you'd go into a worse frame of mind than ever."

"Just goes to prove what I said, little girl. You're too pretty to think." Far ahead of them headlights sparked out of a bend in the road and came around, increasing swiftly and dividing into two bursts of light that swept down on them and flooded the windshield and Bert's grinning face. She ducked at the shock of air and hurtling metal. Her dress had worked above her knees. The draft from the heater flowed up her open legs. Every time he tilted at the charging masses of light and missed by inches, she put her hands over her eyes so she wouldn't see his gleeful face seared, branded white by the headlights that whipped past them like balls of flaming gas.

All of a sudden the Cadillac lunged to one side and spun half way around, bouncing up and down. "Damn," he said. "I think I missed that last bridge."

But then they were rolling smoothly, and, squinting her frightened eyes open, she saw that he had actually turned off onto a side road. Woozy with relief, she socked at his arm. "Hey, be careful," he said. "I'm valuable now." Before she could even smile, with one wrench at the steering wheel he had veered off the road and they were jolting and banging over the unfenced range. The wheels walloped on loose rocks, skidded over the leprous white of a frozen stockpond. Sagebrush raked both sides of the car. "What are you doing?" she shrieked. "Quit, Bert! You're shaking the liver outa me!"

"Whatever suits you, ma'am." He bucked back onto the road by some kind of miracle and stopped. "The hell with riding to hounds, anyway. There ain't no foxes out here."

"You silly thing," she said, holding her throat and laughing. "I had eleven different strokes, I was clear out of this world." But now that they had parked, her shyness came back and with it the old self-reproach. She pulled her dress down over her chunky knees. She fussed with her hair. Oblivious to such matters, he took a drink from a pint of whiskey and said, "Now one for that cough."

"I'm awful," she said. "It's wrong to go sneaking off like this."

"So is stealing apples, but there's no orchard hereabouts so you'll just have to sin the best way you can."

It was the way he had—draped negligently beside her with his boots up on the dashboard—not the ruby cufflinks or the three-carat diamond ring or that he was famous and rich. Weak and small with submission, she moved closer to him. "I'll catch it from George again when I get home but I don't care," she announced. She felt reckless and dreamy. She felt soft all over. He lifted the bottle at the decaying moon, half full of light above the broken spine of a butte, and poured down the rest of the whiskey, spilling it all over the front of his gabardine shirt. "Damn if that news wasn't invigorating," he said. "I'm fresh as a daisy and cranked up to go. We will now proceed to turn this place into a lovers' lane, only just don't holler out and make the cows nervous."

"Bert," she said hesitantly, and then took a big step. "I love you."

"Why sure you do. Damn if I don't feel the same way, Beatrice. I mean Agnes. What is your name anyway? Hell with it. Cuddle up, dear heart, and pet me some."

Accusingly, she said, "I heard you slept with Florence last night."

"I didn't do any such thing. I slept with two other ladies but not with her." He guffawed, his face melted and swaying, but instead of scrapping back at him she drooped. The creamy puffs of her hair sank into shadows. "Just a joke," he mumbled. "I'll give you an ice cream cone and my cap buster for two kisses."

She brought up her face eagerly, a small and gentle moon of love. He kissed her and with a whimper she pulled herself against him, only to see his head roll away, loose, sightless, hanging above his chest in a torn scrap of darkness. A snore dribbled on his lips. Taking him in her arms, she held his ruined face against her breast, caressing the flag of hair on his balding forehead and the wide, humorous cheeks that shrank into such a small, sad mouth. Then, as carefully as possible, she disengaged herself and climbed out of the car, went around and got in behind the wheel. She contrived somehow to turn the car and get back to the highway, but there she stopped, peering first one way and then the other.

"Honey," she said, "wake up, honey." She had to shake him for the longest time before he blinked and made a sunken noise. "Honey, I think we're lost. Do you know which direction is town?"

He staggered out into the road and, twirling slowly on his feet, gazed up at the motionless blizzard of stars. "How the hell should I know?" he said, and pitched forward headlong.

"Bert, Bert!" she sobbed, hauling futilely at him. After a while, still on his back in the icy gravel, he opened his eyes and let one lid dip down in a wink. A crafty expression seeped like oil over his face and he tapped a finger at his temple. "Wait till you see the sugar-cured, eighty-six proof window-buster I thought up while I was laying here. I'm done with negotiations and so forth. As Stalin said to Old Harry Truman, 'Tough shit, Harry.'"

The next day after school, half the children in town were sliding on Watertower Hill. A vast round shape in the winter twilight, nippled with the silver tank on the top, it was alive with bundled figures clambering up the side and, one after another, bellyflopping their sleds into the white courses of snow in the sagebrush. Dogs bounced along, barking. The cries of the children sprang up everywhere, shrill with pleasure, hooting, bragging and squabbling: "Watch *me* now!" "Cheater!" "No fair, Billy, I'm first!" The small ones and the girls went off the lowest fold of hill, squeaking "beep-beep" and gliding on the easy snow. Only the biggest kids, and Charley Trueblood, who would try anything, went all the way to the wind-struck top. There they played "chicken" on the steep, dangerous slides that leaped and streamed down between the savage rocks and brush.

While Buzz Farley and Jerry Olson and the other guys were still daring each other, Charley jumped off at the frozen glow of the street light way, way under him and went smacking and whirling downwards and then skimming over the trampled level at the bottom, gyrating to a stop on his dented washing machine lid.

Debbie Bolton, towing her sled, waylaid him as he started back. "Can I come with? Can I? Lemme come, Charley. We can use my Flyer."

He plodded away, the lid under his arm. "If you do," she said craftily, "I'll swap you three rides on Lady, free!" He slowed down at that; however, he still kept his back to her, pretending to smoke his white breath. Einstein Engleberg sidled toward them and she said, "Go away, snoopy, this is private. No buttin' in."

"Just one single time," she said to Charley. "And you can have five rides on Lady and feed her besides." Stubbing his feet in the snow and snuffling the leak back into his nose, he weighed the proposition, good points against bad points.

"They don't allow girls on top," he said. "Anyhow, you'd be ascared. Dean's ascared."

"He's a big sissy," she replied spunkily. "I'm not ascared. I walked across Railroad Bridge, didn't I?" Her face was valentine-red with the cold. Her breath smelled like a penny sucker. She upped the offer to ten rides and crossed her heart, hope-to-die, that she would keep her word.

For that many rides on Lady he would have taken a hundred punches on the arm. "Stay close behind and don't make any racket," he told her. Ditching the lid in the bushes, he took her around to the back of the hill, past the shacks and the culvert plugged with dead weeds and trash, past the smoking town dump, and sneaked up the rough slope. Debbie kept making too much noise. Then, holding her nose at the smell from the dump, she said, "Pee-yooh!" real loud.

Immediately a voice shot down at them, "Beat it, this is our hill. No girls allowed."

"You shut up, Buzz Farley," she yelled back, "or you won't never ride Lady any more."

"I told you to keep quiet," Charley said in a fury. Buzz was hollering to the other guys. Charley tore like crazy for the top, telling her to get on and get ready as soon as she got up there. Three of the eighth graders were waiting, lined up at the edge, so he turned off just out of reach and led them halfway round the hill, then darted past them like a weasel to the wire fence encircling the tower. "What kinda trick you pullin'?" Buzz said. "Brown trash."

"White trash," he hissed back, slipping along the fence as they spread out and closed in on him. His heart was thumping but he wasn't as scared as he would have been if he'd been on the reservation. They were real tough there. Olson went for his arm to twist it, and he snaked away, dodged between the grabbing hands, broke for the sled and pushed off with half a second to spare. The snow creamed by faster and faster. Locking Debbie tight between his knees and steering with his feet, he peeled off into the long white dive of the slide. It was a lot easier on a sled. She screamed the whole time.

"That was neat!" she cried as they stopped, jumping up and rubbing her butt. Her eyes were shining. "Let's do it again, okay?"

But already the guys were streaking down the hill after him and he took off up the road, keeping a lookout over his shoulder. "Hey, Chief," somebody hailed him and there was Mr. Stephens, breezy and bareheaded, his camel's-hair coat hanging open and a brand new six-foot Flyer at his heels. Charley galloped to meet him.

"Do you want any errands run?" he asked. Twice Mr. Stephens had given him half a dollar for running an errand, and once a dollar.

"I just come to test-drive this thing," Mr. Stephens said. He was pretty drunk. Charley could smell his whiskey-breath from a yard away. "No lie now," he said thickly. "Does your mother really paint buildings at the Salem Army Depot? How about your old man?"

"She threw him out. He lives in a sod hut on the reservation and goes for a walk in the afternoon with the dogs and gets drunk at night. He don't give a damn about nothing."

"He's a philosopher," Mr. Stephens observed and, wavering to a halt, took a sight at the watertower blinking its red warning lights in the sky. "Damn nation, if that's not a mountain. How about giving me a few lessons?"

Charley snatched at the chance to go on sliding protected by a grownup and maybe earn another dollar at the same time. "I'm not ascared," he said. "Come on and I'll show you." He retrieved his lid from the bushes and led the way up, reeling off information in his blurry voice: "Me and the big kids play chicken from the top. Most of the kids are ascared to try 'cause if you hit a hole you really go sailing. I used to soap some cardboard and slide on that till I found this lid. You go slower on cardboard but it's fun. One time the high school kids dragged a junk car clear up to the top and left it go crashing down. It really came apart. All the wheels fell off."

"Sounds like a trip I've took of an occasion," Mr. Stephens panted. He was forced to stop and rest now and then because his wind gave out, and Charley had to help him the last few yards. At the sight of Buzz and Jerry and the rest of them slinking away, Charley felt his heart jump with triumph the way it did when he hopped a freight going real fast, or hung by one hand under the bridge to get the eggs from a bird's nest.

Mr. Stephens sagged down on an old lard bucket and drew out a bottle of whiskey. "I believe the altitude has got me," he said, blowing like an old steam engine. "While I doctor myself, suppose you start the lessons."

Over and over again Charley whizzed down on the Flyer and ran back up. When Mr. Stephens told him he could sure pilot that thing, he said, "That's nothing. Watch." He took his lid and held it behind him, and flipping over in the air as he launched himself, went scooting down on his back, spinning away into the night like a tiny planet. When he puffed back up, though, he found Mr. Stephens on the other side of the tower, just staring down at the derelict boxcars fixed up into houses, the dog yapping in a tumbledown yard, the smashed and worn-out cars, and the charred heaps of the dump fuming up into the cold, rusty sunset. He didn't pay any attention when Charley trotted up.

"Did you see me?" Charley asked him. "Did you?"

"You're a star, all right," he said, but Charley could see that he wasn't having fun any more. "You want another lesson?" he asked him. "I'll take you along this time and steer."

Mr. Stephens allowed himself to be tugged away. As they straddled the sled, he looked at the snow path writhing down in the knotty sagebrush and stones. "Damn, the National Safety Council ain't gonna like this," he said, but he was only pretending to be afraid because when they hit a rock and he landed way off in the brush, he picked himself up looking cheerful again and said, "Deal some more, Chief. Just leave me get the snow out of my underwear first." His coat was torn and there was a thread of blood coming from his eye, but he wouldn't quit. He was real tough. "Let's swap decks," he said after a couple of rides, and, holding the lid behind him like Charley, he threw himself off backwards from the very top. Bang, he jarred into a crater and flew off into the lashing bushes. He staggered to his feet and said, "That sure knocked the pee-water outa me but I'm getting the hang of it."

It took a lot of arguing before Charley could get him to stop and be ridden down. By now it was as black as the ace of spades and the cold was like electricity in the air. Most of the other kids had gone home. Mr. Stephens sat on the sled coughing and slowly pulling off his coat, which was ripped in about sixteen places. "I believe I'll take up another hobby at that," he said, dropping the coat in the snow behind him. "Tell you what. I'll trade you this Flyer sled, which retails for nine-ninety-five at the hardware, for the use of that claim paper in your pocket."

Charley hunched down, on his guard immediately, and began moving backwards. Mr. Stephens had only been trying to get on the good side of him.

"Hey, don't get jugheaded on me. I'm going to finesse the property back for you, Chief. So you and what's his name—that old coot in the hospital—can get to be mining kings like me."

He still didn't believe Mr. Stephens, but his heart began to go faster and faster in spite of himself. The wind swept up the snow and whirled it around them under the street light in brilliant swarms. Mr. Stephens grinned at him, shivering in just his shirt and pants, and said, "Hellfire, I'm backing you against Sam Bolton is all. Truth and justice will prevail—for once. Bertram J. Stephens, champion of oppressed folks everywhere, is going into action." Charley stared at him. He felt like shinnying to the top of the school flag pole. He felt like going down the steepest slide in the world and eating a hundred candy bars and having a boxing match with his father all at the same time.

The next day Bert was as good as his word. With Charley right beside him, he sauntered into the Victory Bar, where he now transacted all his business, and beckoned to his entourage: a scurfy man with a lopsided chin, another who was wearing a limp sportcoat spotted with cigarette burns, and a brainless lout in bib overalls with a little head budding out of wide muscular shoulders. Gleefully he bought drinks all around and said, "All right, you heathens, this briefing session and pancake supper will kindly come to order. Otis, here's the car keys. You take Chief and go fetch what's his name from the VA hospital over in Hot Springs."

Charley and Otis lit out, and Bert said to the man in the sportcoat, "Marv, you're on salary as of now. I want you to hire some recruits for tomorrow at six A.M., sharp. Get twenty or thereabouts, I don't want to be shorthanded. I'll pay twenty bucks a head for each day and all they can drink afterwards. And if their character ain't any better than yours," he added with a canny smirk, "that's all to the good."

He was buoyant again, exhilarated. "That's enough funeral music," he shouted to the grey-faced war vet who was groping sentimental songs out of the organ and singing in a weak, nasal voice. "Flush a march tune outa there, Billy Boy. 'Under the Double Eagle' or something on that order."

"You betcha, Bert," he smiled over his shoulder. After a few tentative smears of sound, something like an off-kilter march emerged and wobbled upward like a ragged kite. "Now that's stirring," Bert said and beat the time with his hand. "Faster! That's better."

Next he sent for his writer, as he called his publicity man: a putty-grey health bug with a personality like a cold sore. Almost transparent hair seeped back from his veined temples. His diet consisted of wheat germ, dried fruit, and several quarts a day of mineral water from Hot Springs; because he'd been a staffer on newspapers for thirty years, he had a genuine dread of alcoholics and of Bert in particular. "How's your bowels, Earl?" Bert greeted him boisterously. "Listen, I want you to leave off everything and get some articles on old Zeke Butler in the Rapid and Denver papers. Discoverer of uranium in the Black Hills, filed the first claim and stuff like that."

"I'll get on it as soon as I wrap up the story on the office you bought from U.S. Mining."

"No, no, this here is top priority," Bert said. Lolling in the iodine-colored booth, he rapped out one command after another. "Also, there's a bulldozer in the garage for repairs. Tell Harry I want it fixed by this evening and on to a truck—hire the truck, I don't want a company truck for this." Earl made a note with one of his gold-headed pens. "Lord, my temperature when I get to figuring," Bert said, and ordering a bottle of beer on the double, he spilled it, foaming, into his boots to cool his feet. "Aah, that's better." Earl made a disapproving sound and turned to leave. "Hold on," Bert said, rolling back under the cracked and taped-up window, a skin of thin light on his raw, gloating face. "Another thing. Send a telegram to Bob Werden as follows: 'Bad news, flying to New York to see you. Signed, Bert.'" With a guileful wink he chuckled, "That'll make him foul his britches! . . . And one more. Leave a note for Wally when he comes in from his day's toil. Quote: 'Steaks is twenty-five cents apiece in South America, Lard. How about going down there with me?' Unquote. That boy is busting a new set of clothes every week with his gluttonous habits," he laughed. "For a man with a saving nature like him, South America is the only solution." Earl waited for more instructions with sour patience. Mockingly, Bert said, "Now scat," and went squishing over to Billy at the organ, jocular, expansive, lighting a cigar.

Thunk-thunk-ding! The target game was lit up and a stubby,

freckled rascal with greasy hair crawling over his collar was aiming the gun and squeezing the trigger. Billy was practically in tears. The target game next to his Hammond organ was the tragedy of his life. "Hershel," Bert called to the lout in overalls. He snapped his fingers and pointed. Showing the rim of gums above his teeth and nodding, Hershel clomped over and jerked at the electric cord under the target game. "Hey, I put a dime in there!" the freckled man squawked and looked to the bartender in vain for help. "It ain't legal."

"Thanks a million, Bert," Billy said, splurging joyous music from the tusk-like yellow keys. "Say, what's all the activity about this morning?"

"I'm gonna chop off somebody's stinger," he replied. "A so-and-so of poor character that has to be restrained. You know me, I believe in good fellowship and peace all around, but sometimes it's necessary to be firm. It's my duty." Leaning on the organ, he took a gully-washer of a drink and asked Billy to do his imitations—a train whistle, a pussycat, a rooster—listening with a judicial air and applauding after each of the inept noises that could have been anything from the slopping laughs of an idiot to the death scream of a tiny animal.

Then Charley and Otis came in with Zeke Butler: a small, shuffling, bloodless ghost in a suit and coat three sizes too large. The brim of his hat wandered above his face and ears. He didn't seem to know where he was.

"Pleased as all hell to meet you," Bert said, picking up the frail husk of a hand and shaking it. Zeke Butler took off his hat and mumbled, "I think I'll set down. My feet are troubling me." It looked as if the old boy was over the hill to nowhere; however, with a few minutes of rest he recovered wonderfully.

"I figured I was at the end of the line," he began to speak in a pale voice. "Yessir, I'd given up on the whole doggone thing. What's the name of your friend again, Charley? You have a good friend here." Though his breath was still like a fluttering pulse, there was a watery shine of hope on his dim eyes and he declared, "This is the best medicine I could have. Yes sir. I bet you remember what I taught you, Charley. Sure you do." More and more vigorous, he told Bert all about his valuable and interesting collections. Poking his face out eagerly, he said, "I'd be just too glad to show 'em to you, Mr. Stephens. Right this minute."

"In due time, in due time. The reason I got you out of the hospital, Dad, is because you have to appear out there in the canyon. Chief ain't sufficient by himself. I'll bed you down in that house down the highway that calls itself a motel and Otis will see to all your wants."

"Surely. Did Charley tell you how Sam Bolton cheated me? There's a story. I was at his mercy, Mr. Stephens, and he never hesitated. The damnable crook." He stretched out the folds of his neck, sputtering, and his false teeth roamed in his loose mouth. "He's a sharp one and no mistake."

"Cheer up, Dad," Bert grinned. "For shrewdness, cunning, and all other types of that, Bolton strictly ain't in it. What's gonna happen out there tomorrow morning, you and Charley are only the originating point of it. The fallout from this one will be fantastic."

At four o'clock the next afternoon Vivie and Sam were pounding along Red Canyon Road in the jeep. "Oh Sam," she wailed, "they're all over everywhere, kicking down our stakes and burying in our discovery holes. It's awful! They're nailing up paper, too, and back-dating all the claims with Zeke Butler's name on them, dated back to before we started."

He muscled the jeep around a shaly cliff at bone-rattling speed. The news had hit him like a swinging fist and his heavy face was trenched and savage. His hair thrashed in the rush of cold air under the canvas top.

"If I hadn't of set out for town, we wouldn't have seen them at all. As it is, they've been at it since sunup. That *darn* old coot! I'll wring his neck," she said violently. "He's got a slew of men, Sam, they must've tore up I don't know how many claims. It's completely crazy! We filed on every foot of that, legal, and he knows it, but he's just taking over everything!" It was all so unexpected, so underhanded and *dirty*. Weeping with outrage, she chattered, "I was driving past Old Woman's Creek, you know, where he had his so-called claim, and it was like—Sam, what's happening? It *can't* be happening!"

The road fell off sharply and climbed up again. A mile ahead in the cold glycerine light, orange pillars lifted from the center of the valley floor, shattered, broken off at the top. Even from this distance she could make out the feather of dust above the canyon wall where the bulldozer was working, and it was like a blow on the heart all over again. "There, over there," she sobbed.

It was too awful. The jeep was bouncing through frozen sagebrush and the squeak of the dry, tortured springs reminded her of the peep-peep of the baby chicks being carried out to the pigs. After more than forty years, the memory of that terrible morning was still inside her—the Ohio farmyard with blossoming plum trees and plowed soil rolled over in plump rows and her father with the bushel basket of rustling, cheeping little creatures. They were culls from the brood just hatched, and he dumped them over the top rail of the pen, ignoring her tears and the pummelling of her desperate fists. The hogs charged through the mud and snuffled them up while she stuffed her fingers in her ears and cried and cried. The chicks were so soft and yellow, such tiny warm live things.

Zeke Butler was sitting in a truck where the creekbed twisted down out of the pines and snow-caulked faces of rock. Sam yanked the door of the cab open and said, "Call off those men, damn it. You're breaking the law."

"You better," she pitched in. "This is our property, old Buster. You can be sued for every penny you'll ever have."

The shabby old invalid blinked at them, his face like a rag dried to a grey shrivel. Then he piped up, "It's my claim! You figured you could diddle me out of it, didn't you?"

"*Your* claim!" Sam said. "That was settled long ago, fair and square. It didn't amount to beans anyhow. And what's one claim got to do with all this? You're sabotaging half the canyon . . ." All at once he broke off with a grunt, holding his arm and pivoting clumsily on his sound leg.

Twenty feet away, in the bare dirt under a cedar, the Indian kid was stooping to pick up another stone. He flicked his arm. The stone banged against the side of the truck not a foot from Vivie's head.

"You! Come here," she barked and took out after him, floundering in the snow-crowded brush, the hood of her parka shaking back from her head. "What's the idea, you little skunk?" She chased him up the tumbled watercourse until she was out of breath, but he kept the same distance away, slipping like a brown shadow through the dusk. Eerily silent, implacable, he turned and sniped at her with rocks that came out of nowhere and punched holes in the cloth of snow, spanged off boulders, whizzed into lashes of red grass right beside her. Pain burst in her thigh and then it went numb.

Yelling threats and flinging rocks back at him, he finally had to return to the truck. "A gyp operation like this ain't gonna work," Sam was saying to Butler. The old crackpot muttered about his precious claim, and meanwhile the bulldozer continued to huff and puff in the high distance. Men were crashing through the trees and axes whacked into trunks, pebbles clattered down, voices answered each other—and there was nothing she and Sam could do! It was just tragic! Another stone buzzed past her face. "You wait'll I get my hands on you," she yelled and fired a stone at him with all her might.

One by one, the crests of rock above the canyon were losing the sun like pink and yellow fruit dropping in the wind.

Just then a man came crunching down the sharp-angled haul road, a flashlight swinging in one hand. "Can I help you folks?"

"Is that you, Marvin Wittaker?" she flamed. "You're trespassing on our property. You know that, don't you?"

"You're mistaken, ma'am. Mr. Butler owns all this along in here and we're just seeing to his property for him." With a cocksure air that was simply insufferable, he whipped the beam of his flashlight at them: glass-white splinters cut into her eyes and dwarf shadows scuttled back and forth.

"Don't get smartalecky with me," she said in a passion. "You haven't drawn a sober breath in ten years, you drunkard. I'll pop you one in the mouth."

Deliberately, he hawked and spat on the road. Sam, with a growl, went for him in a blind, limping charge. Laughing fit to kill, he made a leisurely retreat and Sam was forced to give it up. His anger was like the hiss and flare of high-tension wires blown down. "Come on, Vivie," he said, hobbling away. "By God, I'll get enough law to hang them."

The following morning before sunup, he set off for Rapid City to get an injunction, and she and Frank drove out to the property to hold off Butler's men. All day long, until Sam arrived with the injunction and a sheriff, she and Frank kept the crew at bay. "It wasn't that easy, either," she said when they were back in their trailer. "Me and Frank got there first like we planned, and right at daylight here they came—except for Zeke Butler, he never made an appearance. There must've been two dozen of 'em, but we had rifles and they didn't. We got in front of the dozer and I told them to stay back if they knew what was good for them. I said, 'You have no right here. I can shoot you, it's perfectly legal.' Then Marv Wittaker came braving up. Shaking in his shoes but acting the big shot. Frank was very hot-headed, he was all for a shooting war then and there, but I said, 'Keep still, I'll handle this situation.'"

She was crackling with pride and happiness, as if a thousand sparklers and pinwheels were going off inside her at once. It had been the most thrilling, the most romantic and wonderful thing imaginable, and telling him about it made all the more *real*. Too exhausted even to eat, Sam slumped on the edge of the bottom bunk in the smoky light of the lantern, slowly massaging his crippled leg and nodding from time to time, but she was drunk with excitement, aging and fallen-breasted but glorious, smiling with her wide generous teeth as she acted it out, relishing every single bit of it.

"The afterwards was just terrific. Wittaker said it was their dozer and they had a right to come and take it away, but I knew what he was up to, so I told Frank to drive the jeep to that narrow place up further, where the big rock is. Just like I figured, in a minute here they came a-grinding toward us. I blocked the rest of the gap myself and *dared* them to hit me. I made Frank put the rifle away again and told them off from here to Christmas. I said, 'You hit me and you're all going to jail. You're not getting paid that much.' The little cuss running the dozer drove up *this* close to me, thinking to scare me, only he couldn't. Marv Wittaker was screaming, 'Run over her! Run over her!' But the fellow said, 'If you want her run over you'll have to do it yourself' and down he crawls. There wasn't nobody going past that spot if I was to die for it, and they all knew it. Wittaker kept blabbing his mouth but his bluff had been called and pretty shortly him and the whole gang went off. Oh, they said a few things first, like where did I leave the grandkids, and if I wasn't a woman it would've been a different story. It was just talk, though. They'd shot their wad, they didn't so much as sneak down the canyon and try to kick over more stakes. And Zeke Butler must've thought better of it, too, because they didn't show their face again."

A check of the canyon the next day revealed that nearly twenty claims had been hacked up and scrambled. In spite of this, and though there was still a court case to go through, she was in an ecstasy of triumph. "I can't wait to get old Butler in that courtroom," she told Sam. "He don't have a leg to stand on and he knows it."

"Umm," he said. He was strangely inattentive, subdued and brooding. The more he thought about it, the surer he was that the whole affair stank like a skunk. For one thing, it wasn't like Zeke Butler to hit below the belt like that. It wasn't characteristic of him. For another, where had he gotten the money to pay the crew? And when the sheriff had served the injunction on him in the motel, he'd had a lawyer there, waiting. Zeke Butler didn't have the resources for a campaign of this size; he had to be a puppet, the front man for a larger operator.

And that could only be Bert Stephens. Sam felt as if he'd stepped through solid ground into empty space, into nothing at all. He could just see Stephens' ferocious satisfaction, the face contorted with laughter and the slick grey eyes with chaos in them . . . For the first time in his life he was up against somebody he might not be able to handle. Not because Stephens was so ingenious, though he was that, or because of the way he struck, like a bomb out of the sky. He was so sinister because there were no limits whatsoever; the man would do anything, anything.

In fact, at this very minute he might be getting himself another decoy and a crew to attack again! In a frenzy of haste Sam organized the Black Hills Protective Association, with over sixty uranium producers, ranchers, and businessmen, to guard against claim jumping. Both canyons bristled with revolvers and rifles.

But instead of more raids, articles about Zeke Butler began to turn up in the newspapers, lauding him to the skies as the discoverer of uranium in the region and the *first one to file a claim!* Sam was reeling. Like Vivie, he'd thought that getting a permanent restraining order against Butler would be a mere formality; now he wasn't so confident. Who could guess the effect of propaganda like that on the case? He hired an expensive mining lawyer from Denver and, too obsessed to work the mines any more, spent innumerable hours memorizing every claim, every landmark in the canyon, every drill hole, and every road he had constructed, in preparation for his appearance on the stand.

"Sam, you're wasting energy, time, and money in all directions," Vivie fumed. "I swear, you're not hardly rational any more."

"It's Stephens, all right," he said, bent over maps and photographs and claim papers. "And not a living thing we can do to prove it. That's what's making these grey hairs." Though his eyes were burning and the words and numbers wavered together in the lamplight, he had to keep going. All his life he'd had a very photographic memory; he'd been able to go straight to a particular piece of scrap machinery after five years. Now, all of a sudden he'd begun to mix things up, to forget dates, forget whole stretches of canyon. He wasn't whipped, there was plenty of fight still left in him, but something had happened. It was like something had busted inside him.

Bert, on the other hand, was in fine fettle. After a session with the lawyers in the motel room, Butler quavered to him, "Do we have a chance in court, Mr. Stephens? I couldn't follow that double-talk of theirs."

"Hellfire no," he said airily. "That's just the beauty of it. Now don't look so miserable, you'll be took care of. In return for your services, I'll bankroll any kind of museum you want to put up. I'm dearly fond of museums and public libraries, I use to keep warm in them in the winter."

The old codger spluttered, "I won't take charity."

"You think about it," Bert said, and insisted on taking him and Charley to the Western Cafe for a victory supper and barbecue.

At the door of the cafe, however, Charley hung back and mumbled, "I can't go in there. They don't like Indians in there."

"Damn if that cuts any cheese," Bert said and proceeded to buy them both a restaurant meal, ramming through the cold hostility of the counter-full of chewing men and the surly, unwilling service of Mrs. Binder. Charley ate two hamburgers and two orders of french fries, which he improved with splotch after splotch of gory red catsup. "I had a hamburger in a restaurant once," he said. "In the bus stop on the way to Pine Ridge."

"That's dandy," Bert said. Minute by minute he felt his victory bleed to death, and without his knowing it, his knuckles went into his mouth, into his gnawing teeth. Mrs. Binder, her fat hips bulging out like the arms of a sofa, asked if that would be all and slapped the check on the table. He smiled at her. "You didn't do it right, lady," he said. "I'm gonna build a zoo on this property. See if I don't."

Outside, telling Charley to take Mr. Butler back to the motel, he walked away down the first street he saw. He didn't even feel like a drink. Everything was spoiled and sour and pointless again. But then, as if by a kind of mercy, it began to snow—not an ordinary snow but the kind that happened only infrequently and that moved him in a way nothing else could: soft, soft flakes coming down in motionless air. They brushed his face. They made a quietness, a white silence in the short, ugly streets going nowhere. They covered the raw dirt and grass, the paths on the lawns exposed like twisting nerves, and filled into the torn darkness around the bushes and trees. For a few moments, surprised by a sweet and lonely joy, he watched the children run and swing into the air on the chain of the flagpole by the school, orbiting like tiny shrill planets through the snow-fluttering light. Then he went on. At the end of the street was the open country, deep and silent. Under the last light he came upon an anthill, a pure symmetrical cone of white in the weeds, and he stared and stared at it before climbing through the barbed wire fence into a pasture. Now there was darkness, gentle all around him, and he lifted his face into the delicate touch of the flakes, becoming the whiteness falling out of the sky, becoming silence.

March 1, 1953

After a period of baffling silence about Stalin, the Russian radio suddenly announced that he had suffered a brain hemorrhage. For four days he lay in a coma, a squat moustached man with a withered arm and two toes on one foot grown together. The name "Stalin" symbolized him: "man of steel." While Lenin and Trotsky had directed the revolution, he had waited in the background, collected disgruntled elements, organizing, serving on committees. Luck favored him. When Lenin died, Trotsky happened to be ill and Stalin eased him into obscurity, then exiled him. Eventually one of his assassins killed Trotsky in Mexico City by splitting his head open with an ax.

It was a summary of Stalin's technique—maneuver, wait doggedly, then purge. In less than four years he executed ten million kulaks in a grim campaign to unify and nationalize the swarming peoples of the Soviet Union. He was just the opposite of the intellectual Trotsky; he was the mediocre genius, the stubborn planner and committeeman. Patiently, by craft and by murder, he built a monolithic Russia out of the scrambled pieces of the revolution. He made the Soviet Union a world power—and a police state. As he lay dying in the grey fortress of the Kremlin, an age of Russian history was dying with him, the age of brutal consolidation.

On Thursday night, the Soviet government announced: "The heart of the comrade and inspired continuer of Lenin's will, the wise leader and teacher of the Communist Party and the Soviet people—Joseph Vassarionovich Stalin—has stopped beating."

And the world wondered uneasily: What was happening? Now what?

XXIV

"It could mean the end of the Siberian death camps and the MVD," Paul said. "Who knows, we can even hope for a softer line in foreign policy."

Winken, Blinken, and Nod were aghast. "One Stalin is like another," they huffed. "What's Malenkov?" they puffed. "Nothing but another Stalin!"

"Not only that," he continued, "we might finally get peace in Korea. But only if we put our house in order, too, and cut out the Moscow trials we're holding in this country . . ."

"Wait, wait, hold on," Winken said. He looked like a high-shouldered maiden aunt in a flannel suit—a consumptive maiden aunt. His eyelashes were very long but so white that the lids seemed naked. "You're talking appeasement, Paul. Surrender! You want to throw away at the peace table the lives of all the young men who've died in Korea!"

"That's right. Intentionally or not, you're following the Party line," Nod said, cocking his bearded face. "It's Kremlin-directed thinking, spread by agents and their dupes to create doubt about American policy."

Blinken sucked on his briar pipe and said that personally he didn't doubt Paul's loyalty to his country; however, that sort of talk *was* giving aid and coffort to the enemy.

"That's it in a nutshell."

Paul said, "You couldn't have picked a better place for it," and turned away in disgust. To argue that nothing more could be accomplished in Korea was "Pink-thinking" or "Trojan Horse tactics." The campus was a madhouse. The hounds of McCarthy were on winter's traces, baying now at teachers, and to be less than 200 per cent American was to be un-American.

Black Friday continued. He poured himself another drink and stood alone in the hive-sound of voices and the smells of overbaked ham and perfume, cheese dip and deliberately aromatic pipe tobacco. On the walls were enlarged and colored photographs of the children and a large busy mirror. In the fireplace, as homey as a TV dinner, yellow gas flames were leafing out of an imitation log. Dr. Frankenstein Bush was observing, "The entire Math department is a little pink if you ask me." The picture window was ticking with windy sleet and somebody said that cyclone warnings were out as far away as Oklahoma and northern Texas.

While Bush and company made the world safe for the American Legion, the faculty wives were gossiping by themselves in one corner of the room. The bride of Frankenstein, who had been playing hostess with a gay party expression plastered on her blank face, had perked up as soon as the magic words had been spoken: Cindy, pediatrician, fifth month, toilet training, "he was so funny singing 'tinkle-tinkle little star' while he was on the potty . . ." It unnerved the hell out of him the way she gave you the fake interest, like a deafmute at a community sing, if you spoke about anything else. The last time he had come over, she and Bill had just sat there for hours, watching the kids play "bump-over" with the chess pieces and talking baby talk to the youngest ones and memorizing the highlights in their chatter. Carol, who once upon a time had described a roomful of young professors on the way up as "thirty thousand dollars-worth of priceless minds," who had been a whiz in math and the only lady second baseman he'd ever met with a major league arm, who'd rattled off the names of the Marx brothers as Groucho, Chico, Harpo, and Karl . . . A sorrowful weight dropped over him and suddenly he was ambushed again by the thought of Lucy. Sweating, he fought to get clear.

Closest to him was Miss Nordvall, a muscular hairy-armed woman who took her tape recorder to places like Madagascar to record tribal customs. However, like everybody else in the University, she was obsessed with the communist menace. "Soft thinkers are a greater threat than card-carrying members of the Party," she boomed. "It's the gravest danger to America right now."

"What about the laxative habit?" Paul inquired.

At once he was pelted by acrimonious voices. For a while he still felt remote and disoriented, but the dispute was mercifully hot, urgent. His anger grew. Bush spluttered, "There's one way to settle this. Joe Stalin is dead and I propose a toast to it." Lifting his glass of ginger ale in the swampy light, he said to Paul, "Will you drink to that or not?"

"Sure," he said with unexpected agreeableness. "After all, it was Stalin who killed off communism as a world-wide movement by making the party an instrument of the Soviet Union instead of class warfare. Thanks to him we have East against West instead of have-nots against haves." Clicking his glass against Bush's with a thin-eyed smile, he said, "To Joseph Stalin, the best friend the free-enterprise system ever had."

Bush pulled his glass away, spilling ginger ale on the carpet, and the toast faltered to a stop, dangling like a broken leg. It was the last straw as far as he was concerned. A very convivial occasion was going to pot, to rack and ruin, all because Morris had butted in where he knew he wasn't wanted. And why? To embarrass him and get revenge because his contract, for very good and sufficient reasons, had not been renewed. From the moment he appeared at the annual department party, he'd been a gadfly, a veritable spectre at the feast, refilling his own glass time and time again—although he knew perfectly well that one or two sociable drinks was the custom—and causing friction at every conceivable turn. Claiming the freedom to dissent was one thing and referring to Senator White as "a rat in shining armour" was another. And calling his colleagues "dyed-in-the-wool sheep."

"Carol," he said hectically, motioning her to come with him. "I can't go on," he whispered. "I really and sincerely can't. That Morris, I've picked up the pieces so many times after him . . . Human nature can only stand so much. He's turning the entire party into a fiasco."

All she did was tell him not to fret. "These people know him," she said. "It's just Paul."

"That's just it, it's not. He's drunk besides everything else and stepping on everybody's toes around him without one speck of provocation! And I'm on thet hot seat! I've smoothed it over and tried to pour oil on troubled waters until I'm at my wit's end—which I told him. And do you know what he said? He said, what a trip that must have been! How's that for bad manners? I'd ask him to leave the house except I know he'd just laugh in my face. He actually would!"

"Well, start serving the ham then, and I'll give you a hand as soon as I can."

He flushed. She was his helpmate, his loyal partner in thick and thin, and, instead of rallying to the cause, she wasn't even paying attention; she let her eyes stray away from him, drift. Then he saw her hand go to her breast and she said, "I really can't help now, Bill. The baby is going to wake up in a minute."

Instantly he was contrite, tendering his sincerest apologies. They exchanged an intimate look. Then she kissed him lightly on the tip of the nose and started up the stairs with Betty O'Connor, the young wife of one of the graduate assistants. Her rich, weighted breasts grew heavier and tingled as she went into the bedroom toward the baby. Jimmy was sound asleep in the other crib, tangled up in furry stuffed dogs and teddy bears, one of his small arms sticking out between the pink bars. The baby was wide awake, lying on her back and kicking her chubby legs. "There's my precious. Were you waiting for your mommy?" She smiled, bending over her, and the baby, becoming one rosy smile, ran her little legs in an ecstasy of welcome. "Oh, she's beautiful," Betty said, and after Carol had changed her and put on a fresh shirt and nightie, she let Betty hold her until she began to fuss. Then, switching on the small lamp by the chair, she settled herself in the cozy womb of light it made and Betty leaned on the rocking horse, watching intently, reverently. "We're going to start a baby as soon as Dave passes his prelims," she confided, and while Carol unfastened her blouse and brassiere they talked about waiting to start one and how *left out* you felt. Tenderly, gaily, she said to the baby, "Does she want her dinner? Are you hungry, sweetheart?" Her breasts were swollen tight. She loosened out the cup of the bra and, deep in the round holding of the lamplight, gave herself to the eager mouth, feeling the sweet pull of it and the release in her breast, gazing down at the tiny hand that lay on the sliding white plumpness, and patted, and stroked, stroked. Sweat came out on the baby's temples, in the delicate breaths of hair, and her breast was full and white and nourishing, held sweetly by the baby hand which divided into such perfect little fingers. Having Betty there, hushed with longing, made it less routine, gave it a deeper emotion and meaning. It was comforting, it was lovely and rich, it was warm, it was everything there was, here in the pooling light with the other children asleep in the next room and Betty very still, very still on the rocking horse. Her other breast was beginning to leak and she tucked a diaper into the bra, matter-of-fact about it under Betty's rapt, inquiring look. Slowly the baby's eyes glazed with bliss, her hand went limp, and she was asleep again before she was burped and put back in the crib.

Going back downstairs, Carol couldn't bring herself to any sense of reality about the party. She felt softened and blurry, submerged in contentment, in a soft white dream worlds away from the bickering voices of the men. Still, keeping her promise to help with Paul, she threaded her way through to him and asked why he never came over any more.

"I'm just going through a phase," he said.

Half-heartedly, she persisted: "Did I tell you what the children call the baby? They call her Mister Fats!"

"That's nice." His dark stare was fixed on Bill, who was talking about the responsibility of colleges and universities in the cold war. "It's up to us," he said fervently, "to orientate the young people entrusted to us toward our national ideals. It's a conditioning process, you might call it. The orientation of the next generation to accept the goals of our society and government."

Paul said acidly, "Excerpts from the *Mice Trainer's Handbook*."

Bill glowered at him and continued, "Even if an individual isn't a Party member, they can still be communist oriented. They can do very serious damage in the classroom with their slanted lectures, sabotaging young minds. You can talk all you want to about academic freedom, but it's been far over-abused in my opinion. Which Senator White has pointed out. He hit the nail exactly right when he said we have to whet our precautions to a keen edge. According to his latest figures, at least three thousand American professors have been involved in at least one suspect organization. One thing is sure, though. This university is not going to turn into a Harvard or a University of Chicago, absolutely riddled with Jew-leftist clubs and teachers that have to take the Fifth Amendment. No sir, the administration is going to leave no stone unturned."

"Or unthrown," Paul said.

Bill whirled on him, red-faced and stammering. "I was not addressing you, but since you want trouble, all right. You wait till tomorrow and you'll get some. The meeting of the entire faculty tomorrow morning has not been called for nothing, I promise you that. The stooges of international conspiracy, like you, are in for a little surprise."

"I see. A purge from sea to shining sea, huh?"

"Go ahead and scoff to your heart's content," Bill said. His voice rose, and all over the room the sounds of eating and the stutter and hiccup of china and silverware died down. "Go ahead! But it hasn't been forgotten what you did, applying to the Committee on Student Activities to form a book-burning club."

"You mean the Libraries for America Society? What could be more patriotic than that? We're going to have weekly bonfires of dangerous books, roast some weenies and wind up with verses one and two of 'Columbia, Gem of the Ocean.'"

"I know your tactics from of old," Bill said dangerously. "Tell us—everybody here—tell us open and aboveboard. What's your *real* object? Is it really to have no pro-communist books on the shelves? Is it?"

"Our goal," Paul said, "is no books at all."

It was a pitched battle now and Nelson and Throneberry tackled him, too. Carol plucked at his sleeve, signalled to Bill to change the subject. "Just one thing more," he choked. "Just one. I hate to think of all the damage you've done to young minds in the classroom, Morris, I really do. It's only locking the stable after it's too late, I realize that, but at least the next school where you apply for a position will be forewarned about you. Your letters of recommendation will be very clear about that. The youth of America has got to be safeguarded."

"Like Teddy?" Paul said.

The stillness in the room went blank. For cataleptic seconds, while Paul sprawled on the couch with the glass of whiskey on his stomach and cigarette smoke trickling from his lips, the room was like the mouth of a fish swallowing air after the brain had died. The mention of the dead boy was all the more frightful because, during Hell Week, eight fraternity men had been expelled for breaking into a funeral home and painting a clown's face on one of the bodies. Then, in the shocked gabble that started up, Bill ordered him out of the house. He left, but the party was crippled; every effort to revive it hitched, ran down, and came to a stop like a toy merry-go-round with a broken spring.

As Carol and Bill cleaned up afterwards he refused to be consoled. "I told you he'd cause a fiasco, didn't I? And what was your reply? 'It's just Paul,' you said. But even I never dreamed he'd stoop that far! It was absolutely beyond the pale. It would be absolutely criminal for anybody to mention a tragedy like that—but *him*. Of all the people to bring it up. I don't see how even he could do that . . ."

She said, "You know, I never did get it straight about that boy. It was right before Callie was born . . ."

"I don't want to talk about it! Enough trouble is enough for one day. I was perfectly justified in allowing them to prospect on their free time. If Paul Morris had done his job, a fine young man would still be alive today."

"You mean *you* let them prospect, Bill?" She had stopped scraping bits of ham and congealed potatoes into the garbage can.

"Of course I did," he said indignantly. "They were entitled to do what they pleased on their time off, and at the same time they were contributing their bit toward finding the most critical strategic material there is."

She set the plates down on the sink. Her eyes were dark and strange. Quietly—too quietly—she asked how, then, had Paul been at fault.

"You don't understand," he told her. "He was my second-in-command, Carol. I delegated responsibility for those boys to him and the second they set foot out of the camp they were in his charge. And did he keep a watchful eye on them? Did he accompany them on their prospecting, which any responsible person would have? He most certainly did not. He loafed in town in the evening drinking beer, that's what. The entire summer, from start to finish, he did nothing but aim his jibes at me and undermine discipline with the net result of the tragedy . . . that happened."

She still wasn't satisfied! Appalled, he followed her back into the living room and watched her pick up glasses and ashtrays. He looked at the red valley gouged into the ham. He looked at the creamy white cheese dip, hacked and scraped and dried into crusts around the edge of the bowl. "I don't understand your attitude," he said finally. "Not one bit. We went over this at the time."

Her face—the dear knobby skinny face he loved—was cold and unyielding. "How was Paul supposed to watch boys tramping all over the hills?" she asked. "Did you even tell him to?"

"Yes!" he shouted. "Yes, yes, yes! Can't you get it through your head? He was against them prospecting from the first. Every day we had a quarrel over whether it was right, of all things. I would certainly have ordered him to go along if it would have done any good. The very, very most I could get out of him was to watch them in town where he could drink beer. If he'd only gone along with them they wouldn't have taken such undue chances and gone off by themselves into dangerous places. Now do you understand? I certainly hope so, because this is very painful to me, Carol. As you well know."

"And so you didn't renew his contract." Her face was utterly closed to him now; her mouth was pressed together. It was as if, somehow, he had stumbled into darkness.

"Certainly not!" he told her, panicking into rage. "Obviously you don't comprehend the situation. Since you don't believe in me and trust me, either, I request that you kindly drop the subject. No!" he shouted, "I positively won't hear any more about it. Not another word. I have my principles too, for your information, and I intend to live up to them. Paul Morris gets no contract as long as I'm head of the department!"

Black Friday was followed by Black Saturday and promptly at ten A.M. the faculty convened in the Little Theatre. Decor: imitation Mount Vernon, tall and white. Flags with golden ropes and heavy, prod-shaped tassels. A grand piano on the stage, shut up like a hearse. After a vague non-denominational prayer and the pledge of allegiance, the Dean of the Humanities took the podium and bumbled, "To sum up the situation for you: An anti-subversive bill is going to be introduced at the next session of the state legislature. Frankly, an investigating committee from outside is inevitable and the question is, should we take a good long look in our closet right away—call it a private little cleanup campaign—and if we so decide, what sort of machinery we should set up for self-investigation . . ."

His hand sawed in the powerful light and chopped up and down, always a little out of step with what he was saying, like the hand of a badly run puppet. Sitting behind him, flanked by solemn deans and vice presidents, was the Chancellor of the University, commonly referred to as "Silent Willie" or "The Sphinx." He was a squat, grey nonentity, a third-rate politician who had inched to the top by careful maneuvering and organizing, but he could drive a juggernaut with the best of them. The dean paused with an arch expression to indicate that he was going to deliver himself of a joke, and said, "We intend to make sure there's no color blindness in *this* institution." All around him Paul saw the painfully eager laughter skitter up. The captured faces were bleached with light, identical, uniform, anonymous, all witnessing to the gospel as preached by Joe McCarthy.

The "free and open discussion" was a grisly spectacle: professors and scholars falling over each other in their hurry to welcome investigation, censorship, the purge. Only a few spoke up, uncowed, against the massacre of individual liberty. On the other hand, Paul admitted, he had no right to criticize anyone. For after all, what was he? A lame duck faculty member without a contract for next year, living a posthumous life in the department until June. What did he have to lose? It took no courage for him to stand up and call the whole business an insult. "We're allowing ourselves to be bullied by politicians trading on mass hysteria," he said bluntly. "Terrorized into taking the knife and emasculating ourselves."

Up on the stage the savants and administrators sat in their pudgy chairs, solid, impervious. Smoothly the dean said, "If there are no more comments, we'll put the matter to a vote. The motion has been made that a committee of department heads be formed to look into the loyalty status of all members of the faculty. Do I hear a second? All those in favor signify in the usual way . . ."

As simply as that, he was brushed aside and the liquidation begun. It was democracy by the firing squad now and the hangman was singing "Yankee Doodle." As simply as that. One more lost crusade, he thought drearily, one more Holy Land unrecovered to add to Wally, to Teddy and the other boys on the dig, to Carol, to Lucy . . . He was very tired suddenly, so leaden that for a minute he was defenseless against the sorrow, undiminished by its hopelessness and by time. Ordinarily he was able to live around her, at least when he was not trying to sleep, but he never knew when it would happen, when some little thing or nothing at all would release floods of dreaming memory and he would be sitting beside her against the grain elevator in the rich dusty smell of corn and oats, or feeling the wild flurry in his chest when he caught sight of her walking toward him, her face light and high on her skinny neck. The way she said "Et-ruscans . . ." His mind was sick with the bright running pictures; he moved through the tweedy mob like the corpse of himself. Outside, the steps and sidewalks were gritty with sand. The lean dark trees were plated with ice from last night's freezing rain and they moved stiffly, painfully in the grey wind, clashing their brittle twigs and cracking open, breaking off splinters of ice. From across the grey lawns the chapel bell bonged twelve discords with hideous disintegrating echoes a fraction of a pitch off, like all the keys on the player piano behind the cafe crashing down together, again and again and again.

Fleeing from what had come afterwards, he hurried to the office for a set of tests he hadn't finished.

Bush was in his cubicle at the front of the long deserted room, but the light was not turned on. In the greenish glow that came from the tinted window his face looked bloated and ill. There were dark green discolorations under his eyes.

"Hel-lo," Paul said, stopping in the doorway. "I don't believe you were there to hear about the new Five Year Plan. I made a speech."

Bush breathed hoarsely. He gave Paul a look of hate, but then his shoulders and his face seemed to go soft, one of his hands moved erratically, scuffed in the litter on his desk, and he threw two pieces of paper, clipped together, toward Paul. "Take it," he said in a ravaged voice.

Paul glanced at the contract, then at Bush's woeful face. There was only one conceivable explanation, and he could imagine the domestic earthquake that had led to this. "My, my," he said. "And I thought the only miracles took place in Galilee. Bill, I accept with pleasure." Crisply he signed both copies, placed one in front of Bush and folded up the other for himself.

"And the dig?" he continued. "How about the dig? Make a clean sweep of it, Billy. Do the generous thing all around. Tell you what—I'll go for room and board as a common field hand since the Smithsonian won't rehire me."

Sitting in the green light, Bush stared at the chrome miniature of a B-25 bomber squatting on his papers.

"God bless you, Bill. Now cheer up, it isn't so bad. You know I won't sign the loyalty oath come January first, and the man with the ax will knock at the door."

"Then why . . ."

"What's one death sentence more or less? And this one is too good to miss—a martyr's death, maybe even the stake! It's the nicest thing you ever did for me, Bill."

Feeling decidedly better, he walked across the campus to thank the author of his good fortune. A pale flicker of music came from the parlor of a sorority house. The icy trees dripped and water skinned down the creaking trunks. Carol, shaky and exhausted, was putting a snowsuit on Jimmy, who wanted to go out and play with the others. Just then Bill Junior and Eleanor straggled in, their overshoes mucking big blotches on the linoleum floor, and said it was too cold to stay outside. Jimmy went into a decline and could only be comforted by bread and butter with sugar on it. Food spilled and the refrigerator door slammed, Cindy couldn't find her crayons and the TV began hooting and roaring in the playroom.

But tired as she was, Carol didn't seem as flattened out and blank. "How was the faculty meeting?" she asked him.

"The Super Patriots were deciding what color our fair school is going to be. He shrugged.

"Umhum. Color it dead then," she said. It was astonishing. It was the way she'd been before the juggernaut of five babies in seven years had rolled over her. Somehow, inexplicably, illogically, the quarrel about Teddy's death had waked her up, shocked her back into consciousness. Nevertheless, it wasn't fair to let her exonerate him like this. In a ragged, embarrassed voice he told her about Lucy and said, "I could have kept them scared and quiet but then they saw me with her and that was the ballgame."

She was not impressed. "It wasn't right to blame you for not watching them," she pointed out. "And then to fire you."

"For God's sake, I tell you we both duffed out. Sainthood is a small club and neither one of us is a member. Anyway, a lot of it was bad luck."

After a while he convinced her that her marriage was not a sin, or even a shame. However, she was so worn out by now that she lost heart about herself and wouldn't be encouraged. Off in the other room Eleanor, with the ravishing grown-up air that little girls can get, was putting a raft of dolls to sleep in the bookcase. Cindy was squatting on an orange beachball like a bird on a gigantic egg and watching intently, her blue eyes the color of her corduroy overalls. Jimmy cranked his tricycle into the rows of dolls and was promptly socked in the nose. Blubbing, he kicked at the beachball on his way to tell mother and a three-way squabble took place. And meanwhile, the baby was gurgling good-naturedly, but insistently, for attention. "Get in there and watch TV with Billy," she screamed at the children. "All of you! Or I'll smack you." Then she broke into tears.

As soon as she had taken care of the baby, Paul made her lie down for a nap and closed the drapes over the light. "Sleep," he said in his best hypnotist's voice. "You are getting very slee-py. Your eyelids are get-ting heavy . . ."

She only wept into the pillow. "Remember what you said?" she quavered, sitting up again. "You said, there was an old woman who lived in a shoe, she had so many children her mind fell off." She half-laughed while big tears shook out of her dark eyes. "It's true, too. It is."

"All is not lost," he assured her. "You just temporarily misplaced it."

"But the children! You said—you said I was Mrs. Peter Cottontail and I was making creatures without souls. What am I supposed to do?"

"Well, for one thing, you hear that?" He paused and through the wall came the goofy songs and con man's patter of Bonzo's Circus on TV. "You might start by not chaining those kids to a picture tube. It's the lowest common denominator since zero."

He was profoundly touched by her renewed struggle, the stone rolled back from the tomb and the winding sheets left on the floor, and yet even as he looked at her tear-stricken face, it was Lucy who really mattered to him—Lucy, remembered like the dead. All his wretchedness came back. He thought of the old player piano with its rusty wires scattering dull clanks at random when the roll slipped. The irrational clatter burst in his head again, maddening, like the blind freakish mutations of genetics, like the combination of accident and will and cause-and-effect in everything. It was annihilating, all the billions of accidental lives, each one a buble of sound streaming upward and bursting into death, a tiny separate universe struggling and crying out. In this chaos of noise what could you do? Start a theme and variations; he knew what to do, but his heart was numb and aching. He had written her a dozen letters and finally she had answered: she was pregnant with Sam Bolton's baby and please go to hell.

But if Carol—if she could—irrationally, what had happened to her gave him the beginning of something like hope for Lucy. He sympathized with Carol; he administered words of good cheer, but it was all disconnected and far away from him, meaningless. By the time he left he could think of only one thing: was there a chance after all? Bolton must have gone on to other things by now. He no longer flinched at the thought of Bolton and Lucy, of Bolton's baby; but was there any chance? Hope of some kind, after all the mistakes and surrenders? Hope in spite of the certainty he'd be fired soon, in spite of her shame and pride? And the unborn life inside her, usurping her, amoral, before all conscience or consciousness, willing only itself, feeding on her body blindly and growing—could that be saved too? Like her lovely quick mind, the shining fervor that had come into her face . . .

The summer dig was not just archaeology but a chance to go back there, to see her again, to persuade her to marry him and give it a try. But was there any chance for her? He walked to the student hangout halfway up the hill and called Mrs. Harbaugh long distance. It was sweating embarrassment all the way. At first she didn't remember who he was and when that had been established, he stammered imbecilic questions about Wally, Bert, Sam Bolton, about everybody except Lucy. The conversation limped. Her dog yapped in the background.

"Lucy," he blurted out finally. "How is she? Is she okay?"

"Well, I been sorta outa touch with her," she said. "About as good as you could expect, I guess. She helps out in the cafe and babysits for Helen Mencke. She enrolled to go back to school only the mothers of the other girls didn't like it and so she had to quit. And that's about all I know."

He walked outside. The campus was quiet in the early spring darkness and along the streets and up the boggy lawns the shining trees raised a silver architecture of branches. Lucy was in a bad spot, and it would be three months before he could see her in June. But if she could do that, if she could try to go back to school when she was pregnant, there had to be some sort of chance, a seed of hope to nourish and make grow.

XXV

Helen was in the tub with the baby, giving her a bath. Voluptuously she surrendered to the warm soapy water. The wet slippery little body slipped against her breast, against her slippery wet legs, and she hugged her, sliding back and forth with her in the tub. Little spring peeper. Little mouth budded up, kissing, taste of Ivory. Nice day for it. Warm wind from somewhere melting everything, letting it go. Tickle the baby's white tummy till she squeals, little mirror laughing, same face, same creamy skin, little arms and legs with a body just something to hold them together. Well, you wait, honey. You'll see. Shaggy cloth, sopping soap melting off little neck. "Close your eyes now." Hair wet into curly copper wires on neck. Thin, but she's only a baby, Sandy's hair heavier. Like mine. George at least gave them curly hair. Straight hair's such a nuisance—when Bert threw me in the stock tank and I told George it rained over in Buffalo Gap. Did he believe that? Bad. Sin—oh, forget it, done holding back and worrying. Let it go, relax, slide. Things happen, I can't tell Mamma that of course, but well—things happen. Lucy is wrong. She always hated Bert anyway.

George's voice from out in the drugstore—who's the government going to award the mill to. Now the trial. Bert and Sam Bolton, jackals at each other's throat, he says. He better not take sides, that's for sure. "Sandy, take your clothes off and get in with us. That's right, hang it up like a good girl." Legs tangled up in the soapy warm water riding up and down, slosh and splash and tickle. Whee. "Scrub a dub dub, three girls in the tub—Scrub a dub, Sandy—how nice, you're washing her back. Get that spot on your knee there." That trial, now. We lost, of course, but we celebrated just the same as if we'd won. By then I didn't care any more what George thought. "Are you done, Sandy? All clean?" Twinkles of water dripping off her. "There's your towel, on the potty." Damn George anyway, he's an old woman. Well, hooey. If he don't know how to keep his wife, who

373

am I to tell him? Wish he'd hit me once. Like to see him try. Yes. I would. Buddy gave me a black eye that time I let his kite string go, I wasn't any bigger than Sandy. George just mopes around and won't eat what I cook. He has snacks at the cafes, though, he's not suffering. But not at Mrs. Binder's cafe any more, the things Bert does! George gets back at you so mean, shooting those poor dogs of his to punish me. "Now be still, Teecie, while Mommy washes. Here's your soap. Hold on! Oh, where is it? There now." Hurry up, get ready. "Yes, Sandy, I know the rug's wet but you have to leave it there till we get out of the tub. Tell you what you can do to help. Go in the bedroom and tell me what number the big hand is on. Thank you, Sissy."

Hurry up, lift the dripping little nakedness out of the tub, wrap it up in the towel, receiving blanket, she's bigger now but eight-thirteen was a pretty big baby. Dr. Harris said I didn't think you had it in you, Helen. Buddy likes Bert, that I know. And vice versa, Bert made him his foreman the minute he heard his mine had petered out. The first day on the job Buddy drove the bulldozer and cracked the dust out of that old cafe Bert bought from the bank and evicted Mrs. Binder out of. She couldn't hardly stand it, she'd been sure he was just pulling a joke. But he stood there and supervised with a bottle of gin in his hand, laughing and carrying on and saying to Mrs. Binder she had refused to serve her last Indian, and Bud dirty up on the bulldozer grinning and crunching the boards to splinters. Everybody in town was sore but Bert just laughed and said, "Us Indians are done holding back. Custer messed with us too and we learnt him a lesson." Lucy is wrong about him. Poor thing, though. Hanging around school when it lets out and asking kids what the assignments are.

"Here, Teecie, you want some of my powder? You too, Sandy? Yes, your petticoat is pretty." A mean thing to iron, well Mamma can do it, she's always saying they have to be dressed like ladies and they'll act like ladies. Poor Mamma, if she knew—well I guess I *am* bad. Well, let her try being married to George Mencke for just a little while if she thinks he's such a hot lover. Imagine Mamma in bed with George! Two old women!

"Now you girls sit there and play on the bed while Mommy gets dressed. Here's your little dishes, have a party." It's going to be a party from here on, I deserve one after being married to George. George can't make anything but girl babies. Couldn't keep up with Bert's parties if I got pregnant, I'm round as can be then, but it would be a boy, his boy. He'd be a heller to raise. I said, "You think your harem will let you go?" and he said, "I got a girlfriend expecting twins in Dallas and a wife and six kids in Omaha, but pack your grip, little girl." This blue wool jersey, the kids won't mess it up and it goes with my eyes. Slippery-sleek nylons on soft legs. Tight, but firm, nice. Heels. "All right, let's brush hair, girls. Where's your other shoe, Sandy?" Put the toothbrushes in the bag and the hairbrush in the purse, coats on, boots are too much trouble on the train, money, lipstick, comb, thank goodness we're rid of the diaper bag. Leave keys. And shake the dust from my high-heeled shoes. "George, we're ready!"

Old pudgyface dropping his shoulders down to the bag—my God, he's crying. He knows! But if he thinks that old trick's going to work again he's very sadly mistaken. He knows. Well, buts to you, nuster, I'm not having any. "Got your pockie-book, Teece? There's old Susy, Sandy, don't forget her or you'll never sleep a wink at Gramma's house." That's right, keep it up, talk to the kids, don't take any notice of the tears dribbling down his face. That's his wedge.

Only two blocks to the depot, swirl of tires in the muddy alley, slippery-sloppy mud, warm wind from somewhere. "Well, hello, Mr. Jorgensen, are you working the run to Alliance today? Yes, isn't it nice? I hope it stays warm like this, I'm not taking the girls' heavy coats. My mother won't be able to take them out if it don't stay warm." George will talk to him. He's wiped his face and blown his nose, I'm safe now. They're talking about the poor snow-cover and the prairie fires are gonna be bad this year. George thinks it'll freeze up again. George is wrong as hell. I'll have to think of some excuse to get out of Mamma's house tonight to meet Bert at the station or maybe he'll be waiting for me there and we can just drop the kids off and go. When we get settled in Denver I'll come back and get them. Here comes the train, the big train on the warm wind bang bang bang, he'll be waiting

"Earl, you look nervous," Bert said, sprawled out in the back seat of the Cadillac.

"I'm not nervous, Mr. Stephens. It's my stomach, I got a nervous stomach and when I break my regimen like this, especially out of the clear blue . . ." He went on griping as he drove past the fifteen-dollar wedding mills like dwarf chapels with blazing signs and tubby steeples outlined in neon. At the motel next to one of them, a clerk was dumping garbage into the glaring red door of an incinerator; flames gushed at him out of the blowing sparks. The mountains all around had turned black in the orange and green sky and a bloated moon floated over the blinking, flaring, car-rushing highway. On both sides there were pawnshops and used car lots, pink motels, expensive stores. Downtown, the Golden Nugget and Lucky's were going full blast. A neon cowboy winked a blow-torch eye, and cascading signs splattered a dry, searing rain of light on the sidewalks. Doors opened on slot machines, row on row of them, clattering and rattling like a mill, like an office full of typists. Rows of women fed coins into the slots and pulled the handles; oranges and bells and cherries blurred into metal rainbows and stopped; coins shattered into a tray down the line and the slots went on racketing like cashregisters, stuffing the packed air with more and more and more noise. Bert told Earl to park the car and they went into the Golden Nugget. In the bar, a guitar band was twanging and a cowgirl in a tight blue suit glittering with metal fringes, her long hair swaying under her hat, was wailing "Blue River." The gaming room was jammed. Long mirrors multiplied the crowds at the blackjack and crap tables, multiplied the sunburst chandeliers and red carpets and housemen chanting like auctioneers and strolling guards with two-gun holsters on their hips.

"I still don't know about coming to Vegas," Wally said again. "I mean, at least we could've told her. We could've left her a letter or something."

Bert watched the dice skim, kick against the wall and snap out of motion on the green felt printed with numbers and pictures of dice. "Five and no field, who'll bet the field, the number is four, four is the point," droned the houseman. Wally subsided. How could he criticize Bert for not running off with Helen Mencke? And anyhow it wasn't any of his business.

A fifty-year-old woman in a girlish dress stacked chips on DOUBLE SIX and said drunkenly, "I'm gonna kiss the devil tonight." The shooter crapped out and the houseman spilled a handful of red-and-white dice for Bert to pick from. His hair sliding on his wet forehead, he put five 100-dollar chips on the pass line and swept the dice down the table, flipping and hopping up: five. "Thirty-two, dice," he was hollering. "Say hello. Five, dice, hit a lick. Phoebe!" The flying dice landed and stopped together like copulating grasshoppers: a four and a one. Then he threw a seven right back and let the $2000 ride. The table buzzed, chips went down on the squares. "Eleven, that's a winner," chanted the houseman. Shouts spouted up as Bert gunned the dice and the houseman, chanting "two fives, your point is ten, ten is the point," retrieved the dice with a long limber stick and hooked, cuddled them and pushed them back to Bert. The director, his pockmarked face grey and still, sat behind columns of chips; the bills he sank out of sight in a slot. "Seven out and pay the don't," the houseman droned and the charging, blood-lust excitement collapsed.

Restlessly clicking chips in his fingers, Bert moved to the blackjack tables, played three hands at a time for a hundred dollars apiece, then switched back to a dice table and whipped up another commotion. He was like a Texas twister bouncing down here and there all over the countryside. His black nightclub suit was stretched out of shape; his eyes were like open sores, and between bets his small hands kept shuffling and riffling chips, itchy, irritable. There was nothing joyous about this carnival, not a trace of the old rollicky high spirits he used to have when he gambled. His puffy face, Wally noted, was sealed off and cold in the middle of a rampaging 300-dollar pass. In a few minutes he went next door to the Las Vegas Club and then had Earl chauffeur him out to the Sands and the other places on the Strip. Wally tagged along, watched for a while and then waddled back to the restaurant or the cafeteria, glazed and slow, torpid with food but ready for another meal, famished.

He ate and ate, he couldn't stop eating and no longer tried to. The casinos served fine meals for next to nothing and he put away two or three steaks at a time, then a helping of spaghetti maybe, and after that a milkshake and a massive wedge of devil's food cake with white frosting, cramming the food down at the cave of emptiness inside him. An hour or two later he was gorging on barbecued beef sandwiches and french fries, belching and sweating in a frenzy of eating. His thighs bundled around each other when he walked. The flesh had accumulated under his arms like sacks of pudding. He was aware of a vast Humpty Dumpty wading beside him in the windows, floating like a blimp in the drowsy mirrors. It was a freak, a sideshow freak with a face half smoothed of features, with bellies of fat under the chin, with swollen breasts and wallowing hips. Then the shameful thing drifted away and the thought of it smudged and smeared, dissolved, and he went on slipping deeper, deeper into avalanches of sleepy fat. Even the tastes of food registered vaguely, marshmallows, flapjacks, the chuckwagon breakfast of ham and eggs and fried potatoes. He couldn't cross his legs any more. He wore a size twenty-two collar. Once in a while, in their suite at the Desert Inn, he still made a sluggish attempt at one of his proud books, *Famous Composers,* but the words didn't mean anything: there was somebody named Berlioz who had written *The Damnation of Faust* . . . *Romeo and Juliet* was a botch, a shapeless lump . . . somebody named Brahms said that in different circumstances Beethoven would have been a master criminal . . . He was hungry again, his stomach was a frightening void, and he rushed downstairs, a frantic heap of wobbly flesh trundling toward the buffet.

"Lard, you're gonna bust like a balloon and scatter pork chops all over Nevada," Bert said unpleasantly. He put $50 down on ten the hard way, collected $400, and said, "You know what goes into baloney?"

"No, can't say as I do."

"I did some time in a packing house and I know. It's unborn calves and guts, Fat Man. Do you still feel like bearing down on the grub?"

He was worse tempered than customary, Wally decided, and it

occurred to him that something must have happened. Shortly thereafter Earl showed up, his camera slung over one shoulder, looking as if he didn't relish developments at all.

"Well," Bert said to him. "Quit standing there and playing with your tongue. Did you or didn't you?"

"I'm working on it, Mr. Stephens. Senator White's coming in. All kinds of big wigs are coming in for the Atom Test and I think I can tie you in with one of them. That should make page one of the *Times*."

"It better. That bastard continually needs another lesson. He just only *thinks* he's gonna be the big pecker, Earl, and you know why? Because you're gonna chop him off at the short hair."

Wally's interest faded. It wasn't anything but Sam Bolton doing some growing now that the trial was behind him, opening more mines and building himself an office in town, and Bert in his present exasperated mood was having a wide-open fit.

Earl ventured to remind him of the time he'd placed an item in the *Wall Street Journal* and Winchell had picked it up.

"That's what you're for," Bert said. "Now get moving or it'll take more than mineral water and pure air to fix your ailing colon."

He was like an infected place just about to burst. To the best of Wally's knowledge he hadn't slept for three days but still he kept going. In the Flamingo or somewhere he picked up with a woman with watery eyes and a purse full of twenty-five dollar chips. The ends of her lacquered hair were like sharp copper wire. Every time her boyfriend came up and bummed her for fifty dollars more she said in a loud voice, "I love you madly but you smell." Wally, who didn't care for dirty talk, had never in his life heard such a foul-mouthed woman. All the while she and Bert played blackjack, she continually told filthy stories to the whole table, and after each one she giggled hoarsely and licked her blurry lips. "You wanta hear a poem?" she said. "Here goes. 'Nymphomaniacal Alice, Used a dynamite stick for a phallus, They found her vagina, In North Carolina'— Hit me," she said to the dealer. "That's twenty-one, darling. Am I something or not, Bertsie?"

"For a one-legged girl you are the best," he said. But his cocky teasing was out of sorts and discontented, and pretty soon he got up and made a phone call. Stumbling out of the booth he said thickly, "I have stopped being playful. This is a fight to the finish."

Murky and slow, Wally heaved away without bothering to ask him what he had in mind. Nor was he surprised, a day or two later, when Bert took him to the Sky Room, winking a bloated red eye, and Bob Werden leaped up in a booth and came gibbering toward them.

His jittery eyes went wide, then carefully didn't notice Wally's size.

"Here I am, spring it on me," he laughed. "Go ahead, give me a bath in my own blood." Pretending to wash under the arms, he called to himself in a fond mother's voice, "Don't forget, scrub behind your ears, Bobby." Then the maternal tone twisted into accusation, his neck twitched, and he said bitterly, "You got me out here for a joke again, right? Like the telegram saying the mine was kaput. I tell you, that one got me right in the acorns, wow! You know, Bert, you invented the trapdoor, you really did."

Bert grinned at him. "I was just testing you out. The way I figure, for ten dollars you'd get in bed with your grandmother at the Pendleton Roundup."

He bugged out his eyes. "What's wrong with love?" he asked. "But no kidding, just give me the bad news. I've got it! That typical American town they're building out there in the desert to drop a bomb on—I've been selected as Mr. Average Citizen, right? I get a cocker spaniel, a newspaper, a rocking chair, and I sit in my little vine-covered cottage at ground zero. Oh well, everybody ought to do their bit for civil defense . . ."

Wally drifted away to the enormous window. The shameful thing floated toward him in the glass, cheeks stuffed tight with fat, a sagging wall of breasts and stomach. Through it he could see, down in the heated pool, a few people fluttering and thrashing in the poison-blue water.

"Hey there!" Bob Werden said, clapping his shoulder. "Stay with us chillun, you're the swinger on this deal. Is it honest-to-God true?"

Wally blinked at him. Bert put in evenly, "Like I said, he changed his mind. We're gonna make a corporation out of it and sell stock."

Coming to the surface for a minute, Wally frowned at him. That was a plain out lie; there'd been no talk of selling stock, and in fact he hated to think about any aspect of uranium. Before Bud Robel had taken over as foreman, he had run the mine purely as a job of putting out ore, just any kind of indefinite ore, silver, gold, copper or whatever.

"Boy listen, no kidding," Werden babbled. "Now is the time to go public; uranium stocks are BIG now. I got my finger on the public pulse." Swelling himself out, he pressed a finger to his wrist and looked grave. "Hmm, this is serious. I'd advise you to cut out starches and fornication with the opposite sex—not funny, huh? You're right, but listen, this is terrific. I got the brokers all set, everything. The issue will go right through the roof, I guarantee it. And it's Honest John, Wally! The mine is a sweetheart!"

He was kissing the air all around him when suddenly, without a word being said, he broke off. "You don't want it, I can tell. You were putting me on, Bert. Playing musical chairs with the little deaf boy again." He gave Bert a tragic and murderous look and, stretching out his neck, tuned up off key: "Mi-mi-mi."

"Don't worry yourself, he's in," Bert said, a glare like the tips of white-hot wires in his eyes. "And with the money, we're gonna get control of that mill and freeze Bolton's nuts to the pump handle."

It was just going from one mistake to a worse one, Wally said to himself. It was a shame, but everything was coming apart anyhow, sliding faster and faster while he looked on, numb and helpless. When he signed he felt bad about it.

"Great!" Werden cried. "Now remember, till I give the word we have a little secret. Mum up and pray the market holds steady. Those penny stocks are gonna blow up and take the whole kaboozie with them one of these days. By the by, you guys really ought to clear out of Vegas. That Operation Doomtown is nothing to fool with. What if there's a teensy mistake and the fallout comes this way? You ever hear of leukemia?"

"Shoot," Bert said. "That's your bad conscience talking. Besides, I like this town too good, it fits my personality."

"Have it your way but you know not the day or the hour. One miscalculation and bingo, it gets you right in the apples!" A look of horror which was only half joking bulged out his eyes and he held his hands over his testicles and babbled, "Generations unborn, wow! You never can tell, there might be another Rockefeller down there or a Gypsy Rose Lee."

An hour after he'd gone he was only a sleepy discomfort, a feeling of shame that Wally could hardly identify. His stomach was like the Grand Canyon. He ate two lamb chops and then mashed open the baked potato on his plate, folded in pat after pat of butter, and crammed it down. He breathed heavily. His face was greasy and his eyes were stunned and drifting. In a vague way he wished he could leave town. It wasn't that he was worried about fallout from the blast; he was tired of hanging around and he wanted to get back to Esther and the boys. Why had Bert made him come along anyhow? The casino sign was a boiling stream of white. "Roll up eight—eight now—six and no field," the house man chanted. As usual, Bert was firing the dice and people were buzzing and pressing closer, their faces sucked into the crater of smoking light. He won 6500 dollars in ten minutes and then complained, "This is getting boresome. I'm too rich to gamble, there ain't no flavor to it."

It was the chance Wally had been waiting for. "Let's pull out," he suggested.

"You look different, Sunshine," Bert said. "You been putting on weight?" And with that he strolled off into the bar. Wally trailed after him, too apathetic to be hurt. Maybe by accident and maybe not, the woman who talked dirty was in there and pretty soon she was whispering and blowing in Bert's ear to tickle him. "Keep sugaring me up," he told her. "I'm getting in the mood, you're beginning to look tasty." The plump white pearls on her ears glowed lewdly. Giggling, she took off her high-heeled shoes and hooked her bare feet, bristling with red toenails, around his leg. "Let's just step upstairs and see what ails the baby," he said muzzily. "Why Bertram!" she said as if amazed. "What big ideas you have." But immediately she picked up her shoes and, dangling them in one hand, swayed with him to the elevator. What happened up there in her room must have been unfortunate because when he came back he was a bad-looking sight. His face was grey and clenched and he fought for air like a man about to throw up. "Scotch," he said to the bartender.

"We both had enough of this town and to spare," Wally said. "I'll get Earl and check out of the hotel."

Bert made a grimace, gnawing on his knuckles. "Not yet," he said in queasy gasps. "A picnic ain't . . . over till they shoot off the fireworks."

"You mean the atom test? You want to stay for that? What for?"

Wally didn't get a reply so he said, "Well not me. If it's suitable with you, I'll head back myself."

For one terrible second Bert looked at him, his eyes like clots of blood. Then he swung around and threw his glass of scotch into the bottles of whiskey behind the bar; glass detonated like a grenade; he cursed and staggered down the mahogany counter, raking all the ashtrays off into the well. The bartender dived for cover and pressed a buzzer. The guards with the cowboy guns moved in swiftly, and then all hell really busted loose. Bert kept kicking and flopping around and screaming, "Arrest me, you motherfuckers." It was all Wally could do to get him outside in one piece.

Dully he added one more to the downhill slide of surrenders. Bert wanted them to stay for the test and since there was no budging him, let him have his head. As far as making sense out of it went, he had given that up long ago. But then, suddenly, without any effort at all, there it was: the pieces of the jigsaw puzzle gathering dust in a corner of his mind fell together by themselves. The viciousness, the drinking, the way he acted with women—all of it. What it amounted to was that Bert couldn't stand life, the cruelty and the sickness, the bad breaks, the pain. And so he tortured himself, inflicted pain on himself and everybody else just because he couldn't bear it, none of it, not even love.

There was no helping him, not now or ever, but you didn't abandon somebody with cancer.

Anyhow the test was coming up soon. The official name for it, somebody said, was Operation Shamrock because it was due on St.

Patrick's Day. TV cameras were being set up on four mountain peaks, and the gaunt old town, glittering like cheap glass in the sand, was filled with civil defense officials, more than two hundred newspaper men, brass hats of every description, and any number of tourists who had driven and flown in to watch. Atomic scientists were playing slot machines at the Sands. In honor of the occasion, a beauty shop on the Strip was featuring an atomic coiffure. Soon the approaching test was just about the only topic of conversation. Details about it swam in the dim air with the banging of slot machines and the nasal drone of stickmen at the crap tables: it was to be three-fourths as large as the Hiroshima bomb and the idea was to find out what would happen if an average American city was hit by the enemy. Along with the usual menagerie of rats and dogs and so forth, they were going to use actual houses with store-window dummies dressed in real clothes, cars parked outside in front and everything.

"Come on, Lard. In your enlarged condition a walk'll do you good," Bert said. His moodiness and dissatisfaction had vanished and he was in very good spirits as they went over to see the mannikins for the test stored in a justice of the peace's chapel. Lethargic, sunk in a stupor like snow settling over everything, Wally gazed through the window at the mother in a pink nightgown holding a stiff baby in her lap, at the motionless children loaded with buckshot to life-sized weight, at the jumble of men sitting rigid in the shadows.

Roadblocks were set up around Camp Mercury, seventy-five miles northwest of Las Vegas.

The test was due at five-twenty the next morning and hotel guests either left pre-dawn calls or stayed up all night. The Early Bird Atom-Watchers Club got together. People parked out along the highway, most of them with six-packs of beer and picnic baskets, and in the casinos the steady, twenty-four-hour-a-day excitement was swollen with a nervous expectation that kept increasing every hour like flood water building and building behind a dam. Bert was drinking hard and arguing with an old-timer who wasn't impressed by this baby blast. "You take that Operation Ranger in the winter of '51," he said. "Now that one really whistled a tune on our venetian blinds. Broke windows all over town and set off the burglar alarms." His teeth had rotted down to the gums and he wore glasses with a hearing aid in them, a sort of thin tube that ran down to a pink plug in his ear. A drink-girl with a loaded tray was saying, "They have to do it for science. President Eisenhower said that civil defense is lagging." The slot machines went on clicking and clacking and people crowded six deep around the crap tables, swarming in front of the painting of the Great Steamboat Race and the lush nudes billowing out their creamy flesh on beds and velvet divans. At each end of the carved and gleaming bar, two gilt figures burst out of the polished wood and surged up together: a horned man with bearded legs grappling a naked woman and dragging at the upward strain of her arms and body. It was a filthy sight. "Seven out and a new shooter," droned a house man. At the roulette game middle-aged ladies placed chips all over the green table, stretching their corseted bellies over the squares as they reached. The wheel turned on its axis in long, noiseless, oiled revolutions; the numbers and colors melted together and the ball whirled under the rim, orbiting dizzily like a tiny dying planet, running against the band of slowing, slowing numbers and rattling at last into a slot. "It don't bother me," a woman sporting a shamrock and a green top hat declared. "They say it's only like a flashbulb going off and after a while there's a jolt." Bert was disputing about the number of minutes it would take the sound to reach Las Vegas after the flash. The waiting stretched tighter and tighter. It was standing room only. Some people, pickled to a fare-thee-well, were singing as if they were going down on the Titanic. Some were betting on the time and checking their watches. The action at the tables was hot and heavy. Only one person seemed to be unaware of what was coming; she was an old, old woman in a wheelchair, raising her claw of a hand as high as she could to put quarters in a slot machine. Every few minutes, too weak to go on, she let her head sag and her hands trembled in her lap. Then she started up again, almost dead but with this one craze left, violent, insatiable, pulling the handle and pulling the handle, again and again and again.

"It's about time for the bomb," somebody said. Abruptly the gambling stopped. People tore outside, a lot of them with their drinks in their hands. Stupefied with eating and fatigue, Wally mopped up the steak juices with his bread, chewed and swallowed, and waddled after them, carrying his legs wide to get them past each other.

It was pale and cold. The mountains were grey on grey and the molten pour of the neon signs was dulling in the ash-colored light. At the end of the golden street, the shield-like sign of the Union Pacific station burned in front of a slag-grey mountain. Mindless, inert, Wally stood like a sleepwalker in the crowd until the sky singed white like high-power lines knocking together. The street was black on white, a photographic negative of itself. Some joker shot off a gun. Seventy-five miles away in the desert the typical American town had disintegrated, the dummies had melted into their flaming clothes, and a tidal wave of sound and wind was rushing toward Vegas. Everybody was waiting. A drunk lurched up the sidewalk waving his arms at the white sky, and blinking his swollen eyelids, Wally saw that it was Bert.

Ashamed of his fatness, of the belly jouncing with every step, of the gross flesh swinging like bags of water under his clothes, Wally ran after him and caught him. "Lead off in that hymn," Bert wheezed. Helpless, Wally watched him laughing, laughing in spasms, in choking heaves, wave after wave of laughter vomiting out as if everything in his brain was collapsing and emptying into the laughter. His face was warped and his eyes filled with anarchy were slick in the white light. And he was laughing.